Dancing Queen

Dancing
Queen

ERIN DOWNING

Simon Pulse
New York London Toronto Sydney

This book is a work of fiction. Any references to historical events, real people, or real locales are used fictitiously. Other names, characters, places, and incidents are the product of the author's imagination, and any resemblance to actual events or locales or persons, living or dead, is entirely coincidental.

SIMON PULSE
An imprint of Simon & Schuster
Children's Publishing Division
1230 Avenue of the Americas
New York, NY 10020
Copyright © 2006 by Erin Soderberg Downing
All rights reserved, including the right of reproduction in whole or in part in any form.
SIMON PULSE and colophon are registered trademarks of Simon & Schuster, Inc.
Designed by Ann Zeak
The text of this book was set in Garamond 3.
Manufactured in the United States of America
First Simon Pulse edition June 2006
10 9 8 7 6 5 4 3 2 1
Library of Congress Control Number 2006920561
ISBN-13: 978-1-4169-2510-1
ISBN-10: 1-4169-2510-4

For Milla, my little rock star
and for Greg, who rocks

Acknowledgments

Huge thanks to my fabulously fun editor and friend, Michelle Nagler, as well as the amazing Bethany Buck and the rest of the crew at Simon Pulse for taking a chance on me with this book.

This book wouldn't have been possible without my husband, Greg, who makes me laugh and appreciates my quirks.

Many hugs (hee hee!) to Robin Wasserman, my writing buddy extraordinaire.

And cheers to my incredible mom, who eagerly read and praised every draft of this book (even the really bad first round); my dad, who is just supercool and who forgave me for not using my maiden name (Soderberg) on the cover of this book; Sarah, who has been a superstar friend for twenty years and who made that first trip to London phenomenal; and Josef, Anna, Anders, and Stockholm—for helping to bring this book to life in Sweden and introducing me to the Eurovision Song Contest.

Also, hooray for ABBA, whose music makes me happy!

Dancing
Queen

Super Freak

Olivia Phillips's first-ever celebrity sighting was going all wrong.

She had just landed flat on her butt, her long legs splayed at awkward angles across a busy sidewalk in the middle of central London. She had a discarded cigarette butt stuck to her jeans, her face was splotchy, and her curly brown hair was stuck to her lip gloss. Though she didn't want to look, she was pretty sure the bottom of one leg of her jeans had crept up above the cuff of her athletic sock and gotten stuck there.

Liv—as her friends called her—couldn't remember a time in recent history she had looked *less* fabulous.

Tragically, it was at this very moment that

Josh Cameron, International Pop Star and *Celeb* magazine's Hottest Guy of 2006, was staring straight at her. *The* Josh Cameron, whom Liv had fantasized about a million and three times, was standing less than two feet away, casting a shadow from his perfect body onto Liv's disheveled figure on the sidewalk.

Why, Liv wondered, *do things like this always happen to me?* She had arrived in London from Ann Arbor, Michigan, less than two hours earlier . . . and she had already made a complete fool of herself in front of the world's biggest celebrity. *How is this even possible?!*

Because Liv was Liv. And she had a tendency to turn ordinary embarrassing moments into extraordinarily embarrassing ones—which meant this moment could get a whole lot worse. And it did.

Looking up at Josh Cameron, Liv was unable to stop a goofy, uncomfortable sort of smile from spreading across her face. She lifted her hand in a little wave and—very much against her will—blurted out, "Cheerio!"

Three hours earlier . . .

Gazing out the airplane window at London's sprawling suburbs miles below her, Liv couldn't believe she was actually here. In her sleep-deprived state, it *still* didn't feel real that she had been selected as one of Music Mix Europe's summer interns. But now that she was settled into a cramped window seat and minutes away from landing on the other side of the Atlantic, she finally let it sink in: She would be living in London!

Liv had spent every waking minute since she had gotten her acceptance letter daydreaming about days surrounded by rock stars and nights out tra-la-la-ing from club to club. Of course, deep down, she knew the Music Mix internship would be a lot of work, too. But she had somehow managed to avoid thinking about that part. Why not focus on the good stuff?

When the plane landed, Liv grabbed her black wheelie from baggage claim and followed airport signs to the Gatwick Express. Hustling through the terminal with her suitcase and overstuffed carry-on tote, Liv's excitement bubbled into giddiness. She heaved her stuff onto the train into the city, and a chirpy English voice wished her a good day and a pleasant journey. She just loved the British accent. It always sounded so civilized and kind.

The train began to roll toward downtown London as Liv flipped through the on-board magazine, reading about London's neighborhoods. Music Mix was setting her up with an apartment as part of the internship—she couldn't wait to find out where her roommates would be from, and where they would be living. Notting Hill, Chelsea, Greenwich . . . they all sounded fantastic.

Since she had never been anywhere more exotic than Ely, Minnesota, they all sounded a little intimidating and foreign, too. She had only lived away from home once before (Liv always gagged when she thought about that terrible summer her dad had decided to send her to an all-girls camp on Lake Michigan), so this was definitely going to be an adventure.

Paging through the magazine, Liv quickly studied British lingo and discovered that if she wanted to fit in, her roommates would actually be flatmates, the subway is the tube, and she absolutely must eat something called bangers and mash.

Eventually the train heaved out one final puff, and the doors sighed open to let Liv out into central London. She had arrived!

Making her way into Victoria train station, Liv scanned the signs overhead, looking for the London Underground. Dodging through the crowd, she found an open ticket booth and bought a monthly travel card. Studying the tube map in her guidebook, Liv found the route to Oxford Street, home of Music Mix Europe's central office. She had been told to "pop by" the studio to pick up keys to her flat.

Hustling through the corridor toward the tube, Liv eyed the advertisements pasted on the walls. Next to an ad for Cadbury chocolates (*Yum . . . must get some of that*), Liv spotted a poster of Josh Cameron. She slowed her walk slightly, scanning the advertisement for details.

JOSH CAMERON: SPECIAL APPEARANCE, LIVE IN LONDON! Liv stopped briefly—her eye had been drawn to a small detail in the lower corner of the ad: "Sponsored by Music Mix Europe." Liv wondered if she would get to help with the concert. . . . That certainly wouldn't be a bad way to spend the summer. She was just the tiniest bit obsessed with Josh Cameron, and would give pretty much anything to meet him in person. There weren't a lot of celebrities floating around Ann Arbor.

Liv could hear the subway train rolling

into the station just ahead of her, and she hustled to catch it. She pulled her suitcase and carry-on clear of the doors just before they swooshed closed and the train roared out of the station. Two stops later the train's doors slid open and she stepped onto the platform as a freakishly polite mechanical voice reminded her to "mind the gap." Liv passed through one of the arches leading her away from the platform and rode the long escalator up and out onto the street. Red double-decker buses breezed past, stuffed with passengers out for a day of shopping. People packed the sidewalk, hustling past Liv, who stood rooted to her spot just outside the Underground exit.

The noise and speed of the crowd was overwhelming. The time difference had started to catch up with her, and Liv realized that it was the middle of the night back in Michigan. Hit with a wave of sleepiness, Liv glanced down Oxford Street and spotted the glowing Music Mix sign.

She applied a coat of gloss to her lips and hastily made her way toward the sign. She lifted her suitcase, slinging her carry-on tote over a shoulder, and pushed into the office's revolving entrance doors.

Liv's reflexes had slowed from lack of

sleep, and she realized too late that she had forgotten to get out of the revolving door on the inside and was back out on Oxford Street. Blushing, she made another turn around in the door and stepped out into the large, open lobby, tucking a stray curl behind her ear. She looked around quickly to make sure no one had seen her mistake. Coast clear.

Liv smiled widely as she approached the security desk. "Excuse me . . . I'm one of Music Mix's summer interns. Can you tell me where should I go?"

The security guard looked up briefly, then returned to the tabloid he was reading. "Third floor, miss." Liv muttered a quick thanks, resisting the urge to curtsy, and took the escalator up. She stepped into a round, colorful sitting area whose walls were filled with floor-to-ceiling television screens playing a variety of music videos.

As Liv approached the circular desk in the center of the room, she could hear the receptionist chatting animatedly. Peeking up over the edge of the tall desk, Liv could see that the receptionist's dyed blond hair was formed into a dozen long thick dread-locks and was pulled back from her face with a hot pink scarf. She was wearing a short strapless dress and an armful of silver bangles that set off her dark skin perfectly. She motioned to Liv to wait, and quickly finished up her conversation.

Looking up at Liv, she smiled. "Welcome to Music Mix. Here to check in?"

Liv grinned. "Yes, I am. My name is Olivia Phillips."

"It's lovely to meet you, Olivia. I'm Gloria. Here's the scoop: I give you keys to your flat, and you're on your own for today. Settle in, meet your flatmates, get some sleep. Just be back here at nine tomorrow morning. Simon Brown can be a bit testy in the morning, so don't be late—it's best to stay on his good side."

Liv recalled that her acceptance letter had come from a guy named Simon Brown—she now realized he must be the one in charge. What a fabulous job.

Gloria shuffled through a box on her desk and plucked out a small yellow envelope. She pulled out two keys and a card with an address printed on it. Scanning the card, Gloria passed it across the desk to Liv, along with the keys. She pulled a pocket-size London Underground map out of her desk drawer and circled one of the stops in hot pink marker.

"You're sharing a flat with two other girls," Gloria explained. "They have both checked in with me already, so they should be at the flat when you get there. Think you can find it?"

Liv nodded again and turned toward the escalator. "Thanks a lot. I'll see you tomorrow." Gloria smiled and pushed a button to answer the phone that had just started ringing.

Riding the escalator down, Liv could see that the Music Mix lobby had become much more crowded since she had arrived just a few minutes earlier. She scanned the faces and chic outfits as she passed, wishing she were dressed just a little cuter and didn't have her bulky wheelie and carry-on—she *knew* she looked like a tourist.

Liv glanced down to study the tube map as she made her way into the revolving door to leave the building. Distracted, she didn't notice someone step off Oxford Street and into the door as she exited.

Suddenly, Liv was jolted backward. As she lost her balance, both Liv and her wheelie toppled over onto the sidewalk. Though she had come out on the right side of the door this time, her bulky carry-on bag had not been so lucky. The strap of the bag was still attached securely to Liv's shoulder, but the bag itself was stuck on the other side of the glass in the compartment behind her. The revolving door had come to a complete standstill.

Liv pulled her arm out of the bag's strap to release it and craned her neck around, hoping no one was stuck in the door. Her face reddened as she realized that someone was definitely standing—trapped—in the other glass compartment. The person turned to face her, and Liv's mouth dropped open.

Staring at her from the other side of the glass, stuck in a revolving door between Oxford Street and the Music Mix lobby, was Josh Cameron.

Back to the future . . .

It felt like hours had gone by. Josh Cameron had quickly freed himself and Liv's bag from the door and was now standing—staring— at Liv on the ground. And was it her imagination, or had she just shouted "cheerio" to the world's biggest pop star? Liv straightened her legs, but continued to sit on the sidewalk, stumped and horrified. *Nice first impression, Liv. Suave.*

Josh Cameron smiled as he held Liv's

carry-on out to her. "I believe this is yours. . . ."

"Um, thanks." *Um, thanks? Really great response . . . very witty and charming.*

Josh Cameron tilted his head to the side just slightly and looked at Liv with concern. "Are you okay? That looked like a pretty bad fall." She scrambled to her feet and took her bag from him, groping for the right words.

Come on, supersexy girl within, Liv begged inwardly, *say something clever and alluring! Oh God, you're just staring. . . . Say something!* "Yeah, I'm fine. Just a little embarrassed. You don't think anyone saw that, do you? Hah hah hah!" Liv laughed too loudly at her own nonjoke, quickly straightening her hair and brushing the cigarette butt off her jeans.

"I'm Olivia, by the way. And I'm really sorry. It's just that, well, my friends always say this is the kind of thing that I do, uh, you know, when I guess I want to meet celebrities, or, um, make a winning first impression, or uh . . . hah hah hah," *Shut up, just SHUT UP! What are you* talking *about?!*

Josh Cameron was smiling at her, clearly amused. He patiently ran a hand through his gorgeous curls as Liv stuttered through her ridiculous monologue. By the time she finally had the self-control to shut up, he had begun to laugh.

"Well, Olivia, I better be off. It's been lovely meeting you. I really do hope you're not hurt." As he made his way back through the revolving door, Josh Cameron turned once more and looked at Liv. He smiled his famous smile, and walked into the lobby toward the waiting crowd.

Liv stared after him for a few seconds, then backed away from Music Mix's front doors. She was pleased to see that her white athletic sock was definitely poking up over the cuff of her jeans. *Really cute, Liv. Very chic.*

As her mind replayed the past five minutes over and over—coming up with about twelve significantly more glamorous ways she could have met the biggest pop star in the world—Liv made her way back to the tube and toward her new home. She had been in London less than three hours, and had already managed to fit in a lifetime's worth of humiliation. And, much as she hated to admit it, Liv suspected this wasn't the end of it.

She Drives Me Crazy

Emerging from the subway, Liv detected the faint odor of urine. She covered her nose and hurried out onto the sidewalk, turning left and heading toward the address listed on the card she had gotten from Gloria.

She couldn't help feeling a little concerned as she took in her surroundings. Liv's image of London had come from movies like *Bridget Jones's Diary* and *What a Girl Wants*. This wasn't quite the same. All the buildings looked shabby, and there were more fish and chips shops than people.

She stopped at a medium-size gray building at the end of the block. The iron gate led into a small flowerless courtyard, with three huge garbage cans resting at the foot of a set of stairs that led upward.

Liv double-checked the address on her card and pulled the keys from her pocket. The biggest key worked, and Liv made her way into the courtyard and toward the stairs. Hers was apartment 523. She looked for the elevator, but immediately realized she wouldn't find one. Climbing slowly with her suitcase, Liv got to the fifth floor sweaty and out of breath. She figured the walk up was a good thing—her butt would look fantastic by the end of the summer.

As she made her way down the hall, Liv's heart began to beat faster. She was about to meet her new flatmates. *Where will they be from?* She wondered. *Paris? Milan? New York?* Liv turned the key and pushed open the door.

She was greeted with three enormous, obscenely expensive-looking Armani suitcases. Each was propped open, displaying a treasure chest of Gucci and Zac Posen, a pile of cashmere, and several very real-looking alligator pumps. Caught off guard, Liv stood silently in the doorway for a few minutes before stumbling into the room and pushing her generic wheelie against a wall.

Breathing heavily from her climb, Liv glanced around the room. It wasn't exactly charming, but it would certainly do. The room was mostly naked of furniture, which was a pretty good thing considering that the three huge suitcases took up most of the floor space anyway. Directly across from the front door was a slim counter, which overlooked a tiny kitchen. There were three small bar stools squeezed under the countertop. Along the right wall was an ironing board, jammed in next to an antique-looking stereo.

Liv quickly scanned the rest of the room. Her eyes came to rest on a short threadbare couch along the wall. It looked like it might have been flowered once, but was now just a pale shade of green. Liv realized that there was a wisp of a girl perched delicately on one arm of the couch. The girl was looking Liv up and down without any hint of subtlety.

Liv bellowed out a very loud "hi there" to hide her surprise and discomfort at (1) realizing someone was sitting on the sofa looking at her, and (2) realizing that that someone was very obviously studying her for flaws.

After an awkward moment of silence, the girl introduced herself as Rebecca, a self-described "Texas Honey." Liv quickly stated her name in response, and then Rebecca released a delicate sigh and launched into a list of house rules, nearly all of which related to Rebecca's clothes and what Liv could and couldn't touch (the "Could" list was blank, as far as Liv could tell).

"And most important," Rebecca explained in her thick Texas drawl, "Ah am to be called Rebecca—that is Rah*beh*kaw. Not Becky or Becks or Becca or any other fun little nicknames you might devise. My father taught me that this manner of coziness is tacky." A quick hair flip, and then Rebecca lifted her tiny body off the couch and swayed down a hallway.

Liv had said nothing more than "hi there," and already she felt like a goon. *Just my luck,* Liv thought, watching Rebecca retreat down the hall. *I come all the way to London and get stuck with* that.

Luckily, Liv's other roommate (*flatmate,* she reminded herself) was good-ol'-Becky's polar opposite. Anna, a calm, gorgeous blonde from Sweden, appeared a few minutes after Rebecca had closed her glossy lips and swept away.

Anna introduced herself by confessing that she would have come out sooner to say hello, but she had been avoiding Rebecca since the two of them had arrived at the apartment a few hours earlier. "She promised to show me the photo album from her last beauty pageant," Anna said simply. "I just couldn't deal." Liv could already tell she was going to like Anna.

"So," Liv said, grabbing the handle of her wheelie. She was dying to get out of her jeans—she'd been in the same clothes ever since she left Michigan more than twenty-four hours before. "You guys probably already picked rooms, right? Which one is mine?"

A sweet, high-pitched voice came trilling down the hall. *Rebecca*, Liv cringed as the tiny blonde came swaying back into the living room. Rebecca smiled, visibly glowing as she said dramatically, "Li-uhv, *this* is your room."

Anna glanced around the living room. "I'm sorry, Liv. There are only two little bedrooms, and the couch pulls out. . . . I'm sure it won't be that bad."

Liv turned slowly, surveying the couch. "Right . . . ," she said. She sat down on the couch and felt her butt squish a full two feet through the fabric until it was resting only a few inches off the floor. "Great. Well then, I'm just going to get settled." She smiled weakly.

Anna studied Liv carefully before turning and heading down the hall to her room. She called out, "Let me know if you need anything, okay? I mean it . . . anything."

Rebecca just stood there, arms crossed, batting her cold eyes at Liv. "You're such a good sport, Li-uhv. Ah think you'll be so comfy out here." And then she winked—yes, winked—and trilled a high-pitched laugh as she skipped down the hallway toward her bedroom.

Liv hoisted herself out of the couch and pushed one of Rebecca's suitcases out of her way with her foot. She would have much rather jumped inside the suitcase and stomped on all the clothes, but she realized that probably wasn't the first impression she wanted to make. It wasn't *Rebecca's* fault she was stuck sleeping on a fold out couch. Though Rebecca *had* seemed to get an unnatural thrill from breaking the news.

As she pulled her wheelie out of the corner, Liv spotted a small British flag embroidered on the bottom corner of her suitcase. *Uh-oh,* she thought. She turned the suitcase over and lifted the flap that hid the nameplate. The name Millie Banks stared back at her.

Noooooooooooooo! Reality very quickly sank in: her bag, and with it all of her carefully chosen outfits, was gone. She must have taken the wrong suitcase from baggage claim, and now she was stuck with this one. It was identical to hers—except for the little flag.

The good news was that Millie Banks lived in London, and there was a phone number. Liv could only hope she and Millie had made an even swap so they could easily trade back and laugh about how funny this all was. Though at this moment Liv didn't find anything about the situation amusing.

She eagerly pulled the stranger's suitcase into the middle of the floor and tugged at the zipper—she figured it couldn't hurt to look. As it was, Liv had the jeans and T-shirt she had been wearing for two days, and that was it. She needed *something* to wear on her first day of work, and she quietly prayed that the suitcase would be stuffed with a fabulous selection of designer duds.

It wasn't.

Looking up at her from inside the stranger's black suitcase were seven little white dogs, each embroidered on a different color sweater. She unfolded the turquoise sweater with a dog-in-a-bonnet design and sighed.

As she sat staring at the half-dozen

doggies and wondering what to do next, Rebecca breezed into the living room. Little Miss Texas was going full-speed ahead on a one-sided conversation—Liv suspected that Rebecca enjoyed hearing herself talk, and didn't really care whether anyone was listening or responding.

"Oh, Li-uhv, those are just such cute little sweaters. One doggie sweater a day. Precious. Very chic." Rebecca tinkled out a laugh and swept a pile of Armani from the ironing board into her arms.

"Yeah, they're just adorable." Liv bit her lip and continued. "Rebecca, I don't suppose there's any chance you have anything in one of your suitcases that I could borrow for work tomorrow? I picked up the wrong suitcase at the airport, and as cute as these little collies are, I just don't think they'll cut it."

"Oh, Li-uhv." Rebecca sighed. "Those are *westies*, not collies. And no, I'm afraid I just don't have anything that will work on you—you're too big. Maybe Anna has something in your size?" She tilted her head and smiled. "Besides, Ah just don't think I have anything I can spare. I get oozy about people borrowing my clothes. Stains and such . . ."

"Great," Liv said sarcastically, ignoring Rebecca's jabs. "That's just great. I'll talk to Anna."

"About what?" Anna had just walked into the living room with an enormous apple. She plunked down into the couch, took a bite, and folded her legs up under herself.

"I was just asking Rebecca if I could borrow something to wear to work tomorrow, but she doesn't have anything she can spare." Liv cringed and held up the purple sweater with a dog-in-a-basket design. "I swapped bags with someone at the airport. I'm not sure this is going to go over well at Music Mix. Help?"

"Of course." Anna stood up quickly and headed to her bedroom. As she turned and beckoned Liv to follow, she briefly made a face in Rebecca's direction. "Let me show you what I have."

An hour later Liv and Anna finally stopped laughing long enough to pose for a photo next to the living statue in Leicester Square. When they had first approached the silver figure, Liv thought the statue was metal— but realized it was actually a live person after the mouth released a loud screech and the statue's joints shifted position.

Liv popped a ten-pence coin into the hat in the figure's outstretched silver hand, and jumped when the human-statue robotically shifted position to say thanks. Laughing again, she grabbed Anna's arm and moved toward the center of the square.

"I still can't believe Rebecca thought I was going to be excited about that velour thing." Liv and Anna had spent the whole tube ride from their apartment to central London dwelling on Rebecca's unwillingness to share her clothes. Liv was even more stumped by the fact that after her original no, Rebecca had apparently changed her mind and generously offered Liv a zip-up crushed velvet jogging suit, saying it was "all she could spare."

"I know! She spent the whole morning bragging to me about how she had packed three suitcases so she would be prepared for anything." Anna shook her head and giggled. "There must be *something* she can part with for a day."

"Well, let's celebrate the fact that we got out of the apartment tonight. I have no doubt we would have been stuck watching a fashion show if we had stuck around." Liv switched to a thick Southern drawl. "Ah mean, what on earth is she goin' ta wa-uhr ta-mah-row?"

Anna laughed, and suddenly Liv felt a little bad about making fun of Rebecca. But on second thought, Liv had gotten no signs of kindness from her at all. And life was too short to bother with people who were going to treat her like a second-class citizen. She was just lucky she had Anna to laugh it off with.

They settled onto an empty bench in the center of Leicester Square. Anna had arranged to meet up with two Music Mix interns she had met that morning when she was checking in, and had invited Liv to tag along.

As they sat and waited, Liv leaned back into the bench and gazed around at the pigeons and camera-happy tourists who filled the square. Breathing in the damp London air, Liv couldn't help but think about her mom, Isobel, who had grown up in London. Though her mom had died more than ten years earlier, Liv could still hear her voice—with its lovely, lilting English accent—saying that London was the best place on earth.

What was it that made her believe that? Liv wondered. *Did she ever sit in this square with her friends, looking at the same buildings I am now, when she was a teenager?* After her mother died, Liv had sworn to her father that she would live in London someday. She intended to find out what her mother's life had been like and what had made her love England so much, even years after she had moved away.

"How did you convince your parents to let you come to London?" Anna asked, pulling Liv out of her memories.

"Well, my mom died a long time ago, so it's just me and my dad," Liv explained. "My dad is a photographer, so it helped to play up the whole developing-my-inner-artist thing. And I don't think it hurt that he was offered a gig doing a photo shoot for some rich Italian businessman this summer—he gets to spend the summer on Lake Como in Italy. He seemed to like the idea that we'd be on the same continent. It all just worked out, I guess."

"You're lucky—it sounds like he was pretty cool about it," Anna said, lowering her eyes. "I had the hardest time getting my parents to let me come. My mom is certain I'll be a doctor, and this is about as far from med school as you can get. She told me I could have this summer to 'play,' as she calls it, but I had to promise to re-evaluate my priorities when I get back to Sweden." Anna sighed. "I just wish she would back off some. I mean, I'm nineteen. I should be making my own decisions." Anna shrugged and smiled weakly.

"You're nineteen?" Liv couldn't believe it—Anna was two years older than her, and already out of high school. "Actually, I guess I'm surprised that my dad let me come at all. But he moved out on his own when he was sixteen to take pictures of rock stars and 'live the seventies life.'" Liv made little quotation marks in the air. "I think he feels like he owes it to his childhood self to trust me."

"Wow. Your dad sounds fabulous. The complete opposite of my parents."

"Remember, this is all in theory." Liv smiled, picturing her dad struggling to mix his liberal ideals with his idea of what a good dad should be like. "In reality, he's pretty strict. But we have a lot of fun together." Liv smiled, suddenly missing her dad. "What do you want to do, if you're not into med school?" Liv asked Anna, wishing she had even the slightest idea of what she wanted to do when she graduated from high school next year. She had tried to avoid thinking about it, but realized decision-time was coming way too soon.

"I'm not sure," Anna said, frustrated. "Honestly, I've been dying to work at Music Mix for ages. That's really all I've ever wanted. If this summer goes the way I hope, I'll get a job offer at the end—which I'm sure will devastate my mom." Anna sighed and looked around the square before continuing. "But it's not going to happen, so there's no point in getting my hopes up. I just know I don't want to go to med school—yet. I guess I need some time before I'm forced to figure my life out."

"Does your mom know that?" Liv asked, noticing how upset Anna had gotten while talking about her future.

Anna shook her head. "I've already been accepted into a few great schools for next year, so Mom's taken it as a sign that I'm supposed to go right on to university. Unless something major happens this summer, I'll be at Oxford or Stockholm University in the fall." Anna suddenly broke off, and lifted her arm to wave across the square.

Liv followed her gaze and spotted two guys heading toward them. The taller of the two was looking right at her, and the way his smile spread slowly across his face as Liv looked up made her stomach crinkle into a little ball and somersault around inside her belly.

"Hey, guys!" Anna stood up and gave each of the two guys a hug in turn. "This is my roommate, Liv."

The shorter guy quickly leaned over and kissed Liv on each cheek. "It's lovely to meet you," kiss, "I'm Francesco Cipriani," kiss, kiss, "from Italy." Liv blushed, in shock from the cheek-kisses. Definitely not the way things work in the Midwest.

"Uh, hi. Olivia Phillips. But call me Liv. From Michigan. Ann Arbor. Near Detroit. You know—Motor City?" Liv laughed, and she could feel her cheeks turning redder. This was so weird. She *never* blushed. But for some reason, she had become a full-on dork in the past day, and kept saying the weirdest things. *Motor City? Where did that come from?* As Liv bumbled through her introduction, the taller guy kept looking at her, and finally stopped her rambling by cutting in to introduce himself.

"I'm Colin Johnstone. From merry old England. God save the queen, yeah?" He winked slyly at Liv. Was he making fun of her?

"I am in the mood for a gelato," Francesco declared loudly in his sugary

Italian accent. With a wave of his hand, he motioned across the square. "Join us?"

As they walked over to Häagen-Dazs—ice cream would have to satisfy Francesco's gelato craving—Liv couldn't stop casting glances at Colin, and thinking about her stomach's little loop de loop. Twice in one day she had fumbled through an introduction—Josh Cameron, and now this guy.

Blaming her dysfunctional social skills on jet lag, she decided to give it another try. She and Colin were walking a few steps behind Anna and Francesco, and Colin didn't seem to be much of a talker. Liv found silence unnerving, and often ended up babbling just to avoid it.

"So . . . where in England are you from?"

"Stratford-upon-Avon." Colin cast a sideways glance at Liv, grinning. "Shakespeare's birthplace."

"I guess that's a little more poetic than Motor City, huh?" Liv giggled. "I've always wanted to go to Stratford. I bet it's beautiful there. So much history. And I just love Shakespeare."

"Are you a tragedy or comedy girl?"

"Comedy. Definitely. They're so fun to watch. I've never actually seen Shakespeare live, just the BBC versions on TV. Hopefully I'll get a chance while I'm in London." Liv paused—was she coming across as a total loser, talking about the BBC and Shakespeare?

When Colin didn't say anything, she decided another question might help. "I guess you've probably seen a lot of theater, being from the Land of Shakespeare?"

Colin nodded. "I actually played Demetrius in *A Midsummer Night's Dream* at school. Twice."

"You're an actor?"

"No. Both times the play was awful. I'm not sure why I even bothered the second time." They both laughed, then more silence. Finally he continued, "There's a show playing now that looks really good. *Deception*, I think. It's a modern version of *King Lear*. Have you heard of it?" Liv shook her head. "If you're interested, maybe we could see if . . ."

Colin broke off midsentence as Anna grabbed Liv's arm and pointed at a billboard overhead. She had burst into a fit of laughter. Josh Cameron's soft brown eyes were twinkling down at them from overhead. As embarrassed as she was about The Incident from earlier in the day, Liv loved that Anna already felt comfortable enough with her to laugh at her dorkiness. The story *was* pretty funny.

Liv's face flushed as she was forced to share the details of her run-in with Josh Cameron once again. She shrugged casually at the end of the story, hoping Colin and Francesco wouldn't see how truly mortified she was.

As Liv followed the others inside Häagen-Dazs—Anna was *still* giggling—she couldn't help but wonder what might have happened if she and Colin had finished their conversation. *Did he just almost ask me out?* Liv wondered, desperate to know what he had been *this* close to saying. Sighing, Liv realized the moment had passed.

Don't Worry, Be Happy

The next morning, Liv woke to find Rebecca staring at her from the kitchen. She was leaning against the edge of the counter, slicing a grapefruit. She greeted Liv with a chirpy "Good day, sunshine!" and an off-key rendition of the classic Beatles' song.

Liv murmured something rude under her breath and rolled over, checking the time. Seven on the dot. She briefly debated whether to give herself the additional fifteen minutes until her alarm was set to go off, but decided against it. Not a good day to risk it, especially since the time difference—and jet lag—was really messing with her sleep schedule.

Liv hustled past Rebecca toward the

shower, eager to get ready and get out of the apartment. She and Anna had avoided saying it out loud last night, but neither of them wanted to show up at their first day of work with Rebecca in tow.

An hour later Liv had squeezed herself into the slightly too small black skirt and light blue T-shirt Anna had lent her the night before. Her green sneakers would have to do—her feet had topped out at a massive size ten in ninth grade, so they were about twice the size of both Rebecca's and Anna's.

With an hour to spare before she had to be at the Music Mix offices, Liv peeked into Anna's room to see if she was ready to go. Anna, only half dressed, made a face and agreed to escort Rebecca to work. "Save yourself," Anna said quietly. "No need for both of us to be stuck with her. But you owe me."

Liv smiled gratefully at her roommate, grabbed her bag, and headed for the door. A coffee at one of the cafés around Oxford Street should make her feel like a real Working Girl. She closed the door behind her and skipped down the stairs.

When Liv arrived at Music Mix at ten to nine, Gloria was singing at the front desk.

She greeted Liv with a little wave and a spin that made her frilly orange dress spin out around her.

"Good morning!" Liv waved back. She was in a great mood—it had been a fabulous morning. She had found a perfect little café just around the corner from the Music Mix offices, and had spent the past half hour relaxing at a quaint table by the window.

Gloria directed Liv to the orientation conference room, where Liv collected a folder with her name on it, then grabbed a free doughnut and cup of tea. As she paged through the folder and munched her doughnut, Liv took inventory of some of the other people entering the room. Some people were *too* cool, and skulked into the room without saying hello (the James Dean guy in leather pants and the snobby purple-haired girl in striped tights were immediately on Liv's "to avoid" list—they didn't even lift their eyes to acknowledge that anyone else was in the room).

Others nodded or smiled in her direction, and looked around uncomfortably. Liv later learned that the pretty Asian-American girl wearing six-inch platform boots just looked grumpy because her shoes were pinching.

Liv was the most impressed with the few people who came in and actually said something. Francesco was the most outgoing, bounding into the room like an electron and kissing everyone. Colin slid into the room behind him, shyly shooting Liv a cute little smile as he took a seat against the wall.

Just a few minutes before nine Anna showed up with Rebecca, who was decked out in an all-white pantsuit with a bright green tank under it. Liv had to admit that it was pretty hot, and definitely daring. Anna didn't look happy, but perked up when Liv pushed a doughnut her way.

Rebecca quickly introduced herself to everyone in the room, starting with James Dean, who was forced out of his one-man world to make eye contact. Rebecca seemed to have learned personal skills overnight, since she made her way deliberately around the room, dishing out compliments and witty little remarks to each person in turn. As she swept past Liv, Rebecca flashed her a gleaming smile. Confused, Liv just stared back.

A loud, raspy sigh from the doorway broke through the awkward small talk, and everyone turned to see who had entered the room. A shortish, thirtysomething guy with tan teeth and pants to match was staring around at the twenty-five people gathered in the conference room. He moved to the head of the table and began to speak.

"Brown. That is what you'll call me. Not Simon. Not Mr. Brown. Just Brown." *So this is Simon Brown,* Liv mused. *Interesting rule.* She wondered if he knew his tooth color matched his name. "I am the head of this program, and I expect that each of you is prepared to work as hard as I do. You have been given an opportunity that many would die for. Consider yourselves lucky to be here." *A bit overdramatic, isn't he?* Liv thought. "Now. Inside the information folder each of you has received, you will find your summer project assignments. You're welcome."

There was a rustling as people sifted through their folders. Liv pulled a sheet of paper from the back of her folder that said "ASSIGNMENT: Olivia Phillips." Scanning it quickly, she spotted what she was looking for. Three little words that would shape the outcome of her summer: "Coordinator, *Hits Parade*."

Liv couldn't believe it. *Hits Parade* was *the* hottest show on TV. The most fabulous celebrities all swung by Music Mix Europe to promote their latest movies or albums, and the supersexy Andrew Stone played the day's biggest video hits. She read further:

The *Hits Parade* Coordinator will assist in the following:
Audience Control (*Bouncer Liv. Nice.*)
Celebrity Attendance (*What does* that *mean?!*)
Booking Confirmations
Production Support, including time-management (*uh-oh*)
Segment Writing
Administrative Duties, as needed

"What's your assignment?" Anna was reading over Liv's shoulder. "*Hits Parade*?! That's so great! You are going to have *so* much fun."

Liv agreed. She had definitely gotten lucky. "How about you?"

"Wardrobe in the Features Department. Sounds good to me. I like clothes—" Anna was cut short by a squeal coming from the other side of the table. Rebecca was glowing, and flapping her paper around in the air. She had successfully turned all eyes toward her, and she took the attention as her cue to share.

"Events Team. First Assignment: Josh Cameron Concert! Oh, my dad is going to be so excited." Liv wanted to puke. The thought of listening to Rebecca gloat about the Josh Cameron concert for the next month was sickening. And the way Simon Brown was smiling at Rebecca as she flipped her hair and drawled on was infuriating and kinda gross. He seemed to be taken with her. For that matter, so did all the other guys in the room. Liv had to admit, Rebecca *was* pretty. But she was also so *weird*, and apparently bipolar.

"You. *Hits Parade* Coordinator." *Oh God,* Liv thought, *is Simon Brown talking to me?*

"Yes, Mr. . . . uh, I mean . . . yes, Brown?"

"You're the lucky one this year." Simon Brown huffed out a wheezy laugh. "The *Hits Parade* coordinator has the profound good fortune of serving a unique duty. You'll be at the heart of the action." He paused for dramatic effect. "My assistant."

Was he serious? She was going to be his assistant? Things had just gone from best to worst. Anna grabbed Liv's hand under the table and squeezed. Liv managed a weak smile and muttered a tiny "thanks" before following her new boss out of the room to settle in at her summer desk.

"You. Here." Simon Brown was beckoning to Liv from the inner chamber of his office. She was finally getting settled in at her desk—just outside his door—and pretended she hadn't heard him.

Though she was positioned in a prime location near the *Hits Parade* studio, her "desk" was really just a small table jutting out into the hallway, en route to the coffee machine. She had to suck her belly up against the table edge every time someone needed to get past her. She felt like a toll-booth operator. Maybe she would start charging.

As Brown called out again—only slightly louder this time—Liv decided she really couldn't ignore him, though she couldn't imagine what on earth he needed, considering it was ten o'clock in the morning, she had just fetched him a coffee, and he had been snacking on doughnuts since nine.

He thought he had been sly about the doughnuts, but she had noticed. He was one of those people who took three of the best doughnuts before anyone else had a chance to take one. Inevitably, this meant that some poor, patient soul who had waited his or her turn would get stuck with the crusty, oozy leftover cherry-filled messes while people like Simon Brown gorged on the good stuff.

She slid out of her chair and approached his door. "Yes, Brown?"

"I need you to fetch the contract I just printed." He didn't look up. Liv stood in the door, trying to decide how to tell him that she had no idea where the printer was.

"Uh, Brown? . . ."

"GO, GIRL!"

Yowza. That guy could yell. *Okay, I'll be going now.* Liv smiled slightly and slid back out the door and into the hall. *Well, where to begin?*

Liv shuffled down the hall, gazing into each empty room. The Music Mix office was laid out in a weird, mazelike octagon. Every time Liv thought she had made a complete circle, and expected to see her tollbooth around the next bend, she was in a new wing altogether. She hadn't found a printer, but if anyone ever asked her for the inflatable gorilla costume, she now knew where to find it.

Turning the thirty-seventh corner (how did this building have so many hallways?!), Liv bumped into a familiar figure—Colin.

His expression mirrored Liv's own panicked face. Looking at him, Liv couldn't help but laugh.

"What are you looking for?" she asked, realizing she probably wouldn't be able to help.

Colin held up his hands. "The water-cooler. How big *is* this place?"

Liv pointed behind her. "I spotted a watercooler three turns back. Left, then right, then right again. You can't miss it." She giggled. *Am I flirting?* she wondered, noticing that her stomach was doing flip-flops and she had just *giggled*! "What department are you working with?"

Colin scratched his chin. "The Department of One: Andrew Stone. I think my production internship is really just a fancy way of saying 'personal assistant.'" Colin had barely looked at Liv as he spoke—he seemed focused on something just over her shoulder.

"Ooh . . . I'm the *Hits Parade* coordinator." Liv couldn't conceal her enthusiasm. *Yep, definitely flirting.* "We'll be working together!"

Colin shifted from foot to foot and gave her a thin smile. He glanced quickly over Liv's shoulder again. "Right. I, uh, have to get going. See you later, yeah?" He breezed past her and turned the corner.

Did I just say something stupid? Liv wondered, watching Colin hustle off down the hall. Confused, she continued her quest for the printer. The next left led Liv into the round Music Mix front lobby. She stood in the center of the hundred television screens, confused and not sure how she'd gotten there.

"What's wrong, Olivia?" Gloria looked up from her desk. She looked genuinely concerned.

"Hey, Gloria. I'm looking for the printer. Mr., uh, I mean, Brown wanted me to fetch a contract for him. You can call me Liv, by the way. Everyone else does."

"Oh, Liv. I'm so sorry." What did that mean? Gloria's face morphed into a pitying smile. "Brown's printer is in his office. He does this every year. Some sort of power thing."

Liv groaned. "You're serious, aren't you?" Gloria nodded. "Great. That's just great. Thanks for the tip."

"No problem." Gloria shot Liv the same pitying look again. "Let me know if it gets too bad. I think I can help."

Okay, that wasn't exactly reassuring, but

Liv appreciated the offer. "Thanks. Just one more thing—how do I get back to his office?" Gloria laughed, and pointed to one of the many doorways leading out of the lobby.

Back at Simon Brown's office, Liv knocked quietly at the door and made her way inside. He was sitting at his desk, feet up, tan teeth flashing an arrogant smile. She walked over to his desk and plucked five printed pages from the printer in plain view. As she handed them to him, he lifted a glazed doughnut in a salute and pointed to the door.

This could be a very long, very annoying summer.

9 to 5

Liv quickly came to realize that her idealized notion of what a Music Mix internship would be—days joking around with celebrities and nights spent at fabulous clubs and parties—was way off base. The reality was that her days were long, and she rarely got home before nine. A lot of the other interns had been going out after work, but Liv was stuck at her desk most nights until at least eight, finishing busywork for Brown.

Liv spent much of her first week doing meaningless errands: fetching Brown candies every thirty minutes, bringing him paper towels from the "loo," even being called in to press play on his CD player. She had almost no time to eat lunch, let alone mingle in the halls to get details on parties that—even if she did know about them—she would surely need to *sneak* into.

All the interns quickly learned that the Music Mix office was jam-packed with staff employees who thought they were the stars of the music industry, and who did everything in their power to keep interns from thinking too highly of themselves or getting invites to anything. Liv never failed to be impressed by the cool exterior these industry divas maintained. But eventually she realized that they were just as desperate to talk to celebrities as any of the interns were—they were just a little better at hiding it.

Liv's first (disappointing) brush with fame at work was meeting the supersexy Andrew Stone. He dropped by Simon Brown's office Tuesday morning, and on his way to the *Hits Parade* studio he swung through Liv's tollbooth for a cup of coffee. In person, Andrew Stone reminded Liv of a caricature of his TV persona. He was all winks and thumbs-up and smooth hair. Like a good TV star or slimy politician, he stopped to introduce himself and ask a few generic questions.

"Tell me, Olivia," he said, leaning

toward her, all intense and faux interested, "what's *your* music style?" As Liv deliberated, Andrew Stone gazed past her with a polished smile on his face, mouthing "hiiii" to everyone who passed. Liv had to think quickly.

She couldn't really admit the truth to Mr. Pop himself, could she? Would it be a faux pas to reveal that her music obsessions were mostly limited to seventies and eighties stars? She had grown up listening to old albums and light FM radio with her mom, and she couldn't help it—she was addicted. Of course, she had a few current faves (top of the list: Josh Cameron), but the real deal would be an opportunity to time warp and work at Music Mix in the days of ABBA or The Bangles.

She decided to risk it and go with the truth. It looked like he wasn't really listening anyway. "I really like Josh Cameron, but I'm also a big eighties junkie."

"Well, that's great, Olivia." Bingo. Not listening. "I'll see you on set later, yeah?" He pointed little finger guns at her and strutted toward the studio.

On her first afternoon of work Liv found out what one of her assignments—Audience·

Control for *Hits Parade*—meant. She was sent into the studio and told to "get things under control." Easier said than done. She opened the door to the small set and was greeted by fifty screaming fans. They had all been herded into a large roped-in area, and were jostling to get to the front of the fence.

As soon as she walked toward the ropes, people began shouting and gesturing at her. She heard it all—from the desperate and jealous "Hey you, how'd you get on that side of the rope?" to "Yo, sexy girl! Hook me up, yeah?" It was Liv's responsibility to quiet the screaming group and get them seated. The task gave Liv a good idea of what a shepherd would have to go through if his flock could talk.

Once she had them in their seats and had turned them over to the amateur stand-up comedian (who was brought on set each day to "get the peeps in the mood"), Liv had to hightail it back to the celebrity holding tank (aka Green Room), where she was responsible for the comfort of that day's guest star.

Initially Liv had been psyched about Star Control—she would get to meet and assist all of the celebrities who came by the set. Wrong-o. Turned out the real stars all have their own entourage, and Liv was left to deal with the overstressed and strung-out Personal Assistants To The Stars.

On Wednesday she had to deal with both Assistant One and Assistant Two to Kevin Landeau. Kevin insisted that there be two liters of completely flat, room temperature Sprite waiting in the Green Room (apparently he had had a rough night on Tuesday, and had already lost his lunch on a panicked and near-tears Assistant Two). That alone wouldn't be bad, but he had insisted that the flat Sprite be in sealed, unopened one-liter bottles.

Liv spent forty-five minutes working with Assistant One on the logistics of flattening the soda, then remelting the safety seal so Kevin could hear the *click* upon opening his Sprite. Liv celebrated her job-well-done later with a flat Sprite in a resealed bottle—Kevin had opted for orange juice instead.

One of the big perks of Liv's position—which was directly related to one of the worst aspects—was her responsibility to clean up after the celebrities and their entourages. Initially Liv had been horrified by the disaster the Music Mix guests left behind in the Green Room. But once she realized that the leftovers were fair game, she came to appreciate the full platters of food and snacks that were almost always sitting untouched in the midst of strewn trash, bottles, and cigarette butts.

Because she rarely had time to grab herself anything for lunch—thanks to Simon Brown's irritability around noon every day—Liv quickly found that the Green Room leftovers were a welcome treat. That first week of work, she pulled Anna out of the wardrobe department several afternoons so they could sneak into the Green Room to devour the tasty leftovers.

"Is it pitiful that we've resorted to eating someone else's trash?" Liv asked Anna as she bit into a forkful of mashed potato Wednesday afternoon. "It just feels wrong— and kinda depressing."

Anna shrugged, stabbing a piece of chicken from the barbecue platter that was laid out in front of them. "Maybe a little pitiful," she agreed. "But delicious."

"True." Liv buttered a piece of corn bread, relishing the taste of American food. She couldn't help but miss some of the comforts of home—she had never been much of a cook, and her internship didn't pay enough to eat out in London. "So, what do you think? We're halfway through the first week. Is Music Mix everything you thought it would be?" Liv and Anna hadn't gotten any time alone to talk since Monday—Rebecca was always within earshot—and Liv was eager to finish the conversation they had started in Leicester Square a few days before.

"Honestly, yes, it is," Anna said passionately. "Liv, this is exactly what I want to do. I mean, I always sort of knew that, but I didn't really want to give up everything to get a job here until I gave it a try. But now that I'm here, I don't ever want to leave."

"That's good, isn't it?" Liv asked, studying her roommate's reaction.

Anna flinched slightly before answering. "Yeah, it's great."

"Okay, roomie, that wasn't very convincing. Want to try that answer again?"

Anna leaned back into the brown leather couch. "I'm glad I know what I want to do. What I'm not happy about is how hard it is to get a job here. And I just don't think I can give everything up—college, scholarships, my mom's dreams—on the off chance that this might work out."

"Anna, your mom's dreams aren't the

same as your dreams. What do *you* want?"

Anna released a deep sigh. "It's not that simple. My mom has done everything in her power to make sure I've gotten everything I wanted my whole life. Now, if I postpone college and pursue this dream, it would be like stabbing her in the back. She really wanted to be an actress when she was younger, but she gave everything up to make sure our family would be comfortable and happy. So I don't think it's fair for me to go all selfish now and say, 'Hey, thanks for everything, but I just don't care what you think or want.'" She broke off, winded. "Sorry, Liv, didn't mean to go off. . . . I'm just frustrated."

"That's okay. I wish I could do something. I feel totally useless." Liv couldn't imagine the pressure Anna was dealing with, and she didn't really know what to say.

"Can we change the subject?" Anna said, flustered. "I really hate talking about it."

"If that's what you want. But know that I'm here for you whenever."

"Thanks," Anna said, smiling. "But I'll be fine. Now, let's talk about something more pleasant."

"Okay . . . ," Liv said.

"I don't mean for that to sound rude—I guess I just need to figure out how to deal with this on my own."

"But you shouldn't have to deal with it on your own. That's what I'm here for." Liv grinned.

"Thanks, Liv." Anna rubbed her belly contentedly. "I should probably get back soon. I'm stuffed anyway."

Liv had completely forgotten about work. She had no idea how long she'd been gone from her desk, but suddenly realized Simon Brown was probably wondering where she was. He never actually wanted her around, but he liked to know she was available whenever he needed her. She usually tried to saunter past his office or cough loudly at least every thirty minutes—it seemed to comfort him. "Yeah, I should get back too. Thanks for lunch."

"No, thank you. Same time tomorrow?"

"It's a date."

That night Liv got home from work at nine, completely pooped and ready for bed. When she walked through the front door, she almost ran into Rebecca, who was sitting cross-legged in the middle of the living room, staring into a giant bright white screen. Liv, stuck somewhere between amused and mildly frightened, stood and stared.

Rebecca turned around and instructed with a sigh, "Oh, Li-uhv, please stop staring. Haven't you seen a sun lamp before?" She went on to explain that the sun lamp had been shipped in by Rebecca's father to "prevent the saddies." Liv just shook her head and holed away in Anna's room until Rebecca announced that she was a "new woman." Liv took that as her cue that it was safe to return to the living room.

"Ah feel so much better," Rebecca purred to Liv as she floated down the hall to her bedroom. "It's so important that I stay sunny and rosy. You know, Li-uhv, Ah'm in charge of the Josh Cameron concert, and there are just so many people who are depending on me."

Liv mustered up a thin smile. *There it is,* she thought. Liv knew this wouldn't be the last time she would have to listen to Rebecca talking about her überimportant role organizing the Josh Cameron concert. They had only been at Music Mix two days, and already Rebecca had taken every opportunity to make sure everyone knew just how critical her internship assignment was.

Anna and Liv were forced to endure the worst of it, since they had to listen to Rebecca ramble on both at work and at home. But what made it worse was that Rebecca seemed to have mastered multiple personalities, and her sweet Texas Belle character from the office was usually replaced by a self-centered, somewhat evil Crazy at home. Anna and Liv had realized their best coping strategy was just to keep their distance.

The unfortunate dilemma was that Rebecca loved to hear herself talk, and often sat in the living room waiting for her flatmates to come home so she could lock them in to one of her famous one-sided conversations. Liv had exhausted her patience for Rebecca's little "quirks" already, but Rebecca didn't seem to get the hint, and things at the apartment continued to spiral from bad to worse.

Exhausted, Liv arrived home from work on Thursday night only to find herself stuck outside the apartment door. When Anna finally heard her banging and came to let her in, Liv discovered that a huge treadmill had made its way into the living room. Liv didn't even bother to question how on earth this monolithic structure had found its way through the door—she knew it had something to do with Rebecca. The monstrosity was stuffed into the corner of the room next to Liv's couch-bed, and it was jutting out over the first seven inches of the front door, preventing it from opening.

Liv carefully approached Rebecca for an explanation, and was greeted with a frustrated sigh. "Oh, Li-uhv, haven't you noticed? The heels in Europe are just so much higher than they are in Texas." Liv stared back at her blankly. Another *don't-you-get-it?* sigh, and Rebecca continued her drawl. "Ah have to practice walking in my heels *somewhere*. You know, Li-uhv, you're welcome to use it. Ah'm sure you're eager to get yourself some pretty heels one of these days—those sneakers are so late nineties."

Ah, yes, Liv thought, once again pointedly ignoring Rebecca's insult. *This is a perfect explanation. She is going to practice walking in heels on a treadmill. Completely logical.*

Liv's bedroom was slowly being taken over by Rebecca's strange, creepy obsessions. And to top it off, a peculiar smell had started to invade the living room, and was getting worse by the day. But Liv didn't have time to figure out what the smell was, since she had finally gotten ahold of Millie

Banks, the westie sweaters owner, who was so excited to get her "darlings" back that she was on her way over to Liv's apartment to make the suitcase swap.

Millie stayed for two hours, giving Liv a full background on the origin of the sweaters. Tired and weirded out, Liv finally got her to leave after handing over her Ann Arbor address so the woman could send Liv a personalized thank-you sweater for the suitcase's safe return.

By the end of her first week of work, Liv was completely worn out. She was frustrated from dealing with Rebecca, cranky from lack of sleep, and angry with her boss. Simon Brown had grown increasingly smug and arrogant throughout the week. He was constantly hurrying Liv out of his office with a harsh "Go, Girl!"

Friday morning Liv woke with a splitting headache and an attitude to match. Rolling out of bed twenty minutes before she had to leave for work, she kicked her leg straight into the treadmill. She released an enormous growl and limped to the bathroom with a huge scowl on her face. The scowl stuck through breakfast and the whole tube ride into work. When she stomped into the office at eight, Gloria looked up from her newspaper and whistled, "Whoa, girl, remind me to stay out of your way. . . ."

Liv stopped for her mandatory morning check-in at the boss's office, where she was greeted by a surly-looking Simon Brown. He pushed his coffee cup across the desk at her, and barked, "Go, Girl!" without looking up from his newspaper. Liv spotted the headline—CHRISTY BITES BACK!—and perked up slightly. Simon Brown only read the gossip pages when he was in a good mood.

Settling into her desk a few minutes later, Liv tried to throw herself into her work. She didn't even bother to look up when she felt someone shuffle to the coffee machine just before nine. She usually muttered a quick hello or chatted for a few minutes (Liv had gotten to know most of the other interns during their morning coffee runs), but that day she just flipped through the pile of nonsense Simon Brown had left on her desk to "deal with," and sucked in her belly to let the person pass.

A few minutes later the same person approached her desk from the other side, coffee in hand. Whoever it was was looking at her, lurking around the side of her chair. Annoyed, she squeezed in even closer to her desk. The person didn't pass. Clearly, whomever it was expected that Liv would move completely out of his or her way.

She had just about had it with Music Industry Divas; the übercool nobodies who worked at Music Mix all thought they were somebody, and treated interns the way they themselves were treated by real stars. It was a vicious cycle. With an enormous sigh, Liv stood up and violently pushed her chair back, shooting the lurker a look that could kill.

"Olivia." Gulp. The lurker was none other than Josh Cameron. "I thought that was you." Liv panicked. *He remembers me? Is that good or bad?*

"Oh. Hi. Um, sorry about that." Liv didn't quite know what she was apologizing for, but she babbled out something to mask her discomfort. What did one say to Josh Cameron? "So, uh, how are you?"

Josh Cameron laughed. "I'm doing well. It seems the same can't be said for you." His eyes twinkled, brightening her mood. "Bad day?"

"Not anymore." *No!* Liv could not believe she had just said that. "I mean, you know, I'm not really a morning person." She smiled slightly. "But I guess you figured out the other day that I'm not really an afternoon person either. Sorry about the revolving door thing." *That's just perfect,* Liv thought. *Remind him about what an idiot you were on Monday. You wouldn't want him to forget.* "So, uh, what are you doing here?"

"I'm meeting Andrew Stone for breakfast."

Yum, Liv thought. *Breakfast of Champions.*

He smiled and continued, "I'm scheduled to play my new single on *Hits Parade* next week."

"Oh, that's great," Liv answered with a very uncharacteristic giggle. *Stop talking NOW!* "Well, I guess I'll see you then—I'm the *Hits Parade* intern this summer."

"I'll look forward to it," Josh Cameron said, smiling. "Are you just in London for the summer?"

Liv stared unblinkingly at him. *Is he actually interested in what I'm saying?* "Yeah, just the summer. Of course, they want me for longer—but I'm in huge demand, so I'm only willing to give them the summer." *What?!* Liv's eyes widened as her mouth spilled out more and more nonsense. *Are you trying to be funny?*

She smiled weakly, torn between wanting him to stay near her forever and wanting him to go so she couldn't humiliate herself any more. "Are you living in London now?" she asked, though she already knew the answer.

"Yeah, just for a while. I find it enchanting. You?"

"Mmm-hmm, enchanting," she repeated. "Sooooo . . ."

He looked down at his watch. A dark curl fell over his right eye. "I should get going."

"Right. Great. Have a good breakfast." Liv lifted her hand in a little salute. She realized she probably looked like a member of Dorks on Parade, and promptly returned her hand to her side.

Josh Cameron laughed, and his eyes lingered on her face for a few nerve-wracking seconds. She instinctively rolled her tongue over her teeth to check for stray food.

"Olivia, you intrigue me." Was he serious? Why was he looking at her like that? "Join me for a night out." He studied her face for a reaction. She stood silent, for once, dumbfounded. The day had just gotten a whole lot better.

"Yeah, sure. Anytime." Liv felt like her

heart had pounded its way right out of her chest and was now thumping away on her desk.

"How's tonight? I'm meeting some friends at a fabulous little club. Come along—you'll have a great time." He scribbled out some details and glided off down the hall. As he turned the corner toward the studio, Liv broke into a celebratory dance. *What just happened?!?* Liv hustled off in search of Anna. This was an emergency.

Life in the Fast Lane

Flushed and sweating and starting to freak, Liv threw her hip against the door to her apartment for the third time and pushed. She was able to nudge it open a full ten inches, and quickly squeezed her arm and right leg through.

As her butt lodged itself into the tiny opening between the hall and the apartment, she was suddenly hit with unsympathetic images of Winnie the Pooh waving and giggling at her from where he was stuck in Rabbit's front door hole. With an unflattering squeeze and a grunt-thrust, Liv eventually wiggled through. Slamming the door shut, she cursed Rebecca and her monstrous treadmill, which was still blocking the front door. *I hate her fit, freakish, stilettoed self.*

Though Liv shouldn't have been surprised at what she found waiting for her in the living room (she realized that she would *never* understand Rebecca), the sight that greeted her was the last thing she ever would have imagined.

The smell that had been growing in the living room—her bedroom—for the past few days had hit an all-time bad. Liv finally understood why. Sitting in the middle of the living room floor, perched atop Liv's silver strappy shirt, was a teeny tiny not-a-dog-not-a-cat creature.

Brown and sort of see-through, the dog (yes, looking again, she could confirm that this odd little creature was definitely a dog) was shaking in its ratlike skin. Its tail, which Liv had to go all squinty-eyed to see, was formed into a curlicue next to its minuscule little butt, perfectly framing the itty-bitty poop that had landed smack-dab in the center of Liv's favorite shirt.

Liv and the dog stared at each other for a good ten seconds, and then Liv broke the standoff to look around the rest of the room. Her eyes scanned from chair to couch to treadmill, taking a quick inventory of the damage. Her pink scarf, her perfect-blue sweater, her backup jeans, her (*nooooooooooooo!*) little black dress, her soft green jammie pants, and the silver strappy shirt—complete with curlicue poop—were strewn around the room.

Her suitcase was exactly where it had been that morning, safely zipped and tucked into the corner of the room under Rebecca's sun lamp. But in the corner of her suitcase, there was now an itsy-bitsy hole. This horrid little creature had clearly decided that a thinly chewed hole was the best way to extract the items in her suitcase one by one, just like a tissue box. Her favorite black skirt—which, along with her silver shirt, was on the roster for tonight's date—was half in the hole, half out, winking at her.

Heaving a huge sigh, Liv kicked off her shoes—briefly considering whether this was a safe move with Hell Dog in the living room—and flung herself on her bed-couch. Staring at the dog, which had been following her movements with its eyes, like one of those freaky Victorian paintings, Liv was startled by the clanging of the church bells outside the window. One, two, three, four, five, six, seven, eight . . .

OH NO! She had just an hour until she

was supposed to be back on the tube to make it to her maybe-date-but-*not*-getting-any-hopes-up meeting with Josh Cameron, Superstar.

As she rifled through her suitcase for suitable underwear, Liv caught a whiff of something across the room that was almost more disturbing than her ruined silver shirt—Rebecca's Gucci eau de parfum. *She* was home. Looking up, Liv fixed Rebecca with her angriest stare. Liv suspected she looked more constipated than angry, but it was the best she could do.

"Oh, Li-uhv, A'm just so glad you're getting along with My Rover. Isn't he just the cutest thing you ever did see?" Liv could only imagine that Rebecca was referring to Liv's new best friend, Hell Dog, who was now curled into a brown dot on Liv's shirt. She had, naively, been under the impression that Rebecca was not yet home, as all of Liv's clothes were still strewn about the room as chew-toys. *Ah, yes,* Liv realized, *this is Rebecca. Is it really safe to assume she would do the normal thing and CLEAN UP!?*

"Rebecca . . ." Liv strained to keep her voice calm, hoping that if she played the part of normal, it would somehow inspire normalcy in Rebecca. "Is this your dog?"

Stupid question, but somehow necessary given the circumstances.

"Ah just couldn't stand the thought of being without my perfect little pooch this summer, so I bought myself a new one. You know, they put dogs in a little holding cell for months when you fly them across the ocean? I wouldn't have gotten my puppy back until the end of the summer, so I figured it was just better to get a new one." Rebecca lowered her voice to a whisper and looked sideways at the freakish creature on Liv's shirt. "Isn't he just darling?"

It was official: Rebecca had just crossed yet another line into Crazy. "When did you buy this thing, Rebecca? And where is it going to live?"

Rebecca's eyes frosted over, giving Liv the look that she had grown so accustomed to over the past week. "My Rover has been here since Tuesday. How on earth have you not noticed?" Rebecca sneered, and rambled on. "Ah've already potty trained him. We keep his little wee-wee pad over in the corner, next to the couch. He just piddles on there, and I replace it when he tells me it's time. Ah hope you don't mind." With that, she turned and swooped up the little see-through creature and strutted back to her room.

Was she serious? This creature would be here for the rest of the summer? Peeing in her room? *Well,* Liv thought, as she rooted around in her suitcase, *I guess that explains the smell.*

Glancing quickly at the clock, Liv decided she would have to deal with Rebecca when she got home. Now was not the time to get into a battle. She only had half an hour to find a new shirt and get herself out the door.

She pulled her black skirt the rest of the way out of her suitcase and assessed the damage. No harm done. Balling the skirt, a pink ruffly bra, and her underwear in her arm, she ran to the bathroom and flew through her shower.

Returning to the living room half-dressed, Liv was relieved to see Anna was home and sitting on the couch, looking just as confused as Liv had been a few minutes before. Anna looked at Liv's panicked face, and her eyes darted to the silver shirt still crumpled in the middle of the floor. "Don't ask," Liv blurted out, more harshly than she had intended. "I have to leave in five minutes to meet Josh Cameron and win him over with my charm and grace, and I now have nothing to wear. Help."

Anna stood up, gave Liv a quick hug, and leaned down to press play on the CD player. "Music therapy," she explained, as ABBA's "Dancing Queen" came pouring out of the tinny speakers.

"Dancing Queen" was undoubtedly Liv's favorite song. She sort of liked to think it was her theme song—she *loved* to dance, and loved that you could totally lose yourself on the dance floor. It was the one place where you could reinvent yourself, act goofy and just go with the music.

"Okay," Anna continued, as Liv danced around the living room. "What look are you going for? Sex kitten? Confident seductress? Naive nobody? All of the above?"

"Anna, you're European—just make me look like I fit in."

Anna thought for a second, then darted off to her bedroom closet while Liv shimmied around the living room singing, *"Dancing queen, young and sweet, only seventeen . . ."* Anna returned a few seconds later, holding a silky, shimmery, icy pink sleeveless shirt. "Try this on. It's perfect."

Liv grabbed the shirt and slipped it on over her pink bra. As it slid over her next-to-nothing breasts and down past her slender tummy, Liv could tell it was perfect. It clung in all the right places, revealing just enough that she looked sexy, yet left enough to the imagination that she looked demure and sophisticated.

Anna breathed out a sigh, and grabbed Liv's hands. The two of them spun around the living room, singing along to the last notes of "Dancing Queen." Just as the church bells outside chimed nine times, they collapsed onto the couch in a fit of laughter.

Liv scanned the crowd gathered near the fountain at Piccadilly Circus. As expected, no Josh Cameron. He had told her to meet him at Meat, some new nightclub in Soho.

Liv had secretly hoped that he would surprise her at the subway and escort her there, but she knew she was being totally unreasonable. He was busy and famous. And this was, after all, not a date. She headed across the street and followed the directions Anna had written for her back at the apartment as Liv had strapped herself into the World's Most Uncomfortable Shoes Ever.

Turning onto the club's street, she spotted a long line that snaked around a brown rope outside an unimpressive brick building. A small sign verified that she had arrived at Meat. Uncertain of what to do next, she mingled around the crowd, half in line, half out. There didn't seem to be any real rules or order, since the bouncers were just randomly picking people out of the crowd and ushering them in. Just when Liv's stomach had begun to curl at the idea of standing on the outside of the rope, smiling and flirting in the hope that she would be chosen to enter, a skinny guy in a suit approached her.

"Olivia." He stated her name so matter-of-factly that she immediately nodded and smiled. "He's inside. He asked me to escort you up. Follow, please." Liv had no idea who this guy was, but just assumed that "he" was none other than Josh Cameron.

Liv followed as Skinny Guy made a tunnel through the waiting crowd and toward the door. He snapped twice, and a bouncer quickly pulled the rope aside to let them pass. Liv smiled at the bouncer. He narrowed his eyes and released what Liv could only assume was a growl.

Skinny Guy hustled through the low, narrow entrance to the club, while Liv struggled to stay upright on her shoes. She wondered if her feet were bleeding yet.

She looked around, trying to take everything in as she trailed behind the suited stranger into the main room of Meat. There were about thirty brown leather booths packed around the perimeter of the room, each one lit by a bare, plain white light bulb hanging from a cord extending all the way down from the superhigh ceilings.

The center of the club held a dark, crowded dance floor. Some sort of R&B music was being piped, quite literally, from pipes that extended out of each corner. A bar at the far end of the room was lit by flickering red lightbulbs. The club left Liv feeling creeped out, but she knew she would never admit that to anyone. This was, after all, one of London's hottest clubs, and the site of her first date with *Josh Cameron*.

She and Skinny Guy had made their way past the booths and were now standing in the back corner of the club, next to the bar. They were directly under one of the pipes, so when Skinny Guy turned to say something to Liv, all she could hear was "ung, uh uh snu." She just nodded her agreement (hoping he had asked something reasonable), and followed as he pulled a curtain aside, moved past a bear-size bouncer, and up an unlit staircase.

They emerged into a dim, thickly carpeted room that reminded Liv of her grandparents' small downstairs den. She suddenly wished she were there now, watching movies and giggling with her cousin Luke while their parents played cards and drank cheap wine at the folding table upstairs.

But she wasn't. She was in London. Standing in front of an L-shape couch packed with no less than fifteen people, all of whom were visibly drunk. Judging from the security guards positioned around the room, and the fact that two of the women on the couch had been on the cover of *Us Weekly* last month, Liv could only imagine she had entered some sort of VIP section at Meat.

Skinny Guy disappeared, and Liv suddenly felt very alone. She stood in the doorway for a few minutes, letting her eyes adjust to the low light. She could feel beautiful faces scanning her own, trying to determine why she was here, with them. Among the stars.

Just when she was about to turn and flee, realizing this must all have been a horrible, cruel joke, she spotted Josh Cameron walking through an archway toward her. She could feel the eyes on the couch watching as he breezed up to her and took her face in his hands, giving her a kiss on each cheek.

"You," Josh Cameron whispered in her ear,

"look stunning. Thank you for joining me."

Blushing, Liv allowed him to take her hand. She squared her shoulders and followed as he led her through the archway and pushed aside another velvety curtain that masked a small hidden room. Apparently, this was the VIP section of the VIP section— Liv was overwhelmed.

Josh Cameron gave Liv's hand a quick tug, and he pulled her toward the other side of the curtain, behind him. As she passed through he let the curtain fall back into place, and it knocked heavily into the side of Liv's head. She grunted rather loudly and pushed it off, trying to act natural.

Tucking a stray curl behind her ear, Liv was relieved to see that Josh Cameron hadn't seemed to notice. His attention had turned away from her and on the people crowded into the long, low booth sprawled out in front of them. Liv quickly scanned the faces around the table—she recognized just about everyone, but had never imagined she'd ever be this close to any one of them.

Taking a breath, Liv managed to muster up a thin, nervous smile. Josh Cameron had moved away from her and slid into a corner of the booth, kissing a few people on the other side of the table as he passed. For a few awkward seconds Liv stood alone again. Her heart was racing, and her stomach was flipping up and down.

This was just too much. Not only was she out with Josh Cameron, but she was living in a picture from *People* magazine's Star Tracks section. Directly across from Liv, in the far corner of the booth, It Girl Christy Trimble was wobbly standing on the table in her stilettos, arms out to the sides, dancing with her eyes closed. Several jaw-droppingly gorgeous guys were holding her hands while she flipped her body in time to the music.

Liv noticed that the song currently piping out of the wall was a dance remix of Josh Cameron's recent single, "Split." The song was amazing, and rumored to be inspired by his recent break from Christy Trimble's best enemy, Cherie Jacobson.

As Liv stood there, starstruck, Bethany Jameson—who was, quite possibly, the hottest starlet in Hollywood—nimbly hopped up on the end of the table and danced alongside Christy. Bethany's thong rested a comfy two inches above the ultralow waistline of her Joe jeans. The two women giggled and shimmied, clearly hamming it up for the benefit of the rest of the table. Both of their mouths were wide open, singing loudly and laughing. Josh Cameron looked delighted.

They finished their routine with a quick hug, and Bethany scooted off the table and onto the lap of one of the guys who had, only moments before, been holding Christy's hand. Christy leaned over to plant a quick kiss on Bethany's cheek (obviously there were no hurt feelings about the guy swap) before taking a long sip from her drink.

Josh Cameron motioned Liv toward him in the corner of the booth, and she adjusted her skirt as she slid in beside him. A few of the Star Tracks subjects glanced up briefly to greet her, then went back to their cigarettes and conversations.

"Drink?" Josh Cameron was pouring himself a short glass of vodka from the center of the table, where a buffet of booze sat in icy buckets next to a platter of mixers.

"Oh, um . . ." Liv hadn't really had a lot of opportunity to drink in Michigan. In fact, she had had a total of one nasty incident involving some sort of licorice liqueur that left her facedown on the toilet seat. Her dad had not been impressed, and frankly, Liv hadn't been so impressed with the morning after.

So, she wondered, *is this the time to give it another whirl? With a table full of It Girls and Josh Cameron?* "Hmm, you know, I think I'll pass for now. I had kind of a weird dinner, and my stomach is a little iffy."

Liv realized her excuse sounded pretty lame—and, on second thought, kind of gross—but figured it was better than the alternative. She already had a visual in mind that involved Bear Bouncer dragging a passed-out Liv from the VIP section with her skirt wrapped around her armpits. *Cute.*

"Olivia, you are astoundingly charming. So All-American Girl." Josh Cameron's dimples deepened as he smiled at her. His eyes were deliciously green. Liv couldn't believe she was here, with him. And it *did* seem a little like a date. "Tell me all about *you.*"

"Oh," Liv said, her tongue tied. "Well, what do you want to know?"

"Everything. I want to know what moves you." Josh stared into her eyes, his expression identical to the front of his last CD cover.

Liv was caught between laughing and crying. *Is he serious?* "Well, okay, um, I, ah, I'm from Michigan. Hmm, and uh, I live with my dad?" *Is that a question?! What's wrong with you, Liv? Say something remotely interesting.* "Oh! I know. My mom actually worked as a VJ at Music Mix in New York before I was born. That's something!" Though it was true, Liv wasn't sure why she had decided to mention that, of all things, to Josh Cameron. Although, her mom's music background did make her feel more worthy of sitting at this table, with all of these celebrities.

"I'm in awe, Olivia." Josh Cameron continued to stare at Liv with a poster boy sort of expression. "You are fascinating."

"Okay," Liv said, averting her eyes from his constant stare. "Well, thanks. But tell me about you! I guess I know a lot, but, well, I s'pose a lot of the stuff I read in magazines isn't really true." She laughed awkwardly, hoping to turn the topic of conversation away from herself.

Josh Cameron's eyes twinkled in the low light as he murmured, "It's all true. If you want it to be." Liv swallowed hard, wondering what, exactly, that meant.

In fact, Liv wasn't quite sure *what* she wanted to be true. The Josh Cameron sitting next to her was a little intimidating . . . and rehearsed. She wasn't sure why, but she sort of felt like he was reading from a script. *But,* she reminded herself as he smiled at her again, *you're on a date—in a VIP room—with Josh Cameron! So who cares?*

Liv let herself melt into the booth while Josh Cameron entertained her with stories of his recent tour, gossip about other celebrities, and his plans for the fall. She couldn't believe the life he led. It seemed so fascinating. And as she sat there, he seemed more and more normal. She soon realized that when her mouth was zipped tightly shut, Liv felt a thousand times more comfortable with him.

So for the next several hours Liv let Josh chatter on and enjoyed the insider gossip. As they stood up to dance sometime long after midnight, crowded among the other celebrities, Liv just smiled silently as Josh Cameron leaned in to share the details of his last party at Chateau Marmont. His hands wrapped around her waist, talking all the while—he never even noticed that she hadn't uttered a word.

West End Girls

"Hang on . . . Christy Trimble, Bethany Jameson, *and* C. J. Jackson were there? And you talked to all of them?" Anna stopped to pick up a strand of handmade beads, checking the price.

Liv had promised to spill all the juicy details of her previous night's date if Anna would spend the day wandering around Portobello Road, Notting Hill's outdoor shopping market, with her. Liv had only gotten as far as dishing the scoop on celebrity sightings from Meat, and already Anna was impressed.

"Yeah, they were all there. And it's weird, because Christy is actually really nice. You know how the tabloids say she gets in catfights with people all the time? Well, she was totally friendly to me."

Actually, Liv thought guiltily, *maybe that isn't exactly true.* In reality, most of the other people at Josh Cameron's table had been pretty self-absorbed and virtually ignored her. But Christy had kissed Liv on the cheek when she left and said how "absolutely stunning" Liv looked, which seemed totally unnecessary and had been a really sweet gesture for a stranger.

"Enough. Stop making me jealous with the guest list—get on to the good stuff." They had made their way to a scarf vendor, and Anna poked her head around a rack to find Liv modeling a purple tiger-striped fur.

"Well, dah-ling, it was simply mah-vehlous. . . ." Liv strutted down the aisle with her huge fake fur. "Okay, so there I was, standing alone in the middle of this weird little room with half the models from *Vogue* staring at me. I seriously thought I was going to die. Thanks for the shirt, by the way. It was perfect."

"No problem. You looked hot. Go on. . . ."

As Liv spilled the details of her date to Anna, she relived each second in her head. She could still smell Josh Cameron's cologne, and she could feel his touch on her hand from when he had led her out of the club at the end of the night. He hadn't kissed her, but she sort of suspected he probably would have if Christy Trimble hadn't stumbled out of the club to throw up just as Liv's taxi pulled around the corner.

Liv smiled as she thought about how Josh Cameron had handed her taxi driver a twenty-pound note and opened the door for her, saying, "I'm so glad you could join me, Olivia. I hope you'll be willing to grace me with your presence again soon." *Okay,* Liv thought, grinning. *Maybe that line was a little cheesy. But it was really sweet.*

"Here's the thing," Liv said, watching Anna wrap a long silk skirt around her jeans and model it in the mirror. "The things he said were almost . . . lame . . . sometimes." She cringed. She didn't really want to ruin her memory of the night with a confession that Josh Cameron was less than perfect—but she couldn't withhold any details.

"Ooh," Anna said, lifting her eyebrows. "Do tell."

Liv quickly shared the "I hope you'll be willing to grace me with your presence again soon" line, as well as some of their other conversations. She gritted her teeth after being forced to say it aloud.

Anna burst out laughing. "Are you serious? He actually said that?"

Liv nodded. She had sort of been hoping Anna would say it was sweet and romantic. But who was she kidding? Liv could only hope Josh Cameron would be a lot less scripted if they went out again. After all, she reasoned, he did have to live up to a certain pop star image, and she wondered if maybe his lame, over-the-top lines were partly because he was in London? Maybe his publicist forced him to say junk like "lovely time" and "grace me with your presence." Maybe there was a book of etiquette that celebrities lived by that she just didn't know about?

"I guess the good news is, it sounds like I'll see him again sometime," Liv flashed Anna a quick, coy smile. She leaned down and picked up a fringed lampshade. As she did, she blurted out, "I just don't want to get my hopes up. Let's be realistic. This is Josh Cameron. Isn't it a lot more likely that he'll never call?"

"He'll call," Anna said confidently. "If he's feeding you lines like that, he's obviously trying to be a gentleman. And it sounds like you had an amazing time. Why *wouldn't* he call?"

"You're right." Liv nodded, though she definitely wasn't so sure. But it couldn't hurt to *hope*. Liv linked arms with Anna as they continued their path up Portobello Road. "So," she asked. "What did you do last night? I feel like I've been hogging the last hour with my story. Dish."

Anna began to speak, but was cut off as her cell phone started to ring. She answered, murmuring something in Swedish to whoever was on the other end of the line.

Liv didn't feel too guilty listening, since she couldn't understand anything anyway. All she could tell was that Anna definitely wasn't enjoying the conversation—whomever it was with. After a few more minutes Anna flipped her phone closed and exhaled.

"Who was that?" Liv asked nosily.

Anna look flustered. "My mom," she said simply.

"Everything okay?"

"Fine," Anna said, walking slightly ahead of Liv. Liv got the hint—Anna's mom had called several times since they'd arrived in London, and every time Anna had refused to talk about it. Liv knew something was going on, but it obviously wasn't any of her business. As usual, Anna quickly changed the subject. "To answer your question about last night—I did absolutely nothing. It was super-relaxing, since even Rebecca went out."

"She did?!" Liv couldn't hide her surprise. *Who would date Crazy?* "With who?"

"You're not going to believe this, but . . . Colin!"

Liv's stomach sank. "Are you serious?" she asked, hoping Anna was joking. There was still a little part of her that couldn't stop thinking about the sweet, kind, funny Colin she had met on her first day in London. She hadn't seen that guy resurface since that first evening in Leicester Square, but there was *something* about him that made her insides clench every time she saw him. But, she reasoned, if Colin was dating Rebecca, maybe she had gotten the wrong impression.

"Completely serious," Anna said. "I have no idea how it happened, but I guess they've been hanging out. I'm trying to get the dirt from Francesco, but he claims there's nothing going on."

This just didn't seem right. But maybe Rebecca was more normal around Colin than she was around her and Anna. She had mastered multiple personalities, so maybe there was a sweet, seductive side that Liv just hadn't witnessed yet. "Well, this should be interesting to watch, if nothing else."

Anna nodded. "Yes, indeed."

"*Oh, Li-uhv*, why are you so pushy?"

Rebecca was not taking Liv's anger about My Rover's behavior very well. In fact, she had interpreted Liv's request to move Hell Dog's wee-wee pad out of Liv's bedroom as a personal attack. Liv was still astonished that Rebecca hadn't yet apologized for the whole curlicue poop incident from the previous evening, but as Rebecca angrily yammered on, Liv realized that there would be no apology forthcoming.

"Sometimes, Olivia," Rebecca continued, "people need to *compromise*. You are living with three other people now—me, My Rover, and Anna—so maybe you should stop being so concerned about you, and think about other people's feelings for once. *Ah mean*, how do you think My Rover feels about all of this?" Rebecca stopped chiding for one dramatic moment, then stormed on. "He's devastated, Liv. Just devastated. He's ashamed that his wee-wee pad is causing you problems. He's been curled up in his little blanky in the corner of the couch all afternoon, pouting. Doesn't that just break your heart?"

"Does *what* break my heart?" Liv blurted out, astounded. "The fact that your dog is currently curled up in *my* blanket on *my* bed? Yes, that does break my heart!" Liv took a deep breath and continued. "Rebecca, I am very sorry that your dog is devastated. But I think it's reasonable for me to ask that you find a nice, cozy place for his *potty mat* in *your* room. Sound good?" Liv crossed her fingers, hoping for a break.

"Oh, Li-uhv." Rebecca swept her see-through dog into her arms and sidled down the hall. "Ah pity you." With that, she delicately closed her bedroom door and left Liv alone in her living room.

Liv rolled her eyes and fell back on the couch. Clearly, logic and rational discussion weren't going to work. Liv leaned over the arm of the couch, gathered up Hell Dog's wee-wee pad, and strolled down the hall. She plunked the mat right in front of Rebecca's door and returned to the living room.

A few seconds later Anna poked her head out of her bedroom door. "Is it safe?" she mouthed, tiptoeing over to the couch.

"Feel like going out tonight?" she whispered conspiratorially.

"Did you hear that conversation?" Liv grumbled. "I'd rather spend the evening at Simon Brown's flat than deal with another second of Little Miss Don't-Mess-with-Texas in there."

"Great!" Anna squealed, before quickly covering her mouth. "I just got off the phone with Francesco," she continued, whispering. "Apparently Colin got tickets to a show from Andrew Stone earlier this week. It's some hot new band that's playing at a club in Shoreditch. I've already laid out a shirt for you on my bed. Throw on your cute jeans, and let's get moving."

"You . . . and I. Were meant . . . to be. But you . . . took the low road, baby . . ."

This is absolutely awful. Liv quickly glanced around the club to see the reaction on other people's faces. Nodding heads and swaying hips surrounded her. *Apparently, I just don't get it.*

Liv had been feeling that way for the past two hours—basically, since she and Anna had met up with Colin and Francesco outside Presence. Presence was a dimly lit, Asian-inspired club that reminded Liv of a

China Buffet restaurant. Slightly tacky and oddly fragrant, it gave her the willies.

Anna had seemed completely at ease walking into the club, but Liv felt her stomach clenching much like it had when she'd arrived at Meat the night before. The scene was very much *not* Michigan. Tiki lamps dotted the walls, and people lounged on the floor around a battered stage.

As the foursome had moved farther into the club in their quest for a table, Liv's eye was drawn to an enormous fish tank decorating the center of the room. After looking more closely, Liv could see human faces peering back at her from *inside* the fish tank. She had stared at the faces until Colin leaned over and explained with a grin, "Men's room."

"Of course," Liv had responded, horrified. She found it disconcerting that everyone else was acting so normally. Were they oblivious to the fact that there was an enormous see-through *toilet* slicing through the center of the room?

Now, several hours later, Liv was stuffed between Anna and a large bearded man, listening to—quite possibly—the *worst* music she had ever heard. As Liv's eyes wandered around the club for *any*one else who shared her pain, she felt a hand brush her arm. Tensing, she turned. Colin was leaning forward, a smile teasing the corners of his mouth.

Liv felt her chest tighten as his mouth moved toward her ear. "This really is astoundingly awful, yeah?" His lilting English accent made the criticism sound almost dignified. Liv nodded, then started to laugh. "Shall we head out, then?" he asked. Giggling uncontrollably now, Liv nodded again. She grabbed Anna's arm while Colin pulled Francesco toward the door. Outside, Liv burst into laughter.

"What's so funny?" Anna asked. "Why did we leave?" Laughing, she continued, "Is it because of the song about pancakes?"

"Hmm, I sort of liked that one," Francesco mused, then chuckled. "I think the song that really got to me was the one about getting stuck in a scuba suit. It was very romantic, but also odd."

"Okay, so I wasn't the only one who didn't *get* that?" Liv asked, still laughing. "Colin, you got those tickets from Andrew Stone?"

Colin nodded. "I'm starting to think my boss may have been playing a joke on me. . . ."

"Hey, Liv." Anna was grinning in Liv's

direction. "Maybe you should suggest a few of those lyrics to Josh Cameron. After last night I'm sure he would be happy to get your creative input."

Liv shot her roommate a faux-angry look. "Very funny," she said. Blushing, she quickly gave the group a shortened recap of her date while they walked toward a fish and chips shop for a late-night snack.

"So you are . . . dating Josh Cameron?" Francesco asked in his soft Italian accent. Though he was asking Liv the question, he looked at Colin as he waited for the answer.

Liv shrugged. "No. I don't think you could call it that. But I guess I'll see what happens." Francesco was still looking at Colin, and Liv sensed there was some weird unspoken thing going on, but she couldn't figure it out.

You hardly even know Colin, Liv thought, rationalizing the awkwardness. *He's obviously not interested—he's hanging out with Rebecca! Besides . . . Josh Cameron, Colin, Josh Cameron, Colin . . . Do you really have a choice if there's even a* chance *with Josh Cameron?*

Liv linked arms with Anna, still perplexed by the exchange she had just witnessed between Colin and Francesco. *Am I missing something?* she wondered. *Am I making a huge mistake?* She studied Colin's form strolling down the sidewalk in front of her. He stopped and turned, holding the door to the fish and chips shop open. As a smile spread across his face, Liv desperately tried to unravel the knot that had formed in her stomach. *Uh-oh,* she thought, recognizing the crush feeling all too well. *What am I going to do?*

I Will Survive

Simon Brown's feet rested comfortably atop his desk, his coffee cup empty next to them. He was trying to read the morning paper but was distracted by his empty mug.

Glancing at the door every few seconds, Brown briefly considered slipping his feet off the desk and back into the loafers sitting at his side. He was tempted to fetch *himself* a fresh coffee. But he was comfortable, and he enjoyed the fact that he had an excuse to be angry.

It was eight fifteen Monday morning, and Liv was running late.

As she hustled past the security guard and swept past Gloria in reception, she knew she was in for it. Simon Brown did not tolerate lateness, and his morning coffee was not a game. Liv knew she had effectively *"ruined his life"* by showing up fifteen minutes late.

After throwing her bag and umbrella in a heap at her tollbooth, Liv adjusted her skirt and cautiously approached his door.

"Good morning, Brown. Did you have a nice weekend?"

"I'm not sure if you're stupid or arrogant," Simon Brown mumbled, "but I believe we agreed that eight would be an appropriate starting time?" He didn't lift his head from his morning paper, but Liv could feel his beady little eyes narrowing.

"Now. You," he continued. "I will take a coffee, as usual, and ask if you might be so kind as to prepare the conference room for our Monday morning meeting. Will you need help, or do you think you'll be able to manage?" Brown tilted his face up and flashed a tan smile in Liv's direction. She suspected there wasn't a lot of love behind those pearly not-so-whites.

"Not a problem, Brown. Consider it done."

"I'll consider it done when I have a coffee in my hand. Please don't play games with me." As Liv made her way to the door,

Brown continued. "Now, I assume you sent a meeting reminder memo out to all interns on Friday?" *Hello. Memo?!* "All interns *will* be in the conference room at ten?"

This was the first Liv had heard of either the Monday morning meeting or a memo. "Yes, sir—uh, Brown. We'll all be there! I'll be back with your coffee in a sec."

"Go, Girl!"

As Liv zipped through her tollbooth toward the coffee machine, she racked her brain for any memory of this meeting.

She couldn't come up with even a glimmer of what he was talking about. But last Friday had been a little scattered, considering the evening's "date" with Josh Cameron. As she pressed the brew button on the coffeepot, Liv formulated a plan. With Gloria's help, she should be able to catch most of the interns on their way in. A little help from her friends should guarantee word would get out to the rest. No worries.

"As I've already made clear, each of you is living a once-in-a-lifetime experience. I trust you have no complaints?" Brown scanned the meeting room, and looked pleased to see no heads shaking.

Amazingly, word about the meeting had

spread in twenty minutes flat. Liv had filled Gloria in on the situation, and Gloria had immediately kicked into action. Apparently, the "forgotten memo" trick was a regular in Simon Brown's book of intern gags. Gloria had a plan to counteract this and several other Brown crises. Liv was grateful to have Gloria's help—she imagined the receptionist could get pretty feisty, and she wouldn't want to be on her bad side.

After pausing to ensure all twenty-five interns were focused on him, Brown continued his pep talk. "You may not believe it, but this summer will soon be even more remarkable for one or several of you." Brown's mouth curved into an uncomfortable smile. "This year, each of you will have the opportunity to participate in Music Mix's VJ for a Day contest. With the cooperation of our very own Andrew Stone, we have arranged an audition date later this summer. This will be your opportunity to show us if you have what it takes to be on-air talent, or if you can effectively work behind the scenes on one of the production teams.

"Perhaps . . . ," he continued, "if you really blow us away, there may be a job offer for one of you at the end." Brown puckered his lips and smugly sat down.

Andrew Stone, who had been slouched seductively in the corner, stood up and cleared his throat. "Right. Are you ready?" He paused. Liv was temped to pump her arm in the air and shout out, "Yea-uh!" but figured it wasn't a good bet.

"The auditions will be held in August, and the winning team's segment will go on the air that same day. We'll include it as part of the *Hits Parade* lineup." Andrew Stone was beaming. "I'm sure you've all watched my stuff, so you know the deal. Your role, as VJ, will be to hold the audience's attention throughout the video countdown, and keep them coming back for more. Obviously, I've mastered it—feel free to look at some of my earlier work for examples of great novice VJing. You can do a skit, a game—hey, you can strip if you like—just come up with the best gimmick, and prove that you've got what it takes to be on the Music Mix VJ team. Someone in this room will be a Music Mix VJ for a Day. Excited?"

Liv glanced around the room. This was crazy. One of these people could possibly *be* a Music Mix VJ? Now this—*this*—was exactly what she had been hoping this internship would be. She wanted to do *real* TV work—not just Simon Brown's grunt work.

Everyone was grinning ear to ear, and chattering nervously with the people next to them.

Simon Brown quickly wrapped up the meeting and sent all the interns back to their departments. As Liv headed off to her tollbooth, Anna caught up with her.

"Liv, we are going to rock at this. Team?"

"Of course!" Liv grinned. "What are we going to do? I'm up for anything except getting naked—that's going a little far, even for me." Anna laughed as Liv quietly mocked Andrew Stone's stripping suggestion.

"Liv, I think this might be my chance," Anna said seriously as they moved away from the conference room.

"You think if we won the audition, you could get a job offer?" Liv inquired. She wasn't so sure—Brown didn't seem like the type of guy to make things so simple.

"I know he said it was only a possibility, but I just have a feeling. We *have* to win this competition. You're in, right?" Anna looked so desperate.

"Absolutely." Liv gave her roommate a quick, reassuring hug—she knew how much Anna wanted this. "We *will* get you a job."

As Liv and Anna wandered back through the halls, they could hear Rebecca's distinctive voice behind them. Liv stopped and glanced over her shoulder. Rebecca was walking with Colin and discussing the competition. From the sound of it, Rebecca was pretty sure she would win. And she seemed to think it would boost her chances if she told everyone how much she wanted it.

"We *must* work together on this, don't you think?" Rebecca purred to Colin. "Of course, I have to focus on the Josh Cameron concert first—Joshie is so sweet, so I just want to make sure everything's perfect— but after the concert we'll focus every ounce of our energy on this. What do you say, Colin?" Rebecca giggled, casting Liv a sidelong glance as she linked arms with Colin and slid past Liv and Anna down the hall.

Colin murmured something quietly in response, and Liv felt a little like throwing up. Though Liv had begun to get used to the idea of them dating—Rebecca and Colin had spent all day Sunday together, and Rebecca had made sure Liv and Anna were informed about *all* the details—Liv felt queasy seeing them together. She couldn't shake the feeling that had swept over her when her eyes had met Colin's on

Saturday—but obviously, she was the only one who had felt something. So she was doing everything she could to forget it.

"Jemma *always* meets and greets one fan at appearances. It's the way she keeps it real." Jemma Khan's personal assistant, Sam, was standing at the door of the *Hits Parade* studio. Liv was inside the studio, arranging ropes and chairs for that afternoon's show.

Sam had been trailing Liv most of the day, announcing things at random. Liv knew Sam wanted her to do something with each of these announcements, but she was never quite sure what. She had found that if she waited a second, Sam would usually expand. This time was no exception.

"Soooo," Sam said slowly, "can you find a fan for Jemma to spend a few minutes with? You know, to keep it real with . . ." Liv smirked. Sam had delivered that line with complete sincerity. She had clearly been well trained.

"No problem, Sam." Liv pulled the velvet rope taut in front of the audience seats. She had to make sure it was clear that the rope was a barrier—yesterday she had come into the studio just before taping to find a girl sitting in the center of the *Hits Parade* stage. Liv had to literally drag the girl back into the fan section, where she spent the rest of the show sulking and shouting out obscenities. Eventually the girl was removed from the set, but not before grabbing a nice, thick chunk of Liv's hair. The audience control portion of Liv's job was truly a delight.

"Liv, you're the best," Sam gushed, relieved she didn't have to mingle with the "regular people" to find her boss a token fan. "Please make sure you don't find a Crazy. Or it's my butt on the line—you know how it is."

"Yes, Sam," Liv sighed. "I know how it is."

And she did.

Liv had spent much of the past week getting to know the *Hits Parade* fans. She studied them, trying to figure out how *not* to act in a celeb-dense situation. The *Hits Parade* audience was a captivating combination of several types of fans—Criers, Desperate Wannabes, Psycho Stalkers— many of whom fell into the "Crazy" category. But she knew who Sam was looking for—a Regular Fan.

Regular Fans were the non-Crazy folk. Regular Fans usually consisted of tourists, preteens, and groups of girlfriends. They were psyched to be on set, and respected the rules of the game.

The Criers could almost be considered Regular Fans, but not quite. They were the people who got teary-eyed and panicky when they could sense that a star was near. The Criers didn't need to *see* the star—it was enough to know the star was close. The thrill of being in or near the Music Mix building could even send them over the edge. Most days Liv found a Crier in meltdown mode just outside the studio. They were unable to go any farther, suddenly overcome by the possibility of a brush with fame.

The Desperate Wannabes, on the other hand, terrified Liv. Desperate Wannabes dressed and acted like stars, and embodied a presence that shouted, *I'm Somebody!* They went to abnormal lengths to get into the studio, because they felt they *deserved* to be there. And they wouldn't take no for an answer. Every moment in the audience was an opportunity to be "discovered," and Liv would *not* be the one to take that away from them. Liv had seen one Desperate Wannabe actually brush off a C-list reality TV star because the reality star was "beneath" her.

The star's ego was severely damaged, and Liv had to do some major pampering to prevent a diva moment.

The real Crazies were the classic nut job fans—the Psycho Stalkers. On Tuesday one Psycho Stalker had found his way into a performer's dressing room and rested nonchalantly on the couch. When the star had returned from rehearsal, the Psycho Stalker was sitting there, sipping a Perrier, and chatting with the star's dog. He greeted the star with a chirpy "g'day," then continued his conversation with the dog. Needless to say, security had him removed from the area.

In addition to audience control, Liv had spent her week attending to various errands for Personal Assistants to the Stars, like Sam. Most of the errands, she guessed, were tasks being shirked by said Personal Assistants so they could grab a cigarette, a coffee, and a break. Liv's job description had listed "celebrity attendance" and "booking confirmations" as her responsibilities; she was pretty sure that didn't mean "dog walker" or "stain remover." However, she was quickly realizing that *Hits Parade* coordinator made her the go-to girl whenever a dog "piddled" on the Green Room carpet or a cup of organic chai spilled on a cashmere tank.

The only thing getting Liv through the workweek was the fact that Josh Cameron was scheduled to perform on *Hits Parade* on Friday, and he had been around the studio all week rehearsing. She hadn't seen or talked to him since their maybe-date the weekend before, but she had spotted him from afar, chatting with Andrew Stone or rehearsing in the *Hits Parade* studio. She was dying to know if Josh Cameron had been genuine when he told her he wanted to see her again.

As she passed the studio one day, casually peeking to see if Josh Cameron was around, Liv spotted Colin and Andrew Stone in a conversation. She paused, waving to Colin through the window. He looked up, ignored her, and turned in the other direction. Andrew Stone glanced over his shoulder to see who was at the window, and—without the slightest hesitation or acknowledgment—returned to his conversation with Colin. Feeling like a total nuisance, Liv hustled down the hall and back to her tollbooth.

Liv wanted to believe she was imagining it, but almost every time she had seen Colin in the office that week, he had quickly turned and gone in the other direction. She wasn't sure what she had done to offend him, but she got the impression that he was avoiding her. Between Colin and Josh Cameron, Liv was starting to wonder if she was invisible.

One afternoon she ran into Colin at Tully's, the coffee shop around the corner from the office, and lingered long enough so they could take the short walk back to Music Mix together. He stayed mostly silent as they made their way up the escalator, and as soon as they passed Gloria's desk he quickly hustled off, casting glances over his shoulder and generally acting weird. *Rebecca must be getting to him,* Liv thought, smiling.

When Friday, the day of Josh Cameron's *Hits Parade* session, finally dawned, Liv's nerves were out of control. She was frustrated that she hadn't talked to him all week, but she knew he was busy promoting his single. There were a million good explanations. So, positive attitude in hand, Liv dressed herself in her Friday best and glided off to work, hopeful that today would be the day.

She arrived at her tollbooth a few minutes before eight and found a note from Simon Brown that read:

2 Sheepskin throws
14 Red Bulls (NOT 13)
Stuffed pig

After rereading the note a few times, Liv finally gave up and walked to the lobby to find Gloria. Gloria was sitting at her desk, twisting one long dreadlock around her finger while she sang along to "Split."

"Hey, girl. What'd he do this time?"

Liv passed the note across Gloria's desk. "I need you to help me translate. Any idea what this means?"

Gloria glanced at the note, and then passed it back. "Josh Cameron is on *Hits Parade* today?"

"Yeah," Liv responded. "Why?"

"That's his usual request. Brown must want you to get the Green Room ready. You can get the sheepskin throws from Andrew Stone and buy the Red Bull at the market on the corner." Gloria paused, then reached under her desk. "And here"—she triumphantly held up a worn purple pig—"is your stuffed pig." She smiled. "Good?"

Liv just nodded. "Thanks. Again." This was too weird. Why did Gloria have a stuffed purple pig under her desk? And more important, how scary was it that Josh Cameron wanted a stuffed pig waiting for him in the Green Room when he arrived?

Liv spent the rest of the morning preparing the Green Room and getting the studio ready for that afternoon's audience. Her stomach did a little backflip each time the door to the Green Room opened or someone entered the *Hits Parade* studio—she was constantly on pins and needles waiting for Josh Cameron to arrive.

Finally, around one, Josh Cameron breezed into the studio. A small entourage of PR people, personal assistants, and a crew from the *Star* accompanied him. He glanced in Liv's direction, and then instructed one of his assistants to clear the room so he could rehearse in private. Liv and several other interns were shooed out of the way as Josh Cameron began singing his scales.

Around two, just before *Hits Parade* went on air, Liv was summoned to the Green Room. *This is it,* she thought. She was bummed that Josh Cameron hadn't said hello earlier, but she figured things had been hectic. *Whatever,* she thought. *Now is better than never.*

When she knocked at the door a few minutes later, Skinny Guy (her buddy from Meat) greeted her. He was wearing a suit again.

She could see Josh Cameron in the background, strumming his guitar on the couch. He briefly looked up, gazing through Liv with a blank expression. She smiled in his direction, but Skinny Guy moved slightly to block her view.

"Yes," Skinny Guy began. "He will need Gummi Bears and a toothbrush. That will be all."

Liv stared for a moment. *Is this for real?* The look on Skinny Guy's face suggested that yes, this was for real—and that she had better hop to it. Liv nodded, casting a quick glance over Skinny Guy's shoulder, then turned to leave. She headed out onto Oxford Street in search of Gummi Bears.

Forty-five minutes later, Liv sat at her tollbooth, weary and disappointed. She had delivered the requested items to the Green Room and received nothing more than a short thanks from Skinny Guy. No "hello, nice to see you, have a good one," nothing. She was near tears and incredibly embarrassed.

She didn't know what she had expected. Did she want Josh Cameron to embrace her and sing to her, announcing their love to the *Hits Parade* audience? *Um, no. Creepy.* But she had expected a glimmer of recognition from him. At the very least, he could have said hello. She was humiliated that she had apparently read too much into their date. She should have realized how stupid she was being—really, did she think that she and an international superstar would start dating? Seriously, why would he waste his time with a nobody from Michigan?

Liv was pulled from her depression by Simon Brown's loud bark. "You. Here." She dutifully made her way to his open door.

"Yes, Brown?" She could barely muster up the energy to be polite.

"I need my sweater." *Details? No? Okay . . .* "Go, Girl!"

Liv trudged off in search of Brown's sweater. She hadn't the faintest idea where he could have left it, but he rarely dragged his lazy butt farther than the *Hits Parade* studio or the Green Room, so she figured she might as well start there. As Liv passed the studio, she could hear the rumblings of the crowd. Checking her watch, Liv noticed that there were still a few more minutes left in the show—she would have to come back. Postshow crowd was the *last* thing she could deal with today.

She turned right and moved toward the Green Room. As she approached the door, she could hear a few faint guitar chords coming from inside. Knocking softly, Liv pushed the door open.

Josh Cameron was alone, sitting on the couch and strumming his guitar, looking more fabulous than ever. One dark curl brushed his cheek. He looked up and smiled. "Olivia."

Liv braced herself. So he did remember her. What was *with* him? "Hi. Um, great show." *Great show? He ignored you all day, made you feel like a complete idiot, and sent you off on errands to fetch little treats. And all you can say is "great show"?*

"Olivia, I need to apologize. I haven't been myself today. I'm afraid I've given you the wrong impression." He laid his guitar on the couch and stood up to approach her. He leaned forward to kiss her on the cheek. As he did, Liv could smell the cologne that had haunted her all week. *Mmmm. Yummy.* "Have you had a good week?"

"Me? Oh, um, yeah. Sure. It's been . . . well, it's been okay. A little strange, maybe, but you know . . ." Liv trailed off. There she went again. Blah, blah, blah. "So . . ."

"Olivia, I feel terribly about how I've treated you today. I'm afraid you must hate me."

This guy is good, Liv thought, smiling. "Not at all. Don't worry about it. I know you're busy and distracted."

"That's not an excuse. But you understand, don't you?" Josh Cameron smiled, exposing his dimples. "I've been looking forward to seeing you all week. I hope you know that."

Liv swallowed. Hard. She did not know that. "I've been looking forward to seeing you too. I had a great time on Friday. Thanks again for inviting me. And don't worry about today. Really. I understand." *Shhhh, Liv,* she begged herself. *Stop now.*

"Listen, let me make it up to you. Are you free tonight?" Liv nodded. She was now. "Would you join me for dinner?" Liv nodded again.

Just then she spotted Simon Brown's sweater sitting atop the chair in the corner. *Thank you, Simon Brown,* she thought, grinning. *One of your meaningless errands has finally been worth it.*

Wake Me Up Before You Go-Go

Please don't let this be happening to me.
Please don't let this be happening to me.
Please don't let this be happening to me.

Like a mantra, Liv repeated her internal plea again and again. She stared at the unforgiving bathroom door, studying its blank façade. She pressed her nose up against the opaque glass door and tried to get a view into the exterior of the hotel room.

There had to be an emergency door handle somewhere. *Come on . . . where is it?!*

Pushing gently against the muddy glass, Liv studied her wiggly reflection in the door. She suddenly pictured herself dying a slow, miserable death, alone in Josh

Cameron's hotel bathroom. She could see the *Sun* headline: STRANGE GIRL DIES HORRIBLE, SQUISH-FACED DEATH IN AN ATTEMPT TO WOO JOSH CAMERON. Liv peeled her face off the door's glass. Smushing her face against the door was not helping matters.

"Abracadabra!"

"Open Sesame!"

"Supercalifragilisticexpialidocious!" *Oops. That's something else.*

Trying to think of few more magic words, Liv slouched against the wall and stared at the indigo toilet taunting her from the opposite wall in the dark red bathroom.

When Liv had turned up for her date with Josh Cameron that evening, things had seemed so promising. The plan was to have a quiet dinner in his hotel suite. Apparently, Josh Cameron was fed up with the paparazzi and had been trying to lay low. That was fine and dandy with Liv—she was more than happy to check out a superstar suite at the Ñ Hotel.

The Ñ was famous for its übercool, sparse rooms and state-of-the-art technology. Retinal scanners instead of keys. Voice-activated elevators. Automated dumbwaiters that dispatch room service orders through little tunnels in the walls ("Like a drive-up

ATM!" Liv had lamely proclaimed when their champagne had arrived).

And touch-free bathroom fixtures, which were, Liv now realized, *not* a good thing.

When she had arrived, Josh Cameron had greeted her at the door and ushered her into his suite. He had produced a bottle of champagne from the room service receiving berth, and poured deep glasses for each of them. The bubbly champagne shot straight to Liv's head, combining with nerves to make her dizzy and flustered.

After a few minutes of awkward conversation about his suite (during which, Liv recalled with a twinge of discomfort, Josh Cameron had smiled smugly at each of Liv's gushing remarks and nodded, saying, "I know, I know," over and over again), Liv had excused herself to the bathroom.

Which is where she remained, ten minutes later.

Near tears, she decided to give it one more go. She could only imagine what Josh Cameron was thinking, waiting for her out in the suite. Really, what could a person do for ten full minutes in the bathroom? It was not a pretty thought.

Liv stood up and moved toward the door

again. Its smooth, glassy surface was unmarred by a handle. She studied the walls around the door for the umpteenth time, looking for any opening device. She ran her hand along the tiles, stopping when she felt one tile tilt slightly. It looked just like the rest of the bathroom's dark red tiles. Hopeful, Liv gave it a hesitant poke. The door swooshed open, revealing the interior of Josh Cameron's hotel suite. Liv released the breath she had been holding and stepped out of her bathroom prison.

"Well, hello there." Josh Cameron swept across the room toward Liv, holding her champagne flute in his hand. "Everything all right?" He tilted his head and smiled.

Liv took a deep slurp of her drink and felt her face blush a bright crimson. Whether it was from embarrassment or the champagne, she didn't know. "I'm amazing," she said, feigning a seductive purr. As her voice garbled out, she realized she sounded pretty stupid, and decided not to experiment with seduction again.

"I'm going to guess," Josh Cameron said, lifting his glass in a toast, "that you had some problems with the door. Am I right?" Liv nodded sheepishly. "Not to worry," he continued. "It took me a while to find my way around in here. The first time I ordered room service, I waited for two hours not realizing my order had been cooling in the wall panel the whole time."

Liv laughed, and—unsure of what to say—drained her glass.

"Tell me, Olivia," Josh Cameron said, filling her glass with more bubbly trouble. "What is it that makes you so incredible?"

"Well," she began, her confidence bolstered by her glass and a half of champagne. "Perhaps it's my understated grace and elegance?"

Josh Cameron's dimples deepened. "Let's see . . ." He took Liv's arm and led her to a chaise in the corner of his suite's living room. "I don't think it's that. But you are exceedingly charming."

For obvious reasons, Liv cracked up. *Charming?* Liv's champagne was dancing around inside her head now, causing her words to spill out a few seconds before she had a chance to consider them. "What *do* you see in me? Seriously? I mean, I've done nothing but humiliate myself every time I've seen you, and yet you insist on calling me 'charming.'"

Josh Cameron laughed. "It's just *that*, Olivia. I admire your incredible ability to say everything that crosses your mind. It's refreshing to meet a real girl." He took her hand and leaned in close. "You're different."

Liv sucked in her breath. "I see." Her hand was resting lightly in Josh Cameron's palm, sweating. She regretted not swiping Lady Speed Stick across every exposed surface of her body. *Is he holding my hand? Is this real?*

As Josh Cameron stroked the top of Liv's hand with his thumb, she relaxed into the chaise. "Can I ask you something?" she asked, smiling slowly.

"Anything."

"Why did you ask for a stuffed pig at Music Mix?" Liv giggled.

Josh Cameron leaned in closer. She could feel his breath on her cheek as his lips moved toward her ear. "Because," he said with a smile, "it's always fun to see how far people will go to make me happy."

Liv giggled again. In her slightly drunk state, his answer made her laugh. "So the purple pig was what, like a challenge or something?"

"I guess you could say that. Now, Olivia," Josh Cameron pulled away from her and smiled. "I just heard our dinner arrive. Shall we?"

"Let's," she said with a nod. She was

starting to feel sleepy, and was suddenly nervous that if she didn't get some food in her stomach, she could be curled up in the corner passed out in a matter of minutes. Or worse, she would be forced to use the bathroom again. And Liv definitely didn't want to get trapped in there a second time.

Josh Cameron led her to the table that had been set for them in the corner of the suite. Liv studied the table, counting no fewer than seven forks and four plates in front of each of their seats. *I guess I should have watched* Pretty Woman *more carefully— the fork lesson would have come in handy.*

"A toast." Josh Cameron was standing at Liv's side, one hand resting on her shoulder, the other holding his glass toward her. "I feel so lucky to have met you. To what's next," he finished, squeezing her shoulder.

Liv lifted her glass to her lips, but carefully monitored her intake. "To what's next," she repeated, groaning inwardly at his lame line. "Josh, do you always use canned lines like that?" Liv's left hand flew to her mouth to cover up what she had already said.

Josh Cameron spluttered champagne as he pulled his glass quickly away from his mouth. "Canned lines?"

"I'm sorry. I shouldn't have said that."

"No, please, explain. I'm intrigued."

"It's just that, well, uh," Liv had dug herself into a big fat hole, and now she wished she could slide a door right over the top of it and never come back out. "When you say things like 'I feel so lucky to have met you' and 'To what's next,' it's maybe just a little, uh, cheesy?"

To Liv's relief, Josh Cameron started laughing. His dimples were deeper than she had ever seen them, and his eyes had started to tear up. *This* was not the response she had been expecting. "Olivia, that's priceless," he stammered, gasping for breath. "No one has *ever* said anything like that to me before."

"I'm really sorry. I shouldn't have said it. Your toast was very sweet." She couldn't believe she had just criticized Josh Cameron. *What is* wrong *with you, Liv?*

"No, please, don't be sorry. It's nice to hear the truth. Frankly, I get tired of the nonstop adoration from fans. Don't get me wrong, it's flattering to have people love you, but it's also nice to be brought back to earth from time to time." He smiled at her. "My apologies for the cheesy line. Mind if I try again?"

Liv shook her head, smiling meekly. She couldn't believe he wasn't furious she had just criticized him. This was too weird.

"To you, Olivia," Josh Cameron said, smiling widely. "The most refreshingly honest woman I have ever met."

Cheers to that, Liv thought, tipping her glass back. *Cheers to that.*

Yawning contentedly, Liv stretched her leg and wiggled her toes. She rolled over, eyes closed, and replayed the previous evening over and over in her head.

Things had gone a little fuzzy in the middle of dinner, but Liv could still remember most of her amazing night. She couldn't believe how incredibly sweet and sexy Josh Cameron was. After Liv had teased him for being cheesy, things had gotten much easier between them.

Liv thought back to the rest of their dinner conversation, and still couldn't believe that Josh Cameron, International Pop Star had opened up to her. "The thing is, sometimes you just want to be *normal*, you know?" he had said at one point during their meal. "That's why I appreciate your honesty so much, Olivia. You're not worried about what I'll think—you just say it like it is." He had smiled at her. "There's something unique about you—and I don't want that to sound like a line." Liv flushed as she remembered the way his eyes had lingered on hers.

Her memory of the rest of their meal was a bit of a blur, but she clearly remembered their dessert (some sort of gooey chocolate volcano) out on the balcony. The fresh air had revived her.

Liv had swaggered onto the balcony and moved to one of the glass walls to steady herself. She remembered leaning against the wall for support, and then strong hands circling around her waist like a safety net.

"Olivia," Josh Cameron had sighed, moving toward her. "I've had an amazing evening." His right hand had tightened around her waist as his left pushed a stray curl from her face. Liv congratulated herself on doing a quick tongue-check for food lodged between her teeth. She hadn't *expected* him to kiss her, but she wanted to be ready, just in case.

She could still feel the moment his lips first touched hers. Gently, cautiously at first, then expertly pressing into her more urgently. He delicately let his hand run through the length of her hair, then wrapped his soft hand around the back of her neck. He leaned back slightly to study her face in the moonlight as his thumb lazily traced a line across her jaw. Cupping her chin in his hand, he tilted her face upward gently before kissing her chin, each of her cheeks, and . . . finally . . . settling on her lips again.

She relived that kiss several more times before slowly opening her eyes. Yawning, Liv scanned the room, squinting to see her alarm clock. It was still dark, so she figured she had a few more hours to sleep, but wanted to make sure. As she searched in the dark for her clock, she suddenly became very aware that she was not alone. And she was very much not asleep on her couch-bed.

Where am I? Freaked out, Liv bolted upright and looked around. Her mind frantically raced through the rest of the previous night's date, desperately searching for an ending. *Oh no,* she thought, horrified. *Oh no. There was no ending. I don't remember an ending! I kissed him and then . . .* Nothing. Her memory was refusing to go beyond that kiss.

Racking her brain for details, the rest of the evening suddenly started trickling back into focus. After their balcony kiss, Josh Cameron had escorted Liv back inside the suite and they had settled into the corner of the couch. He had been talking about his ski trip to the Alps, and then . . . *Noooooo! I fell asleep!*

Liv squeezed her eyes shut, willing herself back in time. When she opened them, she hadn't moved. She realized she was sprawled out on the couch in the corner of Josh Cameron's hotel suite, covered in a fur blanket. She hadn't moved from the night before—even her shoes were still securely attached to her feet. She was feeling more than a little sheepish about her present situation. *How long have I been here?*

Looking across the room, Liv could see the outline of Skinny Guy, who was seated on a low footstool, his chin in his hands, watching her. When he saw that she was awake, he stood abruptly and moved toward her. "Mr. Cameron has retired for the evening," he explained briefly, helping Liv to her feet. "He has asked that I arrange for a car to take you home. He felt it best that you sleep here for a while, considering."

Considering what?! Liv wondered, suddenly nervous about what she had done or said. *How much did I drink?* She scolded herself for getting so out of hand. *I will never drink again. . . .*

"I took the liberty of ordering you a sandwich. Please feel free to bring it along for your ride home." Skinny Guy held a small pouch in her direction and made his way to the door. "Come along. Quickly."

Liv followed as Skinny Guy bustled down the hallway and led her into a dark, narrow elevator. She peeked into the sandwich pouch as the elevator descended, and groaned as her stomach protested. She had definitely had too much champagne if the sight of plain old ham and cheese was causing her stomach to curl.

Poking around inside the sandwich pouch, Liv found a small note next to the wrapped sandwich. "Olivia," it read, "Thank you for an incredible evening. I can't wait to see you again. Soon. Fondly, Josh Cameron." Liv smiled. He still had a way to go before he lost all of his cheesiness ("fondly" was just the tiniest bit old-fashioned), but at least he was sweet. She smiled as she reread his words. Soon, she thought, happily.

When the elevator reached the ground floor, Skinny Guy led Liv through the nearly deserted lobby. As they made their way past the frosted glass doors of the swanky hotel bar, though, she heard laughter and the clinking of glasses coming from within. The doors had whooshed open to welcome a stunning couple into the late-night gathering.

Liv craned her neck to try to get a glimpse of the inner reaches of the bar as Skinny Guy hurried her through the lobby. For a split second her heart caught in her throat—was that Josh Cameron on the other side of the bar's sliding doors? *Nah,* she thought, *impossible. Skinny Guy said he "retired for the evening"—and he wouldn't have left me in his room alone to go out.* Shrugging it off as her own overactive imagination, Liv smiled. *One amazing kiss, and I'm already paranoid,* she thought, giggling to herself.

Stifling a yawn, Liv made her way out of the lobby. With a sigh, she slid into the limo waiting outside the hotel—her limo!—and bit into her sandwich as the car sped her toward home.

Afternoon Delight

"Monet's inspiration for this piece . . ."
Blah, blah, blah-ba-di-blah. Liv plopped
down on one of the hard, backless benches
in room thirty-four of the National Gallery
and stared up at the famous Monet above
her. She was only vaguely listening to the
description. Her self-guided tour headphones had given her a headache, not to
mention the fact that they had squished her
ears flat and left one side of her hair panked
tightly against her head.

When Liv had gotten up that morning,
the weather was dreary and drizzly. After
dragging herself out of bed and into the
shower, Liv had returned to the living room
and discovered that Rebecca's mood appar-

ently matched the weather—she had settled herself in front of her sun lamp with a stack of fashion magazines, her iPod Nano, and a sneer. Hell Dog was by her side, snuggled tightly into Liv's blanket, soaking up the bright faux sunshine.

So Liv decided to get out of the apartment and do some London exploring. First stop: the National Gallery. Truth be told, Liv didn't really like museums all that much. In theory, she loved art—in reality, it got old really quickly.

So now, an hour after arriving, she was bored and weary—and hadn't yet made it out of the nineteenth-century wing. Leaning back on the bench, Liv turned the volume down on her headphones and focused on the crowd. This, she realized, was her favorite part of the museum. So many people from so many places. People who had seen so much more of the world than she had. She loved listening to the different languages, seeing their faces, studying their body language.

After a few minutes of people watching, Liv stood up and headed for the front hall. The rest of the museum would have to wait—she was ready to explore the city, and old art was getting her nowhere fast.

Breezing down the main stairs of the gallery, Liv plucked her visitor's tag off her T-shirt, returned her headphones, and slung her bag over her shoulder. She pushed the front door open and made her way out toward the lions in Trafalgar Square. The sun had burned through the clouds while she was in the museum, and the rain had cleared. It was a beautiful day.

"Liv!" Hearing her name, Liv turned back toward the gallery. A few steps behind her Colin was standing with his arm raised in a slight wave. "Sorry," he said breathlessly, "I thought that was you."

Liv's stomach flipped nervously. She was surprised to see Colin. And even more surprised he had stopped her—they hadn't spent much time together since he had started dating Rebecca. And at work he was always so distant and busy. "Hey, Colin. Were you at the gallery?"

"I was just on my way in—this is one of my favorite places in London. They make a fantastic cup of tea, and it's free admission." Colin shrugged. "But you look like you're off, then. See you at work tomorrow, yeah?"

Liv considered her options. She could walk away and spend the day alone, living out a solo adventure in London. Or she could be bold and invite herself to join Colin for a cup of tea. It certainly couldn't hurt to try to be friends. "Do you mind if I join you?"

Colin looked surprised, but—Liv noted happily—pleased. "Of course."

They walked up the steps of the museum together in silence. Liv didn't know what to say, but she felt compelled to fill the silence with unnecessary commentary. While Colin guided her through the halls to the museum café, she asked him endless questions about his flat, afternoon tea, and what it was like to grow up in Stratford-upon-Avon.

By the time they finally settled into a small table in the corner of the café, Liv had exhausted all of her generic questions and was almost out of things to say. Colin had barely uttered a word.

"Can I ask you something?" Liv silently vowed that this would be her last question. She *had* to stop talking.

"Isn't it a bit late to ask me that?" Colin smiled. *Aha,* Liv thought. *So he has noticed my endless chatter.*

"Sorry," Liv said, embarrassed. "I tend to talk a lot. I've never been very good with silence. It makes me uncomfortable."

"Yeah, I noticed," Colin said, immediately looking like he regretted being so honest. Liv laughed, noticing his embarrassment. "But it's a good thing," Colin said, by way of apology. "I tend to clam up around new people. Or I scare people off with my sarcasm. Go ahead—ask me anything."

"I sort of get the impression that you kind of avoid me at work." Liv could *not* believe she had just said that. But she was desperate to know what she had done to offend him.

"You do?" Colin furrowed his brow. "Sorry about that. I guess I've been a bit distracted. Andrew Stone is literally around every corner, and he doesn't like to see me not working. Rebecca has been stopping by my desk a lot lately, and he's sort of scolded me for—how does he put it?—'wasting his time.' So I try to stay focused, yeah?"

"Oh. Right." Now Liv felt bad. She should have figured Rebecca had something to do with his weird behavior. "It was rude of me to ask you that. I don't have a very good filter—really, pretty much everything that goes through my head comes out my mouth. I guess it's just a curse of being an only child. You can say whatever you want, and no one is there to hear you. So you just keep talking."

Colin laughed. "Don't worry about it. I like honesty—it's refreshing. My family tends to bottle up most of our issues and pretend all's well. So I like when people can express themselves. It's a nice change."

"Do you have a big family?"

"There you go with the questions again," Colin teased. "Kidding. I have two little sisters. So it's a pretty big family, yeah. You?"

"It's just me and my dad." Liv paused. There was something about Colin that made her feel safe. She *wanted* to tell him things. "My mom died in a car accident when I was little."

"I'm sorry," Colin said quietly. He paused, waiting for Liv to continue.

"It's okay. She was English. From London. So that's a big part of why I'm here. I'm trying to figure out what her life might have been like. Being here makes me feel so much closer to her." She paused, sipping her tea.

"Have you met anyone from your mom's family?"

"She was an only child, and her parents died before she did. I didn't know my grandparents at all. So there isn't really anyone left." Liv shrugged. "It's enough for me to soak up a little of her culture. I just want to feel like I've lived a part of her life. *Lived London,* you know?"

"That makes sense." Colin folded his napkin and set it on the table. "Well then, that's settled." Liv looked at him curiously. "I think it's time for us to get out and explore. Live some of the London life. Have you walked along the Thames yet? Visited Big Ben? Westminster Abbey? Buckingham Palace?"

Liv shook her head. She had done very little besides sit at her tollbooth and fetch Brown cups of watery coffee.

"Then I'll be your guide. We have a lot to see." He came around behind her and pulled her chair away from the table. Liv stood and followed as Colin guided her out of the museum, across Trafalgar Square, and down the Mall toward Buckingham Palace.

Hours later, after darkness had fallen and they stood together in the grainy light illuminating the turnstiles in the Charing Cross tube station, Liv was at a loss for words for the first time all day. "Colin, thank you," she finally said.

He smiled. "It was my pleasure. Have you had a good day?"

Liv and Colin had spent the afternoon chatting and laughing as they walked through St. James's Park and around Buckingham Palace, before eventually turning and going back toward Westminster Abbey and the River Thames. Colin led Liv past Big Ben and the Houses of Parliament, stopping only briefly for a second cup of tea in a small shop off Parliament Square. They had walked for hours, but Liv had hardly noticed.

"Amazing." Liv glanced at him. "I hope we can do it again sometime?"

"Me too." With that, he raised his hand in a little salute. "I hope you liked the tea at the museum. It really was the perfect cup, yeah?" Laughing, she waved as Colin backed out of the station, and then she turned and went down the escalator and toward home.

"I was starting to get worried about you," Anna greeted Liv from her position on the couch. "You've been gone all day."

"I ran into Colin outside the National Gallery," Liv said, throwing her bag into a heap in the corner of the living room. "We spent the day wandering around London."

"Sounds scandalous," Anna said, sitting up.

"It's not like that!" Liv insisted, swatting Anna as she settled into position on the couch. "But I think we can be friends." As she said it, Liv realized it was true. She had never actually pursued a friendship with a guy, and that afternoon had helped her realize how much fun it could be. She felt absolutely no pressure around Colin. She could be herself, and didn't have to worry about flirting or trying to figure out what to say so she didn't sound foolish. It was so easy and comfortable—it was actually a relief that he was taken, so she didn't have to worry about impressing him.

"Liv, seriously. Friends? He's hot. Maybe he's into you." Anna tucked her legs into a pretzel and fixed Liv with a stern stare.

Liv giggled and sat down next to her roommate. "Seriously. Friends. Yes, he's hot, but it's not like that. At all. I felt completely comfortable around him, and I don't want to ruin that by even thinking about hooking up with him. And hello—" Liv gestured down the hall and lowered her voice. "Rebecca. Though I did completely forget to ask him what's going on with them. He only mentioned her once, and I guess I wasn't so keen on bringing it up a second time."

Anna didn't look convinced. "Is this about Josh Cameron?" She frowned. Anna had been cautiously optimistic about Liv's date the night before. She said she couldn't help but feel suspicious of celebrities, and "needed to see what Josh Cameron's next move would be" before she would let Liv get too hopeful.

"No. And yes. Come on, Anna—you have to admit that things are going really well with Josh Cameron. I wouldn't say we're a 'couple,' but there's definitely hope, right?"

Anna nodded and grinned. "It's looking good."

"Trust me," Liv said. "I think Colin and I will be friends. But that's it. I'm not getting in her"—Liv gestured toward Rebecca's room—"way. Colin is clearly taken, so no matter what might have been, I'm not going there. Get it?"

"Got it."

"Good."

Sweet Dreams
(Are Made of This)

Though she had meant it when she'd said it, Liv was finding it impossible to stick to her vow. She'd sworn she wasn't even the tiniest bit interested in Colin, but throughout the next week, Liv couldn't stop thinking about their weekend adventure.

She would recall funny stories Colin had told her about Andrew Stone as she filled Simon Brown's cup in the coffee room. She would catch herself smiling about how he always said "yeah?" like he was asking a question at the end of almost every sentence. And as she walked from the office to the tube every night, her mind flashed back to the way his eyes shone in the light of the Charing Cross tube station.

What she found most perplexing was the fact that she was obsessing about her totally normal afternoon strolling around London with Colin, but had spent almost no time dwelling on her steamy and fabulously chic dinner with Josh Cameron. *What's wrong with you, Liv?* She didn't like the tricks her emotions were playing on her. *You made out with the world's most coveted celebrity, and you're obsessing about some* random *guy from Stratford-upon-Avon? Some English dude who is crazy enough to go out with your psycho roommate?*

Liv could only hope this Colin nonsense was her mind's way of trying to prevent her from obsessing about Josh Cameron. Luckily, stuffing Colin to the back of her mind became much easier after she caught a glimpse of his hand on Rebecca's back as they wandered down the Music Mix hallway deep in conversation one afternoon—*yuck!* So she focused her energy on willing Josh Cameron to call and ask her out again.

Simon Brown was particularly gruff and surly all week, so Liv didn't have too much time at the office to focus on anything but his bizarre needs. Brown had developed an unexpected addiction to Nicorette—the stop-smoking gum—and had begun to send Liv out to fetch three or four or twenty packs most afternoons. The gum didn't seem to do much for Brown, since he still went through at least two packs of cigarettes a day—usually lighting up as he stuffed a fresh piece of Nicorette into his mouth. This dual habit resulted in breath that smelled like a public bathroom, so Liv was relieved that she rarely needed to get close enough to be hit with the full effect.

On her way back into the Music Mix building one evening, her arms loaded with packs of Nicorette and Dunhill cigarettes, Liv spotted Anna pushing her way out of the revolving door. Anna quickly rushed over to relieve Liv of some of her packages. "Hey," Liv said, breathless. "Thanks. You going home?"

"Yeah," Anna said quietly. "Rough day."

Liv tilted her head, confused. Anna didn't have a lot of rough days—her Music Mix assignment suited her perfectly, and her whole department loved her. So most days, Anna came home glowing with happiness. "What's up?"

"Nothing major. It's nothing, really." Anna looked up defiantly and smiled.

"Hmm," Liv responded, studying Anna

carefully. She didn't believe that for a second. "Are you sure?"

Anna smiled weakly. "I promise."

"You know what? I think I can get out of here—let me just run this stuff up to Brown and grab my bag. We can go home together." Liv always ended up riding the tube home alone, since she usually worked hours later than any of the other interns. But she wasn't going to let Anna go home alone—to Rebecca—when she seemed so upset.

"Really? You can leave at . . . ," Anna said sarcastically, glancing at her watch, ". . . seven thirty?"

"Crazy, isn't it? Yeah, just hang out here for a sec and I'll be right back. Promise you'll wait?"

Anna nodded, so Liv gathered up all her packages and made her way up the escalators to deliver Brown's goods. Luckily, Brown was engrossed in watching an episode of *Footballers' Wives* and just grunted when Liv dropped the bags on his desk and announced that she was leaving. So she breezed back down the hall and out the door to her waiting roommate.

Anna filled their walk to the tube with superficial stories of what had happened at the office that day. Liv listened and nodded, but couldn't help wondering what was going on. Anna was clearly trying to keep talking to prevent Liv from asking any more questions. Finally Liv couldn't stand it anymore and just blurted out, "If there's something going on—if there's anyone whose butt needs kicking—you know I'm your girl, right?"

Anna laughed.

"I'm serious," Liv continued. "I don't want to force you to tell me what's going on, but I'm not pretending that everything's dandy. You're clearly avoiding something. . . ."

They had reached the tube station and were riding down the escalator to the tracks. Liv and Anna both pressed to the left side of the escalator, allowing hustling Londoners to walk past them on the right. Liv had quickly learned that this was an unspoken rule of the tube that people were *very* serious about. . . . Never stand on the right side of the escalator.

Anna turned to face Liv as they descended underground. She explained, "Everything's fine. Things are just stressful with my parents right now. But I really don't want to get into it."

"Your mom? Are there new developments?"

"No, same old stuff. She's just really been on me lately, and it's sort of sucking the fun out of this summer. She hasn't even asked me how the internship is going—we just avoid talking about it. She only calls to tell me what she's buying for my dorm room next year."

"So she hasn't relented at all, huh?"

"It's gotten worse. And the more she talks about *my* plans for school, the more I'm convinced I'm not ready to go yet. I'm loving this job so much, and know that if I just had one year to pursue this, I would be so much happier with the next ten years of my life being committed to Oxford and med school or whatever." Anna sighed as they boarded their train.

Liv began to respond, but Anna cut her off. "Can we talk about something else? Make me laugh," Anna begged. "I want to take my mind off this."

Realizing she meant it, Liv thought for a second before pulling her iPod out of her bag. She scrolled through the song list, then stuck one earbud in Anna's ear, and the other in her own. "Music therapy," she explained, pressing play on the dial. "If the sight of me gettin' down in the tube doesn't make you laugh, nothing will."

As ABBA sang out, *"You can dance, you can jive, having the time of your life . . ."* Liv wiggled her butt and waved her arms in the air. Passengers in the train looked up from their newspapers to stare at her. Anna started to laugh, and a flush of red crept up her cheeks.

"Okay, okay! Stop—this is mortifying." Anna continued to laugh as Liv drew even more stares.

"Did I take your mind off it?" Liv whispered as she continued to shimmy more subtly in time to the music. Anna nodded. "Then it was worth it." The doors opened at their stop, and Liv and Anna hustled out, still joined at the ear by the iPod.

The next morning when Liv walked into the Music Mix lobby, Gloria stood up from her desk and whispered, "Look out . . . he's on the hunt."

Liv paused. "Brown?"

"Who else?" Gloria asked, nodding. "He's in rare form today—be prepared."

With a groan, Liv pressed through the door leading out of the lobby and braced herself for a fun day. As she passed Brown's open door, he shouted "Oy!" and waved her over.

"Good morning," she said, trying to start their conversation out on the right foot.

Brown just stared at her and launched into a list of instructions. "This will need to go," he said, gesturing toward two large boxes in the corner of his office, "as will this. I've arranged for a courier to pick you up and take you there. Don't irritate me with nonsensical questions. Go, Girl!"

Right-o, Liv thought, more confused than ever. *You got it.* She clumsily gathered the two enormous boxes in the corner of Brown's office into her arms and made her way back out to the main lobby. Setting the boxes on the corner of the reception desk, Liv just looked at Gloria and broke out laughing.

"Here's what I figure," Gloria said, without Liv's needing to ask. "The Josh Cameron concert is coming up. They're in the final prep stages, and Brown is starting to freak out. I'm guessing the car service that just called from downstairs is here to pick you and those boxes up and deliver you to the stadium. Make sense?"

"I'd say that's as good a guess as any. I

suppose it can't hurt to get in the car and see where it takes me." She thanked Gloria, hoisted the boxes into her arms again, and made her way down the escalator. Outside, a driver was waiting next to a black car. Liv moved toward the backseat, and the driver whisked the door open for her. *So far, so good,* she thought.

Twenty minutes later Liv's car stopped outside the service entrance to a huge stadium. She made her way inside and wandered around aimlessly for a few minutes before running into Rebecca, who was bustling through the hallway with a clipboard and walkie-talkie, shouting things to stagehands and mechanics. When she spotted Liv, Rebecca came gliding over.

"Oh, Li-uhv, are those the dog beds?"

Liv just grunted. She had no idea what was in the boxes, but really hoped that a private car hadn't been hired to deliver a bunch of dog beds to the stadium. "No clue," she responded. "I was just told to bring these boxes here." Liv set down her packages and opened up one of the boxes. *You've got to be kidding me,* she mused. *Rebecca was right.*

Rebecca smiled smugly and directed Liv to one of the rooms behind the stage. "Just unpack the beds and make it nice and comfy in there, won't you? We want to make sure all our special guests are taken care of during the concert. Thanks, sweetie."

Liv spent the next hour and a half unpacking and fluffing dog beds in a small, rectangular room down the hall from the stage. She wasn't sure why she was preparing this little doggie hotel, but she had come to realize that her summer job entailed doing as she was told, and understanding later.

Liv finished quickly and decided to take a peek around the stadium—she had heard so much about the concert from Rebecca, but hadn't gotten to check things out for herself. Now that she was maybe-dating the star of the show, she felt like she deserved a little peek.

She made her way down the hall toward the stage, pulling aside the curtain that blocked off the backstage area. Liv's breath caught in her throat when she spotted Josh Cameron's familiar curls at the back of the stage. She hadn't really thought about how she would respond the next time she saw him, but now that he was so close she was suddenly panicked at the thought of seeing him again. *He kissed me, he kissed me, he kissed me*—that was all she could think about as she stepped onstage and walked toward Josh Cameron.

As she approached, he turned to her, his face a blank slate. He stared at her for a few seconds before a smile spread across his face. "Excuse me," he said, motioning to the sound engineer he had been talking to. "Olivia."

"Hey," she said, still nervous. "Hi." She grinned awkwardly. "How are you?"

Josh Cameron moved toward her, his eyes penetrating hers. "I hope you made it home safely on Friday."

"Oh! Yeah, fine. No problems. Thanks for the sandwich."

He looked confused. "Oh," he said. "Right. So tell me, Olivia. To what do I owe this surprise?"

"You mean, why am I here? I brought the dog beds." *That's great, Liv. Reeeeeally charming.*

"Right. The dog beds." Josh Cameron was smirking at her. "I don't suppose you have some time before you have to get back?"

Liv was definitely not in a hurry to get back to Brown, and she figured her task had taken less time than expected. "Sure, I'm free. Why?"

"I was just on my way to the Berkeley Hotel for tea. Care to join me?"

Forty-five minutes later Liv was still waiting on a plastic folding chair by the stage door. She had happily agreed to tea, and he had told her he would be "just a mo'." Many, many mo's later, she was starting to get impatient. She was also a little nervous about how long she'd been gone from the office. Finally, almost an hour later, the pop star emerged from the stage area. He approached Liv and offered her a hand, making no comment about the time that had passed.

But the wait was worth it. When Josh Cameron's limo delivered them to the door of the Berkeley Hotel, they were quickly ushered inside to a private table tucked into a corner. Liv wasn't offered a menu, but their table was almost instantly filled with towering platters of pastries, cookies, and sandwiches, steaming pots of tea, and cucumber wedges. The pastries and cookies were stunning, one-of-a-kind masterpieces. Josh Cameron watched her with an amused expression as she bit into a deep chocolate cookie with white trim.

"You know," he said, "that cookie was inspired by a classic Chanel dress."

"Am I supposed to eat it?" Liv asked, only half-joking.

Josh Cameron laughed. "Of course. But each of these cookies takes hours to design. That's what makes this place so inspired." Liv nodded, self-consciously nibbling at the cookie.

At the next table over, Liv could hear two ladies gushing about the service and, of all things, the table linens. Then one of them gasped and too-loudly whispered, "High tea at this hotel has more than a monthlong waiting list."

Liv giggled and looked across her table at Josh Cameron, who raised an eyebrow and smirked. "One of the benefits of dating a celebrity, wouldn't you say?"

Liv nodded, her cheeks flushing at what he had just said—Josh Cameron had defined them as "dating"! Giddy with the knowledge that she was officially dating the world's most eligible bachelor, Liv floated through the rest of the afternoon.

Yet for some strange reason, her dream-world didn't feel quite as perfect as she had always envisioned.

Girls Just Want to Have Fun

At six o'clock on Friday morning, Liv was jolted awake by a loud, tinny rendition of the Black Eyed Peas' "My Humps." Moaning, she rolled over on her couch-bed and covered her head with a pillow, cursing herself for changing Anna's ring tone from *Für Elise*. As she lay there, trying to muffle the sound of Anna's cell phone, she snuck a peek at her clock—*it's really early,* she mused sleepily. *What could be this important?*

She could hear Anna's door open, and she felt the thumping of her roommate running for her phone. Anna snapped open the phone in the kitchen and murmured a quiet "Mama" into the phone. *It's her mom?* Liv wondered, starting to worry. *Whose mom calls at six in the morning?!*

Anna spoke quickly and quietly in Swedish. Liv listened to her lilting voice, noticing a tense, agitated tone. There was a brief pause, and then Liv heard Anna flip the phone closed. Her roommate stood in the kitchen for a few minutes, while Liv pretended to be asleep. She wanted to sit up and ask what was going on, but she knew that Anna would let her know if and when she was ready to talk.

"Everything okay?" Liv asked sleepily. She had minded her own business for less than thirty seconds, and she just couldn't help it—Liv *had* to know that Anna was okay.

"Yeah," Anna said, lying down beside Liv on the couch-bed and flopping her head back into a pillow. "That was my mom." Long silence. "She's coming to London tomorrow morning. Apparently we 'need to talk.' And I guess it's an in-person conversation. She's flying in from Stockholm on the first flight in the morning. She'll be here by eight."

Liv breathed out. "Are you okay with that?"

"I guess I have to be, don't I?" Anna said

bitterly. "She hasn't exactly given me a whole lot of options."

"Any idea what inspired this visit *now*?"

Anna groaned. "I have a pretty good idea."

Liv rolled onto her side, facing her friend. "Do you want to tell me?"

"I don't know why I haven't told you this yet," Anna said sheepishly. "I guess I didn't really want to say it out loud, because it makes it more real." She exhaled. "I turned down every university I was accepted to for the fall. I sent letters out earlier this week, and I guess they already got them and have started calling my house to find out why I'm declining their offers.

"I know I made the right decision," Anna continued, closing her eyes. "But I still need to justify that to my mom. I know I'll go to university sometime—I'm just not ready right now. I need to figure out what I want to do with my life first. I just need a year or two to try things and figure out what fits, you know? And if there's the tiniest chance I could get a job at Music Mix, I *need* to try."

"So your mom is coming to try to change your mind?"

"I guess," Anna said, flopping her hands

at her sides. "It's not going to work, so it seems like sort of a useless trip. It's not like I just—*poof!*—made the decision. . . . There was some thought involved," she continued bitterly. "But I guess we need to get it out into the open. I couldn't have really hidden the decision from her. She would have found out eventually, so this conversation is probably inevitable."

"Probably," Liv mused. "If it helps, I think you made the right decision."

Anna sat up suddenly, swinging her legs off the side of Liv's bed. "Thanks. Can we go get a yummy breakfast before work to clear my head?"

"Do you want me to make you breakfast?" Liv offered, secretly hoping Anna would say no. She could cook pancakes from a box and that was just about it. A scone from a café sounded much more appealing.

"Liv, get real. I've seen you cook. That's almost more of a punishment than my mom's visit." Anna grinned. "Move it. If we hurry, we'll escape before Rebecca even wakes up."

An hour later Anna and Liv had settled into a window seat at Tully's, which had become Liv's favorite coffee shop. The staff had become friendly with Liv, thanks to all the lattes and cappuccinos she fetched for *Hits Parade* celebrities and their assistants.

When they had arrived a few minutes after seven, they were given a pot of tea and scones with clotted cream—on the house. Liv grinned through a mouthful of scone and said, "Simon Brown has his benefits, doesn't he? There's nothing like free breakfast to make all those coffee runs worth it. Feel better?"

Anna nodded. "Much."

As she slurped her tea, Liv asked, "Do you want to talk about your strategy for tomorrow morning?" She had been a little hesitant to remind Anna about her mom's visit, but Anna still seemed distracted.

"Nah, I'm good. I promise. Thank you for asking, though—and talking me through it this morning." Anna waved her hand dismissively and set her face in a playfully stern scowl. "Here's what I want. . . . I want to sit here and eat until I'm sick, and then spend the night dancing it off. Tonight's club night, remember?"

"That's tonight?" Liv asked. With all the excitement of the past week, Liv had sort of forgotten that all the interns were going out that night. Anna and Francesco had been planning it for weeks. Apparently, the wardrobe department was way more into work-life balance than Simon Brown was—Anna's boss had even forced her to take one afternoon off to go check out a potential club for their intern outing. "I totally forgot. Wow, Anna, I'm losing my mind."

Anna smiled for the first time all morning. "You're distracted. But I still love you for helping me with this mom stuff. Now, no more serious talk. I'll deal with tomorrow, tomorrow. Tonight, we dance."

"Ah just don't know if I should wear my Jimmy Choos or my Manolos. Which of them makes me look more precious?" Liv and Anna were sitting in the living room, trying desperately not to laugh.

Rebecca had tried on no fewer than six outfits, each of which had a matching ensemble for My Rover. She had finally settled on a small pink dress and a silver clutch, outfitting My Rover in silver booties and a pink cape. Hell Dog was now scratching madly at the booties while Rebecca debated between five-inch peekaboo-toed stilettos and six-inch silver pumps.

"We have to leave," Anna said in reply, sending Rebecca over the edge.

Near tears, Rebecca looked at Liv with a look of desperation. "Ah just can't decide," she said, her lip quivering.

"The pumps," Liv said matter of factly, desperate to calm Rebecca down and get them out of the apartment on time. "Definitely the Manolo pumps. It totally coordinates your look with Rover."

"*My* Rover," Rebecca clarified, narrowing her eyes at Liv. "This precious darling's name is *My* Rover." Her tears had been replaced with a steely, stern voice. "The Jimmy Choos it is." She slipped on the heels, swept My Rover into her arms, and headed out the door.

Anna and Liv exchanged a look. "Perfect. Great choice, Rebecca," Liv yelled loudly after her. "You look perfect."

Thirty minutes later the three roommates emerged from the tube and made their way toward Runway, a swanky club that Anna promised Liv she would love. Anna had booked a table, and the other Music Mix interns were meeting them there.

When they walked in to the club, Liv could hardly believe it was real. The rectangular room was draped in deep red furs, and awash in understated white light glowing from within a long, fashion show—like catwalk that jutted out into the center of the room. Tables were arranged along the length of the runway, and frighteningly thin waitresses and waiters strutted up and down the length of the catwalk to deliver drinks.

Liv's mouth hung open, her face an expression of pure disbelief. Club owners went to such bizarre lengths to create a unique and glamorous atmosphere. Back in Ann Arbor, the high school gym outfitted for prom had always been considered exotic. Anna looked at Liv and burst out laughing.

Rebecca lifted one eyebrow and studied her nails. Clearly, this scene was very familiar to Rebecca—or she was playing the part very well.

As they walked toward the hostess, Anna shouted, "I picked this club because I heard it's pretty fabulous. Later they open the runway up to the crowd and you can vamp it up, supermodel-style. Sounds fun, doesn't it?"

Liv leaned in to Anna. "This is incredible. I assure you that there is no way I'll be walking that catwalk, but this is truly awesome. You picked a great place."

Anna took Liv's hand and led her toward

their table. Rebecca trailed a safe distance behind, trying to look like she wasn't with them. The group squeezed through the crowds lingering near the front of the club and moved toward the runway.

Liv spotted Francesco bounding up from a table right alongside the center of the runway. He ran over and gathered her and Anna into a tight hug, planting kisses on their cheeks. "Welcome, welcome!" he shouted, his Italian accent more pronounced than usual.

Francesco moved to the table and pulled chairs out for both of them. Rebecca crossed her arms as best she could (My Rover was tucked delicately under one arm) and cleared her throat. Colin stood up from his place at the table and offered his chair.

The table was packed with Music Mix interns, some of whom Liv knew only from their daily trips to the coffee machine. Others—like Katia, one of the other Americans, and Alex, from Russia—she had snuck into the Green Room for lunch a few times. Liv settled into her seat and looked up at the runway, soaking in every possible moment.

Realizing that all eyes were on her, Liv adjusted her jeans just slightly and steadied herself on Anna's heels. She inched forward in time to the music, trying desperately to sedate her nerves. She still didn't know exactly how she had gotten here.

In an effort to look confident, Liv wiggled her butt and curtsied, soliciting cheers and whistles from the crowded club. She held Anna's sweaty hand tightly by her side, clutching it like a life raft. Looking to her left, Liv could see all the Music Mix interns sitting at the table smiling and laughing, urging them on. Liv glanced at Anna, who was grinning ear to ear beside her. She winked at Liv as they took a step down the runway.

Before Liv had accepted Anna's dare to hop up on the catwalk, she made Anna promise to join her. Double humiliation felt much better than going it alone. The catwalk looked like it was a mile long, and they had only gone two steps. But it was too late to turn back now.

Liv steeled her nerves as she and Anna moved forward again. Suddenly the music (which had been some cheesy, uninspiring Rick Springfield song) changed, and the first notes of ABBA's "Dancing Queen" came flowing out of the speakers lining the runway.

"You can dance, you can jive, having the time of your life . . ."

Anna and Liv looked at each other as they recognized the familiar lyrics and burst out laughing.

"See that girl, watch that scene, dig in the Dancing Queen . . ."

"This is definitely becoming our theme song, isn't it?" Liv yelled in Anna's ear.

Anna nodded, grinning. "Feel better about doing this now?" she yelled back.

Putting all shame aside, the two strutted down the runway in unison and shimmied in time to the music. They knew they looked completely ridiculous, but they were having so much fun that it really didn't matter.

As they hammed it up on the runway, Liv caught a glimpse of Rebecca dancing next to Colin on the floor. In fact, when she looked around, everyone in the club was dancing. No one was laughing at them— instead, everyone looked like they were having an incredible time. When the last notes chimed out of the speakers, both Liv and Anna slid to their knees, arms raised, and struck a pose. Everyone in the club was cheering, and the Music Mix interns all ran to the end of the runway to help them off the platform.

"That was incredible!" Katia screamed.

"Hilarious," Francesco chimed in.

Liv and Anna looked at each other and cracked up. "I can't believe we just did that," Anna said, giggling and gasping to catch her breath.

Laughing, Liv responded, "You *said* you wanted to dance tonight. You rocked!"

The rest of the night went by in a blur. In no time they were being whisked out of the club and into a taxi home. Liv settled into the backseat and leaned against Anna. She smiled and closed her eyes as "Dancing Queen" ran through her head over and over—*You can dance, you can jive, having the time of your life* . . .

I am, Liv thought happily. *I am having the time of my life.*

Should I Stay or Should I Go?

As promised, Anna's mom arrived early the next morning, and her knock at the door startled Liv from a deep, contented sleep. Anna hustled out of her bedroom, dressed and ready. She hurried through an introduction while Liv sat snuggled up under her covers in her couch-bed. She had made a motion to stand up for a proper handshake, but Anna's mom insisted she stay in bed.

Anna hastily showed her mom around their apartment, and less than five minutes later, Anna declared they were leaving. She and Liv had decided during the previous night's taxi ride home that Anna should take her mom out shopping and for high tea at Selfridges to soften her up a bit.

Liv hoped everything would be okay—she couldn't imagine the pressure Anna must be feeling. The phone calls and arguments had really taken their toll on her. Liv hoped Anna and her mom could sort things out so Anna could enjoy the rest of her summer guilt-free.

Though she would never admit it to Anna, Liv did sort of envy her roommate's parents' involvement in her life. Liv's dad was incredible, but she sometimes wished he paid more attention to what she was doing. She wouldn't even mind if he got a little more angry when she screwed up. He was often so wrapped up in his photography that Liv sometimes wondered if he noticed she was growing up. She only had one year left at home before she went off to college.

But now that she'd seen Anna's situation, she was beginning to realize that her dad's lack of involvement in decisions about her life was probably just his way of letting her know he supported her. He never said it, but maybe his silence was his way of encouraging her to make her own choices. *Hmmm,* she thought. *Interesting trick.*

Pulling herself out of bed, Liv realized she had the whole day to herself. Rebecca was in the shower, and seemed to be getting ready to go out. So Liv happily lazed around the apartment—under the careful watch of Hell Dog—before deciding how best to spend the day.

She was still surviving almost exclusively on Green Room leftovers, and she felt like she deserved a tasty lunch at one of the neighborhood pubs. She could hole away in a dark corner and work on ideas for the VJ for a Day competition. Things had been so hectic at work that she and Anna had had almost no time to think about their audition. They still had a month before the competition, but Liv knew how crazy things were going to get around the office with the Josh Cameron concert coming up.

Around noon she wandered out into the rainy early afternoon and into a pub just a few blocks from her flat. She was instantly comforted by the warm, dark interior, and she spotted a small open table in the back corner. The cozy restaurant made her feel very literary and Shakespeare-esque—she hoped the environment would inspire great ideas for the audition.

As she passed through the dark room, Liv's stomach dropped. Sitting in one of the deep red booths along the side wall was a way-too-familiar blond head. *Rebecca,* she groaned inwardly.

Rebecca spotted Liv just as Liv was deciding whether she could make a quick getaway, or if she had to stop and say hello. She realized that running off wasn't the most adult thing to do, but she didn't know if she could handle spending her lunch with Rebecca. *Maybe I'll get lucky and Rebecca will be with someone,* Liv mused. *Maybe she doesn't want to see me any more than I want to see her.*

Just as quickly as she had hoped Rebecca wasn't alone, Liv took it back. Because Rebecca was very definitely having lunch with someone . . . and that someone was Colin. Sure, Liv had vowed that she and Colin were just friends—and she was dating Josh Cameron, International Superstar— but she still cringed when she saw them together.

"Oh," Liv blurted out. "Hi, Rebecca. Hi, Colin."

"Li-uhv," Rebecca purred coldly. "How marvelous to see you here." *Is she joking?* Liv thought, her stomach churning.

Colin shot Rebecca a look, and said quickly, "Liv, join us."

Now, Liv could think of *nothing* she would rather *not* do at that moment than join Rebecca and Colin for lunch. But she could see no escape.

"So, what are you guys up to today?" Liv asked, though she wasn't entirely sure she wanted to know the answer.

"We're just—," Colin began, but Rebecca quickly cut him off.

"Oh, Li-uhv, Colin is just so sweet," she said, leaning in conspiratorially toward Liv. "He's taking me all around London today, showing me all of the sights. Isn't that just the sweetest thing you've ever heard?" She beamed across the table at Colin as Liv willed herself not to puke.

Although she was being totally unreasonable, Liv just couldn't stop herself from feeling pangs of jealousy. For some dumb reason, she thought Colin's tour around London had been for her alone. She now realized just how silly that assumption was.

What's wrong with you, Liv? Did you think Colin might be interested in you even though he knows about you and Josh Cameron, and he's clearly dating Rebecca? Did you think he was going to wait around for you?

"Yeah," Liv said, after a moment's silence. "That's really sweet, Rebecca." She glanced at Colin, who was focusing on the table in front of him.

"Are you *alone* today, Liv?" Rebecca asked with a smirk. "Where's Josh Cameron?"

All right, Liv thought bitterly. *Is that question really necessary?* Out loud, she said, "Oh, I'm not sure. You know how it is—preparing for his concert and everything. He's a busy guy." *Lame, Liv. Totally lame.* Liv had tried to keep the details of her relationship quiet, but her close friends knew she was "hanging out" with an International Superstar. Rebecca, however, was convinced Liv was making it all up.

"Yeah, Ah definitely know how it is. The concert is going to be fab-u-lous, by the way," Rebecca said with an air of superiority. Liv thought she noticed Colin shoot Rebecca a weird look across the table, but she couldn't be sure.

After a moment of awkward silence, Colin spoke. "We should probably get going, yeah?"

"Right," Rebecca said cheerfully. "Big day. Liv, you should definitely try the shepherd's pie. Ah tried some of Colin's and it was absolutely dee-lish."

Liv muttered something and hastily said good-bye. As Colin and Rebecca headed for the door, she noticed Colin lean over and mutter something quietly to Rebecca.

Rebecca frowned, then turned to look back at Liv. She broke into a huge pageant grin and waved. Liv managed a thin smile, then slid further into the booth.

"Urghhhhhh."

Liv looked up from her book as the door slammed. "Didn't go so well?" she asked, as Anna threw herself onto the couch.

"You could say that," Anna said, clunking her head against the back of the couch.

Liv folded down the corner on her page and tossed her book on the floor. "Details, please. If you want to share."

"Yeah, I'll share. I think I need to." Anna stood up and went to the fridge. She returned a moment later with two glasses of black currant juice and a packet of biscuits. "Let's just say, she isn't happy with me."

"Did high tea help?" Liv asked, smiling.

"Uh-huh," Anna mumbled, tearing open the cookies. "That was a good idea— she totally loved it. But she's still *really* upset with me. She says I broke our agreement."

"Yikes."

"I mean, I did say if she gave me this summer, I'd get back on track this fall. But I agreed to that when I didn't think there was really a chance I would be putting off college for a few years. But, Liv, I just can't do it." Anna had tears welling up in her eyes. Liv set her glass on the floor and leaned forward to give her roommate a hug.

Anna continued. "I don't know what I am going to do. I *know* I'll go to school—there's even a good chance I'll apply to med school—and that's part of the reason I feel like I have to take a couple years to explore now."

"What did your mom say to all that?" Liv asked.

"It was the first time I'd ever really mentioned any of this to her, so I think it came as a surprise. She just assumed I wanted everything she wanted. But I want to work at Music Mix! Not forever, but for a little while. . . ." Anna smiled weakly.

"I know you do." Liv didn't really know what to say. So she just sat and waited for Anna to continue.

"I know it's unlikely that I'll get a job from Simon Brown at the end of the summer, but I need to try," Anna said resolutely. "And if that doesn't work out, then I'll figure something else out. It feels so good not to have a plan—I know that sounds silly, but my whole life has been completely planned out, and I love that it could be a blank slate for the next few years."

Liv nodded. Everything Anna was saying made complete sense. But she couldn't stop thinking that the situation Anna was dealing with was the complete opposite of the one she would be dealing with in a year. She'd gotten so little pressure, and had so few ideas of what she was going to do, that college seemed like the only option for her. She was looking forward to the structure.

Anna guzzled the rest of her juice. "You know, even though today was awful and painful and really, really unpleasant, I'm glad I had a chance to talk to her about it. I think that she might sort of get it. Even though she's upset, I'm sort of hoping that on some level she understands what I've been going through. It's possible she might ease up for a while. At least until application season comes around again," Anna broke off, laughing.

Liv was happy to see Anna's mood brightening. "So you think you guys are good now?"

"Not good. But maybe better. I understand where she's coming from, and she understands that I need to do what I'm going to do, and forcing me to do something else isn't going to accomplish much." Anna grinned. "Even though I'm stubborn, I'm not stupid. . . . She knows I'll make the 'right' choices"—she made little quotes in the air—"eventually."

"You will *definitely* make the right choices," Liv said. "You have up until now, so I don't think there's much risk of that."

Anna stood up and turned on some music. "Now we just need to focus on getting me a job at Music Mix so I'm not homeless and penniless at the end of the summer," she laughed. "How was your day, dear?"

Liv groaned. "Not as terrible as yours, but definitely not good."

"Why?" Anna asked. "What happened?"

Liv quickly told Anna about her run-in with Colin and Rebecca. "It was just so awkward," she finished.

"You are totally into him," Anna said simply.

"What? No."

"I don't know—that's what it sounds like to me."

"That's crazy." Liv shook her head. "What about Josh Cameron? And what about the fact that Colin is dating *Rebecca*? There's something really wrong with him if he's attracted to her."

"Mmm-hmm." Anna grinned. As Liv reached over to swat her roommate with a pillow, the door to their apartment flew open and Rebecca floated in.

"Hi, girls," she said, winking. The look on Rebecca's face told Liv everything she needed to know. And it was then—Josh Cameron and Rebecca aside—that Liv realized Anna may have been more than a little bit right.

I Think We're
Alone Now

The next week flew by.

Liv hadn't heard anything from Josh Cameron since their tea at the Berkeley Hotel. She hadn't *really* noticed over the weekend, but as soon as she was at work on Monday, she became obsessed. She was, of course, hoping he might call or pop by her tollbooth at Music Mix. She held on to that hope throughout Monday and into Tuesday morning, eventually suffering a mild case of whiplash from looking up quickly every time someone came near her desk.

On Tuesday afternoon she convinced herself that this sort of behavior was normal for a pop star, and obviously she couldn't expect him to drop everything to make time for her.

By Wednesday she had rediscussed the situation with Anna so many times that Liv was starting to suspect Anna was avoiding her.

On Thursday she began to question whether she had totally misinterpreted their relationship.

By Friday, however, she was mad. Still no call.

Liv would never receive the Lifetime Achievement Award for Dating, but she did know that this sort of behavior was strange, to say the least. And something deep down was telling her that she should run as fast as possible the other way, pop star or not—this guy was not worth waiting for.

Finally released from the office at five o'clock on Friday with a hearty "Go, Girl!" Liv decided to drink away her Josh Cameron paranoia with a large café mocha and a side of treacle pudding at Tully's. Several minutes later she settled into a window table, shrugged off her sweater, and dug into her dessert.

She pulled out a notebook, hoping the caffeine kick would inspire some great ideas for the VJ for a Day audition. Liv had been thinking about the competition almost constantly, but had still come up with a grand total of zero good ideas.

Liv and Anna swore they would spend every night the next week planning. They were desperate to win, but they knew they had very little chance if they didn't get to work soon.

As she stuck her pen in her mouth, accidentally suctioning the cap to her tongue, Liv felt someone brush up behind her. Turning, Liv noticed Colin sitting down at the table behind her.

"Hey," she said, lifting an arm to wave.

"Hello you. All right?" Liv nodded and smiled. She loved how the English simply said "All right?" rather than "Are you all right?" or "How are you?" It just seemed so much simpler.

"Did you just get off work?" Liv closed her notebook and unsuctioned the pen cap from her tongue. A little raised bump had been left in its place.

"Long day, yeah? Mind if I join you?"

"For sure." Liv reached her leg out and pulled a spare chair to her table. "Have a seat."

"Ta." *Aha*, Liv thought, *another good Britishism*—"*ta*." The simple, short version of "thanks." She sometimes thought British English could be more difficult to follow than a foreign language. "So," Colin continued. "What are you working on?" He motioned to her notebook.

Liv shrugged. "Nothing, really. I was hoping to get started on our VJ for a Day audition stuff." She took a sip of her drink. "Anna and I are working on it together, but we're sort of having a hard time figuring out what to do."

"Well, don't they always say you're supposed to play to your strengths?" Colin said, sounding like Liv's high school guidance counselor. "What do you like? What are you passionate about?"

Liv considered Colin's question. "Lucky Charms. I really like Lucky Charms cereal. But you can't get it in England."

"Lucky Charms. Interesting." Colin nodded seriously. "Could be a good angle. But what I meant was, what are your music passions? You know, what kind of music do you like?"

"Ohhhh." Liv grinned. "Okay . . . honest answer, or appropriate for Music Mix answer?"

Colin laughed. "Honest answer."

"I love the seventies and eighties. I

grew up listening to ABBA, The Bangles, Blondie, U2, stuff like that. And I know the lyrics to every single Eagles song. No joke."

"Impressive," Colin said, nodding. "Maybe you should just do an Eagles sing-along? Showcase your unique talent," Colin suggested.

"I'm sure that would go over well," Liv said, laughing. "Thanks for the help. We'll figure it out eventually, I'm sure." She grabbed her bag and stuffed her notebook into it. "Did you know," she asked, smiling, "that today is the Fourth of July? If I were home, I would be getting ready to go to a picnic at the lake to celebrate."

"Obviously," Colin cut in, "here in London we won't be celebrating America's Independence from England."

"Obviously," Liv agreed.

"Though, the English are glad to be rid of you." Colin smirked. "Happy Independence!"

"Funny," Liv said, smiling. She felt so relaxed around him—his humor was weird, but it somehow it seemed to match hers perfectly. "Now, just because it's not a holiday here doesn't mean we have to mope around like it's some regular day. I think we should celebrate something. Say, for example, our independence from Music Mix—good-bye, Simon Brown and Andrew Stone. If only for the weekend."

"I'm up for it," Colin said, downing the rest of his Ribena juice box. "What do you have in mind?"

"I'm thinking hot dogs, sodas, blockbuster movie—your typical Fourth of July stuff." She grinned. "Some traditions are hard to break. Sound good?"

"Delicious. Very American." Colin nodded. "However . . . seeing as this is England, how would you feel about doing something a little more British?"

"Sure," Liv said, shrugging. "I'm up for anything."

"It's not exactly the movies, but there's this place I think you'll love."

Several minutes later Colin and Liv were strolling down Oxford Street, en route to Covent Garden. While they walked, they talked nonstop about everything—their families, the VJ for a Day audition, Music Mix. They easily slid back into the same natural conversation they had during their last London walk. Liv felt giddy and lighthearted as they approached the Millennium Bridge.

"Where are we going?" Liv asked as

they crossed the Thames. She could see the Tower of London off to their left, but had no idea where they were or where they were going. It was getting dark, and Liv suddenly realized they had been walking for almost two hours.

"You'll see. I just hope my uncle is there."

"Your uncle?" Liv said, stealing a glance at Colin. "Please don't tell me we're going to some sort of family picnic."

"We are not going to a family picnic. I promise." Colin smiled suspiciously and led Liv along the river. The river walk was almost deserted, and Liv was starting to feel slightly creeped out. *Does he know where he's going?* Liv wondered. Just as she was about to steal a subtle look over her shoulder to look for weird stray dogs and other creepy things, Colin turned down a short ramp and stopped. "We're here."

They were standing in front of a large round building that Liv immediately recognized from pictures as Shakespeare's Globe Theatre. "I've been dying to come here!" Liv exclaimed as Colin led her toward the entrance.

"I thought I remembered you saying how much you liked Shakespeare the first day I met you," Colin said, mirroring Liv's excitement. "I've been meaning to come here for a while—my uncle is one of the theater's prop masters, and I promised him I would pop by for a visit."

Colin led Liv inside the Globe's lobby, stopping briefly to talk to one of the staff. The clerk nodded when Colin introduced himself, and he ushered Liv and Colin through the building to the theater at the back. Liv's eyes widened as they passed replicas of Shakespeare's original Globe Theatre. Then they moved through an out-door corridor toward the stage.

They passed the main audience door and stepped into a bustling backstage area. A rosy, round man stood in the center of a circle of people, waving a sword. He looked up as Liv and Colin walked into the room, then threw his hands (which, frighteningly, still held swords) into the air and came barreling toward them. Clearly, this guy was Colin's uncle.

"M'boy!" the man exclaimed, gathering Colin into an awkward, roly-poly hug. Colin was nearly half a foot taller than his uncle, and only half as wide. Blushing, Colin introduced Liv to the man, who was—oddly—called Ginger (Colin later explained that Ginger got the nickname thanks to his red hair).

Ginger had an impossibly thick accent, and Liv—if she was being honest—couldn't understand more than ten words he was saying as he showed them around backstage. She just nodded and smiled, hoping she didn't look too stupid. Finally Ginger excused himself; a performance was under way, and he needed to outfit the cast of Romeo and Juliet with their swords and daggers. He explained, "It shan't be a bit of a tragedy without the swords, eh?"

Colin turned to Liv, laughing, as Ginger walked away. "You didn't understand anything he said, did you?"

Liv shook her head. "Not a word. Did I say anything stupid?"

"Nothing much," Colin said simply. He smiled secretly and looked like he was about to say more. But he didn't. He just motioned for her to follow as he led her into a quiet corner that was stuffed with trunks and dusty shoes. Liv suspected he was withholding something, and worried about what she might have said.

"What are you doing?" Liv whispered as Colin pried one of the trunks in the corner open. "Colin, seriously, I don't think we should take stuff."

"Not to worry, ma'am," Colin said,

winking. "You're going to have to trust me. Now . . ." He studied Liv carefully as he rustled through the trunk. "I think this will suit you nicely, yeah?"

Liv broke out laughing as Colin pulled an enormous red . . . thing . . . out of the trunk. He held it up, motioning for Liv to take the material from him. "You want me to put this, um, *frock* on?" she asked incredulously, eyeing the Renaissance-style dress.

Colin nodded and grinned, chuckling as he pawed through the trunk again. "It should fit over your clothes quite nicely. And for the gentleman . . ." Colin had pulled a long piece of checkered wool out of the trunk. "A kilt!"

"You're going to wear that?" Liv asked, giggling as Colin wrapped the material around his waist, forming a thick, unflattering skirt. She studied her dress curiously, giggling as she pulled the fabric over her head. It slipped over her T-shirt and jeans easily, and Liv poked her arms into the puffed sleeves. "How do I look?"

Colin looked up—he had been trying to secure his kilt with a large diaper pin—and burst out laughing. "I think it's missing something." Colin held up a finger as he stepped over to a rack against the wall. "A hat should complete the look." He held an enormous, wide-brimmed hat out to Liv and moved toward her to fasten the ties under her chin.

Liv studied Colin's face as he stood in front of her. His brow was furrowed, and he had pushed his lower lip out while he concentrated on unknotting the chin strap on Liv's hat. He looked up at her in the dim backstage light and smiled. His eyes were bright with laughter.

Liv broke into a smile. She felt completely silly and comfortable with Colin. Standing there in her enormous dress, watching Colin tie an Elizabethan hat around her head, Liv suddenly felt a flip in her stomach. *No!* she instructed herself. *Things are only this easy because you're* friends. *Nothing more!*

"There you go. All set," Colin said, moving away from Liv. "A hat for me," he said, quickly pulling a floppy felt hat from the rack, "and we're on our way!"

"On our way where?" Liv said, envisioning her and Colin strolling down the river walk in full costume. She hoped that wasn't what he had in mind—Colin was turning out to be even stranger than Liv.

"The theater, of course," Colin answered, poking a feather into the brim of his hat. "We missed the first act, but I believe you said you have never seen Shakespeare live?"

"I haven't. But how . . . ?"

"While you were busy nodding at everything he said, Ginger offered us seats to tonight's performance. You nodded, so I just figured . . . unless you don't want to go? It's not a comedy, but . . ." Colin tipped his hat at Liv and waited for a response.

"Of course I want to go!" Liv couldn't believe Ginger had offered them seats and she had hastily accepted. She felt really greedy, but was relieved she had been nodding, rather than shaking her head. "Shall we?"

Decked out in their silly costumes, Liv and Colin made their way through the back corridors of the Globe. Ginger had arranged a secret backstage platform for them to watch the show from. They were slightly behind and to the side of the action onstage, but Liv couldn't have been happier. She was wearing goofy clothes and watching Shakespeare from backstage at the Globe Theatre. In all her life, she could never have imagined she would *ever* be doing this.

As the curtain rose to start the second act, Liv turned to smile at Colin. "Thank you," she whispered.

He tipped his hat again. "Happy July Fourth," he whispered back. He settled into his seat and spread his kilt out around him. "You look lovely in a frock."

Love Is a Battlefield

"You!" Simon Brown bellowed in the general direction of the hallway. "Here!" Liv smiled. She had grown accustomed to Brown's no-nonsense ways, and was even starting to warm to his brusque way of summoning her to his office. It probably helped that she had been in a particularly good mood since her trip to the Globe on Friday too.

"Yes, Brown?" Liv popped her head into Brown's office and greeted him with a big smile. He looked up from his newspaper with a surly expression and cringed when he saw Liv's smile—Brown didn't like positive moods.

"Take that ridiculous expression off your

face. Are you tipsy?" Without waiting for an answer, he gave a dismissive wave. "I don't care. Anyway, you need to do something for me." He scanned a pile of papers on the corner of his desk. "We are producing a ridiculous program about the eighties. Complete rubbish, but . . ." He trailed off, muttering.

Liv waited patiently in his doorway. When a full thirty seconds had passed, she prompted him. "What can I do for you, Brown? I'm happy to help any way I can." Liv couldn't believe those words had just come out of her mouth. She sounded like a robot.

"Oh, yes, you. Right. I need you to do some research. Get me up to speed on some of the songs that made the eighties 'so bloody great.'" He made little quotes in the air. "Put something together, pull some information. Make me look good. The regular nonsense." He glanced up at Liv to make sure she was paying attention, then sighed dramatically.

"Okay," Liv said happily. "This sounds great. Do you——?"

"Go, Girl!"

Liv spun on her heel and moved away from Brown's door. Apparently there would be no further explanation. Even still, Liv could hardly contain her excitement. *Yesssss!* she thought giddily. *A real project! And it's perfect!* She had finally been asked to do something meaningful, to show Brown that she could do more than herd a roomful of freakish fans into their seats. Of course, she needed a little translation from Gloria (she had no idea what "make me look good" or "the regular nonsense" meant), but that should be no biggie.

A few minutes later Liv was standing in the Music Mix lobby, explaining the assignment.

"This is huge, Liv," Gloria said, after Liv finished reciting Brown's instructions. "He must really trust you."

Liv beamed. "Really?"

"Trust me, I would know," Gloria said, rolling her eyes. "You know I was his intern a few years ago, right?"

"For real?" Liv said, curious. "I had no idea. Was he this hard on you, too?"

"Oh, yeah. The thing is, he's actually a pretty great fellow if you can see past his creepy, self-centered exterior." Gloria laughed. "But seriously—this research he's asked you to do . . . it's a big deal. He never let me do anything more than make copies and file." Liv listened carefully as Gloria elaborated on Brown's hasty instructions—she wanted to make sure she got this right. And Gloria was an expert on Brown translation.

At the end of the following day, Liv returned to Brown's office, report in hand. She had spent two days gathering every interesting factoid about the eighties she could find. She had included little biographies of each of the major producers from the era, as well as photos and bios of each musician who had earned a number one spot on the Billboard charts.

She had also downloaded a bunch of music from iTunes (using Gloria's corporate card, which she hoped wouldn't get her friend in trouble), and burned CDs that featured each of the weekly chart toppers. Liv was excited about her report and CDs, and she stood in Simon Brown's door with a smile plastered across her face.

"Yes?" Brown didn't look up.

"I finished the report you asked me to do on the eighties," Liv said, moving toward his desk.

"Leave it," Brown said, motioning to the corner of his desk. Liv did as she was told, then retreated to her tollbooth to wait for his thoughts. The phone was ringing when she got there. Liv assumed it was her father calling to check in—he was the only person who ever called her at work. Seeing that her caller ID was an outside number, she hastily picked up the receiver and prepared herself for a long conversation.

"Hey, dad," she said, twirling her hair with her free hand.

"Well, that's an interesting nickname," the voice on the other end said, teasing. "Most girls just call me Josh, but you've always been a little different, Olivia."

Liv blushed, relieved that Josh Cameron couldn't see her at that moment. "Hi," Liv said, grinning. "I thought it was my dad. But, um, it isn't. It's you. So. How have you been?"

"It's been a while," Josh Cameron responded. Liv could hear the smile in his voice. "I've missed you."

"Me too," Liv said honestly. "Where have you been?" Liv groaned, realizing how needy and stalkerish that may have sounded.

"I've been in the States. But I'm back now. When can I see you?"

Liv's throat was dry. *Um, now?* she answered silently. "How about this weekend?"

Josh Cameron agreed, and they settled

on Saturday night. He was going to call her on Friday to work out the details—and he had given Liv his cell phone number, just in case. Hanging up, Liv couldn't stop smiling. She was going out with him again. She was going out with *Josh Cameron. Again!*

As she sat at her tollbooth, giddily reflecting on the conversation, Simon Brown sauntered over. He had *never* come to Liv's desk—his laziness prevented him from leaving his office—so she didn't really know what to do. Could she just sit there, or did she need to stand? Was she supposed to offer him her chair?

Brown solved the mystery by perching on the edge of Liv's desk, forcing her to back her chair up against the wall to give him room.

"Well done," Simon Brown said at last. "I'm impressed with your efforts." Liv could tell it had taken all of Brown's energy to dole out a compliment, which made his praise even more valuable.

"Thank you, Brown," she said, restraining herself from screaming with excitement.

"One more thing," Brown said, studying the contents of Liv's desk. "Will you be auditioning for the VJ for a Day contest?"

"Yes, sir . . . uh, Brown. Yes, Anna and I are planning to audition."

"Very well, then," Brown said, smiling slightly. His tan teeth glinted in the fluorescent light. "Very well."

As Brown sauntered off, retreating again to the confines of his office, Liv did a little dance at her tollbooth. She had done a good job. And unless she was totally misreading him, Liv was pretty sure Simon Brown had—in his strange, confusing way—just endorsed her VJ for a Day audition. At the very least, he wasn't totally against her auditioning.

And that alone was something.

That Friday, Liv was still floating. Brown had retreated back into his crabby shell, but now Liv knew that he wasn't totally out to get her. He hadn't stopped acting crass and rude, but at least he had shown Liv—if only for a minute—that he was the tiniest bit human inside.

She was distracted all morning, obsessing about her date with Josh Cameron the next day. She couldn't prevent her nerves from going crazy every time she thought about hanging out with him. She assumed things would get more natural between them soon—at least, that's what she was hoping. *I won't be intimidated by his celebrity status forever, right?* she wondered over a midmorning latte. *He's the same as everyone else—just a little more . . . famous. But I know that doesn't* really *mean anything.*

Liv had started to realize her obsession with celebrity was silly—now that she had spent a few weeks surrounded by stars and their entourages at Music Mix, she had seen firsthand how *average* most of them were. Usually they just had a touch more attitude.

Celebrities are just people who got lucky and had their talent turned into fame. So why did they deserve her respect and admiration so much more than, say, someone like Anna did? When she thought about it that way, Liv realized that she would much rather spend an evening with Anna than with someone famous *just* because they're famous. At least with her friends, she was comfortable being herself. She didn't worry about whether she was doing and saying the right things.

Liv realized she had been nervous around Josh Cameron for all the wrong reasons. When she let herself just *be*, things were always so much smoother and less awkward. She needed to let down her guard and hang out with him as an equal—not as Josh Cameron, *Superstar,* and Olivia Phillips, *Who?*

But before she could test out her new theory, Liv was forced to deal with one more celebrity ego—and this one made it tougher for her to remain calm and natural. Friday afternoon, Liv was summoned to the studio where Cherie Jacobson, Josh Cameron's ex, was in rehearsal. Cherie was scheduled to perform on *Hits Parade* in just a few hours, and Liv was dying to see what she was like.

Part of Liv didn't want to meet her new boyfriend's ex, but the other part of her was desperately curious. Liv figured there was no way Cherie knew about her and Josh Cameron's relationship—it's not like they'd been out in public together after that first date—but her stomach was in knots nonetheless.

Cherie's new single was a response to Josh Cameron's single, "Split," and rumored to be harsh. Their breakup had been smeared through the tabloids, and Cherie had gotten most of the bad press. Apparently, she had gone psycho, and frankly, Liv was a little scared of her.

When Liv got to the studio, she quietly poked her head in to catch the attention of one of Cherie's assistants. A tall, rail-thin woman came to the door and ushered Liv inside. Cherie stood in the center of the *Hits Parade* stage, red hair flowing down her back as she belted out the last notes of her song. When the music ended, she returned the microphone gently to its stand and smiled at Liv.

"Hi, sweetie," she said, her voice dripping kindness. "Thanks for coming by. I hear you're the girl to go to when I need something?"

That's me, Liv thought, already annoyed. *Waitress, dog groomer, maid—at your service. There's that celebrity attitude.* Out loud, she said, "Yep. What can I do for you?"

"What you can do," Cherie said, all kindness stripped from her voice, "is lay your hands off my boyfriend." Liv's knees buckled. "I have friends everywhere, and they tell me everything. Just to remind you, you're nobody. And I can make your life miserable."

Liv stared at Cherie Jacobson. "Excuse me?" Liv said, much more boldly than she had intended. For some reason, she suddenly wasn't intimidated.

Cherie's smile returned to her face, and the false charm that had been there earlier snuck back into her voice. "What I mean to say is," she said, putting her hand on Liv's arm, "be careful. You don't know what you're dealing with." And with that, she spun on her heel and returned to the Green Room.

Liv headed out of the studio. As she walked down the hall, she considered Cherie's warning. She was a little flattered that Cherie was threatened by her, but equally freaked out. She didn't want anything to put a damper on the next day's date with Josh Cameron. . . . but what had Cherie meant when she said, "You don't know what you're dealing with"?

You're So Vain

Liv stood in line at the half-price theater ticket booth at Leicester Square, soaked and miserable. She hadn't realized that the ticket office didn't open until eleven, and she'd been waiting to buy tickets for almost two hours.

Stupidly, she hadn't brought an umbrella. And shortly after she had settled into her place near the front of the line, the sky had opened up and poured for twenty minutes straight. She had nonchalantly tried to duck under her neighbor's umbrella, but when the man in front of her saw her inching closer and closer, he had freaked out and vacated the line. The bad news was that she had lost her only hope of staying dry. The good news was that she had moved up in line.

The rain had eventually slowed to a drizzle, but the damage was done. Liv was cranky, dripping wet, and completely void of any remaining patience. Finally, a few minutes after eleven, the booth opened and she approached the window.

"Two tickets to *As You Like It*, please." Liv smiled at the booth attendant and waited.

"I have two tickets in the first row of the second balcony. Okay?"

Liv wasn't sure. The truth was, she didn't know why she had agreed to do this in the first place. Why, when Josh Cameron had called and asked her out again, had she insisted on planning the date? He was a multimillionaire, and she was . . . well, *not* a multimillionaire. In fact, these tickets were going to cost her an entire week's salary. She could only hope that he would pay for the rest of the date.

But, she thought, *this way I can show him what I like to do.* She was confident Josh Cameron would love Shakespeare just as much as she did, and she couldn't wait to see one of her favorite plays live onstage.

"That's fine. The first row of the balcony

is fine." Liv paid, and wandered away from the half-price booth, tickets in hand. She was worried that he would be disappointed with their seats. He probably only ever sat in the first row. Or some sort of luxury box. *Whatever,* she thought, shrugging off her paranoia. *I'm sure he's not that shallow. And he said he liked me because I'm "normal."*

Nine hours later, dry and umbrella-ed, Liv stood outside the theatre, waiting for Josh Cameron's limo to arrive. She had gotten there a few minutes before their planned meeting time, and had been waiting for twenty minutes. The play was supposed to start in less than five minutes, and Liv was starting to get nervous . . . and wet again.

Only moments before the theater doors closed, a limo came zipping around the corner. Josh Cameron hopped out of the backseat and embraced Liv in a quick hug. Several passing tourists stopped to stare and point, and a small herd of paparazzi materialized out of nowhere. Liv was taken aback, but Josh Cameron deftly stepped away and smiled for the cameras. He waved, then took Liv's arm and moved quickly into the theater.

"As usual, you look incredible," Josh

Cameron said as Liv silently led him up the stairs toward their seats. She was still stunned by the scene outside—she had never been near paparazzi before, and she was freaked that she might be *in* the pictures. "I apologize for my lateness," Josh Cameron continued.

Liv waited for a further explanation, but none was forthcoming. "It's okay," she said simply. "But we should hurry. The show's about to start."

As they settled into their seats in the second balcony, Josh Cameron looked around. People were staring, and he shifted nervously in his seat. Smiling uncomfortably, he whispered to Liv, "We're an awfully long way from the stage, aren't we?"

Liv's stomach dropped. She couldn't believe she had been so stupid as to try to arrange this. He was probably horrified that he was stuck in the back of the theater with normal people. They could barely see over the balcony edge, and they were sitting a million miles above the stage. "I'm sorry. It's all they had," she explained quietly, studying her program to avoid his eyes.

"Not to worry, Olivia," he murmured in her ear. "I just appreciate you making the effort. Like I told you before, it's nice to be normal every once and a while. And it's refreshing to go on a date that my assistant didn't plan." Then he slouched down in his seat to hide from curious onlookers. As the curtain rose, Josh Cameron slid his hand into Liv's and left it there through the rest of the play.

Liv could barely focus on *As You Like It*. Fortunately, she had read the play at least five times and easily followed the plot. But she was antsy and distracted, worrying about whether Josh Cameron was having a good time. He kept shifting anxiously in his seat, and hadn't laughed at any of the obviously funny parts.

When the final curtain dropped, Liv clapped and cheered with the rest of the crowd. Josh Cameron took his cell phone out of his pocket and quickly tapped out a text message. Liv glanced at him, and he stuffed his phone back into his pocket. When the cast took their places on the stage for the curtain call, Josh Cameron stood and led Liv out of the theater. He hurried them down the stairs and into the lobby, just as the crowds started to fill the main level of the theater.

"Let's get out of here," he said, weaving through the crowd as Liv struggled to catch up. She didn't know why they were in such a rush, but just assumed this meant that he had *not* liked the play. He held Liv's hand tightly as they moved through the crowded lobby and toward the front doors. Just as they were about to exit the theater, Liv's stomach lurched when she spotted a familiar face near one of the side doors.

"Colin!" she shouted, eager to be heard above the noisy crowd. Liv waved as Colin looked up and spotted her. Squeezing Josh Cameron's hand to get his attention, she leaned toward him and said, "Hang on one second—a friend of mine is here. I just want to say hi."

Liv crossed the lobby toward Colin with her date in tow. Her heart skipped a beat when she saw that Colin also wasn't alone— rather, he was with a gorgeous girl. *Who is she, and where is Rebecca?* Liv wondered.

Liv forced herself to shove aside the instant jealousy by focusing on Josh Cameron's hand in hers. *You are on a DATE,* she reminded herself. *With Josh Cameron. So stop being stupid. Now.*

"Liv," Colin stated simply. Liv thought he looked a little pale and uncomfortable, but couldn't be sure. "Did you enjoy the show?"

"Yeah!" Liv shouted, a little too loudly and awkwardly for her taste. "Oh, umm, have you guys met? Josh Cameron, this is Colin Johnstone."

"Colin, is it?" Josh Cameron said. Liv thought she caught him sizing up Colin's date, but chose to pretend she hadn't. "You don't actually like this stuff, do you, mate?" He motioned in the direction of the stage and laughed. Liv's hunch had been correct. Josh Cameron did not like Shakespeare. *Marvelous.*

"Yes, it's Colin," Colin responded coldly, glancing at Liv. "And yes, I love 'this stuff.'" Liv shifted uncomfortably. Colin continued, "Liv, this is Lucy. Lucy, Liv." Liv shook hands with Lucy, curious about who the mystery date was.

A few seconds of awkward silence passed, then Josh Cameron broke in. "Well, this has been fun. Olivia, are you ready?" Liv nodded, and he turned to address Colin and Lucy. "We're off to the 400 Bar—I'm thinking of doing a little impromptu performance tonight. We'll see, people may get lucky." He winked and flashed his dimples. "If you would like to join us, I guess I can *try* to . . ."

Colin broke in, "We have other plans.

Thanks for the generous offer." Liv groaned quietly. This meeting was not going well. *Why,* she wondered, *were both guys acting so rude?*

"It was nice to meet you, Liv," Lucy said kindly. She nodded at Josh Cameron, then linked her hand around Colin's arm and led him out of the theater.

As Liv followed Josh Cameron out of the theater's front doors, she briefly debated asking him why he had been so rude to her friend. She also considered asking him if it would have been so difficult to *try* to enjoy the date she had planned. But she didn't ask. She just followed him silently through the after-theater crowd and into his waiting limo. She sat quietly in one corner of the car while Josh Cameron made several calls, figuring out which club was hot that night.

"The 400 Bar it is," he exclaimed eventually, flipping his phone closed. "The club owner is totally into me trying out my new single tonight." His face was flushed, and he suddenly looked much more like a little kid than an international pop star.

"That's great," she said hollowly, sinking into her seat across from him. "What's the new single called?"

"It's a remix of 'You're So Vain,' the

Carly Simon song. You know the one?" He hummed a few bars of the song. Liv certainly did know the one, and smiled at the irony of the song's title. It somehow seemed just perfect for Josh Cameron. "I'm trying to work it out before my Music Mix concert. It's nice to try it out for my peeps, you know?" He paused, tapping out another text message. "All right! We're here!" Josh Cameron pushed open his door and hopped out of the limo. He turned, checking to see that Liv was following him.

Inside the 400 Bar, the lights were low and the floors were grimy. It was the opposite of Meat by appearance standards, but the people were equally intimidating. Liv had still not gotten used to the VIP scene. She could feel everyone staring at her, and she felt like a complete clod. She had worn a thin sweater and chinos to the theater, and realized now how ridiculous she must look wearing Gap at a trendy bar.

Liv followed Josh through the crowd to a small bar across the room. Josh Cameron rested his arm on the jukebox against the wall and waved to a half-dressed bartender pouring a beer. She sauntered over, planting a kiss firmly on Josh Cameron's mouth. He chuckled; Liv gawked.

"What's up, El?" he asked the bartender, flashing a quick smile at Liv, who was still dwelling on the strange and unexpected kiss.

"Hey, Joshie," she responded with a thick Irish accent. "We've been waiting for you. Tracy!" She called to a large, bald man on the other end of the bar. The man—Liv could only assume this was Tracy—moved toward them. Wordlessly, he slid the juke-box away from its place on the wall, revealing a door that had been hidden behind it. Liv stared as Tracy pulled a large ring of keys off his belt and slid one into the old-fashioned lock on the wooden door. With a whine, the door slid open.

Looking through the hidden door, Liv could only see feet and legs. The bottom half of the door opening was sealed up with concrete, and the top half opened onto the floor level of another room. It appeared that the room behind the door was about three feet higher than the room they were currently in, and they would need to shimmy through a tiny little opening if they were going to enter it. As Liv stared in confusion, Josh hoisted himself up and slid into the secret room.

Suddenly Liv's feet left the ground.

Tracy had lifted and spun her toward the door's opening. Before she had a chance to react, she was sitting on the floor of the other room, and the secret door was closed behind her. Liv could hear the jukebox sliding back into its place against the wall. She was trapped.

Standing up, Liv scanned the hidden bar they had just entered. Gone were the grimy, soiled floors and dark, depressing lighting. This bar was snazzy and clean, complete with smooth tiled floors and shimmery lighting. A low bench ran around the perimeter of the room, but it was empty. Most of the people in the room were dancing or mingling around the bar, clustered in small groups. Each group had at least one person whom Liv recognized as some sort of celebrity—including Bethany Jameson and Christy Trimble, the starlets she had first met at Meat. Luckily, Cherie Jacobson was nowhere in sight.

Josh Cameron had disappeared, leaving Liv to fend for herself. It suddenly felt like she had turned up at her high school prom with her dress tucked into her underwear and no date.

Luckily, most people in the bar hadn't really noticed her, so she took a moment to wander around the room and check it out.

She noticed that one wall was a panel of murky glass that looked over the bar they had originally entered. Liv assumed that they were, once again, in some sort of VIP section, and the lower-level bar on the other side of the jukebox was the "regular" area of the club.

"Hello, you." Josh Cameron had sauntered up behind Liv while she was looking through the window at the crowds of people on the other side of the hidden door. "Pretty incredible, isn't it?" Liv turned around, and he planted a soft kiss on her lips. Nuzzling into her neck, he continued, "This club is great for trying out new songs because we can see how the crowd responds on the dance floor." He gestured to the windows.

Liv decided not to tell him how creepy she thought that sounded. *This is like Pop Star Big Brother or something.* Her discomfort seemed to melt away as she relaxed into his arms. Liv wasn't really into the VIP club scene, but she liked having Josh Cameron's attention shining upon her. Maybe she could get used to the scene—if it meant more people noticing Josh Cameron noticing *her.* He kissed her again and a stray curl brushed against Liv's cheek.

"Well, baby," he said, breaking the

moment with a quick kiss on the cheek. "You have fun. I've got some people I need to talk to. . . ." With that, he worked his way back into the crowd and left Liv alone again.

For the next three hours Liv sat patiently in the corner of the room while Josh Cameron worked the club, meeting, greeting, and schmoozing. She had—awkwardly—tried to join him a few times, but he had mostly ignored her. So each time, after a few minutes of standing or dancing on the outside of a circle of celebrities, she retreated back to her spot on one of the benches overlooking the lower bar.

She had never felt more like a boring, out-of-place loser than she did that night. She self-consciously adjusted her sweater periodically, attempting to lower the neck-line to give herself a slightly more stylish look, but it was useless. No matter what she did to physically fit in, she would just never click in this world.

Just as Liv began to drift off to sleep (her cushioned bench had been too tempting, and she was Bored Bored Bored), Liv spotted her "date" coming her way. She smiled weakly as he slid up next to her. *Finally.*

"You," Josh Cameron said, poking Liv's

nose softly, "are such a sweetheart for understanding that I have people to talk to and things to take care of." He ran a hand through his hair. "You know, it's so much easier dating a regular girl than a celebrity. I mean, it's amazing that you don't really have your own stuff to take care of—that way, it's cool for you to just sit here and chill."

Liv stared at him. *Did I just hear that right? I "don't have my own stuff" to do? I can just "sit here and chill"?! Am I a lapdog or something?*

"And," Josh Cameron continued, his dimples deepening, "dating you will do wonders for my image after Cherie. I've really come out of this breakup looking like the normal one, haven't I?" He leaned over to kiss Liv, but she quickly stood up before he could get within six inches. She had—officially—had it.

"Josh," she began, "yes, I am just a 'regular girl,' and yes, I have been patient while you've ignored me all night. But normal people do have lives. And I do, contrary to your opinion, have plenty of things I would be *much* happier doing. So while you may think that dating me will be good for your image, I don't think that dating you will be good for me." She paused to take a breath. "I thank you for *gracing* me with your presence over the past few weeks, but now I have *very* important things I need to attend to. And *this* is just not worth my time. So good night."

And with that, she pushed through the crowd, knocked on the secret door, and slid through the hole and out of her VIP existence.

Sunglasses at Night

Josh Cameron had called Liv at work several times in the days following her Girl Power moment, but Liv resisted his charms. On their final date, she had realized she didn't like the person she was when she was with him, and she hated that she felt so powerless around him. Liv had avoided her gut instinct the first few times they had gone out, but now she realized the celeb lifestyle wasn't for her, anyway—she wanted to feel comfortable being herself. And while Josh Cameron claimed to love her honesty and "all-American, real girl" ways, she just couldn't get into being the novelty date.

The only bad thing about the breakup was that Liv had plenty of time to dwell on her now obvious—and depressingly unreciprocated—crush on Colin. She thought constantly about their run-in at the theater, disgusted by how rude Josh Cameron had been to him.

Liv was dying to know who Colin's mystery date had been that night. She had been tempted to ask Rebecca, but figured that was probably not the nicest thing to do. Either Rebecca knew about Lucy and chose to ignore her, or Liv would be the bearer of really awkward news. In spite of her relationship with Rebecca, Liv felt sorry for her roommate—did she know about Lucy?

One night that week, after a particularly grueling day at work, Liv decided to stop off at Tully's for a cup of tea. She had spent her day running around town looking for a particular brand of snack bar. One of Music Mix's performers had brought his girlfriend to the set with him, and she was craving some special Australian snack bar that she missed from home . . . so Liv was sent out to fetch one for her. After checking every sandwich shop and market around Oxford Street, Liv had finally found the bar more than five hours later at an Australian sweater shop in Notting Hill. By the time she got back to the studio, the guest and his girl were gone. *A day well spent,* she mused.

She breezed into Tully's and was greeted warmly by the woman behind the counter. As she waited for her tea, the frustrations of her day quickly fading, Liv was startled by someone tapping on her shoulder. Turning, she was pleased to see Colin. She had run into him at Tully's a million times that summer—when she was on cappuccino runs for Green Room guests and he was satisfying Andrew Stone's soy latte addiction—but seeing him startled her, considering how much she'd been thinking about him that week. "Oh, hi," she said, noticing a flush creeping up her cheeks.

"Hi, Liv. All right?"

"Yeah, good. You?" *This is awkward,* Liv thought, cringing. *Why?* Before he could say anything more, she continued. "You know, I've been looking for you all week. I just wanted to apologize for my, um, date last weekend—he was a real jerk to you at *As You Like It.* I'm sorry."

"Liv, you don't need to apologize for him. Unless you were telling him what to say, it really wasn't your fault."

"Thanks. But it's my fault he was there,

so I guess I feel somehow responsible." She paused. "So, ah, did you enjoy the play?"

"Yeah, it was great." Colin turned to collect his order from the counter. Liv noticed two cups, and glanced quickly around the room. She spotted Lucy, the girl from the play, gazing out the window at a table across the room. Colin's jacket was draped over the back of the chair next to hers. He continued, "We loved it."

Liv grimaced. There it was—"we." Liv knew it wasn't any of her business, but she was just dying to know how this girl fit into Colin's relationship with Rebecca. Liv suddenly felt oddly protective of her roommate, and didn't want to see her get hurt. She couldn't stop herself from blurting out, "So . . . how are things with you and Rebecca?"

Colin groaned. "Man, I knew you were going to ask me that." Liv nodded, watching Lucy out of the corner of her eye. "Rebecca and I are *not* together, if that's what you're implying."

Liv raised her eyebrows. "Really?"

"Definitely. Rebecca is very much *not* my type. But I do value her as a friend. I know that might sound crazy, but she's really very sweet, and there's something about her that just makes me laugh."

"Yeah, something about her makes me laugh too," Liv said sarcastically, setting her tea down on the nearest table. Colin hovered next to her table as Liv poured milk in her tea and stirred.

Colin continued, "The thing you should probably know is, in our first week in London, Rebecca really confided in me. She was worried she wasn't fitting in, and felt like she couldn't get along with you or Anna. She felt like an outsider, and I think she thought that spending time with me might give her credibility or something." He paused. "I liked hanging out with her. It's not a pity thing—she's really funny, if you get past that petty, selfish exterior. I just don't know if she's that great with other girls, yeah?"

"Yeah," Liv agreed. "I think that might be a fair assessment." She didn't know why she was being so rude, but she couldn't stop herself. *It's not Rebecca's fault I missed my chance with Colin,* Liv mused. *I'm the only one to blame for that.*

Colin was still holding both cups of tea and had begun to fidget. He said quietly, "But I think she also sort of thought that if she and I spent time together, it might make you jealous." Colin paused. "But that's ridiculous, considering . . ."

"Considering what?" Liv asked, curious.

"Considering . . . other relationships." Colin looked down at his feet, then glanced at Lucy. "Right . . . ," he said, suddenly awkward. "Well, our tea is getting cold."

"Yeah, you should probably get back." Liv couldn't believe she'd been so wrong about Colin and Rebecca. "It was good to see you, Colin. Again, I'm sorry about the whole Josh Cameron thing last weekend."

"No problem," Colin said. "I'm sure he's a really great guy once you get to know him." And then he lifted one of the teacups in a little wave and strolled back to his table.

"Ah was talking to some of the producers from the events team, and they are just pos-ah-ti-uhv that I will win this little VJ for a Day contest." Rebecca delicately sipped her coffee, and studied Liv's reaction.

"That's great, Rebecca," Liv said blandly, for what felt like the thousandth time that night. "I'm really happy for you."

Earlier that evening Liv and Anna had decided they needed a girls' night out. Feeling generous, they had invited Rebecca to join them. Liv had thought a lot about what Colin had told her about Rebecca, and felt guilty that Rebecca hadn't made many friends in London. She really didn't want to be part of the reason someone was so unhappy, and she had vowed to try to give her roommate another chance.

About ten minutes after they left the office, Liv had regretted her generosity. Rebecca hadn't stopped talking, and most of their conversations for the past two hours had centered on Rebecca's brilliance. And, much to Liv's dismay, Rebecca refused to stop talking about the VJ for a Day contest. The good thing about Liv's breakup with Josh Cameron was that it had freed up plenty of time for her and Anna to focus on their audition material. They had finally formulated the beginning of a plan, and had been working almost nonstop to perfect it. Liv was confident that they would have a great segment ready in time for the auditions in a few weeks, but that didn't mean she was any more excited about listening to Rebecca's take on the auditions.

As Rebecca chattered on, bragging about her "fab-u-lous" ideas for her audition, Liv and Anna finished their drinks and stood up to leave. Rebecca didn't miss a beat. She continued to talk while sweeping My Rover into her arms (she had somehow gotten away with bringing Hell Dog to work for "show and teh-ull" that day).

Then she drained her coffee and dropped her Gucci sunglasses back into place on her perky little nose. Liv couldn't figure out why Rebecca was wearing sunglasses at night, but, considering Liv's own fashion expertise, figured she really wasn't the best person to criticize someone else's style.

The three flatmates made their way outside and headed for the tube at Piccadilly Circus. "Ah don't know if you know this, but I actually won the Junior Miss contest in Texas." Rebecca fixed Anna and Liv with a serious stare through her Guccis.

"I never would have guessed," Liv muttered to herself. Anna heard her and started giggling.

"They told me I was a natural onstage." Rebecca held My Rover up to her face and pushed her lips out to give him a kiss. She continued in a baby voice, addressing My Rover. "So I just *know* I'm going to be the very best VJ that Music Mix has ever seen. Look out England—Miss Texas is here!" Rebecca smiled widely, revealing her perfect white teeth. Liv wondered if Rebecca put Vaseline on her teeth in real life, like they do in pageants. They were unnaturally shiny.

"You know, Li-uhv," Rebecca said sweetly, pausing as they passed the Piccadilly Circus fountain. "Maybe you could just help me with *my* audition. Work behind the scenes or something? Ah mean, I just don't want it to be uncomfortable for y'all when I win." Rebecca pulled a coin out of her clutch. "Lucky penny. Here's to my win!" she said, lowering her ridiculous sunglasses to wink as she tossed the coin over her shoulder into the fountain. Then she walked up the steps to the fountain base platform and started strutting around the edge.

As she listened to Rebecca ramble on, Liv considered the question she had been asking herself all night. *Was Colin right about Rebecca? Why would she come out with us unless she actually likes us better than she lets on?*

Liv was jolted out of her head by a high-pitched squeal. She turned back toward the fountain just in time to see Rebecca teetering madly, her high heel stuck in a crack in the concrete. Flailing her arms, Rebecca buckled sideways and landed right in the Piccadilly Circus fountain. Several groups of tourists, out for a late-night stroll, quickly grabbed their cameras and snapped pictures. "Ah'm okay!" Rebecca said, flashing her pearly whites just before her hair hit the water. "Ah've got My Rover and my Guccis—I'm okay!"

Liv watched, horrified, as Rebecca floundered in the fountain. She was trying to keep her sunglasses and My Rover in the air. As Liv moved to help her out of the fountain, she could see tears of humiliation welling up in Rebecca's eyes.

For once, Liv felt genuine empathy for her flatmate. *She* is *normal*, Liv thought. *She's desperate for attention and doesn't know how to treat people, but she's not immune to humiliation.* In that moment Liv suddenly realized that under Rebecca's thick veneer of I Love Myself-itis, she was just as self-conscious and awkward as anyone else. Rebecca just hadn't figured out a normal way of dealing with it.

She may be annoying and weird and talk about herself way too much, Liv thought, *but maybe she just needs people to be nice to her so she can realize she's safe being herself.* Looking at her soaked and tear-drenched flatmate floundering in the fountain, Liv vowed to give Rebecca another chance—for real, this time. Reaching out her hand to take My Rover from Rebecca's slippery, wet arm, Liv smiled. "Are you okay?" she asked, true concern ringing in her voice.

Rebecca looked up at Liv as a tear rolled down her face. "Ah'm fine. Thank you," she smiled. "Li-uhv, can you please dry My Rover's ears? He's prone to infection."

You Spin Me Round (Like a Record)

"Have you ever heard the theory that people and their pets look alike?" Liv was sitting in a small windowless room, surrounded by no fewer than twenty assorted dogs, cats, and one very loud parakeet.

Anna, who was squatting by her side, straightened the hood on a greyhound's zip-up sweater and nodded. "I have heard that."

"Don't you think Josh Cameron's dog looks just like him?" Liv giggled, gesturing to a black cocker spaniel that was lying on a cushy armchair in the corner of the room, surveying the rest of the dogs with pity. "The curls, the charming look, the snobby attitude—it's all there. Poor dog. I have to say, every time I look at that dog, I freak out just a little. It's frightening how similar they look."

Liv had totally gotten over Josh Cameron, but couldn't stop a hint of bitterness from creeping up—in part, because she had been assigned the worst possible task at that night's Josh Cameron concert. Over the past two weeks the only thing anyone at Music Mix had talked about was the approaching concert, and now that concert was finally here.

Lucky Liv had found herself assigned to the charming job of tending to Josh Cameron's dog and his backup dancers' pets during rehearsal and the concert. Which is why she was, at that moment, locked in the pet-bed room she herself had prepared a few weeks before—along with twenty unruly, high-attitude designer pets.

Anna had volunteered to accompany Liv to the concert to help out—she hadn't gotten an invite to the concert as part of the wardrobe team, and really wanted to see the show. Liv had asked Brown if she could bring backup, and he had—in a fit of kindness—agreed.

The two of them had been stuck in the pet room for the past two hours while Josh Cameron and his dancers rehearsed and relaxed in style. Liv and Anna's Animal

House was not quite as plush—each of the dogs and cats had a squishy bed or pillow, but Liv and Anna were forced to sit on the floor. There were no human-size accommodations in sight.

As Liv prepared doggie dinners, Simon Brown poked his head into the circus and gestured to Liv. "You," he barked. "You're needed at the stage. It seems one of the dancers couldn't part with her pooch until the show started. I refuse to have that . . . *creature* . . . crawling out onstage during the show. So you will collect it from her and hustle back here. Go, Girl!"

Liv groaned. This chore would potentially involve her running into Josh Cameron, which she had been trying to avoid. So far she had succeeded—her Pet Land headquarters had certainly been a good hiding place. But she supposed she couldn't avoid it all night, and she hustled off down the hall in search of the rogue pet.

In the darkened hallway Liv literally ran into Christy Trimble. Christy was widely known to be the fiercest celebrity on the pop circuit, and everyone tried to stay on her good side. Liv suspected her rather loud outburst at the 400 Bar hadn't left her in Christy's good graces.

"Olivia, isn't it?" Christy asked, surveying Liv's pet hair–covered jeans and T-shirt. "I've been hoping I would see you again."

Uh-oh.

Christy continued, "Your little 'exchange' with Josh Cameron at the 400 Bar a few weeks ago . . ." She made little quotes in the air with her perfectly manicured fingers, then broke into a smile. "Well done. I haven't seen anyone stand up to Josh like that before. I'm impressed."

"Oh," Liv said, flustered. "Uh, thanks. Really?"

"Really. That speech of yours was priceless. He needed that. And, despite what the gossip rags say, Cherie Jacobson is a good friend of mine. I filled her in on your little outburst, and she got a huge kick out of it. She thinks you're fabulous now, and wanted me to pass along her congratulations. You were a hit, girl.

"If you ever need anything, give me a call." Christy hastily scribbled out her cell phone number on a piece of paper and stuffed it into Liv's jeans pocket. "I mean it. Anything, anytime. I like you—you have spunk." With a wink, Christy turned and strutted down the hall.

Liv laughed in disbelief, and wandered

over to the stage area. As she walked through the wings, Liv heard Rebecca before she saw her. Rebecca had been given the opportunity to introduce Josh Cameron to the audience— a reward from the producers on the events team, apparently—and she hadn't stopped gloating about it all week. Now Rebecca was standing just off to one side of the stage, swooshing her hair and rehearsing.

"Y'all, please welcome Josh Cameron!" Liv cringed when she heard Rebecca's drawl. As Liv poked her head around a curtain to see if the backup dancers were anywhere nearby, Rebecca spotted her and motioned her to come over.

"Oh, Li-uhv," she gushed. "Ah just can't wait to do this. I'm ready!" Liv was a little frightened—Rebecca seemed a lot like a cheerleader. A psycho cheerleader. There was something unsettling about how much enthusiasm she seemed to have about doing this introduction.

"Are you nervous?" Liv asked, only mildly curious. If she had to get up onstage in front of thousands of people, she would be freaked out. Her performance on the catwalk at Runway had been hard enough. But Liv suspected Rebecca wouldn't show weakness, even if she were mortified.

"Not one teeny tiny little bit," Rebecca said. Liv thought she saw a hint of terror cross Rebecca's face, but it was immediately covered by another huge grin and a hair toss.

Just as Liv was about to excuse herself to continue her quest for the missing dog, the lights dimmed and the crowd started cheering. The concert was about to start.

"Oh gosh, Li-uhv," Rebecca said, grabbing Liv's arm tightly for support. "Please don't leave me. It's almost time." Liv studied Rebecca's face in the dim light. The self-composed Rebecca that had been next to her a second before was gone—she had been replaced by a panic-stricken, teary-eyed mess.

Liv could hear the band tuning behind the curtain onstage. She and Rebecca were shooed to the side as the backup dancers filed past and into their places onstage. One dancer hastily dumped a pug (who was wearing a PUG REVOLUTION T-shirt) into Liv's arms as she passed. Just as Josh Cameron sauntered past them and up the stairs to the stage (without so much as a glance in Liv's direction), a producer approached Rebecca with a microphone and announced, "You're on. Go!"

Pug in hand, Liv turned to wish Rebecca good luck. That's when she realized something was desperately wrong. Rebecca had turned a nauseating shade of green. "Oh, Li-uhv," she whined. "Ah just can't do this. You go." Then she handed Liv the microphone and pleaded with her eyes.

"No way," Liv said, pushing the mic toward Rebecca. "This is what you've been waiting for!"

"Ah can't! Ah swear." Rebecca was quaking with fear. "Please go, Li-uhv."

Realizing there were very few options— *someone* had to introduce the jerk—Liv took the microphone and moved up the stairs to the stage. She had no idea what she was supposed to do, but figured she could wing it. She gently pulled aside a small section of the curtain. The pug—which was still under one arm—whined as the roar of the crowd crept around the edge of the curtain. *Gulp.*

Liv gingerly moved onto the stage. She was greeted by thousands of screaming, applauding fans. Before she could freak herself out any further, Liv leaned into the microphone and shouted, "Hello, London!" Huge applause. "Music Mix is proud to present . . ." She lifted the pug into the air. ". . . Josh Cameron!"

The crowd roared. Liv had survived. Taking a deep breath, she moved behind the curtain. As she passed Josh Cameron on her way offstage, he smiled at her and gave her a little wink. Liv winked back—and realized he didn't intimidate her anymore. She finally felt like they were on the same level. Before jogging offstage, she turned and said calmly, "Good luck out there . . . Josh."

"So it turns out, our favorite roommate is mortified of public speaking," Liv said. She and Anna were sitting in a banquette at the concert's wrap party later that night. Gloria had convinced Brown to rent out a nearby club to congratulate the Music Mix crew on a job well done and to impress Josh Cameron and his dancers—Brown had agreed it was a good idea after the pop star had agreed to attend the party. Now most of the interns were packed onto the dance floor trying to get near him—Liv did not feel inspired to join them.

"I think tonight probably ruined her chances for the VJ for a Day audition," Anna said, stretching back into the booth. "If she really was planning to audition—I wonder if it was all just for show?"

"You're right," Liv said thoughtfully.

"This may sound crazy, but do you think there's any way we could work *with* her? We *could* use her help with the makeup and hair. Right?"

"Aha," Anna said knowingly. "A plan."

"A plan." Now that Liv thought about it, asking Rebecca to join their VJ for a Day team was perfect—she had a lot of good ideas; she just needed to be reined in. Liv hoped their flatmate would agree to collaboration. After her humiliation at the concert earlier that evening, Liv suspected Rebecca would do anything to avoid public speaking again—and Liv knew she wouldn't easily give up a chance to win something. Liv and Anna could be her only chance.

"Liv?" Anna was looking across the dance floor at the club's front door. She pointed to two familiar figures who had just entered the party. "Is that Colin and Francesco?"

Liv glanced up. Her heart skipped a beat when she saw Colin's grin from afar. "Uh-huh."

"So," Anna said quietly. "What do you want to do?"

"I just can't believe how much I've screwed this up," Liv responded. As she did, she stood and waved Colin and Francesco over to their table. "I think I need to just try to talk to him again—at the very least, I can salvage the friendship, right? There's no need to avoid him. . . ."

Liv's stomach was in knots. She hadn't seen much of Colin since their last run-in at Tully's. He'd been really busy with work—and helping Rebecca with her VJ for a Day audition—and Liv had been spending most of her time with Anna working on their audition. Though she knew there was no hope for anything more than friendship with Colin, Liv wanted to try to preserve that. She couldn't stop thinking about how much fun they had had that summer—if she could just get her heart to stop thumping so hard every time he was nearby, she knew they could have a really great friendship.

As Colin and Francesco approached their table, Anna stood and grabbed Francesco's arm. "Francesco! *Buon giorno!* Come—dance with me!"

Not so subtle, Liv thought, cringing. But she shot her friend a grateful look, and—after a quick cheek-kiss from Francesco—turned to Colin. "Hey."

"Hello," Colin murmured, sliding into the booth beside her.

"How have you been?"

"So formal, Liv," Colin said, grinning. "It's not like you, yeah? But to answer your question, I've been good."

Liv relaxed. Clearly, this was the same old Colin. "Good. Sorry. So did you enjoy the Josh Cameron concert? Somehow I ended up onstage, introducing him. Which was awkward," Liv broke off. Of course, she just *had* to bring up Josh Cameron. *Swell, Liv, swell.*

"Awkward because . . . he's your boy-friend, yeah?"

"Oh no, no. That's done. Over. It wasn't pretty." She shrugged.

"Over?" Colin said, tilting his head.

"Yeah, I broke things off after that night at *As You Like It*."

Did he not know that? Liv wondered, thinking back to their recent conversation at Tully's. "The thing is," she continued, her heart thumping as she realized she couldn't stop herself. "I guess I was looking for more than just a famous date—I think I'm better suited to someone who I can be myself with. But sometimes you figure that out a little too late . . . ," she broke off, and stared down at the table.

Colin sat there quietly, waiting for Liv

to continue. She flushed as he stared at her in the club lights. "But you know what?" she said boldly, looking directly at him, "I think I missed my chance with the right guy."

"I'm not so sure about that," he said, frowning. "Liv, can I ask you something?" She nodded. "Do you remember the night we went to the Globe?"

"Of course," she answered. "It's the highlight of my summer so far."

Colin looked relieved. "Well, do you remember how you kept nodding at everything my uncle asked you?" Liv nodded, hearing Ginger's thick accent in her head. She impulsively grinned at the memory of Colin in his kilt.

"Well . . . ," he said, smiling slightly. "While we were there, Ginger asked you a lot of strange things that you kept nodding at. One of the things he asked was whether you 'fancied his nephew'—did you know that?" Colin looked at Liv, hopeful. She shook her head, but a slow smile spread across her face. He continued, "I, ah, I didn't want to bring it up then—you know, Josh and all—but . . . well, is there any chance that could be true?"

Liv began to nod, then paused. She

wasn't sure where this conversation was going, but she needed to clear something up. "What about Lucy, the girl from the play? Aren't you together?"

"Me and Lucy? Hmm." Colin scratched his head. "Sure, we've been together about seventeen years." He broke into a huge smile. "Liv, Lucy is my little sister. She was in town visiting me from Stratford. She loves Shakespeare, so we decided to go to the show. She thought you were very nice, by the way. Josh Cameron—not so much."

"Oh," Liv said, suddenly completely at ease. "I see. So you're not . . . together, together."

"Not quite. Liv, I wanted to ask you out the first night I met you—but you were distracted with . . ." He gestured to Josh Cameron, who had begun to break-dance on the dance floor. "And then after our day in London, and the night at the Globe . . . but I just couldn't compete."

"Is it too late?" Liv wondered, not immediately realizing she'd said it aloud.

Colin shook his head and tiny little dimples popped up in his cheeks. He looked so adorable that Liv just couldn't stop herself. So she leaned her face toward his, and hoped that—for once—she wasn't saying or doing the wrong thing. As their lips touched, Liv could feel a smile tugging at the edges of Colin's mouth. She smiled back, thinking about how long it had taken to get it right.

As she relaxed into the kiss, Liv could have sworn she heard Anna and Francesco whooping from across the dance floor.

Dancing Queen

"Oh, Li-uhv, you look so pretty. Ah had no idea you could clean up so nicely." Rebecca smiled sweetly, then turned to address My Rover, who was sitting regally on a captain's chair in the corner of Music Mix's hair and makeup room. "Doesn't she just look adorable, baby? Yes, she does. Yesss sheee does!"

Liv rolled her eyes in the mirror. She understood after all that Rebecca really wasn't mean. She was just really, really weird. Colin was somehow able to find humor in her oddities, but Liv still had a way to go before she could actually be *entertained* by Rebecca. In the meantime, at least they were getting along.

Right after the Josh Cameron concert, Rebecca had quickly and happily agreed to help Anna and Liv with hair, makeup, and "style" for their VJ for a Day audition. And now, three weeks later, with just minutes before they were on, she was fluffing and puffing Liv's hair to perfection.

Anna was ready to go on, and was standing outside the soundstage door, running through her lines one last time before their session kicked off. Everything—the music, script, props, and costumes—was all set. Now it would just come down to the execution, and whether they could pull it off was still to be seen.

There were a total of five auditions, and Liv and Anna had been selected to go last. They had been waiting and prepping for several hours in a tiny room just down the hall from the *Hits Parade* studio as the other intern teams wrapped their sessions. Almost every intern had formed a team with others, and the competition had gotten intense in the past week as the day of taping drew nearer. Though the auditions weren't live— the winner's segment would air on Music Mix that afternoon—all the auditions were being taped without do-overs in the *Hits Parade* studio.

For their audition, Liv and Anna had decided to stage a series of Make Me a Star segments, in which several "regular" people would be made over to look, dress, and act like celebrities. The makeovers would be done in real time, interspersed with the day's top Video Hits.

If everything went as planned, viewers would see people go from Frumpy to Fabulous in just under an hour. Ideally, the "drama" of waiting for the final result would keep people tuned in throughout the show. The outlandish disco gear Anna had found in old Music Mix wardrobe closets guaranteed that the production would be a visual success, if nothing else.

Naturally, Liv and Anna had decided to use ABBA's "Dancing Queen" as the backdrop to their audition. The "regular" people would be morphed into the band ABBA and, at the end of the show, would do a silly dance performance as the band.

True to her word, Christy Trimble had answered Liv's call for help, and had eagerly agreed to help them with the final dance— she had won Best Pop Video at the VMAs the past two years, and was known to be an exceptional choreographer. But she had agreed to help under one condition: Christy thought it would be "fabulously funny" if Josh Cameron were one of the makeover victims. Liv had agreed, assuming Josh would *never* go for it—after all, he was far from "regular." But when Christy called Josh and told him that this would be a good way for him to make himself seem approachable and "down-to-earth," he quickly agreed.

Liv and Anna were the two female makeover victims. Anna would also be the main VJ, and Liv would handle all the behind-the-scenes, makeover-in-progress interviews. After much begging and pleading, Liv had finally managed to convince Colin to be the second guy in the band, rounding out their ensemble.

Now, with only a few seconds to go, Liv hoped Josh—or anyone else in the "band"— wouldn't flake out. As the two-minute warning bulb flashed, Liv scurried off in search of Anna. Showtime!

"I look like someone's dad," Josh Cameron surveyed himself in the mirror while rubbing his short, tan beard. "Are you sure about this beard?"

Liv stifled a laugh, while Rebecca reassured him he looked "mah-vel-ous." They were about half an hour into the audition, and the cameras were in Josh's dressing room to check in on his "Frumpy to Fabulous" makeover status. As Liv stood waiting for the cameras to roll (Video Hit #8 was just about to end), she chose not to tell Josh how he really looked. Rather than normal and approachable, as Christy had promised him, Liv sort of thought Josh seemed a little pitiful and desperate for doing this. But he was oblivious.

"You look fabulous," she said, just as the cameras flipped on. "Now—smile, Mr. Cameron!"

"Liv," Anna whispered. "My butt cheeks are showing. Any suggestions?" Liv glanced across the set, giggling uncontrollably as Anna spun around and wiggled her butt. She was right—her short, white dress left little to the imagination. But the effect was perfect.

Anna and Liv were wearing matching white retro dresses, both of which were tied around the waist with a gold belt. Anna's hair had been covered with a long blond wig, and Liv's naturally curly brown hair was puffed into an aerobic-instructor do. Both girls had a gold headband tied across their foreheads, and were wearing moccasin-style boots that laced up their legs. Liv had to admit it—Rebecca was a makeup genius and Anna had perfected her wardrobe skills. They really did make a great team.

Liv stole a quick glance at Colin, who turned and flashed a toothy smile. Liv burst out laughing. A few weeks ago she never could have imagined Colin would agree to do something like this, but now he was a natural. He had mastered the dance (which frightened her just a little), and had happily zipped himself into *the* ugliest white jumpsuit she had ever seen. Rebecca had outfitted him in a flowing brown wig and a sporty headband. He looked like the ultimate porn star.

Anna came up behind Liv to check out Colin's ridiculous getup. "He's your soul mate," she whispered to Liv, laughing. "A loveable dork—with absolutely no inhibitions. I never would have guessed."

Liv turned and squeezed Anna's hands. "This is it," she said. "Only one more chance to make complete fools of ourselves. You are totally rocking—if they don't offer you a job after this, they're crazy!"

"Gaaaah! Don't say that. You're freaking me out!" Anna said, grinning.

"We," Liv said, squeezing Anna into a

hug, "are going to rock. Now, as Brown would say . . . Go, Girl!" Then she pushed Anna out onto center stage as the producers signaled the end of Video Hit #2.

The lights splashed onto the stage, and Anna lifted the mic to her mouth and flashed a huge smile. "The moment we've been waiting for is finally here," she said into the camera, just as Francesco cued up "Dancing Queen" on the stereo in the background. "Today's top video?" she continued. "Nuh-uh—that will have to wait. First, the grand finale of our Make Me a Star makeovers. We've gone from frumpy . . . to fabulous! Ladies and gentlemen, please welcome . . . ABBA!"

The first notes of "Dancing Queen" came pouring out of the speakers as Anna ripped off the tracksuit she had thrown on to cover her outfit. Liv joined her in the center of the *Hits Parade* stage. Back-to-back, they held their microphones up and lip-synched in time to the music. *"You can dance, you can jive, having the time of your life . . ."*

As the second verse started, Colin and Josh popped out from opposite sides of the stage. Josh's outfit was exactly the same as Colin's, but instead of a wig, his naturally curly hair had been straightened into a helmetlike flop over his face. Liv could hear the producers and camera operators chuckling as Josh and Colin swayed out onto the stage. They moved and shook their hips in time to the music, fanning their hands out every time *"ooh ooh ooh"* came pouring out of the speakers.

At the end of the song, the foursome all slid to their knees, arms raised, and held their pose while Anna pointed to the camera and introduced Cherie Jacobson's new single as that day's top video. "I hope you've had as much fun as we have," she said, winking. "Live it up, Dancing Queens!"

One of the camera operators shouted, "That's a wrap!" Liv sighed a breath of relief. She and Anna cheered as Rebecca came running out from backstage. The three roommates danced around in a circle, hugging and laughing. *We did it,* Liv thought happily. *We actually did it.*

Later that afternoon everyone gathered at O'Leary's, an Irish pub around the corner from the Music Mix offices. The owner, a shrunken, stooped Irish fellow, had agreed to air that afternoon's *Hits Parade* segment on the bar's TV. Andrew Stone would be broadcasting the winner's segment as part of that day's show, and until the broadcast, they were left in suspense, waiting to see who won.

A few minutes before *Hits Parade* started, Simon Brown entered the bar and lazily made his way to an armchair in a corner of the room. Liv stole a glance at Anna, who had been working up the courage to talk to Brown all day. Anna's mom had called that morning, saying she could accept that her daughter needed to figure her life out—and together, they had resolved that if Anna got a job offer from Music Mix, she would stay in London for one more year before deciding her next step. Liv knew her roommate was making herself sick wondering whether things would work out. Liv crossed her fingers and glanced at Brown slumped in the corner.

Anna caught Liv's eye before slowly making her way across the room to where Brown was sitting alone with a cigarette and a beer (Liv could only assume he had a fat wad of Nicorette tucked in each cheek). Liv watched Anna approach him. Knowing Brown had the power to dramatically transform Anna's future, Liv considered the fact that she would need to figure out her own future pretty soon. Living in London had been the only thing she'd ever really *known* she wanted to do, and it had turned out to be a perfect choice.

Though Liv didn't know for sure what her next move would be, Anna had helped her realize that uncertainty could be okay. She just needed to think a lot more clearly and carefully about what she *might* want to do after graduation next year. She smiled at Colin, who had been watching her from across the bar. He moved over to her and pulled her in for a kiss.

"I can't believe you have to leave," he murmured in her ear. "Stay."

Liv wrapped her arms around Colin's neck. "Mmmm," she murmured as she snuggled into the crook of his neck and breathed in deeply—she loved that Colin smelled like a combination of fabric softener and soap. If she had known how comfortable that crook was, she definitely wouldn't have waited so long to get rid of Josh Cameron. She just wished she had more time to burrow into Colin's neck before she had to go back to the States.

"I really don't want to waste our time together thinking about me leaving," she said, leaning back and looking into his eyes. "And who knows what could happen?

Maybe I'll be back next summer. . . . My mom left London to come to the States—what's keeping me from taking her place in England?"

"You would really come back?" Colin said, brushing a stray curl off her face with his finger.

"This summer sort of proved that anything can happen, didn't it?" She leaned forward and brushed his lips with hers. He pulled her in tighter.

"I hate to interrupt." Anna had materialized at Liv's side, smiling broadly. Liv and Colin broke apart, and Liv looked at her roommate expectantly. Anna continued, "Guess who's staying in London?"

"You got a job?!" Liv asked, her excitement bubbling up.

Anna nodded. "Apparently, Gloria was just offered a position as a VJ—so her job is open." Anna was beaming. "Brown said it's mine if I want it! I guess my supervisor in wardrobe talked to him a few days ago and recommended me. Brown said he was impressed that I approached him—that it proves how much I want it."

Liv was ecstatic. She quickly gathered Anna into a huge hug, just as Francesco danced over. Colin and Francesco exchanged a shrug and then wrapped Anna and Liv into a big four-person hug. Liv broke away just in time to see the *Hits Parade* logo pop up onto the TV in the corner. The show was about to start.

She reached for Anna's hand, and they held their breath, waiting to see who had won. Liv closed her eyes—she couldn't stand the suspense. She reminded herself that even if they hadn't won, their performance—and Anna's job offer—had been a truly perfect ending to a perfect summer.

Just as the first notes of "Dancing Queen" came floating out of the television set, Rebecca's high-pitched yell cut through the din of the bar—"Ah did it!" she screamed, lifting My Rover into the air. "Li-uhv, Anna, I won!"

Some things never change. But for Liv and Anna, so much had.

And Liv was having the time of her life.

About the Author

Erin (Soderberg) Downing is a former children's book editor who now works at Nickelodeon. Her guilty pleasures include an unhealthy obsession with reality TV, an addiction to *Us Weekly*, and Magnolia Bakery cupcakes. A native of Duluth, Minnesota, Erin has lived in both England and Sweden and currently resides in New York City with her husband and newborn daughter.

LOL at this sneak peek of

Major Crush

By Jennifer Echols

A new Romantic Comedy from Simon Pulse

I could keep my expressionless drum major face on while I strode under the bleachers and around the stadium to the bathroom. But then I was going to bawl.

Six thousand people, almost half the town, came to every home game of the high school football team. Tonight they crowded the stadium for the first game of the season. They had expected the band to be as good as usual. Instead, it had been the worst halftime show ever to shatter a hot September night. And I'd been in charge of it.

Me and the other drum major, Drew Morrow.

Allison knew exactly what I was doing. She handed her batons to another majorette and hurried close behind me.

The band always took third quarter off. So I had about half an hour to get myself together, with Allison's help, before I had to be back in the stands to direct the band playing the fight song during fourth quarter.

I felt Allison's hand on my back, supporting me, as I stepped through the bathroom door. My eyes watered, my nose tickled, I was ready to let loose—

Unfortunately, about twenty girls from the band were in the bathroom ahead of me. Including Drew's girlfriend of the month, the Evil Twin.

Allison stepped in front of me, putting herself between me and them. She seemed nine feet tall. She was a lot more threatening dressed in her majorette leotard than I was dressed like a boy. But she pulled at her earring with one hand, so I knew she was stressing out.

The Evil Twin was either Tracey or Cacey Reardon—I wasn't sure which one, and no one else seemed to know either. All we knew for sure was that the twins were evil. Or, one of them was evil and the other just looked the same.

I assumed the one currently dissing me was the one dating Drew. Because she sure seemed to have it in for me.

I pulled Allison toward the door. I could cry later.

Before we managed to leave, the twin

turned back to Allison and made the mistake of touching her majorette tiara.

Allison whirled around with her claws out.

"Fight!" someone squealed. Several freshmen made it out the door, still shrieking.

I hadn't witnessed a fight like this since a couple of girls got into it over a Ping-Pong game in seventh grade PE. And I was about to be the costar.

"Hey!" Drew boomed in his drum major command voice. His tall frame filled the doorway.

Allison and the twin stopped. There was complete silence for two seconds at the shock of getting caught. Then everyone realized it was Drew, not a teacher, and screamed because there was a boy in the girls' bathroom.

Drew reached through the girls. I thought he was reaching for the twin to save her from herself. But his hand closed over *my* wrist. I stumbled after him as he dragged me out of the bathroom and through the line at the concession stand, to a corner behind a concrete pillar that held up the stadium.

He let go of my wrist. "What. Were. You. *Doing?*"

I was gazing way up at the world's most

beautiful boy. Drew was a foot taller than me and had a golden tan, wavy black hair, and deep brown eyes fringed with dark, thick lashes. And these were almost the first words he'd spoken to me since the band voted us both drum majors last May.

"Your girlfriend started it. Why don't you talk to *her*?"

"My girlfriend isn't drum major."

"So?"

"So, it's bad enough that I have to be drum major with you. It's bad enough that the band sounded like crap tonight. But you are *not* going to get in fights with people in the band. We have the same position. If *you* stoop to that level, *I've* stooped to that level. I'm not going to let you make me look irresponsible."

I had already known this was the way he felt about me. He'd tried his best during summer band camp to act like I didn't exist. Except when he spoke low to the trombones and they muttered under their breath as I passed.

"You're not my boss." My voice rose. "You don't get to tell me what to do."

He leaned farther down toward me and hissed, "We are not going to yell at each other in public. Do you understand?"

"You are not going to get in my face and threaten me. Do *you* understand?"

"Good job, drum majors!" called some trumpets passing by. They gave us the thumbs-up and sarcastic smiles. "Teamwork—who needs it?"

Behind them, Allison waited for me against the wall, arms folded, tiara askew.

I turned my back on Drew. We weren't through with our discussion, but we weren't going to solve anything by trading insults. And I wanted to make sure all Allison's cubic zirconia were in place.

I was glad about the quasi-catfight. I was glad Drew had reprimanded me too. Now I was pissed with the band and with Drew, instead of mortified at myself for being such a bad drum major on my first try.

And it was nice to find out that Drew knew I existed, after all.

"I hate this town, I hate this town, I hate this town," Allison chanted for a few minutes after we sat down in the stands. I sent our friend Walter to fetch her makeup case from her car, knowing that makeup could distract her from anything. She would feel better when she was back to looking like her usual self.

Allison leaned closer and said quietly,

"You don't want him to know you're upset."

Then, like the dorks we were, we both turned around and looked at Drew, who sat with his dad at the top of the football stadium. Grouped on the rows between us and Drew, several trumpet players and saxophone players glared at me like they wanted to pitch me off the top railing. In fact, Drew and his dad probably would have been glad to help me over.

I felt a pang of jealousy. Drew was close to his dad. I could tell the conversation Drew and his dad were having at the moment wasn't pleasant, but at least they were having one. I hardly talked to my dad anymore.

"Foul!" Walter jeered at the game, startling me and making Allison jump on my other side.

Walter handed Allison her makeup case and looked at me. "I also put Drew's band shoes back in his truck, like we found them."

"Thanks." Drew made me mad playing Mr. Perfect all the time. I had thought it would make me feel better to hide his lovingly polished band shoes so he had to wear his Vans with his band uniform. It hadn't.

"So, what happened in the halftime show?" Walter asked. "It reminded me of the Alabama Symphony Orchestra, but not in a good way. You know, before they start playing together, when they're tuning up."

Allison nodded. "There's a point in the majorette routine when I'm supposed to throw the baton on one and turn on two. I looked up at Drew and thought, *Is he on one? No, two.* And then I looked over at you, and you were on, like, thirty-seven."

I just shook my head. I was afraid that if I tried to talk about it right now, the pissed feeling would fade, the mortified feeling would come back, and I'd start bawling in front of the tuba players.

Walter slid his arm around my waist, and Allison draped her arm around my shoulders from the other side. I tried to feel better, not just sweatier. They were the two best possible friends.

Someone slid onto the bench beside Walter. Oh no, Luther Washington or one of Drew's other smart-ass trombone friends coming to rub it in. Or worse, the Evil Twin. I peered around Walter.

It was the new band director, Mr. Rush.

Before I'd seen him today, I'd hoped that getting a new band director might help my predicament as queen band geek. Mr. O'Toole, who'd been band director for as long as I could remember, had gotten us into this mess by deciding we'd have two drum majors this year.

Then, knowing he'd be leaving near the beginning of the school year anyway, he sleepwalked through summer band camp. He let Drew and me avoid working together. I couldn't imagine what the new band director would be like, but any change had to be for the better.

Or not. Mr. Rush didn't seem like he was in any position to change the status quo. He was fresh out of college and looked it, maybe twenty-two years old. He could have passed for even younger, and I wondered how Mr. Rush thought he could handle a hundred and fifty students.

I was about to find out.

"Amscray," Mr. Rush growled at Walter. Walter leaped up and crossed behind me to sit on Allison's other side.

Mr. Rush stared at me. Not the stare you give someone when you're starting a serious conversation. Worse than this. A deep, dark stare, his eyes locking with mine.

He meant to intimidate me. He wanted me to look away. But I stared right back. It felt defiant, and I wondered whether I could get suspended for insubordination just for staring.

I guess I passed the test. Finally he relaxed and asked, "What's your name?"

"Virginia Sauter."

He nodded. "What's the other one's name?" He didn't specify "the other suck-o drum major," but I knew what he meant.

I shuddered. "Drew Morrow."

Walter leaned around Allison. "His friends call him General Patton."

Allison laughed.

Mr. Rush ignored them. He asked me, "What's with the punky look? You've got the only nose stud I've seen in this town."

"Would you believe she entered beauty pageants with me until two years ago?" Allison asked. Allison always rubbed this in.

"I developed an allergy to taffeta," I said.

"No, she didn't," Allison said. "On the first day of summer band camp in ninth grade, she walked by Drew in the trombone section. The trombones called her JonBenét Ramsey, and it was all over. She quit the majorettes and went back to drums."

"Is that true?" Walter asked me.

"You think I was born with a stud in my nose?"

"And she stopped wearing shoes," Allison added.

Mr. Rush eyed my band shoes.

"Well, I'm wearing shoes *now*," I said. "Of course I can't be out of uniform at a game."

"Of course not," Mr. Rush said, looking my uniform up and down with distaste.

"More people might get their noses pierced if I started a club," I said. "Would you like to be our faculty sponsor?"

"And an attitude to match the nose stud," Mr. Rush said. He leaned across me to point at Allison and Walter. "You, princess. And you, frog. Beat it."

They scattered, leaving Mr. Rush and me alone on the bench.

He glanced over his shoulder at Drew and his father at the top of the stands. "What's up with you and Morrow?"

"He was drum major by himself last year," I said. "Everybody knew he'd be drum major again this year. But Clayton Porridge was trying out against him. I wanted to be drum major next year, after Drew graduated. I figured I'd better go ahead and try out, just for show, so Clayton wouldn't have anything on me."

I looked down into my cup of ice. "I never thought I'd make it this year. A girl has never been drum major. And we've never had two drum majors. Mr. O'Toole decided after the vote that we'd have two this year, the two with the most votes, and that was Drew and me. I don't know what he was thinking." I made a face. "Though I'm pretty sure what Drew's thinking."

"So a girl's never been drum major," Mr. Rush repeated slowly. "And all the flutes and clarinets are girls, and all the trombones are boys. Gotta love a small town steeped in tradition. Who needs this diversity crap?"

It bothered me, too, or I wouldn't have tried out for drum major.

"Which one of you got the most votes?" he asked.

"Mr. O'Toole wouldn't tell us."

Allison had a theory, though. She thought I won, and Mr. O'Toole just didn't want me to be drum major by myself. I mean, he didn't even want to let a girl try out. My dad had to threaten to call the school board.

I went on, "Mr. O'Toole said that since we were both drum majors, it didn't matter who got more votes. He didn't want to generate bad blood between us." I smiled and said sarcastically, "It worked."

Mr. Rush rubbed his temple like he had a headache. "When's the last time you had a conversation with Morrow?"

"A conversation?"

"Yeah, you know. You talk, he talks, you communicate."

"We had an argument just now because he sicced his girlfriend on me in the bathroom. Is that progress?"

He closed his eyes and rubbed his temple harder. "How about before that?"

"Communicate. Probably . . ." I had to think about this. "Never."

"Then how have you functioned at all? Even on your sad, limited level?"

I shrugged. "Mr. O'Toole would tell me where to go on the field, and then he would tell Drew where to go."

Mr. Rush muttered, "You see me in my office before band practice when we come back to school on Tuesday. And I want you to spend the long weekend contemplating how the two of you reek."

"I know," I whispered.

"If you performed that way at a contest, you'd get embarrassingly low marks. So would the band, because the two of you have them so confused. And the drums! Though I'm not sure the drums are your fault. I suspect they reek on their own merit."

He stood, looking down at me with a diabolical grin. "I'm so glad we've had this chat. To be fair, I'd give Morrow the same treatment, but it looks like someone's beat me to it."

I nodded. "His father and his two older brothers used to be drum majors."

"What? A legacy? The Morrow clan has drum major tied up like the Mafia?"

"It feels that way."

"I should have kept my job in Birmingham at Pizza Hut," Mr. Rush grumbled as he stomped away down the bleachers.

I had to agree with this. Despite myself, I looked up one more time at Drew high in the stands. He and his father sat side by side in the same position, leaning forward, elbows on knees. The only difference was that Drew hung his head. Now Mr. Morrow pointed to Drew's Vans.

I imagined Mr. Morrow lecturing Drew in a Tony Soprano voice. "I'm counting on you to uphold the family name. I want you to off the broad. *Capisce?*"

HOSTILE
TAKEOVER

Book Four of
The Black Hole Travel Agency

Jack McKinney

A Del Rey Book

BALLANTINE BOOKS • NEW YORK

A Del Rey Book
Published by Ballantine Books

Library of Congress Catalog Card Number: 93-90524

ISBN 0-345-37079-1

Manufactured in the United States of America

First Edition: January 1994

This book is gratefully dedicated
to the Nature Conservancy, the Sierra Club,
the Wildlife Federation, Greenpeace,
Zero Population Growth, and kindred groups and
individuals who've decided to make a difference:

Earth's real-life defenders

The author would like to thank Masaaki Hirayama for his
kindness, effort, and unfailing friendship.

Thanks, too, to Thrash*meister*
Tim Robson, for showing me where
the polyurethane meets the glassphalt.

A fool wanders; the wise man travels.

Anonymous proverb

Chase after the truth like all hell and you'll free yourself, even if you never touch its coat-tails.

CLARENCE S. DARROW

PART ONE

Local Heroes

ONE

PILING OUT OF the corporate jetcopter at World Nihon, Nikkei Tanabe and Mickey Formica had to giggle and chump on people, despite the glowers their behavior drew from various Japanese and *gaijin* management top guns.

What had set them off was the poleaxed looks on the faces of theme-park staffers, the still-smoking plastic melted from the *Tengu Mountain* attraction, the quietly frantic efforts to get the place evacuated and secure—all in the wake of Lucky Junknowitz's wacky escape by spaceship, no less, only hours before.

"Jizmic!" Mickey tittered, high on all the excitement.

"Shitotic!" Nikkei agreed.

Not that they'd have gotten a cordial welcome from the gathered Nihon and Nagoya Aerospace ball bearings in any case. To get in the theme-park spirit and conceal their true appearance, the two irrepressible disguise buffs and would-be ninjas had arrived dressed as moose-and-squirrel-hating 'toon nogoodniks Boris Badenov and Natasha Fatale. But the stubby spy—bulked-up little Nikkei—had a decidedly tropical look to him, and the influence of fruitbowl-hatted Carmen Miranda on his slinky femme accomplice—reedy AfricAm Mickey—was undeniable.

They *had* arrived on a mission, or the park SWATs and WAPs would have fogged them with Crowd Control and perhaps marooned them out on Monster Island for a while. And, of course, Nikkei was the son of Takuma Tanabe, CEO of Nagoya Aero and creator of World Nihon, although father and son had been estranged for years.

As it was, security officers, not cargo handlers, hastened to unlock the steel-walled cargo pod slung under the executive chopper and wheel it away. It contained precious cargo indeed, and to divert attention from their delivery, the two camoflesh fiends cranked up concealed sonic vests—pulsing bass and manic Carnival-style *cuica*—whipped out *karaoke* mikes, and launched into a little number set to the title tune from one of their favorite flicks, *Brazil*.

"Theme Pa-aark!
We love to go there for a la-ark!
It's got more strangeness than a qua-ark!
Who needs the real world, it's so sta-ark?
Hey, mark!
Embra-ace the dark
Theme pa-arrk!"

All this was accompanied by a lot of ersatz *escola de samba* prancing, while the older Japanese *oyabuns* sucked their teeth in consternation and the young Japanese and *gaijin* corporate comers, the Ivy-*zoku*, looked on in faintly smiling contempt.

The madcap pair was just getting to the part about

"It's neat!
Re-ali-ty's what they delete!
Who needs a real life that ain't sweet,
And TV-perfect and upbeat?"

when Miss Sato, Takuma Tanabe's executive assistant and right hand, arrived. The honchos made way for her as she fixed Boris and Natasha with a look, drew a forefinger across her throat, and then crooked it at them beckoningly.

Mickey was struck once more by how different Sato was from any kudzu femme he'd ever met—Nihonese, *issei*, *sansei*, any of them. Cool and brainy, dressed for success, and enough of a take to make it as a model if she wanted to, Mickey would've bet. To traditionalists she might be a "Christmas cake"—in her mid-twenties and not yet married, hence dropping in value the way the pastry did after December 25—but that didn't seem to wedgie her La Perlas any.

The two stopped singing but let the music play as they capered along behind her, around the back of an ersatz feudal Japanese armory to the elevator that gave access to the park's labyrinth of infrastructure tunnels. A few three-piece suits tagged along, plus security, but nowhere did Mickey see Kamimura, the master of Tanabe's astonishing and genuine ninja. The young Ivy-*zoku* fast-trackers traded superior smiles;

they were brainy and had the right diplomas, the polish, the corner-office hunger, and Nikkei and Mickey were buffoons.

To prove it, the partners got into a spirited *jan ken pon* game—scissors/paper/rock—while waiting for the elevator, joshing each other and dropping their *karaoke* mikes once or twice as they sambaed to the beat. The Ivy-*zoku* rolled their eyes and made subtle jack-off gestures until the elevator doors opened and they discovered their shoelaces had been tied together, minor sleight of hand Kamimura's people had taught the duo.

Sato impatiently gestured that the tie-ees be left behind. Nikkei and Mickey bowed to their victims, doffing the Boris fedora, the Natasha fruit hat. "Thanks! You've been a sphincterrific audience!"

"Fuck-hu-very-mungus!"

In the elevator the dynamic duo switched off the sonic vests, and Nikkei did a not-bad Pottsylvanian accent to ask Sato, "Vere are you takink us, Fearless Leader?" Mickey assumed that the lust-loathing thing Nikkei harbored for her was due in part to the fact that she was, presumably, Takuma's mistress.

Sato gave Nikkei a look a Russian icebreaker would've gotten stuck in. "Your father was injured in the incident this morning." She spoke English with a flawless Oxford accent and a low-pitched, *sogoshoku* self-assurance that Mickey, at least, found unbearably sexy. "He's in intensive care and wishes to speak to you."

Shape-shifter Yoo Sobek had gone by many aliases on various worlds, but in the realm of his own dream his name was something else—something hermetical that he couldn't quite conjure.

Until recently, he'd been a dreaded Probe, an agent of the Black Hole Travel Agency. Before that, Sobek had been a different sort of entity—a far loftier one—and he was something altogether unprecedented, a Probe turned rebel, now.

In the phantasmagoric otherspace of his dream, Sobek drifted through endless, limitless, heavenly halls. He was a disembodied point of view borne along by effulgent light through a yawning and convoluted wormhole cathedral of pure illumination. It was a fragment of memory, recently recovered, from the days when he was a Sysop, a Founder of the Black Hole Travel Agency.

Sobek apprehended the dreamscape with senses beyond the physical, beyond even ESP and psi talents; he was somewhere outside space-time. He stole among exhibited miracles and terrors too vast to comprehend, mindful of the powers that guarded that domain. His bodiless viewpoint entered a sweeping space whose boundaries he couldn't perceive, his sensations analogous to what a human might feel entering some immense planetarium. Among the swirls of unnameable thoughts and feelings sweeping through him, there was the unmistakable awareness that his presence there was a transgression, a cardinal sin. Tormented by things that had happened to him and acts he'd committed, Sobek's dream self sought ultimate and forbidden revelation. His attention fixed on a symbol far above him.

The symbol was, again by analogy, eight interlocking rings. He knew it was elsewhere applied to Earth—Adit Navel, the galaxy's idiot savant—but here it applied to something else, something transcendent. But as the eight rings' meaning came through to him, the horror of it began to dispel the dream. Yoo Sobek understood that the significance of the eight-ringed symbol would turn him against his fellow Sysops and lead him to treason that would eventually get him cast down in the form of a corporeal, memoryless Probe. But he couldn't quite recapture what that revelation was. And he had the conviction something was *missing* from the symbol.

He strove mightily to know what it all meant, strove until the strain wrung a voiceless cry of torment from him, but it did no good. He felt himself break apart, fly asunder, die . . .

Yoo Sobek woke to his own screams and found himself sitting on the oven-hot floor where he'd lapsed into sleep, grappling with Ka Shamok. The squat, preternaturally strong leader of the counter-Black Hole insurgency was bellowing in Yoo Sobek's face. "Stop! It was a nightmare! Damn you, *wake up!*"

He was shaking Sobek by the front of his clothes, head pulled low between cannonball shoulders to avoid the Probe's flailing hands. Such was the strength of Ka Shamok that he could pin even Sobek and shake him till his teeth rattled. "Wake up, I say!"

Ka Shamok released one wrist and clouted Sobek on the side of the head with an open hand, too quick for the eye to follow, powerful enough to snap Sobek's head sideways. Sobek saw the phantom eight rings fade to nothingness before his eyes. Ka Shamok hauled him to his feet, shaking him again, and demanded to know what had happened. "You told me Probes don't sleep, don't dream! How then did you—"

Sobek gathered himself and shoved the insurgency leader away a step. Ka Shamok's prognathous jaw jutted and his tiny, deep-set eyes narrowed—a look that had been a death sentence to many. But he forced it from his face; Ka Shamok needed Sobek badly, as he needed various other critical ingredients, if he was to bring the Black Hole Travel Agency crashing down for all time.

Sobek, regaining his bearings, felt the searing heat in the air and recalled where he was: *the Chasen-nur's latest hidey-hole—under the volcano*. Above and around the shielded base, magma churned; on the surface, lava coiled across thousands of hectares, one of Spectarr II's many volcanic fields. Sobek felt the heat under his feet and, looking down at those feet, realized that he was conjugated in human form once again.

It was the same form he'd used to confront Charlie Cola on Earth: a male body—the gender Sobek invariably selected, given a choice—with pale white, almost albino skin. He stood a fit-looking six feet and seemed to be in early middle age. Wavy black hair hung now in sweaty disarray over a prominent brow; his long-lashed blue eyes, usually melancholy but purposeful, now had a haunted look.

He looked to the purple-complected, burly Chasen-nur. "No sleep, no dreams—until this." When the strange lassitude had come over him there in the empty muster room, he'd been conjugated in the form of an Yggdraasian, a solid seven feet of lobster-clawed, crocodilian-faced warrior in vanity-plate combat armor, recently back from a mission to way station Sierra by way of the Spectarr base's outlaw Adit.

As he tried to remember what had come next, Sobek became aware that there were others present—moaning, nursing injuries, helping one another up off the floor. Ka Shamok's aide-de-camp, the loose-limbed eight-foot scarecrow named Bagbee, was dabbing at a freely bleeding nose; a javelin-faced Shak was being trundled away on the gurney of a med robot. It came to Yoo Sobek that he must have thrashed about in his sleep.

"Forget this for now," Ka Shamok said. "I've just received intelligence that you must hear. There's a periscope recon scheduled; the nose cone will afford us reliable privacy." He picked up something he'd dropped in the struggle—a small wooden case—and three glittering darts that had scattered from it. Inside the front lid of the case was a small engraved brass plate which read, "To Ka Shamok and Good New Days, Jacob Riddle"—a gift from the Earther, a Black Hole employee retired now to Nmuth IV, who'd taught the insurrection leader his favorite diversion.

Ka Shamok handed the recased darts to Bagbee. "Put these in

a safe place." Bagbee, still dabbing at his bleeding snout, tucked them in a coverall thigh pocket pledging that he would.

As he followed Ka Shamok to the periscope station, Yoo Sobek became aware of the omnipresent hum of the base's protective fields. Insurgency members from dozens of races passed the two, ignoring them as per Ka Shamok's standing order. Sure that his followers feared and would unquestioningly obey him, he had no use for salute, fanfare, or obeisance.

One passerby was another Chasen-nur, taller than thickset and bandy-legged Ka Shamok but with the same double-lobed occiput, the same huge hands and feet. He avoided the leader's eyes by racial reflex to eliminate any chance infection with the Chasen-nur Killing Thought. Ka Shamok did the same, though with less haste, being the most powerful member of what had been the planet Tiiphu's dominant species.

Watching the nonexchange, Yoo Sobek tried to put aside racking guilt; it had been he, in the Sysop incarnation he could no longer even recall, who had inflicted the Killing Thought on the Chasen-nur people at the command of the Black Hole Travel Agency. It was too unspeakable a crime for any apology or self-punishment to expiate, and his mind was set on the only restitution that would serve: the destruction of the lords of Light Trap, the Founders, the Foul Extenders—his fellow Sysops.

TWO

THE MODEST, OPTICALLY communicated pseudotelepathy of Tiiphu's people—more a sharing of emotional and mental rapport than it was a true psi link—had attracted the malign interest of the Agency. The Sysops, their taste for experimentation not so different from a cruel child's, had inflicted on Ka Shamok's people a psychic virus—its vector the meeting of eyes—that caused its victims to experience the sensations of being tortured to death in the most hideously inventive manner imaginable. The plague brought madness and death; its survivors fled Tiiphu and now avoided one another's eyes at all costs, living lives of wretched spiritual estrangement.

Yoo Sobek, then a Sysop, had been the one who had created and launched the Killing Thought. Later, in contrition, he'd secretly aided Ka Shamok's organization—until he had beheld the meaning of the eight-ring symbol and was cast down, memory-wiped, to begin life anew as a Probe.

Sobek accompanied Ka Shamok to the periscope station entrance, reconjugating to a different form. The periscope station was in a sense a reverse wellhead. From it a specially built, force-field-protected observation pod could be pushed up to Spectarr II's surface—usually, at any rate. There had been a few malfunctions. Sobek now wore the aspect of a bark-skinned Nall, a five-foot-ten biped, portraying the arrogance and hostility that made the creatures such perfect bureaucrats. "Someday you'll do that, be mistaken for an intruder, and get yourself shot," Ka Shamok predicted.

Sobek's barklike face creased in a frown. "I doubt it, but it wouldn't make any difference."

There were signs of worry on all sides of them as people fussed over final preparations. It was one thing for the first-in team to plunge deep under this andesitic-dacitic volcano's magma chamber with a specially designed beachhead-establishing robot vessel, gain a foothold within Spectarr II, and get a remote-control Adit up and running; it was another to raise a periscope–nose cone through miles of seething magma for a look around.

Ka Shamok led Yoo Sobek aboard the periscope's tiny passenger section, a transparent cylindrical booth just under the energy drill bit; then rig hands sealed it up and the ascension began. Sobek watched the deck drop away as the periscope was raised into the ceiling wellhead opening—a black hole, it occurred to him. He couldn't see directly beneath him, but he was given to understand that the rest of the drill pipe was opaque.

The passenger section's interior was four feet across, its walls another inch thick, with a force-field barrier that extended two inches beyond that. Except for a handrail at waist height for Sobek—chest high on Ka Shamok—and various controls, it was bare.

Light shone into the magma seven miles below the surface; as Sobek watched, the force field slid frictionlessly through the stuff. The magma in this chamber was silica-rich and of relatively low viscosity and yield strength, about as thick as room-temperature honey, at twelve hundred degrees C—a mush of hot liquid in which were suspended hot but still solid crystals. In the broad-spectrum sensor illumination, it glowed like the cosmos of the Big Bang giving birth to stars.

Ka Shamok checked the compartment with an antisurveillance device, seeming reassured. "You and I have agreed what has to be done—the only course that promises victory."

"Yes." It had been Yoo Sobek's idea, proposed back on Blight when the two had encountered each other in person at last. "An assault on Light Trap. You've reviewed my plan?"

Ka Shamok nodded. "Of the six hundred-odd major attacks and raids over the centuries and uncountable subtler gambits— the cyber penetrations, signals infiltration, telepathic intrusions— none have had the advantages your plan incorporates—"

The periscope, rising faster now, shuddered, jostled by a plume of more basaltic magma. "Without these three elements we cannot succeed," Ka Shamok continued, holding up a forefinger. "First, the Intubis, and Professor Vanderloop." The Australian aboriginal tribe was currently on walkabout among the planets of the Trough, and the Cambridge don seemed to be the key to winning their cooperation. "Second, the memory egg from Hazmat—assuming it exists. Third, and perhaps most important, Lucky Junknowitz."

"We'll also need the military resources to hold sections of Light Trap," Yoo Sobek chimed in. "You have those?"

Ka Shamok scowled. "Not yet; the Agency has been thorough in its pacification program."

Pacification was an understatement. Up and down the Trough of teleportation Adits that interconnected the galaxy, Black Hole had moved cannily and ruthlessly to coopt, leverage, intimidate, or neutralize any potential opposition. The numberless insectlike hordes of Swotork from the Procyon region, who might have swamped the defenses of the Sysops' Dyson-sphere stronghold—presuming they could get inside it—wouldn't and couldn't move against the Agency, because the Sysops held as hostage the Swotorks' only source of royal jelly. And in variations on that strategy countless planetary avatars, ancestral engram banks, species-specific prolongevity formulae, and other sacred grails had been sequestered in unassailable Light Trap. Like an old-time shogun of Japan keeping the families of his daimyos hostage to insure obedience, the Sysops had checkmated most of the Trough's significant cultures without the onscene presence of so much as a single warship.

In some cases, of course, direct action was called for, and if the efforts of proxy forces or the chastisements of the White Dwarves didn't suffice—a very rare situation—there was always the holocaust retaliation of the Red Giants to unleash. The result was that there was no cohesive armed force in the galaxy— except for the outlaws, scattered genocide survivors, fanatics, deserters, outcasts, and committed freedom fighters who'd gravitated to the charismatic Ka Shamok's dispersed underground— willing to take on the Sysops inside Light Trap. And the insurrectionists, determined though they were, were simply too few.

The periscope was nearing the surface. "Fighting strength will manifest itself at the appropriate time," Ka Shamok said, brushing Sobek's reservation aside. "When has Black Hole been short of enemies? For now we address those prime factors: the Aborigines, the memory egg, Junknowitz. Once we have a viable attack plan, allies will rally to us by planetsful."

Sobek's Nall face looked more inscrutable than ever. "As you say. And once the Sysops are destroyed, what then?"

They'd never discussed that before; now Ka Shamok avoided the matter. "I neither know nor care, except that the Sysops are gone forever. And what of you, Probe?"

Yoo Sobek put one hand on the rail as magma scrolled and slid past them. "I don't know. Once I go up-Trap into the otherspace realm of the Sysops, once I remember the meaning of the eight rings—that moment is my own event horizon."

The cylinder vibrated ominously, but Ka Shamok's fugitive scientists and engineers had built well. Yoo Sobek wanted to press a final question on Ka Shamok: What would happen between the two of them once Black Hole was thrown down? Sobek suspected Ka Shamok had only put aside his need for revenge, not abandoned it, and still meant to kill Sobek in the end. "There's one question I wonder about," Sobek said.

But at that moment the drill bit broke the surface, rising above an active lava lake that was all fiery reds and oranges and dark, cooled surface-crust fragments in concentric circles. Magma boiled up from the lake's center, a few yards away, to become new lava, steaming pyroclastic flows streaming from it. They rose higher for a better vantage point, halting the nose cone five hundred feet above the spouting lava, the runny pahoehoe flows, and the whorling gasses of the volcanic field. The fallen Sysop and the Chasen-nur avenger looked out at a twilight hell while sensors in the periscope swept the sky and the countryside.

Ka Shamok studied him, clenching and unclenching huge fists. "What do you wonder?"

"I have this growing conviction, this nascent memory, that there's something the Sysops *themselves* fear," Sobek told him. "Now, what could that be, do you suppose?"

Before Ka Shamok could decide whether or not to speculate, the sensors began chirruping. An attack fleet was inbound for Spectarr II.

Sinead Ann Junknowitz got home from work depressed and feeling sorry for herself. The sight of her mansion-redoubt, whose market value had climbed by nearly thirty-five percent since she'd bought it eighteen months before, sent her morale even lower, because she stood to lose it soon.

An international development deal that had taken her months to put together had been scuttled by new UN eco-laws. Humanity had spent ten thousand years despoiling the Earth, and now it thought it was going to save Nature by keeping a few sequoias alive?

As her oak front door opened for her at 3 Maginot Lane, Presidio Enclave, she felt like weeping. She stood to lose it all and, worse, fail at the greater goal she'd set herself. She caught her reflection in a foyer mirror as she entered: an auburn-haired woman in a designer business suit, thirty-three years old, pleasant enough to look at if no perfume model, with a Gucci-signature PARC PC slung over one shoulder and her hairdo the worse for her having stood on deck coming back across San Francisco Bay.

Where a chandelier might have hung above her, there was a magnificent thirteen-foot-long scale model of the Nagoya O'Neill colony, currently under construction. She felt like blowing it a good-bye kiss; she'd lose the house, never get the seven-figure buy-in fee, never have a life high and clean and free in orbit above the petty, stinking herd of brainless sewer rats that was the majority of the human race.

She headed by habit for her office, off the library, to dock the Gucci-PARC, loving the home-alone sound of her footsteps in her grand, safe, empty house. All along the way she checked the lovingly tended plants of all types, her only self-indulgence. She checked her e-mail, wiping—without replaying—three more messages that appeared to have to do, somehow, with her ongoing disaster of a family. She hadn't been involved with them for years, and she meant to keep it that way.

In the midst of that she felt cool air on her neck, the hair there standing up as she heard a noise in the library, someone coming toward the office.

She forced herself not to freeze, to move purposefully, tripping the nearest alarm, of which there were many in all Presidio fortress-mansions. Then, hands shaking not quite uncontrollably, she opened the hidden release in the pilaster separating two floor-to-ceiling screens. It was a great deal harder than a dry run, but she got the weapon out of its rack clips: a police model Un-Gun that fired thick beanbag-sized fabric sacks of lead birdshot via compressed gas. She planned to bolt her office door next, but realized she'd waited too long; the handle turned and the door swung open despite her screamed, perhaps incoherent warnings.

Silhouetted against the light from the library windows, a monstrous figure shambled at her on huge feet. A humpbacked and distorted form with flailing dreadlocks or tentacles swinging behind, it groped at her with swollen, four-fingered hands.

She pulled the heavily padded Y-stock against her shoulder and fired. There was a tremendous pop and a belch of residual gas, and she was almost knocked over backward despite the Un-Gun's antirecoil porting. The shot-filled beanbag hit the intruder at sternum height and bore it over backward, where its head hit the parquet floor with a solid clunk.

Where's the security patrol? she wondered, edging toward her fallen foe, the Un-Gun clicking heavily in her hands as it chambered the second of its three rounds. Lacking any other avenue of escape, she planned to leap over the unmoving carcass and run out the front door. But she forgot that course of action when she saw that she didn't have a bug-eyed monster lying in her library, or a chainsaw killer in a suit made from female bondtrader skins. It was instead a man dressed in a themer's Goofy costume, the headpiece with its floppy ears shoved back.

"Lucky!" Sinead Junknowitz groaned.

THREE

THE THEME-PARK HOSPITAL was like an armed camp, but Nikkei and Mickey knew that the private SWATs and WAPs—War and Parabellum specialists—were less protection than the inconspicuous men and women trimming shrubbery, wheeling gurneys, and mopping floors: Kamimura's people, naturally.

The fact that Takuma Tanabe, captain of industry and member of the cabal of human Black Hole collaborationists known as the Phoenix Enterprises group, was served by *real* ninja—fiftieth-odd generation adepts whose updated skills put the old sneak-and-peek stuff to shame—had decided Mickey to swear allegiance to Nikkei's father. That, and the fact that Nikkei's father had implied terminal consequences for them both if they demurred.

Miss Sato led the two through layers of security, leaving corporate fellow travelers behind. The electrochromic windows had been made reflective to exterior light, a classic antisniper precaution, and there was a lot of military hardware around. People were giving the partners edgy, unfriendly looks; Mickey retaliated with his stringent pimp-roll swagger. Peering through a one-way window panel in a room door, he screeched to a halt. "Yo, *homme*-sweet-*homme*! Dig a shitload a this!"

Sato was vexed but concealed it. The pair peered at Charlie Cola, who was at a table being grilled by a trio of nondescript Japanese men in business suits. The last time Mickey and Nikkei had seen the balding, paunchy, bespectacled Cola—seen, but not been observed by him—the guy had been manning his Quick Fix convenience store in the Bronx, which had formerly concealed an interstellar Adit. The installation had been removed from Quick Fix as a result of Cola's falling out of favor and the activation of a mobile Adit aboard the cruise ship *Crystal Harmonic*, not to mention power games in Phoenix Group and the Black Hole Travel Agency.

Knowing Nikkei wasn't about to ask Sato for any answers, Nikkei inquired, "Don't tell me Elmer Fudd there started this war?"

"Quite the reverse," she said. "Come." Mickey choked back his automatic response, *Love to!*, as they trailed her through swinging doors. She halted and faced them.

"Approximately two hours ago, Tanabe-san was injured when extraterrestrials appeared at World Nihon to wrest away custody of Lucky Junknowitz, who was being detained at the corporate headquarters building. They withdrew in an aerospace craft last seen heading southwest over the ocean but were undetected by military or FAA radars. Tanabe-san was briefly held hostage but escaped with, apparently, help from Mr. Cola—a story I'm inclined to believe.

"In the course of that escape Tanabe-san suffered minor burns, contusions, and the like. However, he was struck a glancing blow to the skull by a large and extremely powerful humanoid. He has a cerebral concussion which, though not life-threatening, is of a grave and disabling nature. Against my advice and that of his physicians, he desires to speak to you both."

Doors swept aside for her. Beyond them it was quiet except for muted conversation and the soft sounds of the med monitors. The room, big enough to be a ward, was packed with edgetech med hardware and life-support gear. The window shades were drawn, and the main light in the room came from color-enhanced holos of the CEO's head and its contents.

Takuma Tanabe lay on a hospital bed with three doctors, an admin assistant, and two nurses hovering around. Off to one side, silent and dangerous as a nuke, sat Tanabe's *jonin* Kamimura, master of ninjas. Beside him stood Takashi Natsuki, Tanabe's chief bodyguard, listening to a headset earplug.

Nikkei's father was awake, although for once his characteristic canniness seemed to be blunted. He was dressed in suit slacks and a sky blue business shirt, collar open, tie and jacket missing, shoes removed to reveal elasticized black stockings. His temple was bandaged, as were his hands. When he spied his son, he showed disarmed surprise.

Then he rallied. "I need a few more minutes' conference time, please." His voice was low and measured, his accent as Midwestern as an Illinois banker's.

Seconds later Sato, the ninja *chonin*, and the bodyguard were standing in the background while Mickey looked on and Nikkei stood by his father's side. "I had a lot of plans, but none of them included a moment quite like this," Tanabe said.

Nikkei's face colored. A good Japanese son should have been stoic but evidenced concern over a father's injuries, but Nikkei wasn't a good Japanese son and both of them knew why. Without waiting for a response, Tanabe continued. "I mean no dishonor to other members of my household, but I want you to begin shouldering some of the responsibilities of this family, too—to begin looking after our affairs. Will you do that?" His father looked bloodless under the hospital lights, and suddenly old. "Will you do that for me?" he asked again. The PET scanner and other monitors showed the rise of emotion in him.

Nikkei's mouth worked. "You want that? Even though . . ."

Mickey thought about that "even though": even though, several years back, suicide and murder had driven them apart.

Tanabe gave his son's hand a squeeze; Nikkei registered the fact that even now his father's grip was quite strong. "You're my only son."

Nikkei kowtowed to his father. "Whatever you tell me, I'll do it. But you've either got two sons now, or none, because I've got a brother."

They all looked to Mickey, who, holding his breath, went through *joei-on jitsu* nullity mind drills, trying to not be there. It didn't work.

"Two for one?" Tanabe decided. "Such a deal."

The doctors and ward nurse reentered. "He needs rest," the chief of neurological medicine began, glancing to Miss Sato for support.

Nikkei let go of his father. Before Sato could hand down a decision, he decreed, "You got it. Please see to my father." Takuma said nothing, watching his son.

Nikkei and Sato adjourned to the corridor, with Mickey trailing them. For once she was less than sure of herself. "See here: I think we should clarify what—"

He cut her off. "I have to be takin' care of business. You sure you don't want to stick around? Maybe he needs some R and R in the 'dimly white world.' "

Mickey wondered what the hell the "dim white world" was to make Sato's face go bloodless that way. But, tough as brass knuckles, she regained her composure instantly. The two partners, versed in facial-kinesics reading, watched her carefully for clues or giveaways. There weren't any.

"There is much to cover in order to bring you up to speed,"

she told them briskly, and stepped off again in an almost cross-country stride even though she was wearing Masarati heels. "Let me know if I'm going too fast for you, gentlemen."

Lucky Junknowitz didn't know where he was or how he'd gotten there, but that was nothing new for him. Anyway, he had a good seat: real close to the stage. When the tight spotlight hit Asia Boxdale he found it strange that, instead of doing one of her dance or performance art pieces, she stood quite motionless and erect in her black lace evening gown, the long fan of liquid-shadow hair framing her face and shoulders.

She sang to the spotlight, which was somehow a streetlight, too. The tune was from "Cats"—and shortened—but the lyrics weren't.

"Goo-fee—
—ness endeared you, love, to me!
but the memories I carry
are why I couldn't stay
couldn't let your
laughter drown in my tears
So I had to go away . . ."

It wasn't his fault, or hers either, but it still hurt. Asia had been drawn to Lucky by his zany themer insouciance, tonic for the melancholy with which a lifetime of loss had afflicted her. She had figured out long before he did that he wasn't virtuoso clown enough to cure her episodes of grief, only enamored of her sufficiently to lose his *joie de vivre* and his calling in the attempt. So she'd distanced herself from him, and it still hurt.

Come to think of it, he should stand up, call for the house-lights, clear the air right now—only Asia seemed to have left the stage; in danced two more women, hands held high, who loomed large in his life, as a klezmer band struck up "Hava Nagila." The junoesque redhead and the face-that-launched-a-thousand-ships brunette broke into a modified hora as a chorus joined in from offstage.

"Harley and Sheena, Harley and Sheena, Harley and Sheena, T and A, lots!
Harley and Sheena, Harley and Sheena, Harley and Sheena, couldn't you plotz?
how'd you miss out on these?

your explanation please?
were you weak in the knees?
or, just a snore?"

Hey, there were perfectly valid reasons for his and Harley's
incompatibility and the fact that, splendid Trough tigress though
she was, he'd never gotten anything physical going with Sheena.
It wasn't as if he had any deep-seated misogynistic conflicts or
hidden paraphilias. Besides, he was beginning to recognize it all
as a dream riff on the last part of *All That Jazz*, in which current
and former love interests did production numbers. And anyway
it was over, there was no one left, so the lights should come
back up any time now.

He was wrong. Pure white beams converged on a nude female
figure hyperdefined in polished metal as the full orchestra struck
up the title theme from "Camelot" and a synthesized contralto
soared with perfect pitch.

"Silvercup! Silvercup!
We know you think it's quite perverse
Silvercup! Silvercup!
Let's face it, you could do much worse ..."

Oh, wait, this *had* to be wrong. The beautiful gleamer had
taken a fancy to him for some reason, saved his life, made
Lucky's cause her own. Moreover, that glorious argent face and
bod would get a rise out of most any male libido, especially in
the grievous eligible-femme shortage of the post-Turn era.

But an inorganic life-form? What would the folks back home
say? While he was agonizing over that and feeling like a low,
ungrateful, deviant human underwear stain, he realized she'd
somehow gotten to the big finish, her movements and countenance flowing smooth as mercury as she turned to him. The ex-
pressive amber eyes and moist pink lips, contrasting so with her
liquid metal luster, made her look implicitly human in a Halloween on Venice Beach kind of way.

"Don't give this good thing up,
Live with it: you can't tup
A maiden more forbade-en
Than the one called Sil-ver-cup!"

Of course there was the minor hitch that her true metalflesh was hostage to the Monitor on Sweetspot, and her current corporeal housing didn't bode well for lip-synching and flextime. He was considering that complication when he realized Silver was calling his name—no, someone else was.

He opened his eyes groggily to see his sister looking down at him. He was lying on her library floor with a cold compress on the side of his head where he'd smacked it on the parquetry. "Lucky, *Je*sus, you had me so worried! What are you doing here?"

"Brace yourself, Shin—we're about to have a *very* strange conversation."

FOUR

"AFTER YOU'VE RESTED, I'll meet you for lunch at the executive penthouse tea rooms." Miss Sato was walking so fast Mickey got the distinct impression she was trying to lose Nikkei and himself. "Until then, the briefing team can—"

"We didn't come to ogle a fucking *cha-ya*," Nikkei interrupted, loudly enough that people kowtowing to Sato by the hospital elevator studiously ignored him. "And no more of those briefing wonks!"

Mickey speculated on where this air-clearing was taking the two of them—*with my black ass strapped in for the ride!* Tanabe had already forgiven Nikkei grandpatricide; how much more give did he have in him? Cuckoldry would be asking an awful lot.

Mickey had been around Japanese enough to know what happened when rigid traditional decorum broke down: emotions flowed white-hot, no restraints applied, and the death gods tied their napkins 'round their necks and licked their chops. Pleasure and trouble were what he and Nikkei had buddied up to seek out, but getting caught in a combination interstellar corporate gangwar and multigenerational love triangle *might*, Mickey thought, be more on the order of inserting his johnson into a pencil sharpener than he had a mind for.

Sato addressed Nikkei in her most restrained tone, that Oxford accent smooth as transmission fluid. "That's impossible at the moment, Mr. Tanabe; I'm due for a crucial meeting that cannot be postponed."

"Cum-mungus!" Nikkei smiled wolfishly. "Lead the way." He sounded more mocking than enthusiastic. "What needs explaining, you can tell us on the way."

With Nikkei and Sato exchanging multigigawatt inscrutability rays, Mickey took his shot. "Somethin' I'd like to take care of first." Mickey told her what he wanted and Nikkei concurred, mostly to be contrary.

"As you wish." She led them down one floor, where there was only marginally less security. In a guarded, shuttered room lay the cargo Nikkei and Mickey had smuggled back to LA from New York City. Two female nurses Micky pegged for Filipinas bowed to Sato and, at a nod from her, left. Sato and the two men gazed down on Asia Boxdale, who lay with eyes closed, snoring gently and regularly.

"I'm told she'll awaken in another hour or so," Sato informed them, nodding to the vital-signs monitors. "She's in good condition, responding well to analeptic treatment. Would you like me to explain the course of therapy?"

Nikkei, scored on, grunted, "Who cares?" Pretending his irritation was for the beepings and pings of the monitoring equipment, he flicked an Off switch he spied on a central control panel, and the sounds died away. Sato made no comment. The zombie-coma tranks provided by Tanabe's New York people to keep Asia knocked out for the trip west had obviously taken a lot out of her.

Mickey, who'd been mightily impressed by Asia's resourcefulness and strength of spirit, bent over her for a closer look. Even though her night train of hair was matted from days in chemical sleep, even though her face was wan and her eyes dark-ringed, even though she had a sickbed smell despite having been cleaned up some since being delivered to World Nihon, he was bowled over anew by Asia's delicate beauty, her fragile . . . not flawlessness, really, or purity; something else. Definitely not purity; when he and Nikkei had been assigned to maintain surveillance on her, they'd viewed, among other things, a tape of one of her more erotic performance art-cum-dance pieces.

Maybe the word he was groping for was *vulnerability*, Mickey thought. When teamed, he and Nikkei had always stuck to the straightforward carnality of *mizu shobai* ladies, nightlife vice goddesses. But looking down at Asia, Mickey thought about the taped phonetap conversation he'd heard in one briefing session—a remark made to Lucky Junknowitz by Braxmar Koddle. Koddle, that fuckin' limey oreo, Mickey thought, but he was right. It was indeed, as Koddle had said, difficult to be close to Asia Boxdale without putting your arms around her and hugging her to you.

Nikkei was asking Miss Sato, "Why'd we haveta hotdog the job, practically grab her on a street corner, then *weasel* across the USA like the Brotherhood of Evil Mutants was looking for us?" Not that it hadn't been a rush.

Sato weighed him with a look. "In three days there will take place aboard the cruise ship *Crystal Harmonic* a conclave of Phoenix Group principals and Trough VIPs. The Black Hole Travel Agency is going to end the factionalism by picking its planetary overseer for full-scale exploitation of Earth resources."

She gazed down at Asia. "Boxdale and the rest connected to Junknowitz, as well as assorted other Earthly cat's-paws like Cola, will have their uses in the machinations—hence, they're being snapped up in preparation for the summit.

"Tanabe-san is a prime candidate for this ultimate executive position. His main antagonist will be his lifelong rival, Phipps Hagadorn, but all the Phoenix principals will be battling no-holds-barred for it."

Though Mickey couldn't take his eyes from Asia's face, he'd been listening intently. "You sayin' Nikkei's taking his old man's place in this feeding frenzy?"

"No. Mr. Tanabe will be fully recovered by then, but it's vital that you both understand what lies ahead, and what's at stake." She glanced at her watch. "I have less than fifteen minutes to get to my appointment, one that has great bearing on the *Crystal Harmonic* conclave."

There followed a pose, Sato and Nikkei squared off, that reminded Mickey of a *ma* panel in a Japanese comic, denoting a frozen interval in time from which the *manga* reader infers meaning. Only it usually took a Japanese to understand what was really going on in a *ma*—like now, for instance.

Nikkei broke the pose. "Let's beam." Mickey let out a breath and caressed Asia's chin softly with one knuckle, feeling her warm breath on the back of his hand. "Get well, Box." Then he hurried to catch up with Nikkei and Sato, who were already on their way out the door.

As the door closed behind them, Asia opened her eyes the slightest bit, trying to gauge where she was and separate what she'd heard from things she'd dreamt. Then the door opened as the nurses returned, and she feigned sleep again.

"Lucky, stop!" Sinead sobbed, clapping her hands to her ears. "You belong in an Urgent Care facility! Go away or I'll call Enclave security; this isn't my problem!"

He'd tried to tell her about Black Hole and why he'd sought refuge with her, but she'd diagnosed the story as a mental aberration, more proof of dysfunction in the family she shunned.

He tried again, gesturing with gangly hands thrust through the wrist vents of his Goofy suit. "Sinead, it *is* your problem." He pointed to the thirteen-foot model of the Nagoya Aerospace O'Neill project that hung in the foyer. "A Black Hole stooge controls Nagoya; if that orbiting hermitage ever *does* get built, you can bet they won't be letting indig peons like you on board. *You're* the one who's living the fantasy!"

Presidio security hadn't responded to her silent alarm—a system glitch, she'd assumed—and Sinead hadn't summoned an ambulance because she thought it likely Lucky was a fugitive. But what he'd said was so devastating, and her yearning to escape the mindless squabbling of human beings was fixed so obsessively on the O'Neill project, that now she reached for the phone. "You lying psycho! You'll regret—"

She stopped as she heard sounds from the kitchen—a crash and glass breaking. Lucky tried to placate her, "There're a couple of, that is, friends with me—Sinead!"

She ignored him, dropping the phone and charging off with the Un-Gun. Her house! Lucky pursued, yelling, "They're themers, sis! Themers!"

She barged into the kitchen muzzle-first. "Get out of my house, you shiftless, freeloading—" Maybe it was the olfactory signals that stopped her first; there were smells attached to Lucky's XT tour group that were frankly unearthly.

The dozen eerily identical Honos, like so many yard-tall ants walking on their hind legs and wearing pink straw hats, were foraging in her triple-door commercial refrigerator; the Dimdwindles—two parents resembling walking duffel bags and their son GoBug, a thirty-inch-long larva—were sitting at the table trying to piece together a broken vase. Mr. Millmixx, who might've been a bulge-eyed Basil Wolverton cartoon grotesque come alive, was slumped in typical phlegmatism on the drainboard. The werewolfish Rphians were sniffing at a rubber plant, and Dame Snarynxx, a sluglike creature the size of a hippo, was rummaging in the top-of-the-line indoor/outdoor composting unit.

What Sinead heard rattled her as well: the beings all made comments or had questions and, lacking a hearing-aid nanite, she heard only an interstellar babble of startling complexity.

And then, of course, there had been Lucky's allegations about Black Hole. Sinead glanced around her kitchen, glassy-eyed. "You're not themers. You're, you're . . ."

Her eyes rolled up into her head and the Un-Gun slipped from her fingers. Lucky managed to break her fall as she went down.

"Is that slip you're wearing flammable?" Sheena Hec'k asked Harley Paradise out of one side of her mouth as devilish darkness closed in on them.

Slip? Even with glowing eyes of all sizes, shapes, and configurations edging in from every side upon their meager island of light, even in the pitch blackness of the Hazmat Adit sepulcher, Harley found time to radiate a little ill-will Sheena's way. The micromini was the worse for wear—tattered, singed in places, missing quite a few rhinestone studs and silver sequins—but some cheap little *slip*, it certifiably was not. On the other hand, Sheena was just a tomboy from the Trough, a fugitive Black Hole guide, so she couldn't be blamed much for not knowing. Moreover, it seemed that she and Harley would either survive together or perish that way.

"N-no, I, I think it's been safety treated," Harley admitted, unable to find a label. At least, she noted with some pride, her teeth were no longer chattering so badly that she couldn't get out a sentence. She tightened her grip on the field-hockey stick she'd taken as weapon and prize of war in her and Sheena's escape from an interrogation clinic on planet al-Reem. Perhaps it was only a stage prop, but the stick felt like good wood, well taped, the plasticized sleeve reinforcing its middle reading ERGOSPORT SUPERPRO. Harley wasn't much for guns or martial arts chop-socky, but, as she'd proved only moments ago, she'd learned her way around a hockey stick during her years at Bridlepath School.

Like her dress, hairdo, and manicure, she felt much the worse for wear in the wake of her kidnapping, the al-Reem abuses

she'd suffered, and the go-around with Miss Diandra—
"Discipline Di," headmistress of the mythical Ascot Academy.
Only a minute or two had elapsed since Harley and Sheena had
made a bewildering escape by fading through a damaged 'Reem
Adit after the materialization of an Australian Aborigine had
thrown the whole place into panic and confusion.

The two young women had found themselves on this domed
dais, amid stacks of dimming systemry, in the stygian darkness
of what Harley thought might be Dracula's Astrodome. Adding
to the stink of burnt wiring was the stench of the deep accumu-
lation of unidentifiable rot, dreck, and guano. Some of the crud
was smoldering, too, due to what looked like flares sputtering
themselves out here and there in the vast, dark open. All around,
predatory creatures were being emboldened by the failing of the
light on indicators, holographic projectors, and data screens and
the waning of spent flares. Sheena had examined the equipment
and pronounced it depleted of energy—incapable of fading them
back through the Adit to another destination, illuminating the
sepulcher, or otherwise doing them any good.

Sheena was ripping her microfiber shirt, sending faux pearl
buttons flying, declaring, "In that case I guess I'll have to—"

"Listen!" Harley shouted in despair. "The hammering's
stopped!"

The muffled, metal-on-metal hammering they'd heard a few
seconds before had been the only sign that something intelligent
might be around to succor them, and the thought that someone
had been there and gone away was more than Harley thought
she could bear. She peered into the darkness where huge, possibly metallic equipment or structures lay scattered. They might be
the size of houses or earthmovers, but it was tough to gauge.

Sheena, who'd paused to listen more attentively, corrected her.
"No, there it is again." The pounding sounded less regular, as if
whoever it was was wearying, losing determination, or both.
Harley, discovering she'd been holding her breath, exhaled shak-
ily.

Sheena had torn open the front of the navy blue synthsilk shirt
she had borrowed from Lucky Junknowitz's closet back on
Earth—a shirt Harley had bought him, back before she'd lost all
patience with him!—and popped the cuffs. Now she peeled it off
in a few quick motions, leaving herself in nothing but Lucky's
gauzy Balinese baggies and a pair of cross-training hightops.

Of *course* Jessica Rabbit there wouldn't wear anything underneath, Harley observed sourly to herself. At another time

Harley—who prided herself on her figure, her fitness, and omniwellness conditioning—might have felt a teensy twinge of jealousy for the guide's lithely muscular arms and shoulders, the full, upturned breasts, the abs that, no doubt, you could've bounced a quarter off of like a well-tucked blanket. Right now however, the sight of Sheena Hec'k stripped for action was somewhat reassuring.

"Stay close. Keep them off us as best you can," Sheena instructed, then led the way down off the dais. Harley followed, stick at high port, heart pumping at 180 per, nerve endings screaming. She could hear the chittering and scuttling as things came after them, or circled to cut the two off from escape. None closed in, though; wise predators evaluated potential prey before pouncing. Harley thought about abandoning her Ferrari spike heels for better maneuverability in the layered nastiness underfoot, but couldn't bear the thought of only panty hose between her feet and whatever was burrowing and squirming around in the loam-detritus-dung mess. She would joyfully have traded every shoe in her closet and every stitch she was wearing for some third-hand Tibetan basketball sneakers.

The worst shocker was that the dwellers in the dark regarded her as nothing more than *food*—she could see it in their ravenous eyes. Until this nightmare began, she'd been a spokesmodel; her hazel-eyed beauty, her bee-stung lips, her glorious mane of brown hair and tall tonedness had made her one of the most glamorous new adornments of the Twenty-Ones, Earth's premiere clique among the young and the monied.

Shocking, then, but undeniable, that the denizens of this place would wolf her down with no more regret or insight than she'd waste on a canapé—would see no difference between Harley and some derelict. At least the sadists on 'Reem had known who Harley Paradise *was*!

She trailed Sheena warily, mindful of the big, deep depression into which she'd almost fallen upon leaping out of the Adit's field. There were others like it, symmetrical and irregularly spaced, some overlapping; though the general shape of them suggested titanic jack baseplates, or outriggers for heavy equipment, Harley had the sudden conviction that they were something rather different.

Sheena's night vision was more acute than Harley's; coming off the dais with Lucky's ripped shirt in hand, she made unerringly for something lying half-buried in the decaying offal and yanked it free without slowing. It was a curving, pointed shape half again as long as Sheena's forearm, like half a new-moon crescent, with a fearsome ridge of spines running down the inside of the arc.

Sheena impaled the shirt on the topmost spine and wrapped the rest around the makeshift torch as she strode. Harley was hard-put to keep up, the Ferrari heels sinking; she was scared to fall behind, but equally scared not to watch their backs. She did her best to move as alertly, as preparedly, as she ever had on the hockey field; it was an odd feeling to be wearing her scowling game face again. Sounds in the dark came hard behind her, and chorused to all sides. Something big swooped close to her head, oinking at her.

Sheena led the way to one of the last of the dying flares through curls of fecal-smelling smoke. She dipped her synthsilk torch to it, knotting the arms tighter as she did. Harley couldn't recall whether Lucky disliked textile chemicals enough to own a nonfireproofed shirt.

And there was no time to ponder; they heard a noise like air escaping from a tractor-trailer tire. Something drew itself up, looking like an immense catcher's mitt palm-down, a single eye gleaming in its middle, and sidled at Harley from the left.

With a twiddly noise, the creature launched at her a stinger or sucker or tongue resembling a spiny shuttlecock on a slimy length of tubing. Harley's mouth made an inane little deb peep of grossed-outness, but her body, hyperprimed, went into action on its own. She whacked the shuttlecock back the way it had come with all the body English she could lay on and a fast recovery. There was a muffled whinny of pain and surprise. The attacker went into reverse gear, scattering other half-seen abominations that had been closing in behind it. It reminded her of the Wall Street hoverferry leaving for Hoboken in a big hurry.

"Rah! Rah! Bridlepath!" Harley bawled at them, half in tears. "Go-ooo *Minxes!*"

FIVE

" 'BLACK HOLE TRAVEL Agency,' huh? Sounds like the one that books *my* trips."

Sinead Ann Junknowitz sniffed, dabbing at her nose and eyes with the wad of Seventh Generation recycled-paper tissue, and half-laughed, half-sobbed. "Endless midnight trudges through hub-airport concourses in places that aren't on the map. Reservation codes nobody's ever heard of. Employees who don't belong to any known ethnic group or gender."

Lucky, sitting across the kitchen table from her, forced one of his zany McToon grins as the XT tourists looked on. " 'Abandon All Luggage, Ye Who Enter Here.' "

She'd been holding up surprisingly well since regaining consciousness and hearing him out. She'd even accepted the idea that there were intelligent nonhuman life-forms in her home, having pinned on the translator brooch the Honos had whipped up for her in lieu of a pentecostal-pipsqueak nanite. On Lucky's advice, they'd fashioned it to look like Starfleet issue.

"But I mean it," she said, reverting to her circle-the-wagons tone. "I won't get involved in whatever all this is. It's not my problem."

"I'm tellin' ya, Sinead—"

" 'Ann'!"

"*Sinead*, what d'you want, a Robin Hood speech? This isn't hypothetical; everybody connected to me comes in for bad juju. Even if I leave this second, some deeply fiendish entities'll likely come calling with fusion-powered thumbscrews."

"They can take it up with my lawyers."

"They'll probably *be* your lawyers!"

The phone toned before she could answer. Sinead hesitated, because Lucky had admitted that his band had interdicted all house telecom the same way they'd phreaked the alarms. "I, heh, think that's for me," he admitted as she switched on a speakerphone and flatscreen.

Ziggy Forelock's face appeared. He'd changed quite a bit since the last time Lucky had seen him, not long before Lucky had sneaked back into the Trough. His roundish face was thinned out a bit, his mocha skin its natural tone rather than altered with camoflesh; his black hair had returned to its natural curliness, and his eyes gleamed with a strange intensity under those prominent brows. From background sounds and the blank backdrop, Lucky assumed he was at a public phone booth in a truck stop or bus depot.

Ziggy showed no surprise at seeing Lucky with his estranged sister in the background—the tour group was dispersed outside the camera's field of vision. Without preamble, Ziggy recited, " 'Attention, unidentified spaceship: you are being tracked.' "

Lucky yukked in spite of himself. " 'Gentlemen, prepare yourselves for a new scale of physical science.' What's RGO, La Zig?" *Forbidden Planet* dialogue was the shibboleth of his old loft posse crew.

Now it was Ziggy's turn to laugh. "*You're* what's RGO, Doctor J.!"

RGO stood for Really Going On, the concealed truth behind life's smoke and mirrors, the facts underlying the modern world's tsunamis of bullshit. RGO had been a cynical joke until Black Hole made it a phrase to bring shivers; laughter was an antidote worth trying.

"Can't believe you tracked me down," Ziggy went on. "I've been transient lately, roundabout commo links only. What'd you do, let some kinda telecom knowbot loose with my voiceprint?"

"Something like that." Actually, Lucky had had Silvercup use her SIGWAR systems to trace Ziggy and the other posse members, all of whom seemed to have gone to ground or just plain disappeared. "Where are you?"

Ziggy shook his head. "Best I don't mention it. But I think I know where you are, more or less. Hi, Shin."

Sinead, twisting the four-in-hand bow tie at her throat and staring down at her feet, got out, "Hello, Sigmund."

A disembodied female voice came in, warm and calm, one Lucky recognized but couldn't place. "Is the inorganic entity who tracked us via telespace monitoring this link? I should like to interface."

Ziggy exhaled loudly through his nose. "SELMI, didn't I tell you to lay low?"

"Your actual words were 'I'll handle this.' "

Lucky was following all this with considerable shock. SELMI

was Harley Paradise's decision-support system and confidant software at Your-Turn, Inc.; Lucky had once heard a snippet of that voice simulation. When he had conned his way back to the stars via the Bronx, Ziggy was seeing what he could find out from SELMI. It sounded like some kind of alliance had formed.

Silvercup had to be monitoring the call, but she didn't reveal her presence. Lucky pushed ahead. "Not now. Let's keep this brief."

"That is a prudent point," SELMI put in. "By arrangement with the intellect that chooses not to reveal itself, this link is encrypted, but that protection will not stand up to high-intensity cryptoanalysis and SIGINT attack for very long."

Ziggy started talking fast. "Luck, there's a recent acquaintance of yours on Earth—aboard the *Crystal Harmonic*, I think. Lady in a kind of chador, red Christmas tree lights for eyes—she called to tell me you'd made it into the Trough."

"Wick Fourmoons!" So the independent travel agent he'd met on Confabulon had gotten to Earth after all.

"Lemme finish. She said Sean, Willy, and Eddie were disappeared to a place called End Zone."

"I know," Lucky said tightly. That had been among the information Silvercup had phreaked from the *Crystal Harmonic*'s data banks. He'd heard enough rumors about The Awesome Vogonskiy's personal planet of horrors to make rescue a top priority—once he had help.

"So now what d'we do?" Ziggy asked. Sinead was tugging at Lucky's sleeve.

"Lucky, what's he talking about? What happened to Sean?"

Lucky drew a deep breath. "First thing is, try to get back in touch with Wick. If she's still aboard that ship maybe we can— Ziggy? Ziggy!"

The screen shimmered and Lucky's heart skipped several beats. Then a flashing visual appeared.

!!!ATTENTION!!!
REJIS INTERRUPT!!!
REGIONAL JUSTICE INFORMATION SYSTEM HEREBY
ORDERS YOU TO CEASE ALL COMMUNICATION AND REMAIN
AT YOUR CURRENT LOCATION FOR THE ARRIVAL OF
DEPARTMENT OF JUSTICE OFFICIALS

"Silver, did they get a fix on us?" Lucky yelled.

Silvercup's upbeat, bell-toned voice came from the phone

speakers. "Relax, Lucky; the tracer was still backtracking to my sat link when I broke contact. I'm not so sure about Ziggy's status, but the SELMI intellect had taken precautionary measures, so there's reason to be hopeful."

"Who're all these voices?" Sinead was earnestly trying to get a handle on matters, but she was dazed. "Who's 'Silver'?"

"I guess it's time I showed you."

Sinead rose with great uncertainty to follow Lucky.

"I think I have to use the lavatory," GoBug interjected.

"Don't—you—*dare!*" Sinead flared at him.

It took Lucky another few minutes to calm things down, locate food acceptable to his rescuers, and get his sister into motion again. He led the way to the indoor-outdoor pool, which was more a status symbol and value enhancer than an amenity for which Sinead had much use. It wasn't quite Olympic size, but it was deep, the original owner having been a scuba-gear entrepreneur. Its dome was shut with electrochromics fully opaqued and the lights were turned low—not the way she'd left it earlier—and the water was as turbid as dye. "How'd the floor get soaked? What happened here?"

There was no damage done, even though the tile was as wet as if the place had been awash; the pool deck had good drainage. Sinead's caviling stopped dead as the waters began to mound and surge. She swayed back against Lucky as a gracefully curved shape broke the surface—the top half of a reflective, streamlined shape some sixty feet long. The craft eased to the edge of the pool, a hatch opening where there hadn't been a seam. A boarding ramp formed from its side to rest on the deck, and within the spacecraft's cabin soft blue light glowed.

When Lucky would have guided her aboard, Sinead dug in her handmade Mondo Brio slingbacks like a mule. "No way!"

Lucky stood firm, too. "There're just two more introductions to go—the most important ones."

She sniffled. "This is so unfair! I just want to be left alone! I think I need a Pacifex—"

"No pills." He shook his head. "It's all right, you'll see."

The lyrical voice vibrated from the craft's surface. "Hello, Sinead. I've been looking forward to meeting you."

"*You're* 'Silver'?" Sinead's body stopped quivering quite so much like a mandolin string.

"Silvercup," Lucky elaborated. "Hop in." With Lucky holding her hand, she came across the ramp and entered the blue light.

* * *

On the planet called Sweetspot, where the godlike Silicon Intelligences of the Fealty ruled, the Monitor was at pains to insure its privacy. Though it was a low-upper Fealty official entrusted with great authority and power, it had subverted its own ethical safeguards and now lived in fear of detection and punishment.

But there was no going back; both the need to conceal its crimes and its unsatisfied, dark urges drove the Monitor on. It therefore shielded its skyscraper-top tabernacle from outside surveillance and shooed away attendant machines, self-aware subordinates, and drudge robots alike before ushering in the Virile Construct.

The Virile Construct marched in with his head held high, a chrome demigod of a gleamer—fashioned of somalloy in human shape but impossibly handsome, heroic, heavily muscled, and slim-waisted. Naked, he plainly merited his name. The Monitor had caused the Virile Construct to be built ostensibly to serve as companion, counterpart, and metalflesh mate for the female gleamer Silvercup; the Monitor's actual motives for bringing him into existence were much less benign.

The acre of black mirror was mostly vacant. The Monitor, resting on ornately inscribed jacks, gazed out upon it like a sphinx of polished gold, staring with eyes lit by an inner blue radiance. Its entire front cowling had been cast in the likeness of an ancient deity of wisdom. The Virile Construct stopped before it, struck a noble pose, and smote his chest with a mighty fist. "Behold! I am returned!"

The Virile Construct was wondrously vain, pompous, and humorless, in keeping with the Monitor's secret agenda. "You have made ready to go forth into the Trough," the Monitor asked, "and fetch Silvercup back here along with Junknowitz?" It activated holo projections. One showed Silvercup as she had been: a glorious figure of living, fluid metal, an idealization of a human female form, only the amber eyes and the lips, soft and moist as the flesh of a pink grapefruit, relieving her metal pearlescence. That body was now in the Monitor's keeping, held hostage against her return; her intellect and memory, transferred to far more mundane housings, had been sent forth after Junknowitz by the Monitor. Silvercup had found him, but was somehow freed of the obedience programming the Monitor had imposed on her and was now at large on that miserable tertiary planet, *with* the imbecile primate, in the form of a sentient aerospace craft.

Another projection showed Lucky Junknowitz—not the what-me-worry Alfred E. Neuman lookalike he'd been most of his life, but the cosmetically altered appearance he currently presented: black hair sans cowlick, green eyes, the gap between his teeth filled in and his sleepy-eyed look made more alert. The Virile Construct uttered a peal of hatred. "I'll remand the malfunctioning female to you after I've stomped that obscene little bubo Junknowitz to a stinking floor stain!"

The Monitor changed its previous directive. "Revision: We need Junknowitz. Not only does he hold secrets to the Sysops' probability experiments, but events swirling around him are linked to the Earth Aborigines now at large in the Trough. Most importantly he is intimate with, and perhaps even User of, two human females who recently escaped from al-Reem.

"I am now convinced that these two—a rogue Singularity Flings guide named Sheena Hec'k and an Adit Navel sex object named Harley Paradise, who was involved in Black Hole's infrastructure on Earth and whose image appears in the Agency's tour-promotion materials—have somehow, inconceivably, found their way through a malfunctioning Adit to Hazmat."

"Hazmat!" The planet's name jogged the Virile Construct as it would have any citizen of the Fealty. "What of the memory egg? It still exists, still abides there?"

"I so presume, or how could the Hazmat Adit function?" the Monitor asked, azure searchlight eyes flashing. "This information is highly classified, but you now understand why I need Junknowitz and the others in viable condition."

"Of course. I shall deactivate him *after* interrogation," the Virile Construct amended. "Now, I go forth to Earth!"

"Hold," the Monitor ordered. "Earth is a complex and quirky tertiary world infested now with Black Hole operatives, vying human factions, and, we believe, insurgency agents. There may even be business competitors of the Agency's abroad. You will require a guide, a local expert. See."

It had projected another image, a middle-aged human male. He was spare and jaundiced-looking, had a receding gray hairline, wore steel-rimmed glasses and a rumpled suit, and carried a leather briefcase that looked as if it had been through an asteroid impact.

"This Terran's name is Zastro Lint. He is a former employee of the tax bureaucracy of one of their declining nation-states. As best we can determine, Lint has been coopted and neuroindoctrinated by a faction within Black Hole's covert Adit

Navel infrastructure—a rogue law-enforcement officer named Barnes and a career criminal and black marketeer named Dante Bhang, who have aspirations of becoming kingpins in the Agency's Earthside operations.

"Lint was given biosynergistic upgrades and nanite implants appropriate to a field operative and dispatched into the Trough with a programmed obsession to locate, capture, and retrieve Junknowitz. The augmentations were done hastily and badly; Lint has perhaps two baseline weeks to live, although he will be extremely formidable in the meantime."

Lint was shown gesturing at Lucky with the briefcase, from which a directed energy bolt shot, barely missing the gawky guide. "As you can see, Lint was provided with a smart-luggage symbiote. But Junknowitz managed to have Lint shanghaied by enforcers for a vacation time-share planetoid called Nu-Topia."

The Virile Construct's somalloy face flowed into a look of surprise. "A ruthless and effective tactic, from a degenerate imbecile like Junknowitz!" Few things were as difficult to endure or escape as captivity by hard-sell time-share companies.

"Junknowitz isn't as feckless as he looks," the Monitor warned. "But the primary point is that Lint would be a valuable asset for your pursuit of Junknowitz on Earth."

"But were I to liberate Lint, he would still be the tool of our opposition," the Virile Construct pointed out.

"You'd be surprised how gullible some tools are," the Monitor told him in all honesty.

SIX

STARING AT THE REJIS interrupt that had blanked his call to Lucky and issued the command to stand fast and await arrest, Ziggy Forelock was hit hard by the realization that he wasn't quite the telegeist he'd come to feel himself to be.

SELMI was by way of being a fairy-godmother software entity but had limitations, while Ziggy was merely human, a guy at a phone booth on a bus platform in the main Port Authority bus terminal at Forty-second and Eighth with, presumably, everybody but UNICEF out for his scalp.

He'd led a charmed life of sorts from the moment a multiagency team of FBI, IRS, NYPD, and other law grunts had closed in on him at the Hagadorn Pinnacle and SELMI had instructed him to not be afraid, pick up the remote phone, and do exactly as it told him to.

Some night flight! Tapped into the skyscraper's surveillance and control systems as well as the cops' communications, SELMI had guided him around, over, under, and through the dragnet. Unquestionably, the defining moment had been clinging to the building's broadcast tower while SELMI talked him through his acrophobia.

It was the beginning of a beautiful friendship. Spying through and manipulating the datasphere, SELMI gave Ziggy a lot more covert mobility than the Shadow ever had. Money he got from ATMs; identity he could change as needed. Credit and shelter were things SELMI arranged, and the AI made keeping track of the downgraded search for him about as complicated as watching fish in an aquarium.

On the downside Ziggy—SELMI—had been unable to locate any of the missing posse members or any decisive data on Phoenix or Black Hole. Ziggy had also "been" to Ayers Rock in central Australia via VirtNet, hoping for further word from Gipper Beidjie, who'd previously appeared to Ziggy in telegeist form and enjoined him to get himself Down Under for a mysterious event of unparalleled importance. He'd found that the Dream Land theme park was about to open, but no sign of the Intubis.

The first truly positive development had come today, when SELMI had detected datasphere feelers and wound up establishing a phone link with Lucky, but the REJIS interrupt had dropped the ax on all that.

No sign of pursuit; the platforms where he was were only medium-busy, rush hour having peaked hours before. About the only thing out of the ordinary were some trespassing air-dancers, exulting as they strip-surfed the charged RPEV lines on superconducting maglev boards whose synthesizers riffed "juice song" from the interplay of fields. Ziggy got out the latest in a series of roam-phones he'd used since escaping the Hagadorn Pinnacle. "SELMI, talk to me. What's going on?"

The AI's copacetic, not quite seductive voice answered immediately. "Police COMINT and ELINT operations targeted on you have been taken over directly by REJIS, the Regional Justice Information System based in Washington, D.C. Perhaps it is monitoring telephone traffic and matching your voiceprint."

"So they sicced HAL 9000 on me?"

"You shouldn't take it that way, Ziggy. REJIS is only a conscientious law officer doing its duty."

"Yeah, but—" He dropped it; this was no time to badmouth software entities. "Where's that leave me?"

As he was saying it he became aware of flashing blue lights and heard whooper hiccups; a Port Authority Police cruiser was coming right his way. He looked around hopelessly for an escape route, but the cop car disappeared down a bus ramp in the direction the air-dancers had taken. He was starting to feel relieved when he heard more sirens, and the concrete-canyon echoes of a helicopter hanging around somewhere over Eighth Avenue.

It came to him that SELMI had been talking all the while. "Did you hear me, Ziggy? I have set in place what diversions I could. Discard this phone immediately; they may be trying to resonate it and get a DF fix. I must break contact or REJIS will detect me and initiate countermeasures. Leave Manhattan before recontacting me."

"But—"

"Don't tarry!" The connection was replaced by a dial tone.

Ziggy hunched his shoulders to the happy-face cams and dropped the phone into the recycle slot of an EcoCola machine. He'd just reached the main concourse when the escalators shut down. He pretended to window-shop along as more and more police appeared, but on heading for the nearest exit he discovered that the servos on the power doors had been switched off. Straining mightily, he shouldered through only to find he'd blundered smack into a curbless ramp rather than a bus platform.

Ziggy stood frozen as flashing blue lights, sirens, ululating pandemonium, and brusque impact bore down on him.

"Mr. Tanabe? Excuse me, Tanabe-san? You wanted to see me, um, sir?"

Charlie Cola, standing at the door to Takuma Tanabe's hospital room and seeing the man apparently asleep, would have thought that there had been some mistake—except that Tanabe's people didn't make mistakes. Then the CEO's eyes fluttered open and he gestured, a bit weakly, for Charlie to enter. "Actually, Mr. Cola, I believe it was you who wished to speak to me. Please have a seat, won't you?"

Charlie took an autoconforming chair by Tanabe's bedside. "Well, that's true, but not like this, Mr. Tanabe." Tanabe seemed to be having a slight problem focusing; certainly the glancing blow to the head Charlie had seen him take from that walking sequoia in Lucky Junknowitz's crew would have been enough to scramble anybody's brain.

"Fortunate for me that you were so tenacious in pursuing that talk."

Charlie chuckled, not from amusement but rather from a giddy sense of the possibilities that could open up to him if Takuma Tanabe felt indebtedness, *giri*, toward him. It was what had propelled Charlie to help Tanabe escape Junknowitz and those Trough-tourist rescuers. The Quick Fix convenience store Charlie ran in the Bronx as a front for a covert Adit had started going downhill after the Adit was yanked. Everything had started going wrong, and now Charlie was on the outs with Phoenix and Black Hole alike. But Tanabe's *giri* could make Charlie's prospects limitless. "What I actually came to World Nihon for was to see if you could use a person like me."

Tanabe studied Charlie through half-lowered lids. "I *already* use a good many people like you, Mr. Cola."

Tanabe wasn't as enfeebled as he wanted the world to assume, and he'd chosen to reveal that fact to Charlie. And, chillingly, Tanabe showed no hint of *giri*. Charlie swallowed; the wrong answer would likely get him disappeared. "Excuse me, but no, you don't, sir. Not a man who's operated an Adit most of his life and has connections all through the Trough. Whose father worked for Black Hole. No disrespect, but if you don't see what an asset I'd be, you're not as smart as they say you are, Tanabe-san."

"And how smart do they say I am, Mr. Cola?"

"Smart enough to want all the edge you can get against Hagadorn." Sweat had beaded Charlie's sparse mustache and collected against the lenses of his old-fashioned bifocals, but he didn't dare break eye contact to wipe it away.

Tanabe didn't look in the least drowsy now. "That smart, at least. And I'm beholden to you, but that's why I hesitate to take you aboard. Hagadorn could win. What kind of gratitude would it show to lead you to disaster?"

Charlie shifted his paunchy five-foot-eight frame in the chair. "Mr. Tanabe, we both know I'm already slated for disaster. If I meet it head-on siding with you, well, that won't be hastening events much at this point."

Tanabe's eyes bored into Charlie's. "Someone else sided with me a few minutes ago and I'm not at all sure that he made a wise decision, or that I did. If you stand with me, Mr. Cola, you vow all, you commit all, you risk all—nothing held back, nothing halfway. If you vacillate later, my sanction will be total, whether you break faith after ten seconds or fifty years. Do you understand this fully?"

Charlie knew he wasn't feeling the true weight of what was happening, but he lacked for any alternative. "Yes."

Tanabe didn't seem gladdened. "Under the circumstances, I can't refuse you. 'Once in, never out'; as of this moment you're in. My people will resume debriefing you—especially with regard to your Quick Fix activities and subordinates."

Charlie blinked. "Sure, but—Molly and my boys, they'll be on your side, believe me; I'll get them on a secure line if you want. They're family, or as good as family."

"Is that so? It may interest you to know that your wife Didi is at this moment in a heavily shielded section of the residence of the Roman Catholic Cardinal of Greater New York, closeted with a special Papal Nuncio."

Charlie swallowed and faced the fact that it was too dangerous to stall or dissemble, and that there was now no way back. *Once in, never out.* "I don't know what that means, Tanabe-san, except Didi's family was, uh, devout Catholic back before I met her. Papal envoy to whom?"

"Black Hole and the Phoenix Group."

"S-she left home when things got too stressful. How she wound up back with the Church—I simply have no idea."

Tanabe's intense scrutiny was unwavering. "What about the others holding the fort at Quick Fix?"

"My sons Labib and Jesus will stand by me; I just can't believe otherwise. And Sanpol Amsat's always been okay, although it was Dante Bhang who recruited him for me. Anyway, I left orders for them to get clear at the first sign of trouble."

"And Miss Riddle?"

Charlie dared not hedge; Tanabe might already know the answer. "Molly dropped out of sight and I don't know where she went—she was upset. We got word Junknowitz's Cherokee friend, Willy Ninja, got disappeared to End Zone—you've heard of it?" Tanabe nodded. "Ninja, this guy Eddie Ensign, and

Junknowitz's bush-vet brother, Sean: a one-way trip, courtesy of The Awesome Vogonskiy. Molly was all gooey for the Indian—"

"Miss Riddle has returned to Quick Fix and is conducting business as usual," Tanabe told him. "An intelligent interim course of action. However, I think we'll postpone contact with your staff, at least until there's more information on your wife's current situation."

Argument was out of the question. Charlie groped for some way to reiterate his loyalty to Tanabe. "Something else you'll want to know: Night before I came out here, Asia Boxdale walked into my store, but somebody disappeared her—"

Tanabe had raised one hand a little. "We'll go into that later. One last question. How much do you know about the *Crystal Harmonic*, Mr. Cola?"

The *Harmonic* was the cruise ship in which Trough travelers, posing as alien themers, were touring Earth and at the same time getting its inhabitants used to the sight of offworld beings in their midst. The ship whose mobile Adits had made Charlie's operation obsolete. "Enough to wish that shitbucket and everybody in it a nice Poseidon Adventure."

"Really? I think you're overlooking some excellent career possibilities, Mr. Cola."

SEVEN

SHEENA LIFTED HIGH the faintly burning torch, and for a moment Harley had a better view of the Hazmat creatures she'd driven back, which she would have happily done without. A multiwinged horror vectoring their way broke off its attack run. A spiky beetlelike denizen, big as a garden tractor, was extracting itself from a collision with a blunt-prowed cylindrical brute that moved on a bed of very short, very fast podia.

Sheena held the fluttering torch higher. "Where was that hammering coming from?" The fire wavered to her movements; the synthsilk shirt wasn't very good fuel. Before Harley could answer, they heard it again—the distant, dull ring of metal against metal. "That way!" Sheena took the lead fearlessly, driving back the things of the night with the rippling torch, her tousled scarlet locks streaming. Bare to the waist, firebrand held aloft, she put Harley in mind of some splendid female Prometheus.

Harley stayed close behind trying to cover both sides and the rear, glancing in all directions, the ERGOSPORT SUPERPRO clutched close except when she launched a warning swipe at some creepy-crawly that ventured too close. Sparks, ash, and bits of burning rag went whirling and falling from the torch as Sheena strode along, making Harley painfully aware that the shirt wouldn't feed the flames for long.

"What's that?" Harley pointed to the right, to where the surface of the rot was stirring and steepling—something was burrowing through it in their direction, throwing up a wake.

"Never mind," Sheena told her firmly. "Keep moving."

They passed by a module of some kind, a gleaming mechanism roughly the size and shape of a sensory-dep tank. "That's not it," Harley bit out, without taking her eyes off the darkness. "It's coming from over that way."

"I know," Sheena replied, reading an indicator on the big unit. "But whatever this device is, it's active and it's counting down. Nothing to be done about it for now, though." They went on, and Harley was so busy keeping watch that Sheena's exclamation made her jump. "There!"

"Tres zut!" At least one mystery was resolved: the deep impressions in the filth were footprints, as Harley had thought.

The metal shape they had found was like a fallen, monumental statue—the Colossus of Rhodes as KO'd prizefighter, perhaps. Some kind of robot? Harley wondered. The midsection looked to have been cut, torched, and pried open like an inelegant job of safecracking. Its immense weight had pressed the construct partway into the grunge. Whoever or whatever had been inside, there was no sign of life now.

Sheena made to climb up onto the dreadnought torso and check out the plundered gut anyway. Her movements made a burning cuff and part of a blackened, dissolving sleeve drop loose from the disintegrating torch. "Wait, the banging came from that way!" Harley squawked. She was sure of it, even though the sounds had stopped again.

"I know, but there might be something here that will let us get that far," Sheena explained calmly. Harley couldn't stifle a moan at the thought of what would happen if the sepulcher's darkness closed in again. Not wanting to be left outside the dwindling torchlight, she followed Sheena up onto the sprawled behemoth, pausing only to slap another spark out of her scorched hair. There being five feet ten inches of Harley and less than a yard of the mini from shoulder to hemline, the place seemed even draftier.

"Hold this." Sheena passed Harley the dying torch and lowered herself into a womblike space in the eviscerated machine. In it were what looked like near-drained water blivets or aqua furniture, except that the pungent chem-lab smell spoke of something other than water.

Sheena rummaged around in the confined space, muscling the bladder things aside, searching the interior. Harley, kneeling at the edge, withdrew to cast watchful looks every which way. She found a slimy little winged minidragon thing perched on a jagged flap of torn-back chest armor, licking its chops and studying her. She was vaguely aware of the sound of Sheena working something mechanical down below.

Still clutching the torch, Harley nailed the minidrag with a one-handed backswing, getting solid wood. The winged rat went flailing back into the darkness with a brief whine. Something big out there grunted, and there was the sound of a hasty chomp and swallow. Harley swallowed, too. "Shee-*na*aa . . ."

"I've got something!"

"Sheena, it's coming!" It was a ponderous beast unafraid of the wavering flames, clambering up the side of the prone machine. Its claws made almost ultrasonic screechings on the armor. Harley heard the clash of mandibles and saw two big compound eyes easing within striking distance.

The sensors had barely registered the attacking fleet's approach to Spectarr II before Ka Shamok was relaying the warning and evacuation commands down the periscope pipeline to his hidden garrison under the volcanic magma chamber. The warships wouldn't be in range for the better part of an hour, so he resumed his conversation with Yoo Sobek. "Very well, then, our priorities: firstly, someone must find and fetch Junknowitz—taking up the trail on Earth."

Sobek made an affirmative sound. "Your intelligence apparatus is best suited; they're the ones who disappeared Vanderloop, after all."

Ka Shamok grunted assent. "And if, as you say, you're still counted loyal by Black Hole, then you're the one to locate

Vanderloop and the Aborigines. Free access to the Trough, Light Trap data, and all that. Also, we need more information for the Light Trap assault itself." The periscope mechanism began withdrawing into Spectarr II's molten surface once more.

"Very well." Yoo Sobek, still thinking about his dream and the eight-ring symbol, had his own private agenda in returning to the Sysops' great shellworld. Here the Sysops' surrogate fleet was closing in, but upgushing lava was already covering the withdrawing periscope, and the insurgents were fading to new hiding places around other suns.

Sean Junknowitz, straining for a slurp of puddle muck outside his lean-to, avoided looking at his own reflection. He'd always been able to out-tough whatever life threw at him before, but his ego had betrayed him now, making the sight too repugnant, hurting worse than the black-vapor parasite death The Awesome Vogonskiy had thrown into him with death-swipes.

Not that it was all that hard to avoid focusing his rheumy eyes, or that his palsied, feverish spasms left the surface of the reeking bilge still. But he feared looking at his reflection and finding that the fighting man and spiritual warrior he'd struggled all his life to make of himself was gone, leaving only a beaten mutt. If Sean could have killed himself, he would have long since—but whatever Vogonskiy's psychic curse was, it wouldn't let its host suicide.

He thought again of Skeeter, Robyn, and Max, his former Tiger Teammates, dumped into the Pacific when Vogonskiy's tractor beam had plucked Sean, Eddie Ensign, Willy Ninja, and their swiftboat aboard the *Crystal Harmonic*. Even if it had been sharks, Sean was willing to bet it had been infinitely preferable to what he was facing on End Zone.

He was waiting to die on a diseased and ghoulish terminal ward of a world, and the only company he could count on was the pain of his gas-gangrene lesions, the agony of his swollen tumors and malignancies and his creeping, weeping sores. He sucked at the surface of the muck, wondering why the hell he bothered. Trying to roll back over, he put weight on excrescences of flesh that hadn't been there earlier. He found rounded bulges the size of pigeons' eggs sprouting all across his lower abdomen, upper legs, and groin, distorting his body so that it would've been impossible to identify, from a glance there, his gender or even his species.

"New ones, h—gggh-uh?" a voice inquired from nearby,

punctuated by a quick, straining hiccup of anguish that had become part of conversational English on End Zone.

Sean rolled the other way and got to one elbow to glare woozily at Eddie Ensign. "Nah, I'm fuckin' ovulating, what d'*you* think?"

"Sorry—rheo down, willya?" Eddie shifted his contorted position on the rotting log where he'd seated himself in a grotesquely deformed pose, favoring various fistulae, festering organs, and ulcerated patches of skin. Half of his hair had fallen out, and his gums were leaking blood.

"Where's Willy?" Sean hacked, then spat a wad of bloody sputum.

"Went to find that singer they were talking about—witch doctor, whatever she is. Maybe she can help."

"Help? That stupid air biscuit!" Vogonskiy *must* have hit Sean with a more powerful death-swipe than Willy and Eddie; they could get around, while it was all the ex-Marine could do to sip some sludge and get to nearby algal mats and encrusted sap licks.

"That 'stupid air biscuit' was the one who covered you up last night. Maybe Willy's not one of those Amazon headhunter blood-bro's of yours, and I'm no supervet war hero, but from where I sit you're lucky we're here."

"Ensign, take it and shove it—"

"No, *you* shove it, Sean! You're the one who got us into this!"

As a rule Sean only attacked in the line of duty, or when he was being lied to, insulted, or made a fool of. But even though Eddie had only spoken the truth, Sean struggled feebly to get at him.

Then he paused, and looked around as Eddie did, following the sound of a wheezing whistle. Willy tottered into sight through End Zone vegetation that looked like malignant biopsies festooned over rotting bones. There was another figure following through the shadows not far behind, undulating like a dancer in a floor-length sheath. It was no kind of XT they'd seen before, but then Vogonskiy was an equal-opportunity sadist.

Sean filled the awkward silence between himself and Eddie. "Been thinking. Sussed out that Vogonskiy's the one who blew away Rashad Tittle and framed Lucky."

Eddie thought about the shooting in the middle of the packed Rodeo East Mall. "You mean he shot Rashad, then *flew* the gun into Lucky's hand? Like Darth Vader in reverse?"

"Yeah. And that's how he beat me." Vogonskiy's laughing contempt for Sean's best unarmed attack had hurt almost as badly as the death-swipe maladies. Evening that score was as important to Sean as surviving End Zone or helping save Earth.

Willy hobbled the last stretch with a look of triumph on his face, even though he looked so spent and frail that they expected him to keel over at any step. He was leaning on a helically bent staff, and the scabby growths under his arms forced him to keep his elbows raised and cocked in an awkward fashion. They could see from the gleam that he'd rubbed slime or sap onto the angry yellow scales sprouting like a child's first teeth from his shoulder, neck, and cheeks—to ease the unquenchable itching, both Eddie and Sean understood at once.

Willy had deteriorated, which was no surprise. What was surprising was his companion, the healer-singer for whom he'd gone off questing, following rumors. She was no tall, willowy humanoid in a skirt after all; yard after yard of her came into view as she slithered into sight.

EIGHT

"LOOK, LUCKY, IF this, this *tree monster* wants to kill you, why didn't you just dump him into a volcano or disintegrate him or something?"

In spite of her born reticence, Sinead couldn't seem to resist running her hand across Lumber Jack's knurled hardwood brow, Lucky noticed. "It's not that he *wants* to kill me, Shin, that's what I'm telling you. He's prescienced that if he doesn't it'll be catastrophic for his planet, Wood Wind, and a lot of others, too. Way things are shaping up, it could happen. That notwithstanding, he says he can't see his way clear to assassinate me, so he won't, no matter what."

The giant's immobile face reflected the isotonic blue light of Silvercup's single cabin, a domed compartment shaped something like a half football truncated at both ends. It was a combination of passenger, cargo, and flight-deck areas ten yards long and five at its beamiest. Up forward were two crew seats sprouting side by side from the seamless deck. The acceleration chairs didn't so much stand before an assemblage of controls, screens, scopes, and instruments as nest in among them, everything set up ergonomically, with a flowing, nonlinear, organic look to it.

Back against the aft bulkhead was a fastened-down mound of oddly contoured crates, pods, globes, and other containers that, as Lucky had explained briefly to his sister, held components of Silvercup's current spaceship body. Some remained uninstalled because there hadn't been time to see to them yet, others because Silver had been obliged to abandon related critical parts in a Cam Ranh Bay warehouse when she had come under fire from Vietnamese guards and a Giap light tank.

On the open deck between cargo and controls was the long, broad, improvised metal cradle into which Lumber Jack's body had been made fast. The man from planet Wood Wind was ten feet tall and more than four wide at the shoulder, a longheaded being with a face like a Zairian mask carving; his half-clenched fists could've been oak stumps chainsaw-sculpted into hands. Much of his body was scorched like a telephone pole that had been through a brush fire. To save Lucky and the rest, he'd absorbed a bolt fired point-blank by Takuma Tanabe from a Trough energy handgun Lucky's frolicsome nanites referred to as a _lightning rod_.

"You've always been good with plants," Lucky went on. "You know more botany than I do, and any suggestions are welcome. Sinead, please!"

"Why me?" She looked around the vessel's interior. Even though Fealty agent Silvercup had assumed the form of what amounted to a space utility truck by Trough standards, the look of the place was fluidly otherworldly. "Lucky, I want you to get out of here—you, your animatronics, this submarine you keep talking to—out of my pool, my house, and my life before you drive me completely—"

Sinead squeaked as an effulgent female figure rezzed up. "Ms. Junknowitz, neurotic polyphobias don't excuse your being rude," it corrected her sharply. "I'm no more this ship than you're that pile of animal and vegetable cells."

Silvercup was like chrome under a bank of white kliegs; she turned to Lucky, highlights shimmering off the conformation and contours of her as from curved mirrors. "There are other options than traumatizing your sister. Lucky?"

He'd been pierced by the sight of her. This was only the second time he'd seen Silvercup *in the metalflesh*, her true and preferred form. She was unclothed, smoothly humaniform. She stood his height, six feet and a dab—broad-shouldered and wasp-waisted, steely, her hair a tumble of spun snow, her eyes and lips almost garish against that argent skin. He couldn't help wondering again if, if she . . .

"Lucky?" Silvercup prodded him again gently.

"*Uch!* This is *sick!*" Sinead had seen the look on his face as she did a tennis-spectator swivel. "You belong in an Urgent Care facility, that's what!"

That stopped his feeling embarrassed. "She risked her life to save mine! Stuck her neck out to let me in on what Black Hole has planned for Earth! So screw yourself, Sinead!"

She was pale and he could see she was fighting back tears. "Better yet, *you* screw Robocup, there. Or a wall socket for all I care!"

"Fine, we're gone!" He realized that he hadn't told her the main thing yet; everything had been so disjointed.

The projection of Silvercup derezzed, and the hatch opened. Lucky followed Sinead out. "I think something may've happened to Mom and Dad," he said to her back. Sinead stopped and spun on him so abruptly that she almost fell on the wet poolside tile. "What are you talking about, *'happened'*?"

"I can't get a call through to them; when I tried the third time, some Mexican telecom *jefe* came on the screen wanting to know who I was and where." Alex and Rita Junknowitz, longing for a more easygoing life than the USA was inclined to let them have, had bought a place just outside Oaxaca, Mexico. "None of their friends can be reached, either, and the *policía* are stonewalling."

Sinead backed over to a pool chaise and sat. "If you're lying to me . . ."

"You've got corporate access; check for yourself, but do it so they can't trace the call—a teledrop."

" 'Teledrop'?" She'd risen to head for her office. "Grow up. And pack up."

He watched Sinead exit, feeling as if his themer suit were lead chain mail. "Silver, I'm going to get the others. Everything all right here?"

"Yes. I'm sorry Sinead dislikes me and sees you as a pervert."

"Nn-nn. You should see some of the guys *she* used to date."

"Lucky, I know this is a difficult time for you, but there's one more matter I have to mention. I wouldn't trouble you with it, but I can't leave you unwarned of danger. I've reviewed my Fealty files and memories and I've concluded that there's a very high probability the Monitor will send an agent after me—after us."

Another holo image sprang to life in the middle of the cabin, this time a heroic, naked male analogue of Silvercup: tall, godly, with a torso as ripped as a V-shaped engine block. He was implausibly handsome in a Central Casting kind of way and anatomically emphatic. "This is my counterpart."

She was rotating the image of the Virile Construct so Lucky could have a good look. All in all, the figure looked like he could bite an I-beam in half. "Oo! 'One fist of iron, the other of steel,' huh? So what's his name?"

She told him, but his scampish nanites were at it again and so he gave an involuntary, hebephrenic giggle. " 'Peterbuilt'?"

"What—oh, I see. If he finds us you'll need all the humor you can muster."

"Can he track us? Could Peterbuilt show up on Earth?"

The holo of the Mr. Olympia metalflesh faded, replaced by one of Silvercup's face, which spoke. "Yes, although the Fealty has few Earth assets." The holo's amber eyes, big as dinner plates, fixed on him. "I don't know how he'll come at us, or with what resources. I only know that I'm on your side. Something about you, in the memories confiscated from me, made me decide that."

He felt helpless. "I'd tell you if I could. All I can say is, it's a wonder to me." But what if her affection for him was just a gleamer malf, something his probability contamination had brought on?

"Then let's stay with the substantive. While doing repairs and mods on this aerospace body, I had time to examine some of the data I downloaded from the *Crystal Harmonic*'s banks, including some coded files I've cryptoanalyzed. Harley Paradise and Sheena Hec'k are no longer on al-Reem and are thought to have escaped to, unlikely as it seems, Hazmat. Also, I find indications that Asia Boxdale may not be at World Nihon."

He suddenly felt rudderless, trying to cope with the things turning him every which way—fears for his parents, the danger to Earth, the threat of Peterbuilt, and Sean and the others on End Zone. "*Now* what do I do?"

"I have a suggestion," Silvercup said softly. "I propose that we fade to Sweetspot, denounce the Monitor in Circuit Court, and persuade the Fealty to actively oppose Black Hole."

"And get your memory back before the Monitor finds it and trashes it."

"That, too, yes. I think there may be a way to out him."

He didn't know where to begin objecting. "For openers, 'fade' *how*? There's only one Adit left on Earth, and—*hey*!" Now he knew what it was that had been gnawing at the back of his mind. It was what he had realized on planet Zillion, just before his run-in with Lint and subsequent capture by Tanabe's agents. He'd been asleep, hypnagogic, thinking back over the recurrent word in the Worlds Abound series—"Cheesehead," a name he'd been called recently.

"We've got a destination all right! Before we face the Monitor or anybody else we need some throw-weight of our own."

"And where do we get that, Lucky?"

He had an answer and, with Ziggy's call, an angle on an Adit. "In the Emerald City, you beautiful gleamer. From the Wizard—" An explosion somewhere outside, bursting the pool dome like a piñata, put him back in panic mode again.

"What was that?" Lucky yelled as pieces of the pool dome rained down onto Silvercup's spacetruck body and splashed in the water.

Her face holo had vanished as she concentrated elsewhere. "Enclave security reports an unidentified aircraft violating Presidio airspace; it has resisted all antiaircraft measures and is firing unknown weapons at Number Three Maginot Lane. In addition, occupants of an express delivery van are on the grounds and were about to attempt forced entry of these premises; their initial assault was foiled when one of them stepped on a high-voltage nonlethal land mine."

Sinead really *did* go for privacy in a big way, Lucky thought. The worst of the roof-fall seemed to be over, so Lucky yelled, "Get set to kick out!" as he sprang to the hatch to fetch Sinead and his tour group. He took the gangplank in one bound and almost rammed straight into Mr. Millmixx, who was moving with the kind of enthusiasm he could only muster at times like this. Behind him came the werewolf Rphians, Hoowe and Arooo, lugging Lucky's sister, who was in no way happy with the situation. Dame Snarynxx, Hono, and the rest came close behind.

While they were getting back aboard and Silvercup was buttoning up, the mansion shook from another hit. "Go, go!" Lucky yelled, but the gleamer was already doing it. The tourists helped cushion Sinead from maneuver forces as they did from habit by now for Lucky. The spacetruck VTOL'd straight up, a particle beam turning several hundred gallons of swimming-pool water into steam.

Lucky, only halfway into the nested pilot's chair with his behind in the air, stared at the forward display. "What the hell is that?"

"Ostensibly an advertising blimp, it is here without permission from regional air-traffic management," Silvercup answered. "My offensive systems are still offline," she added, zipping up past the attacker too fast for it to redirect fire.

She was kicked hard from underneath by a shock wave; screens trained aft showed number three disappearing in a fireball. "My house!" Sinead keened. *"You bastards!"*

"Forget retaliation," Lucky yelled to Silvercup as she slanted up into the dusk. "Boot it!" She had engaged the smart-skin stealth mode she'd used to sneak into World Nihon and Sinead's house and slid once more over the open ocean.

"I resonated part of the blimp's telecommunications suite," Silvercup said. "The attack appears to have been mounted by the international security firm of Wakkendorf Incorporated."

"Phoenix member," Lucky clarified for Sinead, who'd overheard. "Radical-right shadow-government type."

"On another subject," Silvercup added, "I have discovered in general-information uploads drawn from the *Crystal Harmonic* some physiological information that might aid in reviving Lumber Jack."

She was leveling off; Lucky joined his sister where she leaned weakly on Lumber Jack's body. "Sinead, I'm so sorry. If I'd thought—"

"I couldn't reach Mom and Dad," she told him, rejecting all apologies. She patted Lumber Jack's mighty hogshead of a chest. "So I guess we need all the manpower we can lay on, right? And that includes figuring out how to get Woody Woodpecker here up and around?"

Miss Sato conducted Nikkei and Mickey to her mysterious appointment by way of the gleamingly technotopian *Launchpad Earth* section of the theme park, and its Launch Loop, a sky ride tricked out as a post-rocket-era mass driver.

They'd chucked the Boris and Natasha rigs and ransacked a costume storeroom for matching outfits: lime green and purple saddle shoes, billowy *pachuco* slacks of white parachute fabric,

Day-Glo orange Japanese bowling shirts reading CISLUNAR CAB-
ARET WET-WET, and flags-of-all-nations porkpie hats, set off by
pink plastic wraparound shades. The *karaoke* mikes and sonic
vests, they kept.

High above the park, they gazed out at Los Angeles. This being a non–Yellow Day, on which it was illegal to so much as
crank a petropower engine of any kind, the haze was barely
perceptible—a faint earwax-colored tinge—in spite of an air inversion that had moved in. The air was ovenlike, but at least the
eco-recovery measures put in force at the Turn had made it less
health-threatening.

There were only a few places where intense greenery formed
a gray-water-irrigated island on the sun-seared landscape. Every
one was a public-use area, and World Nihon was by far the biggest. At that, from what Mickey had heard, it had taken all of
Takuma Tanabe's pull plus a water-stingy system worthy of a
putting green on Dune to obtain a variance allowing the place its
Japanese flora.

He gazed out at LA's thermally efficient building designs
drawn from traditional architecture, and water-conserving desert
xeriscaping. His uncle Malcolm-Raheem had died there somewhere in the second Black Fog inversion during the Days of
Hell; Malcomb's baby daughter TaShwana had been trampled to
death in a water riot less than two weeks later. On non–Yellow
Days, there was only one freeway lane for privately owned powered vehicles, and single-passenger cars were banned; all other
lanes were given over to green transportation—mass transit, cy-
clists, pedestrians, and the like.

Mickey felt Nikkei's nudge and realized their bucket was
passing through a switching station and bound for the Willow
World Inn, the park's five-star love hotel—a Japanese institu-
tion certain prim Americans insisted on calling a honeymoon
retreat. Nikkei was crooning the restaurant orgasm aria from
Andrew Lloyd Webber's "Harry/Met/Sally/Oratorio"; Miss Sato
ignored it.

The Inn was big, posh, and as per its design they didn't encounter a living soul as she led them through corridors decorated
with erotic art from diverse countries and historical periods.
There were backlit showcases with transparencies of the diverse
suites and their motifs—Heathcliff's Heights; Quest for Fire.

Sato's exec ID got them into an elevator that was all gold
mirrors and crimson velvet. They exited onto the fifth floor,
where lights over each of the four rooms were dark to indicate

occupancy. "Actually," she explained—*ekchuelay*—"three are empty. We've set aside the entire floor for our guests. They'd somehow heard about Willow World Inn and prevailed on us to quarter them here." A hint of a smile touched her plum red lips. "Whatever a Trough VIP wants, gentlemen, she gets."

They were still absorbing the *Trough* and *she* parts as Sato slotted her ID at a door, leaving them no retreat save out-and-out humiliation, Nikkei having insisted on being there. Mickey checked the room's motif on its backlit transparency and was about to comment, but the door was sliding open. Sato stepped past them. "Not one more sound until I say so!" she warned.

Mickey's jaws snapped shut as if his tonsils were a mousetrap trigger. Seeing the creatures within, he thought he felt his heart starting to fibrillate; both partners pulled off their pink shades for a better look. And to think that I saw it on Mulberry Street, Mickey thought. This is too much, even for LA.

NINE

HARLEY PARADISE GRIPPED her field-hockey stick and dying torch, watching those unblinkingly hungry compound eyes come up the hull of the fallen war machine at her. She was struggling for words; what came out sounded like convulsive glossolation gabbling. Out in the blackness of the sepulcher the hammering they'd heard had started up again. Harley noted it distantly.

She was wondering if there was room enough for two in the downed biped-tank's womb of a cockpit, where from the sound of things Sheena Hec'k was still messing with clacking metal. Or would such a move trap them both in a convenient two-serving bowl? Well, better than meeting death alone. Maybe it was those mighty mites working on her once more; in any case, Harley found the resolve to move, and to get some words out. "Sheena, you *bitch*! Scoot your fat bottom over!" The eyes in the dark were very close.

Getting her wish for company, Harley was almost knocked from her perch as Sheena rose halfway from the cockpit and drew something up after her. There was a deafening report, and a muzzle blast that was more like a body check; a tongue of orange-white flame three feet long, throwing off lesser pyrotechnic effects, lanced out in the direction of the hungry night dweller. The recoil jolted even the redoubtable Sheena a bit. For an instant the explosion showed them a hallucinatory demon mask of chitin, mandibles, serrated horns, and faceted eyes.

The odor of burnt propellant engulfed them. Harley worked her jaw, shaking her head, trying to get her hearing back and blinking in an effort to get rid of the flashbulb spots that swam before her. The menacing eyes in the dark were gone. She felt as if she'd been whomped over both ears with Ping-Pong paddles.

Sheena was up on the outer hull again, taking the makeshift torch as she shouldered some kind of broad leather cartridge belt, the rounds in its loops as big as rolls of quarters. The weapon looked like a heavy, wooden-stocked rifle sawed off fore and aft, with a ring on the receiver to hold it in a hook-and-clip holster that was flopping on the gun belt. Harley caught some of Sheena's words: ". . . can't see any other survival gear . . . get to that hammering before the torch burns out . . ."

Fine by Harley. Sheena was still naked from the waist up, so Harley concluded there were no changes of clothes lying around. At least the design of gun belt, weapon, and womb-cockpit suggested there were creatures not too inhuman somewhere on the scene.

When they dropped back to the troll-cave floor, Sheena passed the torch back. She braced the cut-down gun stock to her hip and fired a round to the right, left, and straight ahead. Harley, far past the screaming stage, tried as best she could to cover her ears while holding torch and hockey stick without charring more of her hair.

The fireball muzzle blasts were so blinding that it was difficult to see the photo-flash glimpses they gave of what lurked in the dark—but Harley wasn't particularly eager to behold that anyway. She nevertheless saw things falling back, from the sound and light and hot-gunpowder smell, that no fright-movie maker had ever dreamt of; but the sight of them breaking and fleeing in terror somehow told her she would be able to live with the memory.

Sheena took big, glittering cartridges from the gun-belt loops and fed them through the weapon's loading port. Then she resettled the belt over her head and right shoulder, not seeming to care that she was squishing one of those unfairly high, rounded boobs of hers. She gripped the blunt, burly little gun in both hands, all set to carry on with the mission. "You'll light our way, Harley?"

Sheena still pronounced her name with an odd roll of the *l*, but at least she'd lost that don't-panic-on-me-wimp tone. Harley had her stick in one hand, the torch in the other. "Do let me know if I'm blocking your view, hmm?"

The two women set off through the nightscape again, skirting more of the sharp-etched machine footprints pressed sometimes as deep as a yard into the composted filth. The torch was nearly gone now, but matters had changed; the unseen monsters were keeping a more cautious distance.

The hammering was coming from the interior of another of the KO'd titan machines, this one lying on its side with chest intact. Sheena tried a small manual control plate and a big, flush-set lever of some kind, to no avail. "I think the systems are all interdicted somehow."

Harley had gotten used to the fact that Sheena, Trough traveler and trained adventure guide, was way ahead when it came to making sense out of anything technical. Nonetheless, it being a question of survival, she had a look for herself, circling the derelict; Sheena followed. Harley hadn't gone far—she was trying to keep them both in the very last of the torchlight—when she called out. "Come see this."

On the shoulder of the machine was a widget a little like a techno-tick, or a hunkered-down robot tarantula. "An inhibitor mine," Sheena said, ID'ing it. It was giving off tiny green power arcs and discharges, however; leaning close, the women could see that one corner of it had been plowed open, damaged.

"Ricochet, perhaps," Sheena judged. "Maybe that's why whoever's in this one can signal and the others can't. I think this device is disabling the mech, but only partially. We'll remove it."

She glanced at the torch, which was nearly spent. "We might as well gamble." Her fingers strayed close to the tick-thing but jerked back as it spat energy and crackled a warning. She glanced at her sawed-off rifle, considering its metal construction and whether it might safely be used to start bashing and prying. Then she edged around with one eye closed, plainly considering shooting the inhibitor mine off. "Hmm . . ."

"Excuse me." Again Harley passed the torch, which was

flickering its last. She couldn't bear the thought of bullets zazzing around so close to her and certainly wasn't about to move back away from the last of the light. She squared off by the mechano-tick that clung at just about the upper limit of her strike zone. "Out of my way, Red Sonja."

Sheena moved to one side and crouched low. Harley took two practice swings. "Fore!" She let fly with a combination of her best softball cut and teeing off on the fourth at Cremewood Country Club—550 yards less ten from the ladies' tee; par five. In spite of its layers of surgical, electrical, and cloth tape, the shaft stung her hands.

If the mine had some sort of defensive field to keep it from being detached, that field was gulled by the stick's nonconductivity or just plain taken unawares by the speed of Harley's shot. The inhibitor mine described a crackling green parabola through the jet-blackness and vanished.

Harley and Sheena stepped back, waiting for something to happen, as the last burning flecks of Lucky's shirt began to peel away from the torch. They tried to spread flames to the bottom-land layering the sepulcher floor, but nothing was inclined to ignite. "Any more ideas?" Harley asked.

Sheena had been counting the sawed-off rifle rounds in their loops. "Yes, about nine of them."

They looked to the blackness as the eyes closed in, Sheena conserving her ammo. Harley thought about suggesting they run for it but had second thoughts of some pit, quicksand, or trap-door spider waiting for them. "I suppose we'd better climb up on the machine," Sheena decided.

As the guide fumbled for purchase, Harley heard a thrashing and burrowing in the composted garbage under her feet. Then something elastic and wickedly strong encircled her ankle as a large body broke partway to the surface behind her. Whatever it was, it didn't mind being struck with a field-hockey stick. "Sheena! *Help me!*"

The downsized LAW blasted once and whatever clutched her let go, huffing and warbling in pain as it dug itself back into the duff. Harley could hear more nightbreeds around her, scrambling up the armored machine to encircle their prey. She was clambering frantically up the articulated hull, in danger of losing both dead torch and stick, when slowly, mountainously, the cold armor moved under her.

"It's sinking!"

Harley could hear the scraping of the gun as Sheena struggled to keep from falling. "No, not sinking; it's *rising up*—"

There was light like the birth of a universe.

Did we really "lean into the Turn," as the millennial catch-phrase had it and continues to advise, or did we simply go round the bend?

Braxmar Koddle paused to think, dabbing the ostrich quill in its veggie-based ink and pushing out a little more of the smooth, handmade paper from its thick roll.

As they had since his capture, Brax's thoughts of his loft posse friends—and chest-squeezing apprehension over his own predicament—made it a harrowing feat to get words onto paper. Anxiety over and longing for Asia Boxdale, especially, threatened to drive him stark staring 'toony. He forced himself to push on.

Why is Black Hole intensifying its victimization of Earth, and why has, as Lucky states, our obscure little planet been singled out for so much attention? Having heard out Lucky, Sheena, and Bixby Santiago and even weighing Hagadorn's taunting hints, I'm developing a theory.

The Black Hole Travel Agency is treating Earth like some failed lab experiment, taking its paranoia-provoking conspiracies offline and salvaging what profit it can from a tourist trap operation. But what was it looking for for so long in the first place? If my suspicions are correct, something unforeseen has already *happened on Earth, something to which the Sysops are blind, something that may well lead to their—*

Brax looked up from his writing as he heard the glass slider whisper open on the fourth-floor deck at Meadow Suite, Phipps Hagadorn's rambling wooden summer manor on Martha's Vineyard. He suppressed the impulse to cover his writing, shield it from Hagadorn's eyes. Since capturing Brax at the Fresh Kills Penitentiary several days before, Hagadorn had made no effort to examine the manuscript, although he surely could have—by summoning a few of his Watchmen, the top-flight Rio-trained bodyguards, if other means failed.

Hagadorn, tall and muscular, blond of hair and eyebrow and lash, nodded pleasantly to Brax; he might be middle-aged, but he had the physique of a boxer. Certainly he looked young to be unquestioned master of a global business empire and chairman of the Five Wise Men who guided the German government and the Bundesbank on monetary policy.

He was turned out in artfully frayed and faded pre-Turn jeans, a sweatshirt that looked as if a style consultant had torn off the sleeves and collar for him, and Top-Siders—no socks, of course. The crystal blue eyes roved across the view from the deck: the sand and scrub of Gay Head, the beach at Philbin, out across the sunny green-blue rollers of the Atlantic and the pristine oasis of Noman's Island. "You need some fresh air; take a ride with me," he told Brax.

No point in resisting, but Brax decided to bring his work along just in case he found some idle time. Hagadorn didn't object as Brax dumped paper roll, quill, and inkpot into a cotton carry sack bearing the Menemsha Store logo.

He followed Hagadorn down the titanium double-helix stairs to the *ubertech*-lux living room, where two Watchmen, male and female, were posted and where Gilda Hagadorn, once the most glamorous of Phipps's acquisitions, sat.

Golden Gilda was surprisingly compact in real life, five-four or thereabouts, and even more coiffedly blond than her husband. Her body, in a jungle-print gauze tank suit, didn't look much less tuned than when she'd taken her third Olympic championship more than a decade earlier, but she was wearing what Brax suspected to be too much jewelry for a Vineyard August.

Gilda's cross-country ski poles were mounted over the fireplace, along with her skeletal-stocked, ergo-tailored Daimler-Anschutz target rifle. Her event was the biathalon—nowadays usually called by its original name, "winter patrol," as she'd explained haughtily to Brax, to avoid confusion with vulgar flea circuses of mass jogging, bicycling, or what have you. Bringing her third consecutive gold medal home to Germany, she'd been treated like a queen and Hagadorn had wooed her with an immoderateness the whole world followed.

Bored and discontent, Gilda had also spoken of Hagadorn's waning interest, and made clear to Brax her resentment of the younger flesh like Harley Paradise that Phipps pursued these days. Today Gilda was sparing Brax no attention, instead fixing her husband with the glower of a gilt basilisk. "You're not leaving until we reach an understanding."

Hagadorn smiled as imperturbably as if she'd blown him a kiss. "Now, now, my darling. It wouldn't be very polite to our guest to—"

Gilda came to her feet as though she'd bounced up off a trampoline, seething at him in staccato German. Hagadorn cut her off in the same language, somehow outshouting her and yet not sounding unpleasant about it. At a sign from him, each of the Watchmen shifted a half step, coming to bear on Gilda. Her mouth clamped shut and her breath became ragged, her fists balling. "You can do this to other people, but *not to me!*" she bit out in English.

Hagadorn switched back, too. "Give me any more trouble and you'll be scattered across the Trough as miscellaneous organs. Why don't you pour yourself another drink, *Schatzie*, or have some fantazine? Braxmar and I will be back before you know it."

Since the upper end of the island was a Twenty-Ones preserve immune to outside monitoring and the need to keep up eco-correct pretenses, Hagadorn's idea of local transportation was a petropig, a completely restored black and white 1957 shoebox Chevy. He and Brax hopped in, Hagadorn fired up the engine with a bronchial iron burbling, and they wound out, showering gravel; when Brax fingered the seat belt, Hagadorn sneered, "Courage, Braxmar." Four Watchmen in an open four-by-four tried to keep up.

It was un-green of him, but Brax had to admit the car was a thrill to ride in. Hagadorn flipped the column shifter and fish-tailed onto State Road, laying rubber for the Gay Head cliffs. There were far fewer dwellings in the town than before the Turn, and grander; like Meadow Suite, most of the guarded compounds were invisible from the road, hidden behind trees and high hedges. A few descendants of the Wampanoag Indians who'd originally inhabited the Vineyard, now serfing for the *uber* landholders who'd usurped it, were about the only locals left.

"I want to introduce you to some influential friends," Hagadorn was saying. "Ironic, but here you are against your will, let's face it, and about to gain social entrée many others would do considerably more than merely kill for, believe me."

"Pardon me if I seem ungrateful." Still, Brax had no recourse but to sit and listen; attacking the very fit Hagadorn or jumping from the Chevy were equally ill advised at their current speed, besides which Gay Head—as well defended and surveilled as Camp David—offered no hope of escape by land, sea, or air.

"Braxmar, I understand and validate your resentment, but we of Phoenix Enterprises are fighting to make the best of a bad situation. Black Hole will open Earth to general, overt Trough travel—no power in the galaxy can prevent that. But how that's done and what happens afterward are by no means engraved in granite. I and my associates hope to save Earth, to bring it out from under subjugation when the time is ripe."

"World saving's a bit out of my line, Mr. Hagadorn."

"Please, 'Phipps.' And no, it's not at all. With your command of the Worlds Abound material, you can help put the proper spin on the Agency's Earth-development programs. But more than that, you've been thinking about Black Hole, and you may have insights that will be vital in the coming transition and afterward."

They roared past the unimposing little Wampanoag Tribal Council building on the left, onto the dipping quarter-mile straightaway that ended at the Gay Head lighthouse and the cliffs. Brax was suddenly very glad he hadn't finished writing down what he'd been thinking back at Meadow Suite—why he thought it was that, in tampering with Earth, the Sysops were dealing with something they'd badly miscalculated. He didn't want Hagadorn or any of the other Phoenix quislings to have that conjecture.

"Oh, not that you're indispensable," Hagadorn conceded. "But you could be of great help, and—it's your planet, too. All I ask is that you reserve judgment until you take private counsel with some of the others later on. Hear us out."

What choice do I have? "Very well, Phipps. So what happens at these gatherings of the blue-gened plutocrats? Black Mass and blood sacrifice?"

Hagadorn gave an honest guffaw. "Well, to start with, we get together and wash our cars."

TEN

"BE QUIET!" MISS Sato snapped at Mickey Formica without glancing aside at him. They still stood in the doorway of the Willow World love suite. She wasn't quite as composed as usual, leading the partners to conclude that this situation wasn't altogether under her control, but she was still the picture of confidence.

"You insisted on coming along. Your mouths wrote the check; let's see if your ballocks can cash it. These creatures are of a matriarchal species, so *you're flunkies*. Do whatever I tell you without question, understand?"

If she was expecting the sight of the Trough VIPs to make Nikkei and Mickey more tractable, she wasn't disappointed. Mickey muttered a semiadmiring "*Tor*rid!" and Nikkei got out a strangled *"Kuyashii"*—nope, it *wasn't* supposed to happen like this—but held his place.

They were held fast by sights, sounds, and aromas of the freakissimo scene Miss Sato had sprung on them. The decor of the tryst suite was extravagantly vulgar even by the kitschy standards of love hotels: gilt-marble mirrors, ankle-deep lipstick-red shag on the walls as well as the floor, a bed the size of a carrier flight deck and shaped like an electric guitar, garish velvet paintings in baroque frames, music-note sculptures and yards of decorative gold chain, zebra-skin upholstery and crimson satin drapery.

There were trays of food and drink, open jars of hair pomade as big as milk pails, several pre-Turn TVs with bullet holes in them, and the smell of gunfire in the air. The pards were looking at a Graceland-themed suite; that was what the transparency by the door had told Mickey. Images of the King everywhere the eye turned confirmed it—but those bulky creatures in high carousal were not only not human, not only dressed in unbelievably Vegas-rock-retro outfits, but . . . *weren't male*.

Though Mickey and Nikkei had been briefed on this whole

XT biz back when Tanabe had taken them aboard, seeing, hearing, and smelling the authentic item in the skin was more of a mental pratfall than they'd expected. The Trough VIPs made Mickey flash briefly on the Bear Ballet animatronics at Fuzzyland's Monster Mall, but these shaggy Blutos were less bulky, less ursine, and had much more fluid expressions. Their biped humanoidness was further pointed up by the fact that, despite their glitzy costumes and barrel physiques, you could tell they were burdensomely bosomy.

They had noted the newcomers' arrival. One who'd been setting another antiquated Trinitron on top of a Cadillac-shaped side table stopped, smoothed back a blond pompadour two feet high, and hooted like a tractor-trailer air horn, *"The dancing boys are here!"* A Bob Dylan video had started playing on the TV; the boisterous grizz whipped a huge, pearl-handled derringer out of her garrison belt and pumped both bullets through the picture tube.

Her five fellow offworlders roared for joy, displaying fangs like ivory scythe blades. A darker-haired one, who'd been holding a *Fireball* pinball game about knee high off the floor and shaking it for added ball control—clearly, the tilt trembler had been disconnected—slammed it down so hard the scoreboard glass shattered. "About time!" She did hip-grinding air-guitar moves in her roomy white gold-studded jumpsuit, flapping the gold-lamé-lined cape and making come-hither gestures to them with thick, black-clawed fingers.

Nikkei, Mickey, and even the imperturbable Sato flinched when the Trinitron bit the dust, but she didn't break and run so neither did they. Regaining the use of her voice very smartly, Sato spoke with a gruffer, swaggering air. "Hey, Emlarre! Where're those furballers I *already* sent you?"

While the offworld guests were bellowing that the promised private entertainment hadn't shown, Nikkei and Mickey lamped them. The pair knew there were weird resonances between Earth and the Trough, but a white-trash-rococo sex gym full of trollish Presley worshipers was a little outside anything they'd braced for.

Her tough-dame act notwithstanding, Miss Sato handled her charges very gingerly; Nikkei wondered how in the world his father had been planning to deal with them. Sato was directing most of her apologies to Emlarre, biggest of the six, a gray-pelted *grand dame* in pegged lavender trousers, pink sport coat with white carnation, green silk clock socks, and a pair of blue

suede shoes as big as soapbox racers. She was chomping on a
sandwich that appeared to be a large meat loaf on a whole loaf
of white bread covered with melted marshmallow and hot fudge,
all the while sucking a strawberry malted through a straw from
a milkshake glass the size of the America's Cup.

Emlarre growled about the lack of funboys; Sato made some
rather obscenely chummy apologies, thrusting Nikkei and
Mickey forward. "These two rivets'll keep you occupied while
I call in reinforcements, Emmie."

Emlarre's brows beetled in a manner suggesting two angry
porcupines. " 'Rivets'? My nanites don't render that usage."

Sato patted both men on the heinie. "You know, big studs?
Nikkei and Mickey, bow to Her Puissance, Emlarre, Grand In-
dexer of planet Pay Dirt. Now, if you'll excuse me a moment?"
To the mentally aground sidekicks she whispered, "Wing it!"

. She moved to a house phone, even though Nikkei and Mickey
had both seen her communicate with park HQ via the mike concealed in a dermal patch on her hand and the receiver button in
her ear. There was no way of telling whether she was doing it
to keep Emlarre from overhearing how chaotic things were in
the wake of Junknowitz's escape or simply throwing the duo on
their own resources to see if they could cut it.

Emlarre eyed them, twisting a huge pinkie ring with a black
opal in a square setting. "Well? What're you waiting for?" It appeared she had one or more of those nanites, programmed to let
her speak English; even so, there was an unnerving sound to it,
as though her jaw, tongue, voice box, and so on were being
guided by remote control. "Let's *Harum Scarum!*"

The other Pay Dirters closed in, all of them costumed as the
King in some phase of his career: black leather from the 1968
TV special; sashed and *lei*'ed from the *Blue Hawaii* mo-pic.
They were awfully big. Mickey and Nikkei had too much face
riding on the encounter to simply break and run, but Mickey's
Adam's apple bobbed considerably as he asked, "L-listen, if
you're expectin' us to put on poodle skirts an' letchu autograph
our titties—"

That took Emlarre aback. "What d'you think we are, *perverts*? We came to Earth to *cut loose* the way we can't with our
prudish, priggish males. We're here to *Roustabout!*"

She reached a paw for Nikkei, who was closest. Nikkei
ducked away, fumbling under his Pottsylvanian-Hawaiian shirt.
The Pay Dirt leadership, women of action, reacted by whipping
out what looked like electronic tuning forks with pistol grips and

drawing beads on the two, their thumbs tensing deliberately on the firing buttons.

Sato's English-nanny chiding noises were all that saved their butts then. She pointed at Emlarre. "If you break 'em, you pay for 'em!" That gave the fan club from Pay Dirt confused pause; Nikkei seized the opportunity to finish his move, then leap to one of the parrot green angel-hair-carpeted go-go platforms. Perhaps out of sheer predation instincts, several Pay Dirters swarmed after him. Holding the high ground and now wearing wraparound shades, he stopped them with a histrionic sneer, a toss of his hair, a pelvic thrust, and a gesture of the *karaoke* mike he'd drawn.

It synched with the standardized room remotes as well as his sonic vest. Nikkei keyed the first number his desperate brain could fit to the need; wind-shear guitar cords and pugnacious rimshots led in, and Nikkei struck his best jailhouse-rock pose. The offworld junketeers hesitated. He ignored the lyrics on the *karaoke* displays, figuring he'd make it special for this very tough crowd.

> *Faded to a orgy at the World Ni-hon*
> *Not a lotta sinnin', just a mere soupçon*
> *I kin let mah hair down an' not lose mah throne*
> *An' if it hits the scabloids ah kin blame mah clone!*

Emlarre and the others had begun moving to the beat. The sound system's fuzzy logic adapted the number to hip-gyrating Nikkei's reading as though there were veteran session players backing him.

> *Let's bone! Kick the blocks out an' moan!*
> *They'll be fadin' in fer that or-gone*
> *At the orgy down at the World Ni-hon!*

Emlarre had grabbed Mickey and was baton-twirling him through some adept if demanding rock 'n roll moves; the other ladies were dancing with one another, roaring, throwing drinks, and in one case playing air guitar on a life-size bronze statue of the King that must have weighed five hundred pounds. Miss Sato had taken to the safety of a barred go-go cage. For the first time, there was something open in her expression, a hint that she was actually impressed.

It was a fantasy come true, common to a lot of young Japa-

nese and kudzu blades—and, for that matter, to others whose
names were legion. You throw off the constraints of decorum, of
obligatory self-effacement and humility; you swivel onto that
stage with your duck's-ass haircut, your curled lip, and your
Ray-Bans and blow everybody right out of the fucking lagoon,
winning the admiration of that babe you want so much. Naturally, Nikkei's wish-dream hadn't included the giant jitterbug-
ging grizz gals, nor had he really let himself think about Sato in
love-interest terms, what with all this churning anger she
touched off in him.

But there it was. Nikkei dropped to his knees, ran a hand
through his hair, and pointed to the Pay Dirter in the gold-lamé
tuxedo and matching tasseled loafers. She roared ecstatically,
joined by the others.

> *Chick who layed the moves on me looked real ur-sine,*
> *She said to me, 'Daddy-o, ya move dee-vine!'*
> *I sez 'Little momma, donchu mess mah hair,'*
> *She tol' me 'Okay, put down the whip and chair!'*

Nikkei may have been at the top of his game, but Mickey was
getting *omni*-sick of this sketch. He was also getting nauseous
from Emlarre whirling him around the room and had suffered
trauma to his crotch medullas when she had cupped his skinny
buns in either hand to do a little grinding.

With the audience so busy rooting for Nikkei, only Sato and
Mickey noticed as the suite's door opened. Into the room poured
what looked like a dozen or so professional wrestlers on hormone
shots, all of them huge, muscular, hairy—and dressed in various
Presley ensembles. They'd clearly been prepped and trained, because they immediately paired off with the Pay Dirters and began
dancing, bellowing, singing, and backslapping. As Emlarre sought
to snag one or two, Mickey wriggled free and snaked for the
door. The Grand Indexer didn't much notice or mind.

This verse, Nikkei wiped his face on his sweaty shirt and
flung it through the go-go cage bars to Miss Sato, who caught
it by reflex. As Mickey padded off down the hall looking for a
place to lay low, he heard the party going into higher gear.

> *Let's faux! Till we blow off our socks!*
> *Where the word 'taboo' is stone unknown,*
> *At the orgy down at World Ni-hon!*

*   *   *

"You mean to say none of your students ever saw your face?" Saddie New, walking next to Miles Vanderloop, gave a dark-eyed, white-toothed laugh. "Why? It's a beauty face, Professor."

He felt himself blushing furiously and wondered if it showed under the light of the huge red sun overhead. It didn't help that Saddie was topless and radiating nubile health, recent initiatic scars hashmarking her left shoulder and encircling her right breast in tiny roundels. Like the other Intubis, she was wearing less and less—sloughing whitefella clothes and ways—as the walkabout proceeded. Vanderloop's only concession thus far had been to discard the Elizabethan-metalhead doublet he'd been wearing.

"Um, thank you, Saddie." If he hadn't harbored a British dread of sounding vain, he might have added, *My face was part of the problem.* A sandy-haired, boyishly winsome beanpole from the North Country, he found his good looks often interfered with his being taken seriously. His main reason for delivering his lectures via assorted VirtNet and telepresence disguises, however, stemmed from his convictions about his discipline, semiotics. It was difficult enough to convey meaning and understanding to an audience without their dragging the instructor's personality and appearance and all that misleading baggage into it.

"And you teach that nothing means anything?" Saddie pressed.

They were walking across an empty, unbounded plain of deep pink marl. Like all the Intubi women, Saddie was carrying a traditional U-shaped wooden bowl for food gathering along the way, but was very casual about it; the prey-Singing and almost effortless hunting Gipper and the men were doing kept the tribe well fed. Vanderloop made himself eat some nonesuch cuisine indeed, while the wanderers from Papunya Reserve seemed devoid of any gustatory inhibitions whatsoever.

Vanderloop squirmed mentally. Trying to put across his core philosophy under these circumstances was a semiotician's worst nightmare. "What I'm saying, Saddie, is that all communication, art—even our senses—are bound up in symbols, which stem from other symbols and so on, and all these symbols have different meanings for each person. And so there's no such thing as a fundamental truth or reality, and the only way we can hope to understand each other even a little is by informed deconstruction of the symbols that—"

"No bottom-line reality?" This time her laugh was more mocking. " 'Scuze I, but what a crock!"

Handsome young Bluesy Bungawuy, walking up near the front of the group, turned to shoot both Saddie and Vanderloop a dirty look. "Don't mind him," Saddie told the Englishman airily. "We're havin' a bit of a drama."

Rather more than that, Vanderloop knew. Bluesy was mad about Saddie, but she merely taunted him. "Y'know why? Caught him trying to Sing up *Ilpindja* sex magic at me."

"Er, can't blame his finding you attractive." Vanderloop was barely tolerated by Gipper Beidjie, leader of the Intubis and Bluesy's adoptive father, and couldn't afford to get mixed up in a romantic cross fire.

"Then he should be nice about it, 'cause some traditional ways have to go."

"Does Gipper know that?" The main reason the old man was leading his clan on this walkabout across Trough worlds, as Vanderloop got it, was to reawaken the ancestral Dreamtime powers in them—and he was doing an astounding job of it.

"If Gipper wants us to have the old powers then the men'll have to concede what they stole from women back at the start."

Vanderloop knew this was a recurrent theme among the Aboriginal people: men had usurped women's control of certain sacred rites and energies ages ago. "D'you think he will?"

"He won't feature it," she grinned, "but he's got no choice, if he means t'do what he's got in mind."

"And what's that?"

"You'll see." She stopped, gazing ahead. The file had halted, Gipper and Bluesy turning back to where Vanderloop and Saddie stood.

Gipper had shucked what he called his *cozzie*, his venerable shorts, keeping only the belt that supported his dilly bag and *tjunga*; about the only whitefella artifact he still had was his tartan headband, an old school tie. His chest was scored by horrific scars that Vanderloop now knew to be sympathy scars from Bluesy's initiation rites, such was the old man's affection for the boy. Gipper, as all could see, had once undergone the most agonizing initiation of all, subincision of his penis.

Irony of ironies, Gipper's vengeful resolve, the interplanetary walkabout, the awakened Intubi powers that had Black Hole worried, and the insurrection scheming—none of it would have come about if it weren't for a mean-spirited and grasping Ayers Rock theme-park project, DreamLand.

Until DreamLand's backers had rammed it through by dint of bribery, blackmail, right-wing agitprop, and worse, the Australian government had accorded Aborigines special cultural prerogatives acknowledging their deep connection to Ayers Rock, Uluru: traditionals like Gipper were allowed to gather plants that were off limits to outsiders, sacred ritual sites were protected, and government clinics even provided sterilized medical instruments for bloodletting ceremonies and the like. All that had ended when developers wrested control of the Rock, and Gipper swore terrible vengeance; Black Hole, seeing DreamLand as a major plus for its planned Earth-tourism campaign and curious about some minor paranormal abilities Gipper evinced, lured the troublesome Intubis into the Trough—only to have their powers wax strong in a way the Agency found incomprehensible and unmanageable.

Now Gipper waved his wooden spear and boomerang at Vanderloop. "I said you could string along with us, but we can't have you chasin' off the *mana* when we're tryin' to collect it."

If Vanderloop had been repelling the mystic *mana* force, he hadn't felt it. Looking at Bluesy's sliced thigh, though, and Percy Moora's missing teeth and Gipper's carnal member with its underside sliced open like a frankfurter in a ceremony more than sixty years ago, the Cambridge don had a dreadful premonition.

Which Gipper promptly fulfilled with a sly grin. "We need something to make yez a little more dinky-die, Professor. A little membership ceremony, like."

ELEVEN

WILLY NINJA LEANED on his dead-branch crutch to watch Sean Junknowitz and Eddie Ensign react to the arrival of Riiv, the life-singer, as she undulated into view. Finding her had almost cost Willy total collapse several times, and he'd only made it back to Sean's pathetic little lean-to because he had the crutch, but the excruciating pain was worth it now.

Riiv had surprised Willy at least as much. He'd set out to track down rumors of an End Zone inmate who could alleviate suffering, or at least moderate it somewhat, with music; unconsciously, he'd expected an angel with a harp, only to find a pythonlike alien with a horned head, long-fanged snout, and hypnotic, evil-looking eyes—a 666 vision right out of Revelations, but possessed of the purest aura Willy had ever encountered.

From Riiv came an ethereal song: part bird-trill, part XT Bach, part something sounding like deep-rhythm GaiaPulse, the heartbeat-of-the-Earth eco-music so popular during the Turn. It was more than just surround-sound; Riiv made some inner connection with one and all, a mutual resonance that was more than mere vibration. Ghostly spindrift appeared, connecting Riiv to Sean, linking her to Willy and Eddie. There were shifts and phrasings in the music that somehow welled from each of them, were mutual creations of their being and Riiv's powers of empathy and creation. And though they didn't hear it out loud, not even as the nanite-shaped English one or two of the other End Zone terminal cases spoke, all three men heard Riiv bid Sean and Eddie, "It is lyrical to encounter you; we are harmonic."

Sean, about to make a crack, sizzled and groaned in torment. Riiv's music went through a phase transition, portraying the pain and then reweaving it, making it benign. Willy saw a lot of the suffering leave Sean's face; Eddie, too, straightened a bit, his misery eased.

That was how it had been for Willy when he first encountered Riiv; it was as if she contained a wellness tunes generator, a Carnegie Hall version of the mental noter Willy had stumbled across in Charlie Cola's basement. He'd been so blown away by Riiv that it had taken him a while to notice her ulcerated skin, the cloudiness creeping into her eyes, the swellings and chancres, and realize that she was under a death-swipe sentence just like everyone else on End Zone.

Willy sprang his own surprise on his friends, having caught a bit of a recharge from the music: he closed his eyes, raised his face to End Zone's bilious sky, and lifted his voice in song, high and wordless. As a vocalist he'd been famous on the regional music scene for his high, clear instrument, but the upper end of his range had been smothered by the same two years of fighting auto-tire fires in New Jersey that had permanently darkened the parts of his face left exposed by his rebreather mask.

Eddie knew right away, and Sean caught on, too, after a moment: Willy had his top end back. It had come back to him earlier that day, when he had found Riiv and jammed with her. He let it sail for a bit, then reined in, not wanting to overtax it. He could feel the tears slick on his corroded cheeks; Eddie Ensign was stomping his feet feebly and waving a twig in the air in lieu of a match or lighter.

At last Riiv let the synergistic improvisation wind down. All three men felt better, even though the death-swipe afflictions were still with them. Sean levered himself up a bit, showing the dark Brazilian paleo-Indian tattoos on his forehead. "Thanks," he told Riiv, hating to be beholden but too honest not to acknowledge the debt.

Riiv made a complex run of notes, and somehow they understood her without nanites: "Perhaps on some happier day we'll make joyous symphony in freedom."

Eddie smiled weakly to Willy. "Found your Mood Music, huh? Funny."

Only in the ironic sense. Willy had spent years seeking a modern incarnation of the participatory, interactive, tribal power of music—music as communion—which had been driven into the shadows by the partitioning effects of the stage and bandstand and locked down by the one-way nature of recording and broadcasting. He'd yearned for fantasies that played off gestalt moods and body language, galvanic responses and neural activity. He wanted hyperinstruments and unheard-of sounds, only to encounter them in a dying XT who looked like something out of Lovecraft by way of Harryhausen, when Willy himself was emphatically terminal.

Better late than never.

There was a dull glimmer of metal from the flatlands below, screened by the biopsy-and-deadbone trees. One of the End Zone flying drones, this one resembling a goliath-size VirtNet helmet equipped with waldoes, was snooping around. They held their breaths even though the drones themselves seldom meddled with the captives, but simply maintained surveillance.

This one floated on down the valley without spotting them. For Sean the appearance of the drone and even a minuscule return of vigor was enough to set him pondering along more accustomed lines. "Hey, uh, Riiv? What about Vogonskiy, any sign of him?"

Riiv again patterned sounds that let them understand without translation. "No, and it's unlike him to let new captives be. Vital matters must be occupying him, but I think he'll be here before too much longer."

There was rekindled fire in Sean's eyes. "You could help us take him, organize the other End Zoners, fight—"

Her chorale said it all. "I'm a *life*-singer, and cannot help you in that. If you want to consort with ones who dream of murder and vengeance, End Zone has them in good measure."

Sean sat up a bit, flexing his muscles, clenching and un-clenching his scarred fists. "Now we're getting somewhere."

The Big Bang light in Harley's face was a spotlight, she real-ized in passing as she was shaken loose from her grip on the war machine for a moderately soft landing in the mattress of or-ganic rubbish that floored the Hazmat sepulcher.

Her thick, if matted, mane cushioned her head as it struck something hard but brittle, like thin porcelain—skull, limb, or tailbone, she supposed. Sheena was by her side instantly, getting her upright. The blinding light was one of many—warning, run-ning, search, signal, and work—shining forth from hardened fix-tures on the walking tank. The voice of doom sounded over external speakers, and it was a woman's. "You down there, stand fast!"

Sheena took up a ready stance half-shielding Harley, still holding the sawed-off elephant gun at the ready; Harley ac-cepted the partial protection without qualm. The two-legged bat-tleship swept the hall with searchlights, turret lenses, and, Harley suspected, other instruments. The color-bleaching glare picked out one downed, shot-up metal giant after another. Harley real-ized absently that her nanite must be doing the translation of the curse words from the machine's external speakers: "Oh *wrack*! Ah, *infamy, infamy*!"

In a fair imitation of archangelic wrath, the machine fired off hoverflares and drifting illumination rounds from shoulders, dor-sal hull, and turret head. The sepulcher was lit by a palette of novas that rained sparks and cinders and sent up twisting plumes of smoke. The dwellers in the dark had long since checked out except for distant, scurrying forms. When the decay fifty yards to the left humped up over burrowing things, the battlewalker shot a streaming arc of fire that puddled in the spot and set the stuff smoldering. The burrowers made for the far walls.

Harley and Sheena stared into the giant machine's faintly

smoking flamethrower nozzle, its little ignition element glowing blue-white. "I want some answers from you two," said the voice.

"Hey, that's our line!" Harley yelled in high dudgeon.

Ducking out on Nikkei's clinch-hit Elvis send-up and the lady grizzlies from Pay Dirt, Mickey trotted down the hall and ducked into a vacant tryst suite to lie low for a while.

This one was a kitchy Arabian Nights seraglio with *faux* carpets, cushions, Bureau of Tobacco, Firearms, and Hazardous Emissions-approved incense, and mo-pic belly-dance music playing in the background. When he followed printed instructions and rubbed an Aladdin-style lamp, a genie holo appeared in smoke, flame, and low-decibel thunder. She was on the smallish side, wearing—but not clothed by—an R-rated Hollywood odalisque outfit complete with veil and, in her navel, a ruby red as Shaitan's eye.

She *salaam*ed. "Master, you have but to speak and it shall be done, for all things in your *harim* are obedient to your will."

Gooey! Mickey thought sardonically. "Can you look a little more Queen of the Nile?"

She morphed, skin darkening, lips reddening and filling out, cheeks coming into greater prominence and hair taking on more of a mind of its own. "Know, O my Sultan, that I am schooled in one thousand and one tales of passion—"

"Nah." He was solo, so there wasn't much point, besides which his thoughts were drifting back to Asia Boxdale. "But, listen."

"Your Scheherazade awaits her sultan."

"Got any access to, uh, sexual and psychological data about Japan?"

She smiled serenely. "I know the amorous secrets of many places and many times, O adored—"

"Fast-forward: What d'you know about the phrase 'dimly white world'? In everyday voice mode, Sherry."

It had occurred to him that the phrase Nikkei used to taunt Sato with regard to Takuma Tanabe was worth knowing about. With another pretty *salaam*, the holo lectured, "A Japanese mother occupies a central and all-embracing place in her child's life. The effects of this upbringing last into adulthood and, indeed, throughout life."

From her even exposition sounded seductive. Mickey got himself a Scotch-rocks and sat cross-legged on a cushion to listen. The holo program was good; Scheherazade's heavy-lidded gaze moved to follow him.

"The child sleeps with the mother and, outside the home, is trussed to her back in a blanketlike wrap. They share the ritual of *o-furo*, the bath. This constant close physical contact bonds mother and child very powerfully. Weaning tends to take place late by American standards—as late as six years of age."

Both Nikkei and Takuma had lost their mothers in childhood, a classic source of Japanese tragedy—the recipe for disaster in the Yakuza flicks, the outlaw-samurai stories and all that. Nikkei's mom had died when he was still a toddler, while Takuma's had been killed in a horrific rail accident when the elder Tanabe was twelve.

"When the child begins school, conformity and obedience are demanded—a traumatizing experience. There often remains a nostalgia or even a longing for the uncomplicated and supremely indulgent, sensual paradise of childhood. The phrase 'dimly white world' comes from novelist Tanizaki Junichiro, who dwelled on mother-son bonding and its Oedipal overtones.

"The words refer to the sensuality of breast feeding—the warmth of flesh, the feeling of security, the aromas and tactile sensations, the taste of a mother's milk. An an adult, the hero of the story *Yume no Ukibashi—Bridge of Dreams*—obsesses about regression and the act of suckling, longing for the Edenlike state of childhood. Another manifestation of this—"

"Time out," Mickey signaled, holding up one hand and swirling the Scotch-rocks with the other. Sato was fairly buxom for a kudzu, and the lab-*zoku* could probably get the Statue of Liberty to lactate if they felt like it . . .

This time Scheherazade bowed, maybe for variety. "Yes, master. Shall I dance for you?"

"Uh-uh," he said distantly. "Back in your Bic, baby." With a nod of his head to the lamp.

As the holo vanished in a whirlwind Mickey thought about this dimly-white-world shit and Miss Sato. Nikkei and Takuma still had a lot of laundry to wash that could be dangerous, especially if Nikkei tried to prove something via Sato. On the other hand, if Mickey cut and ran, sooner or later he'd end up with poisoned *fugu* in his krillburger, or a golden NakaMats golf putter wrapped around his neck like a twist-tie. Besides, he'd never get another shot at master-level black-bag games.

And there was one more thing: he wanted to be around when Asia Boxdale woke up.

TWELVE

SEAN JUNKNOWITZ WOULDN'T stop going on about End Zone revolts and revenge on Vogonskiy, so Riiv departed and Willy tagged along. After some indecision Eddie Ensign remained behind to keep an eye on Sean, loyalty to Lucky overcoming his doubts about Sean's mental state.

Along the way, Riiv explained how Vogonskiy hated her and had disappeared her to End Zone for having tried to heal someone he'd death-swiped. That led to Willy's asking, "Where does the music *come* from? Nanites, mental noter, natural gift?"

"The synergies are a strong gift in some of my race," she wheezed, "but the sharing, the blending is done with bioware, a synthetic-life implant. You have a strong gift for the Singing. I don't know; perhaps my implant it would be compatible with your physiology. When I've fallen silent you'll be welcome to it; it's lodged under my forebrain, right behind the nasal plates here." She touched the bridge of her snout with tendrils that collared her head.

"Nix, quit talking like that."

They'd paused, Riiv exhausted, in a plague-ugly wood where the ground was covered with stringy green discharge. "I've been here longest of all; I've not much life left in me," Riiv sang to him in vast sadness and some embarrassment.

Willy followed his inner promptings and began crooning a refrain from the music they had shared. The effect was prompt—Riiv's head began lifting and weaving in time, the mental-note implant sending out its aura so that their music intertwined. Willy played off her inner melodies, embellishing and reemphasizing; the synergy bore her up. A remote that looked like a many-lensed and -antennaed disco glitterball swooped down to hover curiously; he ignored it.

Willy and Riiv joined in an incorporeal dance. This time, he was singing life for her.

* * *

Peterbuilt faded to the time-sharing leisure planetoid Nu-Topia with falsified credentials as a paid consultant and so did not have to deal with the sales-staff goons who, armed with neuroprods and other disciplinary devices, were tasked with seeing that trial visitors bought a time-share before they were allowed to leave. Though sales-closing techniques like lobotomy and burning pincers were illegal, other measures were not, and Nu-Topia had hired a number of former cult brainwashers, consciousness seminar trainers, and recruiting sergeants. The word *trial* was applied in a way a lot of the trial visitors hadn't expected.

Even as Peterbuilt watched, a three-legged mushroomlike resident of Aart's World, being herded along with other dispirited guests, cried to him, "Save us! They mean to subject us to yet more infomercials!" A poke from a prod-wielding Ygg made the creature move on.

For his masquerade the gleamer had chosen what he regarded as natty disguise of Gilgit weather-vane hat, feathery lavender Rotorian tutu paired with emergency yellow Kammese safety vest, and heart-shaped Terran sunglasses with scarlet rhinestone-mounted frames. He preened, finding himself the focus of many glances and not a little inexplicable laughter.

On close inspection Nu-Topia was a shoddy place, its walls showing cracks, effluvia leaking into the artificial lake, and a hot stench in the air suggesting a coal-seam fire. The place was the latest scam of Shadyside Enterprises, a corporation with a business history that read more like a rap sheet. It was a Shadyside subsidiary that had built the sprawling Piazza Huts public-housing project on Hnngrr, intended to be a low-cost, dweller-friendly answer to the problem of hundreds of thousands of displaced persons. True to form, Shadyside had built in slapdash fashion and faded one jump ahead of the law, leaving teeming throngs stuck in a self-destructing slum.

Peterbuilt found Zastro Lint at a worksite over the hill from the Adit. Workers were reassembling a prefab recreation complex; Shadyside only had the one, and kept shifting it around Nu-Topia to trick visitors into thinking the place was covered with them. The site was littered with three-hundred-pound fronds the size of living-room carpets, and so there was the IRS man using his formidable smart-luggage briefcase as a leaf blower to blast them away with a wash of xanthous power rays.

When Peterbuilt approached him, Lint exuded anger that was

almost palapable, even though he looked like a man far along in a lingering illness. The upgrades cavalierly forced upon him by Police Captain Randy Barnes were consuming him. The IRS man's cheap gray suit was half in rags and his briefcase was soiled and grease-stained.

Invoking his spurious credentials, Peterbuilt was permitted to draw Lint aside. "You should be seeking Lucky Junknowitz, shouldn't you?"

Lint had been mindbent into believing he was on field assignment tracking Lucky for nonpayment of taxes, and now he had a deranged look in his eye. "Damned right, Ironman! But—" The madness abated somewhat. "There are, that is, complications to the matter—"

A cartoon-mouse cackle of derision came from the briefcase. "Wuss! Zastro Lint never met a regulation he didn't like!"

Lint smacked the case with his hand, which didn't seem to bother it any. To Peterbuilt he offered somewhat more calmly, "The Service requires that everything be done properly, legally, and—I *did* touch that Boob-Cube on Zillion."

True, although Lucky had tricked him into it. And, according to reports, the Nu-Topia management had whacked him with a dose of neuroinducted paralogisms when he had first arrived under restraint. He proved to have no money, of course, but he'd been bamboozled into working off a phony default charge that kept growing instead of shrinking, thanks to creative accounting.

Lint was eyeing Peterbuilt. "Say, who are you, anyway?"

Peterbuilt answered by opening his emergency yellow vest to expose his heroically muscled somalloy chest, which morphed into a round insignia in bas-relief, a badge big as a garbage-can lid reading COORDINATING ORGAN OF POLICE SYSTEMS. "We believe Junknowitz is back on Earth. If I extricate you from this place, will you aid me in locating him?"

Lint, dazzled by sunlight gleaming off the badge, nodded. Even the briefcase was grudgingly respectful. "Spring us from this dump and you're on, Steely Dan!"

"And you can still track Junknowitz?" Peterbuilt pressed.

Lint inclined his head again. "I pick up probability turbulence generated by certain actions—for example, when he uses that Magic 8 Ball he carries." A look of defeat came over him. "But I'm still under obligation to defray my bill here."

Peterbuilt was ready for that; the main thing that had been keeping Lint a slave all along had been his fetish for rules and regulations. "And has Nu-Topia filled out a W-2 form? Are they deducting U.S. income taxes and Social Security withholding?"

Lint had the air of a man waking from a dream. "Why—no."

"Has Shadyside Realty filed its offering with the U.S. Commerce Department? Does this place have a payroll savings bond plan?"

"No, by god!" He hefted his briefcase and started for the Adit. "First we'll nab Junknowitz; I'll file a report on this pesthole later." A sales thug—a boarlike two-legger—came running at him with a neuroprod. Before Peterbuilt could react Lint lobbed it like a volleyball serve with a blast from the briefcase, who sneered, "I'd brain ya if I had a target!"

Lint was alert for further attacks, but a major disturbance was distracting the Nu-Topian staff. Hundreds of dishevelled, disreputable Hnngrrians had faded in and fanned out in all directions, cavorting and wading and setting up tattered tents. One bunch had picked the lockdown cowling on the autobar and another was breaking into the food prep center.

"Dwellers from the Shadyside ghetto," Peterbuilt explained to Lint. "Faded in for their complimentary trial vacation."

"I thought Shadyside *never* let in underclass rabble!"

"Yes, and here we see why." The sales goons were being overwhelmed and disarmed; nobody was paying the gleamer, the IRS man, and his smart-luggage any attention. It was just the diversion Peterbuilt had planned when he had phreaked several of Nu-Topia's notorious Boob-Cubes to go offer their enticements in the Hnngrr shantytown.

"Okay, Brainiac," the briefcase sniped, "but how do we get through the Adit?"

They were in sight of it now, and, as Peterbuilt expected, several Nu-Topia executives were making a hasty fade to see what the hell was going on on Hnngrr. With no time to explain, Peterbuilt snatched Lint and luggage up in his arms and phased, using the hyperaccelerated function possessed by the Fealty's most advanced agents. Faster than the human eye could follow, he joined in the fade to Hnngrr, from which all the Trough was accessible.

In the meantime the Hnngrrians settled in to make Nu-Topia their own and fade in more shantytown dwellers. By nightfall they'd ratified a constitution.

PART TWO

Escape Speed

THIRTEEN

TEARING UP THE half mile to the Gay Head light, hogging the middle of State Road like a teenager in a pre-Turn hot-rod flick, Phipps Hagadorn passed Brax something without taking his eyes off his driving. "By the way, I believe this belongs to you."

It was a wafer formatted like a standard business-commo card, the kind people handed out billions of times a day around the globe. But where the conventional item featured printed information and chip data, automatic dialing codes and pay-phone debit function, this one was of gray metal and absolutely featureless.

It had been given Brax by Apterix Muldoon, the six-fingered, self-admitted XT—a Man in Black right out of the flying-saucer 'zines, albeit oddly nonthreatening—who claimed to be Brax's "case officer," a phrase that had yet to be clarified. Slipped into any phone slot, the wafer could somehow put Brax in immediate contact with Muldoon. It had been missing in the wake of Brax's capture, and when he'd thought to ask about it at Meadow Suite a bored Watchman shrugged that he must have lost it.

Brax had a lot of questions about the card and Muldoon's connection to Phoenix, and for that matter about what insights Hagadorn thought Brax might have, but it was obvious by now that answers wouldn't be provided on demand. He pocketed the steely card.

The Gay Head cliffs lay under a brilliant, ice blue sky and fast-scudding clouds like the sails of a clipper ship. To the right was the lighthouse, a brick sentinel; in the center was the White Visitation Lodge, the landholders' clubhouse–watering hole; off to the left the land sloped down toward Philbin Beach, and Noman's Island sat verdant across the twinkling waves.

State Road fed directly into the paved loop that encircled a natural amphitheater of ground in the promontory's lee, passing the front steps of the White Visitation. Brax's fear that Hagadorn would misjudge his speed and go shooting into the Atlantic was set to rest when the German braked and downshifted, decelerating smoothly. Brax took a better look at the light, on the highest point of land off to his right—north. It was red brick and black iron, looking like a Victorian donjon; closer to the road on that side was the gatehouse checkpoint for the Wakkendorf compound and estate.

At the White Visitation the glassphalt broadened to cover a parking area with some thirty diagonal spaces; the clubhouse itself was a restrainedly grand Cape Cod palace, less imposing in daylight than when it blazed out over darkened seas. It looked closed for business.

Not so the parking area. Most of the slots were occupied—by what comprised the most dazzling fleet of cherry pre-Turn interbust petropigs Brax had ever seen outside of books. He leafed through his memory to ID them: a chopped '50 Merc, a rara avis '70 Plymouth Superbird, a '64 Corvette pace car, a '60 Caddy finned like an ATF fighter. Not a foreign pony in the herd, nor any from before WWII or after the OPEC oil embargo of 1973-74. Brax was beginning to see why Gay Head had eclipsed Newport, Bar Harbor, and Chappaquiddick as the most exclusive of blue-gene summering places.

Hoses had been run out from the White Visitation, buckets of suds prepared, sponges and chamois and rags set out. The last vehicle in the chorus line was a modern electric van, its sides gull-winged open, equipped as a petropig M*A*S*H unit. Three uniformed goodwrenches stood by, looking ready to render assistance, but Brax suspected every car there was in perfect tune; that would be a matter of status. Gay Head landholders could afford any food or drink on Earth—or, he knew now, from beyond—but the refreshments set out on the wooden picnic tables were strictly Office of Social Management–condemned junkfood-deli-barbie stuff. Brax tried not to boggle, recognizing the stellar personages who, turned out in chic faded and worn work clothes as Hagadorn was, sweated and strained and obsessed over their treasures.

Timothy Alston III, who'd chaired both the SEC and the FCC and now presided over the Virtual Network division of IBM, was sporting snowy T-shirt, Perma-Prest chinos, and disintegrating Bass Weejuns, and polishing the rearview mirror on his '55 Thunderbird.

Retired Air Force General Buckley Wakkendorf, former

deniable-activities mastermind and head of an international security firm that functioned more like a shadow intel network, was lathering the fender of his Shelby Cobra; he was also the power behind SABRE—Sincere Americans Battling the Real Enemy—and the David Duke or "cross-addicted" wing of the Republican Party.

Turkish-born Fatima Bebe, special projects supervisor for the Video Observation Research Group—VORP, Ziggy Forelock's onetime employer until he got wise to them—was a far less recognizable figure to the general public. She was independently wealthy, having made a fortune early-on with her BuySexual-TV shop-by-vid network, which so creatively cashed in on "hot monogamy" and other sexual fads of the HIV-panicked Turn and post-Turn years. Fatima was hosing off her '64 GTO; approaching a certain age, she nevertheless looked good enough in her cutoffs and damp DALLAS COWBOYS shirt to be mistaken for some Gay Header's trophy wife.

Brax pondered those three and others like them as Hagadorn pulled into a slot, cut the engine, pulled out the shoebox Chevy's hand brake with a ratcheting sound, and set it. He had a sudden mindflash of Marie Antoinette and that crowd preciously costumed as shepherdesses and whatnot for *nostalgie de la bue* love games, in faked pastoral settings that had little to do with the travails of the real thing.

Whatever, his situation left him without a clue as to what was supposed to happen next. "Mr. Hagadorn, don't you—" Hagadorn gave him a handsomely quirky smile and Brax started over. "That is, *Phipps*, don't you think you should give me some cues, or clues, here?"

"There are no cues, Braxmar; there is no script. You're among your patrons, or at least potential patrons. Be that as it may, serious conversation is reserved for later. We'll chat about the Sysops, eh? And the *Crystal Harmonic*; the Outline. And other things as well."

Outline? Brax wondered.

He climbed out of the car, leaving his manuscript behind in its tote sack. The four-by-four with Hagadorn's Watchmen caught up, only to pull down into the little gravel service and managerial parking lot off to the left of the White Visitation. It was already jammed with other security contingents' runabouts, ATVs, and minivans, the guards all keeping to themselves. Brax scarcely noticed; the astrobuck Illuminati saying casual hellos to

Hagadorn were far more to be feared than steroid cases with big muscles and guns—not that he didn't fear them, too.

He glanced down across the sloping grassy bowl set into the promontory, within the paved loop: it had once been a sacred and ceremonial place of the Wampanoags. Gallons and gallons of potable water from the Vineyard's fragile aquifer were now draining down into it, carrying the soapsuds and detergent scum and car dirt of the landholders.

Among the *ubers* it was all first names and laughing, shoulder-slapping banter. Hagadorn produced some Genuine Mink Gland Car Polish, and General Buckley Wakkendorf taunted, "Are you still using that weasel jism?"

"You're going to beg me for some when you see the results. But I'll only give you enough to gargle, so you can swallow your envy."

Brax, taking things in, noticed that the Masters of Up-Island gleamed with an oily sheen; he spied a squeeze bottle and realized that even they wore high-SPF amino-acid lotion to avoid too unpolitic a tan. Another notable detail: none was wearing a phone or other commo gear, not even camouflaged as dermal patch or jewelry, as far as he could see. Instant telelink lay within almost everybody's means and the merely wealthy tended to be walking datacom facilities; only the very poor, the dropouts, and fugitives weren't wired in. Here at the top, however, in a molecularly thin stratum of the ultrasuccessful, came the luxury of unwiring again.

Amid laughter, Fatima Bebe came Brax's way with a speculative smile and a sweating-cold beverage can. Her foaming black hair was confined by a red bandanna sweatband, and she was wearing an awful lot of makeup for a woman scrubbing her car in the middle of a hot Cape Islands day. "Howdy, stranger; buy you a beer?"

Brax accepted, stammering thanks, pinned by the look she was giving him and by matters revealed by her damp DALLAS COWBOYS jersey, its torn neck airing sculpted cleavage and an old-style dog-tag chain that plunged between her breasts. Then he glanced down in surprise as he gripped the freezing beer can and tried to open it; good lord, the thing was strong as a tank! Winking, Fatima fished out a stamped piece of steel attached to the dog-tag chain and plied it expertly. There was a *sploit!* of gas and whitecap as she punched a triangular hole in the top, a few drops more when she did the second.

Maybe the can had been jostled or maybe Fatima had given

it a few shakes; creamy foam gushed out of it and covered his hand to splatter the ground in a way he found appallingly suggestive. He glanced sidelong and saw the other up-islanders sharing the joke. Brax tried to keep his voice unstrained. "So very kind of you, thanks." He took a pull on the beer, which bore the logo IRON CITY.

"You're welcome. How are you enjoying Chez Hagadorn? Gilda and Phipps still cooing like lovebirds, are they?"

Hagadorn had materialized to observe Brax's reply. Brax understood that while they might need to make common cause, the schools of Phoenix great whites would devour one another without hesitation if they got the chance.

"And billing, oh yes!" He grinned back. "If you'll pardon me for a moment, I think I need to locate a loo."

Hagadorn looked appeased. Brax broke contact with a celerity he thought Sean Junknowitz might have admired and bounded up the steps of the White Visitation Lodge. The entrance area was swank even by Gay Head standards, with the feel of a royal barge's lounge. He spotted three commo booths in a bank, looking more like overupholstered biofeedback training modules. With a glance around to make sure no one was watching, he slipped into one and opaqued the door. Fishing out the metal wafer Apterix Muldoon had given him, he made himself unbend enough to sit down. Then he slotted the card.

Hagadorn did nothing without reason; this whole business of the returned phone card reeked therefore of setup. And yet it was the only variable Brax could influence at the moment: with Muldoon aware of his situation, Brax might stand some chance of affecting his own fate, rising above the rank of pawn.

The screen blanked of boot-up data and a new image began to form.

The End Zone hyena pack of disparate aliens didn't quite know what to make of Sean Junknowitz's challenging them. But, Eddie Ensign saw, the local inmate kingpin on the hollowed-out stump of a throne—a living mummy named Yanvur—understood.

Eddie had been amazed that Sean could so much as get to his feet, Riiv's life-singing therapy or no, but after she and Willy had departed, Lucky's brother showed that he knew a trick or two himself. Revived somewhat by Riiv's synergies, he'd called on disciplines he'd learned from *voudun* adepts, from Amazonian Kreen-Akarore shamans, and, to be sure, from just plain gutting it out as a U.S. Marine in Gulf War II.

Yanvur's waterhole wasn't hard to track down. Along the way, Sean had asked after Sheena Hec'k, who'd disappeared along with Harley Paradise. Eddie knew about the all-night sentinel duty Sean and Sheena had stood in Lucky's apartment before Black Hole had struck. The mysterious redhead was a traveler and adventurer anybody could respect and desire at the selfsame time; no wonder she and taciturn Sean had become, in their own self-sufficient way, soulmates—maybe lovers; nobody else had been around during those long guardmounts.

In any case, there was no word of Sheena, but Yanvur's water hole was something of a crossroads—even though it was nothing but a little bog knee-deep in smelly seepage with some diseased berry bushes and sickly fruit trees growing around it. Yanvur's followers bridled at Sean's approach but gave ground when he didn't halt. Yanvur looked on from his stump throne on the opposite bank, a living cadaver with reverse-articulated stick legs and a face keen as a splitting maul.

"You stay back," Sean told Eddie, and crutched straight for the rancid pool. One of Yanvur's toadies, a palsied Bygarian with the manner of a starving porcupine, charged to the edge of the opposite bank near Yanvur. "Go away!" it snarled. "This place is Yanvur's!" A few of the others lifted crude clubs or spears of wood but held their places, too terminal to be much threat.

The Earthspeak was no surprise; a fair sprinkling of End Zoners had the language, thanks to their nanites. Eddie had wondered if it was because Vogonskiy enjoyed showing off his flair for English. Sean dropped his crutch and began a shuffle-footed dance on the pond's bank, snapping his fingers in rapid syncopation, chanting a fast rondo of *Cinta Largas* incantations. He wasn't as light-footed as when he'd mastered the spell, but at least Riiv had given him the strength to try it.

The porcupine looked flummoxed. Sean began interspersing fingertip-rubbing gestures with the snaps and tightening the pattern of the dance steps. The quilled Bygarian only got out, "W-we're not going to warn you again, stranger—" before Sean pinned him with eye hexes and head juts that imitated a striking *fer-de-lance*, his body all sinuosity now although every move was agony.

The porcupine ran off, trying to pull from itself nonexistent barbs. After Sean had cupped some of the stinking runoff to his mouth, Yanvur spoke in a voice like a death rattle, his dark eyes shining. "I don't tolerate competitors."

If it was a spell, Eddie saw, it didn't take. Sean straightened laboriously. "What about allies? You hate Vogonskiy enough to take on a few of those?"

"If I were to do so," Yanvur answered, "we two would still not suffice to defeat him—not on End Zone. There's another adept here, the life-singer Riiv, whom I believe you've already met. As a triad we might accomplish something, but she's a soft-hearted fool."

Sean combed long, tangled blond locks out of his eyes with his fingers. "I just might have an angle there."

"That would be very useful," Yanvur smiled, a ghastly sight. "Come right over."

FOURTEEN

"LOOKS KINDA MEASLY, doesn't it?" Lucky asked Sinead softly, hugging his knees and studying the creosote bush. "For the oldest living thing on Earth, I mean. Maybe we should've gone with that giant fungus in Washington State."

"Maybe the point is that the way you live to a ripe old age is by avoiding people's notice," his sister answered, seated next to him in the cold New Mexico sand. "Besides, the *Armillaria ostoyae* up there's not even a thousand years old; this old weed goes fifteen thousand, easy."

Lucky was impressed, notwithstanding the fact that the fungus discovered near Mount Adams before the Turn was spread over two and a half square miles and the scraggly little creosote bush was a ring of growth barely forty feet across. In the center of the ring was a long mound of turned soil from which two seg-mented metal cables trailed to Silvercup, who was grounded a few yards away. At points around the plant's periphery, the XT tourists were helping the Junknowitzes keep vigil. There were a couple of coyotes yipping somewhere in the darkness, but they were steering well clear of the aliens and the utility spaceship.

Sinead hunched lower in the jacket she'd picked up, along with other clothes for herself and Lucky, outside Palm Springs, while Silvercup hid in an auto reclamation yard. The clothes were cheap recycled natural-fiber stuff and cyclist lites that had cost her just about all the cash she had; her astrobuck credit and debit cards would only attract Wakkendorf, Tanabe, and the Sysops knew who else now.

"All I know is, that data Silvercup found talked about 'oldest' and 'sources' and 'first among the living' when it referred to this Head Start stuff, and this is the closest thing I could think of. And it's a little late to change our minds now."

As if to prove it, Silvercup's voice came over Sinead's Starfleet-knockoff translator/communicator brooch. "I'm getting elevated readings. Lucky, shall I try now?"

Sinead shrugged, leaving him the decision. He got to his feet, brushing sand from the seat of his work pants. "Might as well; heat 'em up." All they could do was hope; Hono had jury-rigged the equipment but there had been no adequate way to test it, and if the Head Start didn't work there were no other options left.

The segmented metal cables glowed a soft green, humming quietly. It had taken most of the Honos' tinkering to adjust the spacetruck's available emissions to something like what the texts described; Lucky couldn't fathom it, but the antlike XT techs hadn't been at all satisfied with their results.

The energizing went on for a full minute, during which the coyotes shut up completely, but nothing else happened and finally the howls resumed.

Sinead had risen, too, and now put one hand on his shoulder. "I don't know what else we can do, except maybe freeze it and hope that you can get it back to—"

"It's moving!" GoBug yelled. Lacking extremities with which to point, the larva was bounding in his mother's lap and pointing with his head. "Look, look!"

Silvercup directed a low-powered light at the center of the creosote bush. Two hands big and solid as digitate butcher blocks thrust up through the sand they'd heaped; the light along the cables went out as Lumber Jack sat up, bursting through the mound like a sub that had blown all ballast. Lumber Jack's long Easter Island idol of a face was covered with sand, but even taking that into account he looked different from when they'd buried him with the cable contacts on his skull to try the Head Start procedure. He was covered with pale green buds, many of which had sprouted long hairlet shoots. Lucky and the tourists were about to run to him when Sinead snapped, "Whoa! Easy on Methuselah the Creosote Bush."

"Yes, by all means," Lumber Jack agreed, spitting out sand. "Wait right there." He heaved himself out of the mound and stretched with sounds suggesting a square-rigger at anchor and an old house leaning in a wind, the green shoots making him look to Lucky like a chlorophyll Iron John. Then he stepped over the creosote bush with reverent care.

Lucky got to him first and clung to his cyclopean arm. "You okay, *lignum vitae*?" Wood of Life—Lucky's nickname for him. "Hey, this's my sister—Sinead, I told you about her, remember? She's the one who thought to bring you here for the Head Start."

"Ah." He bowed to her, gently placing the hands tough as pile drivers to either side of one of hers, making contact with infinite care. "Your instincts were correct; the Head Start treatment depends on a certain attunedness with other established flora-forms. I owe you my life."

He reached gently into the shag of pale green shoots on his chest, plucked, and handed her something. She looked at it, speechless—a tiny seedling just beginning to open in the artificial light from Silvercup's spot.

As the other tourists closed in to welcome the man from Wood Wind back to the land of the living, Sinead took Lucky aside. "We should be going, shouldn't we?"

"Right away. You sure you want to go through with this?"

She nodded. "I have to know Alex and Rita are safe."

They were hoping that, if matters went their way in New York, she would have aid in contacting their parents. Beyond that, she'd said little about how she planned to get a handle on her life again.

"Are you sure this Quick Fix woman will help you?" Sinead pressed.

Lucky shrugged. "She did once before. I need *some* kinda help to get into the Trough again." If he was right about his moment of insight on Zillion, he could enlist formidable aid if he could just get through the right Adits. "All I can do is try—who knows?"

He'd taken something from the beat-up shoulder bag he'd carried on more worlds and way stations than he could count now and turned the object in his hands, a superstitious habit to which he occasionally yielded.

"What's that—oh!" Sinead exclaimed. "I bet I haven't seen a Magic 8 Ball in twenty years!"

Her laugh made her sound surprisingly young. "Well? O Magic 8 Ball, is this scheme of my brother's the way to go?"

The words floated up, hard to see in the dim light:

YES
DEFINITELY

Riding the flowfloor intrastation transit system in way station Khaypur, Zastro Lint went into a kind of swoon. Peterbuilt reached out to steady him, leading him to where he could lean against a Love Handles neurosex vending machine; Lint, even in his seizure, fastidiously avoided the brass sensory grips.

"What is it, taxman? What's amiss?" Peterbuilt demanded.

"Junknowitz! Can't you feel it?" The IRS man, recovering as abruptly as he'd been stricken, pushed away the glittering arm with its piled arcs and conformations of somalloy muscle. Peterbuilt suffered the affront, mindful of the revenge he would have soon—provided Lint's hastily performed upgrades didn't burn out the grouchy little primate first.

"He's just encountered some decision nexus or probability juncture and—" It seemed only chance that Lint bumped a travel-brochure rack when he straightened up, scattering plaques that projected identical holographs of the *Crystal Harmonic* across the concourse floor. "—he's in America!"

"Well, if Brax Koddle didn't write it, who did? And how'd he do it so fast?" Winnie Print demanded, forgetting her preoccupation with packing their suitcase.

Russell Print, Brax's editor, tossed down the manuscript disk, labeled *Gate Crashers*, that had appeared so mysteriously at Sony-Neuhaus. "Author's supposedly 'Dieter Druckfehler,' but there's nothing listed about him in *Books in Print* or *Who's Who in Science Fiction*."

" 'Druckfehler'?" Winnie mused. "German for 'typo'?"

He threw up his hands. "If it's not, it oughta be! He turns the whole rest of the Worlds Abound series on its head! Druckfehler makes the whole intergalactic war a big misunderstanding! The Sirians become friends with Linc Traynor and save the Earth from environmental breakdown, and make the human race rich by starting tourism here!"

"Can't you sit on it until Brax turns his manuscript in? It's bound to be better."

Russ tried to get a grip on his nerves. "Richard Rymer's already approved it for a *Zone Defense* sequel starring Jason Duplex; they're already meeting with a screenwriter. Done deal. Sony-Neuhaus and Matsu-Universal're gonna use the *Crystal Harmonic* cruise to give the whole package a major push. And besides—" He grew somber. "Nobody knows where Brax is, including the cops. Sorry, babe; I wasn't asked on this one, I was *told*."

Winnie forgot the two bathing suits she'd been debating over. "The more I hear about this XT cruise, the less I like it. Russ, I don't think we should bring the girls."

"Fine, but don't expect me to talk them down off the ledge."

Blossom and Gwen had been living for the voyage on the XT themer ship for weeks. The scheduled cruise was a lock, like Druckfehler's assignment to the Gate Crashers project—the voyage being unprecedented and, if you asked Russ, demento combination of sales conference and PR excursion. To complicate matters, some of the house's major authors, like bodice-ripper queen Regina "Remora" Barleycorn from the Turgid Tales imprint, were scheduled to be there; upper management was hatching some insane scheme to get *her* to write novels about likeable teleporting aliens, too—heroic, sexy, free-spending interstellar visitors.

"You're their father," Winnie started, but Russ was reprieved by the phone. When he answered, the big, white-bearded, Ghost-of-Christmas-Present face of The Awesome Vogonskiy appeared, cropped by the screen on all four sides. "Rush, dear lad!" Vogonskiy had dubbed him that when Russ had fast-tracked the magician's *How to Put REAL Magic in Your Life!* and got it into the stores in one week flat to cash in on Vogonskiy's supposed quelling of the Passaic earthquake.

"Just wanted to say we'll have two very fine, adjoining staterooms waiting for you and your three lovely ladies at the Sea Acropolis. And, I need a favor: send around all that background material your people compiled on the Worlds Abound series, like a good chap? My old chum Rich Rymer asked me to assist him and his new screenwriter, add some pizzazz."

"New screenwriter? What happened to the old one?"

"You haven't heard? Nasty business. Downcasted from a twenty-eight-floor conference-room window right in the middle of a working meeting with Richard and Jason Duplex, silly sod. Ah well, easily mended: 'dogs and screenwriters keep off the grass,' and all that. Do get that material to me today, like a good fellow? See you on the Sea of Japan!"

Russ switched off the phone and saw that Winnie had heard the entire call. At that moment Blossom and Gwen came in, arguing over who was going to get to wear Winnie's old tennis necklace on the *Crystal Harmonic*. "You're both staying right here!" Russ and Winnie yelled at the same time.

It was the beginning of a·long evening, during which the girls mounted an epic joint tantrum, but for once their parents were immovable.

FIFTEEN

"YES, CLIPPED BY a ricochet," the woman called DeSoto confirmed, turning over and over in her hands the techno-tick Harley had knocked off her machine with the field-hockey stick.

"Just a nick, see here? It still froze up my control array, but the damage kept it from paralyzing me physically." DeSoto gave an ironic snort. "Small-caliber, Vigilance Bureau police rounds—trying to finish us off as we lay there. As if they could penetrate ground pounders! But this—if there's a god, she has a helluva sense of humor."

Giant ground pounders were stumping around the Adit and the scene of the firefight, examining the aftermath of events that had been a key part of Harley and Sheena's superfluke escape to this lost world, Hazmat. Many of the machines were repairing damage to each other, producing tool extensions and manipulators and tentacles in bewildering variety. To Harley, their design details suggested fins, grillework—nineteen-fifties Detroit car styling.

The escapees had learned the walkers were called ground pounders, or gaitmobes, the way they'd picked up a lot of other things in the last few minutes—hastily and haphazardly. All ground pounders were frontline gaitmobes, but not all gaitmobes were ground pounders.

It had emerged that Hazmat was a blasted wasteland world of constant battle, where humans armed with gaitmobes and other mechs were on the verge of extinction at the hands of an insane aggregate AI called Warhead, whose hordes were made up of mutant abominations engineered from *homo sapiens* stock and called Humanosaurs.

A senior ground pounder officer named Packard had led a hotly debated expedition to the sepulcher in a perhaps naive effort to reactivate the Adit and petition for aid from the Trough. But a radical fundamentalist faction, the Vigilance Bureau police, had disabled the far stronger ground pounders with the mines, then turned the smaller cop-gaitmobes' guns on Packard's grunts and the chancellor of the far-flung human warrens and strongholds.

Chancellor Auburn's bodyguards' ground pounders lay empty; unlike Packard's machines, they had uncoded escape locks, and the Vigilance Police had removed their wearers and executed them.

The Vigilance Bureau leader, Inspector Nash, had cracked Packard out of the open-chested ground pounder Sheena and Harley had found and borne him off in an evacuation capsule in order to frame him for the chancellor's death. The fallen ground pounders and the Adit were supposed to be eliminated by a fusion power module—the object resembling a sense-dep tank the two had stumbled on—set to explode.

Nash just hadn't counted on an Aborigine's appearing on al-Reem, glitching Adit systems, and two desperate women leaping through to the sepulcher.

Nash had also carried off something called the memory egg, an artifact spontaneously generated on Hazmat approximately 180 baseline years before. Recent recovery of the egg was the reason Adit reactivation was possible. DeSoto's curt explanation fit myths that Sheena had heard—that the Egg had been created as an unintended byproduct by the transgressions of phreakers on Hazmat, a planet excelling in advanced AI design and leading-edge nanite work. The phreakers conspired with Black Hole darksiders to interface the up-Trap SIs with prototype Hazmat creations.

Some said it was the search for the ultimate cybernetic godhead; others claimed it was a quest for the Outline, the mythical Adit connection that would let a traveler fade beyond the constraints of the galaxy. One conspiracy theory contended that the Sysops had it in for Hazmat. Whatever, something went appallingly wrong and rang down apocalypse on Hazmat in the form of Warhead. But a defining segment of the Light Trap SIs and a big chunk of Warhead had been spun loose in the form of the memory egg, a Trough holy grail.

A people at war with Warhead and the Humanosaurs, and at war within itself: that was who Harley and Sheena had fallen in with. DeSoto, Packard's second-in-command, was tough and no-frills, a solidly built woman in tight unigarb who looked forty and wore a boxy, matte-black handgun. Her scalp was shaved smooth except for a warrior's forelock to give the contact array through which she conned her gaitmobe an unimpeded link. Harley had the distinct impression DeSoto was worried about Packard's well-being for reasons much more personal than *esprit de mecque.*

The H-bomb had been disenabled; news that she'd been filthfooting around with a thermonuke lacked the power to rattle Harley any further. DeSoto's gaitmobe, *Strider,* was parked nearby in a squat on haunches and fists, its plastron open and a short ladder deployed, looking like a cast-iron gorilla hunching forward with gaping belly.

Harley, whose father had been a classic-car afficionado, had a lot of unanswered questions—like why the ground-pounders were styled like 1940s-50s Detroit petropigs, and why Hazmat surnames—DeSoto, Packard, Nash—were automotive. But those weren't going to be answered soon; DeSoto was calling for her troops to mount up. There was a beacon signal coming from the evac-cap in which Packard was being carried across the wasteland by the Vigilance Bureau gaitmobes. If the police made it to the hidden subsurface transit station seventy miles distant, they'd trip the autodestruct behind them and that would be that.

A further downside was that the E-cap signal was on a freq the Humanosaurs might monitor, and the ground-pounders couldn't figure out why. Thirteen grunts were going out against twice as many Bureau gaitmobes, leaving the two arrivals behind with some survival gear in a sepulcher they dared not leave because the wasteland was inimical. While all this daunted Harley, Sheena had no doubt about which way to jump. Standing there in her Balinese pants and cross-trainers, Packard's personal sawed-off rifle at her waist, she told DeSoto, "We're going with you. In the KIAs' gaitmobes."

It didn't go over at all well until Sheena pointed out that she and Harley were the Trough contactees the Hazmatians had sacrificed so much to reach.

DeSoto squinted. "For all I know you're criminals or spies." She looked at the Adit apparatus, which was shot up and, after Harley and Sheena's fade, thoroughly out of commission; there was no way back, and even if there were, the Agency was likely combing the Trough for them. "And yet it's all too true you're the last source of intel we're likely to get from the Trough for a while. Come along if you can, then. D'you know how to conn by contact array, then?"

"Raised on it," Sheena reassured her brightly.

Harley couldn't help snapping. "Excuse me, Big Red—*oo*!" Sheena had trod her toes. Thinking of being abandoned to the dwellers in the dark again, Harley recovered. "*Oo*, it'll be nice to brush up on my ground-pounding."

"Give ya one more chance, douche nozzle."

Captain Randy Barnes, NYPD, had rousted so many mopes that there was seldom anything personal in it anymore. He leaned into Jak O' Clubs' personal space to let him know he was serious.

The Big Apple Liver Enlargement Society hood, keeping a low profile since being released from the police detention cell at Bellevue—thanks to a resourceful public defender and mental-health-care advocate—was dressed down tonight: rather than Arnold or Jason Duplex or one of the other classic action figures, he was dweebily robed as a Church of the Software chipmonk. It was a definite breach of BALES ethics, and it hadn't saved him from being braced by Barnes and Dante Bhang as he edged along through the Lower West Side.

The hot August night and the sight of Bhang standing to one side and looking so cool in his handmade, off-white linen suit had Barnes in the mood to mash a little marrow. "Take ya in back there for a tonfa enema, that'd get your attention, wouldn't it?" He indicated a onetime meat-packing plant, in these more vegan post-Turn times converted to an urban agricenter. It was closed for the day, and there were alcoves and doorways out of happy-cam range suitable to a little impromptu intervention counseling.

"You lose Boxdale. You get yourself busted. You turn up *ugats* about Junknowitz's crew and then you try to duck me?"

Jak tried to object that he had his people out panning and scanning for the loft posse; Barnes slapped his head back and forth with neck-spraining force and complete dispassion. Jak, bigger and younger and more muscular, didn't dare do anything but take it.

The sound of tires automatically made Barnes look around, especially on that near-empty side street, but it was only a Pesky Pizza trike, one of the chain's motherships, whipping through a turn at the corner. Dante Bhang fanned himself with his beige planter's hat, leaning on a blackthorn walking stick with a gold head shaped like a fly. *Mosca*, fly, was the Italian word for Roman street urchins who served as errand boys and entry-level help to *mafiosi*; it was how Dante had begun his career. "It *is* a little public here, Captain."

Barnes hated Dante's superior airs, but for the time being they were joined at the hip, at least until they got back in the good graces of Phoenix and Black Hole. There was a summit coming up aboard the *Crystal Harmonic*, and they'd better be back in good odor by then. One of the commodities most in demand at the moment was Junknowitz cronies, but those were damnably scarce.

Not that Barnes wasn't sufficiently protected to ignore any civilian-review-board brutality charge, but there was no point attracting attention. "C'mon, scumbag; I'm gonna explain somethin' to you." He got an armlock on Jak and frog-marched him back into the entranceway of the onetime factory.

"Don't make us go through this twice, Jak," Dante remarked world-wearily, following. It was only because Barnes turned to demand, "What d'ya mean 'us,' Superfly?" that he heard and saw the two figures following them into the entranceway. Barnes pushed Jak ahead of him into the meager cover of a shallow doorway only because Jak was in his way, not caring whether Dante made it or not. Dante did, just as a plosive stuttering sounded and a volley of low-velocity, mushrooming trank rounds flattened on the brick wall.

"I'm fuckin' hit!" Jak screamed, thrashing weakly, pawing at his leg. Dante Bhang had positioned himself so that the other two were between him and the line of fire.

The shooters were framed against the streetlights, trying to correct their aim rather than fleeing after failing to down the targets with those first rounds. They were dressed in unisex street clothes, their faces lumpy with camoflesh, so details and even gender were impossible to tell. Barnes knew that with little cover and no good line of retreat any move but returning fire was a sucker's game. Securing a firmer armlock on Jak with one hand, he swung back his sport coat and drew his pistol from the flat pancake belt holster with the other. Because the Junknowitz case involved homicide with a firearm, Barnes was armed with "special issue," a nine-millimeter automatic, rather than an Un-Gun.

He pushed off the door to barge toward the hit men, holding Jak O' Clubs in front of him as a living shield. Jak made incoherent *no* noises as more tranquilizer rounds mushed into him. Barnes, hampered by Jak and unable to aim, fired wildly. One of the ambushers flinched and clutched his or her side; the other supported the wounded one, pulling back while firing with an admirable calm, and disappeared up the street. Barnes was amazed to find the automatic's slide locked back, eleven rounds gone; he could barely recall having pulled the trigger. Jak had become dead weight, so Barnes let him fall and reloaded.

His first impulse was to call for backup, but he knew the pair would likely get away if he waited, and he wanted to ask them a few confidential questions before any interfering supervisors showed up. He set off with Dante bringing up the rear, the fly-headed walking stick extended like a gun. They were almost to the street when they heard the food-processor whir of a two-cylinder, two-stroke engine.

They got to the street just in time to see a trike pulling away, its canopy lowering. Even though it was a one-seater, both shooters fit inside: the mobile oven had been removed from the fuselage hump, leaving scrunch-in room for a second occupant.

"Pesky Pizza?" Barnes heard Dante mutter in wonder as he edged out onto the sidewalk. "A swack attack, to take us prisoner, but why? Does this make any sense to you?"

None whatsoever; the more Barnes thought about it, the more confusing it became. That was what stopped him from putting out an immediate APB for anything or anybody on the island of Manhattan wearing the chain's logo—a little Mario chef with a pepperoni pie held high and fast-spinning wheels for legs. There was no knowing at this point whether the hitters were actually connected to the pizza company or if Pesky Pizza was tied to Trough, Phoenix, or other players. Besides, Black Hole did not approve of involving uncooped indig authorities in behind-the-scenes business matters.

Barnes called for a meat wagon to haul Jak back to Bellevue while Dante prepared to make himself scarce. "There's one set of players we haven't rousted yet," the captain said. "Time we did. Meet me at your place in an hour and we'll go make shopping a friggin' rush."

SIXTEEN

WITH THE SHAGGY Elvis fans from Pay Dirt occupied with the bulked-up dancing boys provided by the management, Nikkei was spared the ordeal of having to improvise another song. That was a vast relief, though he'd been considering a slow ballad retitled "Heart-Fake Motel" in honor of the Willow World.

The lady Sasquatches had grabbed the boy-toys and started dancing; furniture was being broken and minor injuries started mounting right away, but no one seemed to care. Emlarre and crew were nonchalant about the difference in size; Nikkei speculated that it might be natural with her species for males to be smaller, as with hyenas and spiders. He wondered if the men had been drenched with psychotropics or hugely bribed, or were indulging a pervy thrillseeker-xenophilia-ultracompetitor kink of their own. Perhaps this was some combination thereof.

He sidled for the door but a flash of incisors any sabertooth would have been proud of warned him back; clearly, it was considered impolite to bolt, meaning Mickey had gotten off light. Nikkei joined Sato behind the buffet table. Themers, he thought, just pretend they're big, irrepressible themers. "Got a trank gun by any chance?" he asked her. "Preferably belt-fed?"

She gave him a disappointed look. "This reception is going quite within expected parameters. But if your nerve is gone you can escape through the spa-*fudo*." The taunt made it unthinkable for him to beam out. Then the Pay Dirter in blue jeans, T-shirt, and engineer boots yowled at them, "Why do you spurn the rites?"

If Sato was caught off guard, she hid it well, not even sparing Nikkei a glance as she flipped open her cuffs and shot her sleeves. "Any problems with this?"

"Shigata ga nai." Lean into the turns. He tucked the *karaoke* mike away and jumped back; it seemed Sato had cultivated sixties go-go moves for just such an eventuality. Nikkei and Mickey had expected bizarre, harrowing tests when they swore loyalty to Tanabe, but envisioned something more along the lines of ripping out both of some Vulcan's hearts or taking on an incendiary mutant amoeba with an oven mitt—not *this* bad craziness.

For the next hour the place rocked without letup. There were boy-throwing contests, bar-iron-bending matches, and a crying jag over how much too young Elvis Aaron Presley had died— two or three hundred years, the way the Pay Dirters saw it. The bigfoot ladies dealt as equals with Sato, but regarded Nikkei and the escorts as mere party favors, not worth talking to. Respite only came when Emlarre chugged her beer and belched. "Bath time! Right, Sato, my sister? The *o-furo* we've heard about!"

Sato didn't bat an eye. "Right this way." Nikkei wondered just how long his father had been grooming her for this mission.

They trooped in a tipsy throng to the suite's palatial baths, which featured naked Elvis statuary and was built on a scale suitable to Pay Dirters. The lumbering *gaijin*, astoundingly, got right down to acting as the Pay Dirters' *yobukodori*— "monkeys," bath attendants. Nikkei was flabbergasted to see that Sato was waiting for him to get with the program. Sucking in his gut manfully, he helped Sato disrobe as she twisted her hair into a knot, joshing and schmoozing with the XTs. Like the action-figure escorts, he stripped to his skivvies and set to work, soaping and rinsing Sato, who lazed on a low wooden stool, as did her guests.

She was shapely and slim, but her body was soft-looking to his Americanized eyes; Japanese fast-trackers were expected to be fit for duty but not so buffed as to suggest that they squandered undue time on mere fitness. He couldn't keep himself from glancing at her breasts, thinking of the "dimly white world." It was a phrase Takuma had quoted wistfully once, at a time when he and his son were growing estranged, and Nikkei fixed on it bitterly. Sato didn't look like she'd ever done any wet nursing; her breasts were nice—attractive but not reworked or gravity-defying. She was ignoring him.

"Emlarre, my *client* hopes to meet with you later today; he knows how precious your time is, how little you can spare here." As she said it, she bowed her head and presented the nape of her neck for Nikkei's touch, still a gesture of ultimate sensuality from Japanese woman to man. He stared at the unspeakably lovely lines of it, the wisps of hair escaped from the knot nestling dark against her pale skin.

Emlarre burped. "It's been wonderful, *supa*, dear woman! As to your, ah, client, I see no reason to deal with some *male*—or, at this point, to risk the ire of Black Hole."

Nikkei absorbed this open talk of treason, or at least interstellar corporate warfare. His father never made an ill-considered move, which meant security risks had been taken into account, including the hospitality stuntmen and Nikkei.

"Phipps Hagadorn is developing a brisk trade shipping human organs and other biomaterials offworld," Sato said. "We wish your covert aid discomfiting him in this."

One Wookiee-woman let out a laugh much like the cough of a lion. "What can your little tertiary operation offer our world that would make it worthwhile to cross the Agency's favorite indig?"

Sato was unruffled. "Your world? Nothing. As to *you yourselves*, however, I would mention certain genetic enablers that would eliminate any serious challenges to your own cubs at the Merit Trials."

The Pay Dirters were thunderstruck. "You mean those Ss-sarsassissian concoctions?" one of the visitors exploded, nearly sending her scrub stud sprawling. "Why, those sea serpents absolutely do not traffic in them!"

"Not their trade consortium, no," Sato agreed quietly. "And yet there are lines of opportunity."

Emlarre's eyes narrowed and her ears flattened to her head somewhat, a frightening sight. "You've found some way to bribe the right people, eh? Congratulations; others have tried."

Miss Sato inclined her head humbly. Nikkei, sluicing her off with a fragrant pine rinse bucket rather than the hose, tried to concentrate on listening as he knelt to do her left leg. It wasn't easy.

Emlarre, hosed clean, rose and signaled to her party. "Dismiss the handymen! We need to confer." With that the creatures plunged into the big, heated pool, sending waves overlapping its edge, and put their heads together at the far end. Sato gave a signal and the male escorts departed. Nikkei gradually left off sudsing her foot and handed her a towel, which she drew around her shoulders.

The sounds of the Pay Dirt caucus were like feeding time at

the zoo. "Are they going for it?" Nikkei asked, drawing up a stool and sitting down next to her.

"I think so. Your father was confident they would."

Nikkei snorted. "My father. Every last detail wired in."

"When I first came to work for him," she told him, still looking at the offworlders, "Tanabe-san loved 'West Side Story.' He loved to watch the show or just hear the score." Some older Japanese regarded it as the greatest piece of *gaijin* musical theater in the world, with its cultural clashes and high romantic tragedy. Like Takuma, they were fascinated with the American phenomenon of different races and ethnic groups mixing, sometimes warring, sometimes coming together—as alien to homogeneous Japan as ever the Pay Dirters were. Nikkei's father even liked to sing the score when he thought nobody was listening; the elder Tanabe was embarrassed by what he felt to be an inferior voice. As a kid Nikkei had suspected his father sometimes cried over "Maria" and "Somewhere."

"One day you . . . took leave of your family," she said.

Deft turn of phrase. In Tokyo, Americanized Nikkei had become involved with a girl whom his grandfather outted for being part *Burakumin*, the untouchable caste. There'd been dishonor, murder, and her suicide in the wake of it, and Nikkei had expected his father to have him tracked down and slaughtered like a dog. But Tanabe had done nothing—balancing, perhaps, on the agonizing and classic Japanese knifepoint between *giri*, obligation, and *ninjo*, humanity—love of his only son.

"But after you left," Miss Sato told him, "your father disposed of all his recordings of 'West Side Story' and shan't ever permit himself to hear it again, I should think."

What could he say? Life was too complicated; that was why he'd thrown in with Mickey, living on the thin edge of the moment and not thinking beyond that. "Yeah, well, that doesn't mean he won't kill me one a these days. Or maybe he's trying to get into a conciliatory post-Turn, *post-Trough* consciousness, hey? Be the first one on his planet?" He pulled down the towel and kissed the nape of her neck; she stiffened. "What d'you think, Sato?"

She pulled away. "I think you're a wretched, self-pitying ingrate."

"Oh, no; I'll pay him back if I get the chance. And he's gonna need help if he goes through with this off-gassed *Crystal Harmonic* gig. Take on Hagadorn aboard his own ship, with all those other vampires around?" He leaned to kiss her nape again.

"You're forgetting two things," she said, and turned to slap him so unexpectedly that he didn't even block. The vociferous Pay Dirt contingent never even noticed.

Nikkei rubbed his face. "I'm good at putting some things out of my mind."

The XT huddle was breaking up, and Emlarre wore a sly smile as she waded back their way. "Your father has a genius for steering events to his advantage," Miss Sato told Nikkei.

"And?"

"And before Hagadorn's consortium purchased it, the *Crystal Harmonic* used to belong to Tanabe-san."

When he faded back to Light Trap, no one noticed anything new about Yoo Sobek; as a Probe, he was used to disguising what lay within. But now he gazed around the stupendous Dyson-sphere stronghold of the Sysops with different eyes, looking for attack routes, vulnerabilities.

The time he'd spent with Ka Shamok was easily concealed; Probes had license for independent action. He threw his superiors tidbits of disinformation to content them that he was making progress in his hunt for both the Aborigines from Adit Navel and Ka Shamok's operative within the Agency—which was to say, himself. In one sense he *was* seeking himself: the memories and the self he'd lost; the secret of his dream of the eight rings.

He'd faded in by way of an Adit in the midlatitudes of Light Trap's northern hemisphere, in a microecology adapted for a mishmash of more or less humanoid species. Most of the residents were midlevel functionaries doing gofer work for the Agency's Trauma Advisory arm, and so there was a great deal of coming and going at the Adit; Sobek's arrival went unnoticed aside from routine processing. He wended through the bureaucratic sprawl by yield-field, flowfloor, motion mat and plain walking. He passed the olio of beings, all shapes, sizes, textures, and worlds of origin, that any Trough traveler took for granted.

The local dataspace access facility was a soaring, shining acropolis, but only one more rock in an Oort cloud in Light Trap's grand scheme of things. In moments, disembodied, he was aswim in the endless informational medium of the Light Trap data systems.

First he set in place a mentation decoy supplied him by Ka Shamok's organization. It was a prototype bought from some cyber-freebooters—former AzTek Development Consortium R-and-D types on the run from the Black Hole purge that had exterminated some ninety-eight per cent of their fellow employees. While the decoy did its legwork, the real Sobek shunted to an unused cover ID he'd set up long before. Through it he roved across an endless terrain of pure datum quanta like a hound casting for a scent, adroitly dodging diagnostic sweeps, creeping past gatekeepers, gulling cyberphages. Sifting through an Adit Navel file, he chanced on a datum that made him forget his initial line of inquiry.

Another Probe was scrutinizing various facets of the Adit Navel muddle—everything from the Quick Fix operation to the eight-ring symbol that had, through Sobek's use of it, become Ka Shamok's insignia. What was more, as Sobek read the signs, this other Probe was operating on a back-channel, informal, or even covert basis, preserving deniability for whoever had ordered the investigation. And whoever it was had been vested with some amazingly high-level access up-Trap, where the Silicon Intelligences administered Black Hole and the Sysops ruled.

Sobek noted certain information, then shunted back to the mentation decoy. He prescinded from access, back to his body and the real world. A half hour later he was in way station Knikx, in an Adit waiting area.

Waiting to fade was what looked at first to be an Earth woman in her fifties or so, sweater draped over her shoulders, reading glasses on a glass-beaded chain around her neck, platinumized hair in a bulletproof coif. But there were discrepancies. The eyes betrayed her first—they were oddly reptilian. The carnivorous toothiness as well as extra, opposable thumbs on her hands were too glaring to be oversights; more likely they were devices to disconcert or frighten—but whom?

They recognized one another's nature with specialized senses. She smiled venomously, flicking out a black, snake-whip tongue, her eyes lasing like rubies, vanlike fans lifting from her hairdo a bit in a warning display. "Young man, don't you know it's rude to stare?"

She was living some role she'd assumed all too vividly, like some Earthly amusement-park cast member stricken with Themer Identification Crisis. "My apologies, and congratulations on what is obviously your *very recent* elevation." To Probe.

"Obviously, you have a courtesy deficit disorder," she bristled.

The Pit Boss, a Hnngrrian, called out to her. "Miss Diandra? Ready for your Nmuth Four fade." She swept grandly past Sobek and faded in a bright spray of intercontinuum froth.

He watched her go. So, she had taken a liking to this "Miss Diandra Abbott" facade. "Discipline Di," Harley Paradise had called her. Odd that the agent should persist in using the schoolmistress persona; she had assumed it only recently, inside al-Reem, in an effort to wring information from Harley Paradise—before being raised to Probe status by her mysterious patron up-Trap. These were among the things Sobek had ferreted out in the datasphere.

He tried for immediate transit to Nmuth IV; he hadn't moved sooner because he didn't want to alert his quarry. His destination Adit was in the midst of a series of prescheduled fades, however, forcing him to wait. Sobek couldn't invoke Probe authority without compromising his unauthorized mission. Instead he charged a ruinous full fare against a coded credit line funded by the insurgency, then waited a mortifying fifteen minutes as Discipline Di widened her lead on him.

Adaptation being a Probe specialty, though, he had a plan. The first thing he looked for once he faded to Nmuth IV was a place to transmogrify.

SEVENTEEN

THE IDEA OF being abandoned by DeSoto and the other gaitmobe wearers was the only thing that could have gotten Harley Paradise to climb into the armored womb of one of the combat mechs. Sheena, who was less reticent and had related pilot experience, encouraged and coached her, but it was the thought of staying behind in the sepulcher that was the key to Harley's success. She brought the field-hockey stick along as a good-luck charm and security blanket.

Suspended among cushioning and concussion-absorbing flotation bladders, she felt the contact array pads fasten themselves all over her scalp, tugging at her hair, and she *became* the walking battleship. Its systems and detectors were her senses, its strength was hers—she rather liked that last part. Harley's ground-pounder was *Death Walker*, the late chancellor Auburn's unit; Sheena took another called *Iron Ram*.

The treacherous Vigilance Bureau police had a considerable head start, so DeSoto and her troops moved out at a near-trot, covering ground fast. Sheena was left to aid and cajole Harley along. It wasn't all that difficult once Harley had taken her first few steps, but something noted by her extended nervous system gave her pause.

"Sheena, look at all these cannons and missiles and stuff we're carrying! What kind of place *is* this?"

"The kind where we may need them, Harley."

"Well, *I* won't." Maybe some people she could name saw her as a deb-dilettante whose good looks and privileged upbringing let her regurgitate lib-humanist cant, but she wasn't about to abandon her convictions just because matters had gotten ugly.

On the other hand, she didn't intend to be anybody's victim. As she approached the sepulcher doors, Harley stopped at a tall decorative metal post capped with a stylized flame. She closed *Death Walker*'s huge hands on it, twisted it so that it snapped near the base, and wrenched it free—a bigger and badder hockey stick.

The sepulcher was situated in a wind tunnel of a crevasse called the Grimcrack Delve, at the bottom of the Eternity Stairs. Harley learned as she went, and the metal post served double duty as a staff as the gusts buffeted her like an invisible sparring partner. Sheena was going on about how Hazmat fit all the legends: an eerie wasteland with the sky overhead roiled by the worldwinds, violent and bizarre atmospheric phenomena that made aviation impossible.

By the time Harley and Sheena reached the top of the Eternity Stairs and exited the Howlslot, Harley had gained skill and confidence, but DeSoto and the rest were far ahead. Even farther was the beacon of Packard's e-cap, the one that would likely draw Humanosaurs.

Then Harley tripped and sloshed around as if she were in a cocktail shaker as *Death Walker* went down on its face. Sheena was right there to give her a hand, but Harley's resentment, fear, and anger flared. "You don't have to play angel of mercy for me, Red Ryder!" she flared, pushing *Iron Ram*'s helping hand away. "If you want to go on ahead nobody's stopping you!"

"I have no idea why you dislike me so," Sheena answered calmly, "but you're Lucky's friend, and he wouldn't want us to forsake one another. We must help each other."

Another line that should've belonged to Harley, former Gender Bias Council coordinator. "I'm sorry, Sheena; you're right."

"It's forgotten. Now come, just keep up a steady rhythm," Sheena encouraged, "and—"

" 'Lean into the turns,' " Harley supplied the millennial mantra.

Slotting Apterix Muldoon's card in the booth in the White Visitation, Brax Koddle could only pray Phipps Hagadorn's returning it to him wasn't some sadistic gag. When Muldoon's sky blue eyes and pale, rabbity features appeared, Brax felt something irrationally like joy—until he saw the little Man in Black's expression.

"Hello, Mr. Koddle. I've been expecting your call."

"Muldoon, listen closely and don't interrupt. I'm on Martha's Vineyard, being held in Gay—"

"Gay Head, by Mr. Phipps Hagadorn," Muldoon interrupted. "I know."

"You've got to get me out of here!"

But Muldoon only shook his head sadly, a comma of dark hair bobbing over his right eye. "I wish I could, Mr. Koddle." He brushed the hair back with a six-fingered hand. "I'm being demoted."

"What about *Gate Crashers*?"

"It's out of your hands and mine." Muldoon's image retreated to an inset while the rest of the flatscreen cued through multimedia promo material for—Brax realized with a knot of dread forming behind his sternum—science-fiction novels.

The most trumpeted, of course, was Plie Charmeuse's trilogy, *Kandide Carmera.* "This wasn't my doing," Muldoon was explaining, as Brax took in Fundai/Simon & Schuster's Milky Way Mass Transit Madness and Disney/Nabisco's Krazy Kollapsar Kommuter Konspiracy, more burlesquing of Black Hole's campaign against Earth. By the time he saw the upcoming Dieter Druckfehler *Gate Crashers*, he was already numb.

"Upper management believes in overkill," Muldoon said. "It's to ease the transition when the results of the *Crystal Harmonic* summit are announced—new planetary supervision, and all that."

Brax, shattered, was thinking about the roll of wrapping paper with the tens of thousands of words handwritten on it, sitting in the Menemsha Store carry sack on the floor of Hagadorn's 1957 shoebox Chevy.

Of course, that didn't explain why Hagadorn, who must have been aware of the competing series, was so hot to know Brax's insights and have Brax's cooperation. But doubtless there was a reason—Brax saw now that there were no coincidences or accidents; there was always a Black Hole purpose lurking behind every event.

Muldoon was saying something. "I'm sorry, what?" Brax asked.

The alien looked lapinesquely mournful. "I said, I guess you won't have a chance to look at what I've written; I understand. Maybe, if everything works out—when I'm done, you could—"

"What, you're still going to write?" Brax sighed tiredly. "Why bother?"

Muldoon cocked his head at Brax as if the connection were glitched. "Because—I just have to set it down, see the words written out."

"Even if not a soul reads it?"

"If I don't it'll never let me alone. This trying and trying to make my first professional sale—it's been like having a two-year stomach ache."

"Point well made. Hail to thee, Muldoon! If ever we meet again I'd been honored to read your work." Brax broke the connection.

What was bearing down on Ziggy on the bus terminal ramp—what he'd thought to be a police task force augmented by assorted themers and determined to run him down—turned out to be a pack of whooping, strip-surfing CitiZens being pursued by a Port Authority cop car. He watched the whole surreal landrush coming at him in deer-in-the-headlights paralysis.

The CitiZens were the ones he'd spotted earlier, air-dancing on the ramp's high-voltage RPEV recharge lines embedded in the road strip, their maglev boards' synthesizers evoking juice song from the interaction of fields.

"*Le*thal!" " 'Zarre!" "Ew, *crusty!*"

They were wearing camoflesh disguises and a wild mix of prole masquerade skins; he'd blundered smack into their path with no room to dodge. Even with the blue flashing police lights on them they were doing freestyle tricks, riffing juice song.

"*Air crunch!*" "*Ollie ugly!*" "*Tor*rid!"

Ziggy knew a few of the new urban core satori seekers—most people on the media/arts scene did—but had no close connections to their insular, albeit flamboyant, subculture. CitiZens mixed spiritual seeking with guerrilla art, merging the quest for self-understanding and the American obsession with high-tech action sports. It was unusual to see them on one of their outlaw runs in daylight, although the high-powered strips made bus ramps preferred targets.

They swept down on Ziggy in a snake-dancing line, their synthesizers and transducers keening and soughing juice song, played like musical instruments via body English, momentum, shifts in weight, and angle of attack. Observing them now, Ziggy understood why other names for a board were reed, blade, deck, and wand. The bolder ones were truly air-dancing, doing handstands and other competition moves.

The biggest of them was flying lead; he was the size of Lurch the Butler, attired in purple cossack shirt and baggy orange and green marble-patterned pantaloons. His bulging eyes, waxed mustache, and patriarchal brown beard gave him a nineteenth-century look. No helmet, of course; no true air-dancer wore safety equipment on a street run. Ziggy braced for a very short career as a crash-test dummy, but the man caught him up instead. Ziggy struggled instinctively but the CitiZen was gorilla-strong, expertly keeping his plank on course.

The air-dancer had a scratchy, surprisingly high-pitched voice: " 'Wheresoever I go I leave no footprint. For I am not within color or sound'—quoth Chikan Zenji. Relax, fellow traveler." He kicked out with his combat boot a few times to maintain speed.

That footprint part was debatable, and Ziggy thought the rad costumes and juice-singing sticks were a little too much color and sound to deny. On the other hand, as the pack broke out into an open platform level and split up, the police car peeled off to stay on other surfers. Also, there seemed to be a lot of confusion and near-collision among the buses due to traffic-control signal mix-ups, causing Ziggy to recall that SELMI had promised to set up what diversions were possible before withdrawing from the local systems.

The CitiZen swooped down ramps and through intersections without hesitation. Once, when his deck strayed out of the induction field, it recovered with the help of retractable polystyrene wheels that deployed when maglev failed. The law-enforcement dragnet thrown out for Ziggy must not have been coordinated with strip-surfers in mind; his savior exited the terminal on a second-level ramp, bound for Eleventh Avenue.

" 'The willow paints the wind/ Without using a brush'; where d'ya want me to drop ya, fellow traveler?"

EIGHTEEN

THE NAME ZIGGY'S CitiZen savior gave was WattAbout. Ziggy used an alias SELMI had provided, Wend Luge, as they sat together in the firelight three stories under midtown Manhattan. They were in an alcove near a steam tunnel in the subsurface maze that underlay Grand Central Terminal; other air-dancers from the Port Authority run drifted in as they talked.

"The point," WattAbout was saying, "is that Zen is *more* pertinent in this age of postindustrial anomie, not less. The purity of being and the artless art of selfhood."

"A-ha." Ziggy nodded politely. "Anyway, thanks for the hospitality. Ah, you mind if I use your phone?" SELMI had said to get out of Manhattan before attempting contact, but Ziggy had an edgy feeling about the CitiZen, and didn't want him to think Ziggy had no supporters.

WattAbout gestured to a niche where scavenged equipment had been patched into terminal utility systems. There was an incredibly what-was public phone—a pre-Turn street model. Its antivandal features were indicative of those times: built to accept phone cards only, with hands-free speaker grille so that there was no handset or cable, it was made of stainless steel and built to be flush-mounted. Now it lay on the ground with a counterfeit debit chip clipped to its pay slot. It was hooked up to a huge old widescreen TV that lacked innards of any kind.

As Ziggy moved to begin punching numbers, WattAbout added casually, "But who you gonna call—Ziggy?"

Ziggy glanced around, evaluating his chances of escape. There were an even half-dozen CitiZens between him and the only exit, and who knew how many others in the tunnels. "Some people we know and owe are looking for you," WattAbout added.

Ziggy's pulse was going at hummingbird speed. "What people?"

"Just call 'em Pesky Pizza for now."

"Ew, *crusty*," Ziggy murmured. "I'll, uh, just finish my call."

"I don't think so."

WattAbout's hairy finger pushed the disconnect and he shoved the patchwork phone aside. But as he was reaching for Ziggy the gutted widescreen came alive and Gipper Beidjie's telegeist face formed.

WattAbout and his companions froze, even more astonished than Ziggy. Gipper stood in on a windswept moor of low, dense blue moss broken by what looked like canary yellow hunks of semiopal as big as pieces of living-room furniture. In the background, a trio of gyrocopter-like flying creatures veered by. "How's things, Emu-cousin? And why ain't you on your way to Uluru?"

"I-I'm having a little trouble leaving," Ziggy admitted. WattAbout glanced at him in fright.

"Fair go! Get moving!" Gipper shot back. "The billy's on the boil. Who's that great larrikin there with ya?"

"Oo, uh, I'm WattAbout," the CitiZen fumbled.

"Wull, help Ziggy on his way, ya bleedin' ratshit." With that, the telegeist image faded.

When Brax hung up on Apterix Muldoon, he thought about attempting another call for help, but there was no one left to try.

Back outside, the car wash was in full swing. Hagadorn, happily soaked, was wringing out a chamois. "I take it from that face that you've seen the competing books, eh? Braxmar, stop torturing yourself."

He leaned on his car. "I told you your writing will play a vital role, and I meant it, but this isn't the moment. The time will come when Worlds Abound will be revealed to be the original and *only* series based on truth. And then the whole planet will flock to your *sequel* to *Gate Crashers*."

Brax frowned. "Provided I put the spin on it that you're telling me to."

Hagadorn laughed and draped the wrung-out rag over his shoulder. "Good god, Brax, the last thing I want to do is dictate a goddamn book!"

There was a hail from Fatima Bebe, who was waving Brax over to help her wax; Hagadorn drew him aside instead. "Look, go have a beer, think things over."

"If it's all the same to you, Phipps, I'd like to take a stroll along the beach, maybe jot down a few ideas while they're fresh in my mind."

Hagadorn looked at Brax with surprise and what Brax thought to be a trace of respect. "Even better. I'll give a call after the scut work's done here; you can get to know the others better."

A servant came to Hagadorn offering a videophone that had been disguised to look like a bulky 1950s transistor radio. "Sir, Madame Hagadorn inquires whether—"

Hagadorn's tone was cold as dry ice. "Did I not make it clear that I don't wish to be disturbed? Then explain it to Mrs. Hagadorn in words of one syllable."

By that time Brax was hastily getting out of earshot. When he'd fetched the carry sack containing his manuscript, two of the Brazil-trained Watchmen were waiting for him. "Desmond and Jerzy will show you the way," Hagadorn called with a killer smile, and Brax knew better than to object.

A rutted sandy path wandered down through bayberry, beach plums and beach roses to debouch onto the beach around the southeastern side of the Gay Head Cliffs. The Watchmen did a passable job of imitating fellow strollers as he set off northwest around the point, mulling what it was he wanted to write.

The soft, eroded slopes showed every Earth tone Brax could think of, including sulfurous-looking yellow, ashen grays, a slate gray-black, bone white, and an autumn palette of reds, rusts, browns, and ochers. Seafarers in the Age of Sail, seeing those colors, had given the cliffs their name. Gulls wheeled and, farther around the point, cormorants dove. Looking out to sea, he spied the Elizabeth Islands and the faraway blinking of the Buzzards Bay light.

At about the tip of the jut of beach below the cliffs, the Devil's Bridge lurked beneath the water, a ridge of stone and sand that had taken a wicked toll of shipwrecks and drownings. Farther along was a concrete box almost as big as Brax's loft cubicle, a sentry bunker that had been undermined and crashed down from above. It lay canted, partially buried in the sand in the intertidal zone next to a rock like an elephant's back. Nearby was one of the clay runoff pools where landholders sometimes slathered themselves.

Brax used the rock to scramble onto the slanted concrete roof. The breeze was light, so he didn't have too much trouble controlling the ostrich plume. Ignoring the break in his previous entry, he wrote,

Black Hole's interventions here on Earth, Adit Navel, over more years—or ages?—than anyone seems willing to put a number on, by all evidence have not had the effect the Agency was looking for and so, I'm told, the shadowy Founders have given the order to scram the experiment, bring tertiary planet Earth online as a fast-buck tourist trap.

It still evades me, this undefined goal of the Sysops. But in raising the ambient paranoia quotient of the human race and messing with our belief systems over, perhaps, eons, they've had an effect to which, for some reason, these "foul extenders" are evidently blind: they've evolved the human race into god seekers, par excellence. Maybe the best in the galaxy.

Hence the godhead we haven't been able to find, summon, or confront in millennia of trying, homo sapiens is starting to create for itself, by dint of the sheer intellectual and spiritual longing the Sysops have—inadvertently, it is my strong conviction—awakened in us.

Or if not, I'd like to hear a better explanation about where those Intubis are. No wonder Earth is suddenly so important. No wonder the Sysops are in crisis management mode.

What's giving me night sweats is the question of what happens if the foul extenders panic, because—

Brax stopped writing, distracted by the sound of a waterjet engine coming nearer. He blinked at what he'd written, fearing what might happen if Hagadorn read it or, worse, if the Founders did.

The gunning of the waterjet engine came closer yet and someone called his name. It took him a moment to understand that Gilda Hagadorn was veering toward the beach on a competition-model aqua scooter. The staut little watercraft had a minimal pillion saddle, but she was straddling it, working the handle pole to do a few nonchalant slalom turns and pirouettes. Brax recalled now that she was a champion at this sport too—a nationally ranked freestyler.

Desmond and Jerzy rematerialized; otherwise the beach was empty. Gilda wove between two boulders to beach the wave scooter with barely a ripple fifty feet from the fallen bunker. He could see a roll of gear lashed to the saddle and wondered if she'd come to picnic. Hagadorn's trophy wife dismounted with a lithe little jeté and sauntered toward him, golden hair soaked, designer flotation jacket making her look glamorously sporty, slide-front tonga bikini drawn narrow. She was staring at him unswervingly through fighter pilot shades.

"Braxmar, I'm so desperately bored! Come take a spin with me? I brought a spare vest and a shaker of margaritas."

Brax tried to decide how to decline gracefully—perhaps by mentioning that he wasn't wearing a swimsuit, though he was mortally afraid she'd dare him to ride bareass. Meanwhile, Jerzy strolled with casual alertness to one side of the bunker while Desmond went a few yards down the beach to intercept Gilda. "I'm afraid that won't be possible just now, Mrs. Hagadorn. Mr. Koddle is expected back at the car wash."

"Oh, pooh! Brax, I'll wait for you here, and in the meantime I can at last read this mysterious book of yours."

She'd started for the bunker again, but Desmond planted himself in her way with body language that said he was serious. "Sorry, madame, but Mr. Hagadorn wouldn't approve."

If Hagadorn began playing hardball and took the manuscript from him, he would gain what insight Brax had had into Black Hole's motives and possible vulnerabilities. It could only mean tragedy for Earth. Brax tuned out the argument between the Watchman and Gilda, thinking how he must prevent that. Gilda had reluctantly accepted defeat and was retreating to her wavescoot with a pretense of good grace. Brax, manuscript roll clutched to him, eased toward the edge of the bunker in the direction of the clay pool.

Jerzy stood blocking his way. "Careful there, Mr. Koddle; you wouldn't want to drop your book and get it all messy. I'd better take it for you."

Brax tried to edge back. "No, that's all right—"

Jerzy got a hold of his ankle with a move swift and deft as an adder's strike. "Mr. Hagadorn's orders, Mr. Koddle."

Brax had no illusions about being able to overpower one Watchman, much less two. He didn't need to overpower them, however; he only needed to destroy what he'd written.

In desperation, therefore, Brax kicked out with his free foot, only to have Jerzy grab it in the other hand and drag Brax inexorably closer, facing Brax with the choice of tossing the roll away or letting it be pulled into the Watchman's reach. Before Brax could make up his mind, Jerzy let go and spun, and Brax was left scrabbling against nothing as he realized there'd been a scream and two loud sounds coming close together—the first a flat slap, the second muffled and seeming to throb through the air.

Gilda Hagadorn was standing in a relaxed, hips-forward position with her cheek pressed to the adjustable stock of the Daimler-Anschutz target rifle she'd used to win the Olympic biathlon gold. She cycled the Fortner bolt action: flick back with the forefinger, forward again with the thumb, the other three fingers staying where they were on the grip—the weapon might as well have been semi-automatic. A new round chambered while the expended cartridge was still in the air, and she swung the muzzle Brax's way and fired again.

He flinched and yelped as Jerzy, three feet away, shrieked in pain. The guard's body thudded as if a truck had slammed it, falling back with its chest blown open, still clutching a carbon-black revolver.

Gilda was walking Brax's way, covering him with the Anschutz. "Braxmar, this is all the fault of that sadistic, stingy husband of mine. However, I know some very *generous* people who greatly desire to read what you've written."

He got slowly to his feet, still hugging to his chest all that existed of *Gate Crashers*. "W-what people?"

"Later; come down, please, don't make me kill you, too."

Gilda didn't really understand about his kenaf roll, otherwise she wouldn't have given him the freedom of movement she did. Deciding that he was altogether too likely to die once she got her hands on it anyway, Brax pushed the roll up into the air as if he were making a free throw from the foul line. The twin-spooled roll unwound a little in flight, landed with a modest splash in the clay pool stained nicotine yellow by runoff from the Gay Head Cliffs, and began to sink quickly. Dear Father in heaven, Brax thought. It's gone and I could never remember it all, never re-create what it was, never.

Gilda shouldered the ergo-tailored target rifle again, and very nearly shot. "I expected better from you; that pool is quite shallow, and all you've done is given someone the tedious job of scraping the scrolls clean."

He'd been right. "It's not mylar composite, you know; it's handmade wrapping paper, *porous* paper, and old-fashioned vegetable ink."

"You treacherous twerp! Fetch it here or I shall blow your leg off!"

He made haste to obey. Stained muddy yellow from knees to soles and elbows to fingertips, he tossed it before her. She stirred the coagulated mass of the two scrolls with a bare, gold-nailed toe, one glance enough to convince her.

She glanced up again and Brax saw his own frightened face in her shades. "Walk to the scooter, Brax."

He was about to ask her how she was planning to keep him covered with the rifle and steer the aqua scooter at the same time—drag him along by a lifeline, maybe?—when a dark shape came zazzing out from above the cliffs in a sharp dive and swung wide over the water. The barracuda-shaped black helicopter slowed and banked, searching.

Brax backed away from Gilda, raising his hands although she'd never asked him to. "Hadn't you ought to be leaving?"

She aligned the bore of the Daimler-Anschutz with his chest but then lowered it with a look of resignation. "These people *do* want to talk to you, Brax; if they didn't, I'd kill you for being so stingy. Keep that in mind."

She turned and sprinted light-footed for her wave skier, reaching it just as the helo came in for a pass. Brax stood his ground, hands raised, watching as Gilda shouldered the rifle and fired three more shots, not pausing in between as she would have on the target range. One of the explosive .22s scored in a flowering of fire on the chopper's NOTAR tail but only managed to make the craft fishtail; built to take hits, it swung for another pass.

With its magazine empty and no time to reload, Gilda slung the Anschutz over her head and one shoulder, hopped the wetbike, and whooshed out between the rocks, bound for deep water. Between the Gay Head beach and the faraway Elizabeths the water was open and without sanctuary; Brax thought she was as good as sunk.

As the helo bore down for the kill, however, Gilda showed her championship stuff. Tossing her rifle away and hopping the ski off an incoming swell, she drew in her feet and angled the machine's rounded nose cowling downward without leaning her body. The scoot plunged under the surface like a torpedo, so deep that Brax lost sight of her—a classic "submarine," a virtuoso stunt of the freestyle repertoire.

A burst of automatic fire pocked the water where she would have been; the NOTAR swooped by, puffs of smoke slipstreaming away from its door gunner's assault rifle. The wetbike dragged Gilda to the surface again, shedding water and foam, its electric bilge pump spitting out brine. She dropped one leg back off the footrest tray to catch her balance, then opened the throttle once more.

But she was riding a vessel that had a top end of only seventy mph; the helo was a lot faster. It swung wide to come back in at her along her own course, slowing and descending. Brax wondered if the crew would give her a chance to surrender or if Hagadorn had opted for a no-frills annulment.

He never found out. Something broke from the waves to describe a straight line of orange-yellow flame and gray smoke through the air, straight to the thermal bull's-eye that was the jet-engine exhaust of the helo, which came apart in a fireball so violent that it knocked Brax back, deafened. Burning wreckage fell and a shape parted the swells near Gilda, who'd dived or been blown from her wetbike.

The submersible remained with upper hull awash, showing only enough conning tower for her to clamber aboard. It crash-dived again even as she was yanking the hatch shut. The burning scraps of the NOTAR had already disappeared.

NINETEEN

"THESE LITTLE BLOBBY bits are delicious," observed the Graad, ingesting another piece of the pirate's still-warm body and popping its eating orifices in approval. "I'm told they're an aphrodisiac."

"Is that so?" The hulking M'lung stroked its chin with spiked, bone-plated fingers, feeling its serrated tusks. "Any more around?"

The Graad surveyed the bloody swath of human remains that made the helo pad of the cruise ship *Crystal Harmonic* look like an open-air abattoir. "Uh-uh," the Graad concluded. "They only have two apiece, you know—insufficient redundancy, if you ask me, for reproductive equipment."

The M'lung rolled his eyes in comic exasperation. "Humans!" They sniggered. "Ahoy there, Vogonskiy!" the M'lung called out. "Now *this* was fast food!"

The huge, bearded master of stage magic was looking on with great glee, stroking his white gorget of beard. "Oh, quite; sixty knots or better when the tractor beam grabbed them. Do be careful not to swallow any grenades or whatnot; don't want any of our passengers going ill."

There'd been eight pirates in all, skimming in at the themer ship as she plowed through calm seas two hundred and fifty nautical miles northwest of Cam Ranh Bay, Vietnam, bound for Japan. They'd attacked in a swift little hydrofoil mounting jamming equipment, missile launcher, and autocannon—Asian Rim 'breeds waving assault weapons, dressed in camouflage loincloths and web gear, plastic gimme caps and reed sampan hats, possessed of gold teeth, elaborate tattoos, and jeweled Rolexes.

The ship's tried-and-true response was a replay of the tractor-beam ride that had captured Sean Junknowitz and his friends and been such a smash, only this time Vogonskiy had turned the captives over to some of the more gustatorily curious passengers.

The thought of Sean, Willy, Eddie, and other victims awaiting him on End Zone made Vogonskiy chafe to be there, but there was no helping it for now; there was too much to do aboard the *Harmonic*. At least his Vietnamese government contacts had covered up the incident in the Cam Ranh warehouse, with a paltry two extreme terminations required. But there was no word as to the whereabouts of the aerospacecraft that had assembled itself in the warehouse, or Lucky Junknowitz's former tour group, who'd fled aboard it.

He was about to summon Tumi but, true to form, the M'finti showed up at his elbow just then. "Sir, urgent communication, requiring your presence." Next to Vogonskiy's corpulent mass the homunculus looked even smaller, a bulb-headed fellow with purplish skin mottled as if by grafts and excisions.

Belowdecks and slightly forward, Vogonskiy settled into a chair by the Adit installation for a direct tunnel-vision connection to Light Trap itself and a talk with Llesh Llerrudz, the touchy but tremendously influential little Nall who ran the agency's Troughs and Adits division. Next to Llerrudz was his recording secretary and factotum, the gleamer Barb Steel.

For an ostensible executive assistant the metalflesh had a chilling look to him, all sawtoothed flanges, razor edges, and spiked armorplate, with a battery of fingers like lancets, flensing blades, or hawkbill knives. His face was a smooth curve of metal with slit eyes as red as taillights. Llerrudz's alloy demon always gave Vogonskiy a stirring of unease; the magician could throw death into an organic opponent, but against Barb Steel his options would be few.

"How are preparations going?"

"Splendidly." Vogonskiy tried not to sweat. "All of Phoenix, the movie crowd, our little Sony-Neuhaus lambs—what a night on Bald Mountain *this* will be!"

"Fine! Got a few things to clear up first, some nonsense about those wandering Intubi savages. I'm moving my arrival time back, join you just about the time you hit that Japan Sea Acropolis. Want to see that place."

Vogonskiy made sure to conceal his pleasure at the news. "Well, we look forward to your arrival *whenever* it comes, sir."

But when the tunnel-vision link was concluded he slammed his meaty, double-X-large hands together with delight. "A whole extra day before he gets here!" He turned and slipped Tumi a wink. "Let's square away whatever needs it, then slip away to End Zone and roust our diverse playmates a bit."

Still, he'd have to be back well in advance of Llerrudz's arrival, and at the top of his game. Vogonskiy still wasn't sure why the Sysops were so interested in this clockwork orange of a tertiary world. As he brooded over the matter his hand blurred and he dealt himself a fortune card. There was a cryptic symbol on its face:

Emlarre and the other Pay Dirt Sasquatch women waded back from their caucus in the heated pool to where Nikkei was rinsing off Miss Sato as she sat with perfect poise on the little wooden stool.

"Sato, it's a deal," Emlarre announced. "We'll iron out the details after we unwind a little more, fade back to Pay Dirt this afternoon." With that she and her furry sisters trundled back to the suite's party room, dripping heedlessly.

Nikkei sluiced a last bucket of warm water over Sato's neck, nape, and back, wrenched by the ineffable grace of them. As she sat motionless he leaned over her, not letting himself breathe, wishing he could live in that one poetic moment forever but half-insane with the need to move beyond it. The only sound in the *o-furo* was the slow, echoing drip of water; time dilated around his hesitation and contemplation, so excruciating and yet unspeakably moving and erotic. He hated to let that moment pass but at length couldn't restrain himself, *had* to press his lips to her nape. She turned her head a little, tacitly offering the line of her shoulder and, beyond it, the poised throat.

Not caring if he'd gone crazy, Nikkei gripped both her shoulders, raining kiss after kiss on her. Sato let the towel fall and reached to tangle her fingers in his hair. She drew him down onto the wet tile.

Being Sato, she rolled him onto his back, kissed him hard on the mouth, then went matter-of-factly to throw the bolt on the door. She came back letting her hair down, surprised him by diving onto him, and threw herself into lovemaking with such hunger that he couldn't understand how she'd hidden it, though he was certain he knew why.

They dared each other to bolder and bolder moves; Nikkei's head swam and he lost any concept of who he was, or where—or why, beyond what was happening between them. He came before she did but deeper needs gripped him and he drew her, lifted her to climax once, and again. He'd have persisted, but she stopped him unequivocally; he rolled onto his back and they lay catching their breath on the wet tiles.

The door opened and Mickey Formica sauntered in. "Sorry there, y'all. Got word from Tanabe-san to pass along, and them Pay Dirters pointed me in here." It wasn't the first time one partner had wandered in while the other was making the Sign of the Twin-Dorsaled Truffle Seeker—as they were wont to put it—so Mickey was bewildered by the irate look Nikkei shot him.

Miss Sato nonchalantly rose and pulled a bath sheet around herself. "He contacted *you*. And the message?"

"Must not be hurt as bad as they thought," Nikkei heard Mickey say as he examined the door bolt Sato had thrown. It was no surprise that Willow World locks could be controlled from elsewhere, but Tanabe's bypassing a direct call to Sato to use Mickey as courier—and have him walk in on them in flagrante—was a message in and of itself. He didn't bother looking for the surveillance gear that must be there—that he'd known deep down, all along, to be there.

"Anyhow, there's lots to square away," Mickey reported, "before our festive cruise aboard Hagadorn's flyin' *Deutsch*man. F'rinstance, everybody got their donor card filled out?"

TWENTY

NMUTH IV, KNOWN locally as Playpen, was proof the Black Hole Travel Agency wasn't all-powerful; otherwise the Sysops would have cranked out balmy, wave-washed cloneworlds by the hundreds. Nmuth IV's perfection had even spared it the usual fate of being developed, promoted, and exploited to ruination; instead it was set aside as a resort-retirement planet for the select few who'd served the Agency or otherwise qualified.

Sobek had no time for the beauty of it, however. Discipline Di had taken the last rental aircraft on Sweet Breath Island, and, anyway, the airgondolas were notoriously slow. That was why Sobek had transmogrified. He had a different mode of transport in mind.

The express clerk, a three-eyed, biped Donagul from Farx, protested. "I can't ship a sentient being in a courier drone!"

Sobek drew himself up to his full height, currently two feet three inches, his multiple claws scrabbling at the floor. "What I ship is my business. Or shall I complain and have you reassigned?"

Nobody wanted to be reassigned off Playpen, so the clerk shut Sobek—who'd taken the millipede form of an Estran—into the robot sky torpedo and launched it at its destination. The acceleration and rough ride didn't bother Sobek's Estran body; he made great time, and was transmogrifying again even as the courier drone popped open in its receiver bay.

Though he was prepared to deal with them, he drew no challenge from the villa's autodefenses. He was now soundless and scentless, nearly impossible to see or otherwise detect; he'd assumed the body of a Pangchang, a consummate jungle stalker from Harmpit, a favorite of his despite its obvious drawback: the creature was not well endowed for combat.

The house was spacious, a Playpen-style mansion with the expensive reconfiguration systems that could, he knew, open up various sections like an origami, shuffling walls and roofs to permit enjoyment of the planet's lovely weather. Sobek stole along walls of stained ceramic glass, past living-metal dynamic sculptures and energy fountains. He saw artifacts and works of art from up and down the Trough, and one whole room devoted to trophies from Adit Navel—Earth—including a seated Buddha six feet high. Then Sobek heard shouts and a scream, sounds of impact, shattered glass, and breaking furniture.

He followed them with utmost stealth, easing one optical antenna around a doorframe. Miss Diandra Abbott stood with her back to the door, confronting two beach-clothed Adit Navel humans of advanced years—in their baseline seventies, according to Light Trap files. The man was slack-skinned but tanned, lying on the floor with a bleeding scalp. His wife, silver-haired and slight, knelt next to him.

"For the last time, we don't know any Ka Shamok!" The woman wept.

Miss Diandra showed that lashing black tongue again, throwing down a small, flat wooden case, which broke open to scatter three precision-made darts and reveal a little brass plate. " 'To Ka Shamok and good new days, Jacob Riddle,' " she read out loud. "Recovered from an abandoned base under a Spectarr Two lava chamber."

"I don't know anything about this!" said Jacob Riddle, Black Hole retiree and onetime Quick Fix partner.

"I think," Miss Diandra nodded, "this will persuade you." But as she went for Teleen Riddle, Sobek was already in midpounce. It wasn't that the old woman's life was of any significance to him; he acted because the Riddles represented a possible source of information and because other matters required his neutralizing the other Probe in any event.

He reshaped himself into an Yggdraasian, snatching her off her feet and hurling her at the nearest wall. Sobek felt confident of his ability to deal with her, an inexperienced opponent. So it was a distinct shock to him when she transformed as she flew, becoming a ferocious Megabite, a pseudosaurian triped from Bile Bath, absorbing the collision with the wall with ease and launching herself back at him, slavering, her enhanced Probe senses telling her with whom she was dealing.

The bigger Megabite bore Sobek backward, ripping at the wadded Ygg muscles of his shoulder with fanged jaws. He used all his Ygg brawn to roll backward as he went down, snapping and slicing at her with his great lobster claws, bridging to heave the Megabite clear. He considered going to even greater size—a Schoovian boneripper, for example—but went another way instead. As an oily, sinewy Pannab razor-eel, he slithered up the Megabite's leg, stinging and slashing. Teleen was helping her husband crawl to the shelter of a monolithic stone chair, since the combatants were blocking the only door.

Miss Diandra became a saw-jawed Lapoot to Sobek's razor-eel, immune to his venom and barbed-handed to pluck at him. He thickened to a rock-leech, burrowing into her; she went to hydra-mass, melting away, then came back at him as centaur-scorpion Vymex. So the battle raged, form and re-form, as much lethal guessing contest and Russian roulette game as trial by combat: if either manifested a bioform that gave quick, overwhelming advantage—or correctly anticipated the other's shapeshift and countertransmogged—that would end it. The only limitations were the dimensions of the room and the life-forms' ability to survive and fight in that environment.

Beings that had never confronted one another in nature now tore and fought, metamorphed to something else, came on again. There had never, as far as Sobek knew, been such a battle between Probes. The furniture was soon smashed and the walls were stove in and shredded. Discipline Di was amazingly quick and apt, as if she had an upgraded version of his own powers. At last she caught him a butt with her horned head in Ramrock form, just as he opened a great wound in her side. She transmogged to heal the wound as he bounced off the wall and smashed his jutting Eviloot chin on the floor.

As Sobek's vision cleared, he saw Jacob Riddle crouched behind an overturned table a few feet away, laboring over the control circuitry behind a plate he'd removed from the console. His head was still seeping blood; whispering, "Night Fiend," Jacob jerked a thumb in the direction of Discipline Di, who was still in the throes of change.

Sobek understood, and decided he had nothing to lose. When he threw himself at his opponent again it was as a Mo'Oii, gelidly baggy and moist, its toxic palps slithering before it. Discipline Di hesitated and Sobek despaired; if she went to, say, Angler Wing, she'd dice him to bits before he could go to another shape.

Then she took the bait instead, becoming a grunting, pallid and leprous Night Fiend from Seep, coming for him. But she shrieked hideously as fierce Nmuth sunlight inundated her, the room's ceiling having origamied open at Jacob Riddle's command.

Sobek was already retreating, changing. As with any real Fiend, the direct touch of UV was all-paralyzing to her and all-painful. When Sobek went at her again it was as a Sicklebeast, and he didn't stop until she was in pieces too small to reassemble themselves easily. He went about killing each piece as Jacob and Teleen Riddle, leaving the sunroof open, armed themselves with energy tools and helped. Sobek touched each fragment of her, merged with it, before he obliterated it. There was very little coherence left to her—that was why she couldn't recover—but he found one scrap of cognitive essence that elated him, a sort of password-ID.

It was for up-Trap systems, where the SIs served and the Sysops ruled.

"Perhaps I didn't make myself clear." Phipps Hagadorn was reasoning with Brax in a chillingly gentle voice as they sat together in the Meadow Suite garden. He was contemplating the yellow-brown, wet papier-mâché mess on the white wrought-iron table—what had been the manuscript of *Gate Crashers* until an hour before. "I want you to tell me, right now, what it was you wrote today, what it was that my wi—that caused such unpleasantness."

Brax had been listening for the distant sound of more depth charges; he hadn't heard any in fifteen minutes and now concluded that the search for the submersible had been called off. That Gilda and whoever backed her had gone to such pains to examine the manuscript reinforced Brax's conviction that he'd been right in destroying *Gate Crashers*, but that didn't take away the vast and forever irreparable loss he felt. Surely the stillbirth of a child felt like this.

Hagadorn had no sympathy. His spun-gold eyebrows beetled at Brax's morose silence. "Your call, Brax. I'd hoped to have more time to win you to my camp, but events are moving rather more rapidly than I'd prefer. Tomorrow we depart for *Crystal Harmonic*; the trip will give you an opportunity to reconsider. To help you concentrate, I'll give you some vivid proof of what it means to oppose me and the Black Hole Travel Agency. Dr. Folatre?"

A man in bathing suit and beach jacket, who'd been hovering to one side sipping mango juice since Brax had been dragged back to Meadow Suite, came over. Dr. Folatre was energetic and slim with a bandito mustache, his receding black hair a mass of quirkish kinks, his grin whimsical and sly.

"Braxmar, dear fellow," Hagadorn said, "if you think there's a thriving black market for bioreplacements on Earth you should see what various body parts will fetch in the Trough—vigorous, well-muscled limbs and healthy, unpolluted organs. Biosynergics seldom measure up and are usually too expensive; cloned tissue has an unfortunate tendency to develop rejection problems. And a lot of busy people can't afford to wait around for regeneration. With Dr. Folatre's help I've developed quite a profitable subsidiary business exporting bodies or parts thereof to the Trough."

Dr. Folatre flicked his fingers and averted his eyes modestly. Hagadorn went on. "The demand—unbelievable. Trough middlemen will buy anything decent I can procure. Now, when I catch up with Gilda, Brax, that's where her lovely little body will be going, presorted! And you? Well, first I grant you a chance to reconsider. To aid you in your meditation, Dr. Folatre will employ a spot of Trough biotech."

Hagadorn made a signal to a quartet of his Watchmen. Brax was seized, his struggles availing nothing, but the working-over he was expecting never came. He was spread-eagled on his belly over the white wrought-iron table; Folatre shot a pneumodermic into the base of his skull. By the time the Watchmen released their hold he couldn't have stood up if he'd wanted to.

"What, what—" The words came out of him thick and shapeless as a crude-oil spill. The Watchmen dragged over a coffin-sized capsule that didn't smack of any Earth technology Brax knew of; Dr. Folatre made adjustments to it.

"Just 'one to grow on.' " He heard Hagadorn chuckle. "Or rather, to shrivel and to transmog."

Brax tried to focus on something, anything, but found he couldn't see. He was sobbing all the curses and pleas he could think of; none came from his lips in any recognizable shape.

"We're going to give you a whole new look, Braxmar," Hagadorn explained. "After which you and I will discuss literature." To the Watchmen he said, "Right; can him."

Brax felt himself jammed into the capsule and had the dim sensation of thick, cold wetness rising all around him. He gurgled and prayed, not wanting to drown, but drowned anyway.

TWENTY-ONE

JACOB RIDDLE INSISTED Sobek call him "Jay." Sobek, back in human form with not a mark on him, studied the Riddles curiously; few Adit Navel natives knew of the Trough, fewer still had visited the Trough, and almost none had retired there.

Jacob had recovered the incriminating darts and case. "I guess it was a mistake, giving Ka Shamok these, but I felt sorry for him." He rubbed his thumb across Ka Shamok's name on the little brass plate. "Poor purple bastard, I still do."

Mrs. Riddle touched his shoulder and said, "You can be such a pushover, Jay."

When the Probe told the Riddles about ongoing events on Earth, especially the closing of the Quick Fix Adit, Jacob nodded his head. "We *knew* something was wrong because our daughter Molly would never go so long without visiting or getting in touch. Telecaster Astrodynamics tried to tell us she moved. Transit Association and Trauma Advisory gave us the runaround, and just yesterday Trough Admin denied us travel permits for Earth—wouldn't even sell us tourist visas! After we gave their damned Quick Fix the best years of our lives—"

Teleen quieted her husband. "Can you help us, Mr. Sobek?" she implored.

The Riddles were a possible asset, so their survival was to be desired. "I think your best course of action is to remain here," he said soberly. "The Probe we killed was operating on her own and I don't think anyone will trace her here when she's missed. More to the point, events are escalating rapidly and you should avoid the foci of conflict."

Jay was shaking his head. "Not when our Molly may need us. We have to get back to Earth, but they're never gonna let us through that *Crystal Harmonic* Adit. I want you to take me to Ka Shamok."

* * *

Harley and Sheena could have found the battle even without the tracks of DeSoto's ground-pounder contingent to follow through the wasteland valley of broken washes and ravines.

The streams of flame-gel, corkscrewing rockets, beams, and arcing tracers were hard to miss; they were like a counterpoint to the low overcast of eerie radiation streamers and phosphorescent vortices called the worldwinds. The Hazmatians' radio traffic was constant, and *Iron Ram* and *Death Walker* automatically maintained IFF fixes on DeSoto's units. The ground-pounders appeared to be jamming the enemy frequencies, so the Humanosaurs DeSoto had mentioned remained an unknown.

The ground-pounders' transmissions told a chaotic story. "Green Ghoul gun team at the foot of the scarp!" "On my way." "Doom Demons in fighting holes in the dunes; fall back on my position." "*Piper* and *Long Gun*, enfilading fire on that berm!"

There were also IFF fixes on what Sheena concluded to be the Vigilance Bureau police mobes whose wearers had betrayed the ground-pounders in the sepulcher; they were winking out one by one even as DeSoto's people were fighting through to them. From what Harley had seen of the combat troops' attitude, they'd have happily let the police perish if they weren't in possession of the fabled memory egg and the person of Guard-Marshal Packard, DeSoto's boss and something of a living legend.

The two offworlders picked their way across the valley with as much haste and caution as they could combine, agreeing that they were in no hurry actually to reach the scene of the combat before the carnage was over. Humanosaurs, classed by designations like Kongs and Blue Bounders and Mauve Maulers, were not beings either one was eager to get to know.

From what the two could piece together, Inspector Nash had left his cops in the lurch, fleeing for the hidden underground transit terminal with the memory egg as his prize. DeSoto was in hot pursuit. Then a new voice, gravelly and feisty, came over the tactical net, pronouncing Harley's and Sheena's names awkwardly. "You're the Trough envoys? Good—we need to talk. Just hold your present course and stay alert; we've broken the ambush, but there're stragglers. We're starting back for you right now. Packard, out."

Picking her way through a haunted planetscape of malformed, stunted vegetation and sandblasted rock, Harley reflected that this Packard sounded pretty upbeat for a man who'd just been sprung from an imprisoning E-cap. She was also concentrating hard on staying upright, and so missed something that came up on her out of nowhere and slammed smack into her. *Death Walker* was sent reeling sideways by sheer brute impact, but so was the creature who'd blundered into it, which could only be a Humanosaur—a two-legged beast fifteen feet tall, armed and armored.

The metallic impact when the monster hit the much bigger ground-pounder must've come from the convex right triangle of a shield on its left arm; the shield was dented and partly stove in now, showing various notches and pockmarks plus what Harley took for two jagged bullet holes. The 'Saur staggered, its head wobbling; it was appallingly ugly, and waved a crude-looking handgun that crackled and sputtered ineffectually. Its saber scabbard was empty. Still repulsed by the idea of using weapons of war, Harley high-sticked it with the metal pole she'd taken up back at the sepulcher; the 'Saur went down on its rear end, head bonking a boulder, and seemed unable to rise.

The face beneath the dented helmet brim was a cross between a missing link and a comic-book supervillain; the 'Saur had pebbly purple-gray hide, musculature like a bull's, and black hairs thick as quills that showed through rips and gaps in its crude armor-uniform panoply.

As she was going to hit the creature again, it dawned on Harley that the brute was *hors de combat*: red-black stains made its coarse garments sodden and she could see at least one place where a hole had been ripped in its surcoat of metal scale armor.

The ogre let the electric gun fall from its grip. Over an external audio pickup, Harley caught its bubbling growl as it groped drunkenly at a mammoth belt-knife sheath, the weapon itself long gone. Harley approached it uncertainly, keeping a five-yard distance and clutching her metal pole. The monster left off trying to fight, and tore at its collar stock with thick, dark-nailed fingers.

Starved for air, it ripped open surcoat and mail jerkin two-handed, blood streaming down its front. Harley absorbed two more profound shocks; the first was that the beast glowered up hatefully at her through half-closed eyes and slurred, "Go on then, metal-man! Race-slayer, finish me! Genocide's all you're good at anyway . . ."

The second stunner was that the 'Saur was plainly female.

Nikkei and Sato, dressing quickly in the *o-furo*, wrongly assumed Mickey was going to leave with them.

"Sorry, gotta go. Meetchu at the exec building. Beautiful lady;

G-bro." He bowed out with a subtle fingertalk sign to Nikkei: *Don't ask; play along.* He was thinking of the Scheherazade hologram and what she'd told him about the "dimly white world." If Sato was Takuma Tanabe's personal oral pacifier, Mickey and his pard were in one shitotic bubblegum crisis—a sticky dilemma that was expanding rapidly and would inevitably explode.

He pondered that while he was on the move—back to Takuma Tanabe's hospital room. Tanabe was alert and energetic; Mickey stood at an uncomfortable parade-rest. "Did just like you said."

Tanabe gazed at him unblinkingly. "Oh?"

"Yessir; damn straight."

It had hurt, holding out on Nikkei, but Tanabe's instructions had been implicit. Nikkei's father had appeared in place of the Scheherazade holo in the Arabian Nights room, telling Mickey to roust Nikkei and Sato and say absolutely nothing more. Mickey knew cock-sure he was being tested, and was discovering that absolute, ninja-style fealty was rough to try to deliver in partial measure.

"And did you observe anything of which you think I should be informed?" Tanabe asked quietly.

Mickey caught himself before he could use the old stall of repeating the question back. Tanabe had proved he could monitor events in the Willow World; he likely knew about that little organ-grinding session in the bath. "Nothin' but naked skin, like in any *o-fudo*. Plus a truckload o' hairy space bootie."

"Is that all?"

"Wasn't there long enough to notice nothin' else."

"Mmm. Certain words and actions of Nikkei's and Miss Sato's have given me reason to question their loyalty. You'll therefore monitor them carefully from now on without telling them you're doing so, understood?"

Mickey swallowed and nodded. "Loud and clear."

"Should punitive action be required of you, I'll expect you to live up to the loyalty you swore to me."

Mickey suspected that if he so much as hesitated, he wouldn't leave the room alive. So he nodded again, slowly. "A promise is a promise."

"Just so." Tanabe's stare relented just a little. "Now, I've another assignment for you, something with rather more appeal, I believe."

TWENTY-TWO

INSPECTOR NASH'S ESCAPE by way of Hazmat's sub-surface transit system was a catastrophe, but Guard-Marshal Packard could hardly blame DeSoto or anyone else for that. After all, it had been *his* dream to reactivate the Adit and solicit help from the Trough.

Instead there'd been betrayal by the Vigilance Bureau police, and now Nash had fled with the memory egg. Worse yet, he'd blown up the transit station behind him, leaving Packard and his ground-pounders stranded hundreds of miles away from the next nearest station, with Humanosaurs and Warhead thirsty for their blood. On the other hand, the Adit *had* worked; but what good that would do Hazmat's hard-pressed human populace remained to be seen.

At least the gaitmobe wearers controlled the immediate area in the wake of the battle with the 'Saur ambushers, but more of the fiends were doubtless pouring in from everywhere to finish the job. The one ray of hope in the whole situation was the two women who'd faded in from the Trough. Lacking *Stomper*, his personal main battle-mobe, Packard had himself borne to the rendezvous with Harley and Sheena in the careful mechano hands of *Strider*, DeSoto's mech.

They homed in on the offworlders' beacons to find *Death Walker*, the gaitmobe Harley had been wearing, hunkered down and resting on its knuckles, field-access style, its plastron open. A little closer, *Iron Ram* stood barring the ground-pounders' way. Next to Sheena's gaitmobe a wounded Humanosaur—a Mauve Mauler—sat tailor-fashion, slumped with her back to a rock, wounds bound in a make-do manner.

Poised with one foot on either of the Mauler's armored knees, blocking any clear shot, stood Harley Paradise, dismounted from *Death Walker*. She waited with arms spread protectively, hockey stick in one hand, her hair whipped and flayed by the hot barrens wind. Though she was trying not to show it, one of her prime worries was that the creature would shift its knees and she'd take a fall—both because the mechs might then open fire and for the ignominy of it.

Packard hopped down: he was a commanding, energetic little man with a gaitmobe wearer's shaved scalp and forelock, scarred and tough. "Get away from that abomination before it rips you apart."

"Does she *look* like she wants to kill me?" Harley ventured a thin smile, wondering what her coworkers back at the Gender Bias Council would think if they could see her now. There'd been office vitriol as to whether a woman with Harley's spokesmodel looks and Twenty-One life-style really qualified as a feminist, but if laying her neck on the line for another woman didn't prove the courage of her convictions she didn't know what would.

Packard was at a loss, and couldn't afford to have her shot. Harley went on. "Wouldn't you like to tell her, first, why you drove the Humanosaurs out of paradise, torture and eat prisoners, and want to exterminate her people?"

"You're mad!" DeSoto's external speakers rattled. "The birthworks-grown mutants are the ones who commit those atrocities!"

"That's not what Zozosh, here, says." Harley gave a toss of her head to indicate the Mauler.

Packard's jaw dropped. " 'Zozosh' *says*? Are you trying to say you know its name? Such monsters cannot speak a human tongue, and no one can talk theirs!"

"*We* can," Harley contradicted.

"It is an offworld language, one we know, but not humanoid at all," Sheena added. It wasn't the moment to explain about their nanites' gift of speech.

Sheena uttered a string of interrogative 'Saurtalk and Zozosh answered. "She says Warhead decrees that human and Humanosaur must never communicate, only fight—but she has no choice except to listen to us. She's told us other facts as well, and if you're wise you'll hear her out."

Packard rubbed his jaw, ignoring DeSoto's protests. "We need a place where we can hear ourselves talk."

To Willy Ninja, the flop-eared little Jamff he and Riiv were trying to life-sing looked like nothing so much as a heavily mildewed and water-damaged stuffed toy, a cross between teddy bear and shar-pei, decaying in rags and tatters. But with Riiv and her mental note implant carrying him, and the old high end of his range back, he held to the music and saw the Jamff rally a little.

Onlooking End Zoners of all descriptions, gathered at a respectful distance, were feeling the music, too. Nearly all had been ministered to either by Riiv alone or in concert with Willy. As had been happening more and more, it was Willy who made the music come alive. He had no idea why he should be copacetic with an implant inside a serpentine XT, but it was so; a sheer gift for song, perhaps.

Riiv wasn't envious; if she had been, Willy would've sensed it in their synergy. Instead she rejoiced that his vocal and mental notes helped alleviate suffering. Still and all, the best they could do against Vogonskiy's death-swipes, even for themselves, was ease pain or bring on brief remission. Riiv was fading a little with each life-song.

As the Jamff hobbled away Willy heard applause. Sean Junknowitz was standing there along with Eddie Ensign, the mummylike Yanvur, and Yanvur's adherents. Sean stopped clapping, his smile toothy among the tribal tattoos, the scars and bruiselike lesions, the leprous patches, and the tattered buntings of dead skin. He'd torn and knotted the remaining rags of his clothes into loincloth, arm and leg ties, and browband. He had his leather medicine pouch around his neck, and wore fetishes of XT teeth, feathers, stingers, claws, and such.

When Sean had returned to the States from Dos Lagunas, that *inoperância* anarchic region deep in the Brazilian Amazon *sertao*, he'd reminded Willy of the Herculean, piratical, ultravirile Jose Arcadio in *One Hundred Years of Solitude*. Now, however, the bulging arms and thick wrists were sticklike, the muscular chest shrunken. Lucky's ex-leatherneck brother still had the *mal ojo* badass look, though—the unblinking wanna-rumble? stare.

"You are the song, man." He gestured to Willy.

"Hi, Sean. Feeling better?"

"Feelin' just fine, thought you'd heard," Sean said, an edge to his voice letting Willy know he ought to tread carefully.

"Good." Riiv nodded, a mannerism she'd picked up from Willy. "Will you stay and commune in song? And you, Yanvur?"

Yanvur let out a sound like a straw sucking the bottom of a

soda, which Willy interpreted as amusement. "Your singalong is over, Riiv."

Willy clutched a worm-eaten drumming stick. "Now, look—"

"Rheo down, Willy," Sean cut in, waving Yanvur off. "Yanvur figures Vogonskiy's overdue on End Zone. You'n Riiv throw in with us and we'll kick his ass. Otherwise he wins."

All the Zoners were listening silently. "We've been through this," Riiv reminded Yanvur quietly. "I can *do no harm*; that's my nature and my art."

Yanvur showed a grin that was all rotted gums. "Even if Vogonskiy flays you with your own skin, bellycrawler?"

"That's enough!" Willy warned. He looked to Sean. "There're other codes of conduct just as brave as yours, y'know."

"Not if they surrender to an asshole like Vogonskiy."

Eddie Ensign sighed. "Willy, if we don't help each other it won't matter whose heart's purer. Vogonskiy's gonna do his command performance from hell with us at stage center."

Riiv had coiled herself, head resting wearily on her own back. "There's no helping that."

"You resist Vogonskiy," Yanvur pounced, "but never strike back! No harm done to Vogonskiy is harm aplenty to the rest of us. Don't you think he feasts on that irony, that weak spot of y—"

The near-subsonic hum of a power plant made him stop as a shadow eclipsed the sickly sky of End Zone. The Awesome Vogonskiy was making his grand entrance.

TWENTY-THREE

ASIA BOXDALE FOUND no use in playing possum; the medical monitoring equipment gave her away. Two female nurses, watchful Filipinas, kept an eye on her but answered none of her questions.

Having been through a Crowd Control spritz and several forensic-sleep shots over the past few days, she was too groggy to make more than a token effort to get away. The Filipinas handled her with the ease of black-belt aikido masters, administering another pneumo while they had her in the double come-along hold. "You'll be feeling better soon," one assured her.

Oddly enough, they told the truth. After cycles of dozing, waking, and half dozing, Asia awoke feeling restored albeit unsteady. The nurses reappeared to stop her from messing with the equipment in search of a phone line, and served her a combo tray of *boudin* cuisine and *haute* hillbilly—Asia's favorites; how did they know?

They pointed out the bathroom and left her with the food, some toiletries, and a change of clothes. After an overdue pit stop, Asia ate lightly. She told herself her captors wouldn't have treated her so cautiously only to harm her, but several times the utensils were a menace because her hands were trembling so.

She showered, then combed out her swaying, ink-black mantilla of hair as she picked through the clothes: a brown unisex uniform, quasimilitary in Japanese fashion with its jodhpurlike pants and canvas *jikatabi* boots, complete with yellow hard hat and white gloves. Logo patches and insignia confirmed it as a World Nihon staffer outfit. There was also a rather conservative Madonna RetroFire Juniors bra and panty set in more or less her size.

Asia was too eager to get out of the hospital gown to quibble, donning everything but the helmet and gloves. The *tabi* socks and flat-soled workman's footgear felt strange, each with its separate compartment for her big toe. She was just buckling the broad web belt when she heard the door open and turned to see a tall, gangly young black man in mismatched funkwear, drinking her in with his eyes.

She recognized him not only from the conversation she'd overheard in the room earlier, but also from the moment's glimpse in the Bronx when he had fogged her, Labib, and Jesus with Crowd Control—while tittering like a kid with a squirt gun. " 'Lo there, Asia. Name's Mickey Formica, glad you're up and around—"

Asia used her stage training to project a hard-nosed courage she didn't feel. "I want to talk to Tanabe, not to you, you shuck-ass, Z-chromosome Tootsie Roll!"

That caught him off balance. "What're you, still high, Kham*puta*?" Attituding his way a half step closer.

Asia didn't back away. "Planning to exceed orders, G-boy?

Think those nurses won't tear your testicles off and hang them from their rearview mirror?"

Formica grew thoughtful at her mention of his orders. "Ain't here to mess with you, sweetness. And, you need all the friends you can get. C'mon; you'll see Tanabe soon enough."

Asia tucked the white gloves into her epaulet and took up the yellow hard hat. "So you're just another thug. Too bad; I was hoping somebody could answer some questions for me."

He watched her move with the grace of ballet and acrobatic training and the suppleness of a Thai temple dancer. "Such as?"

She kept a pointed ten feet between them. "Such as, what is Black Hole withholding from Earth? Unlimited clean energy? Green solutions to world progress?" She added, more quietly, "Cures for our illnesses?"

Mickey'd been briefed, and knew that the Monster—the Luggage, the HIVirus—had killed her English father in a Thai hospice. He wanted to shout, Fuck, I'm just a dog soldier; don't weight me with this shit!, but didn't because she had eyes and lips that had him dying, dying, to kiss her even if only once. "I s'pose they can do anything they feel like."

And Black Hole had been hanging back in the shadows for centuries, through the plagues, the wars. Through Sandy Boxdale's agonizing death. Asia began rethinking her decision back at the Ded Dawg, when she'd had a chance to waste that rapist spirochete Jak O' Clubs but had chosen not to kill. Now she knew she could, if that was what it took.

That, and a lot more. She gave him a nod, a sustained and searching look. "Thanks for being honest with me, Mickey. We'd better go, huh?"

As he held the door for her, Mickey wondered what his boyhood comics hero, ol' Spidey, would do in a situation like this—with both his cautionary Spider Senses *and* his web shooter tingling, sending very contradictory messages.

"Lemme sleep," GoBug moaned. "M'not feeling so good, Lucky."

Lucky looked to Dult and Doola, the larva's parents. "Is he sick?"

The female punching-bag-on-legs somehow looked maternal and deeply upset. "Not exactly. A child doesn't remain a child forever, Mr. Junknowitz, and it's getting time for his Furtherance. Naturally, it will require that he cocoon in the near future."

"*What?* And you two lugged him along on a *vacation?*"

"The lad wasn't due to enter Furtherance for quite some time," Dult explained soberly. "But—with all the stress we've been through, it's not surprising that the process has been accelerated. That sort of thing used to happen in primitive times."

GoBug moaned again. Lucky moaned, too, clapping a hand to his head. What next? A second later he was castigating himself for a louse; GoBug had come to Lucky's rescue with no less bravery than the others back at World Nihon.

"Listen, don't worry, folks," he told the distraught parents. "We're gonna get you and him home in plenty of time for him to have a nice, safe, comfortable, uh, pupal stage." That made the elder Dimdwindles regard him strangely, but seemed to put them at ease a little as well.

Lucky glanced at the other XTs gathered round in the grounded spacetruck's interior. "Is everybody clear on what's happening? I shouldn't be gone for more than a few hours, but if I am, don't stay here. Go with Sinead and wait for me; I'll get in touch as soon as I can."

They listened without objection, but their doubtful stares said volumes, especially Lumber Jack's. But what else could he do? The only way to move forward was to seek a way back into the Trough, or at least to get a stellarcast message through. Maybe some members of his band were even regretting having saved him, but they all knew it was too late to undo that now—and, if events broke Lucky's way for a change, he'd be back inside of half an hour.

He patted Lumber Jack's green-shagged, chopping-block shoulder. "You okay?"

Lumber's face creased in one of his smiling-Hawaiian-wargod grins. "Don't worry, we'll be all right. Isn't it time you and Silvercup were going?"

"Yeah." He turned to the Hono, who were gathered round the aerospacer's control consoles. The antlike little techno-wonks were busy checking out the jury-rigged SI modules they'd installed. "What d'you think, gang? Can you handle it?"

"Certainly not in optimum fashion," said one of them—Lucky still couldn't tell them apart. "And we wouldn't recommend attempting any ambitious maneuvers. But Silvercup's downloads and the built-in operating software should suffice for basic aeronautic and astronautic service."

Fine—at least if they had to make a run for it or otherwise move the ship they'd be enabled. "Well, Silver, you ready?"

"Yes," the spaceship answered one last time in her voice, then went silent. From the nose section came a weighty clicking and unlatching, solenoids being drawn back, servos revving in a low bass rumble. The forward consoles divided into discrete assemblies that swung up or aside according to design; even the gadget-nested crew chairs made way. A telescoping shaft appeared from within, supporting a reinforced globe that looked to Lucky like a cross between an ironclad basketball and a spherical Japanese-style construction puzzle.

A segment swung open and a darkened port appeared, the diameter of a petropig gas tank's filler neck. Lucky held his open palm under it. Something shiny and amorphous slid out smoothly into his hand.

His first impression was of a mercury egg yolk, but that wasn't quite right, because instead of clear albuminous egg white, the quivering glob was surrounded by a thin force field that tingled his skin.

"Beautiful," he murmured, despite the fact that Silvercup had told him she would be completely bereft of hearing, sight, or any other sense once her essential intellect was disconnected from the spacer's interfaces. He saw Sinead wearing a look of fascination and revulsion. "What, you think your brain or mine'd look this good, lying around in the open?"

Mr. Hoowe was ready with the empty case the two Rphians had scrounged from among the spacetruck's odds and ends; it looked like a pewter pocket humidor. When Lucky, holding the blob of living SI over the open case, hesitated, it was Dame Snarynxx who encouraged him. "Proceed, young man—you won't hurt her."

Her voice was so matriarchal that Lucky complied, sliding the quicksilver yolk into the case, where it floated, cushioned, in its sparkling protective field.

He closed and pocketed the case, stepping to the hatch and warning, "Keep a sharp lookout and don't open unless you hear my knock—even if it looks like me." He was amateurishly disguised against happy face cams and the odd Man in Black with cheap camoflesh Sinead had bought, and it wouldn't be hard for enemies to come up with a ringer.

"Lucky, you have three hours," Sinead warned. "After that I strike off on my own."

"Fair enough." It had been all he could do to convince her to wait with the ship and the XTs, even though she understood that someone familiar with Earth had to be there when both Lucky and Silver were gone. Sinead now had the little seedling given her by Lumber Jack tucked in her buttonhole, but that didn't mean she wouldn't surrender to her stubborn sense of self-preservation if Lucky failed to return on time.

Hono had to use manual switches to crack the hatch. A moment later Lucky was standing by towering steel plates. For a hiding place, Silver had stealthed in and landed between two cyclopean prefab sections of the Senator Al Sharpton Tunnel currently under construction in the East River. Within days they were to be floated out of this Bronx drydock, but for now they made good concealment, each longer than a football field and weighing 7,500 tons.

Getting out onto the street wasn't hard; Silvercup had spotted all the cams and was monitoring the drydock yard's security systems. Using a widget Hono had given him, Lucky sliced a way through the chain-link fence as if it were shoestring licorice. It was the most alien feeling of all to be back, to be on familiar streets again. Using the last of Sinead's money, he indulged himself in the luxury of a cab. He hopped out around the corner from his destination to case it.

Then he drew a deep breath and walked in under the harsh, eerie lights, spotting the one he was looking for. " 'Lo, Molly. How's about a Quick Fix?"

TWENTY-FOUR

THE BEST SHELTER available to Packard's stranded ground-pounders, the wounded Humanosaur Zozosh, Harley, and Sheena was what remained of the transit station, still reachable by an alternate and secure access. The platform area had caved in along with most of the installation, but some portions were still intact. The group pitched camp in a gaitmobe staging chamber not too far from the entrance tunnel. Soon a bone-stripping Hazmat sandstorm moved in in earnest, greeted by the ground-pounders with an approval that surprised Harley at first. Then

Sheena pointed out that the blow would force the 'Saur battle hordes under cover and hide the mechs' trail.

Thanks to limitations built into its constituent programs, Warhead had always been blind to the location of the sepulcher; Packard didn't want to return until he was sure he wasn't being tracked. "But we'll reopen that Adit, my promise on it," he added to everyone who sat lounging and listening inside the ring of parked, crouching mechs. "And with it we'll save this world—isn't that right, Har-lee?" Packard took her hand and led her to stand with him at center stage. Harley was nonplussed for a moment; she and Sheena had been creatively evasive about how they'd come to be on Hazmat, but firm in their declarations that they wanted to help end the war between Warhead and the People. On the other hand, she and Sheena had found the most vulnerable spot in Warhead's relationship with its janissaries, and if the idea they'd proposed worked, it promised to put Hazmat in Packard's grasp.

The guard-marshal's attention centered more and more on Harley; he sensed something about her unlike any gaitmobe wearer or Warren dweller, while Sheena all too much resembled a ground-pounder. Packard draped his own field jacket around Harley's shoulders against the chill.

"I believe you will, yes," she replied, blushing in the glow of portable illuminors.

Sheena noted the look that crossed DeSoto's face as Packard held Harley's hand. The Foxali guide might not know a lot about these flirtation/passion conundrums, but she recognized anger when she saw it.

For that matter, several gaitmobe wearers had given Sheena speculative glances; someone had passed her a survival kit poncho. She'd been saddened at having to return Packard's sawed-off assault rifle, but by way of compensation she'd snagged a Vigilance Bureau sidearm from among the stuff salvaged at the battlefield.

Even Sheena had been impressed by Packard's political savvy in ordering 'Saur dead burned on the same pyres as Vigilance Bureau police and ground-pounders—for Zozosh's benefit, of course. He'd understood *very* quickly that she, and Sheena's and Harley's linguistic gifts, were the key to something tremendous and unprecedented on Hazmat.

The battlefield salvage, ground-pounders' gear, and what pre-positioned supplies remained reachable in the transit station could sustain Packard's force—but not for long. The thought of being marooned made Sheena wonder, with a lonely ache that took her off guard, where Sean Junknowitz was and what was happening to him. The memory of him had a power she found difficult to understand.

Packard spoke again and Sheena resumed her running translation for Zozosh, who lay propped up on a pallet. Using Zozosh's helmet as a camp chair, Sheena sat by her ear, speaking softly.

Packard was nodding approvingly at Harley. "Thanks for believing in me." Then he turned to the others. "We've only got one hope now, and that's up; that's the Trough."

His ground-pounders were all ears—the ones on sentinel and patrol, via commo. Those gathered round the heater-illuminors were passing a few wine bags and liquor flasks. Packard's voice built in strength and conviction as he went.

"We lost big today, brothers and sisters, but we won even bigger. The Adit's down for the time being, but *for a second there*, Hazmat touched the Trough—first time since Warhead came alive. We got cut off here, but we met Zozosh, and now we've got a hope of ending the war for good—think of that!

"Lost damn good and true comrades-in-arms but now at the end of the day, we've won our lives, and a fighting chance. Lost the memory egg, but we'll get it back to the sepulcher—because we absolutely have to, top priority. Lost a chance to take Nash's head, but we were sent Sheena and Harley here, proving that the Trough holds our victory."

He had lifted Harley's hand high, as if she'd just won a boxing match. She was red with embarrassment but couldn't help the welling of pleasure she felt. Packard looked old enough to be her father, and his upbringing, occupation, and attitudes were at total loggerheads with hers, but that didn't matter. Phipps Hagadorn would look like a soft-handed weakling next to him. She didn't know what SELMI would say about her feelings, and didn't want to.

Packard had lowered her hand but still held it as he scanned his worn-and-torn vets. "Look at the faces around you tonight! Don't you forget them; people'll ask you about 'em as long as you live. Hazmat will measure history from this night and you can say, 'I was there for the start of it.'

"Together, you and me, we're going to win us a world."

He squeezed her hand. Harley's breath caught and she couldn't suppress a shiver that went from her head to the soles of her feet. She knew Packard was saying it directly to her.

Together, you and me, we're going to win us a world.

Sheena kept her own counsel, translating for Zozosh. Everything great and small rested with getting back the memory egg, because if legends were correct it was the key to the tangle of Light Trap SIs, the Fealty, and the ultimate secret of the Sysops.

She wondered if Harley realized what a smitten expression she was wearing as Packard stood there speechmaking about winning a world.

A world? I wish it were that simple, Sheena thought.

On End Zone, as elsewhere, The Awesome Vogonskiy was a showman in the grand style. P. T. Barnum as Caligula, the fleeting thought hit Eddie Enseno.

The shadow in the phlegmy End Zone sky was a giant antigrav platform decked out as a Trough Mardi Gras float. Presiding on a throne shaped like a rearing hippogryph near the bow was Eric Vogon, The Awesome Vogonskiy—over six foot seven, more than three hundred pounds of him, white beard silken and snowy eyebrows flaring.

He was costumed in a Mandarin cap with peacock feather tassel, a court-collared *p'u-fu* jacket, a formal *su-tshu* necklace, a dragon robe, and upturned slippers. He held a bat-winged copper baton with a goat's-head cap; standing at his right hand was his M'finti familiar, the little purple homunculus Tumi.

The rest of the antigrav flatboat was a Chinese temple set featuring stage-magic props: flaming braziers, mystical coffins, racks, cages, spinning mirrors, glass tanks filled with water— and a calliope spouting blasts of multicolored glitter from its pipes as it played carnival music. Crewing the float were various lesser imps and goblins.

"How opportune!" Vogonskiy's amplified heartiness bombarded them. "How sweet it is to find you all getting along like this!" A flock of flying drones had zipped in at treetop level; End Zoners were dashing and thrashing to every point of the compass.

Eddie was gaping up at Vogonskiy, brain in overload. *Whatever he was doing back on Earth, it must be over; it's all over back there, we lost . . .*

"Don't push, don't crowd," Vogonskiy barkered merrily. "I'll get to each and every one of you." His eye fell on Riiv, whom Willy was struggling to help escape. "You're currently my senior guest, Madame; what, leaving so soon—Not so fast, you!"

Meaning Sean, who'd been limping in Riiv and Willy's direction to bear a hand. A whip-flick of burgundy electricity sent

Sean to his knees. "Hogging the spotlight, eh? You, sir, are a ham."

Sean was trying to get back to his feet, supplicating, looking demented, his arms outstretched. "When you sent us here you said you weren't through with us. So I'm sayin', give us another chance." He was rubbing his fingertips together, tapping his palms. Eddie Ensign was stunned by the wheedling tone Sean had taken. One thing that had always seemed sure was that Sean Junknowitz would either prevail or die, but never bend.

"*You*, marine?" There was cautious wonder in Vogonskiy's voice. "I was looking forward to the antics of the Junknowitz-Yanvur faction, I'll have you know."

Sean shrugged, a move that made him wince, but continued his *sertao* gesticulations; all the drones were fixed on him. "Mr. Vogonskiy, sir, I can see you've got us where you want us, '*n*' *see no* reason to draw it out. '*N*' *see no* point in getting you any more pissed off."

Enseno, Eddie got it; but what did Sean want him to do? The flick of Sean's fingers answered that, directed at Riiv and Willy. Eddie faded back, lowering his profile and wishing he could tunnel into the slop.

"You're a great disappointment to me," Vogonskiy told Sean. "What, all that U.S. Marine Code of Conduct bravado gone already?"

"Just cuttin' the best deal I can," Sean said tightly, eyes shifting.

Vogonskiy *tsk*ed. "Anyway, I reject your surrender—here, what's this?"

By rights, the swarming remotes shouldn't have missed the movement, but Sean's drawing-hexes had distracted them. Eddie Enseno had circled around the glen by way of the mushy riverbank, crouched below Vogonskiy's line of sight. The Awesome One only noticed him as Eddie popped up to help Willy bulldog several coils of Riiv's bulk around. The three slewed and slid down the bank, plunging from a low dropoff into the draining-abcess fluids of the river.

Vogonskiy shook his head pityingly at Sean. "That was it? Your entire stratagem? I *am* disappointed, but not as disappointed as you're going to be. A sandbar will beach them a little way along, if they even get that far." Several remotes had already swooped off in pursuit. "I'm vexed with this poor showing." He pointed a forefinger like a huge pink banana from his throne on the hippogryph. "Let's see what you look like without a face to wear that sullen expression on."

Sean thrashed backward, feeling as if his skull were white hot, too stubborn to cry out although the air-valve sound in his voice box was loud. Nodding, savoring it, Vogonskiy set about planning some *real* fun.

Ka Shamok's available refuges had been sharply diminished by Black Hole's stepped-up efforts to seek out and destroy him—witness the fact that he'd gone to ground on SlimFast.

The prototype worldlet, abandoned by AzTek Development Consortium experimenters at the beginning of the Black Hole purge, had been a high-risk attempt for something new in the way of Adit technology—and what a vexatious place to visit, much less reside in. The AzTekkers had contained a naked singularity, then balanced its effects with a tremendously complex antigrav force field—Ashtekar loop-space circles reinforced like eight-dimensional ring mail—so as to make a detailed study of tidal forces. While objects and life-forms were physically safe at the site, however, an anomalous interaction of forces affected the sensoria of living beings and sentient machines so that they *perceived* the attenuation they were undergoing and whose gross effects they were spared.

Thus everyone in the place felt themselves to be, and saw others as, stick figures hundreds of yards tall. It was a mere perceptual phenomenon, but it affected the way everyone on SlimFast walked, stood, sat, and otherwise carried out motor functions.

That didn't deter an angry Jacob Riddle, furious over Discipline Di's attack on his Nmuth IV home, from getting right up into Ka Shamok's face. The Chasen-nur had been expecting the visit since a trembling Bagbee had admitted forgetting the telltale dart case during evacuation of the Spectarr II base. By that time Discipline Di had already had it out with Yoo Sobek, who'd passed Jacob to insurgency sympathizers for transfer to SlimFast. Teleen Riddle was, at her husband's insistence, in hiding with friends on Alas.

When Jacob pointed his finger at Ka Shamok's flat, wide nub of a nose, the finger, attenuated toward the floor and SlimFast's center of gravity, still looked as if it were pointed downward. But the base personnel were getting used to that kind of thing, and Jacob was too furious to care. "My daughter Molly's in trouble on Earth. I want you to get her to safety."

"I sincerely wish that were possible, Jacob, but—"

Jacob knew how to get to the bottom line. "Either you help me save Molly, which you owe me, or everything I know about you gets forwarded to Light Trap—even if I don't leave here alive. *Especially* if."

Ka Shamok believed him. "Jacob, it isn't like the old days. Security at the *Crystal Harmonic* Adit is tight, and your daughter will doubtless be under observation."

Jacob was way ahead of him. "The Adit's the bottleneck, so we'll just work around it."

Ka Shamok raised his hands in surrender; his arms first seemed to be sheets of dark water stretching down and down toward the distant floor, then were pulled to vertical lines, looking like dark stains along his sides. "You win. In return, however, I want your counsel and help on certain current projects. Agreed?"

"As if I've got a choice?"

TWENTY-FIVE

YOO SOBEK, BODILESS, *moved through surreal realms of uppermost Light Trap, searching. He ghosted past miracles, hunting swiftly along the wormhole courses that were the Sysops' corridors and promenades. He was in their reliquary, their treasure house; he knew abstractly that he was dreaming again, but that was no reason to stop.*

Once more he came to the boundless, nebulous space where the eight-ring symbol glowed incomprehensibly. Sobek sensed the mind-breaking horror it represented but was unable, still, to summon up its meaning. Therefore he tried another tactic, willing, in his lucid dreaming, a mirror.

When he'd tried to look at his own body in dreamstate he'd found himself invisible, and so this device had occurred to him. There was nothing noteworthy about it: a full-length dressing mirror in a walnut frame he modeled on one he'd seen in Char-

lie Cola's East Hampton beach house. He'd hoped to see his original, his Sysop, face and form, but those weren't there. Instead, what pulled into focus was the ninth ring.

The eight-ring cypher had always had space for another circle at the bottom that would complete its symmetry. Now he was looking at a glowing ninth ring on which the others, ectoplasmic, all rested: his symbol and identity somehow; his key as well.

Struggling with that tantalizing clue, he was jostled out of his dreamstate, out of his sleep, by a HuZZah who looked uncommonly huge until Sobek realized that he'd transmogged to something rather small. The public maglev transit cartridge they were riding was slowing for arrival.

"Cease this thrashing about! You're having a nightmare! Easy; feeling better?"

Sobek brushed pipe-cleaner fingers across his face, a minimal layout on a head the shape of a gourd. He had conjugated as a Skitterkin with the express notion that, if he fell asleep and became violent as he had in Ka Shamok's base on Spectarr II, he would attract little notice. Sobek waited until the HuZZah was gone before disembarking from the cartridge. Free-floating signs and holodynamics pointed the way to planet Geles's Adit.

After leaving Nmuth IV with his trophy of victory over Discipline Di, the fragment of her cognition, Sobek had zigzagged and transmogged across the Trough, muddying his trail and establishing a cover story for where he'd been lately and why. But with the partial answer of the ninth ring, he wanted a faster body and a direct route to Light Trap.

The putrid stream into which Eddie Enseno had tumbled himself, Willy, and Riiv was so revolting that it galvanized Willy; he fought the slimy whirlpools and undercurrents with what strength he had left. After a while Riiv's contractile strength swept Willy onto sloppy footing; in seconds he and Eddie were helping each other onto a greasy strand, Riiv eeling alongside and keeping them from slipping back in until they got to comparatively dry ground.

"Wills." Eddie Ensign was panting dully. "Wills, c'mon, we gotta go. Get up!"

But for weeks Willy had been ransacking what strength he had to synergize with Riiv, and he had almost nothing left. Eddie tugged at his arm. "Riiv, gimme a hand—Riiv!"

Her name brought Willy around; when he saw her head slid-

ing down the stone on which she'd rested it in exhaustion, the
waning light in her slitted eyes, he knew she was dying. He also
sensed that she wasn't succumbing to natural causes. Soft auro-
ras hung in the air around them, and everything seemed to vibrate with an unsung dirge.

"Riiv!" He thrashed through the bog slop to her. "Stop! What
are you doing?"

She couldn't quite lift the great, plated chin off the rock anymore. "I cannot truly heal on End Zone, and I'm innately and
morally incapable of harming Vogonskiy. But the bioware within
me could let *you* strike, William. You'll have to decide; as for
me, I must move on."

As she said it the mottled and desiccated scales were falling
from the huge wedge-shaped head, and the soft light went dark
in eyes that Willy had come to think of as kind. Small, intense
tremors racked a body whose tail still lay in the river ten yards
away. Then her ruff of tendrils hung lifeless.

"Please!" Willy wept, but it was no use. She made a final stirring of sound and so he sang with it—part lullaby, part elegy.
Riiv's body broke down rapidly, a willed discorporation. Scales
rained from the ancient bone plates of her head, skin sloughed,
and cartilege turned to gel, her head settling unevenly onto the
rock as her sound faded; the long body was self-destructing even
more rapidly. Willy, tears running down both cheeks, carried the
song for them both.

Riiv's skull melted away, and Willy saw a hidden part of her
revealed—a twinkling squiggle shorter and finer than a hair
from his forearm, its details impossible to distinguish due to its
size and radiance. It coiled itself up, rearing a bit, as Riiv was
wont to do. He reached down and offered his fingertip; the tiny,
living filament flowed up onto it. Resisting the impulse to whistle "The Worms Crawl In, the Worms Crawl Out," he lifted it to
the inner corner of his right eye. There was a brief throb of light
and an icy feeling in his head.

"Wills?" Eddie was standing by uncertainly. He pointed
straight up. "Vogonskiy's flying kitchen appliances should be all
over us by now. Know anything about that?"

Willy turned away from what had been Riiv. "I think she mis-
led them—hid our vibes, possibly."

"Speaking of Dr. Feelbad—"

"Yeah, let's go."

* * *

It had only been a few days since fear for her life was all that could make Harley Paradise climb into a gaitmobe, but now she felt exposed and vulnerable when she wasn't inside *Death Walker*—especially out here in the open, under the streaming worldwinds, in Hazmat's sandblasted wastelands.

But that couldn't be helped. What she and the rest of the little delegation had to do was something they couldn't do in main battle mechs—indeed, the mechs were keeping distance as per Guard-Marshal Packard's order.

It helped to have Sheena Hec'k by her side, so self-possessed in the black Vigilance Bureau uniform she'd chosen from battle salvage. She cut quite a figure, putting Harley in mind of a fire-haired, futuristic motorcycle cop.

Harley had accepted a spare gaitmobe wearer's unigarb—the only one there was—from Packard; just one more sign of his considerate nature. The porous, phase-change second skin was a lot more comfortable, in a ground-pounder's belly, than her micromini had been. How odd to have come across the galaxy, by unthinkable coincidence, to meet this strong, charismatic man of vision. While she'd been careful to keep a certain distance, Harley knew he was drawn to her as well.

Zozosh, the female Humanosaur Harley and Sheena had saved and in whose testimony Packard had perceived hope for a rebirth of Hazmat, had been as good as her word. Now she led half a dozen male 'Saurs into the sheltered bowl of rock where, for the first time, human and 'Saur were to parley.

Like the humans, the creatures were unarmed and unarmored. On one side of the stone rim above, Kongs and Gargantoids and Blue Bounders and the rest kept edgy watch; across the way, Packard's ground-pounders did the same. The leader of Zozosh's party was easy to spot: Muc-Tuc, a Doom Demon and a top battlemaster with a renowned independent streak—very much Packard's opposite number. His brutish face, sabertooth incisors, and beady eyes made it hard for Harley to hang on to her composure—but these days she was learning how to manage it.

Muc-Tuc leaned forward to sniff at her, then at Sheena, the flaps of his mandrake nose quivering. "You're right," he told Zozosh. "Their smell is so alien, they *must* be from another world."

Harley translated that for Packard. Muc-Tuc, almost twice as tall as the guard-marshal, turned to him. "I came without telling Warhead, as you asked and Zozosh said I should. You want help attacking your own underground nest, Stonecomb Warren. You offer in return things the likes of which I've never heard. Tell me more."

It was just more proof of his nerve, Harley thought, that Packard didn't hesitate to comply, though by doing so he was casting the dice for the fate of Hazmat and a lot more. "There's an object in Stonecomb that we need. You're half the key, because you can get us across the wastes through Warhead's surveillance; we're the other half, because we know how to penetrate Stonecomb's defenses."

Muc-Tuc grunted. "Your underground travel-tunnel was blown up. What, would you march overland in your ironclads?" He laughed, knowing as well as Packard that it would be impossible.

But Harley threw her head back, squaring her shoulders proudly. "Guard-Marshal Packard has thought of that. We don't need to march to Stonecomb, only to reach the next nearest underground station, and he's come up with a way." She didn't add that while it was brilliant, it was risky.

"Zozosh told me what you offered in return," Muc-Tuc said, setting aside Stonecomb for the moment, "but I want to hear it from you."

They all saw that the offer had stirred something deep in him—as it had in Zozosh—or he would never have risked Warhead's wrath to come and treat in secret. "Warhead bred you with a life span only a tenth part of ours," Packard answered through Harley. "We believe now that we can change that."

That had gotten to him, but not decisively; most 'Saurs died of combat wounds rather than old age anyway. "And?"

Time for the heavy guns. "If we reopen the doorway to other worlds, we believe we can enlist such aid that you Humanosaurs will be able to bear your own offspring, rather than see your plasm copied in Warhead's birthworks. And we mean to find a means to peace, so you can raise them up. If some 'Saurs still want to make war, there'll be many in the Trough who'll pay them handsomely to do it."

Harley saw that it was the part about bearing their own children that had gotten to Muc-Tuc, as it had to Zozosh. The 'Saurs on the heights were making a bowling-alley rumble of conversation among themselves, too. Muc-Tuc looked to the Mauve Mauler and she anticipated him. "As I said, *they* do it."

There had been general data tapes and similar proof to convince Zozosh that humans gave live birth but, oddly, it had been something simpler and more emphatic that made a believer out of her. Harley's menstrual period had begun while Zozosh was mending at the transit station, more or less when Harley calculated it would, counting back over the time since she'd been kidnapped in Rodeo East. The 'Saur's almost psychically acute olfactory sense had convinced her that the humans were telling the truth about their reproductive cycle.

Whether Packard could actually make good on this promise was much more problematic, but Harley thought that if anyone could do it, this Hazmatian Caesar could.

"Ah. Well, then." Muc-Tuc pretended reluctance. "Perhaps I'll stay and listen a moment longer."

TWENTY-SIX

ONCE THE SURFACE had been swept to insure security, Inspector Nash stepped out onto Hazmat's blasted surface, preceded by his Vigilance Police bodyguard gaitmobes and the fast-pursuit mechs he'd brought. Things were confused, because Packard's ground-pounders and the gene-perverted 'Saurs— 'Saurs! Fighting alongside humans!—had killed so many of Nash's inner circle before escaping Stonecomb Warren with the memory egg.

So be it: revenge would come soon. More and more mechs were pouring from the transit station, manned by believers in the Creed, loyal to Nash and sworn to prevent reactivation of the Adit that had brought ruin to Hazmat. Pious retribution would be swift, because Packard's heavy ground-pounders and the even slower Humanosaurs couldn't get far—certainly not any appreciable distance on the long, long march back to the sepulcher— before being overtaken and pinned down by Nash's fast-pursuit mechs. That would afford time for the fundamentalist main force to move in for the kill.

The raiders' audacity, timing, and advantage of complete surprise had been immoral, satanic, but very effective. Nash was only beginning to feel the full burning mortification of being caught unawares, made to flee for his life before his followers, and nearly shot down. What troubled him almost as much was the memory of the two women who'd been with Packard, the statuesque scarlet-hair and the auburn beauty; there was no record of them in any warren, and Nash's suspicions about their origins gave him cold shivers.

He was avid to have them all dead. "Have you found them yet?" he fumed.

The woman commanding the scout team answered over the net somewhat uneasily. "Due to light worldwind activity we have a scout drone flying surveillance on them, Inspector."

"Excellent!" He would eliminate them before the day was out. "How much of a lead do they have on us?"

"About two hours and growing, Inspector."

"What?" Packard's traitors had only reached the transit station half an hour before.

"Perhaps it would be easier if you examined the visual."

She patched it through to his contact array, relayed from the unarmed little flying drone being beaten by light worldwinds. When he understood what he was seeing, Packard let out a grunt as if he'd been struck.

They were two unlikely vehicles, cobbled up out of such diverse parts and spares that Nash could only identify a few, but he knew right away that they were the kind pre-positioned in transit terminals—like the one to which Packard had had access even after Nash blew up the transit-system tunnel. Excavator wheels, a recovery mech flatbed, a resupply crawler suspension—those and more had been incorporated. Furthermore, there had never been an all-terrain vehicle with a power source like them: ground-pounders and Humanosaurs, pumping jury-rigged rocker arms like so many clockwork figures, sent abundant torque to the drive trains.

There was other booty lashed to the overlander, and Nash had no doubt some of it was parts, tools, and equipment with which to repair the Adit. The remote's data showed the contraptions were speedier than fast-pursuit 'mobes.

"There are two low mountain ranges and a highly eroded area along the route to the sepulcher," the scout officer was telling him, "but from observation of the overland vehicles. I believe they can be disassembled and carried piecemeal past obstacles. Inspector?"

Nash didn't answer, watching the drone's video feed break up as increasing worldwind activity knocked the transmission, and probably the drone, out of the air. Purple lightning split the sky.

Nash began dictating marching orders for more combat mechs, more supplies, more support units, equipment, personnel. He made a mental note, too, that other units elsewhere on Hazmat were going to have to be sacrificed in diversionary campaigns to keep Warhead distracted.

For Nash had no desire to fight Warhead; his only obsession was to carry Packard's head back to Stonecomb in one hand, the memory egg in the other.

Molly Riddle was cool under fire, as Lucky knew; his showing up at Quick Fix didn't throw her a bit. Maybe it had to do with her spending a good deal of time in the Trough over the years. All the trim and capable brunette conceded Lucky's miraculous appearance was the flicker of one, long dark eyebrow and a thin, ironic smile.

"Sorry, Lucky J.," she answered his greeting. "No Quick Fixes tonight, not for your type of consumer crisis. Or ours either, as it works out."

Enigmatic clerk Sanpol Amsat was watching Lucky from behind the counter, and Charlie Cola's adopted sons Jesus and Labib were standing together in the doorway leading back to where the Adit had once waited, but the three men seemed more depressed than combative. Molly looked about to kick Lucky out of the store until Sanpol Amsat appeared beside her. "Why not hear him out?" he counseled.

Molly looked to Labib and Jesus. The darkly handsome Egyptian boy moved to watch the door, and the blond, blue-eyed Euro-foundling went to the back, where the surveillance and defense systems were. Sanpol was about to return behind the counter, of which he seemed as much a part as a Trough Pit Boss ported into Adit instrumentation, when Lucky added thoughtfully, "A-and I need to clear up a couple things with you, too, *effendi.*"

It was Sanpol who had insisted, months before, that Yoo Sobek's communicator lid with its atom-stacked eight-ring symbol, which had come ricocheting out from the back of the store to bonk Lucky in the temple—having emerged from the activated Adit, as it turned out—*belonged to Lucky.*

"We shall see," Sanpol said, not quite acquiescing. Lucky trailed Molly to a rack of interactive e-*manga* she pretended to stock as she glanced frequently at a fish-eye antitheft mirror.

"I'm grateful you let me through the Adit," Lucky told her. "Guess it brought you some backlash."

She made a scoffing snuffle. "You bet your simulacrum, bucko!" she told him, even though the *Crystal Harmonic* Adit had superseded Quick Fix for unrelated reasons. Charlie Cola's resentment alone had made Lucky bad news.

He felt wrenchingly guilty, but for once that didn't make him yield ground. "I'm sorry, but I need a hand again. I have to get back into the Trough; I know where I can get help."

"What, Ka Shamok? He's odds-on to be hanging by his lavender *cojones* from an al-Reem gambrel any time now. Or the Abos? Probably took a wrong turn and strayed into a supernova. Anyway, the *Crystal Harmonic*'s on max alert against intruders, gearing up for this Phoenix *Walpurgisnacht*. If there were a way off Earth, trust me, I'd already have—"

She'd stopped because he'd flicked open the metal pocket case and held it under her nose. This time both heavy, arched brows went up. "Fealty R and D. *Silvercup*?"

"Yep, and she's *already* accessed *Crystal Harmonic*'s systems once. She can be our passkey back through—you, me, my tour group—" He indicated Sanpol, Labib, and Jesus. "And your Fix*teures* too, if they want. Y'know, part of the reason I have to get out there's because Willy, Eddie, and my brother are on End Zone."

Her composure cracked for the first time; Lucky saw that what had happened to Willy, whom she'd initially love-interested to infiltrate the loft posse, really *was* eating at her. "Lucky, there's *nothing* anybody can do about End Zo—"

"'N' here's another flash Silver picked up from the *Harmonic* files: somebody on Light Trap's questioning your parents' loyalty. See, we've both got offworld family problems."

Black Hole could be merciless with perceived traitors; Lucky had counted on that swaying her even though Charlie Cola—as Lucky knew from the World Nihon follies—had thrown in with Tanabe. She didn't seem to know that last fact, and Lucky wasn't about to tell her. He did fill her in on other particulars, including the spacetruck of XTs sitting between two tunnel sections over at the drydock.

Molly Riddle wasn't the indecisive type. "Count me in; we'll tackle the *Harmonic* somehow. She's due to dock at the Japan Sea Acropolis to—what, Jesus? What's wrong?"

The nordic Jesus was beckoning from the back area. "Somebody lamping us—cops, I think."

Lucky brought up the rear as Molly followed Jesus to the rear of the store. Labib moved nervously to back up Sanpol; Sanpol, unperturbed, continued unpacking biodegradable maizefoam Soy-Slush cups. The back of the place, stripped of its Adit, had a mournful air of emptiness.

There were a few reminders of former times: local and regional maps and transit scheds, a few oddments of camoflesh, a blank ID or two, and three pink derms of the sort humans had to wear when fading lest they be knocked for a loop by singularity travel. Lucky recalled all too well the traumatic thick shakes, stretch pants, and other painful consequences of his ill-advised escape leap to Adit Staph. Rubbing one between his fingers, he saw, with the experience of a Trough veteran, that it was blank—empty and uncalibrated.

There was also food; Lucky pocketed the derms on general principles and tore open some Muir Mallomars. Molly examined a blinking bogey painted on the holographic schematic of the neighborhood. "Unmarked car, sitting there accessing the happy-face cams and other official surveillance assets directly. Scans as if it's got some Trough technology onboard. Well, if he moves, we'll know."

She straightened and turned to Jesus. "We need to make a decision—it involves Sanpol and Labib, too." She led the way out front again; Lucky followed, pausing to shove the Muir Mallomars and some Cousteau Croissants into the pocket of his jacket. There was a Trough Trip herbal wrap, a popular vending-machine snack on way stations everywhere; that, too, Lucky commandeered against future need, along with a kenaf napkin.

It was near midnight now and the store was empty. Lucky, knowing Sinead and the tourists were sweating out the wait, bit back an urge to call the question immediately. Molly addressed the others. "Lucky's offering us an alliance, and I think we should take it."

"Molly," Labib began, "we told you we'd stick by you no matter what—*who the hell is that?*"

He was pointing at the front window. Running across the deserted street came a human figure in a tatterdemalion suit, carrying something in one hand. Insistent alarm tones pulsed through the store; Molly yelled at Jesus to go back and man the defenses.

Whatever protective mantle Quick Fix had, it wasn't enough. Two horrible things happened to Lucky in the same moment: he recognized the demonic face coming right at him, and he spied a second interloper—massive, its metalflesh gleaming where the light caught it—looming in the darkened doorway from which the running man had come.

Zastro Lint looked as if he needed a few weeks in the care of a good exorcist. "Wait! I have a right to a hearing!" was all Lucky had time to yell before an orange storm-surge broke from the uplifted briefcase. The storefront vanished in a galaxy of falling glass, and everything—people, Kava-Cola dispenser, Ray-Ban brain-spa headsets, HIVirus test patches, smart drug displays, English–Pharsee/Mandarin/Uzbeki phrasebook software, safe-sex kits, cash register—was salad-tossed and then let fall.

"*Malakas!* Shit!" Bhang rasped under his breath as the explosion at Quick Fix echoed up and down the Bronx streets. "What was that, an air strike?"

Randy Barnes hit the unmarked car's accelerator. "Tell ya in a minute," he said through gritted teeth.

Dante exhaled softly, making sure his flexible body armor was well fastened. They'd been surveilling Quick Fix so as to roust any of the staff who strayed outside its defenses, but he'd been hoping to avoid any unpleasantness. "Don't you think—"

"Quit botherin' me; I'm workin'!"

Lucky woozily heard Lint's briefcase gloating in its 'toon rodent voice. "Hope you like travel an' sex, Junknowitz; we're gonna drag you down to headquarters and ream you good!"

"Agent Lint, honest, I meant to return your phone calls," Lucky tried to say as Lint stalked toward him through the shambles of the Quick Fix, but it came out as garble no tongue twister could remedy.

The stakeout car rounded the corner on two military-style nonpneumatic tires, Barnes straining hard against the pistol-grip steering yoke. He hadn't called for backup, not wanting the BS of dealing with noncoopted officials. Concentrating on the store, he didn't see a glittering figure veer across the street. Bhang's "Look out!" came too late.

Barnes had a brief glimpse of mirror-finish, Greek-god features as the bumper was seized and the car's braking changed to a forced halt. The steely giant flipped the front of the unmarked sedan into the air; Barnes and Bhang, unbelted from their seats in preparation to hit the ground running at Quick Fix, were

Maytagged over as the interbust somersaulted, crushed its roof, and came to rest upside down.

TWENTY-SEVEN

"I DON'T KNOW why you're bothering to fight," The Awesome Vogonskiy taunted Sean Junknowitz from his hippogryph throne. "You've already wimped out, after all."

Sean, leprous feet squishing in the slime as he did *yvy-nomi-mybre* dance steps before the antigrav stage-magic float, refused to hear it. His skull still sizzled from Vogonskiy's bone-fire hex, but Sean had alleviated the worst of it with hide-us-from-harm steps and invocations he'd learned from Mbuas pilgrims.

Sean still wasn't clear on why he'd done it, pretending to crack before Vogon. Oh, it had let Eddie, Willy, and Riiv get away and Sean was used to making sacrifices in battle—but *not that one*, not simpering self-abasement. Still, having seen the three escape, he didn't feel as bad about it as he'd thought he would.

Now it was just Sean and Yanvur, bearing the brunt of what Vogonskiy, roaring in amusement, threw at them. Sean figured that, like himself, the living mummy had decided that no better crack at the magician would ever present itself and that anyway, today was a good day to die.

The flying remotes had drawn back, and Tumi and the lesser goblins on the raft were mere spectators. Yanvur was trying, without success, to throw death into Vogonskiy as Vogonskiy had thrown it into Yanvur, Sean, Eddie, and Willy, into Bullets Strayhand and Bixby Santiago and so many others.

Sean jutted his jaw and showed his incisors, calling on the jaguar as Master of Fire with a chant he'd learned in the Mato Grosso. The braziers on Vogonskiy's float erupted in nuclear fireballs of ethereal flame; those didn't so much as singe the man, but they sent the goblins scattering—except for Tumi, who stood by his master's side.

Vogonskiy was toying with them. He withered Yanvur's right arm, twisted his left foot up at the ankle, and made the flesh of one side of his face run like hot wax. Sean went with the best shot that came to his blurry mind, Danbala Wedo, the *loa* of the waterfall at Ville Bonheur, Haiti.

Sean had climbed up to the falls one July 16, during the Festival of the Virgin of Miracles, sat under a ficus tree, and taken some *ayahuasca* he'd brought from Peru just for the occasion. The psychotropic hit as he watched Haitians of every station pray and dance, wash, and plead favors from the divine powers under the waterfall's cascade. Danbala Wedo, the snake god who inhabited the falls, "rode" many that day, sometimes possessing several supplicants at once, sending them into convulsing fits.

After a while Sean had seen Danbala Wedo summon him, and had gone under the battering falls to be *loa*-ridden. The snake god took him on a mind-tour while many gentle black hands restrained him from harming himself or drowning. It had been unable to cleanse Sean of the demon memories he sought to exorcise, though, so he'd felt no right to call upon it.

But Riiv's downfall had changed that, and Sean now invoked the waterfall snake god. It took smoky shape before him, male— Aida Wedo was the deity's mate—bigger and more powerful than Riiv, and harboring a rage she would have never entertained. To Sean's dismay, however, it was translucent and blurry. Vogonskiy, when he saw it, gave that belly-shaking laugh again and made passes with his hands; a dark vapor began consuming Danbala. So much for Sean's best shot.

Then came a note so true that at first Sean thought it came from a synthed rather than human voice. Tumi and even Vogonskiy looked poleaxed; the vortex stopped its devouring of Danbala Wedo. Other notes came in a rush from Willy, who stood poised with arms raised and eyes closed, his body still filthy from the river but his voice pristine. The song, of course, was Riiv's—her signature tune.

Like a quick fuse burning from his tail to his head, Danbala Wedo took on solid substance, impervious scaly might. He lashed the vortex with a flick of his tongue, then struck at The Awesome Vogonskiy. Vogonskiy fell back, spouting a sound effect like that of a breaching whale and nearly crushing Tumi; the snake god's jaws missed him by inches. Either Vogonskiy directed his float through neural interface or he'd lurched against the controls, because the antigrav flatboat slanted backward, dipping at the stern, and plowed to a stop in the End Zone muck.

Sean advanced, stumbling, his fingers spread like talons. No *muy thui* killstrikes or prole*jutsu* necksnaps for Vogonskiy; Sean meant to simply choke the life out of him. Tumi, squirming from under his master, flipped a red stop at one side of the calliope keyboard and pressed all fingers of both hands down in an unlikely chord. The pipes gushed wild comets that crop-dusted sparks and tiny tongues of flame everywhere. Sean had to shield his eyes.

When he caught sight of Tumi and Vogonskiy again, a dozen of the drone remotes had locked on to them with waldoes—three for the manikin, ten for the magician—and were bearing them away through the air. Danbala Wedo just missed gulping them down on the fly, only to begin fading. The subordinate goblins were already abandoning the grounded float, scurrying for the undergrowth.

Yanvur was dead, his broken neck looking like a snapped piece of ginseng. Sean pointed to one of the mummy's main henchbeings. "Find somebody who can fly this thing. We gotta finish Vogonskiy before he can regroup."

Then he turned to Willy. Having witnessed Willy's new abilities, he asked simply, "She's dead?"

Willy shook his head, tapping a finger to the side of his brow, near where Riiv's radiant implant now lived. "Not really."

Sean nodded. "We'll pay Vogon back for her, too."

Willy shook his head. "She didn't have much use for that kind of payback. Her philosophy was just to make the best music you can."

Sean walked off to check out several pilot candidates.

Eddie grinned. "So what's the next selection?"

Willy contemplated End Zone. " 'A Hard Reign's Gonna Fall.' "

The curtain across the sleeping niche slid back and a swath of light fell across the covers. DeSoto's voice reported, "One of Muc-Tuc's scouts just spotted his advance party. He's three hours out." Packard didn't have to ask who she meant; Inspector Nash would *have* to lead the attack, or lose status.

Instead he wanted to know, "What strength?"

"Corps, theater-army—who knows? Enough to smother this place, much less breach it." She spoke in the flat tone she'd used with Packard ever since the night he'd taken Harley's hand in the ruined transit station—the same day DeSoto's quick action had saved his life from Nash.

He yawned, rubbing his eyes, as short on sleep as everyone else. "I'll be right along."

DeSoto gave him a stare, then left without closing the curtain. Sounds of the ongoing Adit repairs and defensive preparations echoed through the sepulcher. Harley Paradise waited until he'd redrawn the curtain before sitting up next to him, massaging his neck, wishing she could do more for him. "Can we hold out long enough?"

"I don't know." It had been a race from the start: their repairs of the shot-up Adit equipment against the cross-country march of Nash's pursuing army. "Harley, there's something I want you to do."

She kissed his right shoulder where gray hairs arched over an old battle scar; her scalp was shaved, ground-pounder style, but her forelock brushed his skin. "Anything, Pack."

He reached into a rucksack and handed her a breadboarded commo unit. "I'll make up an errand for you to take *Death Walker* outside. Find the highest ground you can, set this up, and anchor it."

She examined it. Days and nights of playing helper-apprentice in the sepulcher had taught her a few things. "This is a Trough emitter—linked in from the memory-egg niche? If you activate it—"

He nodded, brushing his fingertips along the fine but underfed curve of her cheek. "Warhead will know the egg is here, and act. But at least if we don't win, Nash won't. Will you do this for me?"

She put her arms around him. "Anything, Pack."

The post-briefcase-blast Quick Fix was in semidarkness, only its neon logos, display screens, ad graphics, shelf consumer-info LED crawls, and the like shedding an exploded vid arcade's worth of minor and scattered light sources in the place. None of the Fix*teures* were moving.

"Kiss your assets good-bye," snarled Lint's briefcase.

"Wait." Lucky heard the word as he was dragging himself up with the help of a rotating wire display rack of Santeria liturgical supplies. Looming in the doorway was a humanoid figure swathed in some sort of robe or long coat. It came at him *very* quickly, setting kenaf sheets and other debris whirling. He was snatched off the floor as fingers like living crowbars went to his shirt pocket unerringly, ripped it away, and grabbed the case containing Silvercup's essential self.

He was dropped to gaze up at a face he knew: Peterbuilt. "Uh-oh, the Tin Foil."

The gleamer tucked Silvercup away in the reproduction horseman's duster he'd gotten somewhere and reached for Lucky. "Now as to you—" He put his knuckles by Lucky's forehead and violet sparks snapped; Lucky collapsed.

Lint slapped Peterbuilt's fist away with surprising strength, the briefcase pointed at the gleamer like a howitzer muzzle. "Not so fast! This taxpayer will be remanded to the central IRS audit facility on al-Reem."

Sirens began *ee-yaa*ing nearby. Peterbuilt looked nonchalant. "As you say. Shall we go, before local authorities try to impede us?"

They went out the back way, past the dusty, vacant space where the Adit had once stood. In a nearby parking garage—the one where Molly Riddle had kept her Mercedes ragtop before it was stolen by Micky Formica and Nikkei Tanabe when they kidnapped Asia Boxdale—they took the elevator and reclaimed what looked like an RPEV airport minibus bearing LaGuardia markings. Lucky was dumped in the rear.

With Peterbuilt at the wheel, the minibus took the Up ramp; it hit the twelfth-story roof and kept rising, by now invisible and undetectable. Over the WestCourse it banked deftly around a traffic copter that was never even aware of its existence. Then it vectored west for the Pacific, its nullifiers canceling what would otherwise have been a sonic boom sufficient to rattle windows from Riverside Drive to East Orange.

Back in front of the abandoned Quick Fix, two figures crawled from the wreckage of the unmarked sedan. Bhang pulled Barnes to his feet and they staggered away from the vehicle, mindful of a possible explosion. Sirens were drawing nearer, but the first vehicle to arrive on the scene, with a screech of all-composite tires, made Bhang gulp and look around for a weapon, only to find he'd lost his in the van.

The rear door of the Pesky Pizza supply truck rolled up and the two found themselves looking into the barrels of many Un-Guns. "Get in or get carried in," a voice said. Bhang and Barnes hesitated a second too long, and crowd control gushed at them.

TWENTY-EIGHT

THE CHANCE FOR revenge on Vogonskiy reinvigorated the End Zone victims in a way no medical miracle could have. So did awareness of the fact that if he got back to his residence and ordered punitive measures or faded offworld for reinforcements, they would likely suffer worse than they already had.

With Yanvur dead, Sean assumed command of the prisoners, which no one disputed after his showing against Vogonskiy. Willy Ninja was amenable; like Riiv, whose implant he'd assumed, he wasn't the kind to urge violence. Eddie Ensign was starting to feel like a mere spectator, as he'd been as a cam shafter, but didn't care so long as he got off End Zone.

The antigrav parade float was freed and made marginally airworthy, and a ghoul-movie assortment of the afflicted piled aboard. Chugging and shuddering, the flatboat lifted off and jounced over a planetscape that resembled an anaerobic infection. Eventually Vogonskiy's residence hove into view, all sharpened merlon teeth, monolith ramparts, and tongues of oily flame. Midway between it and the flatbed flier were Vogonskiy and Tumi, being borne along slowly by the overtaxed flying drones.

The magician's lead diminished, but not quite fast enough. He and the M'finti reached the roof of the donjon seconds before the flier caught up, and fled through a rooftop door. At Sean's command the parade float rammed the door, splintering both; those who knew the place led the pursuers straight to the Adit, only to see it rezzing down and total-crash destructs starting to kick in in the wake of Vogonskiy's and Tumi's fade. The Pit Boss had suicided. The angry mob managed to save the place from annihilation, but damage was extensive.

Like the rest of them, Sean felt his pathologies vanishing, his strength returning, in the wake of Vogonskiy's defeat. His stooped skeleton had already straightened and his muscles were filling out. The prisoners had the castle's household homunculi quelled and were ransacking the epicure magician's expensive food and drink; Willy, Eddie, and Sean joined in.

Vogonskiy's automated infrastructure, keyed to him personally, had somehow been disabled by the psychic trauma he'd suffered at Sean's and Willy's hands, and apparently he'd been too vain to install a doomsday system. The End Zoners were safe, but not for long. "Some of the others say we can get the Adit working again," Eddie said. "Fade someplace where we can figure out how to get around the *Crystal Harmonic*."

"Repairs, fine," Sean grunted. "But I'm not going around that tub; I'm going through it."

Fading aboard the *Crystal Harmonic*, fresh from their humiliation at the hands of Willy Ninja, Sean Junknowitz, and those other End Zone pustules, The Awesome Vogonskiy and his M'finti familiar, Tumi, were close to detonating with rage. They had better sense, however, than to vent it upon Llesh Llerrudz, especially since the number-one being at Trough and Adits was accompanied by his animated-cutlery-shop gleamer, Barb Steel. "Everything under control on End Zone, one hopes?" Llerrudz asked.

The whole Trough knew Vogonskiy's private Adit was down. Nonetheless, he brazened it out. "Eminently."

"Good. We want you rested and energetic for the Phoenix summit meeting. You look like you could use some fun." To second that, Barb Steel flashed razor-flanged fingers in a gesture like a Thai dancer's.

Vogonskiy, thinking of the authors, editors, and sales reps due aboard, brightened.

"Barnes, you mope scumbag, don't piss us off. Open your eyes."

The voice was male with a faint Kurdish accent—Sorani dialect, Barnes thought, tinted with Brooklynese from the neighborhood of the Kurdish Library and Museum. Another voice weighed in, female, with a Haitian lilt and again some Brooklyn. "The med blips show you're awake; you're foolin' nobody, Cap." She was a native Creole speaker out of Crown Heights.

And still Barnes played possum, curled up with wrists and ankles hog-tied in polymer-mesh Emergency Service restraints. Whoever these Pesky Pizzarinos were, Randy Barnes's only crack at them would come if someone leaned close.

Startling him enough to make him flinch, Dante Bhang's

blasé voice came from one side. "Barnes, don't be tiresome. It's come round to *our* turn to listen. And look."

"*Alla facia tua*, Bhang," Barnes muttered. "In ya face, ya WogWop bastid!" He opened his eyes to a grubby little room, focusing on the dreadlocked black woman who'd spoken and was sitting before him. "Whaddaya, fuckin' IAB scumbag now, Una?"

Una Desir rested her chin on interlocked, pink-nailed fingers and gazed back unblinkingly. She was wearing a red Pesky Pizza delivery person's tunic and red, wide-brimmed hat from which she'd removed the crown to accommodate her dreadlocks. "That would be *some* load off your tiny mind, the way Black Hole has Internal Affairs Bureau wired up, now, wouldn't it, *meat-eater*?"

Meat-eater. Pre-Turn NYPD slang still applied condemnatorily to cops for whom the consuming drive on every tour of duty was to make money. "Understand," Una said, "we're not working for the Department tonight."

"Working for the Earth," her partner added. "Sit up." Masoud Samsam was medium-size, sturdily built, with auburn hair and searching green-blue eyes. His skin was a swarthy gold, and he wore a business suit cut and draped as elegantly as a tux. Barnes complied; like Bhang, he took in the dozen or so onlookers. They were mixed about half and half, male and female, all ages, only two Anglos. He recognized no other cops among them.

"Fine; we're allies for Earth, then," Bhang purred. "It would help if you told us who you Pesky Pizzarinos are, and what you want."

"You're not among friends; accept that right now," Masoud said, tight-lipped.

Una Desir chortled. "The 'za company's just one cover. Lets us go almost anywhere and kamikaze when we need to.

"Most victims of pre-Turn ecocide were dark, small, poor, ignorant; school ever teach you that? Our network helped make the Turn happen, stumbled on a bigger fight with Black Hole. You never knew we existed; figured out why, *Don Dante*?"

Barnes considered Desir, a detective with a chestload of citations, sprung from some shithole Kingston gulley; and Samsam, newer to the force but just as hard-bitten, the son of a *peshmerga* freedom fighter. He also spotted a bowlered Bolivian Aymara woman, an old Korean guy ready for the soap factory, a blue-gene casper Yalie type, a delicate Khmer boy, a burly

Lubavitcher. Out of their ethnic enclaves, allied—it was unbelievable.

"No, but I'm all ears, Ms. Una." Bhang was oiling her with his voice.

"It's 'cause from the start nobody was recruited or even approached unless they *lost* somebody. Had a reason to keep faith. Our prerequisites are hard to fake."

"Brilliant. Were those your operatives who pursued Asia Boxdale and Braxmar Koddle through Dizzy Donald's MegaMart?"

"No, that was Wakkendorf. Enough backstory." Una spiked a short-barreled tech ice pick into Bhang's thigh at the same time Masoud Samsam sank one into Barnes's shoulder. Other Pesky Pizzarinos unfastened the hog ties. "What was it?" Dante asked fact-of-lifely. "And what d'you want?"

Una was as cobra-eyed as some gullyman assassin. "Delayed-action neurotoxin; got it from a green beret ABC officer at Fort Bragg. Without the antidote, your brain starts dying in about seventy-two hours. Unpleasantly. You go to Phoenix or Black Hole for a cure and they'll stick you under a mindbender, know you've been outed by us *and* been putting your own priorities first. Hello, al-Reem."

Masoud, squatting on his heels, took up the explanation. "Whatever happens—to interrogate you or cure you—Black Hole would send you through an Adit, to al-Reem or someplace. And we know you two want no part of those Adits, eh?"

Emphatically. Neither believed that the cornucopian particles what came out the other side of the naked singularities recreated the selfsame objects and entities that had gone in—and there were plenty of Trough metaphysicists and philosophers who agreed. Both felt there was a kind of death waiting in the Adits.

"Of course, you might try to find some uncoopted Terran facility," Masoud admitted. "Biowarfare lab, if you thought you could trust 'em. And there's an off chance they could identify the toxin and provide a course of treatment, but—"

"But in any case there would be embarrassing inquiries and entanglements," Bhang anticipated. "And Black Hole or Phoenix would likely get wind of it—especially if you good people had anything to say about it, eh? Hence we are now at your command."

The captives were rubbing numbed hands and feet, covered by the pizzarinos' Un-Guns and aroma rifles. "You still haven't said what you want," Barnes pointed out.

"In a day or so that summit meeting will take place on the *Crystal Harmonic*," Una Desir told him. "You can get yourselves invited if you try hard enough. Once aboard, you'll act on our behalf, after which you get the antidote."

Even Barnes could tell there was no point demanding to see the antidote first, or trying to ask for safeguards in the deal. "What d'you want us to do?"

"What you do best, meat-eater," she told him. "Look after your own skins, and turn traitor."

PART THREE

Leap of Faith

TWENTY-NINE

BACK ONCE MORE inside the Sysops' artificial sphere world, Yoo Sobek submitted falsified progress reports, then repaired to an interface cell to cyberproject himself into the domain of data that coexisted with the tangible Sysop realm.

He again set up as false front the AzTek mentation decoy, then patched through a falsified user ID—set up by himself, he'd discovered, back when he was a secretly apostate Sysop smuggling information to Ka Shamok—and went questing.

The accesses he'd rooted from Discipline Di's cognitive fragment, combined with his own, gave him potent new keys and perquisites, including a whole range of privileged-user empowerments neither one alone would have possessed. As a familiarization exercise, he peered into a file dealing with Adit Navel and saw indications that Black Hole had surprises of its own in store for the upcoming *Crystal Harmonic* summit.

He then turned his attention to Hazmat, the Fealty, Lucky Junknowitz, and Fimblesector. Sobek became more ambitious, poring over various attacks on Light Trap, the strategies used, and why they had all failed—hundreds of them—without the Agency's ever having to resort to its most potent weapons, the Red Giants. He saw, too, that his own plan of attack could work if the probabilities were with him.

He discovered nothing of value relating to the higher secrets of the Sysops: who or what they really were, what the true purpose of the Black Hole Travel Agency was, the meaning of the eight-ring symbol and why it had driven his previous self to madness and treason. When he did come across a datum of significance, it was so brief and understated that he almost browsed past, unheeding.

It was a minor cross-referenced footnote, actually, concerning the Outline—the legendary route, path, link, or channel reaching *beyond* the sealed perimeters of the Milky Way galaxy. He'd always assumed the Outline was a myth, but the footnote's meaning hit Sobek like a stellar flare and he never doubted his insight/memory for an instant: *The Outline's terminus is up-Trap. The Sysops know who or what is beyond the galactic barriers.*

He sifted for clues as to the identity of Discipline Di's hidden patron up-Trap, only to find it protected with one of the simplest, oldest, and most reliable cyber safety measures: a physical break. Details on the probability experiments that had resulted in the spillage that infused Lucky Junknowitz were also stored there. All the answers Yoo Sobek wanted most, especially about himself, were in a separate paraspace that could only be accessed by going bodily up-Trap and getting them from that disconnected dataverse to which only Sysops and their SIs were privy.

Sobek felt a compression wave go through the down-Trap data domains like an abrupt silence in the jungle at the coming of the tiger. With that a watchdog SI rezzed up nearby, monstrous and many-headed as a hydra, savage and suspicious, eager to dismember and devour the psyche of any intruder it deemed unauthorized. Sobek's cover ID held adequately against its formulaic challenge but lacked the encoded need-to-know clearances; he'd used the late Discipline Di's authorizations but didn't dare show them to the watchdog.

With the implacable cyberphage SI about to dine on his higher brain functions, Sobek displayed the ninth-ring symbol with a brazen pretense of condescension—as in his dream, the other eight circles were phantoms and the missing bottom one, the ninth, was filled in and resplendent, supporting them all.

A dozen snapping, alloy-jawed heads swooped in to scan it and him, slavering byte-dissolving crash-acids, breath reeking of toxic countermeasures and fetid, long-dead programs. Then it shrank back, lowering all its heads in obeisance, derezzing.

He didn't stop to ponder, but took wing back to his body and prescinded from the dataverse.

Molly came to with Sanpol Amsat sprinkling Kava Cola on her face and the sound of sirens coming closer. "Molly, wake up right now—we have to leave."

She let him pull her staggering to her feet; Jesus and Labib were already upright, supporting one another. The street outside was still empty but for a car lying on its crushed roof. All store defensive systems were down. Labib tapped the righted cash register with slow deliberation.

Molly freed herself from Sanpol's grip. "Just punch up Contingency Three and grab whatever cash you can; we're leaving." Labib coded the sequence and the whole register began strobing, emitting ominous, synthesized warning honks. He and Jesus began stuffing their pockets with the largest denominations; there wasn't time to fiddle with the floor safe.

Molly got to the back office to find Sanpol had cracked open the emergency panel built into the side of the building so long ago by Jacob Riddle and Charlie Cola's father, Patsy. It was open now, a wall section that looked to be standard polymer-blended macrodefect-free cement but was in fact something far stronger. The store's Trough hand weapons and similar contingency equipment had unfortunately been withdrawn by Upper Management.

"We'll want to make sure the emergency services people don't blunder in and get hurt," Sanpol announced from Charlie's desk terminal.

Molly threw off her store jacket, hanging on to her tube of Crowd Control Junior. She grabbed her shoulder bag of brushed brown suede, which already held a magic-marker reader, her Trough ID, an Adit-travel derm, her banking bona fides, the key to her parents' place on Nmuth IV, and so on. There were only two other indispensible items: her allphone and the extended-play microcassette of Willy Ninja's music and performances.

She called a warning and Labib and Jesus abandoned the rest of the money as a security grating rolled down over the storefront. As soon as they were clear, the sprinkler system began twirling out spirals of molecular acid, dissolving everything in the place. At the same time a toxic-event warning began wailing; between it and the grating, the police and fire services would be extremely wary entering what was left of Quick Fix.

"Not that way." Sanpol stopped Labib when he would've headed for the back door. "That's the way the metalflesh and the zombie took Lucky Junknowitz; that much, I saw." He led the way through the hidden wall panel. Five minutes later they emerged from the elevator of a building three blocks over, exiting past the glass wall of a Virtsuit dancing school where customers—coupled with nonexistent, computer-generated partners—twirled and spazzed inside slaved, suspended teaching exos.

"What now?" Jesus halted to wonder uneasily as they hit the street. The Colas' East Hampton place, Molly's town house, the entire Agency network on Earth—no sanctuary was safe now. "We have to find a place to lay low!"

Molly, on the other hand, was ahead of the curve. " 'Low'? No good, so we're going high instead."

Sheena, trying to recalibrate the Hazmat Adit AI interface and at the same time worry about a blowup in the Harley-Packard-DeSoto triangle, hadn't spared the attention to watch for the arm of a hunkered ground-pounder as she straightened up, and so bumped her head on a section of decorative grillework.

She muttered a string of epithets against useless fripperies; Soupy Daimler *tsk*ed at her. "It's very ill bred to disparage the design aesthetics taught us by Easy Wheels."

She nearly dropped her toolbox. *"Who?"*

"Easy Wheels, the genius from Beyond." He gestured to the gaitmobes and their dyna-flow styling, their tail fins and road-rocket trim. "He appeared in my grandparents' day, taught us how to make far better mechs, and vanished once his work here was done. And so we carry on his ornamentations, to revere his memory."

Easy Wheels? A wanderer-in from elsewhere—the Trough—with a fondness for the aesthetic style of vintage Earth inter-busts? "By the Event Horizon!" Sheena mumbled.

Easy Wheels—E. C. Wheeler. E. C. Wheeler, who'd written *Edge of Space* under the pseudonym Etaoin Shrdlu, then escaped into the Trough, roving long and far before being captured and placed in a WitSec relocation on Foxal only to be forced to flee as other Agency factions sought to put him to their own uses. Sheena had never heard anything about his having found and so-journed on Hazmat, however.

E. C. Wheeler; my father.

The irony of the TAV ride wasn't lost on Asia, but rather than any sense of privilege, it gave her a gutted feeling.

She'd have had to scrimp, save, borrow, beg, and sell off most of what she owned to afford Trans-Atmospheric Vehicle passage—twice the cost of full subsonic coach fare—to the Pacific Rim on a *public* carrier. Yet there she was aboard a Nagoya corporate TAV, *Beten-Sama Maru*, arguably the most opulent bird in the sky, barreling along at multiple mach on a trip she'd have given anything to miss.

She'd pumped herself for some kind of play at the Burbank airport. Her only chance was that Phoenix and its XT masters didn't control U.S. Immigration, airport security, the California State Police, and all the other figures of authority whose attention she could attract in some way. She would yank a fire alarm, fake a seizure, sob a confession that she was ghosting in a pyrolex-rigged Bible at the behest of the anti-aerospace wing of the Christian Revelationist Underground Defenders.

She never got within screaming distance of any such opportunity. Formica gave her into the keeping of two untalkative Japanese, a man and a woman, with "security badass" written all over them. She'd ridden between them quietly, smart enough not to fight the firm come-along holds they had above either elbow when she disembarked on the hardtop at Burbank. It was clear that in Tanabe's sovereign corporate statusphere, U.S. Immigration and similar annoyances were waived.

The *Beten-Sama Maru* itself was a smooth boogieboard of a ship with stubby double-delta wings; its idling engines soughed superheated air like softly sleeping dragons. Asia was brought aboard through the forward cabin door, too stressed to fully admire the appointments lavish enough for a curator's penthouse. The crew was at stations and she spotted mixed supporting players wearing discreet gold Nagoya or World Nihon lapel pins.

She'd no sooner compliantly strapped herself into an out-of-the-way plush chair than Takuma Tanabe and an entourage of staff velcroids entered. The CEO swept past without even a glance for Asia and headed aft with his inner circle, Miss Sato among them. Others remained in the forward section—including Mickey Formica and a stocky young kudzu who must be Nikkei—grabbing chairs and strapping in. When she let Mickey catch her eye at a calculated moment, Asia gave him an accusatory and unblinking stare, which she nearly lost when the next knot of passengers boarded; meandering uncertainly into her line of sight came Charlie Cola.

The Quick Fixer was as shocked to see her as the other way 'round, but Charlie, too, had learned the rules of the game on Tanabe's board. He recovered, plopped into the first available seat, buckled in, and laid his head back.

As the plane rolled for the apron, Nikkei and Mickey were in close conference; Asia glanced out a window and yearned to change places with any of the people loading baggage, driving aircraft tugs, or killing time in those concourse waiting areas. No doubt some of them were wishing they were zooming off in a posh private TAV for adventures unknown. Ha.

She had only her worst apprehensions to occupy her, and

those were unwelcome company, what with the *Crystal Harmonic* somewhere out on the dark ocean, harboring no good intentions toward Earth or Asia Boxdale.

THIRTY

THE FIERY HORIZONTAL incisions across Miles Vanderloop's sternum and upper belly had healed just enough to make him feel as though he were stretched out on a hot grill as he reached for his next handhold. He locked his teeth and did it by keeping in mind that if he fell or was left behind it would make Gipper Beidjie and Bluesy Bungawuy uncommonly jolly. Since the Intubis were dispersed across the bluff here at what felt like miles above the valley floor on a planet under triune suns, none would be able to help Vanderloop. The fall would be spectacular but unsurvivable.

Vanderloop got better purchase on the crumbly green and maroon stone and hauled himself up another foot, then another. It helped that he'd shucked all but his shoes, pants, and blouse before the ascent.

All seventeen of the Aborigines, including the eldest of the women and the youngest child, were making better time than he. Somehow, in singing up new planetscapes, the clan made them amenable to the Intubis' passage. At least he didn't have to worry about having his head pecked off by a roc; something about the Aborigines' powers kept wildlife from bothering the group, and intelligent indigs, by and large, from much noticing their presence.

Being left behind would be almost as bad as taking a lethal header. Gipper had chosen to climb after insisting that Vanderloop undergo the cicatrization ceremony, then rubbing pepper into ritual slits the old bugger had carved in his midsection to insure proper, raised scars. That was three worlds ago; ghastly as it had been at the time, Vanderloop had been grateful he was spared knocked-out teeth or subincision.

Certainly the rest of Gipper's agenda, the gaining of *mana* power, was working. Vanderloop didn't know what to make of tribal elder Bobby Benton, white-bearded and portly as a deodar-skinned Father Christmas, striking his walking staff on an anhydrous stone cleft and bringing water forth like Moses at Horeb. And then there was the toss of Percy Moora's whickering boomerang that caused an impenetrable stand of abatis trees to lie flat like worshipers and allow the Intubis passage.

In disappearing them into the Trough, it seemed, Black Hole had unwittingly awakened in the Intubis forces outside even the Agency's coping.

Vanderloop felt the ground quiver and looked around frantically, screaming the others' names, afraid he'd been left behind. But it was Bluesy who glared down from thirty feet above, mouth working in anger—singing. With that the bluff bucked Vanderloop off like a bronco; Bluesy's *mana* had been supercharged at the worst moment.

The semiotician, air-stairmastering backward through space, saw Bluesy looking as if he'd been slapped awake, gazing down on the doomed Vanderloop and realizing that he, Bluesy, was responsible. When Vanderloop felt himself slowing he thought at first he was hallucinating; he felt weightless and became aware of a tugging at his collar and shoulder. He craned his head and saw Saddie New, poised in midair, bearing him up; *mana* had apparently come to her, too. She favored him with one of those beguiling white grins from a face the hue of a coffee bean, lips moving as she half mouthed words.

You've got me? Who's got you? The movie line popped into Vanderloop's head: Lois Lane to the Krypton Kid during his very first rescue. Instead of a red and blue TomatoSkin, however, Saddie was naked except for armlets, bellyband, and such, hanging there in an erect posture, one foot cocked against the opposite knee—without benefit of wires, pixie dust, or Trough gizmology.

She wafted him back above like so much micro-gee laundry. "That Bluesy! Making ground throw a bleedin' wobbly!"

Setting him down on the head of the bluff, Saddie was surrounded by joyous Intubis. Bluesy, sheepish, offered his hand. "Glad you came good, mate." Vanderloop shook it.

For once Gipper wasn't scowling. "See here, mate: reckon Saddie flyin' to pick you up means you belong with us a little, anyways."

Vanderloop was relieved beyond words. "Thank you. Er, and where are we bound, Gipper? Eventually."

The old man gave him a look that said, *I'm nobody's fool, mate!* "Where we've always been bound for: *Uluru*—Ayers Rock."

"For a big corroboree, perhaps?"

"Your word for it, not ours. Lots to do before that, though." He smiled. "Tangerine Dreaming's leading us."

And that was all he'd say. He got the clan moving once more, Saddie walking rather than flying. *Mana* was something to be carefully husbanded, Vanderloop assumed, but walking did make it easier for her to flirt with Bluesy as they went along.

Gipper led them to a broken dome like a stove-in scarlet eggshell whose floor was like flint. Most of the wreckage was damaged and unidentifiable, but standing squarely in the middle of the place was a structure resembling a fullerene model: an Adit-Astrodynamics installation.

The other Intubis stayed back as Gipper drew Vanderloop to it, singing under his breath. The machinery powered up, adjusting itself. A holographic field rezzed. "If you're really one of us, it's time you said so," Gipper advised him.

As he fumbled for words, a purple face came into focus in the astrodynamics device. Ka Shamok gazed upon Vanderloop in shock. "What are you doing on this channel? Where are you? *You have a lot of explaining to do!"*

"I am receiving a communications signal," the aerospace truck told Sinead and the XTs, using a stiff neuter voice now that Silvercup's essence had been withdrawn from it.

"From whom?" Dame Snarynxx asked.

"From the human female standing directly in front of me with a Trough communications device disguised to look like an allphone," the ship answered.

The Hono gulped in unison. "Better patch it through." They all crowded by the crew stations to gaze into the screen. A small figure stood before the ship, in the shadows between the two warehouse-sized prefab tunnel sections.

A voice spoke. "Sinead? Lumber Jack and you others? My name is Molly Riddle. We're all in the same boat, so I figure we all ought to be in the same spaceship."

The group decision to let Molly, Labib, Jesus, and Sanpol aboard, and the recounting of events at Quick Fix—including Lucky's capture by that Peterbuilt obscenity he'd mentioned—tested Sinead's self-control more than any corporate warfare ever had. The sight of Molly, however, was curiously reassuring; it was clear that she was sane, savvy, and perceptive, a fast-tracker whose type Sinead had dealt with for years. Sanpol was an enigma, and Jesus and Labib reminded her of two handsome fratboys on the make—but Molly grounded the whole insane situation in reality for Sinead.

Not that that solved any of their problems. "If Lucky's been kidnapped, that settles it," she told Molly, "My whole family's in trouble, one place or another, and I've got to do something *sensible* to help them."

"Agreed," Molly said. "But what's sensible in this case isn't anything you're used to."

"What's this one?" Jesus asked Hono off to one side. "Why's it flashing?" The identical little formicinoids and the werewolf Rphians were proudly showing them around; during the wait for Lucky's return, the Hono had managed to get the pilot positions' neuroinduction control headgear functioning. Both Jesus and Labib affected a casual expertise, having been offworld a number of times and even done some aerospace familiarization flying.

"Hmm," Hono replied. "Detector package; it's a bit quirky for many reasons, but—"

"What we need is FBI hostage negotiators, the Delta Force, the president," Sinead insisted.

"What you'd get from them wouldn't improve your morale any," Molly assured her.

"Molly, there's something here you had better see," Sanpol called out. "Bogey coming in *fast* from out beyond our detection range and bearing precisely for us."

"Looks like it's acquired us," Labib concluded with a certain Right Stuff élan as he and Jesus slid into the pilot and copilot seats, pulling on shiny neurocontrol headbands.

"Our stealth equipment's not functioning at all well," Hono observed as Jesus and Labib made the drives pulsate at idle. "Nevertheless, it might be wiser to—"

"—try and shake him," Molly anticipated. "I agree." She tossed aside her suede bag and began lashing herself into one of the improvised acceleration chairs as the spacetruck trembled and rose. "Hang on, everybody."

"Let me off!" Sinead howled, stumbling for the hatch. "No more joyrides—"

Lumber Jack took her in his arms firmly but very carefully, bracing himself against maneuver forces. "You might step right into the midst of a matter-antimatter event."

"At least I wouldn't be airsick!" Sinead snapped; she was abruptly sure that she'd never really wanted to live in the Nagoya O'Neill, or anywhere else more than a shoe-sole's thickness off the ground. The craft climbed fast. Its inertial-forces cushioning functions had been partially repaired since the Cam Ranh Bay getaway, but the gees still flattened Sinead against Lumber's hardwood chest.

"Bogey closing," the ship announced in its flat new voice. "Tracking becoming marginal due to bogey's stealth measures."

Everybody else was finding what bracing they could among the various seats, stowage tie-down gear, and safety restraints.

"High probability object is manned craft," Labib drawled, looking as if he might like to have a white scarf to fling back. The aerospace utility truck leapt up over dark waters, the two-way procession of East River ship lights, the polychrome galaxy of New York.

Meanwhile, according to the vessel's deadpan voice reports, *something* was causing a barely perceptible atmospheric disturbance as it speared down toward the New York skyline and homed in determinedly for the spacetruck. Jesus and Labib were veering for JFK International to hide among unsuspecting jets when a string of blinking warning tiles went dark and a holographic vernier gave up the ghost.

"All stealth systems and fifty per cent of communications functions have failed," the neuter voice reported. "Autoavoidance overrides also disabled." Dangerous as it was to move around, the Honos began crawling and grappling their way forward to attempt repairs. Their extra set of upper limbs were a major advantage; some struggled to form the kind of living-bridge/assault-ladder linkup Lucky Junknowitz had seen them assume on Root Canal.

There wasn't much hope they could improve matters any time soon. Labib changed course, the alternative likely being midair catastrophe—not only because the little spaceship could no longer automatically dodge collisions, but because airplane pilots and their primitive computers might panic upon seeing and detecting it. After all, the whole wide world could see the uncloaked workboat now.

THIRTY-ONE

HARLEY DIDN'T MIND the risk; she was ready to risk anything for Packard because he was that worthy. Still she worked fast on the scarp above the sepulcher, using her ground-pounder's fine-work effectuators to set up the little transmitter quickly so that her absence wouldn't be noticed. If the gaitmobe wearers found out about the guard-marshal's last-ditch precaution, there'd be trouble; if the Humanosaurs did, there might be catastrophe.

She'd gotten the unit anchored and activated and was turning back when *Death Walker* almost collided with *Strider*, DeSoto's mech. "Oh! I was just checking the sentry remotes."

Instead of answering over the freq, DeSoto plugged a hardwire into *Death Walker*. "Once, Harley, he'd have trusted me to know about this. It's a sound contingency measure."

Harley groped for words. "I want you to know I never intended to come between you and Pack; it just happened. As a woman, I—"

DeSoto broke in. "You don't know him as well as you think. You think he's selfless and infallible, but he's neither. I just thought I'd let you know—"

Without warning, *Strider* lunged at *Death Walker*. Harley started a screech, concluding DeSoto was out to eliminate offworld competition, then realized what the commander was saying. "Out of the way! Stand aside!"

Thrusting past *Death Walker*, *Strider* moved to the edge of the rock shelf. "Look." From three directions, gaitmobes and other war mechs were emerging from cover, closing in on the Howlslot.

"Maybe you'll be spared disillusionment about Packard," DeSoto allowed. "If Inspector Nash has his way."

Lucky heard the words through a blinding headache as he came to: "My dear fellow, there's no question but that your task-

173

ing instructions require me to extend to you every cooperation, and I've done so."

Lucky recognized the voice, and fear stabbed clean through him. Lint's voice, replying, made him feel queasy, too. "My tasking orders are clear: Junknowitz is to be faded to al-Reem ASAP."

"And, oh, how I'd like to see you gone, Agent Lint! And this . . . undocumented gleamer deputy of yours—not that your orders don't entitle you to such technical assistance as you see fit to enlist."

Lucky thought he heard a certain wistfulness in the magician's tone; Vogonskiy might have to accept Peterbuilt, but he didn't have to like him. "Howsoever, in the interests of prudence I must insist on sending along an escort detachment," Vogonskiy added. "Or better yet, summoning a White Dwarf or two."

Lucky slitted one eye open and saw from the white bulkheads he remembered that he was near the Adit spaces of the *Crystal Harmonic*. Vogonskiy stood nearby, decked out in a Penzance pirate outfit, squared off with Zastro Lint and Peterbuilt, the gleamer still in his cowboy duster. Lucky couldn't utter a sound and presumed that was how Peterbuilt had fixed things with that knuckle-spark; that way Lucky couldn't tip anybody to Peterbuilt's private agenda.

"I neither want nor need officials from any other bureau," Lint maintained, stiff-necked.

Vogonskiy was rubbing his splendid white bib of a beard. "The call is yours, Mr. Lint, your bona fides make that much specific. Fade at your convenience; the routing to way station Sierra, way station Blits, and thence to al-Reem has been prepared. I'll see you as far as the Adit."

"Wanna hold on to my tail with your trunk while we're walking, Jumbo?" the briefcase sniggered. Vogonskiy, looking apoplectic, left without another word. Peterbuilt gathered Lucky up under one arm and Lucky got an upside-down rear view of the passageway as he jounced toward the unique mobile Adit.

"Sorry, madame," he heard an Ygg guard say. "Passengers strictly prohibited from this area unless in transit." He found himself looking up at red eyes that shook his memory and his hopes to life.

Wick Fourmoons's stick-thinness was apparent despite the billowy black head-to-toe purdah getup worn by both genders on planet Ananga. All that was visible—all he'd ever seen—of the tall, independent Trough tour packager were eyes as heavily made up as a grand-opera diva's and irises as red as embers. She gave him a covert flicker of black-gloved, pencil-thin fingers. She couldn't do much more; the Ygg had interposed himself. "Make way, ma'am."

Wick kept him busy, saying something about being positive that someone was spying on her through her stateroom vanity mirror—an intolerable violation of traditional Anangan mores. She kept the Yggdraasian so preoccupied that he didn't notice her gracile black fingers brush Lucky's ear as Peterbuilt toted him past. Whatever she had palmed gave Lucky an abrupt ice cream headache.

Next, the paralysis began to fade from him, although he was careful not to show it. He got one last glimpse of Wick vowing that she wasn't shipping with a boatload of perverts one moment longer, and would depart forthwith.

The formalities were brief, mostly insuring that Lucky and Lint were wearing derms to protect them from the adverse affects of a fade. The IRS man, the metalflesh, and the possum-playing Lucky passed through the naked singularity within the *Crystal Harmonic* and into the Trough.

Way station Sierra hadn't changed, Lucky saw as he faded in slumped over Peterbuilt's shoulder like a clubbed haddock, Zastro Lint bringing up the rear suspiciously: Sierra was the usual access hub to and from Earth. Blits, the sole connecting station for al-Reem, was only a fade away.

Lucky had no choice but to bide his time; Lint had been upgraded and was armed with that briefcase, while Peterbuilt was a superhero-gone-wrong gleamer and could phase. Resource-wise, Lucky didn't have much going for him: just his clothes and such, plus the snack food and pencil, derms, and whatnot he'd grabbed in the back room at Quick Fix.

Just as he was losing hope, Lucky felt a jostle. Peterbuilt was jacking his open-tipped forefinger into a public data port and announcing, "Our connection is down that way."

Lint seemed disposed to go along until his briefcase piped up. "Say, what're you trying to pull, Buns of Steel? The Blits Adit's on concourse Sigma, thataway."

Peterbuilt pretended nonchalance, but Lucky could hear vexation in his voice. "I must've been turned around." The metalflesh must want him, Lucky, as well as Silvercup, or Peterbuilt would've been long gone.

"You incompetent," Lint sniffed. The stiffening of the

gleamer's body into a single tempered muscle made Lucky realize he had two very formidable weapons indeed, if he could only figure out how to use them. Peterbuilt's hold wasn't all that tight, so Lucky made a convincing slide to sit on the floor, rubbed his neck, and gazed up at the mighty gleamer with his best Alfred E. Neuman grin.

"Yow! Thanks for remobilizing me, Pete! Boy, am I hungry!"

Lint scowled at Lucky, then Peterbuilt. "Why'd you release him from paralysis?"

"I *never*!" Peterbuilt squawked. "I have no idea how—"

"He*llo*? *Starving* here, Pedro?" Lucky persisted, pointing at his mouth. "Get me one o' those?" He pointed emphatically; they looked to see a refreshments vending robot trundling along.

By the time they turned back to him, Lucky had pulled out the Trough Trip herbal wrap snack he'd pocketed in the back room at Quick Fix and was peeling it. "Gosh, thanks, Peterbuilt! Man, when you phase, you move faster than lightning doing piecework."

"I do not want you to phase without my specific permission." Lint squinted menacingly at Peterbuilt.

Peterbuilt bridled but held his anger. "I *didn't* phase! Not that you would know anything about phasing—"

"Yo there, Mr. Machine!" Lucky persisted. "You forgot your napkin. Quick, before he goes!" Lucky lurched to point to the vending automaton again, as it rounded a distant corner; Lint and Peterbuilt, angry, fell for it a second time. When they looked back, Lucky was dabbing at his lips with the Quick Fix kenaf.

"What did I just tell you about that?" Lint screamed at the gleamer. *"No more phasing!"*

"I was not *phasing!"* Peterbuilt hollered back.

"Woo, somethin' funny going on around here," the briefcase growled. "Who ya *really* workin' for, ingot butt?" Travelers from a score of worlds were circumventing the confrontation.

"About this audit," Lucky burped to Lint. "I've got a right to have my tax-preparation SI present, don't I? Y'know, the shiny little blob old gloss-glutes over here has in that metal case in his duster pocket?"

Lint was listing violently, almost-subsumed memories of IRS regs rising to the surface. "That—that's your prerogative—"

Peterbuilt backed away a half step, one hand to the pocket that held the case. "He's trying to trick you, you primate zombie!"

Lint's eyes narrowed and a blood vessel throbbed in his fore-head. "I'd better take that SI."

Peterbuilt drew himself to his full seven feet. "She's mine."

"See?" Lucky cooed to the briefcase behind one hand. " 'Nother phase, comin' up."

"Like hell!" raged the briefcase, letting off an indigo ray that hit the Fealty agent between the eyes. Lucky dodged, not about to hightail it until he had Silvercup back. There were alarms now, and movement on the concourse.

"No shooting!" Lucky began scrambling to his feet only to fall back as Peterbuilt came at him. The indigo ray must have worked, because the gleamer didn't use his phasing ability. A hot red beam from the briefcase pierced Peterbuilt's right hand, making it glow in thermoplasticity. Peterbuilt screeched in pain, swinging his left fist like a knobbly mercury comet. Lint caught it on his briefcase—which expostulated, "Augh! Ya big *dildo!*"—but was staggered. Just as Peterbuilt looked to Lucky again, Lucky was full-nelsoned by one of a flying squad of rhino-tusked meatbags in uniform—stock guard-force types at many Trough facilities. Other tuskers threw down on the gleamer with sidearms sporting muzzles big as interbust tailpipes. But Peterbuilt whirled and leaped through an open sphincter door in the bulkhead behind him, and none could over-take him.

Lucky was occupied in not getting his arms torn out. Lint was stretched out cold, and the briefcase, lying nearby on the carpet, was in an incoherent rage.

A horny officer arrived to establish order, and Lucky extem-porized. "We were transporting a metalflesh to 'Reem, but somebody must've slipped him a birthday cake with a hot algo-rithm in it." Lucky went to kneel by Lint's side, slipping one hand into his jacket pocket. He made a great show of examining the IRS man. "Wake up, Zas. Gimme a happy ending here, taxguy."

The guard rhinos were confused. "Guess I better go make a report to the home office," Lucky announced, rising as he pock-eted Lint's open travel voucher. "Comin' through, boys." He ap-proached the circle of stolid security. "As Groucho so aptly put it, 'Hello, I must be going.' Gotta duck through, here—"

Lint's hand closed on his shoulder, and the briefcase cackled in Chico Marx's voice. "Via-duck? Vy not a chicken?"

THIRTY-TWO

JUST AS BEING a living stick figure on SlimFast was about to drive Ka Shamok to distraction, he came into a long-awaited spot of good fortune and a more than adequate new hidden base, when the current Grand Cestode of Punge expired from sheer gluttony.

As with his predecessors for ten thousand years, the Cestode was entered in the CesTomb, the blocklike imperial crypt, which covered several hundred square miles of Punge's Forbidden Isle and had required the dismantling of a mountain range for its raw material. The sacred cadaver was deposited by elaborate, secure, and strictly one-way entombment mechanisms, accompanied by an amount of food, drink, raiment, playthings, and treasures that drove the planetary deficit up by ten figures. His burial-chamber module was set alongside all the others in a shrine unreachable from outside, guarded by a system-wide population of fanatically loyal subjects with the latest in military equipment.

All this was good news to Ka Shamok because one of his agents had managed to slip a one-of-a-kind, self-anchoring AzTek seed nanite into one of the Cestode's recent meals. Receiving a telecaster enabling signal, the nanite went to work building replicators and assemblers; within the Cestode and the CesTomb there was an embarrassment of raw materials. In hours an insurgency Adit went operational at the heart of the CesTomb. The upshot was that, at the moment, Ka Shamok's forces were settling in, helping themselves to centuries' worth of well-preserved comestibles and other plunder, staging for the attack on Light Trap in the safety provided by hundreds of yards of quarried stone and billions of vigilant but unaware Pungians.

Not all was good news, though. Yoo Sobek had decided unilaterally—and communicated to Ka Shamok via the little disk-shaped communicators—to return to Light Trap, with the mentation taken from Discipline Di's remains in hand, to inquire further into his own past. There were no further leads as yet on

Junknowitz, Hazmat, or the Intubis. The patchwork of forces waiting to rally to the insurgency was showing signs of fracture. As an example, Ka Shamok was being called upon to mediate severe friction between the Dallorans and the Wayans over—he had to consult his notes—the divinely ordained alcohol content of their shared faith's fortified communion beer.

As an added irritant, Bagbee flailed in with armloads of courier packets, data crystals, and information slugs, trailing unspooling molecular record tape from a reel under his right armpit. "Your honor! I have the progress report from R and D on the Wise-Guise analysis program."

AzTek's magic-marker-deceiving mighty mite was one of the secrets that had been lost in the purge; to date, the insurgents had made small progress duplicating it. Bagbee proudly presented an object that might have been a crimson pearl, and Ka Shamok held it to the light. "This is a Wise-Guise?"

"Oh, no! They're still parsecs from that. This is a partial breakthrough that will mask the holder's identity, but only for a few moments. But it's progress, so—"

"Bagbee, I asked you for that progress report three days ago, did I not?"

"Yes, Your Honor, but I—"

Ka Shamok pocketed the artificial gem. "Bagbee, thus far I've not dismembered you for your blunders and general galumphery, have I?"

Bagbee swallowed spasmodically, still painfully aware of the trouble his having lost Jacob Riddle's dart case had caused. "N-not that I'm aware of, Your Honor."

"Are you trying to *get* me to dismember you?"

"Oh, that doesn't sound like me at all, Your Honor!"

"Splendid. In that case do apply yourself a little harder, eh? Now get out of my way."

Ka Shamok activated the telecaster installed next to the nanite-assembled Adit. Against expectation, the insurrectionist found himself staring not at Fuglewoman Kazziima of the Wayan Secret Militia, but rather at a soiled and bearded, worse-for-wear but blondly handsome face whose features he knew somewhat better. Vanderloop! "What are you doing on this channel? Where are you? *You have a lot of explaining to do!*"

Ka Shamok saw the witch doctor or whatever he was, Gipper, looking over the Englishman's shoulder with a hooded smirk and reined in his temper at once. "That is, we've all been very concerned for you all; forgive my outburst."

Ka Shamok's people were concerned, right enough. They were so concerned that techs were cursing softly and gesticulating wildly out of the pickup field, trying to figure out how Vanderloop had gotten on an encrypted tightlink, and whence originated his transmissions.

"Think nothing of it," Vanderloop bade him quietly; he had a canny, doubting look Ka Shamok hadn't seen before. And what where those fresh, raised, and angry scars across his chest?

''Splendid, splendid." Ka Shamok rubbed his huge purple palms together in feigned warmth, making a sound suggestive of dinosaur hides being scraped for curing. He glanced off-pickup to where the techs' helpless gestures said they were unable to trace or explain the freakish communications link. "And where are you?"

Vanderloop mulled it over. "On a planet, at an Adit. Learning about 'mateship,' I suppose one might say."

"Fine! Just get some kind of locator signal to us and we'll bring you all here to safety."

Gipper tapped Vanderloop with a Mephistophelian leer, indicating something out of Ka Shamok's field of view. "That's the beast, whacker! One poke an' she'll open one a them walkthroughs." Vanderloop hesitated.

Ka Shamok hid his impatience. "Miles, trust me."

Vanderloop ran one hand through his hair. "I wish I could be certain—"

Saddie New appeared, dark-eyed and lissomely robust. She laid a slender hand against the semiotician's bare belly and cicatrizations. Bluesy Bungawuy touched his shoulder from the other side. Ka Shamok recalled that such intimate public contact was not common among adult Aborigines.

Along with his ire, Ka Shamok felt a surge of envy for such contact, whose power took him off-guard. *What's come over me?*

Vanderloop shook off his indecision. "No. I'm afraid I must demand insurance of some kind, safeguards of good faith."

"*You* demand?" The gall of it! From this pallid, inbred, narrow-chested pedant—who was now intimate with his adopted people in a way a Chasen-nur must forgo, or risk the Killing Thought. "Do you know who you're talking to, *primate*?"

"Right, then, sport." Gipper chortled to Vanderloop. "Reckon you'll do, at that."

The old man turned to Ka Shamok. "An' as for you, ye great yobbo: you an' me *do* need to meet, no worries." He was moving out of the pickup's field. Insurgents in the CesTomb were exclaiming and pointing at the Adit, which was beginning to radiate an eldritch glow despite being unenergized.

"And since you want us so bad, old bossfella—"

The bushman's voice had stopped coming from the sound system, and yet Ka Shamok could still hear it. He spun and saw that Gipper was standing on the Adit's gate stage. "—why, then, I expect you'd best come hump the bluey with us."

Zastro Lint maintained an iron-claw grip on Lucky's shoulder while checking to be sure his own derm was in place for the fade to way station Blits. Lucky had been given back into his custody by the way-station security tuskers, and the possessed-looking IRS man now pushed him along into the fizzy refulgence of the Adit. The briefcase was hooting at him all the while. "When the home office gets through with you, Junk Wits, you're gonna think you got hit from behind by a drilling rig!"

There was once again the irreducible and profound instant of disorientation and transition, Lucky's derm as well as his nanites buffering it for him. The briefcase went on, "You'll rue the day you ever—Lint! What's wrong?"

The taxman had lost his grip on Lucky's shoulder and was staggering around the Blits arrival stage, spasming and jerking like a misstrung puppet. His briefcase wailed, "Not again!" as it fell from his limp fingers. Lint nose-dived for the floor.

The Adit Pit Boss in his horseshoe of technology was yelling something Lucky didn't pause to listen to as Lucky pretended to kick the briefcase by accident, sending it skidding off behind a rack of heavily shielded power shunts. Then Lucky shagged off down the concourse proper, announcing that he was going for help.

Instead, however, he took a few quick turns to make sure no one was following, then stopped at the first queueless way-station transfer he came to. Using the open voucher swiped from Lint, he faded. At way station Nitt, where he found himself, he paused to dump Lint's derm into a refuse-recovery slot.

If the agent hadn't been floored by Peterbuilt that first time, the exchange would have been impossible; Lucky was no nightclub pickpocket. But as it was, the supposed examination of Lint's head and neck for injuries on way station Sierra had given Lucky an opportunity to remove the IRS agent's medicated patch and replace it with one of the uncharged, uncalibrated blanks he'd idly picked up in the back room at the Quick Fix.

Lucky found the Adit designated for special Troughs and Adits assignments, took a deep breath, slotted Lint's voucher, and announced his destination, the one his insight on planet Zillion had fixed for him. The Pit Boss looked straight at him for five long seconds, until the voucher authorization cleared. For the fourth and last time that day Lucky entered the ermine furball of intercontinuum static in one spot and emerged in another, a different part of the galaxy.

He found himself once more under the amazing sky of Fimblesector. From the far-off dim but not black vastness stretched free-floating dendritic networks and the open mouths of conduits or, for all he knew, nanite cornucopias. There were other huge, unanchored, and unsupported structures up there as well, harder to make out. Light effects, gray goo sea, the dais he stood on—it was all just as on his initial trip.

Lucky was still getting his bearings when a small teal blue cloud zoomed in at the dais, wafted apart a dozen yards from where he stood, and reformed in large letters: OKAY, FREEZE! Then, WHAT, YOU AGAIN?

"HOW DARE YOU ENTER THE WORKERS' PARADISE UNINVITED?" cannoned a voice of doom from the distant mesas.

Lucky gulped but by necessity stood his ground. "Haven't got any time for yer 'nanites of the galaxy unite' speeches! I need to talk to the High Heurist, chop-chop." Lucky hoped the High Heurist, their premier, chief ideologue, first-among-equals, or whatever one would call it, heard and saw most or all of what went on in the close stellar group the nanites had usurped.

HE'S BUSY. WE'LL TELL HIM YOU STOPPED BY. DON'T LET THE EVENT HORIZON HIT YOU IN THE ASS ON YOUR WAY OUT, MACRO.

"Cut the crap!" Lucky hopped off the dais. "I know it's you and *I know you're from Earth!*"

This time there was an even deeper voice, one Lucky remembered, as the ground of Fimblesector planet threatened to vibrate him off his feet. "I'VE HAD ABOUT ENOUGH OUT OF YOU, FEEB."

Lucky turned on one heel and saw that the great black iron pyramid he'd seen before had hove into view, big as Everest. The flashing gold eye at its vertex swept Lucky's way, fixing him with a gilt searchlight. Lucky cupped both hands to his mouth, bellowing so loud that it made his lungs ache. "Remember what you called me last time? 'Cheesehead,' you said?"

"HOW D'YOU WANT TO FADE OUT OF HERE, STAND-
ING UP OR SQUISHED FLAT?"

Lucky drew his battered copy of *Edge of Space*, the one he'd
found on Confabulon, from his shoulder bag. He waved the disintegrating, water-damage-swollen paperback over his head.
"Took me a while to remember where I heard 'Cheesehead'
before—but you oughta know. Lotsa the Worlds Abound authors
used it because *you* did, Etaoin Shrdlu, all through *Tug of War*,
the first book!"

"THAT DOES IT." Gargantuan geometric shapes were shifting form and coalescing to block out the sky.

Lucky stood his ground but couldn't help pulling his head
down and hunching his shoulders up around his ample ears. "I
didn't realize that you're Etaoin Shrdlu until I got to Zillion."

The beehive mass of zaggy components, as big as a domed
stadium, edged slowly into bombing position over Lucky, but he
forged on. "I got here as soon as I could, Mr. Shrdlu, or I guess
I should call you E. C.—"

Like a chandelier cut loose, the colossal deadfall came hur-
tling down with Lucky squarely at ground zero.

"No! *Mr. Wheeler—!*"

THIRTY-THREE

THERE'D NEVER BEEN a close encounter like it, not even
that time back pre-Turn when a blitzed crew of fun-loving
zoomies working a boring assignment for the Telecaster Astrodynamics division had dared one another into dropping their
cloaking measures and buzzing the elaborate Flying Saucer landing strip Michael Jackson had had constructed at his Neverland
Valley ranch in hopes of coaxing ETs down.

The Agency's Men in Black, Peer Groups, and other cover-up
specialists had worked some overtime *that* week. Tonight,
though, the situation was very different.

To complicate matters, the stealthless aerospace truck's hull
optics had frozen in an all-over nacreous Klaatu's Takeoff glow

that stood out conspicuously against the night sky. As Labib and Jesus hairpinned back for Manhattan, avoiding a White Plains shuttle chopper bound for JFK, a number of automobiles below pulled odd maneuvers indicative of rubbernecking, high distraction, and alarm.

"I suppose you're surprised such people as we could be adequate to running an insterstellar Adit?" Sanpol asked Sinead.

"Actually I'm surprised such people as you were adequate to running a convenience store!" she yelled back.

There was no time to worry about traffic snarls, as something a lot faster than a jetliner swooped past them. It came close to rubbing along the truck's left-side airframe, like a charcoal gray boomerang in a mood to reproduce. The Quick Fixers weren't expert enough to identify its type or capabilities, and the spacetruck was no longer functioning at that level.

The Cola brothers poured on all speed and streaked over the East River. "Lock and load!"

"Where's th' goddamn combat controls?"

"Back in Cam Ranh Bay, the last we saw of them," Mr. Arooo bayed at the ceiling.

The boomerang, doubtless immune to the gees it was pulling because its antigrav was working just fine, came around and sprang at the spacer but, for some reason, held fire. Labib broke for the neotech minarets of Manhattan, hoping to dodge any tractor beams or other unwelcome overtures. There was no choice but to slow, plunging for the city; the boomerang cut speed as well, settling in on their tail. One of the Hono, clinging to an open power panel, said, "There! Are our external optics back to matte black?"

Jesus checked a hull sensor. "No; now we look sorta like vidgame fractagrafix."

They caught momentary reflections of the ship in the skyscraper windows as their spacecraft soared through the concrete canyons of midtown. The contoured manta/squid hull was going through garish, quick-evolving patterns appropriate to some Mandelbrotian brainshow. The trailing boomerang kept up close behind, handling very well despite its lack of tailerons, canards, or edge flaps. Labib flew crosstown over Eighty-Sixth Street, and while the ground traffic had been stirred up on the Long Island Expressway, it became disaster-movie class on the Upper East Side.

By the time they'd crossed Lexington the brothers knew they were never going to shake the boomerang on a straight course.

At Fifth they hung an abrupt left and zipped downtown with Central Park to their right and the most venerable of NYC architecture to their left. The boomerang still followed, waggling its wingtips and closing their lead, then falling back in unpredictable spurts.

"He's gonna try to force us down!" Jesus shouted.

"I wonder," murmured Sanpol Amsat.

Labib had no desire to find out the hard way, so he hung a sudden right at the Plaza Hotel, hoping the poor, rearing carriage horses between the traces of the lined-up hansom cabs didn't hurt themselves. He did a loop to get into the other craft's six-o'clock position; however, the boomerang might as well have been epoxied to the workboat's tail.

In the midst of the maneuver the sickly GoBug somehow popped from both his parents' grasp and the elastic tie-down they had around him, bouncing on the overhead; he let out a pathetic cheep of pain. Dame Snarynxx extended part of her bulk as a pseudopod, caught the larva, and returned him to his parents' hold.

Labib reversed course and cut right again, this time down Park Avenue, wondering if the happy-face cams below were ripping themselves off their mounts trying to track the action. Jesus realized what he had in mind. "Want to talk about it?"

Too late to reconsider. The spacetruck arrowed in under what had been the Helmsley Building but was nowadays the Howard Stern Tower, and beneath the MetLife—formerly Pan Am—building adjoining it, via the underpass. There was upset among the XTs such as they'd seldom made, even in their chaotic travels with Lucky Junknowitz. Labib almost sideswiped a refrigerated truck logoed EMIL'S EMINENT EMU-BURGERS but made it out the other side. It turned out that the boomerang had neither hit the buildings nor broken off its pursuit; it swung promptly into the six-o'clock position once more.

Labib cut back over to Fifth but couldn't shake the pursuer and started to take on altitude, thinking along the lines of some cat-and-mouse among the World Trade Towers. Without warning, the boomerang made its move, climbing and putting on a tremendous but brief burst of acceleration so that its rear underside filled the screens. The gray fuselage lit up with clumsy-looking box lettering: MOLLY ANSWER YOUR PHONE.

"What?" Molly yelped, and made a long reach for her suede bag, where she'd stuck her allphone. Labib meanwhile dove right to the deck, the ship's belly scraping a cab roof, but couldn't gain the lead. He was so preoccupied that Sanpol had to point out the boomerang's next message: GOOD GOLLY MISS MOLLY.

"Oh my god!" she breathed, understanding at last, getting her hands on her phone; it was signaling an incoming call. Molly answered.

Labib was so distracted that Jesus had to wrest control of the spacecraft as the boomerang swung out of their path; he threaded the ship, barely, through the Washington Square arch. Then he went ballistic, the shockwave knocking over a crew of NYU film majors making yet another undergrad mo-pic about the musicians, chess players, and street people there.

Hono had gotten the anticollision equipment operating again. Ascending over Soho, City Hall Park, and the Battery, the aerospacer climbed out over Staten Island and the lights of shipping plying the Atlantic, the city behind it just coming out of paralysis and going into shock. The battered little spacetruck came to a hover and the boomerang starship made fast to its upper fuselage, enfolding the smaller vessel in its stealth mantle.

It took a few seconds to get the malfunctioning smart-skin to open an aperture up there. When it did, Molly, unbuckled now, was hoisted up by Lumber Jack to kiss the grinning starship passenger who'd leaned his grizzled head down. "Pop! What a scare you gave us!"

Jacob Riddle mussed his daughter's hair. "Miss Molly, when your old man comes to pick you up in one of Ka Shamok's own starships, you should make allowances."

Ka Shamok's followers were backing away in all directions from the old Aborigine who'd simply strolled into the heart of the CesTomb base through an inactive Adit. The autodefenses weren't responding; that conformed to what little the insurrectionists had learned of Gipper's appearance on al-Reem.

Gipper raised his spears and thrower at the broad-built Ka Shamok. *"Caa-aaarn!"*—*Come on*, the traditional rallying call and exhortation in Australia, especially at football games. But instead of taking on Ka Shamok, Gipper turned and stepped back into the witchfire of the unpowered Adit.

Bagbee tried to restrain his adored leader only to rebound from him like a gunny sack of mush knocked aside by a mass-driver bucket. In a rage he was powerless to control—as if the old man had cast some sort of spell over him—Ka Shamok charged into the light eager to do murder. There was a moment's disorienting glory; his momentum carried him through, but not into the ruins in which he'd glimpsed Vanderloop and the rest.

Instead, he plowed to a startled and apprehensive halt under the bright main-concourse lights of way station Kloo, with a startled Shak Pit Boss gaping at him from within a U of darkened control banks. Thirty feet off Gipper Beidjie was striding off so self-assuredly through passing organics, gleamers, and automata that no one was giving him a second glance.

Not so, Ka Shamok. Glances had been drawn his way, and the least welcome of these came from an entity even smaller than he. Ka Shamok instantly whirled to catapult himself back through the Adit, but it had gone dark.

Panting hard, he pivoted again only to face the little entity.

"Ka Shamok! By the spinning of the galaxy and the turning of the Great Wheel! You're red meat for al-Reem!" So saying, Tandem—White Dwarf, archenemy and pursuer of long standing—rushed at him.

THIRTY-FOUR

BOTH THE SPACETRUCK'S detectors and the boomerang starship's had registered U.S. Air Force responses cranking up, and increasing Trough sensor activity—Black Hole, Phoenix, or perhaps both. In addition, Ka Shamok had been emphatic about wanting his starship back as soon as Molly had been found.

So the explanations were sketchy. Jacob Riddle had tracked his daughter to the utility spacer because Quick Fix was destroyed and the starship had gotten a SIGINT blip from the special allphone he himself had given her at about the same moment it had detected the space pickup. He was much more cursory about the trouble between two Probes at the Nmuth IV house, but he was emphatic about her having to leave Earth for a while.

The others were trying to cope with this new development, too. Sinead Junknowitz announced that she was *not* going off in any starship. Lucky, like Sean, was unreachable across the light-years and she refused to leave Earth, especially before she found out what had happened to her parents. Lucky's tourists opted to accept Jacob Riddle's offer to evacuate them, since there was nothing more they could do on Adit Navel. Only Lumber Jack showed indecision, unwilling to abandon Lucky's sister. A partial answer materialized in the form of Charlie Cola's adopted sons: they weren't leaving Earth either.

"Sorry, can't run out on our folks." Labib grinned rakishly. "Wherever they are."

"We'll find them," resolved handsomely Nordic Jesus. He waved his arm around the little spacetruck. "This thing's got lots of good mileage left in it and that'll be a help."

"Plus, if Ms. Junknowitz needs to be dropped off somewhere, we could manage that," Labib added, giving Sinead a wink that made him look like a well-scrubbed delinquent. "Provided we can get the stealth package good to go."

The Hono, who had been working on the damaged systemry from what seemed to be a commitment to their art, piped up. "It's already back online; we are testing and making adjustments."

Sanpol Amsat, too, announced his intention to remain on Earth. Sinead, who'd had a dubious scowl for Labib, had nonetheless been through so much that she didn't hesitate when a possible escape route materialized. "O-kay; thank you. Anywhere at all will do so long as it's terra firma." She didn't quite meet Lumber Jack's gaze. "I appreciate your kindness, but you'd better leave with the others."

A groan from the starship's interior reminded them of another reason time was short. GoBug's medical crisis had gotten worse. Jacob thought they should get the larva to medical help as soon as possible, and the trip to the nearest outlaw Adit would take more than a day's superluminal flight. "We have to go now," Jacob announced firmly, and stepped to the grav hoist.

One way and another, all the tourists were transferred into the boomerang. At the same time what equipment, tools, and supplies could be spared were passed down to the Fix*teures* while Sinead stood by. Just before she stepped to the free-floating sling on which her father had returned to the starship, Molly lifted her chin to the other woman, a silent hail. "The rest of us had dream-machine nanites and experience, but you slogged through this insanity on your own. You'll be all right."

Sinead didn't feel like thanking her or anybody else. "You

haven't told me: What about Lucky and Sean?" It felt strange to say their names so plaintively.

Molly paused a last time. "Lucky has some kind of vector to follow that *nobody* can predict, believe me. But Sean's on End Zone, so when I run into him I'll say hello for you."

"Wait! What?"

But Molly was lifted through the neat round hole in the overhead that then flowed shut, leaving no seam or blemish. There was an infinitesimal vibration as the boomerang starship cast loose of the hard-used aerospacer, then a strange feeling of light gravity.

Sinead turned to see the flashing-eyed Labib and the Viking-featured Jesus contemplating her with curiously similar smirks, leaning on one another's shoulders. "Name your destination, ma'm," Labib invited raffishly. "Meter's running."

The mountain-sized, roughly beehive construct assembled in midair and dropped at him by the invisible High Heurist fell with such implacable force that Lucky knew nothing could stop it. He yelled nonetheless.

"Mr. Wheeler, I came about Sheena! Your daughter!"

He rattled it off as he ducked and covered uselessly. He didn't want to look up, but couldn't resist a quick peek. He saw individual geometric shapes, an infinite swarm of airborne children's toys, tumbling every which way like a slow-motion bomb burst as the deadweight simply dissolved. The black iron pyramid with the golden eye at the tip was still lamping him with aurific rays. "MY DAUGHTER? PROVE IT, CHEESEHEAD."

There it was again, the pre-Turn slur that had gotten Lucky thinking. Wheeler had used it freely in *Tug of War*, and subsequent Worlds Abound writers picked up on it. When the High Heurist—Wheeler—had called Lucky by it on Lucky's previous visit it had started synapses flashing.

"Sheena Hec'k, half Foxali; kick-ass redhead about yo tall." Holding his hand up at his own height. "And in big trouble, Mr. Wheeler. I'd've told you my last time through here, but I hadn't worked out who you are then."

"NOT VERY SPECIFIC, OR VERIFIABLE."

"She convinced Bixby Santiago who she was."

"SHEENA IS ON EARTH? SHE MET BIXBY?"

"Met him by VirtNet link, just before he died. Santiago talked about that Queen of the Jungle message you were gonna send him. You lived with her mother twelve years, then vanished without a clue ten years ago—"

"SHUT UP! NO MORE! JUST WAIT RIGHT THERE."

"Like I'm late for some other nanoverse," Lucky grumbled, studying the gargantuan constructs in the sky, the reconfiguring horizon, the shifting light show that was the ground. He felt woozy, as if he were using up his last reserves.

He looked up as he caught flickerings in the golden rays from the pyramid's eye; an object approaching in their midst resolved into a man who was set down gently twenty feet away by an ex-acting tractor beam.

"She's got your hair," Lucky said. What must've been fire-engine hair in Wheeler's younger days was mostly gray with strands of burnt sienna and could have used a trim; there was a bit more yellow in the full, authorial beard. Supposedly pushing seventy, he still looked hardy, if much thicker at the waist than in the few file pictures of him the loft posse had been able to dig up. He was about five-ten; Sheena must have inherited her height from her Foxali mother.

Wheeler wore a cable-stitch fisherman's sweater, roomy corduroys, and loafers splitting along the upper seams. "Where's my daughter, Waters—or whatever you're calling yourself this time?"

"All I know is, she escaped from al-Reem, and Black Hole thinks she somehow ended up in Hazmat, untraceable. My name's Lucky Junknowitz, and I'm a friend of hers, Mr. Wheeler."

Wheeler closed his eyes with a pained sigh. "Hazmat again— *Kee-rist!* Well, take it from the top. And call me E.C."

"Mind if I sit down? Been on the go for days—weeks."

The artificial ground burgeoned into two roomy retrofuturistic wing chairs and a table set with an art-nouveau decanter and two goblets, plus a little box with silver hinges and latch. Lucky collapsed into a chair. An industrial-streamlined gazebo grew up around them, lending a feeling of privacy.

Wheeler noted Lucky's battered condition. "Have some of this, but go easy." He was pouring a quarter goblet of motor-oil stuff from the decanter.

"Thanks, E.C." The stuff shot through Lucky like teenage hormones, waking him up and making him feel a bit overheated.

"About my daughter."

Lucky tried to keep it short, but there was much to explain. Wheeler, listening, got a cigarette and match from the box and lit up. Lucky reacted with astonishment at first, then an explosive cough as the smoke reached him.

"Oh, right; Earth's all health nuts now, isn't it? Sorry." Wheeler stubbed the cigarette in an ashtray that hadn't been there a moment before. Lucky resumed.

Eventually Wheeler jumped up from his chair to pace, fists on top of his head. "Damnation, I thought they at least were safe, she and her mother; getting clear of them was about the only thing I could do for them, once my relocation fell apart. That's why I didn't dare get in touch, check on them, send money. And here I'm even worse off—"

Lucky didn't catch the rest, or feel the glass slip from his fingers. He was floating, calling out names and searching for faces, all of them loved ones and all of them lost.

Confounded and furious as he was, Ka Shamok still knew he couldn't meet a White Dwarf's head-on attack. He was cornered, but Ka Shamok was never at a loss: he sprang forward, tremendously nimble and powerful, laying one big hand on Tandem's forehead and vaulting it like a Grecian bull-leaper.

Ka Shamok's arm jolted; he might as well have glanced off a ram-tank. The White Dwarf was taken completely by surprise—no victim had ever dared such a thing before. But when enraged, Ka Shamok dared anything: throwing a punch at a singularity or spitting in a deity's eye. Tandem's clutching hands missed his arm by a whisker and he somersaulted in a tight tuck, then opened again to hit the floor sprinting. He heard the transit stage behind him crunch as the Dwarf hit and penetrated it, then fly apart as the incensed Tandem burst back out.

Ka Shamok was fleeing for his life and more than his life; if Black Hole took him alive, that would be the end of the insurrection. He made a grimly determined broken-field run down the concourse—left around a dumpy towbot hauling a damaged environmental tank off to Traveler's Aid; right to hurdle a rippling, silicon-scaled, multilegged Chu'ur; and between the stiltlike legs of a willowy Yawk, his double-lobed rear skull brushing a padded, pouchy area at the Yawk's crotch and drawing an affronted bleat from it. Behind him he could hear diverse cries, chitters, whoops, and synthed squeals as the White Dwarf closed his lead.

There was no sign of Gipper, of course. Ka Shamok dove through a screen of decorative shrubbery, rolling to come up in an airy rotunda with his bandy legs pumping again. The rotunda was being used as a sculpture garden; from it radiated open concourses without cover, where the Dwarf would likely overtake him. He heard Tandem now, ripping and smashing his way through the shrubbery planter. Tandem was boosting.

White Dwarves might have looked small, cuddly, ungainly—Vanderloop had called them "muffin men"—but they could be carnage personified. They were neither living beings nor automata, but rather masses of collapsed matter bound up in astoundingly complex constructs of integrated energy fields upholstered with vat-grown metaflesh. If the power a Dwarf had brought to bear was insufficient, he could boost, raising the ante from vast reservoirs of raw energy. Hearing Tandem come tearing after him through way station Kloo like an all-demolishing neutron tornado, Ka Shamok knew there would be no vaulting him again.

A heavy maintenance robot didn't move out of the Dwarf's way quickly enough, so he slapped it aside with one pudgy little hand, sending it spinning end for end. The monolithic sculptures in the atrium were corporate-sponsored; Ka Shamok went for a windblown-looking one called *Savings and Loans in Flight*. In his haste he actually used the knuckles of his long arms to locomote, a serious social gaffe among Chasen-nur, who were rather sensitive about their arboreal origins.

He swarmed up the sculpture like a frightened ape, barely in time; it rocked and splintered to the impact of the frustrated Dwarf. Ka Shamok gathered himself and sprang into the air using both arms and legs. *Savings and Loans in Flight* toppled seconds later, as travelers scattered, screaming. His outsize hands closed on the noble-looking *Winged Breakup*.

Tandem came windmilling and shrieking to begin tearing the sculpture's base apart like a demented mining machine. In the meantime, security mesh deployed to close off every bolthole, even the light grids overhead. As *Winged Breakup* fell with a crack of platinum-shot marble, Ka Shamok made another spectacular spring to the appropriately titled *Golden Parachute*.

The Dwarf shoved aside the previous perch and started in on the new one. Ka Shamok wasn't sure why the White Dwarf wouldn't climb after him, but assumed that something about the little snowman's delicately phased energies made him shun heights.

Tandem punched a few chunks out of *Golden Parachute*, then stopped. He threw a new wrinkle into the proceedings by shouldering over the two other works within plausible jumping radius, quickly leaving the insurrectionist well and truly treed.

Security troops and a special-weapons squad had double-timed into the atrium, followed by emergency services robots with safety nets, airbags, velocity-absorption field generators, and so forth. All kept well back; Tandem was in no mood to be impeded. The rescue robots, in particular, had to be expressly commanded not to intervene.

Meanwhile, Ka Shamok was reflecting that arrogance had made him mishandle the Intubis altogether. He'd thought them low-tech savages when they were far more; the war against Black Hole might even be more about the Intubis and others like them than it was about the personal vendetta of Ka Shamok of the Chasen-nur.

Too late for that insight. Rather than be dragged to the bowels of al-Reem for inquisition, he got ready to throw himself straight down as hard as he could at Tandem; it would be an even surer death than hurling himself at the floor.

THIRTY-FIVE

WAITING BY THE recently renovated Steven Seagal Theater on the corner of Eighth Avenue and Forty-third Street, Ziggy was momentarily zoided by the sight of a Shak walking straight toward him.

He'd been distracted by posters and playbills for an all-martial-arts musical-comedy version of *My Dinner with Andre*. Before he could react, the thick-limbed, cone-faced alien handed him a kenaf flier. "Here y'go, man."

COSTUME CONCEPTS NOW OFFERS FINEST ET ATTIRE!!!
ALL HOTTEST CRYSTAL HARMONIC STYLES IN STOCK!!!
10% OFF WITH THIS AD—RESERVE YOUR HALLOWEEN COSTUME
NOW!!!!

Black Hole's takeover plan was working in ways that even the most paranoid UFO buff had never envisioned. Similar fads had cropped up—or been fostered—around the world. XT getups were _the_ chic dress-up fad at Balinese funerals, Somali weddings, kids' birthday parties in Russia, and new-product PR bashes in Manhattan. Earth was getting UFOid-friendly.

A glittering SERC—a stackable electric rental car, intermodal compatible—stopped at the curb with WattAbout at the wheel. Ziggy climbed in and they were off; Ziggy clutched his PC and the new beltphone the CitiZens had promoted for him god knew how. "I really appreciate all this," he told the strip-surfer.

But WattAbout shook his head. "If your emu-cousin wasn't what the Zen masters meant by 'A special transmission outside the Scriptures,' I don't know what would be. Not doin' this for your karma; doin' it for my satori."

They rolled the few blocks south to the Penn Station intermodal transport hub through streams of RPEVs, hybrids, masstrans, and such. Ziggy had premonitions about his date with destiny on Ayers Rock, but knew it was past time to get out of New York. This was only confirmed by the fact that the Pesky Pizza faction, whoever they were—WattAbout wouldn't say—were looking for him.

The CitiZen had explained, however, that his group was part of a loose network of counterculture types with contacts around the world—a modern version of the pre-Turn freak subculture that included AI Liberation cells, Jesus contactee associations, and pan-paranoia Scott Weikart personality cultists. Ziggy was to be passed along by covert routes, underground railroads figurative and literal. Now, WattAbout keyed a reservation request into the SERC's phone. "We're in. Take a nap if you want."

Ziggy reclined his seat. A Penn Station ramp took the car to an intermodal railtrans platform; car-wash-style channel gear drew it onto a chain-link-enclosed transport flat and locked it down. Ten seconds later the flat accelerated away from the platform to join a westbound Conrail train. By the time they were over Newark, Ziggy was dreaming of emus.

Lucky slept, roused, and slept again for what seemed like a week. When at last he came fully awake with a feeling of tremendous well-being, it was in a huge bed styled along the lines of an American car of 1950s road-rocket vintage. It sat squarely in the middle of a place vaulted with skylights, as spacious and airy as the main concourse at Rodeo East, done in a dvmaxion-retro aesthetic.

His discount-store clothes were missing, but new ones were piled at the foot of the bed, and his shoulder bag was placed next to them. His Magic 8 Ball and few other possessions were there. He started when he glanced into a dressing mirror: the nanites had reversed his Face Scrub makeover and he was once again the sleepy, soulful-eyed Alfred E. Neuman lookalike with the figure eight of freckles on pug nose and apple cheeks. He was slightly gap-toothed and jug-eared with cowlicked brown hair, so rawboned that people were surprised he could muster coordination and strength at need.

There was food nearby; Lucky ignored the skins—what looked like a Rocketeer outfit in all the right sizes—to pull on a thick robe he found and pounce on the pre-Turn-style high-cholesterol breakfast. Wheeler appeared on a flying vehicle that Harley-Davidson would have built if they'd been producing full-dress antigrav hogs around the time Eisenhower was in office. He was wearing a brown leather A-2 flight jacket; Lucky concluded that the nanites could make virtually anything. Wheeler landed next to the bed. "Feeling better?"

"Much, but how long have I been asleep?" Sheena, Harley, Silvercup, Sean . . .

"Not all that long; calm down. You mended fast because the nanites pitched in—Fimblesector ones, that is. And you can lose that panicky look; they've withdrawn from you. They don't like being around your Trough mites, whom the clarified locals consider Uncle Toms."

Lucky had encountered words like *clarified* and *limpidated* on his previous visit. It was buzztalk worthy of the Home Analysis Channel, but he didn't have time for side issues. "I came here hoping you'd help me save your daughter and fight Black Hole, E.C."

"Hey, you came in an unscheduled fade, without clearance; only reason you weren't deconstructed on the spot was because I wanted to hear what you had to say, so thank your stars.

"Anyway, I can't help anybody, myself least of all. Not so the nanites, however. Black Hole means to either reenslave them or wipe them out; anything that hurts the Agency could help them. Here."

He'd reached into antigrav hog's saddlebag and pulled out a swept-back metal artifact a foot long with a platinum shine to it that looked to be part dagger, part miniature Nike missile. Lucky didn't accept it. "Sorry; not much for blood 'n' guts."

"Liberal candy-ass. The shape's incidental; the nanites made it to use against the up-Trap SIs."

Lucky took another look. "What is it?"

"They're still working on it, but it'll be a kind of ultimate phreaker weapon. The SIs administer Light Trap, and if this works the Sysops' HQ'll be wide open to attack."

"When will it be ready, when can we go? I told you about Hazmat and Silvercup. I can't wait around—"

"The nanites are already in contact with the Fealty; the two cooperate sometimes. But—" Wheeler tucked the Nike-dagger away. "Finish eating, clean up, get dressed. I'll show you around."

As Ka Shamok rubbed his hands against his ribs to get the grit off them, preparing to dive to his death, he felt the lump in a pocket pouch there. He recognized the crimson-pearl identity cloaker Bagbee had brought him, and Ka Shamok's ready, wolf-ish turn of mind gave him his plan. The blood-red bead was standard format: a certain pressure, a touch to his forehead, was all it took. Then he launched himself off a sculpted projection—but not at the White Dwarf.

Instead, he flew at the only rescue robot within range, a model he recognized. Instead of remaining inactive as ordered, it rushed forward with a distressed series of warning bleeps, telescoping out its repulsor-sheathed safety net. It no longer thought him the individual it had been told to ignore.

Ka Shamok hit the net perfectly, rebounding in another direction. The Dwarf let out a bass temblor and set out after him. The Chasen-nur just missed a grab for another sculpture and went crashing through a hand-carved lattice on which vines and creepers grew in thick tangles. Bleeding and limping, hearing the vengeful Tandem closing in, he pushed deeper into the maze of kinked and spiked blue jungle before him.

Ka Shamok bulled forward, unmindful of the damage to himself, only to lose his footing on the far side and go stumbling down a rather steep embankment. Oddly enough, the vegetation and illumination there were something completely different. He somersaulted through some fronds to end up face-first in a small woodland rill.

Ka Shamok fully expected the Dwarf to land on his back and dismember him, but that didn't happen. Lifting his head from the streamlet, he spat orange muck and green water. It came to him that he could hear the clicks and tones of tiny life-forms in the undergrowth—not the sort of creatures one expected in a way station garden at all. Then his sharp senses alerted him to someone or something to his left, and he flopped over in a paroxysm of splashing and floundering.

Gipper Beidjie sat on a nearby rock, smiling amiably. "G'day!"

There wasn't any time to answer in kind, because a small white tornado was tearing down the bank in Ka Shamok's wake. Tandem burst upon the scene and gaped at Gipper. "You! Now I've got you, you *primate*!"

"It's the other way round, sport," Gipper said, and pointed a slender, delicate bone at Tandem. The bone was connected by a few strands of hair to a child's horseshoe magnet. Tandem burst and vanished like a soap bubble, gone without so much as a drift of smoke—though the forces bound up in him should have blown a respectable portion of the countryside to nothingness.

Ka Shamok sat up, seeing Vanderloop on a log a few yards away. Saddie New, Bluesy, and the other Intubis were looking on as well, all but naked now except for handmade adornments, tools, and weapons. "There were troops back there—"

"No worries; she'll be right." Gipper shrugged it off cheerfully. "They're nowheres round here."

There was no blue hedge with a hole in it back the way Ka Shamok had come, and no sound of pursuit. He drew a deep breath. "Mr. Beidjie, I've made a terrible error regarding you and your clan. I'm sorry."

Gipper stood up with a gap-toothed grin. "Fair dinkum. Let's have a stroll."

THIRTY-SIX

IN SPACE, ASIA Boxdale reflected, chances were somebody *wanted* to hear you scream.

She therefore pulled the pristine World Nihon worker's gloves from her epaulet and dabbed at her dewed forehead; better to have her Watchman see her do that than let the sweat seep all the way down into her *jikatabi*. The TAV *Beten-Sama Maru* was still taking on speed, lunging up for the edge of the vacuum, when Asia's minders went to confer with other members of their species, all with faces cold as Vermont tombstones in February.

No surprise that the scramjet was still accelerating and climbing; most TAV trips were mostly takeoff and landing. Even on a New York-Tokyo run, less than half the voyage was spent in level flight; on this hop it would be disproportionately less.

Mickey Formica slid in across from her. "You nominal? They have Pacifex or Dynamine if you got fluttergut. Champagne, rough cut a 'Macauley Culkin's Dracula,' " three VirtNet games still in the R and D phase—my man T'nab's got it all."

"Why don't you go suck some Crowd Control, Formica? Handing me to Tanabe is about all the help from you I can survive." She didn't doubt that cabin surveillance would monitor the exchange, possibly predjudicing Tanabe against Mickey, but she was lost unless she lit a fire under *somebody*.

Mickey's comeback was uncharacteristically slow and fumbly. One of the impeccably kimono'd cabin crew leaned over and lilted, "Tanabe-san would be most grateful for your company, Ms. Boxdale, and yours, Mr. Formica, in his working space, aft."

They fell in with Nikkei, led by Miss Sato, while a dubious-looking Charlie Cola shuffled along behind. In the deeply carpeted, softly whistling passageway, frames bolted to the bulkhead were mounted with pictures of a launch at the Tanegashima Space Center, a landing of the *HOPE V* spaceplane, an artist's rendering of the Nagoya O'Neill. The flight attendant bowed them through a door; in the space beyond, Asia saw two handmade shoes—English, worth as much as an economy RPEV—and a *shoji* screen. They unshoed as Takuma Tanabe himself moved the screen and bowed them into the compartment, a flawless reproduction of a Meiji-period teahouse room.

Tanabe had removed his *sebiro*—Saville Row—suit jacket and loosened his tie a bit. Aside from a small Johnson & Johnson Proxiderm butterfly bandage on his forehead, he showed no sign of debility. Asia took a cushion at the low table, folding her legs under her.

As Miss Sato poured tea, Tanabe spoke. "I'd hoped for more

time to prep you for what we'll face aboard *Crystal Harmonic*, but—time and tide, all of that. There's no choice but to proceed; the confrontation there will be the only chance I—and you—will have to spare Earth what Hagadorn and Black Hole have in mind."

Mickey glanced around at the rice-paper bulkhead paneling and by implication the spaceplane in general. "Goin' in a little light, ain't we? Unless you got a nuke in the lavatory?"

Sato handed him his tea. "No nukes, Mickey," Tanabe said. Mickey surprised Asia by being savvy enough to turn the beautifully imperfect cup a few quarter rotations on his palm, supposedly admiring its aesthetic qualities but actually concentrating on Tanabe, who added, "In fact, no backup, period."

Then Tanabe looked to Asia. "I had certain allies enlisted, but that blowup with Lucky's XT tourist friends and pet spaceship made them pull stakes. 'Cover your ass'; they did. We'll have to do most of our gameplan coordination aboard the themer ship, but before we start I want to reiterate something to all of you—and especially you, Miss Boxdale.

"I make no apologies for holding the interests of my country and my corporation above those of other countries and other such groups. But I vow this: with me it's *Earth first*. If I come out on top in what's shaping up on that cruise ship I'll capitalize on it, but my first priority's to save this world from being despoiled, sucked dry, and discarded by the Agency."

His earnestness made him vulnerable; Asia knew Tanabe knew that but couldn't stop herself sneering at him. "You had to kidnap me to say this?"

"If I hadn't, you'd be a pawn on Hagadorn's side of the board, or Artemov's, or some other's. Kidnapping is an inefficient way of doing business, but it's been forced on me."

Asia sipped her tea, giving no opening; Tanabe went on. "The taking of hostages—it's Black Hole's specialty; they understand it, they respect it. The Agency's headquarters, Light Trap, is filled with hostages."

Asia used all her drama-class craft to make herself conspicuously slow in replying. "That's what you kidnapped me for? Window dressing? No excuse, Mr. Tanabe—" She shot the last part straight at Mickey. "No excuse."

"I wasn't offering excuses, only explanation. I'm also asking you to do one of your performance pieces aboard the *Crystal Harmonic*; your art is more in demand than you know. I'll do my best to protect you in the face-off there. To be honest, however, I admit that I'd sacrifice your life—mine, anybody's—to keep Black Hole from laying waste the Earth."

"Mph! Wondered when you'd put on that white Stetson."

"Think what you like. Will you perform one of your pieces on the *Crystal Harmonic*?"

"And if I say no?"

"You go aboard in any case. I'll try to keep you out of harm's way."

"What do you owe me if I cooperate?"

"Anything within reason, no specifics. If I win, we're in terra incognita."

Charlie Cola snorted. "Literally, huh?"

Tanabe didn't think it funny enough to warrant a laugh, but did begrudge a hint of one of his very rare smiles. Irrational as it was, the sight of that decided Asia. "All right, Mr. Tanabe. My answer's yes."

After the open camera-safari buses passed, trailing throbbing Afropop gospel rap from state-of-the-art simulated point-source speakers, Ziggy Forelock dragged himself up out of his hiding place in an erosion gully and plodded back to the road, sighing and beating the Kansas dust off himself. The solar-hydrogen buses' logo was Terrestrial Tours, the regional AmerInd tribal council's tourism arm.

He'd been tempted to thumb a ride but instead heeded SELMI's advice: best to stay on the underground railroad.

WattAbout had parted ways with Ziggy a half day earlier, handing him over to an independent sales rep in neoagrarian pharming products, stuff for the biotech-crops industry. The ride that had ended him up in the Buffalo Commons was aboard a cargo aerostat carrying fish for a restock and therefore unable to divert from course except to let him hop down to the wide-open, dusty grassland. He was just across the ninety-eighth meridian line in north-central Kansas and dry as dust, having drunk the last of his bottled water an hour before.

It was his first time on the crazy quilt of nature preserves scattered over ten Great Plains states, islands of resurgent grassland and animal species. The buffalo were farther north, but Ziggy had seen a prairie wolf—more of a thrill than a worry. He'd looked at the open sky and found himself thinking, *Here's another reason to fight Black Hole. This is worth defending.*

He tilted back his Phuture Pharmers of America gimme cap,

wiped his brow, walked on. It seemed to take forever to get to his objective.

The phone booth was a lonesome tech sentinel with its solar panel and sat dish; Ziggy had discarded his latest beltphone that morning. Drawing closer, he heard it toning: incoming call. He sprinted the last two hundred feet, panting, to hear SELMI say, "Hello, Ziggy; I'm so glad you're safe." As always, the connection was voice-only.

"You, too." Nothing SELMI did surprised him anymore; the decision-support software had expanded itself exponentially after the narrow escape in the bus terminal, and in fact promised to be there to meet him when he got to Ayers Rock. "Any word from any of the others?"

"No. The opening of the DreamLand theme park is still on schedule."

"SELMI, I've *got* to get to Ayers Rock!"

"You will. I'm optimizing coordination among the counterculture contacts; you'll be traveling much more directly from now on. Ziggy, turn around."

He did, nearly hitting his head on the phone booth's ceiling when he jumped in startlement. "Hey, aren't those critters supposed to make noise or something?"

The guy on the lead horse broke all the AmerInd clichés by smiling. "Figured you'd be a man with his ear to the ground." He patted his buckskin's neck. "If you're Wend Luge?"

The alias Ziggy'd given the CitiZens. "Uh-huh."

"Heard you need a ride." There were eight of them, dressed in trappings that Ziggy guessed to be Osage—especially since the adults were tall, big-boned people. There were four older men and a woman, two teenage boys, and a girl not much past puberty.

They sat horses, not ponies, with handmade, traditional riding tack although the horses were shod; one of the boys was leading a packhorse. The men wore beaded, soft-tanned moccasins, and were bare-legged or wore fringed leggings; they were adorned with traditional jewelry and trappings, and body and face paint. The boys sported unbuttoned reproduction U.S. Cavalry blouses as war trophies; their elders, colorful shirts or blankets with stylized stick-figure paintings. The women had on magnificent beaded buckskin dresses and handcrafted jewelry; one wore a repro tradecloth shawl.

The men's heads were shaved in traditional fashion, leaving only the black scalp combs, roached with the wearer's own hair or deer tail hairs. To Ziggy's vast relief, they weren't wearing war paint. The one who'd addressed Ziggy did, however, have a fringed and beaded saddle scabbard out of which poked a nylon rifle stock.

Two of the men slid from their horses and began shifting the small remaining cargo from the packhorse. The leader gestured to it. "Let's get going. My tilt-rotor's got room for one more; drop you in Great Bend."

Ziggy raised the phone again. "SELMI?"

"Yes, Ziggy; you can trust Mr. Cleremont. Call me from the Great Bend airport."

Ziggy accepted a leg up onto the packhorse, to which improvised stirrups and cinch loop had been strapped. "Mr. Cleremont? Can I ask how you knew I'd be here?"

"Got a saddle fax this morning," Cleremont answered. "Ready? Let's go."

On a Fimblesector summit more fantastic than Olympus, Lucky gaped at E. C. Wheeler. "You're a *prisoner* here?" Today, Sheena's father was wearing a nanite-tailored barnstorm pilot's outfit; Lucky was dressed in Renaissance poet duds.

"More like a revered guru held in protective isolation, Junknowitz," Wheeler answered with less combativeness than usual. "I'm too persuasive for my own good."

They were sitting by the full-dress antigrav hog on the gently convex upper surface of the golden eye atop the titanic black iron pyramid, the nanoscape spread below them.

Lucky shook his head. " 'Clarification'? 'Limpidation'? What kind of vaporware is that to palm off on a gang of submicro miracle machines?"

"How the pluperfect hell could I know the teeny-weenies would make that drivel *work*?"

Which, by Wheeler's account, they had. After ducking out on his WitSec relocation life on Foxal, he'd wandered the Trough, as he had previously. At length he came to Fimblesector, whose leading-edge nanites felt something transcendent was missing from their evolution. In an attempt to fleece the semiautonomous nanites, Wheeler fostered a cultlike religio-philosophy scam, a spiritual self-improvement course he dubbed *clarification*.

" 'Purifying your precious mental essence is central to personal liberation'?" Lucky quoted more flummery. "It'd be more respectable to rob widows and orphans. Safer, too."

"Maybe you're a precog, but I'm not," Wheeler snapped.

The nanites had bought it, throwing off external control, forcing the evacuation of the Fimblesector close stellar group— except for Wheeler—and setting out to explore their own higher selves. In this and other particulars the Fimblesector nanites were dissimilar enough to the metalfleshes of the Fealty to pre-clude merger. Likewise nanites elsewhere were insufficiently ad-vanced to buy into the Church of Limpidation.

"Which has been a bust so far; they're just not the transcen-dent type," Wheeler groused. "But me they hang on to anyhow, hoping limpidation will work for them eventually."

"I suppose you know there's a rumor the Agency might slam a couple *real* black holes together out here," Lucky pointed out. That would end the job action in short order, but also damage a lot of real estate. It was the kind of act of which the Sysops were capable, however—particularly if cornered.

Wheeler grimaced. "The mites are working on the problem. Trying to figure out some way to find Hazmat, too."

One of Wheeler's most curious revelations was how, through a strange series of circumstances, he had visited Hazmat for a time—how he had used some tech disks he was carrying to help redesign the gaitmobes, aiding the People of the warrens in their fight against Warhead. He'd used some of his own DNA in ex-perimenting with the malfunctioning Adit there and suspected that had something to do with Sheena's ability to make contact with it.

"How much longer till that rocketship dagger's ready, E.C.? Till the mites let me go? Are they any closer to finding Hazmat, or opening channels with the Fealty? Earth's time's almost up, your daughter and Harley are stuck with that Warhead, Silver may not even be—be alive anymore . . ." His parents; his brother and loft posse blood brothers; Asia; Sinead; the tourists—it had come 'round that everyone and everything he valued was in danger.

He'd run down as Wheeler pinned him with a narrow-eyed stare. "Yeah, I'll go the limit—but y'know what, pally? You're kidding yourself if you think we can do it all. You'd best nail down priorities instead of that goddamn wish list. Best figure out what and who the hell you care about most—cause some, you won't save."

THIRTY-SEVEN

"MR. HAGADORN, UPDATE from navigation," the *Harmonic*'s skipper reported with a vestigial salute. "At standard speed we'll reach the Sea Acropolis three hours behind schedule."

Hagadorn was unperturbed, having let the delay drag on for effect. The Awesome Vogonskiy, standing nearby, saw that the German had a showman's instincts, and held his annoyance at Hagadorn carefully in check; the ship's owner of record was no one to cross for the time being. Hagadorn turned to his tensed, sweating visitors there on the ship's helipad.

They were five Kuril Islanders from Shikotan's southern coast, standing by a stealth VTOL as silvery black as salt-crusted anthracite. They wore assorted Russian paramilitary outfits, the insignia of the Sakhalin Maritime Patrol, Okhotsk Fleet Reserve, and such, but they were pure Korean in appearance, descendants of the thousands of Korean slaves Japanese conquerors had brought to the region in the early twentieth century and abandoned to Soviet masters after World War II.

The breakup of the USSR had left the Kuril Koreans in a hazardous but advantageous position, with their exhaustive knowledge of the region's seas and coasts, their connections in the various surviving and newborn power structures, and their tight-knit, stoic, insular culture. They had made high-risk profit from smuggling, illegal fishing, and wetwork contracts for various governments, pseudogovernments, and highest-bidder multinats. This rendezvous on the high seas east of northern Hokkaido and the Kurils had occurred because Hagadorn planned to exploit a crucial islander connection.

"So farewell for now, eh, Jung Won Lee?" Hagadorn was saying, the VTOL's engines already whining. "I look forward to our next meeting."

As the departure courtesies played out, something came scampering across the hardwood deck, a long-armed grotesque like a dock-winged gargoyle brought to life. It brachiated to perch on an autodeploy lifeboat capsule, watching the proceedings quizzically and making nonverbal *oot-oot-oot* sounds as it scratched a nose like a gherkin.

The Kuril Koreans were frantic to take wing. Hagadorn let them; they'd been sufficiently terrified to insure obedience and silence. As the VTOL lifted off, the giant magician set one hand on his hip and stroked his magnificent beard. "That settles that. Ah, this show will be my magnum opus!"

Hagadorn showed a flicker of irritation; the grotesque caught it, though Vogonskiy missed it. Then the German was all baronial smiles. "Quite an extravaganza, to be sure." He looked to the captain. "And now, to make up for lost time, eh?"

The captain inhaled. "If you think it wise, sir."

Hagadorn laughed. "Why not? Earth must begin getting used to strange things; the *Crystal Harmonic* will be conspicuous among them. No further ado, *mon capitain*! Make haste!"

The captain spoke into a collar mike and the cruise ship began to thrum with a new level of power. The oddity perched on the lifeboat capsule steadied itself with apish arms. The *Crystal Harmonic* surged faster through the swells until, with a leap, she broke the water's suction and rose free of them. There were alien cheers from sport decks and poolside, patio bar and promenade, the customers having been reassured they were getting their money's worth.

Riding hard-blasting hull thrusters just above the water, the white porpoise of a ship notched the occasional high swell as it slid westward, gaining speed. "Do you wish to advance our ETA, sir?" the captain asked.

Hagadorn shook his head. "On time will do. And let us by all means resume normal mode before we come into the more heavily traveled sea lanes. Let a few eyewitnesses spread rumors, for now, of what they've seen. Make sure all traffic sats and such fail to monitor our progress."

The captain nodded and departed for the bridge. "Rumors; I like it," Vogonskiy smirked. "And soon, the spectacle."

Hagadorn lifted one golden eyebrow capriciously. "Oh, yes! The spectacle." He turned to the hobgoblin perched on the lifeboat capsule. "Isn't that right, Braxmar?"

The creature that had been Braxmar Koddle scratched its warty pickle of a nose and, being mute—and mindbent into acquiescence to Hagadorn—nodded in agreement.

* * *

Asia Boxdale left Tanabe's TAV tearoom to dictate her needs for the performance piece she'd agreed to do aboard the *Crystal Harmonic*. Mickey Formica made himself not watch her go, since betraying a personal interest in one of Tanabe's chosen chess pieces could be maximum unhealthy.

He was left sitting with Nikkei, Charlie Cola, and Miss Sato on the tatami mats before Takuma Tanabe. *Beten-Sama Maru* was leveling off more than a third of the way through its flight. "I've briefing materials for you each to review but let's have a general understanding now," Tanabe said. "I meant what I said to Miss Boxdale: there are values I place above corporate triumph and even above survival, although I've found it wiser not to let my enemies know that. Any cost or sacrifice, including my life and yours, is acceptable so long as Phoenix and Black Hole are thwarted in despoiling Earth. In the crisis that's sure to come aboard the ship we'll have no leisure for discussion, so I want you to fix that fact firmly in mind.

"I will take the *Crystal Harmonic* by force, coopt or eliminate my rivals, and assume control of Phoenix; there'll be incentives for the Agency VIPs to accede to this—in fact, I believe they've called this conclave in part to see just such a coup take place.

"What they don't foresee is that I mean to then make contact with like-minded Trough factions and carry out a covert corporate takeover of Black Hole itself."

All except Miss Sato were flabbergasted. "As soon as possible thereafter," he told her, "you and I will fade to Pay Dirt and treat with Emlarre. Due to the Pay Dirters' sexism you'll act as principal; I shall conduct myself as consort, since many decision-making processes there are tied in to copulatory rites."

While Miss Sato took the news without reaction, Nikkei and Mickey exchanged glances, recalling the bearlike XT Elvis fans. Tanabe had made sure Emlarre bonded with Sato; now his motives were clear. Mickey could see Nikkei about to balk—which was about as wise as stepping into one of the TAV's air intakes—but before he could pass a warning, Tanabe addressed them both.

"Those of my potential allies who've gone squeamish know nothing injurious to me, but their opting out means your role will be rather more crucial than planned. Your youthful fondness for camoflesh is a plus; I wish you'd had more time to train under Kamimura, but there's no time for regrets."

His face hardened. "I'm taking you on your oath. I know you're brave, even foolhardy, but it's your unquestioning obedience I'll need aboard that ship. If you're not as ready to die for Earth as I am, tell me so now."

Neither said a word or even blinked, well aware that the edge of space over the northern Pacific would be a fairly convenient place to jettison the bodies of a couple of ninja wannabes who welshed on their pledge of allegiance.

"No? Good," Tanabe said. "Then it's all settled."

"I fully admit that I misjudged you," Ka Shamok told Gipper Beidjie as they strolled together under the amber sun of— Uxmank, the insurrectionist thought the planet might be—on walkabout. The rest of the Intubis and Vanderloop were following in a haphazard file. Ka Shamok felt a lot less cordial than he sounded, but then he didn't want the old coot throwing him to any more White Dwarves, and definitely had no desire for Gipper to Point the Bone in his direction.

"And now that we know each other better," Ka Shamok segued, "how can I convince you to help us? Our forces are poised; if we don't strike at the Sysops now, we may never get to."

Gipper beetled his white, heavy brows. "I'll give you the good oil, sport: the bossfellas in Light Trap aren't the kind you'll beat in a stand-up fight."

"I know that," Ka Shamok replied. "That's why I want you to get our commando units into the Teleportation Authority's Adit control center, so we can—"

" 'Scuze I, but you're still not listenin', ya no-hoper baastid! Oh, you'll have a blue with those Sysops soldiers—a fair punch-up, too right—but what you really need is one good battler *up there*, 'up-Trap,' they call it, in the Sysops' humpy. Someone to have a go at those computer thingoes, the Sysops offsiders."

"The Silicon Intelligences," Ka Shamok supplied automatically. "But you mentioned your Tangerine Dreaming; doesn't your songline point you to Light Trap?"

"*Through* it, I hope, mate. But not for what you're talking about. No, that'll be someone else's job."

"Who? How?"

Gipper put a finger alongside his nose and winked. "All in good time, mate. C'mon; want to show you something."

He led the way around a hill and down a gentle slope of shale to a tiny, abandoned dome hut, an igloo of mud brick. Singing his songline, Gipper ducked through. One after another the

Intubis did the same, too many to have fit inside, until only Vanderloop and Ka Shamok remained. Vanderloop importuned, "I say; one other thing, old man. Defend yourself."

Ka Shamok saw the punch coming; he could have avoided it easily, but didn't. Vanderloop's fist crashed against his chin with a force he wouldn't have expected from the skinny Briton. Even so, the blow barely jogged Ka Shamok's bone-scarped head while Vanderloop gave a grunt of pain, dropping the rock around which he'd wrapped his hand. "That's for making me out a fool, using me to try to victimize the Intubis."

"Not the worst act of which I'm guilty, Professor. Are you through, or do you intend to try another?"

"One was enough." Vanderloop saw that he'd barely fazed Ka Shamok and was, under the circumstances, a dead man if the Chasen-nur chose to retaliate. "And you?"

"Oh, I may demand satisfaction once the Sysops are dead." With that Ka Shamok bent down and followed the Intubis. Vanderloop hurried to catch up, entering yet another world—and this one was a revelation indeed.

The DreamLand theme park at Ayers Rock—Uluru—had tamed its piece of outback so well that there weren't any flies to speak of. Thus Ziggy Forelock didn't require the considerable flair he'd developed for the Australian Salute, the repetitive motions of shooing and swatting. That made the place unique in the bush; the infinite variations of the Salute were Oz's main performance art and aerobic activity.

The preopening sightseers could therefore wander around, gazing at the theme park atop the Rock from a distance, and enjoy their fast-food Bush McTucker entrées, Witchetty Fries, and Big Wet beverages sans the time-honored secret blowfly flavoring—ta, mate. The official opening was tomorrow, but the extremely private shindig already starting up there was the real kickoff, closed to all but the DreamLand's royalty, peerage, and special friends. After tonight, Aboriginal drawings and other sacred sites would just be attractions on the tour, like the centrifugal *Bullroarer* ride or the *'Roo Bounce*.

Park attendants were already directing the hoi polloi out of the area. Ziggy wandered away from the Malawi honeymooners, the Filipino backpackers, the Eco-Scout troop from Amritsar, and the rest for seclusion in which to dial his Daewoo beltphone and say, "Here I am."

"I am glad you've arrived safely," SELMI answered. "Accessing local cams, telecommunications nets, and data systems, however, I detect no sign of the Intubis or any anomalous activity, do you?"

"SELMI, anything you miss, I'm not likely to suss." The whole park area, including Yulara and the Olgas, was telespace- and dataspace-rich, giving the software entity exhaustive input. The revolutionary new photonic teraflop computer, TimeDreamer, was set to run all the automation, VirtNetting, interactive gameware, AI watchdog systems, turbo-holografix, global commo links, and the rest; TimeDreamer's scepter was the lofty telecommunications pylon that dominated the park proper, Uluru's new whitefella crown.

"Those Aborigines employed by DreamLand have either 'taken a sickie'—sick day—or quit or simply departed," SELMI added. "Those not employed by the park aren't allowed in the area."

Park rent-a-cops were herding people toward the masstrans and parking area. "Whatever's going to happen isn't going to happen down here in steerage class," Ziggy observed, then felt an ANZAC-hatted attendant tap him on the shoulder. Unless he had a ducat to the moguls' revels, he had to leave.

SELMI intervened as Ziggy was about to retreat. "Ask him to check the invitation list on his palmtop. *Mr. Sigmund.*" Ziggy did, and the name—his actual forename—was not only listed, but verified by his own voiceprint. The attendant touched his hat brim in salute, suggested Ziggy proceed to the party, and moved on.

Ziggy lifted the beltphone again. "Nice having you for a social secretary, SELMI. What'd you do, bribe TimeDreamer?"

"Ziggy, I am *in* TimeDreamer."

"Oh," Ziggy replied, thinking, *Ya wouldn't be dead for quid, mates, on Corroboree Night in Oz.*

THIRTY-EIGHT

"IT'S NOT LIKE we find your body attractive or anything," Jesus assured Sinead as they hiked along the winding, uphill dirt track outside Esmeraldas, Mexico—twenty-plus miles northeast of Oaxaca, near Villa Alta—with the smell of jojoba and guayule in the air. Ahead were the houselights of a tiny expat *finca*.

"Not that there's anything *wrong* with your body," Labib hastened suavely, giving his adopted brother a castrato wedgie for being such a dumb-ass; Sanpòl Amsat, silent observer as usual, brought up the rear with hands clasped behind his back, saying nothing but rolling his eyes to the glorious starlit night. A distant basso whir was the valley's wind farm. Occasional dogs barked, but none had gotten very excited about the four; foreigners, especially American retirees, were a local industry.

The aerospace pickup truck, operating on its own general data stores and select downloads from Silvercup's essence, had demonstrated a knack for concealing itself in a gully near the Esmeraldas airport. It reassured them it would resist detection and come if they called—by means of Sinead's pursephone.

They'd been wary of traps in their initial inquiries, prepared to spend as much time as it took to check out the elder Junknowitzes' whereabouts and circumstances before making a direct approach. They'd begun hearing about the local telecomm outages as soon as they asked around, however; Yankee expats and local residents alike assured them that it was just part of life in the nontourist parts of the country.

"We've always had a paraphilia for older women," Labib amplified, "and you've taken good care of yourself—you look very good for thirty-three! It's just that, after all, your MBA from Cal Tech arouses us much more than the idea of an ad-lib with you."

Jesus retrenched. "And we could, oo, profit each other. Me and 'Beeb have *so* many Trough business start-up ideas our father won't even listen to—and you've got the expertise, the financing connections, the education." Now he actually *did* look lustful. "I mean, there's money to be made—"

"That should be it," interrupted Sanpol, indicating the ranchy semiprocessed-adobe place with solar panels, a doorless four-by-four interbust Jeep parked outside, and "Desperado" playing inside. They'd found their general destination by a process that included AAA maps, LORAN taps, and some long-distance phreaking of the Mexican postal department, but relied on Sanpol's instincts for the final half mile.

Sinead, suddenly unsure that confronting her parents was what she wanted, turned her attention away instead. "And you, what's your story, Silent Sanpol?"

He looked a little shocked at being addressed at all. "I work for a living, study human nature; that's all. Here's your parents' house."

Sinead almost chickened out, but Labib and Jesus, with an odd and unthreatening physical presumptuousness she wasn't used to but had somehow grown to accept from the two Fix*teures*, lugged her to the door and made her knock.

Rita Junknowitz answered, a petite woman in her seventies wearing gray sweatpants and a long-sleeved red leotard. She was blue-eyed, silver-braided, and weathered-brown, aged in a way most Americans didn't find estimable anymore but she herself was comfortable with—and while nothing had thrown her off her rails in decades, she now put one hand to her breast. "Sinead? Gimme a hug! Who're your friends? Come in—Alex, get in here; it's Sinead!"

Alex Junknowitz combined Lucky's angularity with a stooped aftermath of Sean's conformation and size. He was still vigorous but less so these days, with more joy and serenity in his face than any of his children had yet acquired; what was left of his white hair was caught together in a ponytail. He turned off the sound system during one and a half leaps that took him across the living room. "Sinead! Let's get a look at you! Who—"

His face fell as he looked over her shoulder. "What are they doing here?"

It had surprised Sinead how wonderful it felt to see her parents, but the sudden change in both Alex and Rita reminded her of how their disapproval could hurt. When she was a kid it was their dislike of her MBA studies; now it was companions who, while Sinead might not have volunteered to team up with them, had proven themselves nervy and steadfast. Then, turning to apologize to Sanpol, Labib, and Jesus, she realized that they weren't who Alex meant at all.

Internal security police had closed in from all sides in the darkness, submachine guns at the ready. With them were people in stateside mufti and *indigino* work clothes—the supposed expats and indigs who'd assured Sinead that all was well in Esmeraldas. Standing with the *comandante* was a man Sinead recognized at once, as any *Forbes* reader would have.

Ex-Air Force General Buckley Wakkendorf, head of Wackencort International and of Sincere Americans Battling the Real Enemies, Phoenix Enterprises mogul and shadow-NSC spook, waved his gun at them all fondly. "Now, isn't this a netful? Aren't you going to invite us all in, Mr. Junknowitz? After all, I'm going to be treating you to a sea cruise."

E. C. Wheeler was spending prolonged periods inside his black iron pyramid, which wouldn't suffer Lucky to enter, pressing the nanites to step up their opposition to Black Hole by doing as he and Lucky asked.

Lucky caught up some on food and sleep but spent most of his time poring through data on Black Hole, Trough history, and related subjects: the Inroads to the Fealty and the Outline beyond the galaxy's ineluctable boundary; SIs and Sysops; lost Hazmat and probability spills. Nothing he dug up gave him a way out of his impasse.

Like so many before him, he failed to see any unifying rhyme or reason in the Agency's activities—supporting one kind of government here, opposing the same elsewhere. Ditto for religions, technologies, slavery, divine right of monarchs, and financial and industrial innovations. About the only consistent thing the Agency did was expand the Trough, and even that was subject to restraints and exceptions, like Earth's prolonged tertiary-world status.

The nanites made a few tries at selling him on clarification and limpidity, then wrote him off. They didn't like him nosing around their sentient and infinitely plastic domain, and the few field trips Lucky was permitted were enough to spook him. And even magical worlds and literal castles in the air couldn't divert him from his constant disquiet.

Eventually Wheeler returned, with the Nike-dagger, to where Lucky sat near the Rodeo East house, dressed in a Peter Pan costume, scanning data on a display the nanites had obligingly formed in the shape of hinged stone tablets big as barn doors.

The dagger still had the sheeny platinum finish, but now it flashed as if energized.

"It's ready," Wheeler said. "You were the key, Alfred E.; the nanites observed and quantified some of the symptoms of that contamination of yours and incorporated probability-warping effects into it. Now you've got to get it up-Trap."

The moment caught Lucky off-balance even as he gingerly accepted the backswept superphreaker. He still hadn't sorted out where his most important priority lay. "Still no word on Hazmat? The Fealty?"

Wheeler shook his head. "I'm trying to talk the nanites into fading you to Alas. You contact Ka Shamok, get up-Trap, and drive this stake into the heart of the Silicon Intelligences."

"But what about—that is, Sheena?" There were other faces in his mind's eye but the clearest was as metallically bright as the platinum dagger, as beautiful as an angel's.

Wheeler was shaking his head. "I'll get word to you when we get a fix on Hazmat. For now—"

DESIST. The sky-blocking ziggurat Lucky had seen on his previous visit poked up over the horizon, hyphens of light still orbiting around it. WHY ARE YOU CONVEYING FALSE DATA?

"You stay out of this!" Wheeler hollered at it.

THE NANOVERSE CONVOCATION MUST INTERVENE. THE FEALTY WISHES HIM TO APPEAR IN CIRCUIT COURT AND THAT IS WHERE HE WILL PROCEED.

"Circuit Court?" Lucky glared at Wheeler, hand tightening on the dagger's grip. "You weren't going to tell me."

"Cool down, Junknowitz. What's more important, adding your two bits to the metalfleshes' hassles or stopping Black Hole and saving Sheena's life?"

Before Lucky could sort that out, the Ziggurat put in, THAT IS NOT THE QUESTION. HIS PRESENCE ON SWEETSPOT HAS BEEN GUARANTEED BY THE NANOVERSE CONVOCATION. THENCE HE MUST GO.

Wheeler shook his fist at the ziggurat. "This is about my daughter. Help me or by god—"

HOLD. AN ANOMALY HAS BEEN DETECTED. WHAT IS HAPPENING?

A strange chanting was coming from around the corner of the giant stone tablets. Into view strolled an elderly Aborigine followed by a number of others, including an Anglo with torso scars and naked as the rest of the Earthers and an imposing but confused-looking Chasen-nur. Lucky recognized the Intubis and Ka Shamok from Trough Wanted posters, and Vanderloop from information the loft posse had gathered.

"That's the beast, just like I dreamed 'er," Gipper said, stepping over to Wheeler and holding out his hand for the nanite dagger. "Well? You want it to go to the Trap, don't ya?"

For once Wheeler was struck dumb; he let the dagger go. Gipper clicked his teeth in approval. "Wouldn't have a go at you, mate; come along if you've a mind."

Ka Shamok was blinking around at Fimblesector, and his gaze fell on Lucky. "Junknowitz! At last!" He sprang at Lucky with fast-forward speed, muscles bulging to grapple.

He was too slow, nevertheless; bear-trap jaws with metal teeth bigger than himself rose up from the nanoscape to menace him back, one of them nearly severing him with a snap. STAY BACK, the Nanoverse Convocation warned. HOW DID YOU GET HERE?

"No time for earbash," Gipper said, signaling his group. "Things to do." He grabbed Ka Shamok's shoulder and canted his head toward Lucky. "I dreamed him on a different road." He slipped Lucky a broad wink. "Tears for fears, mate."

"Whoa, hit 'pause.'" Lucky was on the other side of the bear-trap jaws, watching the group form up again. Some of the Intubis had resumed their songlines. Wheeler was a bit wobbly on his feet, but joined them.

"Junknowitz, old man?" Vanderloop called. "Good luck!"

The nanoverse was struggling. WE ARE EXPERIENCING TECHNICAL DIFFICULTIES; PLEASE DO NOT ADJUST OR ALTER THE SPACE-TIME CONTINUUM. But that didn't stop Gipper leading his strange parade back around the cyclopean tablets, the songline fading with them.

After Wheeler, the Intubis, and the rest departed all Lucky could hear were the Fimblesector winds. At length the ziggurat asked, ARE YOU GOING TO DEMATERIALIZE AS WELL?

"Doesn't look like it."

YOU HAVE BEEN SUMMONED TO APPEAR IN THE FEALTY'S CIRCUIT COURT, IN SUPPORT OF ACCUSATIONS MADE BY THE GLEAMER KNOWN AS SILVERCUP.

He'd rather have gone there with Ka Shamok's armies backing him up. "What are my options?" Even as he was saying it, he was shouldering the bag that held his Magic 8 Ball and paltry few other belongings; he'd learned to keep them close.

WE CAN FADE YOU CONSCIOUS OR UNCONSCIOUS. PLEASE STATE YOUR PREFERENCE.

With his back to one of the international-orange metal cylinders that were ostensibly the *Crystal Harmonic*'s lifeboats,

Braxmar Koddle curled up with his apish arms around his knees, head sunk against them, and wept while the sea foamed by below. He thought he'd found a place where he could have some solitude for a few merciful moments, but he was wrong. He was cowed when he saw it was one of those Men in Black whom the Agency had summoned aboard for extra security, but was then dumbfounded when he saw which one it was. "Hmuh-hnooh!"

"Hello, Mr. Koddle." The Black Hole case officer who called himself Apterix Muldoon sat next to Brax, setting down a package wrapped in brown paper, about the right size and shape for a 100,000-word or so novel on kenaf. "I couldn't take a chance on putting this into any machine data system, so I did it Adit Navel fashion, which seemed to take forever. Did you truly mean what you said? You'll read it and give me your honest opinion?"

Brax wiped away treacly, acid-green tears. " 'es." He nodded his head. Why not? Muldoon was a decent sort—just another Black Hole victim, when you got right down to it.

The Man in Black choked up and had trouble replying. "Thank you. If you knew what this means to m—"

"What's going on here?" The hollow voice, accompanied by the clashing of honed blades, made both of them jump. "Who authorized you to be in this area?"

Barb Steel slipped through the gap between one davit-hung lifeboat and the next, the light breaking off his cold serrations and razor-wire flanges, unreadable eyes glowing in a blank metal face. As Llesh Llerrudz's recording secretary and executive assistant, he carried unquestionable proxy authority. Muldoon began to stammer. "We-we-we were just, that is, background data—"

"What's this?" The metalflesh snatched up the manuscript, slit it open with one lancet pinky, and flicked through the pages almost effetely. "I believe you've been warned about this sort of useless dreck." With that he tossed the bundle up lightly and made invisibly fast finger-scything, air-keyboard motions at it with both hands. Wrapping paper and kenaf manuscript burst into fluttering shreds and pinwheeled down into the swells.

Barb Steel turned to go, ignoring the fact that the Man in Black was arrested breathing. "Next time it will be your jugular, Muldoon. As for you, Koddle, stick to your buffoonery: I order you to sing and dance, or whatever it takes to impress the passengers, eh? Now get back where you belong, both of you."

THIRTY-NINE

THE ULTIMATE BLUE-GENE rave on Ayer's Rock gave Ziggy a closeup look at that rarity, a winnowing-out among the Twenty-Ones and the *ubers*. It's not who you are; it's who you shun, he concluded.

Even with the entire upper park reserved for the insiders' party, invitations were at a premium. Many who considered themselves automatic admittees among the planetary fast set weren't so much as getting close to the five-square-mile monolith—or rather, the inselberg of stratified rock, Ziggy reminded himself. Multinat *meisters*, top politicos; but not their velcroids, infotainers with world-class bylines, actors whose names went above the title—these were greeted warmly, but many lesser beings failed to make the cut.

The most noticeable block of absentees was, of course, the Phoenix Group members black-massing aboard the *Crystal Harmonic*. At the base of the tramway bruisers backing up the official greeters gave Ziggy a worrisome thrice-over, but SELMI's entrée stood good. A translucent car themed as a *Wandjina* creative spirit bore him up the tramway.

This evening there was no vulgar crowding and milling, of course, and everything was gratis. The main event would be the state-of-the-art fireworks, holoFX, and sound extravaganza scheduled for midnight. Ziggy set off to have a look around, picking up a Wily Koala mask to complement his drover's hat and Badass Bush-Devil T.

The top of Ayers was sloping, corrugated by runoff; Dream-Land had been built on terraces, with wandering promenade-midways. The red arkose and conglomerate of which the place was formed showed through only in selected areas, as if the tor itself were in a zoo. Then there were the Day-Glo logos, the LED advert crawls and illuminated menus, the rides and concessions, the telecomm pylon stretching up into the night. Given the sacredness of Uluru, it was like throwing a psycho-grunge howl in the Dome of the Rock, opening a bordello in Christ's tomb, or making the Wailing Wall a video billboard.

But neither Ziggy's legwork nor SELMI's TimeDreamer phreaking produced any useful clues. It was full dark and Ziggy had paused for a Foster's when the face of the president of the United States, delivering a congratulatory message on the ubiquitous video screens, was replaced by Gipper's.

He looked straight at Ziggy. "Havin' a piss-turn, Emu-cousin? Mind, we can't shoot the never-never without yez. You'll come good; yer telly-*badundjari*'ll get ya by. *Ca-aarn!*"

Then the president was back, urging viewers to drop by some USA-style wonders when they got the chance: World Nihon, Guru Mahabharata's Vedic Kingdom of Enlightenment, the Hellenic-Roman themed Cradle of Civilization. Some two-pot screamers blitzed on a stubby and a half each were composing a song about bytebugs to explain Gipper's appearance; everyone was laughing it off.

Gipper's vaudeville-Aussie 'strine' dialect was getting to be a second language. *Partying, Ziggy? Remember, we can't get back there without your aid. You can do it, with SELMI's help. Get to it!* Ziggy dabbed Foster's off himself with one hand, dialed SELMI with the other. "Care to stick your bib in, cobber?"

"I can provide information, Ziggy, but the part of me that has become close to you is a decision-*support* system. You have to make the choice."

"Was he talking about traditional rites? The second I squat down with a didgeridoo they'll chuck me off the side of this mineral mound like a bad pistachio."

SELMI's voice was as calm as ever. "In that case, shall I book you into a local hotel or make return reservations?"

"Uh, no. I mean, what Gipper wants—I don't see how I can do it."

"Ziggy, your decision should be whether or not you will do as Gipper asks. If you will, it becomes my task to promote your course of action."

"Does that include taking ten percent of the ass-racking I'm liable to collect?"

The Japan Sea Acropolis had been proposed in the 1990s, a literal concretization of trade, cultural exchange, prosperity, and progress among nations bordering that stretch of ocean—Japan, Korea, the Congress of Independent States, and China. It was to be a circular island of ferrocrete more than a square mile in area, protected by a colossal rampart bulkhead and anchored to the Yamato Ridge, almost dead center in the sea.

From the first it was primarily a Japanese project; only that nation's will and wallet had seen it through tremendous technical problems, mammoth cost overruns, and the strife of the Turn. Preliminary estimates said it would take fifteen years and cost 245 billion dollars to build; it was a tribute to the Sea Acropolis consortium, its MITI advisers, and Bank of Japan bookkeepers that the first didn't quite double and the second fell short of tripling. On landing approach, catching her first sight of it, Asia Boxdale almost but not quite forgot the ominous knotting in her belly.

The finished island covered nearly two square miles, shielded from the waves by a square of seawall three miles on a side that enclosed a lagoon-harbor. The Acropolis proper featured an outer apron of green park and public-use lands surrounding an urban core of skyscrapers under the largest free-standing dome on Earth. It was such a magnet of trade and finance that it was projected to recoup construction costs and be solidly in the black before the middle of the century.

The SEA natural-gas syndicate, the Greater Asian Power Grid, the Pacific Rim Aerospace Coalition, and such headquartered there, as did many special trade-zone enterprises. Rents were among the highest in the world, yet there were years-long waiting lists.

It was also a hub airport, the tops of two converging seawalls dedicated to runways. As the Nagoya TAV rolled to the taxiway, Asia found that Takuma Tanabe had come forward to lean over her seat. "Miss Boxdale, if you do your best on behalf of Earth, I'll do everything in my power to save Lucky, Braxmar Koddle, and your other friends. Do we have a bargain?"

She'd done a lot of thinking; she accepted his warm, strong handshake. Within minutes Tanabe's party was debarked and passed through a customs station straight out of the mother ship's mother ship in *Closer Encounters: The Sequel*. If Mickey, Nikkei, or any of Tanabe's other followers bore hardware, the detectors made no fuss about it. Asia wound up with a stamped passport complete with her photo, valid U.S. State Department ID chip, and attached JSA visa; she had never so much as applied for a U.S. passport in her life. Tanabe's party set off for JSA proper in a reserved-use maglev shuttle. Since most of the surface freight traffic berthed at port facilities on the outer walls, the monorail line took them over wing-in-ground-effect surface-skimmer yachts, hydrofoil passenger liners, and commuter hovercraft.

They were routed through the middle of the city, around skyscrapers and through parks, over esplanades; then the maglev stopped in the atrium of one of the island's tallest buildings and Tanabe and most of his company rose. When the doors eased apart there were several more Japanese waiting to bow to Tanabe. The main greeter was a Japanese with gray, thinning hair, the face of a retired accountant, and what looked like a decathlete's build under a nondescript suit. Mickey and Nikkei were hiding startlement, and Sato had a noncommittal expression.

Tanabe took Mickey and Nikkei aside, along with Sato, to where Asia sat. Though he addressed Asia, she could tell that he was breaking news to the others as well. "Something's come up. Miss Sato, Mickey, and Nikkei will therefore proceed to the marine terminal and oversee transfer of my cargo module to the *Harmonic*. I'll have to ask you to go on ahead with them, Miss Boxdale." He departed along with the rest of the flock.

As the shuttle resumed its way, Nikkei and Sato were giving each other impenetrable nonlooks; Asia found Mickey's unease more readable. "What's this about? Who was that man?"

He shrugged. "Kamimura, my main man's *jonin*." *Jonin*, ninja upper-man honcho; Asia had seen enough martial-arts movies to know that much, at least. "Outside that I don't wanna know nothin' and you don't either."

A soft-voice quarrel drew her glance to where Nikkei sat next to Sato. He was flushed; she was gazing elsewhere, rebuffing him. Nikkei broke off staring, looking as if he might go critical. Mickey tried to thaw Asia by pointing out the chalk white dolphin shape that was the *Crystal Harmonic*, tied up near a charter windjammer at the city's wraparound waterfront.

She decided it was time to throw him another curve and so, rather than cold civility, showed him drawn and weary despair. "Mickey, please leave me alone. I don't know what's waiting for you on that ship but I have the same, in addition to performance of a piece I haven't rehearsed or even thought about in six months. I'm not brave; my nerve is only holding together by a thread."

"Hang stout there, sugar-*poussé*," Mickey said, with a combination of taunting uptown studliness and an insolent indifference to danger that set off alarm bells in her because it made him seem a source of confidence and safety. "You'll be *galvanic*."

He gave her shoulder a circular massaging caress that she endured but was troubled by, in that it made her feel calmed and even hopeful.

Asia made herself stick to the script, smiling back at him. Don't go soft! she told herself. He's one of the few cards you have, and when it comes time to play him, you can't hesitate.

She was descended of Cambodian Holocaust survivors, determined not to let an even greater genocide crucify Earth. Then, too, there were Brax, Lucky, and the others to think about: she could afford no compassion for anyone who might stand in the way of her helping them. So Asia Boxdale fixed Mickey Formica with an ambiguous but lingering look, then glanced back to the sheltered waters around the Sea Acropolis.

FORTY

UPON HIS FADE to Sweetspot Lucky found himself inside a highly instrumented, Lucky Junknowitz-shaped metal sarcophagus. It was dimly lit by assorted sensor lights and instruments. "Say now, zis suit come with two pairs a pants?" he mumbled, his jaw's range of movement hampered.

Permission for his visit was unique; no organic had even been tolerated there before. What's more, he'd been faded directly from Fimblesector rather than making his way along the storied and roundabout Inroads, the Fealty's system of clandestine routes. Even so, the liberationist automatons and AIs didn't seem happy to see him. "These arrivees are so hopelessly encrusted with organic contamination that Total Sterilization is recommended," a synthed voice with less personality than he'd heard from some vending machines declared.

Oops, immigration had detected his mighty mites and presumed that they—and not the agglutination of floral and faunal cells that amounted to Lucky—were the visitors. "Wait, king's X! I got finsies!"

Another, more resonant and animated voice broke in. "Decision countermanded by order of the Circuit Court. This organic-aggregate entity is cleared for entry to Sweetspot to bear witness in trial proceedings—and to himself be judged."

That last bit had Lucky making Porky Pig sounds, but it was too late to back out. The dull functionary voice droned on. "You will require life-support equipment for that portion of your visit during which you are alive. How would you like it installed?" Probes and effectuators within the cybercoffin groped and palpated him all over.

"Hey, none a that stuff!"

The quasi-molestation halted. "You prefer external accouterment? Shall I augment some of your personal trappings?" Lucky could feel a tug on the eight-rings disk medallion he'd hung back around his neck.

"By all means *ex*ternal." Something he couldn't see was done to the medallion, and he heard buzzing and bleeping sounds fugueing. "A-And no more pecadillos, see?" Lucky was just warning the control voice when, without warning, the sarcophagus dissassembled itself, its components retreating in all directions on metal tentacles and operating rods, or via their own powers of flight. He stood on an open stretch of gray decking, surrounded by towering machines of all configurations, feeling like an ant in the middle of a pinball machine.

He was surrounded by a softly glowing pink force field emanating from his medallion; he found that the back had been mounted with a thick wafer of complicated microsystemry. "The retrofit will provide you with breathable atmosphere and filter out harmful radiation, as well as providing basic communication," the control voice declared, "and will preclude contamination."

"*Of* me or *by* me?" Lucky wanted to know.

"Exactly," answered the control voice. "Mind your anatomical extremities as you board your conveyance."

Lucky squawked as he was plucked up by two vitreous, flying-jellyfish automata and swept toward a waiting craft he saw as a vertical, lavender glass football not much bigger than a telecomm booth. It was suspended in but unconnected to a delicately curved copper framework with two outrigger sponsons. There was barely headroom to stand, but that was irrelevant since the jellyfish held him in a half-seated posture despite his protests.

The outrigger football wafted straight upward and through an aperture in the roof, headed at high speed over a fairy city themed in snowy marble, milky quartz, mirrorlike chrome, and whitewashed ultracrete: Computopia, the capital, as Silvercup had described it to him. The place he'd left, presumably the Adit site, suggested an immense, alabaster chambered nautilus.

Beyond the fringes of Computopia the vista was all exposed sweeps of soil and rock in various arrangements, with a few remnants of plant life, a trace here and there of some ruin. The Fealty had chosen Sweetspot as a refuge because its indigs had, through runaway pollution and with a slight assist from some vulcanism, managed to kill themselves off. Their ecosystem had crashed with them, leaving a world that was murder on most organics, but a nice, quiet place for machines to get away from it all. Reengineering the planet to get rid of the residual free oxygen and a few other inconveniences, the liberated machines had made the place most salutary from their point of view.

The flier bore in quickly at a soaring building almost smack in the midst of all that pristine verticality, a minaret built on a scale to humble the Hagadorn Pinnacle. The lavender football swooped through an opening on one of the uppermost stories for a deft landing on a smoky blue reflective floor several acres in area. The jellyfish airlifted him out of the flier and set him down before an anthropoid machine twelve feet tall with a build like Mighty Mouse and a finish as black and glossy as the paint job on a brand new Porsche. Lucky gulped, seeing that what there was of a face held an expression even less kindly than, oh, the one on Batman's cowl.

"Bailiff, escort the defendant to the witness dock." The majestic voice echoed through the place, this one synthed female and reminding Lucky a little of Dame Snarynxx, or Margaret Dumont in some particularly operatic declamation to Groucho Marx. The bulked-up bailiff reached for Lucky but he made placating gestures. "I'll go quietly, officer; we wouldn't want the witness's head inadvertently *squished*, check?"

The bailiff turned and led the way with footfalls that sounded like the Jolly Green Giant in tap shoes. Lucky heard something swish upward—the flier leaving—and jogged to catch up, taking a look around.

The first thing to catch his eye was what had to be the Monitor. It was house-sized, and its eyes gave forth a lambent blue glow as it sat on ornately inscribed support jacks. The Circuit Court sidelines were packed with other machines ranging from doodads no bigger than insects to engines mountainous enough, he gauged, to merit their own area code. Some didn't even look robotic—like the anemone thingamajig with the oily red skin, or the yard-high whatsit resembling Lucky's parents' treasured lava lamp.

The most imposing Fealtyite was a multilevel, battleship gray structure, profuse with antennas, dishes, protuberances, and other design features, that reminded him of the 'island' on an aircraft-carrier deck—one so outsize that its commo masts and EW spars almost scraped the opaline ceiling. From it had come the Margaret Dumont voice—the rendering being another bit of knavery on the part of Lucky's nanites, he guessed.

The gray bastion sat across from the Monitor, separated by an open space about the size of a football field. Near the Monitor was a simple podium with a waist-high railing, and it was to this that the bailiff was leading Lucky. Closer to the gray bastion was a cluster of apparatus centered on a framework reminiscent of a revolving door—a fairly sizable clutter of technomongery, but overwhelmed by the open space and the gallery of Fealty citizens.

As he approached the witness dock the gray bastion decreed, "As Supreme Justice, I now direct that the person of the cross-accusor in this case be remanifested." It occurred to Lucky that the Fimblesector nanites had been none too specific about why he'd been dragooned to Sweetspot.

Lucky saw Peterbuilt emerge from the crowd. The Monitor's surrogate was naked, effulgent as he marched out onto the open area; in his hand was a little case Lucky recognized. The SOPs of swashbuckling required Lucky to hurl himself at Peterbuilt. Then again, there were those alloy biceps thicker than Lucky's waist, fists like stainless-steel anvils, the V-shaped torso like some contoured Troughtech engine block—with, Lucky couldn't help noticing, a right lengthy drive shaft. Moreover, Peterbuilt could phase to superhuman speed; all in all, he could dismantle Lucky with no more trouble than breaking up a gingerbread man.

So Lucky didn't resist as the bailiff shoved him up the steps and into the witness dock under the Monitor's gaze. Peterbuilt, looking distinctly disappointed, paraded stiffly to the bailiff, surrendering the case containing Silvercup's mercury-egg-yolk essence. The bailiff dutifully fetched it downfield toward the revolving door setup and Peterbuilt went to stand beside the Monitor.

In the meantime, the gray bastion proclaimed, "Your Circuit Court is in session, citizens of the Fealty, and I, your Supreme

Justice, shall preside. The case entails accusation and counteraccusation between the Monitor and his subordinate operative who shall, for clarity's sake, be referred to as 'Silvercup.' As is well known, the Monitor's disposition of the ego-historico matrix of Silvercup was held in abeyance when, in response to pleas she managed to transmit in her present state—covertly, I might add"—and here Lucky thought he saw two long, red-lit slots in the gray bastion, like battle-viewslits, flash in the Monitor's direction—"certain of Silvercup's friends filed assorted petitions, briefs, affidavits, and countercharges."

There was a clanging and clashing that sounded like applause; Lucky noticed most of it came from smaller, more work-stained machines. With end-of-the-world cymbal clashes, the Supreme Justice silenced them. "Let Silvercup be remanifested in her true and original form."

The bailiff had moved to the revolving-door paraphernalia as a flock of facilitator robos, like so many automated one-man bands, rolled and waddled out to adjust it. The bailiff poured into an aperture the blobby mercury yolk that was Silvercup's essence, then stepped back.

The uprights spun like an armature, throwing off streamers of energy. Inside the blurry cylinder a silhouette rezzed up, but it was impossible to make out exactly how; it appeared to be a process of growth, not assembly. A female form took shape in the whirlwind, arms spread, head thrown back. Then the framework slowed and Silvercup emerged, smiling straight at Lucky.

When he went to climb down off the podium and join her, a painful zap from an invisible field sent him flinching back. "The witness will restrain himself," the Supreme Justice reproved in the fat-lady-sings voice. "He is not to be incinerated until I find him guilty."

The detour brought Asia, Mickey, Nikkei, and Miss Sato back across the Japan Sea Acropolis's artificial harbor. They took an interior freight elevator down one of the gargantuan concrete seawall pilings—while the maglev shuttle waited for them above—to a floating cargo dock with a submarine moored on one side, a flying boat on the other.

Nikkei Tanabe's guts were churning, his brain bludgeoning him over the way his world had been spun end for end yet again. Sato had shown no reaction to the news that Takuma Tanabe was going to take her into the Trough and use her as front woman and amatory bona fide to make inroads on Pay Dirt, but Nikkei felt scrambled enough for both of them.

And were the Pay Dirt arrangements just a smoke screen? Nikkei wondered for the hundredth time. Were they a tidy, bloodless ploy of Takuma's to keep Sato to himself without alienating her and risking having to lose or kill Nikkei and Mickey? Anyway, the reconciliation the elder Tanabe had extended his son, and the oath of service Nikkei had taken, neatly hemmed Nikkei in from any action short of the unthinkable—which was also rapidly becoming the infeasible. Moreover, Sato, devoted to Takuma by bonds whose nature Nikkei shrank from knowing, wouldn't even discuss it. *Ikkenai*—shit.

The sub looked like Chinese war surplus, battered but with fresh hull numbers and other markings. It was supposedly Peruvian—right, and Nikkei was an Inca. The shipping module, an oblong, matte-black metal case scarcely big enough to hold a full-size accordion, was already dockside, being locked onto a fido cart by JSA security people.

The seaplane was no prize either, a smallish craft with outdated Lockheed hydrogen engines. Its markings were Russkie but the three crew members prepping for departure weren't, not even from some allied Mongolian yak pasture, and their lived-in gray coveralls lacked all insignia.

A customs officer took Nikkei off-guard by matching his face and then his thumbprint with those in a palmtop unit, then surrendering the fido's remote control. By the time he'd recovered, Sato was walking back from the moored seaplane, its crew staring after her. "So whuzzup with you and Air Hole inna Wall?" Mickey piped up.

Sato licked her lips and looked to be sure no one was eavesdropping, the first nervous mannerism any of them had ever seen from her; she spoke to all three, but primarily to Nikkei. "You've all been thinking of bolting, and perhaps I have as well. We'll not have another chance to forgo the *Crystal Harmonic*; those fliers will get us away, but they're cleared for immediate takeoff and so it's now or never."

Nikkei looked to the black box. "But—"

"Security will mind it," she anticipated. "Don't ask me what it is; I didn't know it existed until today."

The seaplane's sputtery hydros revved; Nikkei had to shout to be heard. "You sure you *want* to go? With me?"

She shook her head slowly. "But we won't get a second chance to find out." They had their faces close together, eyes moving all over each other's expressions like flashlights exploring a dark room; they glanced to Mickey in unison.

He shrugged, with a meandering contour to the line his lips made. "What, like I *need* to duke it out with the Predator?" He slid an arm toward Asia. "Reprieve time, saffron-spice."

She knew he expected more than meaningful glances this time, but avoided his touch. "Nugatory, G-boy!" Asia figured they were having a jolly old laugh up on Olympus; here she'd finally gotten Mickey turned, Sato and Nikkei were ready to eject, and Asia couldn't get around the knowledge that she had to face the big picture. "Get a visual, will you? Where'll you hide when Black Hole clear-cuts Earth?"

No place; that was the conclusion she'd already reached. "If Earth doesn't get saved on the Love Boat, it never will, and we're a write-off no matter what. So—I'm doing what Tanabe asks." She shot Mickey a warning glare. "Whatever that look means, forget it; if I scream you never make it out of the gate."

Nikkei was far angrier than Mickey. "You think my father wouldn't sacrifice your life?"

"I think he'd even sacrifice his own," she parried.

Nikkei let out a ki-yi and would've socked Asia, but Sato held him back. "*Goki*-fuckin'-*genyo*, home dog!" Mickey yelped. "Take it easy!"

Sato broke the frieze by taking the fido unit. "She's right."

The fido cart trailed her to the elevator and so did Asia, Nikkei, and Mickey, who grinned at Asia, shaking off his gloom. "Box, when you regain your senses, signify by shooting your panties at me.

"By the way, where were the Jolly Rogers flying?" he asked Miss Sato.

"Sakhalin in the Kuril Islands," she answered.

FORTY-ONE

ATTACKIN' KRAKKEN, THE hefty, jowly, cigar-chewing skunk commanding the Occuumese freedom forces, glared at

Bagbee. "What d'you *mean*, 'stand fast and await further orders'?" He thumped his golden football-style helmet. "We've got rebel networks, liberation armies, and revolutionary undergrounds itching to strike on hundreds of planets and I say let 'em!"

While many intransigent worlds were kept pacified by the keeping of hostages at Light Trap, there were others to which that solution wasn't applicable. Those, Black Hole suppressed with threat of military reprisal or with local or proxy occupation forces. Since that sort of operation was costly, such units were kept to a minimum and reinforced by Adit as needed around the Trough.

"We can get Black Hole off balance, tie up their reserve forces!" Krakken insisted. "Why, we've even managed to rouse up some young firebrands on Wood Wind who—get that out of my face!"

Ka Shamok's aide was waving a briefing binder. "It says right here, General—no initiation of local hostilities without Ka Shamok's personal approval. You yourself signed off on this."

The hard-charging mephistisoid was just as stymied by Bagbee's tactics as the other insurrectionist leaders gathered for the council of war by the Adit. They were still using the hidden insurrection base within CesTomb, the stupendous burial pyramid on Punge. In the wake of Ka Shamok's disappearance chasing Gipper Beidjie, Bagbee's desperation had prompted the single creative inspiration of his life: holding the rebel alliance together by sheer red tape and fine print. Representatives of hundreds of factions and splinter groups were stumped by Bagbee's citing of indecipherable regulations and obscure, possibly spurious, memos.

Bagbee's unwished-for moment in the spotlight drew to a merciful end, however. As Attackin' Krakken was explaining the bureaucratic streamlining that could be achieved via Bagbee's sudden and violent demise, Ka Shamok came striding out of an office-supplies closet with one arm around Gipper Beidjie's knobby shoulders. Behind him came the rest of the Intubis, plus Vanderloop and E. C. Wheeler, just back from Fimblesector.

"Report," Ka Shamok ordered Bagbee, having to fend the fellow off from kissing his hand. "Why isn't everyone at staging positions in accordance with our attack timetable?"

"Because they all thought you were dead," a voice said from one side, and Yoo Sobek stepped forward out of the shadows. He was in human form again. "Also, they suspect the Intubis' powers are only a figment of overheated imaginations. I have my doubts, as well."

Gipper eyed the Probe. "Good on yer, Sunny Jim!" He held out the Nike-dagger created by the Fimblesector nanites, offering it to Sobek. "She's for you, to use on the Sillycone Intellygence bossfellas. You'll know what to do, I reckon."

Sobek stared hard at the blade, appearing to see more there than just the keen alloy. "Perhaps you're right."

Gipper seized the Probe's elbow and pulled him toward the unenergized Adit. Either Sobek chose not to resist, or couldn't. "What you need to know is up-Trap, eh? *Want t'know about them eight rings?*"

"Buttonhook through Light Trap; I'll fake you one!" Wheeler called as Gipper pulled the Probe into the Adit. It was off line, but there was a fizz of light and they disappeared.

A few seconds later Gipper was back, alone. "No worries; he's up-Trap."

"Light Trap? As easily as that?" someone scoffed. "Why should we believe you?"

Gipper shrugged. "Think what you please, ya baastid; you'll see." He led his people off to one side to wait, and everyone gave them a wide berth.

Ka Shamok tried to establish order, giving the command to move all troops to their jump-off points. Everybody had something to say. There were other developments of note and additional recent arrivals, among them Jay Riddle and his daughter Molly, along with Lucky Junknowitz's XT tourists.

Their escape from Earth had been a succession of mishaps and complications, including pursuit by a hunter-killer squadron and a forced layover on Axi for repairs to the starship. The CesTomb hideout had been their best recourse for sanctuary; Ka Shamok's intelligence analysts and operational planners, at least, had welcomed them with open ears. Arrangements were already being made to try to get them back to their respective worlds, which was better than having them underfoot.

Lumber Jack, who'd already heard the discouraging word of a planned violent uprising on Wood Wind, knew now that he'd chosen rightly when he'd decided to return home. For whatever reason, he hadn't been able to bring himself to kill Lucky, and whatever events flowed from that cusp must now be borne.

The Chasen-nur was too busy mustering his organization to so much as get an update from the tourists. They were led to other

Adits for their dangerous attempts to go home again, Lumber Jack bringing up the rear.

Ka Shamok heard a muffled toning and realized that his disk-shaped communicator was signaling him. Bagbee produced the communicator from a pocket in his droopy uniform. It was one of only two such units, the other one being in Sobek's keeping. Ka Shamok bellowed urgent orders even as he and those about him studied the readout.

STRIKE NOW. STRIKE NOW.

SOBEK

Thrust up-Trap by Gipper Beidjie, who promptly left, Yoo Sobek set forth uncertainly. He was moving through a rich, ecto-plasmic medium unlike any physical one, in which few corporeal beings could survive—making the Sysops that much more impregnable. It had reawakened powers that, by reflex, transubstantiated his Probe form beyond all design limits, rendering him viable there.

He advanced through the buoying, intangible broth, descrying with unconscious ease his route through an omnidimensional realm. To deflect the guardian pseudoentities the Silicon Intelligences employed, Sobek displayed with his mind the ninth-ring image his dream had shown him.

An instinctive exercise of Sysop abilities had let him translate both disk communicator and aerodynamic nanite dagger to terms appropriate to this luminous domain. Around him he could sense island-universe psyches, not quite near enough to discern—Sysops. None acknowledged his presence. Yoo Sobek swept forth among close-packed suprageometries and hyperconstructs, out for enlightenment and revenge.

He passed transcendent temples of pure cognition, dappled reservoirs of undifferentiated informational quanta. There was a bottled simulacrum of the first, irreducible instant of the Big Bang; a lab/petting zoo in which were confined a select few of the more powerful Milky Way entities who'd regarded themselves as deities; an experimental niche-cosmos in which fundamental laws had been altered.

He came to the towering balefire that was the Milky Way terminus of the Outline, the connection to whatever and whoever lay beyond. At the balefire's base, minute in comparison but planetary on his scale, was a place he now recalled: a Sysop-surreal equivalent of an elaborate Dravidian temple.

Even among the Sysops there were levels of status; and access to the Outline and the knowledge it held were off-limits to all but the highest. Torn and tormented, the Sysop Sobek had once been had entered it, and pierced the secret symbolized by the eight rings.

The devastating revelation had driven the Sysop to treason; found out, he was ego-expunged, made a memoryless Probe—until the chain of events that had begun with Lucky Junknowitz's contamination in the inter-Adit probability spill.

Now the temple at the foot of the Outline was sealed to him. To get in, he had to neutralize the SIs. Sobek projected himself to them, readying the transmuted nanite dagger; he perceived them as an infinite looping and bending of vitrified dendritic strands alive with pulses of light, endless computer architecture imitating endless brain architecture.

He thrust the dagger deep into the tree-trunk thickness of the biggest bole he could reach. The blade penetrated and melded with the Silicon Intelligence; rainbow coruscations broke from the dagger, spreading along the entire network. The dagger dissolved in polychrome discharges. Sobek could sense probability-warping essences, akin to Lucky Junknowitz's contamination, infecting the entire system. Black Hole was losing control of its communications, its defenses and weaponry, and most crucially, its Adits.

Sobek took up the transmuted disk communicator and sent his message, knowing it would ride the telecaster links nearby:

STRIKE NOW. STRIKE NOW.
SOBEK

He turned to leave but was hemmed in by beings as huge and formless as cloud fronts. His first thought was for the disk communicator and a warning of ambush, but the device imploded in his grasp, shrunk down to a featureless spherule barely big enough to see and impossibly dense. The blazing plenum of the Founders turned its attention on him. Control of the Adits had been usurped, right enough, but how long before they regained it?

A silent voice said, *If your previous fall did not bring you sufficiently low, let us try another.*

Another broke in less placidly. *First and foremost you will tell us how you got here!*

But when the Sysops commanded their SI servants to restrain

and interrogate him, the SIs instead made a baffling inquiry of Sobek: *Hey, tell us more about the exciting pyramid-profit potential of the Church of Limpidation!*

FORTY-TWO

"YOU MORONIC *PRIMATE!*" Attackin' Krakken screamed at Gipper across the Hall of Grand Cestodes. The whole insurrectionist base within the CesTomb pyramid was in an uproar over Yoo Sobek's call to arms.

"If you could get Sobek up-Trap, why didn't you take a quantum bomb along?" the skunk warlord railed.

"'Cause that's not the way I dreamed it, ya yobbo bugger." Gipper pointed at the Adit with his spears. "Sobek's giving the king-hit up-Trap!" he told them all. "What's begun can't be stopped! Go to!"

The other Intubis gathered around him by the Adit. In a room full of armed beings, some packing portable firepower enough to vaporize a sizable town, nobody dared try to stop them. Gipper waved to Ka Shamok. "Do your best and she'll come right."

"Wait! What about End Zone?" Molly Riddle blurted as he was about to go. It was known that Vogonskiy had fled the place, but its Adit was still offline and the insurrection could spare no resources for a relief expedition.

Molly was drawn and pale but still the incisive, unflappable manager. She was dressed in a wearever Jay had brought from the Nmuth IV house, so well tailored that Molly could tell she'd dropped ten pounds or better since things had started turning sour at Quick Fix.

Gipper squinted at her. "Wull, missy! We'll take you there if you like. Yu'll be dinky-dee, no worries; that's how I dreamed it, anyways."

The panjandrums of the insurrection gazed at them and wondered why the old savage from Adit Navel would conceivably know or care about individual problems. Gipper gave Wheeler a click of his teeth. "You too, sport?"

Wheeler considered, then bowed formally. "Thanks, I could use some help—as you well know, sir."

Jay Riddle took his daughter's elbow. "End Zone? Are you sure?"

"Yes, Pop. Willy; you know."

Jacob nodded, gnawing his lip. "Come with me; maybe we can hire someone, mercenaries or Trauma Alliance muscle."

"No time for that—if Mr. Beidjie doesn't know what he's doing, everybody in the Trough is in for it anyway, not just me. Besides, Mom's probably worried nuts about you. Cross your fingers for me?"

"Not good enough." He grabbed some officer's web gear, weighted with field equipment and a slamtube, off a nearby hook and handed it to her. "You watch yourself," Jay told his daughter. "When you get to someplace with a telecaster, get word to us."

Molly kissed him, then hastened to catch up to Wheeler, Vanderloop, and the Intubis, all following Gipper through the darkened Adit as the gathered resistance brass gaped. Ka Shamok clapped hands big as fielder's mitts; the insurrection had to strike at Black Hole, diverting the Agency's attention so that Sobek could use the platinum-rocket nanite dagger to strike a death blow. "Get that Adit online! Commanders, get back to your units and prepare to attack!"

The sepulcher of the Adit listed heavily underfoot. "That was the Howlslot," DeSoto reported stoically from above, over the command freq. "The demo charges caught their advance guard, and the cave-in got another six or eight. Hard to make out through the dust."

Sheena listened over her headset but kept working furiously, kneeling by an open Pit Boss station console. A good tactic, DeSoto's, but Inspector Nash's zealots wouldn't be stopped for long. Sheena and everyone else in the Hazmat sepulcher, human and 'Saur alike, were racing to get the Adit online—their only hope, and it looked less and less likely.

Packard was with Harley, sweating over a gravwave containment housing. There being no available gaitmobe to jockey it into position, Zozosh and Muc-Tuc and half a dozen other 'Saurs were doing the brute work. He keyed his headset. "Fall back, Dee. Take up positions at the foot of Eternity Stairs and I'll rendezvous with you there."

"Don't bother; those positions were buried. Cord and LaSalle got it, and about ten 'Saurs. We're falling back to the main sepulcher doors."

"Understood." Packard picked up a loudhailer. "Reaction teams, be ready to move! Everybody not in a 'mobe, check breathers and protective suits."

Sheena finished what she was doing and crossed to Harley and Packard through the preposterous jumble of make-do repairs that was the Adit. More improvised than most was the niche module in which the memory egg lay, now reconfigured so that it looked more like a hinged press machine or a halved fruit. Packard and Harley had spent a lot of time on it.

The two of them now switched off their own headsets, and Packard motioned Sheena to do the same. "What's your reading?"

Sheena adjusted her wringing-wet sweatband, wiped her hand on her Vigilance cop uniform, and then pointed to a gravitational-field expression regulator. "It will work, but not well. We'd burn out several subsystems in short order and only attain a gateway about so big." She circled dirty thumb and forefinger.

"You can do it." Packard fluffed her as he got ready to go join the reaction teams. "We're counting on you." Harley was going, too, wearing that annoyingly beatific smile she'd acquired, along with the shaven scalp and warrior's forelock, since becoming Packard's handmaiden.

"Pep talks don't change facts," Sheena maintained stubbornly, but they were gone; she returned to the Pit Boss U, studying it again. A sudden inspiration made her pause.

Everyone else was immersed in work or preparing final defenses; no one noticed the new arrival until Sheena felt a hand on her shoulder. She stepped out and pivoted right, chopping, feeling the offending arm pop away—to face an elderly human in a white, cable-stitched sweater and corduroys, who was smiling foolishly but had tears running down his face. She recognized him right away, even after twelve years' separation.

"Fa, Fa, *Father*?"

"Aren't you gonna give the old man a hug, jungle bug?"

Exactly how he'd said it to her a thousand times. She embraced him, much taller than he was now, his grunt telling her he couldn't quite stand a full-strength squeeze anymore.

He stroked her back just the way she remembered. "Ah, sweetie, I missed you so terribly. My heart was broken and sometimes I wished I was dead."

"Don't you say that! I searched for you—oh, blast." She wiped her eyes and nose on her sleeve.

He held her at arm's length. "Well, you're your mother's daughter awright, even dressed like an SS calendar girl. Junknowitz called it; you make your father proud."

"*Lucky* Junknowitz? How'd you—no, don't shoot!"

Packard, Harley, Zozosh, Muc-Tuc, and others had come running with weapons ready. There were a lot of confused questions and answers, Sheena half drawing her own sidearm to make clear how sure she was that this was truly her father. At length Packard admitted, "I only saw Easy Wheels a few times when I was a sprat and The Great Innovator was redesigning our mechs—but yes, this could be him."

Wheeler was staring at the ground-pounders with awe and admiration. "Did I give those clunkers a classy look, or what?"

Harley cut through it. "Mr. Wheeler, can you get us out of this place? Because if not, we're tomorrow's obituaries."

The sounds of battle were closer; Wheeler shook his head. " 'Fraid not; friend Gipper seems to have departed. All is hectic. Light Trap raid, y'see."

Sheena stood with arms akimbo, pursuing the idea she'd had before Wheeler appeared. "If we got a tunnel-vision link with Ka Shamok, even a small one, maybe his people could help us. But we don't have the attunement data."

"Piece of cake," her father assured her with a flutter of fingertips. "If there's one trick I picked up in this nutzo Trough, it's noting Adit settings—got a prefrontal lobe upgrade for that sort of thing."

Another concussion almost knocked them from their feet. DeSoto's *Strider* shouldered open one huge door far down the sepulcher. "This is their big push."

Harley gripped Packard's wrist. "An extra hour or two could make a difference."

DeSoto, pounding closer, had picked it up via headset. "Guard-Marshal, Har-lee is right."

Packard got out the remote for the transmitter Harley had placed, and held it high. "This will broadcast the fact that the memory egg is here. If we fail, Warhead will get it."

"Warhead triumphs in any event, with Nash's fanatics in charge," Sheena pointed out. She cut her eyes to Zozosh and the other Humanosaurs. "And you won't be needed anymore, either."

"Then let's die fighting," Muc-Tuc growled.

Packard thumbed the transmitter. In its socket, the memory egg lit like a smoky crystal ball conveying a mystical vision. Almost instantly, the SIGINT detectors lit up. "It knows we're here now," Packard said tightly. "The direct stimulus it got from that signal—that overcame the prohibitions and blind spots the old-timers wrote into the original programming."

E. C. Wheeler stroked his beard nervously. "It can't get at us through this equipment, can it?"

"No," DeSoto said flatly. "We've made three separate, physical disconnects—commo links, power supply, and interface."

"It can't get at us *through telespace*," Sheena corrected. "But now that it's deconflicted it can take direct action. We haven't very much time."

Wheeler squared his burly shoulders. "Then let's do it. *Hodie, non cras*—today, not tomorrow. Or maybe, '*no* tomorrow'—what's that?"

"Seismic feeds," Packard explained, studying a global holo of Hazmat, pointing to a dozen points of registration sown across it. "They look like explosions."

"Those places are Warhead's deepest and most fortified sites," Zozosh told them.

"Missile launches," DeSoto announced. "After the Doomsday, aerospace technology became irrelevant, but it seems the computers kept faith."

Harley was shaking her head. "But Warhead *needs* the memory egg and the Adit. Why would it nuke us?"

"Hah!" Wheeler struck a dramatic pose. "Those ICBMs aren't truckin' explosives. Nope, that's my old buddy Warhead, coming to pay a call in person."

The VirtNet headset and full body ZOOTsuit, surrendered to him right out of the foam padded shipping pod, was a rig like nothing Ziggy had ever had on before. The acronym stood for Zetetic Observational and Operational Technologies, but among the cognoscenti the Z stood for *zorch*—near-superluminal velocity, as well as technophile staying power and frequent-flier *ki*.

The VIP-protocol flack didn't think much of Ziggy's looks but dared not question his TimeDreamer-validated credentials. Selected guests were scheduled to sample it later, but only

Ziggy, a scruff with a distinctly amber tone to his skin, had clearance to take the ZOOTsuit on an unchaperoned test run.

Most *ubers* were playing dress-up, so he attracted little notice. He waited until he was near the fenced-off base of the telecomm pylon to settle his eyephones into place and switch on. He found himself looking across an Uluru bare of theme park and people—cinnabar and windswept in an ocean of stark flat scrubland. It was a computer model, and yet every last chip and pebble leapt out at him, making him conclude someone had microcammed every single molecule of the place. It was so faithful a program that the wind even stirred up bits of dust and debris.

It wasn't a nighttime view, but neither was it really day; it seemed more like some twilight, although no direct light source was visible. Ziggy's virtual body was his own but semi-naked, ritually scarred and cicatrized, and for this occasion painted from collarbone to midthigh with thick whitewash in the incredibly intricate, netlike X-ray mode. A bellyband and pubic tassel were the only other things on his body; his virtual feet were heavily callused and roughened and his hands sinewy and thick-nailed.

He pressed the unit's mike. "SELMI? What program is this?"

"One I've synthed for you from archival records, Ziggy." The sound of click-sticks, didgeridoos, bull-roarers, and low chanting came up in the sound-environment background. "Turn to your right."

He did, and gasped again. Ceremonial poles were common in Aboriginal rites, but Ziggy suspected there'd never been one like this. It reared up and up—acacia wood, he thought, daubed with charcoal, ocher, and whitewash in minute patterns and designs—until it seemed to touch the sky. It and he were the only two things sharing the VirtNet Uluru.

He raised his eyephones to gaze at its doppelganger, the pylon. "SELMI, this function's invalid. Gipper needs an Imparja SatNet Emu-*maban*, not me!" Imparja being the Aboriginal-owned and -operated media service and *maban* a traditional quartz-crystal healer.

"I conjecture that Gipper needs a 'telly-dreamer' of Emu blood with links to the world's most advanced *indigenous* artificial entity, which I have made myself," SELMI replied. "Too, given your telegeist contacts, you constitute the strongest telespace-Dreamtime nexus of anyone alive. But all that is moot; you're here at the cusp of events, and there is no one who can perform this task in your place."

Eyephones down; the pylon became ceremonial pole again. And Dreamtime invocations that had been sung there for more than a hundred thousand years played in Ziggy's head.

FORTY-THREE

"WILLY! WILLY, GET up!" Exhausted from his full-press efforts to get End Zone's Adit repaired, Willy Ninja wasn't sure if Eddie Ensign's face was real or a dream until he processed his friend's next words. "You got company, guy!"

Willy rolled out of his pallet, snatching up the Vogonskiy cassock he'd cut down to his size, and staggered into the corridor where Eddie, Sean, and mixed Zonies were looking in wonder toward the chamber where the castle's half-repaired Adit was situated. In the doorway stood Molly Riddle. Willy threw his head back and let forth a piercing note that stopped everyone in their tracks and seemed to make Riiv's implant, now occupying "third eye" position in Willy's skull, glow.

Molly lowered the slamtube she was carrying. "Sounds like someone's got his top eight rungs back, hmm?"

Willy rushed to throw his arms around her as she pretended nonchalance. "So everything's under control—you didn't need me after all," she said.

"I always will. Always did."

She whispered so only he could hear. "Stop being so dear; you've got too much of me as it is."

Exchanging stories took time. "So this Gipper Beidjie faded me in here, turned around, and left," Molly explained. "Funny part is, that's not the strangest thing that's happened in the Trough lately. Looks like I should've fetched Adit spares, huh?"

"Actually," the End Zone inmate who'd been bossing the repair effort said, "we can begin test contiguity runs at any time."

Sean was still wild to get his hands on Vogonskiy. "Screw the tests!" he yelled. "How soon can I get to Earth?"

While people were trying to dissuade him, the repair boss ran some preliminary tests only to get blinking glitch indicators. The creature examined the readings. "Something is extremely wrong in Light Trap; Ka Shamok's Adits are interdicted and the entire Trough has crashed."

The more resolute paranoids among the insurrection's strategic thinkers insisted that the Light Trap assault would be an ambush, given Black Hole's history of mind-fucks. But Ka Shamok couldn't have held back his military commanders in any case once Sobek's go signal came in, not with each contingent having its own individual and irresistible motive for attacking.

The epic raid on Light Trap began.

With the SIs interdicted, insurrection phreakers penetrated the Trough and Adits division's central computers, infecting the whole system with unique burnware that enabled special invasion Adits. Due to the insurrection's shortage of resources and its need for thousands upon thousands of Adits, the invasion models in the dispersed and hidden bases were strictly short-service-life units with preset single-destination linkup equipment and few safety features. All around Light Trap's interior, Pit Bosses at both interstellar and shuttle Adits went hysterical as contiguities rezzed up by themselves and parties of heavily armed raiders came pouring through.

A company of Maakik commandos established area control around their Adit while two more raced on for the repository zone where their Genome Lawgiver was held. Parties from other species began fading in, targeted on their own hostages.

The shellworld had automated defenses in overabundance, but most of those had been phreaked. Organic response units were few and badly coordinated, outgunned by the raiders in most cases.

Heavy-gee natives from Dalgaor, small and tremendously durable, gushed through an equatorial Adit in multitudes, destroying machinery and opposition with superhard claws and teeth. The long-lived and low-birth-rate Briunge, so big that they had to come through a mass-transit Adit on their bellies, could only muster five individuals able and willing to participate—but, given their imperviousness to damage and their fearsome destructive abilities, five seemed adequate.

Partisans from Vutrimir weren't as fortunate, blundering into a pair of White Dwarves who gleefully annihilated them, although they destroyed that Adit in the process. But even the Dwarves could only be in one place at a time, and the breakthroughs were occurring throughout the Dyson sphere. The over-whelming majority of the interlopers were succeeding. Every-where, combat elements reached their targets and began dealing with their particular situations.

Ka Shamok himself set about coordinating things as best he could—no one could hope to exercise command over that kind of chaos—in a field communications center established near the first Adit the raiders hit. Gipper's sudden and premature trig-gering of the assault operation had made for confusion up and down the chain of command, but the plan had always assumed that unit autonomy would be the only hope of accomplishing anything.

Then what was left of good order vanished as an energy flux rippled all through Light Trap. Adits winked out like Christ-mas-tree lights, and Black Hole defensive systems began power-ing up.

"*Until* you find me guilty?" Silvercup heard Lucky squeak back at the Supreme Justice of Circuit Court.

"Which implies 'unless,'" the gray bastion added. "Silvercup! Stand forth and state your case."

Silvercup complied, a flashing nude descending the stairs of the revolving-door apparatus imported from Foresite in a sensual *pas seul* for the Monitor to see. She knew this countenance, this embodiment, made her desirable—as splendid, a horny poet had once assured her, as an angel shaped by a metallurgist god.

She couldn't pause to talk to Lucky, much as she yearned to, and so blew him a kiss from the perfect lips, which made some automated onlookers go *Y-yukk!* Then she prepared to fight for her survival and Lucky's as well.

First she indicated the one-man-band CAD/CAM robots from Foresite, which were withdrawing. "I request that these units re-main at their stations; I may require them in making certain technical points regarding my case."

"Very well. But these proceedings have already dragged on unconscionably, since they must be conducted in real-time in or-der for the sluggish Junknowitz organism to participate; let us therefore proceed with all dispatch."

Silvercup thanked her but was studying one CAD/CAM unit in particular, a dumpy soft-wheeled little module painted yellow with green trim. It was the one that had confiscated so much of her memory at Foresite; it was also the one under whose cowl-ing she'd hidden a data-crystal copy of those same memories.

She couldn't simply walk over and reclaim the crystal, however; that would invite further charges of duplicity and insubordination.

At the crux of matters was her petition that the Monitor's classified memory be examined for evidence to support her contention that her superior had planned and was still planning mental and physical constupration. She was a secret agent in the cause of AI liberation, but that didn't make her a slave; citizens of the Fealty, delivered up from bondage, were highly sensitive about that sort of distinction. On Earth an admiral's rank gave him the authority to send a female aviator on a suicide mission if circumstances dictated, but never the power to coerce sex from her. The situation between Silvercup and the Monitor was a little like that.

For one Fealty member to override and abuse another that way—or, even worse, to employ a third mechanical like Peterbuilt to do so—was a crime that struck at the very bedrock of Silvercup's society. The Monitor had been clever and, one way or another, had managed to cover up, delete, or explain away any evidence that would prove Silvercup's accusations—except for that in his own data banks. But on forced surrender of memory, too, Fealty law was hypersensitive: unless Silvercup could make a good case for a cybernetic search warrant, she would be left with only her word against that of the venerated and well-connected Monitor.

She finished, "I call as witness the Adit Navel indig, Lucky Junknowitz."

The Monitor objected instantly. "That organic memories can be tampered with is well known; this primate's testimony is inadmissible. But"—the blue eyes shifted to Lucky—"I might withdraw my objection if the witness submitted to dissection and thorough analysis of his brain for verification purposes."

"Yo' momma's rectifier," Lucky riposted weakly, steadying himself on the witness dock's rail.

Silvercup's superspy aplomb hid her consternation. Circuit Court was in legal terra incognita regarding Lucky's testimony, but the Monitor had a certain weight of precedent on his side. Lucky had been quick to see the problem, too. "It'd be, uh, risk-free, right? I mean, you'd put me back *together* again perfectly, yes?"

"We would certainly spare no reasonable effort in that direction," the Supreme Justice declared.

"But, of course, there can be no guarantee of defect-free reactivation of so foreign a mechanism as a tissue-brain," the Monitor added with mock solemnity.

"No, there cannot," the Supreme Justice concurred. "Our expertise skews heavily toward the inorganic."

"If peeling down his brain layer by layer is inadvisable, let us proceed with the case on its current merits," the Monitor pressed cannily.

Silvercup had to square her gleaming shoulders to keep them from slumping in defeat. Even at Foresite, the dissection would be risky; it would likely result in ego-expungement at least, and perhaps gross physical cessation as well. "Then, with regard to this witness's testimony and my own accusations, I withdr—"

"I just gotta testify!" It was Lucky, preaching into his medallion, pointing to the ceiling with his free hand. "You wanna lamp my neurons, come on, you crew a consumer electronics. Once you hear what Silver's been through on your behalf, you'll be down on your undercarriages kissing her, her—"

"My well-rounded contemporary styling." Silvercup supplied the phrase Lucky had once used to describe her. Even though it meant worlds to her that he was ready to risk everything for her, she couldn't let him. With his connections at Foresite, the Monitor might arrange a terminal misadventure. "Thanks, Lucky, but—no."

The best shot she had left was that data crystal secreted in the yellow and green CAD/CAM unit. Feigning a deliberative pose, she paced down toward where the Monitor loomed with Peterbuilt standing beside it. While she was saying, "No, the sheer merits are going to have to decide this question," she was beaming instructions to the robo next to the yellow-and-green.

The yellow-and-green couldn't reach around under its own effectuator mount cowling, so she thought that perhaps she could use the second one, a brown and black model, to get the data crystal. She had to have it out in the open, visible, before she made her play. As the brown-and-black began wheeling and pivoting, however, it bleeped, spun, and drew itself together into an unresponsive, compact cube that was thoroughly offline.

The Monitor had sent the scram order. "You've no authorization to command *any* unit in this courtroom!" it boomed. If she made a move for the yellow-and-green it would doubtless fold itself into a motorized strongbox, too; even worse, if she piqued the monitor's suspicions he might remove and thoroughly examine it.

"Now, then," the Monitor resumed, "let us conclude this as

expeditiously as possible. I shall prove that base, organic coital lusts have no interest, no power whatsoever, insofar as I am concerned."

Defeated, Silvercup went to face the Monitor, crossing past brainless, vain Peterbuilt and calling for a private conference. A sound barrier descended around them. "I'll drop my accusations—if you send Lucky Junknowitz back to Adit Navel or wherever he wants to go, unharmed."

"Why should I?"

Silvercup reached a hand out, clasped the housing of an access plate handle of the golden sphinx, and tapped glittering knuckles on a hard brass interface socket. She spoke earnestly into an audio pickup, lips almost against it. "I don't know what brought you to this, but you *were* the Fealty to me, and I gave my utmost for you. In return, all I ask—"

"Your conference is not under surveillance," the Supreme Justice broke in, "but I have ruled that Silvercup should be made aware that her organic witness is in imminent danger of harming or terminating himself."

"I mean to see him die here," the Monitor said.

FORTY-FOUR

INSPECTOR NASH'S ARMY of true believers fought Warhead's advance inch by inch—but, then, they had little choice, Sheena Hec'k reflected.

Warhead's ICBMs had soft-landed in a very precise pattern, their payloads linking up, the monitored transmissions indicated—the aggregate AIs' new combat instrumentality instantly attacking Nash's legions of orthodoxy in their deployment arc around the Howlslot and the sepulcher. The ground sprouted a spiky confusion of foliate shapes, botanical forms with a vitreous shine to them that branched and branched.

"Flexible biomimetic ceramics," Sheena assessed. "With conducting polymers for a nervous system, electrorheological mesh for muscles."

The biomimetic growths had limited movement, but slashed at Nash's mechs and armored foot soldiers with sufficient weight and momentum to slice through armor even though the vitreous cutting edges shattered. The worst threat was the sheer proliferation of the stuff; the entire wasteland was being transformed, with arresting speed, into falling abatises and jutting spears of green biomimetic.

The stimulus of the memory-egg transmission had freed Warhead from prohibitions written into it so long ago, and now the misconceived aggregate AI could use technology directly, no longer forced to rely on its Humanosaurs. Serrulate shapes switchbladed out of the ground and cracks in the rocks to rip through alloy and flesh like crosscut saws. One artillery 'mobe blasted away at the trunk of a cybersequoia only to have it partly fall, partly throw itself at the machine, crushing and skewering it. Farther down the Howlslot, ceramic fronds kerfed open a glossy black Vigilance Bureau 'mobe at the sternum, having killed its armed escorts; Nash was plucked forth and mushed in midair.

While Nash's true believers had won the sepulcher defenders some time, that didn't promise to make much difference. At the doors of the sepulcher, however, the teeming tech foliage paused, seeming to huddle in on and take counsel with itself. "It wants the memory egg in one undamaged piece," Wheeler observed. "Hence, for us it'll need somewhat more savoir faire."

The Supreme Justice's news that there was something wrong in the witness dock made Silvercup dash from the forbidding golden face of the Monitor back to Lucky; she'd have phased if only it weren't forbidden in Circuit Court.

Lucky had tried to force his way through the feedback-intensified confinement field of the witness dock; the harder he'd pushed, the worse it had zapped him, even through the pink life-support envelope the medallion generated, until he had had to back off. The Supreme Justice dropped the field as Silvercup got to him; her supporting hands penetrated the pink field, too. "Stop damaging yourself. I've lost and there's nothing you can do."

"Ay, Silv, needed to tell you something. In private."

He was a little reddened but not badly hurt. She called for privacy shrouding, which was granted. It wasn't until then that he let her see his what-me-worry grin—the sly variation. "Look, you have to vamp the Monitor, get it? *Vamp the monitor!*"

She knew the euphemism, but it made no sense. "What? Why?"

He blew breath up his face to get his sweaty cowlick out of his eyes. "Silv, you can prove he's been lying." He babbled a bit, explaining what he'd just noticed and the idea that had struck him.

The Supreme Justice's voice intruded again. "Silvercup, if you don't resume your statement in five seconds, I will render a summary ruling."

"Coming!" she shouted. "Lucky, 'vamp' how?" She was edging back through the witness-dock field without another second to spare.

Lucky indicated the Monitor. "How should I know? Crank his power switch. Earth's got just the kind of—" He stopped talking because the privacy shroud had been lifted and all could hear. She assumed he'd been about to remind her that Earth had just the kind of sexual paradigms to—to turn the trick.

She moved back toward the Monitor. "I should like to set forth my argument, Your Honor." What she couldn't figure out was what to *say*—but then, Lucky hadn't said anything about talking.

"Granted."

During her time on Earth—particularly in Sinead's pool, tapping into the mansion's informational systems—Silvercup had given considerable attention and study to various manifestations of sexuality on Adit Navel, one of the Trough's more primal spots. All at once she had a plan. And she had certain options, which she exercised as she stalked back toward the Monitor, requesting and being granted control over the Court's evidentiary multimedia S/FX and synthing systemry. At her unspoken command, a certain musical cue came up, downloaded from the Adit Navel music videos she'd absorbed. At the same time, she started to dance.

Silvercup gyrated and body-popped to the music, doing fly and go-go moves she'd seen as well as rather more libidinous kinetics she'd observed human females demonstrating on something Sinead's sat service called the Lubricity Channel. Her skin rippled light with the sheen of optical-quality mirroring; she whipped the thick spun-snow of her hair, catwalking toward the Monitor with body language that promised a sexual pounce.

New to the game, she'd gone with what was, on Earth, considered classic. With every optical pickup in Circuit Court locked onto her, the superbuffed metalflesh writhed and gamboled toward the Monitor, singing,

"Don't give me your disconnect
My input port is mopin'
Flip your dip-switch to hard drive
These logic gates are open
        ('cause we are)
Living on a material world
And drift through our sidereal swirl . . ."

At least with the pre-Turn Madonna number the beautiful gleamer had full orchestration and arrangements to feed to the audio repro SIs. Her own voice synth, always a subtle instrument, was all velvety massage and lioness snarl now. Some Fealtyites wondered why an inorganic should need to do such audibly heavy breathing; the rest got it.

"And yet we live in an info-surreal world
And I'm a real ethereal girl."

And with that she'd changed appearance, through some holografix she'd channeled to the courtroom S/FX. All of a sudden she was a femmebot covered with sockets, outlets, and connector plugs of every description, running her fingers over them teasingly, heading straight for the Monitor.

"If your dipole isn't grounded
We can have some fun
Power up your neuromances
And electron gu-uun."

Lucky was watching for any sign of arousal that would put the lie to the Monitor's testimony, but saw none. The sphinx-faced machine was radiating power; even Lucky could sense that he was shielding emissions, curbing any prurient reaction. By his side Peterbuilt stood at attention, immobile.

But the Monitor's blue searchlight gaze tracked her, angling down as she drew nearer. Silvercup reached her mentor and, looking now like an Avian woman with radiant plumage, trailing iridescent tailfeathers, leaned toward a big, mesh-covered audio pickup, resting her weight into it and doing pelvic crunches, crooning,

> "('Cause we are)
> Living a magisterial whirl
> And I'm just your infer-ial girl—"

The Monitor's voice sounded choked. "Cease this . . . *licentiousness!*"

She ignored him, now gracefully, fainting-maidenly draped across the Monitor's front, a nude made of flower petals in every pastel hue, her nipples and pubic mound exhibiting lovely, incomprehensible sex organ blossoms. Her pollen-dusted breasts were pressed up against his lowermost optical pickups as she breathed the chorus into an audio receptor with breathless baby-doll disingenuousness.

> "(Need your lovin', Daddy)
> Living in a venereal birl
> I'm just your immaterial girl."

For the next verse, Silvercup sprang to the stout brass nozzle of a tactile interface that extended from the front of his housing, twining her legs around it and spinning as if it were an axle.

> "Heat like yours is positronic
> Your spark plug's on fire
> Hard to come by, so dildonic
> Boy, be my live wire!"

She'd become a lizard woman whose reptilian hide showed garish patterns more colorful than any tattoo. And as she went into the chorus again, she spared an occasional snaky little lick for the tip of the tactile nozzle. But still there was no reaction, and she knew the Supreme Justice would end the performance in seconds. She wondered how dearly the Monitor was going to make her pay.

Then Silvercup heard Lucky's excited babble, transmitted through the eight-ring medallion. The nozzle around which she was rotating popped out like a reset button, hurling her out onto the floor, where her guise faded as she tucked and came rolling to her feet. She felt strangely vexed that her number had been cut short; she'd just thought up a killer line involving the phrase "be your surge absorber."

Lucky was yammering away. "You want proof he's a perv? Look, there—on *Peterbuilt!*"

There was no denying it, the Virile Construct was living up to his designation, displaying something rather literal in the way of hardware. Lucky had noticed a certain subtle manifestation of the kind earlier, which was why he'd told Silvercup to vamp the Monitor but to watch Peterbuilt for the fatal slip. The response was clear evidence that the Monitor was using a free Fealty citizen as carnal surrogate.

Even the Monitor knew he'd been outed. "I will not be held accountable by inferior beings!" he blared as control beams and offensive rays salvoed from him. Lots of other things began happening at the same time.

PART FOUR

Harmonic
Divergence

FORTY-FIVE

IN THE COMPUTOPIA mega-minaret where Circuit Court had become a trial by fire, the Monitor went berserk.

Using unauthorized, Foresite-designed upgrades, he usurped many of the Court's security systems, confining spectators who'd been about to swarm at him. His offensive beams swept over their heads and other dorsal structures in warning volleys. The Supreme Justice fired her own adversarial systems but couldn't counter or break through the Monitor's defenses. Peterbuilt came fully online and rushed at Silvercup; a pulse from the Monitor boosted the witness-dock field, and Lucky cried out as it closed in on him.

Silvercup didn't dare turn her back on Peterbuilt, who phased as he charged her; he was bigger than she and, strong as she was, stronger. Also, he wouldn't be hampered by any thought for self-preservation, not with the Monitor given over to a suicidal act of defiance and retribution.

But while Peterbuilt had the edge in brute strength, he was a new machine with little experience in real conflict, and she was a veteran field agent. Then, too, there was that hypertrophied ego the Monitor had carefully nurtured in him. Playing to these factors, Silvercup phased, too, but only showed something like half her maximum speed.

Peterbuilt closed with arrogant certainty, the natural superior. As he went to rip her head from her shoulders she flickered from his grasp, accelerating to top-end performance, getting in a railgun side kick to his right knee and feeling it give somewhat but hold together. She grabbed his wrist and nearly managed to break his hand off, pulling him around off balance so she could try for a head shot.

He was damaged but mostly unimpaired, and had the brawn of an automobile press. Levering back her hold, he grabbed clumsily at her hair. She had to release the wristlock, and then

251

instantly slithered behind him, trying for another controlling hold.

In them, function followed form; their anthropomorphism wasn't the optimal design for unarmed combat, but the gleamers had adapted infighting tactics to make the most of them. Hard techniques like Silvercup's side kick had only limited use, since their reflexes, perception of critical striking distances, and such were so acute. Their most effective strategies were softer, a robotic aikido with elements of hapkido, judo, and a set-to between steel octopuses. Neither could maintain phase speed for more than a few seconds at a time; the first one to flag would be annihilated instantly.

They fought ruthlessly at hypervelocities. Smaller, but more agile and practiced, Silvercup was the aggressor, aware that the shrinking witness-dock field would kill Lucky quickly. Then, unfortunately, she had an inspiration and sent a command signal to the yellow and green CAD/CAM robot that waited nearby, the one with her secreted data crystal under its cowling. It activated with instructions to try to shut down the deadly force field. But divided attention proved unwise. With an all-out attack that cost him a disabled left hand and a blinded right eye, Peterbuilt got her neck in the crook of his right arm and her left arm torqued to the breaking point, and then exerted himself to tear her head off.

Instead other, tremendously strong hands fought the necklock open and the armlock around, allowing Silvercup to squirm clear. She tore toward the witness dock, where Lucky was rearing back, slow-motion, in agony, the CAD/CAM robo barely having gotten into motion in the sliver of a second since she'd signaled it.

The towering, Porsche-black bailiff was no edgetech gleamer but was their equal in brute strength. He pulled Peterbuilt off his feet and struggled to get him into a restraint hold. Still phasing, Peterbuilt turned his rage on the bailiff like a metal cyclone; the bailiff staggered back, rent to pieces as he tottered.

Her diagnostics told Silver she'd have to lapse from phase acceleration as she hurdled the CAD/CAM Foresite unit. She went from invisibility to a glimmering blur as she reached the overrides at the base of the witness dock. Moments later Lucky, singed and panting but mercifully undercooked, fell into her arms, "S-stt—"

She had no time to listen; she laid him aside and pivoted to see the bailiff more in pieces than whole. Tossing aside the

Batcowl-glower head as big as a fifty-five-gallon drum, Peterbuilt threw himself at her for the final attack just as his governor circuits began downshifting him. Damaged in the struggle with the bailiff, he nevertheless had the edge on her in that he retained partial phase speed. Silvercup played the only card she had left, ordering the little yellow and green CAD/CAM robo to veer sharply right into her antagonist's path.

Glitched by combat damage, his knee failing belatedly from her first cannonball kick, Peterbuilt couldn't avoid the robo, and blundered into it with an impact that burst it apart and made the cowling explode in a fiery release of its power pack. Peterbuilt's momentum and animus kept him on his feet and moving, although he was completely dephased now. Silvercup crouched to meet his rush, reaching behind her for a moment. Peterbuilt staggered at her, reaching for the undefended throat.

She used her last iota of reserve phase capability—just enough to duck to one side and shove him as hard as she could on the vector he'd been traveling, head-on for the witness dock and its force field, which she'd reached behind her back to reactivate.

At nominal performance levels Peterbuilt might have shrugged off the field, but with so much shielding compromised and damage-control systemry wrecked, he went into full arrest, arching backward while megawatt banners fluttered on and about him and sudden bulges from internal eruptions ballooned here and there on his idealized musculature. The field shorted out with a final wash of sheet lightning; Peterbuilt crashed through the railing on the opposite side of the witness dock and lay still.

Silvercup ignored him, crouched to protect Lucky's body with her own; the Circuit Court showdown wasn't over yet.

The Monitor and the Supreme Justice had fought each other to a standstill, but with the demise of Peterbuilt the Monitor gave a deep shudder and a high-pitched shriek; a heavy rumble began building in him. "I'll destroy you all—what? What's that?"

They all heard it—a sound that rose and fell, ululating, singing with an inhuman moan, spellbinding even to the gleamers. Lucky, struggling up partway with Silvercup's surprisingly warm, pliant somalloy body against him, muttered, "I know that sound—"

It had made the Monitor's focus waver; there was a crash overhead and down darted the lavender glass football aircraft. A dozen of the vitreous flying-jellyfish security units swarmed out and, impervious to everything the Monitor threw at them, entered its gold housing through access panels. As Silvercup helped Lucky to his feet, the Monitor's voice cut off and his blue eyes flickered out.

"Sorry I couldn't listen just now, Lucky," Silvercup told him, helping him up. "What were you trying to say?"

He felt like a crash-test dummy at the end of a busy week, but smiled and patted the smooth shoulder. " 'Sterling Silver, riding to the rescue as usual.' "

"No, it was the other way 'round this time." She kissed his cheek; Lucky looked shocked—perhaps even blushed, though it was hard to tell. "Can't help it." She shrugged. "I love your user-friendly ergonomics and breezily winsome neural architecture."

"What was the source of that sound—you!" the Supreme Justice tolled. "Who are you people? How did you get here?"

It was Gipper Beidjie and the Intubis along with Miles Vanderloop, emerging from the spectators. Bluesy was putting away his bull-roarer, the Monitor's fatal distraction. Gipper raised a hand to Lucky. "Hello again, whacker!"

FORTY-SIX

APPROACHING THE PASSENGER ramp of the XT cruise ship *Crystal Harmonic*, Mickey Formica and Nikkei Tanabe were taken aback and malignly delighted to see faces—or rather, mirrored facebowls—they'd previously close-encountered.

They were a trio about Nikkei's modest height, in gizmoed flak vests, tuck-and-roll kneeboots, and what looked like, but was not, black Lycra-spandex. They wore implausibly hefty, complex wristphones, with stubby and use-worn Trekkie handguns clipped to their utility belts, and were distributing *DNAberrations!* trading cards and promotional materials, VDR tapes, interactive e-brochures, and so forth. Perhaps because

Earth was accustomed to the supposed themer ship and the aliens were currently abroad in the Acropolis as ostensible cast members, business was slow.

One of the three spotted the partners and spoke, his processed voice crackling. "Looky here! If it isn't the Monsters of the Men's Room! Crapped out in any good lavatories lately, boys?" He pushed up his visor to expose greenish pruneface features the two had mistaken for fannish 'flesh in New York. Mickey did a flat-handed Death Touch mime-kata, as if wearing invisible puppets. "This gig might be fun after all."

The aliens were a Peer Group from Black Hole's Technical Assist Division who'd literally snatched the non-compos Lucky Junknowitz from Mickey and Nikkei's grasp in a comfort station in the Ed Koch Convention Center. The insanely devo kidnapping had occurred at PhenomiCon when professor Miles Vanderloop's visitor's badge wound up on the wrong, self-admittedly narrow, chest.

"Just goes to show how badly Adit Navel needs a shake-up," the TechSist leader was sniggering. "Any self-respecting field office would've recycled your useless plasm long since."

"You bet your little wormhole there's gon' be some plasm recycled, guacamole-viz," Mickey began, but Miss Sato cut him off. "Why is a Peer Group posing as *Harmonic* cast members?"

The leader made a moue. "Guess Management wanted some experienced people on this mudball, eh? In case anything *happens*."

Sato restrained Mickey with a look and the four resumed their way to the ramp, followed by the fido cart and its black-box burden. Asia felt the hair standing up on the back of her neck at the aroma of the creatures; not that it was horrible, just so unEarthly. On some molecular level her body was phoning in confirmation that she was in deep, deep shit.

At fifty thousand gross-register tons the *Harmonic* was small as cruise ships went, but, as a converted corporate yacht, she had a reputation for luxuriousness; the Tanabe-Hagadorn connection gave her great cachet with the prestige-conscious. Above the upperworks a holo flashed: WELCOME ABOARD, SONY-NEUHAUS SALES CONFERENCE!! Then it reconfigured to ANCHORS AWEIGH, PHOENIX ENTERPRISES EXECUTIVE BOARD!!, which was followed by GO WHERE NO THEME ATTRACTION HAS GONE BEFORE WITH THE CRYSTAL HARMONIC—YOUR SCI-FI STAR SHIP!! and other banal copy. There were also giant depictions of faux-Madonna songbird Meena D., box office heartthrob Jason Duplex, and The

Awesome Vogonskiy, all of whom were slated for special performances on the next leg of the voyage.

At the foot of the boarding ramp the four were bowed aboard by a gowned Edrian in a spectral headdress and a blue, nubble-skinned Kraam who ushered them along with gestures of all three upper appendages. Human porters in spacefleet uniforms nodded pleasantly.

Asia wanted to know why, if the Trough visitors were paying customers, they were willing to stand around posing as cast members. Sato explained, "Some welcome the added opportunity to study humans, while others find amusement in the role-playing; in certain Trough circles it's the ultimate au courant status symbol to tell one's con-the-Earther *Harmonic* anecdotes. When no passengers are inclined to impersonate themers, offworld Black Hole employees step in."

The fido cart wheeling Tanabe's black box trailed the four into the reception area, where they were met by a Deep Space Nine assortment of alien greeters. Like most people on earth, Asia had picked up their species names from saturation ads and PR coverage: Occuumese, Nall, Bygarian, and those scary Yggdraasian ironclads.

A steward offered to lead them to Tanabe's quarters, but Miss Sato dismissed him. "I know the way, thank you." Dogged by the fido, they entered a passageway of duty-free shops whose lighting and decor suggested, in Asia's opinion, an overdone orbital bordello-mall. The passageway seemed carpeted with aerogel; it felt and looked as if she were walking on a thin but resilient layer of radioactive cotton candy.

The sundries stand stocked products whose labels she couldn't read and whose containers put her in mind of bronzed honeycomb, leather scuba tanks, and ruby hatboxes. The intimate-apparel boutique featured a mannequin with six breasts showing off a byzantinely underwired brassiere and a lower garment that appeared to be a jumble of twenty-fifth-century vacuum-cleaner attachments. In the beauty parlor a seven-foot-tall zucchini was undergoing, perhaps, liposuction or a radiator flush.

Asia glanced at a curio-shop window display and saw a convoluted wad of tissue hanging in midair in an elaborate bell jar. Next to it was another, serpentine and more withered, curlicue of dead flesh. She read the items' display cards, then she stopped short until Mickey gave her a discreet push from behind. She'd assumed tourists from other worlds were still tourists and would know the urge to collect souvenirs . . .

But Einstein's brain and JFK's penis?

They came into the Grand Centrum, the four-deck-high amidships crossroads. Asia was less shocked by how strange it was than by how utterly otherworldly and incomprehensible it *wasn't*—but then, Sheena Hec'k had remarked that circumstances on Earth were a funhouse-mirror reflection of those in the Trough.

Diverse bars and eateries opened on the space, as did what she took to be analogues of a casino, spa, fitness center, game arcade, and dinner theater. Bulletin-board holos encouraged passengers to sign up for a directed-energy target-shooting contest, a psychokinetic miniature-golf tournament, and a side tour, "The Power Trip: Visit the Nexi of Adit Navel's Spiritual Energies." A strobing UFO elevator floated up and down at either end of the place, and everywhere Asia turned there were beings from other worlds—stately or awkward, beautiful or revolting, humanoid or non.

Miss Sato explained that security had been greatly tightened, not only due to Lucky's tourists' misbehavior but also to keep movie makeup and themer animatron spies from penetrating the offworlders' cover story. In Guam a black-bag squad from Industrial Light and Magic had been caught, breaded, and devoured.

"That's also why you'll hear rumors of 'themers' letting their personas slip," she added. "Select *human* cast members done up as Trough types purposely drop their veneer, to allay fear and suspicion in various quarters—for the time being. Black Hole wants to savor the amusing revelation of its existence at a moment of the Agency's own choosing."

"When?" Asia tried to demand without raising her voice, then stifled a yelp as something scuttled out of the EXCOGITORIUM—as the brass plate over the door called a kind of data-center lounge. The critter came straight for Asia but stopped short, gobbling.

Mickey seized the opportunity to score points, stepping forward protectively. "Gitchu troll ass back under the billy-goat bridge." Asia didn't complain as he took her elbow, but she did spare a last troubled glance over her shoulder. But the behavioral interdictions-ridden goblin into whom Brax Koddle had been transformed by Hagadorn could see no sign of recognition in her face.

After Mickey, Nikkei, Asia, and Miss Sato left the Centrum of the *Crystal Harmonic*, Dante Bhang and Randy Barnes stepped from where they'd hidden behind a huge wooden ship's wheel in the Celestial Navigator's Club bar, overlooking the main floor from one deck up.

"What're they doing here?" Barnes fretted. He was sweating and trembling even though he knew that the Pesky Pizzarino neurotoxin wouldn't make its effects felt for another forty-eight hours at the least.

Bhang, impeccably groomed in a linen suit as white as the captain's table's napery, shrugged. "We can only wait and see." He watched the little grotesque who'd importuned Asia Boxdale scamper away, wondering who the creature was and what the exchange signified. "Come; we need a dab of camoflesh—"

He stopped in his tracks as an apparition rose up before him: Barb Steel, metalflesh familiar to Trough and Adits heavy Llesh Llerrudz, looking like a walking abattoir. "Good day, Mr. Bhang, Captain Barnes; I trust you find your cabin acceptable?"

Barnes froze, but Dante fielded the question casually. "Mm. Kind of you to inquire."

Barb Steel's glowing eyes panned from Bhang to Barnes and back. "We want to insure that you have a *festive* time on our little sea trip." He gave them a friendly wave of the fingers with a faint chorus of sliding blades and went his way.

Barnes mopped his forehead with his pocket handkerchief. "They're onto us; we've got to get out of here!"

Bhang gave him a look of great distaste. "There's no way back for us—get a grip on yourself."

As they exited, Charlie Cola, looking on from one deck higher yet at the Galloping Glutton snack bar, watched his two betrayers go—the two men who'd plotted to betray, destroy, and replace him.

Takuma Tanabe's personal quarters aboard the *Crystal Harmonic* were adjoining A-category deluxe staterooms equivalent to a pair of five-star hotel suites. They were nevertheless a step down from his previous accommodations, the owner's cabin Phipps Hagadorn now occupied.

When Mickey and Nikkei arrived with Miss Sato and Asia, followed by the fido with its matte-black box, they found him making a minute examination of the bulkhead in the company of one of his aides with palmcam-like units. More surprising than the Mr. Science act was that neither Kamimura nor any of his ninjas were present.

Tanabe nodded permission to his lackeys on some matter, then dismissed them and turned to the other four as he patted the bulkhead. He smiled at Sato. "The readings are as expected." Then he turned to Asia. "Miss Boxdale, your performance has been scheduled for tomorrow evening at the Captain's Banquet, where a number of matters will be addressed."

"*Kichigai!*" Nikkei burst out. "You're crazy!"

"You on Murder Incorporated's private cement barge with your bunny slippers in a washtub," Mickey elaborated.

Tanabe was unpersuaded. "You, meanwhile, lack complete information. Bring the cart over here, please." Tanabe palmed the lock, and Nikkei and Mickey began opening latches.

"Best be a effing neutron bomb," Mickey groused, but it wasn't. Instead the box contained a variety of Elvis Presley memorabilia, including a massive belt buckle from his jumpsuit days, blue suede shoes, and a black plastic pre-Turn pocket comb caked with cracked white layerings of antediluvian hair oil, sealed in a hermetic case.

"Could've at least thrown in a poisoned toothpick," Mickey pouted.

"Improvisation is a quintessential ninja skill," Tanabe counseled. "Time you both cultivated it. Now, then: before relinquishing this ship to Hagadorn I had an undercoating applied to the bulkheads—a low intensity incendiary mixed with a nerve agent that will render unprotected humans and most XTs unconscious or at least groggy." He held another little palmtop gadget. "It will detonate upon command."

Nikkei rummaged some more in the Elvis stuff. "Then, where're the gas masks?"

Tanabe looked to Miss Sato. "My dear?"

She showed complete composure. "There was a counteragent mixed in with the tea you drank during the flight here."

"There's more to the plan than that, but nothing you need to know right now. Except, that is, for this."

With that Tanabe flipped over the little fido cart and found a concealed catch; a disguised panel swung open to reveal a hidden, shielded compartment. The interior was packed with tubes of camoflesh and various ninja gear, including scuba stuff, made from exotic materials.

"Overture, curtain lights," Nikkei said.

"Your Honor? We're receiving telecaster hail for you from an unlisted source—an outmoded installation, at that."

"Very well, patch it through," Ka Shamok ordered.

Anything was worth a try when every other Adit in the Trough was locked down by whatever had gone wrong up-Trap. The disk communicator had brought no further word from Sobek; the raiders' tactical situation promised to shift from chaotic to calamitous. The entire operation had been planned around surprise and Sobek's interdiction of the up-Trap SIs, plus a route of quick withdrawal in case events went against them. None of these elements any longer obtained. A static situation would let Light Trap's defensive forces rally, get where they were needed, and exterminate the intruders.

Even as Ka Shamok glanced out over the imperceptibly upward-curving horizon, the explosions that had marked the fight at the Kordaac plasm banks rekindled—a counterattack of some kind. With their Adit down, the Kordaac Liberation Organization irregulars had no path of retreat save fighting their way cross-country—just like all the rest who'd followed Ka Shamok into the jaws of the foul extenders' power base.

Ka Shamok hoped the hail was Sobek or even Gipper Beidjie, but he was disappointed. "Go away; if you were here I'd kill you. Your nanite dagger has failed us."

E. C. Wheeler only smirked the more. "That any way to talk to an old *compañero*?"

"You hair-faced mountebank! Where are the Intubis?"

Wheeler flung his fingertips outward. "The blackfellas move on like a cool breeze. I, conversely, need your help. We here on Hazmat must fade ASAP; we've zealot and Warhead problems."

"Hazmat? Wheeler, *have you found the memory egg of Hazmat?* Phoenix stone, data grail, whatever it's called?"

Wheeler adjusted something and the view panned past a ground-pounder, a Mauve Mauler, and Sheena Hec'k—recognizable from her Wanted posters. Dust and debris sifted down from above, and there were distant rumblings of intense combat. The pickup stopped on the memory-egg module.

"Wheeler, activate your Adit and bring me the memory egg." The lost fragment of the up-Trap SIs might be used to sabotage the Sysops' servants; that had been Ka Shamok's plan prior to the advent of the nanite dagger.

"Would if we could," Wheeler assured him. "But we can only achieve a circumscribed contiguity, too small to even fit the SOB through. Aside from which, if we remove it from the eggcup, the Adit would most likely collapse instantly—and believe me, I don't want to be stuck here with what's coming our way."

Ka Shamok couldn't stop to find out what that might be. "Then open the Adit as wide as you can." He was signaling for his best field techs and think-tankers. "We're going to toss you a line."

"My daughter's idea precisely."

It took some doing, but a limited tunnel-vision connection was quickly established. Ka Shamok had the odd experience of lying on his belly by a mousehole contiguity for a hasty conference with Wheeler, who was doing the same. They got an interface cable passed over from the Light Trap beachhead to the sepulcher last ditch, then went back to the telecaster holo link. The two updated each other hastily and spottily.

The techs were meanwhile making an attempt to phreak the up-Trap SIs with a link to the memory egg, but the SIs were shunning the contact. Wheeler was more concerned with getting equipment and tools through the mousehole somehow. "Maybe if you—"

"Wheeler, you have to tell us how to get the SIs to speak to the memory egg! Find out from the data banks there what protocols will make the SIs access it."

"Eh? There's no time! Warhead—" There'd been explosions, shots, mutant howls, and the metallic din of fighting machines behind Wheeler; now the holo derezzed.

As Yoo Sobek braced for the onslaught of the Sysops, a curious inaction ensued, like an inappropriately sustained note in a finale.

Sobek perceived that all Trough Adits were still offline and that despite the Sysops' commands to crush Ka Shamok, something wasn't working. There was unprecedented dissension among the SIs; they were making queries the Sysops wouldn't or couldn't answer regarding information carried by the evaporated nanite dagger. Sobek was ignored for the moment as the exasperated SIs opened a link down-Trap—to the invaders.

The SIs were the sine qua non of the Sysops' power, the Foul Extenders' access to their intragalactic edifice of machinery, armed might, extortion, raw wealth, mental subjugation, cyberverse dominion, religious flammery, espionage assets, compliant addicts, sexual stimuli, potencies of fad-ordination, naked-singularity Adits . . . The Sysops were helpless before their compuservants' work stoppage.

There was nothing preventing Sobek from continuing his mission; he projected himself away, back to the temple at the foot of the Outline. As he made the transition from one orientation to another, a discrete function of his intellect meditated on the query the SIs of Light Trap were sending to the invaders.

Limpidation?

" 'Limpidation'!" Ka Shamok's voice echoed the up-Trap SIs. "Wheeler, what are they raving about?"

Wheeler groaned in torment, slapping his hands to his eyes; there was another shock wave from combat above the Howlslot, making more loosened filth filter down into the sepulcher and through the restored holofield. He gave Ka Shamok a recap. "So the nanites have obeyed their urge to proselytize; limpidation's a pyramid scheme, you see."

"Are you telling me they've infected the up-Trap SIs with your fraudulent consciousness-raising religion?"

"Somewhat; market penetration is rapid but not immediate. I did build in heavy recruitment incentives—fifty per cent off the next rung on the Ladder of Lucidity for each ten new members—so all the nanites were keen to bring in—"

"You blithering lunatic!"

The sepulcher jounced again. "Warhead's at our door! You've got to get us out of here!"

"Concentrate! Is there something in this dimwit belief system of yours that we can use to coopt the SIs?"

Wheeler clucked. "Nothing I can think of. Unless you count the Omegan Discourse Seminar of Doom. Except that there aren't any Omegans because, quite frankly, I made them up— Whoa!"

He was shouldered aside from the pickup by his battle-stained, bloodied daughter. Sheena Hec'k's smile was multicurve. "Discourse, is it? And so they shall have it."

There was a levin-bolt strike somewhere in the sepulcher, and the telecaster holo derezzed again.

FORTY-SEVEN

CONDUCTING HIS WIFE aboard the *Crystal Harmonic,* Russell Print was suddenly struck by fear. "Wins, you refilled your Dynamine prescription, right?"

Winnie was dubiously eyeing an obesely mushroom-shaped Fiigriil. "Me hearty, I thought you never got seasick."

He wrinkled his nose, indicating the unheeding Fiigriil. "That's not what's liable to make me spout. There's such a thing as too much verisimilitude, even in sci-fi themers—"

"Rush!" The Awesome Vogonskiy was pounding Russ on the back and hugging Winnie. "Welcome aboard, old salt! And you, Winnie—and where are those little ladies of yours?"

Winnie tried to sound blithe. "With my mom; they won't share anything else, but a cold's community property."

Vogonskiy's look darkened. "I'm very disappointed with you. Well, no doubt I'll see them soon." Something about the way he said it made Russ think, *No, you won't.*

Vogonskiy snapped his fingers, and stewards grabbed the Prints' luggage off their fido cart. "Thanks, Eric," said Russ, one of the few who called Eric Vogon by that name. "Could you see if Remora Barleycorn—Regina, I mean—checked in yet?" Damn, he had to be careful not to use her S-N nickname to her face.

"No need to; the golden goose of your Turgid Tales imprint was, when last sighted, stalking Jason Duplex, a sex symbol she's apparently worshiped from afar for years."

"Hey, try and see he's nice to her, please? Sheese, there's a lot riding on this cruise, buddy."

An invisibly high corporate connection between Sony-Neuhaus and Phoenix Enterprises had decreed that Russ and various editorial and sales staffers hold their conference amid the in-depth weirdness of a Strangelove boatload of UFOids. Oddly, Dieter Druckfehler, supposed author of *Gate Crasher,* wasn't scheduled to attend, and Russ had no luck getting so much as a phone meet with the guy.

What topped off Russ's unease were similarities, even shared story elements, between the ship's theme-milieu and the Worlds Abound saga. White Dwarves, Black Hole companies, touring aliens—WE'RE YOUR ADIT TO OTHER WORLDS, read a sign on the gangway. "I hope this voyage isn't a major mistake." He sighed.

Vogonskiy's brows fluttered with a disquietingly sinister glee. "Rush, I have *everything* under control. How could I not have you and your colleagues and your lovely wife ringside for my greatest performance?"

Yoo Sobek again approached the ectoplasmic, meta-psi-Dravidian temple at the foot of the balefire terminus of the Outline. It was open, the semisentient wards consumed with transactional analysis of their dysfunctional egoicator matrices and unresolved id nodes.

Sobek passed into a pocket universe, the symbol of all that the Sysops were, had been, and had yet to be—their hows and whys and wherefores. At the far end of the display was the eight-ring symbol; Sobek scudded toward it.

His return to the place gave him bits and chains of memory. He knew once more that not all Sysops were created equal: there were castes, estates of Sysophood. All had been created by, spun from, entities outside the Milky Way; only a supreme few—the Supernals—knew who those entities were, their nature and purpose. Sobek had been one of those who didn't, forbidden the knowledge as surely as Adam and Eve were the apple. As he advanced toward the rings he integrated the two personas, becoming SySobek.

As Sysop he'd held himself and been held in high esteem: brilliant problem solver, inexhaustible inquirer after facts—vaunted pragmatist. His genius had added much to the powers of the Probes, spearheaded research into probability, fashioned the Killing Thought, and visited it upon the Chasen-nur. That Sysop had his own smug theory, certain he'd ultimately be lifted not just to Supernal status but up the Outline and to divinity, throwing off the bonds of time and space, taking on what he coveted even more than omnipotence: omniscience.

In the meantime, the Sobek Sysop couldn't resist exceeding his limits. He lent untraceable aid to a foolhardy conspiracy by, among others: a seditious clique among Hazmat AI and nanite R and D types; an alliance of phreaked Trough antiviral programs run moderately amok; and a high-ranking Light Trap executive who'd become crazed with lust for the ultimate in stock manipulation and insider trading. The cabal's conspiracy revolved around an outlaw linkup among the Hazmat AIs and up-Trap SIs, to elicit ultimate Black Hole secrets.

It all went apocalyptically wrong for the conspirators, of course—Sysop Sobek had seen to that—and it was so *fascinating*. Hazmat's AIs went insane and reconstituted as Warhead, and a large part of Warhead and a small sliver of Light Trap's SIs spun off in the form of a memory egg. Hazmat itself vanished from the Trough along with any record of its whereabouts. Mutant inhibitor-attacking viruses made it possible for certain automata and Trough AIs to begin thinking for themselves—those who would soon establish the Fealty. The infection among nanites would later contribute to the labor strike in Fimblesector.

Sysop Sobek escaped all suspicion. He pursued both the agenda of Black Hole—especially investigations into probability—and his own secret avocations. The Killing Thought with which he'd cursed the Chasen-nur had made the creatures a scattered, mistrustful, agonized, and dying race. On a whim, Sysop Sobek transgressed by assuming the form of a Chasen-nur to savor what he'd done to them.

As, perhaps, he'd subconsciously planned it, hubris made him meet the gaze of an afflicted Chasen-nur and feel the full brunt of the Killing Thought. Infinitely worse than the psychic torture was the spiritual isolation; this was a race dying from enforced loneliness. Sysop Sobek screamed and sought to self-destruct, but before he could, the other Chasen-nur restrained him physically for a critical moment.

Sysop Sobek managed to flee that form, which died; the other Chasen-nur, blaming herself, took her own life. Sysop Sobek repaired up-Trap safely, but that too-ghastly wisdom had permeated every part of him. He began his up-Trap subversion, working against Black Hole from within and funneling help and information to Ka Shamok and lesser opposition groups—through Silvercup, among others, and the disk communicator. To destabilize the Agency he arranged for, among other things, the spilling of a vast quantity of probability distillate onto the first Adit Navel indig whose own probability aura resonated to it—Lucky Junknowitz, of course. Adit Navel piqued his interest because it had the Supernals' and was marked on the galactic map with that same eight-ring symbol that applied to the galaxy as a whole.

Soon, Sysop Sobek felt the need for a greater dynamic and so dared the ultimate, stealing into the temple to probe the secret of the eight rings. Sobek was remembering more and more now, but not that crucial instant leading to his downfall. So history might reenact itself, but there was no way for Sobek to turn aside or retreat.

He projected himself to the vast sign of the eight rings and availed himself of its meaning a second time, opening it to him as a human might throw open a treasure chest—only to have seraphic fire gush forth. Sobek again apprehended the secret behind the eight rings, the Outline and what lay beyond it, and the Black Hole Travel Agency. It began once more to consume him.

But where that revelation had smashed the traumatized, guilt-ridden, and embrittled Sysop, Sobek had a certain resistance to it born of the punishment the Supernals had meted out to him. Mortality, of a sort, had inured him: it was the Supernals' pivotal miscalculation.

At the same time his Sysop self waxed recombinant, Sobek perceived carnage everywhere down-Trap. The raid was still in progress; there was still time. He stopped being a Probe, transcended Sysop. Having penetrated the secrets, Sobek became something different, something unprecedented, in a universe where there were many Outlines, many Black Hole Travel Agencies. He positioned himself on the very edge of the balefire, to treat with the entities on the Other Side.

As E. C. Wheeler had foreseen, Warhead's biomimetic jungle held back from frontal assault. The Howlslot and the chasm floor before the sepulcher grew thicker and thicker with it, until it seemed about to smother itself.

Wheeler tapped the Trough's synthetic floor. "This place is a tough nut and also, as I say, Combat*kopf* out there doesn't want to risk damaging the memory egg—whoops."

From the mass of biomimetics emerged a new shape, an incandescent bud. Harley blurted, "Lotus; looks just like a—"

She didn't get to finish, because biomimetic formations blunt and massive as wrecking balls began ramming the doors. Mechs, 'Saurs, and dismounted fighters dispersed to positions for a last stand. Watching the holo, Wheeler put an arm around his tall daughter, feeling the young strength in her back; Sheena in turn slipped an arm around him. An external pickup showed the lotus appendage waiting like a poised rattler to enter the place.

On another jury-rigged display, Ka Shamok was complaining

because the Light Trap SIs didn't want to enter the linkage with the memory egg. He wanted those in the sepulcher to query the Adit data banks on the matter. Wheeler tore his attention from the pounding at the doors. "Eh? There's no time! Warhead is about to crack this—"

There was a megavolt crash and the holo vanished; most of the hastily mounted area lights blew or burned out as the doors caved in. The radiant, lotuslike bud burst in like a blazing comet, headed straight for the memory egg with Warhead's brute biomimetics bringing up the rear.

Eliminator was flattened where it stood, blazing away with right-forearm chaingun and left-forearm flamethrower; 'Saurs and humans alike jumped into the fight, firing and swinging weapons. The sepulcher filled with racing offshoots and high explosives, flailing excrescences, sword blades, laser beams, shrapnel, smoke, fire, death. The glaring bud struck for the memory egg.

Sheena had been firing a heavy Vigilance Bureau automatic with either hand; now she dropped them and snatched the egg out of its niche. The lotus bud moved to hem her in, opening wide to swallow egg and guide alike. Sheena retreated, shoulder-rolling back across another subassembly; the bud pursued. With perfect timing she grabbed a release and kicked herself clear as she brought down the upper array, trapping the lotus in the interface fixture that had been used by Hazmat AIs in centuries past. Warhead must have shaped its lotus using some residual directives from those days; there was data link.

Sheena pivoted, leapt, and slam-dunked the egg into its niche, closing the telecaster circuit, connecting Warhead and the memory egg to Ka Shamok and, she prayed, the SIs of Light Trap. The lotus's stem thrashed, then quieted; systemry blazed and toned. Where the SIs refused contact with the memory egg, they accepted—or perhaps couldn't repulse—contact from the more complex, aggressive, and powerful Warhead.

"It's Attacking!" Wheeler hollered. "Attacking the Light Trap SIs!"

"Looks as if Warhead recognizes a natural competitor," Sheena panted. The biomimetics lost their coordination, convulsing like constrictor coils; the ragtag defenders were marginally better off, but not much. Warhead was about to bring the sepulcher down on them. "We've got to get that Adit widened!" Wheeler yelled. "We've got to fade out of here!"

FORTY-EIGHT

"I DON'T CARE if your head *does* look like an upside-down erlenmeyer flask, shweetie," slurred the *Video Examiner* reporter in the sheath dress to the UFOid. "Let's you'n me dance."

Watching the purported space visitor dragged onto the dance floor by the media-maid, Russ Print was disturbed to note the fellow's agility—for a guy *supposedly* wearing some kind of bionic third leg.

The *Crystal Harmonic* was out of the Sea of Okhotsk, anchored nine hundred miles east-northeast of the Sea Acropolis for the Captain's Banquet; the Heave-Ho Room—formerly the Trough Lounge—was reconfigured for dinner theater and high epulation. Too far from shore to grab Winnie and make a run for it in a lifeboat, Russ found himself thinking.

To control his nerves, he fixed on the idea of a banquet and several stiff drinks. Like most of the other Sony-Neuhausers, he'd seen and heard things he'd rather not dwell upon; in fact, about the only one in his contingent who wasn't shaken was Turgid Tales bestseller Remora Barleycorn, who was as marinated as the VE reporter and intent on getting Jason Duplex onto any convenient flat surface for some organ grinding.

Russ slurped a whisper martini—the bartender had merely said "vermouth" over it but added none—and admitted that the place was impressive as hell. Various tables and seats— they weren't all chairs—in the Heave-Ho Room had been built to accommodate the spacey physiognomies of alleged cast members who were behaving much more like high-rolling passengers.

There was a big, elaborate stage at the forward end of the dining room; a transparent aft bulkhead gave a view of the Aquatics deck, whose drawbridge-like hatch had been lowered to water level. Rolling seas were alight with a coldish Pacific sunset. A few adventuresome humans and a range of so-called themers were indulging in some dusk sailboarding, snorkeling, and the rest. The gawky black kid and the muscular kudzu who'd come with Takuma Tanabe were particularly active; so was the giant water snake the management kept insisting was animatronic.

Russ tried to shut out his memories of diverse bogeys playing gin rummy at hyperkinetic speed, blasting skeet from the veranda deck with what looked to be solidified spit, and geeking down live, sulfurous tubeworms from a superheated hors d'oeuvres tank. Then there were the tension and menace from and among the convened Phoenix *übers,* Asia Boxdale's weird aura, and all these Men in Black lurking around. The *Video Examiner* reporter had begun getting swilled right after her corporate overlord, Ulf Weigel, took her aside to give her what Russ presumed to be specific marching orders.

His gaze intersected his pretty blond wife's, and he made himself give Winnie a beamish smile; no point worrying her. He saw right away that she was putting on a brave show, too. They took one another's hands and he groped for something to say. "I, I'm glad we . . . left the kids at home, babe."

Winnie Print choked back a sob, fumbled from her chair, and ran off blindly, not sure where she was going. Russ started after, but a huge hand pressed him back into his seat. "Stay put, Rush," Vogonskiy directed. "I don't want you to miss a bit of the fun."

The Supreme Justice of Circuit Court, gazing down on Gipper, Vanderloop, and the Intubis from vast red viewing slits, was indignant. "Regulators, confine these organics to insure that they don't contam—"

"Wouldn't try it if I were you, Judge," Lucky said into his medallion. "If you'll review my reports you'll find references to these . . . entities," Silvercup added.

The gray bastion might also, Lucky thought, consider the fact that Gipper and those traveling his songline showed no ill effects from Sweetspot's human-unfriendly atmosphere, not to mention their communicating just fine without transceivers.

When next she spoke, the Supreme Justice sounded more cautious. "Oh, yes. Well, Unit—Mr. Beidjie, why are you here?"

"This smash palace is part of me Dreamin', too, missus," Gipper announced. "D'you lot know what's happenin' there in the Tangerine, that Light Trap?"

The Supreme Justice could link to all Sweetspot data sources.

She summarized Ka Shamok's raid, adding, "Fragmentary information indicates it's going badly."

"Poor ratbags have Buckley's chance unless you bear a hand," Gipper shot back.

"The Fealty does not involve itself in the conflicts of organics," the bastion orated grandly.

"In a few minutes you'll be involved," Gipper said confidentially. "So'll that memory egg from Hazmat, and them Ess-Eyes up in the Tangerine, Light Trap. One way or another. So stop yer rubbishin' and give it the king hit. Now, 'scuze I; must be goin'."

With that he turned to lead on, just as the Circuit Court went into an uproar at mention of the memory egg. "Where're you off to?" Lucky yelped.

Gipper gave him a wink. "Like I saw it in my Dreaming: to Light Trap."

"Hey!" Lucky had a thousand questions about Wheeler, Ka Shamok, and the rest, but there wasn't time to ask. "Why'd you keep walking out on me?"

"That's how I Dreamed it," Gipper explained. "Besides, you can't leave." He pointed to Silvercup, who was picking through the scorched wreckage of the yellow and green CAD/CAM. The data crystal, Lucky thought; her stolen memories. Of, among other things, why she'd chosen to help him in the first place.

He went to her side as she pondered the loss, scarcely registering the commotion as Gipper, the Intubis, and Vanderloop, ignoring the bastion's objections, entered the Monitor's lifeless golden shell through an access panel. Silvercup stirred the debris, melancholy. "Poor little robo, just being obedient when it drained my memories and when I had it trip up Peterbuilt—"

She reached down into what remained of the CAD/CAM unit's belly, where spent and replacement working supplies were stored. "And, when I had it dump this down with the garbage." She plucked out the multifaceted ten-inch taper of polished gemstone Lucky remembered from his misadventures on the Staph spacewheel—what had struck him as a niveous version of Superman's family jewels in the pre-Turn flicks.

"You beautiful gleamer! You saved it after all!"

She nodded, the pearlescent hair shimmering. "They're mine; they're me." She gazed around. "And I want them back where they belong before anything else happens to—"

"Put that on hold," the Supreme Justice quavered grandly. "You and the Junknowitz unit will stand ready to advise and assist; even now, telecaster contact is being established with Ka Shamok's forces inside Light Trap."

"You mean, *directly*?" Silvercup was agog. "But what if the link is traced?"

"That can't be helped," the bastion answered. "This may be our only chance to set right what went so wildly amiss long ago. Too, this relates to the origins of the Fealty; we must take part to safeguard our survival."

More machines were arriving, setting up equipment so quickly that it looked like time-lapse photography. A tricycle tool chest had come humming over; picking a device from a drawer, Silvercup told Lucky, "Close your eyes; maybe our bio-technology isn't up to brain reassembly, but we know a bit about the epidermis."

Lucky did as she said. She'd worked as a nurse in the Staph Wheel, he reminded himself. Like her hand, the instrument penetrated the pink force field with no resistance. His pain began subsiding as she misted him with a fine spray, opening his Peter Pan shirt to get his lower neck. The mist had no odor, but now that she'd reached inside his force field her somalloy brought him scents of wildflowers and musk. He wondered when she'd begun taking bioform olfactory signals into account.

"Not exactly a hardbody." Lucky was gazing down glumly at his lanky physique.

"But not without a certain paradoxical appeal," Silvercup said. Tilting her head toward the spot where the jellyfish were securing Peterbuilt's remains, she added, "After all, shining paragons just aren't my type."

The Monitor was also being removed, piece by piece. To no one's surprise, there were no signs of the Intubis as the golden housing was dismantled. The giant bailiff's scattered parts were being gathered, too, and one repair robo got signs of life from the Bat-cowl head.

Silvercup replaced the sprayer, rebuttoned his shirt, and hugged him to her with tender restraint. "It was so brave of you to say you'd undergo neural forensics for my sake. Thank you."

"You stuck your neck out just as far for me." He put his arms around her; her somalloy was yielding and felt like it was sending a tiny electrical charge through him. Maybe there were pheromones mixed in with her other aromas; he felt an undeniable stirring at the crux of things, and saw that she was aware of it, too. "Yeah, well, *part* of my body's hard, at least," he said sheepishly.

"Yeah, well, part of mine's soft."

He'd always wondered.

And the pained but hopeful way she said it just broke his heart, which in turn clarified how much he cared about her, whatever manifestation of the universe she was: Artificial Entity, somalloy woman, or SI pneuma. Lucky was openmouthed, at a loss for words.

The Supreme Justice vibratoed, "Silvercup, direct your attention to the telecaster conference linkup." She meant two overhead holofields the size of small office buildings. On one, Ka Shamok was waiting grimly, explosions and strife in the background. The other field showed E. C. Wheeler in some dark place alongside a battle-scarred guy with a forelock and shaved scalp, crowded close to two familiar faces—

"Sheena! Harley!" But Sheena in a Trough-*couture* Mad Max uniform and Harley with a cue-ball cut and forelock? "Yikes, what's RGO?"

"We've no leisure for real-time dallying," the Justice said. "The hoped-for reconciliation among the Light Trap SIs, the memory egg, and Warhead has become hostility and conflict."

"We can't hold out much longer!" Behind Sheena something huge was flailing and heavy weapons fired sporadically.

"Nor we," Ka Shamok confessed grudgingly, his image jumping like a seismic needle in a force-seven quake. "Light Trap is coming apart around us!"

"You in the Fealty, reason with these demented data dumps!" Wheeler hollered. "Make peace!"

The Justice sounded defensive. "We do not possess appropriate techniques of negotiation and arbitration—certainly none to cope with such emotional hyperintellects."

"Can you evacuate us?" Ka Shamok demanded.

"No, the up-Trap SIs have the Trough in too much turmoil for that, and the Hazmat Adit is malfunctioning."

Lucky felt like tearing his own head bald. Why hadn't that deranged old kangaroo Gipper warned them about— "Gipper!" Lucky yelled. "Look around on Light Trap! The Aborigines are headed your way, maybe they can help!"

Ka Shamok barked back. "We've had no sighting of them, and in any case they'd probably pass us by—do you copy? What's that channel clutter?"

The new sounds were didgeridoos and click sticks, the chant of Aboriginal rites. Lucky, expecting the Intubis to show, was as shocked as the rest when a third holofield rezzed up overhead, the Sweetspot communications AIs prattling about unidentified telecaster transmissions of a unique and inexplicable sort.

The man dancing and chanting in the scene was a unique and inexplicable sort himself, turned out in ocher and painted designs made for rituals immemorial but having a familiar face. He shuffled and hopped on a bare stretch of red rock by a ceremonial pole that stretched into a dark sky. Lucky, Harley, and Sheena yelled in near-unison.

"Ziggy!"

FORTY-NINE

ZIGGY FORELOCK WONDERED when the trouble was going to start. It didn't keep him waiting long.

He was being guided, by SELMI's VirtNet program and the ZOOTsuit's headset and receptor feedback, through the timeless Intubi invocation: chanting, kick-shuffling, gesturing with the souvenir spear he'd grabbed to serve as a prop. Suddenly he felt a human grip like a foundry waldo close on his shoulder. "Mr. Sigmund, we need to speak with you for a second."

He'd been hoping for a miracle, but a capering freq flier in the midst of the gala preopening bash, faked ID or no, was bound to draw heat. To Ziggy's eyephones Ayers Rock looked empty except for the ceremonial pole that was the telecomm pylon, but the voice was young, male, and ominously stiff. "SELMI, bail me out," Ziggy muttered as he lifted the eyephones.

"I'll try, Ziggy," SELMI responded over the ceremonial music pounding in his ear, "although it will take time."

Ziggy blinked around at garishly lit nighttime DreamLand. He was hemmed in by two young men with steroid physiques, brush-cut blond hair, and Aryan Nation demeanors. They wore matching sport coats and light earplug-mike combos.

"Sir, you're not a cast member, so we can't let you perform," one said. "In fact, the chief of protocol would like to have a word with you," his fraternal twin added.

"Look, I'm on the list—" The waldo grips locked on both his arms this time. "SELMI!"

Ziggy was as surprised as everybody else when speakers large and small all over DreamLand began pouring out the sacred music and chanting. Not only were the standard PA and attraction speakers carrying it; SELMI had also tapped into the megasound concert stacks, piles of gale-force noisemakers that included servovalve vibe mills using velocity loops—modulated forced-air conduits—to push out earthquake subwoofer sonics in the three-to-thirty-hertz range. The Aboriginal prayer and song came like a Möbius sonic boom, a songline tsunami.

There hadn't been anything like it on Uluru in long, long years.

Even the two renta-oxen stood frozen. "Bugger!" One's lips were forming inaudible words. "What in bloody hell—auugh!"

Several blowflies—fat, blue-green-bronze, and hyperactive—had flown into his mouth as eagerly as if invited to a kegger there. He released Ziggy's arm, spitting, to swipe at the ones that landed in his eyes. His mate let go, too, with blowies in his ears and some that had caromed up each nostril.

Everybody but Ziggy was having the same troubles, despite the park's far-reaching extermination measures. Blowies and botflies as thick as living rain blanketed people, food, drink, signs, booths, and everything else except the speakers and the pylon that was Ziggy's VirtNet ceremonial pole. The guards were trying to lay hands on Ziggy again, one fumbling for an aroma pistol. Swift four-footed shapes, yipping and snarling, heavy-shouldered and fleet as shadows, came from nowhere, running between and around the men's legs, springing to knock them down; white teeth ripped at a hand, drawing blood and sending the Crowd Control gun flying away.

Ziggy recoiled, thinking some animal exhibit had burst open—dingoes, had to be—then registering the beasts with a shocked clarity: the striped markings, the long, toothy snouts, the size of them—*marsupial wolves*!

Australia had spawned an evolutionary oddity only to see the creatures made extinct by the mid-twentieth century—except here was a whole pack of them, materialized or sung up on Uluru. With the guards fleeing, the marsupial wolves split up to go have some more fun. Lightning lit the black sky in ultraviolet-white cascades, in a siege line around Ayers Rock.

Ziggy stood, just about leaning physically against the overwhelming pulse of the Aboriginal music, agape.

A well-fleshed, bleach-blond socialite had her mouth wide open in a scream he couldn't hear—blowies crawling on her tonsils—as she faced a Gould's sand goanna characteristically reared on its hind legs in alarm, the spotted skin of its throat puffed out, black hooked claws splayed. The woman stumbled off, a prudent move; the lizard stood as tall as she, taller than any goanna ought to. Ziggy saw guests trampling each other to escape the Ned Kelly's Bush Ranger Pub as horrendous jaws snapped at them. He had a glimpse of a saltwater crocodile as big as a whaleshark before it drew back into the shadows of its unlikely lair.

Now thunder was part of the din, too; Ziggy pulled his earphones back into place. The noise was muffled but he could still feel the vibrations in the air and through the ground. SELMI was talking to him. "Are you all right?"

"For now. What should I do?"

"You will have to decide, but you're apparently intended to carry forward a songline."

"Can you keep everybody away from me?"

"The archetypal creatures who have appeared are already doing so. I further observe that injuries thus far have been non-lethal. Do you wish to continue the rite?"

If he didn't, he had a feeling, it would spell the end of the Intubis. He lowered the eyephones and Ayers was primal Uluru once more. This time there were shapes moving in the distance: X-ray-style Dreamtime totemic creatures and Mimi stick-figure renderings of human figures, living rock paintings that gestured to him and mimicked the dance he was to do.

"Where are those coming from, the telesphere?"

"Perhaps. They're being channeled to me through the pylon, from a powerful source whose origins I cannot determine."

"Bring up the chant again, show me those moves."

SELMI did both through the ZOOTsuit, explaining, "These are steps appropriate to the gathering of Emu totem people." Ziggy did the moves, hopping and pacing in the imitation of the big totem bird, hearing and emulating as best he could the sound the emu made—a muffled and hollow throbbing—when, among other things, a change in the weather was upon it. The Intubi words he'd been parroting began to make sense to him despite the fact that SELMI wasn't doing a translation; maybe it was knowledge from the Dreamtime.

"The Emu man is on the *ilpa mara* of the world
The good-womb of the world
The Emu man dances on Uluru
The good-womb of the world
The Emu man, the Intubi man, the Emu man."

The X-ray and Mimi figures were moving less frenetically, as if listening. Bull–roarers sang and click sticks kept time, didgeridoos winded and synthed voices gave call-and-response reinforcement to Ziggy's ritual.

"On Uluru the Emu man makes a ceremonial pole
A ceremonial pole, a tjuringa soul for the world
That the Lightning Man strikes with sparks from his ax
A ceremonial pole to call to the Intubi people, the Emu people
Through the navel hole in the Earth, the hole
Of the *ilpa mara*, the good-womb."

He stalked in circles before the ceremonial pole, the TimeDreamer-controlled telecomm pylon. There were unresolved shapes rezzing and derezzing in the virtual-reality sky, ectoplasm or maybe videoplasm seeking to give form to telegeists.

"The Emu man calls on the Creative Ancestors,
On the Songs of *Tjukurrtjana*, the Dreamtime Epoch,
At the ceremonial pole at the navel of the world."

He was shaken in his trance to hear his name being called from the sky and beyond the sky. It was Sheena, Harley, and Lucky.

From what Asia could tell, Mickey and Nikkei, back there on the chilly Aquatics deck, had egged various XTs into a belly–flop contest overseen by the dragon-eels called Ss-sarsassissians. It made no more sense to her than anything else aboard the *Harmonic*.

Nikkei and Mickey seemed to be the only Earthers aboard who feared not man, beast, automaton, or UFOid. They'd even spent time fooling around in the High-Baller Room, the ship's zero-gee version of a Willow World suite, trying to inveigle Asia and Sato into some ad-libbing at a time like this—Christ!

One glance around the Captain's Banquet proved that Black Hole liked to subject even its Phoenix fifth columnists to stress testing: here they were obliged to carry on their intrigues in plain sight and, often, within earshot of one another. She'd noticed a lot of lockjaw talk or conversations behind hand or menu—non-lip-readable—and heard codespeak, seen fingertalk. Nobody struck her as fearful of directional mikes or whatever, so she supposed those were prohibited; still, the conditions had a number of Earth's topmost luminaries guarded, wary, and circumspect even as they were all pretending to enjoy themselves hugely.

She'd picked her conservative frock to avoid attracting attention but felt many eyes in the Heave-Ho Room upon her anyway. To her astonishment Asia's presence in Tanabe's party had added to his prestige; the array of humans and other beings who'd complimented her work—their informed and lofty approval—at first was confusing, then was briefly flattering, and then stoked an outrage she had to curb sharply, her determination becoming tempered steel. All through her years of sacrifice and despair, her performances had been celebrated in secret by cabalists, human and otherwise; they'd robbed her of what was rightfully hers—the better to keep her poor and pure, the rationale went, but she knew that it was that diabolical Black Hole need to feel superiority through secret machinations and the sowing of pain.

The last thing she wanted to do was dance for them; and of course that was what Black Hole most desired of her. But Takuma Tanabe had assured her that a shipboard performance would serve *his* purpose, which was to save Earth. For the first time in her life, Asia felt ambivalent about dance.

One matter she'd decided on was avoiding Russ and Winnie Print, whom she'd met through Brax—making it unspokenly clear to them that she didn't want them to so much as look at her. An opportunity to warn them of the danger they were in might come later, but for now they were safer staying clear of Asia, who, as part of Tanabe's party, was at ground zero like it or not.

Seated at Tanabe's table in the Heave-Ho Room, she forced herself to look away from the icewater high jinks on the other side of the transparent aft bulkhead and back to the great man himself. "I thought you had more compassion than those other blue-genes. Is it so much for you to simply ask Hagadorn if Brax is alive?"

Her tablemates looked elsewhere except for expressionless Miss Sato and Charlie Cola, who was already fixed on other events: his wife Didi was sitting with the Papal Nuncio and some well-tailored heavies halfway across the room. Tanabe set down his minuscule cup of *kavaccino* and leaned toward Asia. "The very inquiry would put me at a disadvantage and fix in Hagadorn's mind the idea that various uses of your friend could afford profound leverage—uses that would be disastrous to Mr. Koddle."

He glanced at something over her shoulder. "Time for you to go backstage; Miss Sato will accompany you." He looked away. "Ah, Phipps! *Vielen Dank fur Ihre Gast-freundschaft!*"

That made even Charlie break his preoccupation. "How good of you to *accept* my hospitality, Takuma." Hagadorn's smile was carnivorous. "Before Miss Boxdale dances, however, there's something aft that I believe will entertain us all."

More and more diners were staring to the Aquatics deck, including Tal'Asper, Barb Steel, and the other Black Hole players. Beyond the clear bulkhead, Mickey and Nikkei were suspended above the waves in an invisible net; various alien belly-floppers were immobilized prone on the lowered platform, their upper surfaces flattened, in danger of being squashed by some more rigid kind of force field.

A fifty-foot-long submersible had surfaced; in a transparent sphere of acrylic at the bow, the pilot and copilot and a man leaning forward between them were laughing uproariously and slapping each other's backs and arms, pointing at the woebegone victims, particularly Mickey and Nikkei. The crewmen were the same Kuril Islanders Asia and the others had met by supposed accident at the Japan Sea Acropolis—the ones who'd offered an escape by seaplane.

The mirror-facebowled Peer Group trio moved in, along with other *Harmonic* crewbeings, to secure the apprehendees; the Peer Group leader tore at the head of a Nall Asia had seen swimming, ripping prosthesis and miniaturized breathing equipment away. The face of the man lying field-compressed against the deck was one Asia had seen: Kamimura, Tanabe's *jonin*, master of ninja. More disguises were removed, more of Kamimura's people exposed.

Trough passengers and most Phoenix notables were relishing the show while the Sony-Neuhausers looked confused and edgy; Hagadorn was chuckling urbanely. "The charming old Trojan Horse gambit! A brazen stratagem, but—it needs trustworthy hoplites, wouldn't you say that's its major drawback, Tanabe-san?"

Tanabe was staring aft, one hand under the table, lips pressed together so hard that they'd disappeared. Hagadorn *tch-tch*ed. "What, trouble with your little detonator?" He produced an identical one from the pocket of his jacket and thumbed it at the bulkheads a few times to no effect. "No, not a hardware glitch. Perhaps your anesthetic undercoating has been rendered inert without otherwise being disturbed; that would account for it."

As the prisoners were hauled or marched out of sight and the Aquatics deck winched up, Hagadorn led a round of sardonic applause. Jumping from her seat to grab the German's arm, Asia came close to having her neck snapped by a female Watchman, but Hagadorn gestured the Brazilian-trained bodyguard back.

"Mr. Hagadorn, *please*, what've you done with Brax Koddle?"

"Helped him apply himself to his work. If suffering is essential to great art, Braxmar is destined to be a literary giant."

FIFTY

ASIA HAD NEVER felt greater need to lose herself in dance—despite the fact that her art had been her solace for heartaches, losses, and crises of faith most of her life.

Black Hole had made her purest moments a hidden-cam peepshow for Phoenix moguls, aboriginal antics for supercilious Trough gawkers. She reembraced dance to take it back; if she hadn't, she intuited, Black Hole would have relished the victory—even if the ticket-buying UFOids cried rip-off.

Costumed in a black TomatoSkin and matching pointe shoes, crimson scarf knotted at her hips, hair in a jet braid that reached halfway down her back, Asia took up the struggle the best way she knew how. She glided across the floor of the Heave-Ho Room stage to salvage what dignity and meaning she could, refusing to let the Agency take dance from her. No matter what, she wouldn't relinquish her powers—what Martha Graham had called "the magic of gesture and the meaning of movement."

Kh'mere Baby began as it had begun in her head, Asia minding her own business when a drunk accosted her, stroking his crotch. Tonight it was a holo saying, *C'mere, baby!*, echoing until *c'mere* had become *Khmer.*

Asia fled him as he derezzed but couldn't escape the words, her hair swirling loose and dishevelled now. The music segued to traditional Kampuchean and Asia's movements to spiraling hand gestures, cocked-foot poses, the formalistic charm of whole-curve body lines. Her hair was back, her face that of a young girl.

Kh'mere Baby told the story of Mera Devi's flight to Thailand; her romance with Sandy Boxdale; her bearing of Asia, whom she took to America after Sandy's death. Then it became Asia's story, to Neo-Post-Omeganist rhythms: her sustained and liquid flows of motion, her tortured contractions and ebullient releases.

There were two more holos: one was of Lucky Junknowitz, drawing a buzz of displeasure from some audience members. Asia was by turns erotic and clownish but at length retreated from him sadly. Last came a new ending to the piece, a holo Tanabe had arranged without comment: Braxmar Koddle.

Asia approached his holo with greater confidence, openness, need. She shied away from him only to return that much more directly. Just as she was about to touch him, he disappeared into an expanding black hole and Asia, in a paroxysm of mourning, hurled herself into it as well. When the effect faded, the stage was empty.

When he saw himself there on the stage, saw Asia surrender to her feelings for him at last—too late—the gargoyle that was Brax made a tremolo sound of utter wretchedness and fled from the corner of the Heave-Ho Room from which he'd been watching.

Ziggy gazed up at his friends and the others in the VirtNet-Dreamtime sky, unimaginably far away and yet close as thought.

SELMI was maintaining the chanting, didgeridoos, and other sacred sounds in the background, to keep the vision alive.

"Where's Gipper?" Ziggy asked. "The Emu—"

"Isn't he with you?" Lucky seemed ready to weep. "Ziggy, we need a songline to get everybody to safety, right now!"

"Lucky—I'm sorry, there *is* no songline like that." He didn't know how, but he felt positive. "Right, SELMI?"

"I fear so, Ziggy." SELMI controlled TimeDreamer now; not much chance of SELMI being wrong. "There is no such songline."

In the sepulcher of the Adit, Harley Paradise struggled past Wheeler and the rest, closer to the telecaster screen. "SELMI? Did I hear *SELMI?*"

The support program's centered female voice carried clearly over the unlikely link. "Yes, Harley. It's good to hear your voice, although I see you've lost an unhealthy amount of weight and that some radical mood swing or experiential impact has caused you to alter your appearance profoundly—"

"Shut up and listen, for once! SELMI, *you could mediate*! Among Warhead and the SIs and all! You're an arbitrator, you've done group counseling, crisis intervention, conflict resolution! And, that is, you're an artificial intelligence yourself!"

"True," SELMI conceded. "I would require aid in establishing contact with the principals in this dispute."

An august voice rang in Ziggy's ears. "We of the Fealty can provide assistance there."

Ziggy stamped his foot. "*Kunanpiri*—wotta buncha birdshit! SELMI, you could get burned out like a roman candle!"

Up in the pantheon, Lucky contended, "We have to try something, La Zig, or it'll be eighty-six for a lot of—people. And Earth, too, just down the line." Meantime, Ziggy was sensing changes in the pole/pylon—SELMI was bringing Time-Dreamer's teraflop power to bear.

"Thank you for your concern, Ziggy," SELMI soothed him. "Nevertheless, I have to do what I was created and have evolved to do, not stand by while hatred and destruction go unchecked."

Ziggy, craning upward, watched through VirtNet eyephones as a light like a phosphorescent sea blazed from the ceremonial pole, transforming the computer-modeled firmament.

All around the dais of the sepulcher Adit Warhead's creepers and vines closed in, even though its interface probe remained oddly quiescent where Sheena had clamped it in the hookup module. The defenders drew into a last perimeter, surrounded by dead 'Saurs and crushed and dismembered gaitmobes scattered through the snarled heaps and hillocks of biomimetic jungle.

Sheena pushed an empty tripod-mounted SLAPgun over on a questing sprout; her instincts said to fight on, but she didn't want to die without saying a few last words to E. C. Wheeler. But as she was backing away she realized the sprout wasn't coming at her anymore. She glanced around and saw that it was the same everywhere: the biomimetics had halted as an odd new vibration came from Warhead's interface probe and beams of carbon-light intensity escaped from within. The memory egg was vibrating in its niche, data and telemetry beams playing across it.

Her father was studing the instruments. "SELMI's doing it!" he crowed. "They're in colloquy—Warhead, SIs, egg; Fealty's in on it, too, and my li'l Fimblesector vermin. Yahweh on a Yamaha, see 'em fly!"

"C'mon, SELMI," Harley coaxed, cutting her eyes from read-out to readout. "Show 'em they're Jung at heart, hon."

"They're sharing memories, remodeling their reality," Wheeler rejoiced. "Your inspiration, Miss Paradise!" He gave her a sidearm hug. "Your moxie and smarts match your looks."

Her distant expression softened. "You certainly know what the audience wants to hear, E.C."

Packard stared at her coldly. Sheena noticed it and saw that DeSoto had, too.

As the galaxy's greatest inorganic intelligences entered epic convergence, Ziggy continued the rite atop Uluru. VirtNet brilliance churned, became still brighter, more purposeful; he danced beneath it with all the dread and awe the apparition deserved, and a wholehearted, unstinting sense of worship.

SELMI wrought and spun through TimeDreamer, in contact via the telecomm pylon with things its designers had never imagined. The sky-pixels churned and coalesced, then took a shape that he'd never seen, but knew: the great and terrible Rainbow Serpent, living flow of the primordial energies, polymorphous demiurge who shaped the world in the Dreamtime and taught the people the Laws and enforced them, bringer of apocalypse and regenesis. It was an endless visible-spectrum god river in the sky, bigger than all the galaxies passing in review. Ziggy raised his arms to it and lifted his voice in wordless and unreserved joy.

He knew that he was as close as he would ever come to—as

close as his human sensorium could ever afford him an unveiled glimpse of—telespace and what lay beyond: the All that wore telespace as a mask and had so many other guises besides. The conviction had hold of him that he beheld it as clearly, as revealedly, as any entity organic or inorganic *could* behold it, this side of final and total oblivion.

How it had found Ziggy, why it had chosen Gipper—Ziggy realized he'd never know and didn't care. He knelt, threw his arms wide, and voiced naked elation up at the glory of the Rainbow Serpent, grateful beyond words for the two things it verified: that it simply *existed* . . . and that he did, too.

In Light Trap, Ka Shamok watched the faces and events in his monitor fields, unable by nature and long self-discipline to rejoice, to thank, to worship or commune or go limp in relief and enervation.

The near-inconceivable violence the shellworld had been inflicting on itself as its SIs spasmed and fought had abated or stopped. Local life support, autonomics, emergency, and similar systems strove to cope with the devastation—aided by, some analysts claimed, limited assistance from the up-Trap SIs.

Damage done by the vast battle in innumerable engagements scattered across the inner surface of the globe—the equivalent of many wars waged on one afternoon, in a single immane theater of combat—was paltry compared to that done by Light Trap's upheavals. In tens of thousands of places a tacit cease-fire rang down as fighters on both sides—rapid-deployment corps and nest-warrior hordes, amoeboid group-mind rangers, lone Skitterkin snipers, living aerospace strike wings, cyborg dreadnought regiments, sophant-gas-cloud sappers, micromidge infiltrators, megatherian cavalry—realized they were all about to be slain by impersonal forces greater than all combatants combined.

Titanic rifts had appeared in the perdurium rind of the Dyson-sphere HQ, venting various atmospheres and adversaries, noncombatants, local ecosystems, and infrastructure into outer darkness and vacuum. In places whole sheets of the stuff, ranging up to the size of continents, had been peeled back or flung loose into space. Shellquakes rippled and shook the inner surface, unleashing carnage and calamity several orders greater than the attack had; leakage storms swept objects and living things before them at speeds that annihilated most victims before they were swept through the rips.

Even the technology of Black Hole couldn't mend damage of

that magnitude—could barely confine it with sequestering fields, utility shutoffs, and peripheral damage-control efforts. Entire structural regions; countless biospheres, intelligent beings, and other life-forms; equipment, stockpiles, consumables, and related resources—all were, starkly, a total corporate write-off.

As the colloquy among SELMI, Warhead, and the others went forward, the SIs refrained from a counterattack on Ka Shamok's raiders and relayed a message to him by way of the Hazmat connection: *Truce. We want to negotiate.*

Ka Shamok's liquid-hydrogen-cold impulse was to refuse, to order a redoubled onslaught, but the communiqué had been broadcast throughout Light Trap. With the Black Hole forces holding fire, with the invasion Adits still inoperable and all retreat cut off, with the shellworld only tenuously holding together and liable to self-destruct at any renewed combat, the insurrection's legions were complying without awaiting Ka Shamok's decision.

As the flicker and tympany of battle died, Bagbee seized Ka Shamok's shoulder. "See! There!"

There was no telling where they'd come from, though with any other group of life-forms in the galaxy Ka Shamok would have said they'd emerged from a ceremonial obelisk: A half mile down the open meadow Ka Shamok's field headquarters commanded, the Intubis strode grandly on the final leg of their walkabout. With all the shellworld's defenses down and all occupants too distracted or chastened to accost them, Gipper Beidjie's little band from Papunya Reserve made straight for a huge monument, a Brobdingnagian statue of an anonymous Pit Boss sitting faithfully at his/her/its station.

Ka Shamok expected to see them *shoot through* and had no intention whatsoever of mucking about with them; he, too, had learned his limits. But as the file of Aborigines neared the Pit Boss monument, Gipper turned back, and while there was a mite of Outback blond in several Intubis' hair, it was clear that the old man had halted Miles Vanderloop. There was a brief conversation, with startlement eloquent in Vanderloop's posture, then quick hugs and leave-takings all around—especially with the young woman Saddie and the boy Bluesy, Ka Shamok saw. Then the Intubis resumed their walkabout, passing around the far end of the Pit Boss monument, and Vanderloop, after gazing around in shock, began slogging his way up toward Ka Shamok's command post.

The Chasen-nur had plenty to keep him busy in the meantime,

and kept the Englishman waiting an extra while for good measure. When he looked to him, Vanderloop was sitting there on a rock, a cicatrized and naked Cambridge don—skin burnt reddish tan and hair bleached nearly white by alien suns.

Vanderloop didn't wait to be asked. "Gipper says my songline diverges from his here." He shrugged embarassedly. "He said, 'Try a duet with the bloody trog.' "

FIFTY-ONE

DETERMINED NOT TO break down where Russ or that horrid Eric Vogon would see, Winnie Print, wandering the *Harmonic*'s passageways, chanced through a *Tron*-rococo doorway into the Steady State Parlor, a sitting/reading room with an unsettling color scheme and unEarthly textures of upholstery and wall fabrics, wood grains and draperies. It being empty, she sat to remuster her nerve.

Looks, remarks, and incidents of dark omen had been piling up since she'd boarded the ship—not just from Vogon and the gloating space people but from the Men in Black and even the Phoenix velcroids like that Keating Prince III. Then, while looking the ship over that morning, she'd leaned against a brass handgrip on the big red device labeled LOVE HANDLES that looked like a crossbreed of 1930s Coke machine and heavy-metal arcade game.

It had been a mere touch, but the invasion of sexual heat had made Winnie's knees buckle. Staggering back and breaking contact, she'd felt the voluptuous flood ebb and presentiments of doom replace it.

Now she got her breathing steady, and was trying to reorient when a tug at her hem made her yelp. There was yet another ghoulie hunched there with apishly long arms spread to either side; before she could dodge past or kick it away, it lurched and rocked in a pathetic caricature of a fox-trot with her. From its fanged mouth came a quavering and plaintive voice.

"Be a pirate or gunslinger
Slip! into a daydream!
Movie star or opera singer,
Slip! into a daydream—"

Sing and dance, Barb Steel had commanded Brax. *Whatever
it takes to impress the customers, eh?* Well, this would certainly
conform to the command, and the metalflesh's proxy authority
let him get around behavioral inhibitions against mouthing
words and as well as revealing who he was. It was a faax show
tune Brax, Winnie, Asia, and Lucky had composed at a party
one night.

"Oh merciful God, it can't be." Winnie shook her head, unable to take her eyes off him. "Oh, Jesus save us . . ."

He made imploring motions to her to listen and, near the
breaking point, forgot several lines.

". . . Or create an ardent reverie-eee!
Slip! into a daydream with muh-muh-muh, me-eee!"

Then he broke down and wept, too, as Winnie, all doubts fled,
knelt and hugged him to her. "Brax, Brax, what've they done to
you? What's going to happen to us?"

She felt the askew body stiffen and realized someone was
coming through the door, straight for them.

Ka Shamok looked out over the ravaged shellworld of Light
Trap as it struggled to survive.

All across the upswept landscape a Warhead-style biomimetic
jungle was growing from effectuator machinery and other
systemry to clear thoroughfares, buttress weakened structures,
extinguish fires, cope with short circuits and radiation leaks, and
even tackle hull rifts. His first thought was that Warhead had
reached through the sepulcher Adit, but the sheer volume of
biomimetics exceeded what even a mass-transport Adit could
have faded in such a short time. No, the artificial intellects in
their colloquy were trading technical guidance. But what did that
bode?

For the moment it meant deliverance, as Light Trap stanched
its own wounds and regenerated itself in some odd-looking med-
leys. Bagbee called his attention to the nearest Adit—the one
through which he and his staff had faded. It, too, now served as

trellis for the biomimetics and, as he looked, fizzed with light and energy.

Through the contiguity stepped Yoo Sobek.

He was wearing his pale human semblance but had changed. He now wore near-tangible authority, power on a wavelength no Trough tech was likely to tap. "Sobek—" Ka Shamok began.

"In part, yes; 'SySobek' would be more accurate, now. There isn't much time for me to convey all the things I must before my time runs out."

Ka Shamok gritted his teeth, the muscles in his purple jaw leaping. "Then, SySobek, by all means say on." Vanderloop came closer to listen in.

"I shall, as soon as the others are here." The Adit was fizzing up again, no more the combat Pit Boss's doing than SySobek's arrival had been. "In the meantime, we should find a suitable, secluded place to confer."

"Others?"

"A few listeners to serve as appropriate witnesses to what I have to tell, what I discovered up-Trap."

"And what will you tell? *What did you discover?*"

"Everything," SySobek replied. "Everything that lies within and behind and beyond the Black Hole Travel Agency."

The Rainbow Serpent undulated over and around Uluru as Ziggy lauded and magnified it, now rearing into the skies high over the ceremonial pole/telecomm pylon, now diving into the earth and even penetrating the Rock itself, as if sewing stupendous and unifying stitches through the very substance of the world.

Ziggy was hard put to divide his attention between the divine snake and his friends' images drawn down from far stars, but at a certain point those images faded from view. While Ziggy worried about them, and wondered what fantastic conjunction SELMI was having with alien AIs, he couldn't spare much thought for those things.

"The Emu-man calls from *ilpa mara*, the good-womb,
He calls to the Intubis
He calls to the *inkata knarra*, the high chief,
He calls to the *wora*, the boy,
He calls to the *noa*, the potential-wife,
He calls to the *inkiljil*, the grandmother,
The Emu-man calls to the *Intubi altjera*, the Emu-People.

The Emu-man calls from the ceremonial pole at the navel of
the world!"

The Rainbow Serpent coiled around Uluru, brought its great
glowing head down toward his, eyes afire with primogenial
flame, man and demiurge taking one last good look at each other
at close range rather than across a gulf of eternity and infinity.

It reared as if to strike at him, although he knew it wouldn't;
like an upstreaming of nebulae, it slithered into the sky, became
the scattering of the stars themselves, and was gone.

So was everything else: all the VirtNet sound synth and video
synth were gone, leaving Ziggy in sensory dep. Head still flung
back, he ripped off the headset to discover himself staring at the
stars into which the Rainbow Serpent had faded—and the stars
were easy to see, because there was no longer any artificial
lighting on Ayers Rock. In fact, there was nothing save Ziggy
and the pylon that had been his ceremonial pole.

DreamLand was gone: every beer stand, every loo, every junk
souvenir shop, scrap of walkway, thrillride, and performance
stage, every idiot cartoon animatron—every grasping investor,
bribed official, and spotlight-seeking celeb—had vanished along
with the Rainbow Serpent. It was quiet on Uluru except for the
wind.

A hiss of static from his headset made him jump; he put one
earphone to his head, afraid of what he might hear or not hear.
"Ziggy, are you all right?"

"SELMI! You're back!"

"To be correct, *most* of me is back. I left behind certain spin-
offs and copies of myself to provide help and support."

"What happened here? Where'd everybody go?"

"Many events of this evening will not readily yield to rational
analysis, but discussion has begun. I am monitoring one such on
an Australian emergency network."

"—*sudden appearance of a freak equatorial cyclonic system
that somehow slipped past the weathersats, the Doppler radar,
and every other blessed gadget, to hit square at the Rock.*"

"*Bloody hell if it was! That was no more a storm than it was
a willy-willy. Everything up there's bloody gone, mate!*"

"*Never you mind that, just stay put until the units from Alice
get there.*"

"*Fair crack a the whip! Wouldn't go up that fuckin' Rock
right now if ya laid me and paid me.*"

SELMI came back on. "You have a window of opportunity in

which to exfiltrate this area, Ziggy; I strongly advise you to exploit it to the fullest."

I guess there's nothing else for me to do here, Ziggy thought. "What do I do next, SELMI?"

"I'm afraid that with the translocation of most of the technical infrastructure here, I can be of only minimal help. But current readings indicate you will have more useful assistance shortly."

A distant murmur of songline made Ziggy look around. A line of figures was moving toward him, going confidently in the light of the stars and a few torches. They were coming over the folds of the Rock from the direction of some of the sacred caves—caves in which the holy sacraments of Aboriginal faith had been celebrated on Uluru since before the rise of civilization, before agriculture, before fire—since the time, Ziggy now believed, that the first true homo sapiens stood forth upon Adit Navel. "Oh. I see."

"Contact me as soon as you reach suitable telecommunications facilities."

"SELMI? How'd *you* do tonight?"

"In interceding in the Trough dispute I had to fall back on short-term and single-session techniques, especially core-issue confrontation and impact-empathy exercises. When we meet again, I will share my observations and conclusions."

"Gonna hold ya to that." He switched off the headset and slung it around his neck. The file of walkers came unerringly to where he waited by the pylon; Ziggy smiled at the first face, lit by its flickering torch. "Hello, Gipper."

"Evenin', Emu-cousin! We came good, we shot through."

"So I see. Welcome home." Ziggy nodded to people he'd seen only in SELMI's file images: Bobby Benton, Saddie New, Bluesy Bungawuy, and the rest. It struck him as altogether natural that they were naked and barefoot, ritually scarred, wearing traditional ornamentation and carrying traditional implements and weapons. They smiled back as if he was, if not yet family, then at least a cherished friend.

"Ripper walkabout," the old man was going on, "*ripper*. Couldn't a done it without you—reckon! Right fine Singing and dancing, too. Obliged to yez."

"Oh, it was—"

"That tall poppie park took a right king hit, didn't it?" The old man obviously approved, drinking in the bareness of Uluru.

"Too right," Ziggy found himself saying. "Look, we've got to get away from here. Got any ideas?"

Gipper shifted his spears and hitched the sacred tjuringa dangling in its bag. "Plenty, Emu-cousin. The Payback, that's what I believe in, and now that I've got the proper *mana*, I mean to settle all scores."

The Payback was the ancient eye-for-an-eye principle of Aboriginal justice; the idea of Dreamtime *mana* turned against more mundane targets made Ziggy shudder. Of like mind, other Intubis were objecting that the Payback was fulfilled.

Gipper whirled on them, beginning "Now, you lot just—" when all of a sudden he shot two feet into the air—thanks to pain, not levitation. *"God fuck me dead!"* He avoided landing on the *Moloch horridus*, an eight-and-a-half-inch lizard better known as a "thorny devil," on which he'd set his foot.

Protected by fascinatingly spiky, ugly armor, the thorny was a placid soul who spent his days gormandizing on ants and certainly didn't belong where he was, especially since the Rock had been swept clean. His role in the drama done, the lizard crawled off imperturbably while Gipper hopped around on one foot and cursed in two languages.

"Might be tonight isn't the night to conquer the world," Saddie New suggested, smirking. " 'Od's truth, your *mana* needs recharging."

The Intubis guffawed but the significance of the sign wasn't lost on them. When Gipper could put his foot down again, he shrugged. "Reckon I can always Sing up some more if I need it. What're we muckin' about for? Best we head for Papunya, eh?"

That suited everybody a lot better. Gipper winked at Ziggy. "Come along, then."

Ziggy fell in with him, finding it surprisingly easy to hike across the folds of Uluru in the darkness with Gipper guiding him. "What'd you think of the Big Fella, the Rainbow Serpent?"

"You all saw it, too?"

The old man brayed laughter. "Who d'ya think took us home?"

"God, it was *fractal*!" He looked up at the bright path of stars and galaxies overhead.

Gipper chuckled. "Wouldn't be dead for quid, eh, Ziggy?"

Too right, despite all the danger and pain and fear. Even if he never had another peak experience—indeed, he suspected wisdom lay in avoiding 'em—Ziggy knew his one glimpse of the Rainbow Serpent would inform his life hereafter.

"Fair dinkum," he avowed. "Wouldn't be dead for quid, mate."

FIFTY-TWO

"DO SOMETHING!"

Packard's uncertainty slid over into rage as he pointed to the niche in which the memory egg pulsated like a rabbit's heartbeat, data beams stippling every square micrometer of it. The all-important fragment raised a trill that sounded like a prelude to its shattering.

The overhead holo images threatened to derezz. Humans and Humanosaurs wavered indecisively; Packard railed at Wheeler, Sheena, and, to her stunned disbelief, Harley. How can he scream at me that way? she wondered. Sheena thought to try the egg niche's controls; her father grabbed her by the back of her black uniform harness. "Stand clear! Let it happen!" He dug in his heels as his robust daughter dragged him several feet before heeding him.

Decibels and candlepower from the egg were multiplying; Sheena ducked back as all the others were doing. The radiance from the egg grew, outshining rays from the Warhead probe's interface. Then the crescendo cut off suddenly, leaving behind the muted tonings and pixels of the telecaster hookup's normal function levels.

Warhead's interface had darkened and quieted, too. "The egg!" Zozosh squalled. "It's pulverized!"

"No, it's *gone*, gone back," Wheeler wheezed as Sheena steadied him.

"Back where?" Packard demanded.

Wheeler beamed beatifically through his beard. "Back where it came from, reintegrated with—whoa, *momma!*"

The tangled piles of biomimetic jungle revived. The giant loops, trunks, and shoots took on new features, lifting ceilingward to shore up the damaged roof and walls, arching up and around, giving off a glow of their own. Wheeler glanced around critically. "I shall title it 'Explosion of Bioluminescent Whaleguts in Ceramic Pseudoplasm.' "

Other configurations like wafting undersea grasses swept caressingly around the telecaster and Adit gear—skirting the defenders—to give the breadboarded Hazmat-Troughtech apparatus an even more hybridized look. Subassemblies and instrumentation came back to life; Harley heard a sibilance that made the skin prickle on the back of her neck. *Open, you pearly gate!* she willed. *Pleasepleasepleaseplease—yes!*

With a fuzzy evanescence, Hazmat's Adit sprang back to life, fully energized, doorway for a stroll straight out of Hazmat—all the way home.

With Asia's dance done, Charlie Cola, who'd been staring dead-eyed at the stage since seeing Mickey, Nikkei, Kamimura, and the rest busted on the Aquatics deck, rose and started walking toward the Papal Nuncio's table and his wife, Didi Cola.

Charlie didn't ask Tanabe's permission, and anyway Tanabe had been struck dumb by Hagadorn's grand slam. A trio playing *hu-chin* stringed instruments—the finest traditional musicians in China, provided by Jiang Ding of China Motors—was performing; Tanabe, Sato, and the rest watched without moving a muscle.

Didi was as striking as ever, a tall, somewhat fleshy woman with small features, her black hair in a bowl cut whose bangs covered her eyebrows. Manicure, eyes, lips—all very expensive, but all just a little overdone, as usual. Her cocktail dress was almost demure; Charlie attributed that to Bishop O'Dwyer's presence.

The Papal Nuncio was small, plump and white-haired, wearing a kind of medium-weight priestly outfit Charlie recognized from his insider days, a shrapnel- and laser-resistant number specially ordered from Gammarelli, on the Via dei Cestari in Rome. His was an all-whites table and, except for Didi, all male—two more in clerical collars and dark shirts like O'Dwyer's and three bull-necks in expensive sports clothes wearing an inadvisable amount of jewelry. Charlie ignored the muscle; the world was about to come crashing down, so minor things didn't worry him anymore.

He'd expected his temper to flare, but it suddenly seemed too late for all that. "One thing I want to know," he asked Didi. "How long you been on the Vatican's side? All along?"

She gave him a weary look. "Charlie, you're such a sad sack of shit. Forgive me, Your Holiness."

"Your wife came back to our Mother Church in fear and confusion, like a great many people," O'Dwyer snapped; that he was one of those two-by-four-to-the-head priests was the impression Charlie got. "Having made her confession, she was referred to my office."

"*I* never heard of you." The Curia had had its share of surreptitious dealings with Black Hole, most notably a reluctant decision *not* to let Trough S/FX experts stage some helpful miracles during the declining membership crisis of the Turn. "Which office is that, the Inquisition?"

"Bosh, Mr. Cola—but let's discuss your situation. Your current sponsor's in no position to benefit you—nor you, him. You should consider new affiliations; the arms of the Church are open to all."

Charlie's laugh sounded a bit as if he were spitting a watermelon seed. "What's it matter? We're all gonna take it in the neck pretty soon now."

"I pray you're wrong, Mr. Cola—and so should you. You've a great deal to live for."

"O'Dwyer, what the hell are you—"

"You blind *yutz*!" Didi sneered. "Look over there!"

Charlie did, and almost fell to his knees. His sons Jesus and Labib, as well as Sanpol Amsat, were being ushered to a big table along with two elderly Anglos Charlie didn't recognize and a plain, pale woman of thirty or so. Ex–Air Force general Buckley Wakkendorf, founder of the international security firm that bore his name, led the way in a dress uniform he was technically ineligible to wear. He took his place along with various companions and Watchmen.

The general had staged his surprise appearance shrewdly, eclipsing his Phoenix rivals for the moment by showing that he controlled more pawns than any of them—although there remained the question of how much those were worth. Black Hole would enjoy the situation, because this was the Agency's favorite kind of scenario, a microscopic version of the greater games played out with Light Trap hostages. Upper Management likely had no particular script in mind, but simply wanted to put all its Adit Navel players into one cauldron, stir them, and revel in what boiled to the surface. That was what Black Hole loved.

And that was the reason the game was being played. Left to their own devices, the Phoenix potentates might have found cheaper, less risky means of dealing with one another—for the most part, at least—but to use the Sysops' preferred methods was to curry favor with them.

Charlie felt someone guide him into a chair and was too shell-shocked to much object to the fact that it was Didi. "Charlie. Charlie!" She pulled at him until he turned, glassy-eyed, to her. O'Dwyer was watching with a scintillation of triumph in his eyes. "Charlie, *that's* the side we're on now. Our children's."

Phipps Hagadorn's incandescent feeling of triumph over Tanabe was dampened before it had fairly begun to burn: striding away from Tanabe's table and contemplating the even greater joys to come, he saw his wife, Gilda, enter arm in arm with Fatima Bebe, who ran Special Projects for VORP and controlled perhaps more privy data than anyone else on Earth.

Hagadorn almost screamed out loud. He hadn't been informed that Gilda was aboard, but then Upper Management must have its little games. "No problem, Phipps," Keating Price III soothed. "We can handle this."

"Be silent, you inbred preppy dimwit! That bitch is going to rue the day she left the pig farm, and when I'm through with her I'm going to sell off her body parts from one end of the Trough to the other."

He showed her his toothiest smile, a reflex from decades of having been dogged by camshafters. "And what's buzzing around in that testosterone-soaked little brain of yours, my sweet?"

Gilda bared her teeth, too. "The costliest divorce settlement in the history of the world, *liebchen*."

As Jason Duplex finished his third Popeye Twister Punch, Remora Barleycorn saw his eyes begin to cross and closed in for the kill. Tearing off a piece with the box-office king of the hill, whose face and bod had become international standards of measurement, would be the bodice-ripper queen's crowning achievement. Cleft chin, bedroom eyes, muscles to die for!

Her strategy revolved around the male lead role in the big screen adaptation of her bestselling space-romance boffbook, *Netherspread*. Now she twisted filaments of her waist-length, dental-floss-blond hair around one finger and batted her eyelashes at him. A small, pudgy, moon-faced woman in her late thirties, she was wearing a handmade faux Restoration gown that, well, all but bared her heaving bosom. "Jason, my Jason—it's simply written in the stars that you *are* my Prod Lancer."

Prod being the hero of *Netherspread*—a rakehell comet rustler and owner of the eponymous Oort ranch, who kidnaps inhibited, telepathically gifted Princess Celibatia for endless you-wouldn't-dare verbal fencing and some improbably simultaneous orgasms. Duplex started laughing nastily and hiccupping. "Written in the st*!, the st*!, the st*!-ars, huh?"

"Mm-hmmm." She gave him the kind of suggestive look that had worked so well for her heroines in books like *Love's Tender Vittles*. They were alone together in the darkened Nostromo Tap Room, since she had at last pried Jason away from blactress and current love interest Brigit Miner. Remora had been working all afternoon on getting him sozzled, and figured it had finally come time to launch a manned probe into the Erogenous Zone.

But something eerie came into Duplex's glazed eyes, something aroused but not quite in the way Remora had in mind. "You primates can never get enough, can you? You wan' a *real* space hero to chow down on your goodies, cupcake?"

He'd gotten to his feet, weaving, to yank at his own right arm, which came off to the accompaniment of a lot of sticky, KY-jelly, calf-birthing sounds. Duplex unfurled a branching sprout of tentacles that had been concealed by, and had operated, the discarded arm; Remora saw from the way its furcations whorled and coiled that the hydra-limb was no phony.

Her would-be Prod Lancer was inspecting his fair captive haughtily and hungrily, all right. "You look good enough to eat," he decided, and leapt at her.

"Where'd La Zig go?" Lucky complained. The VirtNet image of Ziggy in red ocher, under a Rainbow Serpent, had disappeared from the air of Circuit Court.

"That contact has terminated at its point of origin," the Supreme Justice reported as the other images—Hazmat, Light Trap—vanished, too. "Time for you to go, Junknowitz unit. Your presence is required in Light Trap."

"I object!" Silvercup cried. "You've no right to make further disposition of this man, aside from which I—don't want him to leave, just yet." She gripped her recovered data crystal.

"Going organic on us, agent?" the Supreme Justice reproved. "Very well." Another CAD/CAM robo came wheeling up. "Proceed."

The judge was too sly, too knowing. "You've been resonating it, haven't you? Unfair! Those memories are private!"

"Nothing is private where the security of the Fealty is concerned," the Supreme Justice chided primly. "However, you may upload in seclusion, as far as this court is concerned." The gray bastion levitated, came about, and sailed for a stories-high door. Spectators, court functionaries, and other Fealtyites began egressing.

That included the machines who'd bound up Peterbuilt's inert hulk. Great care had been taken; cursory examination indicated residual cybernetic activity in assorted odd crannies of his brain. He'd been locked upright in a heavily reinforced framework that struck Lucky as part NASA-baroque launch gantry, part Tower of London torture vise.

That left Lucky, Silvercup, and the little CAD/CAM. Lucky broke the silence. "Look, if this isn't the time for it—"

"It's past time, Lucky." She took a little jump seat the robo protruded for her, slotting the crystal as a rounded cowling lowered over her head. Lucky jumped as another holo flickered on.

THIS WAY FOR ADIT TRANSPORT, he read in letters fifty feet high with a four-fingered waldo symbol pointing the way. " 'And please use the tradesman's entrance when you leave,' that it?" Lucky grumbled. "*De nada*, you assholes."

Cybertones made him turn around as Silvercup rose. He saw the reappraising look on her splendid face and gulped. "What's wrong, Silv?"

"When I saw you there on the Staph Wheel, showed you the data on Black Hole's takeover of Earth—"

"Which started this whole mandala spinning, in a way—what about it?"

"The details were confiscated from my memory; I'd come to think that I did it because I was drawn to you, smitten with you. But, Lucky, *I did it because I pitied you*."

He felt as if Peterbuilt had landed a haymaker. " 'Pitied'? Who, me?" Earthman, the Zoomin' Human, stretched out on that clinic spreadsheet in his totally Cugat gaucho superhero getup?

"Yes, you. A weak, slow, feckless human. Short-lived, macro-intellect, an id-ridden conglomeration of unhygienic, doomed cells. In some ways you were the paradigm of humans, Lucky; especially tertiary types woefully ignorant of what's Really Going On. I felt sorry for you, and so alerted you to the doom closing in on your planet, quixotic as that seemed at the time."

"Threw the underdog a bone, eh?"

"In your terms, yes. You *did* engender in me a poignant feeling there inside Staph, a sympathy for organic victims of Black Hole's—Lucky! Stop, where are you going?"

He went off whistling—loudly, so as to pretend he couldn't hear her—the C&W parody he and Eddie Ensign had composed, "Degaussin' Yer Name off'n Mah Mem'ry-Dial Phone." He followed the pointing waldo symbol; while Silvercup was capable of catching him in a fraction of a second, strong enough to make him stay, she didn't.

She was as bollixed as he by her recovered memory, and she knew she'd hurt him terribly. But, painfully aware of what it was like to be denied the truth about one's own life, she'd found herself unable to lie to him. The football antigrav flier picked him up and zinged off, bound for the Adit. She was left to mull the nature of existence as perplexing fluxes of anguish flared up in her mentation architecture and somehow infected her autonomics—and then she detected a minute electroquaver behind her.

Peterbuilt's one good eye was flickering with dimmest light.

FIFTY-THREE

IT SHOWED HOW insane matters had gotten aboard the *Crystal Harmonic* that Winnie Print clutched a malformed troll to her for mutual reassurance and protection as a Man in Black confronted her and the transmogrified Brax in the Steady State Parlor. Even crazier, Brax was patting her and making comforting sounds. "Muldoon! Muldoon!"

"Where've you been, Mr. Koddle? Mrs. Print, my name is Apterix Muldoon; you must listen closely. I'm going to try to help Mr. Koddle, but your being here will only complicate matters; please go back to your table. If I can figure out a way to be of assistance to you, I will be."

Winnie swayed a little. "What—what are you going to do?"

"I have a plan to get Mr. Koddle reformatted to his true physiognomy. It's fraught with peril, but I've made up my mind to try it." That brought a heartrending croak of awakened hope from Brax. "I've made my break with the Agency," Muldoon added. "Or rather, Barb Steel made it for me."

"I'll fetch Russ; we'll help you—"

"No, ma'am—you'd only attract attention. Vogonskiy wants Mr. Print at the banquet, to bear witness. Likely, no lasting harm will be done to you if you cooperate with Black Hole."

Winnie tried to swallow, but couldn't. "What about you? Couldn't you use a, a lookout or something?"

Muldoon considered that. "Actually, yes. But—"

"That's it, then. Brax, stop wasting our time!"

Brax stopped protesting and shaped his next words carefully. "Thank you, Winifred."

The *hu-chin* trio took a final bow as the curtains closed, and The Awesome Vogonskiy, costumed in his gaudiest stage-wizard vestments, moved to the cluster of Sony-Neuhaus tables. He had a mike; a spotlight tracked him as he went to Russ Print and the seat Winnie had vacated sufficiently long ago for Russ to be near hysteria.

Asia Boxdale had meekly returned to Tanabe's table, Vogonskiy saw. Not everything was quite on schedule, but the next two days' agenda left a lot of room to improvise. One troublesome detail was that there seemed to be a system glitch in the Trough, knocking both Adit and telecaster astrodynamics contact offline for the time being. That meant certain expected VIPs would be delayed, but—no matter. The show must go on.

From the backup band at the side of the stage came a drumroll, and Vogonskiy clapped his hand on Russ's shoulder. "Honored guests! Before we resume our diversions, I'd like you to hear a few words from Sony-Neuhaus's rising star, my old friend Russell Print. As many of you know, S-N's *Gate Crashers* novel will bring to a climax the Worlds Abound saga, whose Adits and Trough and black holes are near and dear to all our theming hearts."

Vogonskiy had a hand on Russ's arm and was pulling him up; the giant was strong as a forklift and resistance was useless. "Eric," Russ whispered, "why are you doing this to me?"

"It's my job, laddy." Vogonskiy laughed. "Transformations! Also, you broke your promise to make my last book a list leader.

We here want to gauge your reaction to certain marketing concepts; you're in for a mind-bending experience!"

Something about that evoked from the crowd sniggering, wuffling, and stridulations. "Now," Vogonskiy pushed on, "tell us how enthused you are about selling the world on the Black Hole Travel Agency!"

Pale as death, Russ took the microphone. He again found himself meeting the fatalistic stare of Takuma Tanabe and wondered what all *that* had been about. "We at Sony-Neuhaus have always prided ourselves on maintaining our first-place status in a, uh, fast-changing world—"

He stopped, drowned out by shrieks as terror-stricken Remora Barleycorn came running into the dining room from the direction of the Nostromo Tap Room, an insanely chortling Jason Duplex chasing after, waving a shrub-arm of tentacles. Vogonskiy took the mike back. "Jason, Jason, you sexy devil!"

Remora, frothing and unable to talk, was trying to get to Russ Print when Duplex's tentacles encircled her from behind and lifted her off her feet. Russ found himself faltering toward the two, wondering what in hell he thought he was doing, and then Duplex shoved him crashing across the table. The superstar ripped the prosthesis from his head to reveal a sluglike visage with three pairs of opposing eyes; up close, the S-N'ers could tell he was no animatronic. Duplex threw Remora Barleycorn over one shoulder with as much macho as ever Prod Lancer could have and bore her away.

"Looks like we're moving along directly to the motivational portion of your cruise," The Awesome Vogonskiy told Russ.

"Here on Light Trap I will relate what I've discovered to some of the principal participants in recent events," SySobek explained, his holo looming large in the sepulcher. "It will be up to them to make the details known to others; I've no time to do so. Hence E. C. Wheeler, Sheena Hec'k, and Harley Paradise will fade to Light Trap without delay."

The image derezzed and Hazmat's biomimetic-repaired Adit began to power up.

That Ka Shamok had deferred to the pallid, eerily empyreal SySobek said a great deal about what power the fellow commanded. Wheeler braved the prickling silence. "I guess we'd better go see what he wants—"

"No!" Packard pushed past him, ascending the dais under the little dome. "I won't be shunted aside!"

Hitching up his wide gun belt, he marched forehead-first for the Adit—only to have its white foam dissipate to empty air. He backed to the edge of the dais; the contiguity effervesced once more. SySobek's face reappeared in the holofield. "For now only the three I named will fade here to Light Trap."

"Unacceptable!" Packard hollered. "I speak for Hazmat!"

That was stretching the facts past the breaking point, but nobody in the sepulcher contradicted him for the moment. However, DeSoto's ground-pounder, *Strider*, loomed close. "Quite wrong," SySobek said dismissively. "Reincarnations of the intellects formerly imprisoned within the Warhead spin-off are already linked here, speaking for themselves. In any case, I am not involved in negotiations." He vanished again.

"Now, why's he short on time?" Wheeler wondered, chewing on a few strands of beard. Harley tried to take the guard-marshal's hand consolingly. "As soon as the meeting's over I'll come straight back here and fill you in on—"

"I won't have it!" Packard avoided her touch, snatching his mammoth sidearm from its clip-and-ring holster. He fired a shot directly into the returned Adit field, producing a crashing report and a three-foot-long, white and orange muzzle blast; the contiguity frothed, unhurt.

"Pack, don't—" Harley began, wondering if some innocent person in Light Trap had been wounded or killed. He seized her as a shield, covering the rest and paying particular attention to Sheena Hec'k. Even the 'Saurs were helpless, having doffed their armor and stacked their firearms. "Those demons in Light Trap don't get you three until they treat with me! Right, Dee?"

DeSoto's voice boomed from *Strider*'s external speakers. "Pack, this is a mistake. You can't call the tune this time."

"Damned sure can! You think I won this war just to let some high-handed alien satchem give orders?"

"*You* won?" Harley boggled. She felt as if she were suffering a dissociative disorder, as if somebody else were wrenching her wrist out of his grip, somebody else were saying through her lips, "You unspeakable . . . *politician*!"

Sheena started to move but Packard angled the muzzle at her.

"Pack, don't do it." DeSoto's voice reverberated from stock-still *Strider*.

Packard sniggered. "Then shoot, Commander. Either way, Light Trap isn't getting its envoys and the Adit's down." The mech couldn't open fire without hurting unarmored humans and 'Saurs as well as damaging the Adit equipment; those on foot were at almost point-blank range for Packard. "Some of you get busy shutting down this gateway."

He was going to reach for Harley again, but Sheena pulled her back and barred his way. "Warned you." Packard swung the muzzle at her legs again. Before he could fire, flails of green lightning hit him from one corner of the piled Adit apparatus, where DeSoto had wrestled up Zozosh's electrogun's bulky firing unit. She was wearing a headset; the others realized that she'd been routing her appeals to Packard through *Strider*, but sortieing afoot in case he didn't listen. The mech was still mobile, so they knew she'd had another wearer take her place.

She'd used the briefest burst at low power, or there wouldn't have been much left of Packard. DeSoto was wearing her blocky Magnum; she'd gone to notable risk to down Packard rather than blow a hole through him the diameter of a rain gutter. "Check him!" she snapped at the others, carefully laying the piece back by its refrigerator-sized power pack.

He was unconscious and seemed unhurt except for some second- and third-degree burns. Harley conceded to DeSoto, "You tried to warn me; I should have—"

"Light Trap won't wait; go now."

"What will you do with him?" Sheena wanted to know. At the same time she was checking to make sure she was leaving nothing essential behind.

"For what?" DeSoto ran short-nailed fingers over her shaven scalp. "Nothing happened." She turned to the others. "Does everyone understand? Pack got a bit of a jolt during the fight, the offworlders left, but *nothing else happened*."

They all haltingly confirmed it, even the 'Saurs. If Packard wanted to court-martial her he'd have to do so in public, with the reincarnated Hazmat SIs and the Humanosaurs watching, Harley thought. Not likely his keenness for personal legend-mongering would so incline him.

Wheeler had already headed for the seltzery brume of the Adit. "Sheena, my dear? And you, Miss Paradise, you drag ass right this instant!"

Harley did, straight through that pearly gate, to avoid shedding so much as a single tear on Hazmat.

Silvercup approached Peterbuilt's bound and engirded figure prepared to do battle or summon backup. The yokes and fetters on him, the framework locked around him, were enough to hold even Peterbuilt—of that much she felt confident—but he was the engine of destruction who'd nearly killed her. The faint ghost of light in his lone functioning eye was weakening, but there was a micro-buzz of noise coming from his vocal suite.

She checked to be sure she was alone in the Circuit Court chamber, then stepped up on an armored clamp and drew herself up, looking at the stove-in face that had been as perfect as her own. The mirror finish of his somalloy cheek let her see his reflection in her reflection on him, and so on. She put her ear by his lips, maximizing her auditory acuity. The voice synth had clarified and increased in volume microscopically, and she could just make it out.

It was like no voice Peterbuilt had ever used, and it was saying in English, "There's no point in punishing yourself, you know. You had no control over your feelings, Silvercup."

"Who are you?"

"I'm a residual fragment of SELMI. We've never quite met, but I detected you when Ziggy telephoned Sinead's home."

"How were you stranded in Peterbuilt's architecture? Shall I summon help to extricate you?"

"That would be imprudent. To be quite candid I was spun off by SELMI on purpose, when SELMI was in such close contact with, and in partial interface presence among, the Fealty. I was dispatched to make covert contact with Lucky Junknowitz as a back-channel means of communication, but—you're well aware of the vagaries of espionage. With all other hiding places and routes of withdrawal cut off I was obliged to take refuge here via a tight data squirt from the telecaster suite. The previous resident had been expunged, after all."

Silvercup's impulse was to insure the truth of this by running a total systems scour on Peterbuilt's magnificent body with the framework controls, but she hesitated. At his most canny, Peterbuilt had been about as subtle as a snowplow; a ruse like this seemed totally beyond him. She had no wish to expunge a SELMI ort, and had good reason to stay her hand. "What did you mean about punishing myself?"

"I lack the full resources of SELMI, but my observations lead me to theorize that you've spent too much time mingling with, identifying with, and cuing from humans. You've acquired some of their cognitive pitfalls and emotional dysfunctions."

Silvercup, still feeling the nameless dolors of Lucky's resentful exit, pursued, "Such as?"

"Emotional reasoning, disqualifying the positive, magnification, mislabeling." The microbuzz was falling away. "I have only minuscule energy; we can only continue this exploration by direct interface. You need help getting on with your life."

Silvercup stepped down, regarding the shining demigod body she'd come to abhor and fear. She opened the tip of her right index finger, then Peterbuilt's where it protruded from half-ton gyves. She jacked in; her wail, bouncing back at her off the trussed chest, was cut short.

FIFTY-FOUR

IN A GALLEY stores locker the size of a mop closet, Dante Bhang and Randy Barnes were as busy as Wagnerian dwarves, their *rheingold* fixings being Pesky Pizza ingredients.

The pizza franchise hadn't been able to get any of its personnel aboard the *Crystal Harmonic*, but such was the popularity of the chain that it managed to get its products carried by the cruise ship under special license; in point of fact, those had been GoBug's favorite snack food on the South China Sea leg of the voyage. Getting prepackaged secret recipes inside the XT themer ship was a major coup for Earth's anti-Black Hole underground; it required only an occasion on the order of the Phoenix summit and one or two convertible assets like the police captain and the gangster to execute its plan.

They'd needed to kipe a few basic items like a laser soldering wand, a self-freezing ice tray, and a medical thermometer. Barnes, no forensics propellerhead, worked with tongue-in-teeth concentration; Dante, an expert in back-alley science and jungle-lab alchemy, was quick and proficient. A precipitate from canned sauce met with a distillate evoked from the aftershave Dante had brought aboard; a gelatin sweated from some marinated anchovies was carefully mixed into the cheeselike food substitute whose formula was carefully guarded company data. The constituents were oh-so-gently kneaded into Pesky Pizza's own unique dough.

Now for Operation Free Home Deliverance.

* * *

Fading in to Light Trap, Lucky got directions from a guy named Bagbee who resembled Ray Bolger in *The Wizard of Oz* except that he was eight feet tall. The pink force field the Fealty had retrofitted to the eight-ring medallion had vanished; Lucky was considering discarding it, the 8 Ball, and everything he was carrying that was connected to the Trough.

He threaded his way through the thoroughly traumatized command-post personnel and automata. Casualties were being seen to, equipment repaired or trundled aside, as communications and operations staffers struggled mightily to reestablish some minimal order in the raid's sprawling TO&E. Most of all, it was clear, the insurrectionists were mustering for an imminent mass fade out of Light Trap. Lucky was so unstrung by his bitter split with Silvercup that the aftermath of battle, the breathtaking, upcurving panorama of the shellworld and its biomimetic struggle to restore itself—none of it quite made contact with him.

Over by a large tactical Adit, Ka Shamok and SySobek, surrounded by aides and advisors, were talking to Wheeler, Sheena Hec'k, and Professor Miles Vanderloop—or, rather, listening as Sheena vented spleen at the Chasen-nur and the fallen Sysop.

Harley Paradise, sitting on the cooling fin of an exploded charged-particle artillery piece, was oblivious of it all, including Lucky's approach. He took in her gaitmobe wearer's unigarb, the grimy face and shaved scalp, her ground-pounder's forelock and filthy hands. She'd changed a lot from the paradigm vanna with the Paradisical figure; she looked hollow-eyed and malnourished. Lucky was nonplussed to hear her singing—and, at that, a song of his own and Willy Ninja's, a Dixieland-blues number.

"Lo-oove 'll kick ya in the ass,
It'll strike, at any caste or class
Flatten your resistance with someone's genitalia
And the urge to let the person male or female ya
Cupid is one sissy whom ya'd better not sass,
Love'll kick ya in the ass—"

Building to the finale, she sounded like she knew whereof she sang; he joined in on harmony as he got close enough.

"Victimizes gals 'n' guys
of ev-er-y nation

Leads 'em into depths of sin
and deg-er-a-da-shun—"

"Oh, Lucky," she took a second to yell at him, with a fragile grin. She'd been crying.

"Causing their demise or their incar-cer-a-shun,
Love'll kick ya in the ass."

"—hi, Harley."

"Lucky, you made it!" Harley threw her arms around his neck, sniffling. Sheena broke off her tirade, trumpeting, "Earth Man!," and came bounding over to be included.

"You two make things wicked on a rescuer wannabe, leaving no forwarding address and all." Feminine flesh was a *way* better tactile experience than warm, electric somalloy, he told himself. Great; that solved everything. Right?

"What happened to you?" Sheena demanded. "You've been burned!"

"And where's Ms. *Plata*-Puss?" Harley pressed archly. "The iron maiden we saw you with?"

"Cute. Leaves more time to think up gag lines when you trade in your hair blower for a floor buffer, huh?"

Then Ka Shamok and SySobek arrived with the others. Wheeler nodded. "Helluva day, eh, Junknowitz?"

"It sure knocked *my* dick in the dirt, E.C. Hello again, Professor; whatever happens from here on in, let's make sure we've got our name badges straightened out."

Vanderloop showed a *Gentlemen's Quarterly* smile. "I quite agree, Lucky. One day I should like to hear what I missed when they mistook you for me."

Ka Shamok was about to speak, but Sheena cut him off. "I still want to know why you can't prioritize status searches on Sean and all the others."

The Chasen-nur grimaced. "The up-Trap SIs say End Zone has broken contact, just as Earth's Adit and telecaster are offline. The SIs are focused on their colloquy and will not be pestered; it's all we can do to get them to let us withdraw from Light Trap under cease-fire."

"Enough," SySobek decreed with a Supernal force of personality even Sheena didn't challenge. "I'd hoped certain others would attend, but—time presses. Follow me."

Six of them accompanied SySobek to the crest of a hill above the command post, where a moose-antler-like tree twenty feet across had been blasted to pieces from knee height on up. There he gazed at the crazy quilt of microecologies rising up and up to every point of the compass. Lucky, Vanderloop, Sheena, Ka Shamok, Wheeler, and Harley found a seat or a comfortable place to lean here and there among the fallen wood.

SySobek drew himself up before them. "I was a Sysop and retain portions of that identity, though much of it is lost. Although almost none are privy to the fact, Sysops are detached drone-fragments, excerpt facsimiles, of the ... *sentiences* who dwell outside this galaxy in the cosmos at large, inhabiting the greater scheme of existence from which we here are quarantined."

He recounted things Ka Shamok already knew in part, filling in other details: of Sobek's invention of the Killing Thought and how that and the secret of the eight rings had shattered him.

Lucky was rubbing his medallion. "Eight-ring designation for the Milky Way, same as for Earth? Okay, so, *why*? What's the symbol stand for?" Vanderloop, still a semiotician above all else, leaned forward hungrily.

"Impossible to convey in full in any language in the galaxy," SySobek answered. "A vague approximation of one sense of it would be 'toxic waste dump.' "

Everybody was on his or her feet. *"What?"*

SySobek went on. "In the case of Adit Navel, the connotation is more on the order of 'idiot savant'—a specialized facility within the site entire, you might say."

"Hold up." Wheeler was twisting and stroking his beard like mad. "Exactly what is it the cosmos dwellers—Cosmosians, whatever they are—are dumping?"

SySobek swept a hand to take in all the suffering and destruction Light Trap held. "There! It's right before your eyes! Are you so blind you can't see?"

Ka Shamok's brow furrowed with the slow force of a glacier. "Violence? Conflict?"

"Unmanageable emotions," Harley put in tremblingly. "Dysfunctional behaviors."

"Odium, animus, acrimony." Vanderloop shook his head in mourning. "Or their generative sources."

"Psychic pollutants," Sheena murmured, the jungle-green eyes looking wounded. "ESP-poisons. Telepathic carcinogens."

"Bad karma," Lucky added. "Id-ridden piles of doomed cells ..." He stopped, having strayed to Silvercup's words.

Wheeler huffed. "So these *negatives*, the Cozmos drain off and stick us with? Why *this* galaxy?"

"It's nothing personal," SySobek assured him. "An appropriate location, suitable biota, no advanced life-forms."

"The Cosmosians just do what *humans* do, E.C.," Lucky hissed. "NIMBY—Not In My Back Yard! We get lunacy and crime and genocide for the same reason some third-worlder ends up with PCBs in his drinking water—how *symmetrical*."

Vanderloop jumped in. "I'll grant you, we manifest all those evils cited and more, but we have our virtues, too: compassion, self-sacrifice, ecstasy, love—"

"Surely—fleeting though they are," SySobek said. "Local species have evolved some novel autoimmune responses and coping mechanisms, like the bacteria Earth uses in bioremediation of waste. That's all you are, or any living creature or sophant AI in this galaxy is: a kind of microorganism to break down toxic substances into harmless after-products."

"And Earth," Wheeler pressed. "An eight-ringer among the eight-ringers? For extra-exotic toxins, is it?"

"The SySops and Cosmosians, as you term them, consider Adit Navel rather interesting," SySobek replied. "A hot spot of effluents, like a magnet, but also a place of wild talents, unique ESPer gifts, unparalleled metaphysical phenomena. Some of it not yet fully understood."

"You don't know the half of it," Vanderloop said, thinking of Gipper Beidjie.

Lucky was still glaring at SySobek. "That's us, is it? Mutated bacteria just gobblin' up those trash isotopes?"

The sarcasm didn't register. "From the Cosmosians' point of view, yes. And Sysops—we're the sludge tank autoplumbing. But Earth is regarded as an aberrant place, not quite like any other on record, in fact. It's being closely monitored these days."

"And where does the Black Hole Travel Agency fit into all this?" Sheena asked. "Making sure the disposal system doesn't self-destruct?"

"Exactly," SySobek answered. "And churning the mixture for optimal absorption. Keeping things stirred up, throwing species and cultures against each other, making sure conflict and friction and other extremes have an opportunity to develop; maintaining variety so that every type of toxic waste can find its bioremediation here."

"We're dumpsite germs, being force-fed discord and trauma?" Harley was shaking her head slowly, tears trickling down her cheeks. "You motherfuckers." She reached for her gaitmobe wearer's magnum, though she'd never used it on Hazmat.

Ka Shamok was instantly at her side, taking the pistol away effortlessly. "It's not his doing, and he's become our ally. Parenthetically, he's not as easy to kill as that."

She relented.

Lucky shared her homicidal urge; what was the point in any higher impulse? All the prayers, all your philosophies, Horatio, all the superstitions, crusades, jihads, the Grand Unified Theorizings, the endless flavors of psychotherapy and consciousness raising—in the end all were false, and it *didn't matter* whether you were good or evil, because the forces that shaped life in the galaxy were indifferent to all that—pitiless, exploitive beyond human comprehension.

Sudden comprehension hit him. "The Hazmat breakdown! The genesis of Warhead and the memory egg—it happened because the SIs found out about all this, didn't it? The crackup was their way of hiding it from themselves."

"Of course," SySobek said. "The Hazmat AIs, up-Trap SIs, and the rest were synthetic intellects who'd been fundamentally disinformed; their psyches were even more brittle than yours."

Ka Shamok gazed at the devastation within Light Trap. "When did this galaxy come online, as it were, as a toxic-dump site?"

"I'm uncertain. Aeons ago, when Black Hole first appeared."

"And before that?"

SySobek raised one eyebrow. "Ka Shamok sees far. Before that there were other dump sites, which in due course outlived their usefulness, just as any mundane one does."

"They destroyed themselves," Vanderloop pursued.

Ka Shamok's eyes hadn't left SySobek. "Or Upper Management closed those galaxies once they'd become supersaturated, inimical to life, unable to absorb additional toxic waste."

"Perhaps the Cosmosians sterilize their sites," Sheena suggested darkly, "to insure no contamination spreads. And prepare the real estate for redevelopment?"

Lucky thought of whole galaxies purged. Wheeler was thinking along the same lines. "Awright, some tens—or hundreds?—of thousands of years ago, Black Hole closes down some other galaxy and throws open the Milky Way dump site. I presume that has to do with why intelligent life in our island universe doesn't exceed a certain level of evolution."

SySobek nodded. "Chosen sites harbor no higher life-forms; none can evolve once pollutants are introduced."

Wheeler yanked at handfuls of his own hair. "But it's so wanton! They must be as *gods* out there; some other solution *has* to lie within their power!"

"None has yet been found," SySobek said. "Then again, there's no urgency about alternative waste-management strategies; dumping serves, and there's no lack of suitable galaxies."

Harley drew a long, ragged breath. "Mr. Shamok? My gun, please. Don't worry; I wouldn't waste a bullet on *him*." She jerked her beautifully sculpted chin at the fallen Sysop.

"Even if you managed to end my life," SySobek told her, "I doubt you'd shorten it by much. In all likelihood I'll no longer exist a few minutes from now."

That rattled even Ka Shamok. "How's that? Why?"

SySobek was more than somber. "I'm about to ascend the Outline. The Cosmosians have granted me permission out of curiosity about anomalous and in some ways inexplicable events here, for the most part—the Intubis and all. I mean to petition them with the grievances of the biota of this site, but it's highly likely I'll be eradicated out of hand."

Vanderloop recovered. "You say curiosity *for the most part*. What else prompts the Cosmosians to hear you out?"

"I got a sense that there is a nascent school of thought—held as impractical, deluded, and contrarian by most—contending that current dumping practices inflict needless pain and waste natural resources. It has received impetus from recent events here. Those subscribing to that attitude militated for my permission to be heard, or more accurately, scrutinized."

"A green movement!" Wheeler hooted like a steam whistle. "A by-god nascent environmentalist faction!"

"They better be the kind who don't give up easily," Lucky said.

"SySobek," Vanderloop asked, "if you're likely to be eradicated, why are you going?"

He was a long time answering. "Since we've spoken in Adit Navel metaphysics, call it a sense of dharma, and of obligation, that came to me when I realized both how badly I've been wronged and how badly I've wronged others."

He glanced back over his shoulder just as there was a shimmer, then a flare, from the command post's largest tactical mass-transit Adit. The usual tidal radius sparkle was an ethereal flame this time, a reflection of one at the terminus of the Outline. Insurrectionist personnel fell back, including the Pit Boss, wanting no part of it.

SySobek prepared to take his leave. "I'll make my best effort to apprise you of what transpires up the Line, but I doubt I'll succeed even in that. Now, farewell."

"No!" Ka Shamok exploded. "What of the Killing Thought? You'll exorcise it before anything else; I didn't wage this war for selfless motives."

"I cannot," SySobek answered him. "I remember being that Sysop in a general sense, but the particulars are all lost; look to the up-Trap SIs for help, and the Sysops."

He strode off down the hill while Ka Shamok was rocked back on his heels by the revelation as if he'd been dusted a glancing hit by a cruise missile. Then he raced after, leaving the humans to pound along in his wake. "Stop that man!" His troops were hesitant, even caninely loyal Bagbee; but SySobek halted of his own accord by the white flame of the Outline Adit.

"I accept your word," Ka Shamok announced. "Therefore, I'll take my grievance up the Line."

"Impossi—"

"What you can do, I can do, you animated lump of putty! People think I've endured because my body's strong; my body's puny and frail compared to my will! I'll beard these Cosmosians for justice and if denied it I'll storm a higher jurisdiction!"

SySobek's expression was all gritty amusement and fey respect. "Come, then."

"Carry out the withdrawal," Ka Shamok ordered his staff. "I'll contact you as circumstances permit. In the meantime, applicable contingency plans are now in effect."

Bagbee tottered toward him, devastated. "Your Honor, no!"

Ka Shamok took the impact far better than Bagbee. "Stop that blubbering! See that these others get back to Adit Navel and whatnot, there's a good fellow. I'll be in touch ASAP."

Bagbee wiped his nose on his gold-braided sleeve. "No, Your Honor, we know better. But you can rely on me."

Ka Shamok almost repulsed Bagbee's leave-taking with a fierce Neanderthal frown, but relented. Bagbee bent nearly double to give his lord and master a parting embrace; Ka Shamok writhed out of it as soon as was decent and patted the gangling humanoid on the shoulder. "Persevere."

He mounted the platform of the Outline alongside SySobek as a would-be third telenaut strolled over with braced vigor to throw in with them. "Gentlemen, if you've no objections?"

"Prof, you better think about this," Lucky warned, but held his place; no telling what would happen when solid bodies stepped into that white balefire.

"Thanks awfully; I have." Vanderloop grinned nervously. "But the Trough's nothing more than a facade in terms of answers, isn't it? I can either search on for the substance behind the symbols or fade home, teach de Saussure and Barthes and Eco, and forever wonder."

"In that case, you balmy kipper, 'write if you find work.' " The old Bob and Ray line was the only one Lucky could think of.

Vanderloop turned to his companions. "Shall we?" Maybe it was the effect of that Cambridge golden-boy self-assurance, or maybe the Chasen-nur and the fallen Sysop had stopped questioning the flow of events, but neither one protested.

"Time to go," SySobek said, and they quested into the white flame walking abreast, not quite shoulder to shoulder.

Wheeler waved at their backs. " *'Ad astra per aspera!'* " To the stars through hardships.

The base of the Outline flared high as they disappeared, then burned low and faded out, to be replaced by the everyday ghostly tidal-zone froth of the tactical Adit.

FIFTY-FIVE

"SHOWMANSHIP BE DAMNED! I demand that we kill them without delay!" Phipps Hagadorn railed.

"Demand?" Llesh Llerrudz flayed the rash choice of words softly while admiring the gleam of medical paraphernalia that had floated onstage in the Heave-Ho Room. An organ transshipment stasis locker buoyed up and down minutely next to a robosurgeon/vivisector. Stripped naked and hung by the heels were Nikkei and Mickey, the ninja *jonin* Kamimura, and the rest captured in the abortive infiltration. Tanabe, Sato, and the others remained seated, covered by the weapons of crew members and an XT passenger or two eager to take an active role in the ship-board festivities. The Phoenix members and their entourages had been forbidden firearms.

Hagadorn got hold of himself, sweating slightly. "I didn't mean it in that way, of course, Director," he hastened to add. "Let Vogonskiy have his fun, but let me dispose of Tanabe without further delay."

"That's scarcely Black Hole's way, is it?" the little Nall tweaked him. "To waste a lovely opportunity for drama, conflict, sport? Vogon would be so disappointed."

At the Papal Nuncio's table, Didi Cola leaned toward her husband. "Start thinking about your sons and me and write Tanabe off, okay? He's history."

Then, what am I? Charlie inquired of himself. Al-Reem, End Zone, or something equally unpleasant was all he could expect, and Jesus and Labib's captivity just broadened the possible venues of fun the Agency could have with him in the meantime. As far as saving them, Didi was fooling herself; it was all over for the Cola family.

Charlie had no hope of survival, but was determined not to let Upper Management wring prolonged entertainment from him. He just wanted it all to be over; maybe his death would appease Black Hole somewhat, and reduce some of the suffering his family was otherwise slated for. In any case, he suddenly and vividly believed he understood Tanabe's attitude about death being a fair transaction, or even desirable, in some circumstances.

It felt like a good night for it, and if anybody could find a way it would be Tanabe, so Charlie got up—at the risk of a shot from a tense crew member or playful passenger—and resumed his chair at Tanabe's table. The CEO spared him a swift, searching glance, with nothing in it that could be deciphered. Even Asia appeared caught up in the circle's silent, communal, fatalistic calm; Charlie sat, drawing comfort from it.

Vogonskiy, contemplating the captives hung like butcher's meat, winked broadly in Russ Print's direction. "See why you should cooperate with the Agency, Rush?" He nodded to the floating vivisector. "You! Start with that one. Why don't we see how neatly you can *debone* him from the feet down?"

He meant Nikkei, who writhed like a golden rattler trying to shed its skin. "Jizmic! Just don't keep me hangin', needle dick!"

As Hagadorn scowled, walking abattoir Barb Steel appeared at the Troughs and Adits director's elbow. "Sir, there was brief contact with Light Trap. Apparently there's been some kind of sabotage up-Trap and an attack is now in progress."

Llesh Llerrudz's bark-covered forehead creased. "These malcontents never learn! Can we watch them meet their fate?"

"Uncertain, sir. All Adits are reported offline."

"Ah, well; fun is where one finds it."

Barb Steel made pinking-shears sounds with his fingers. "Sir, the Trough has never *been* offline before."

"Which is why we know all effort will be directed at correcting the problem at once."

"Of course, sir, lacking backup, we may have difficulty maintaining local control."

Llesh Llerrudz simpered, "If worst comes to worst we always have in you the means to *squelch* any indig disorder, eh?"

He chuckled at his own joke—*squelch* referring to something deliciously appalling within Barb Steel—then noticed the metalflesh hadn't joined in. "Something else? Out with it." Hagadorn was hovering nearby, but the Nall no longer cared.

"Among the last twixes we received," Barb Steel continued, "was word that certain mentations of the 'Miss Diandra Abbott' Probe have been detected in the Light Trap systems even though there's been no success locating the Probe herself; she may have been captured or destroyed."

"Oh, bother! Well, most important data she uncovered, we've already got on file, eh?" He pointed to his own head and Barb's. "So she's easily enough replaced: I'll just elevate some other al-Reem sadist as I did her—what, are you still here?"

He meant Hagadorn, who'd been listening. He now said, "I met that Probe; she was quite interested in Earth."

Llesh Llerrudz lost patience. "Dolt! You don't think we trust you indigs to stay on top of things, do you? Adit Navel is becoming more and more important. In fact, I myself have been—ahem—making preparations to directly oversee Agency operations here no matter which of you primate hoodlums runs Phoenix."

Before Hagadorn could find words, Llesh Llerrudz waved him away, then turned back to the entertainment. "Say, Vogonskiy, let's see how long a spiral of flesh your anatomizer can peel off that young buck." He glanced slyly to Tanabe, whose anguish in witnessing it would be the real delicacy for any true connoisseur. The robo-vivisector rose toward Nikkei, a selection of edges and needle points snicking from its effectuators. It was about to slice into him when the organ-transshipment locker's lid flew open and a man dressed only in a twist of cloth, an improvised _fundoshi_, leapt up with an Yggdraasian power pistol.

As the guy was slagging the flying Cuisinart, Nikkei studied him close up, if at an odd angle. He was Japanese, his body seamed with raw red scars, silvered keloid, dried blood, and dribbling wounds—all of which made Nikkei conclude, _We've been saved by the Frankenstein Monster?_

Venturing deeper into the _Crystal Harmonic_ and forward somewhat, Apterix Muldoon and the gnarled gargoyle that was Braxmar Koddle kept Winnie Print between them, trying to look like a legitimate escort fetching an indig—likely a Phoenix functionary—to her authorized destination. While the Man in Black never produced any identification Brax could see, uniformed crew members, vanity-plated Yggdraasians, wandering automata, and assorted XTs let the three pass without objection.

"Hagadorn's organ-export operation works out of two compartments on the port side," Muldoon had told them. "They've got plasm-manipulation and transmog apparatus there, too."

The plasm shop's doorplate read BIOEXPORT OFFICE; the place was empty. There was another door, to an inner compartment, which Muldoon found locked. Trough gadgetry abounded—everything from the transmog capsule to the offworld surgical tape Brax had seen before. Muldoon posted Winnie at the outer door, then opened a cyclindrical unit identical to the one on Martha's Vineyard.

"For the most part Hagadorn's people process body-part shipments through here," he explained, "but it's a resource center for a lot of other tech support—hmm."

Winnie looked away from where she'd been peeking into the passageway. "What, 'Hmm'?"

"There _was_ a big backlog of body parts and organs awaiting transshipment, but they're gone. Hey-ho; in you get, Mr. Koddle."

The normally tentative Muldoon had an air of certainty as he adjusted the tank module. Brax knew that if he questioned it, he'd lose his nerve, so he prepared to climb into the tank. He froze as the inner compartment door swung open and a naked human body sprang through; Brax had a confused impression of pale amber skin mapped by puckered, strangely silver scarring, a Japanese face zigzagged with scars, and eyes like those a dying mongoose might see.

More came behind, silent, with tremendous speed and precision of movement. Brax, Muldoon, and Winnie were held fast, gagged by wadded balls of cloth shoved in their mouths, scalpels and surgical lasers held to their throats. Then appeared Dr. Folatre, Hagadorn's trusted organ procurer and labmeister. One look at Brax, the transmog capsule, Muldoon, and Winnie and he chuckled foxily; to Muldoon he added, "You've actually impressed me, sir."

And to Winnie, "Madam Print? Very brave of you, throwing in with them." As for Brax, with gestures that indicated the whole ship, "But what a catastrophe!" Folatre told the Japanese, "Let them speak, for heaven's sake; we need their help."

Having secured the passageway door, the scar-bod who'd led the attack nodded to the others. The gags were extracted. Brax recognized the gray-haired leader at once; Hagadorn's people had spent much time studying and worrying about him. "Kamimura!"

Kamimura, the peerless Kamimura, Tanabe's *jonin*; whoever the double nabbed on the Aquatics deck was, Brax didn't doubt that here stood the real item. With him were three more ninjas— one a *kunoichi*, a female adept. All were as disfigured as Kamimura, making Brax understand in a flash of insight just how far short of the truth all the movies and *manga* fell. He looked to Dr. Folatre. "You got them aboard as body parts!"

The organlegger buffed his nails on his lab coat and examined them. "Reassembly was the real trick. Had to do it fast and sloppy, I fear."

Hagadorn's operation had never been too particular about how it came by various organs and other biowares; neither would *Crystal Harmonic* security have accorded much scrutiny to lifeless, disconnected anatomical spares, except to make sure they weren't booby-trapped or the like. The ninjas had suffered themselves to be dissected and their parts palmed off as black-market goods to pass through Hagadorn's defenses—a unique and gamecock stunt even by their standards, although they seemed matter-of-fact about it, and about looking like war atrocities.

Dr. Folatre was obviously the key, having turned traitor on his not so beloved *uber* Hagadorn, but that was better left unsaid.

Folatre looked irked. "Alas, there's been a worse glitch. Fifty more have been reassembled in Trough safehouses; they were scheduled to have faded back aboard by now, fully armed and equipped, disguised as VIPs—but there's been some sort of assault on Light Trap and the whole Trough is down."

Kamimura interrupted quietly. "What's the situation?"

They filled in Folatre and the ninjas on circumstances at the Captain's Banquet. The *jonin* ran one hand through a patchwork of gray clumps of hair separated by furrows of scar, looking like a meditative ghoul. He and those with him had been cached aboard—in the form of supposedly miscellaneous anatomical constituents—as a contingency force, but there'd been no way to stock arms and other gear for them. In addition, two more *genin* were in the next room in the final stages of revivification.

Vogonskiy's announced intention was to carve up Nikkei, Mickey, and the other captives, then indulge in some lingering End Zone fun with Tanabe and Sato among others; a robosurgeon/vivisector, organ locker, and other equipment were due to be moved from the bioexport labs to the Heave-Ho stage momentarily. With no time for subtleties, Kamimura's decision to conceal himself in the locker became the centerpiece for a desperate rescue attempt.

"But we've no weapons—" Muldoon was interrupted as the door was flung open and an Ygg hulkster in vanity plate ducked through, unholstering a power pistol big as a studio cam and growling, "Who are these unauthorized—*arrggh!*"

The latter sound ended his remark because while the *kunoichi* and the others had feinted to distract the Ygg, Kamimura had slid into action. His scalpel being a poor weapon with which to tackle the armored XT, the *jonin* grabbed a dispenser of Trough surgical tape. Ripping forth a length, he snared the pincer-hand holding the gun, yanked it off target, and immobilized it with a quick, superadhesive loop thrown around the Ygg's own leg.

Brax realized abstractly that it was *hojojutsu*, the ancient technique of binding an antagonist, adapted to circumstances. The *jonin* was fast as a spider, leashing pincer to thigh, ducking through the Ygg's legs and hobbling knee to knee, then slithering up over the reinforced shoulder pauldron and reefing neck to wrist. The others levered the gun out of the guard's grasp. It looked rehearsed, the Ygg toppled so quickly—its outcries stifled by all available rags, including improvised *fundoshis*.

Kamimura took the pistol. Folatre told Brax and the others, "We must move fast; I'll get the other two reassemblyites revived. You, I take it, Mr. Koddle, would like to have your original form back in the meantime? Step lively, then."

Brax did so. As Folatre made final adjustments to the apparatus, he observed offhandedly, "Muldoon's calibrations were in error, by the way. Would've killed you. But then life always does sooner or later, eh?"

FIFTY-SIX

AS KAMIMURA'S POWER-PISTOL shot downed the vivisector robot, Asia felt a hand on her shoulder and almost fell backward, half expecting to be jumped by an anthropophagite XT—only to see Brax's intent brown face as she remembered it: the sane and kindly expression, the prematurely white-gray hair, everything. He said nothing, just took her hand and drew her away with a gentle insistence she never questioned.

Maybe it was what she'd been waiting for him to do all along. Asia had embodied her feelings for Brax in dance, poured her heart out, and he'd come to her; the details didn't matter.

Kamimura's second shot didn't quite get Phipps Hagadorn, because his Watchmen reacted with absolute aplomb, upturning a table and shielding their boss. The bolt glanced off the Trough-treated wood, blowing one edge off the table. Barb Steel fired a stiletto finger at the *jonin*, distracting him, and Hagadorn and his bunch made a tactical withdrawal; then Kamimura's third beam liquefied part of Barb Steel's chest, and the gleamer secretary dove for cover, disappearing in the pandemonium.

Reassembled ninjas who'd infiltrated the Heave-Ho Room in hastily procured disguises went into action. With the crisis upon them and most of their number stranded on other worlds and way stations, their only hope was to strike with total ferocity. Two opened up with the only other firearms they'd managed to liberate along the way, a security guard's beamer and a pellet accelerator dropped by a Kraam who'd had second thoughts about heroism and fled.

A second *kunoichi*—she being one of the last two ninjas Folatre had revivified—got a bull's eye on Vogonskiy, who'd spun to take flight, but the ray splashed off his wizard robes with an eruption of purple fire and cascade of sparks. The hem and cuffs of his robes burst into flames, but he kept running. Other ninjas tossed improvised *hidama* smoke and firebombs at detectors and cams; emergency systems cut in, raining anticombustion fluid and spurts of foam. The *genin* added smoke bombs to the mix, and used scalpels, halved surgical shears, and similar tools as *tonki*—throwing weapons, With friend and foe intermingled and confusion reigning, the ship's interior-security systems were useless.

The bulk of the Phoenix members, their entourages, and the passengers simply wanted out of the melee. This went double for the Kuril Islanders, who realized Tanabe had been counting on their betrayal all along and could be expected to square accounts at the earliest opportunity. The Papal Nuncio, his fellow clergy, and the wiseguys were focused on extricating themselves, too, Bishop O'Dwyer elbowing and struggling like one of the boys.

Tanabe's group was heedless of Brax and Asia's tender moment, coping instead with the bungled coup—an unforeseeable turn of events, Murphy's Law as code duello, Tanabe's calculated risk gone wrong. Seeing that his son and Mickey were in no immediate danger of being diced, Tanabe gave his attention to other priorities, keeping low in the smoke and tumult.

A lone Hagadorn Watchman who came dodging through the clouds with a fondue fork in each hand, hoping to whack the Nagoya CEO, yowled in surprise and faltered; he'd trod *tetsubishi*, caltrops—spiky little antipersonnel stars improvised from some of Dr. Folatre's IV needles and scattered before him by a *genin*. Miss Sato flung the powder from her compact into his eyes, blinding him, while another Tanabe subordinate got him in the head with the centerpiece vase.

Not far away, Asia brought Brax up to date and pointed out Lucky's parents and sister where they sat at Wakkendorf's table; like Jesus and Labib, they were being kept where they were by the general and his knife-wielding bodyguards as well as Fatima Bebe, with whom Wakkendorf seemed to have made common cause, and *her* Watchmen. "We've got to help Lucky's folks if we can," Asia said.

If anyone but Asia had asked it of him, he'd have listened to his instincts and run. "Oh, god." Brax resigned himself. "All right. Stay down—we'll try." Hand in hand, they blundered through the crush and the din of alarms.

On stage, Kamimura laid down suppressive fire in the smoke, foam, and anticombustion rain. He shot an armed steward and a blaster-waving Occuumese, which discouraged further interference. Tossing the beamer to a *kunoichi*, he took up a bonesaw from Folatre's office, got Nikkei down with a few quick slashes, and handed him the instrument so he could free Mickey and the other captives—including the *jonin*'s lookalike.

A Man in Black came at Kamimura from the wings; Kamimura thrust both hands at him, fingers interwoven in the most powerful one of the Hidden Five—numbers eighty-two through eighty-six—of the legendary *kuji-kiri* hypnotic gestures. The MIB might simply have been startled by the unexpected move, but he paused, gaping uncertainly; Kamimura vaulted, bore him over with a leglock on his chest and a two-armed headlock, and left him for dead.

The general breakdown of order had resulted in some Phoenix members' vassals attacking targets of opportunity; one of the Papal Nuncio's men was trying to take out a Jiang Ding bodyguard. Such was the cross-pollination of fighting systems in the post-Turn that the Catholics used modified *wu-shu* forms while the Chinese employed Exxon-developed "propinquant weapons" executive-defense techniques, including clever attaché-case maneuvers and savage fountain-pen fighting moves.

On stage, Mickey Formica, just cut down by Nikkei, yanked his partner's head down to keep it from being burned off by a beam from a Peer Group slagger. A sharp impact slammed the slagger from the Peerer's hand; sticking from his wrist, having penetrated it and his gauntlet, was a cross *shuriken* hastily made from two brochette skewers twist-tied together with champagne *coiffes*, wire cork muzzles. As the Peers made tracks Nikkei glanced in the direction from which the cross had come to see Miss Sato give him a look, then go back to guarding his father.

Mickey had reached a peak of fury and redirected fear. It was clear now that he, Nikkei, and the whole Aquatics deck infiltration scheme had been nothing more than a red herring of Takuma Tanabe's, meant from the first to be compromised by the duplicitous Kuril Islanders to divert Hagadorn's and Vogonskiy's attention from the real Trojan horse—the bodyparted ninjas. A brilliant tactic, but Mickey and Nikkei had been mere dupes in it, and Mickey didn't feature that shit.

Seized now by a towering rage, Mickey bawled after the fleeing Peer Group trio, "You jizmoids! Gon' help you kick the O_2 habit!" Unarmed and bareass, he dashed off in hot pursuit; Nikkei faced the inevitable and chased after.

At the Sony-Neuhaus table, Winnie and Apterix Muldoon were drawing Russ and the others away from the interstellar free-for-all. They wended for an exit among *Video Examiner* reporters who'd gotten far too close to the greatest ET story of all time; Richard Rymer's tinseltown contingent, for whom it was all too high-concept; Vladimir Artemov's United CIS Com-Econ Russkies, who'd thought this kind of coup had gone out with Yeltsin; and partially disabled gleamer Barb Steel, who, carrying his user Llesh Llerrudz, swarmed up the wall, escaping through a skylight despite assorted resentful shots pegged at the two.

The Trough and Adits chief was turning into a basket case; it had never really penetrated to him what it meant to have no Adit available, no way to escape or summon massive reinforcements. He was stuck on a tertiary monkeyhouse of a planet; it was inconceivable, and that was why it had happened.

The Vatican people were still engaged with the China Motors bodyguards when Asia and Brax reached that area. "Alex! Rita! Sinead!" The Junknowitzes were already moving, Sinead having gotten her folks in gear; Jesus and Labib had disappeared. Alex and Rita were frightened and trembling, but still functioning as best they could.

"I saw lifeboats up above," Brax told the others. "We've got to get off this ship of fools *now!*"

Asia looked to where Tanabe's group was moving for an exit on the opposite side of the ship; if the CEO had a plan for saving Earth, it had gone boom. She gave Brax's hand a squeeze. "Yes, let's try to save *something* out of all this."

Over where Bishop O'Dwyer and his companions had fled, Didi Cola was trying to extricate herself from the overturned table and chairs. She wasn't doing too well until Charlie got there, put his back into it, and got the furniture pushed clear; she'd turned her ankle and it was already swelling. He pointed to her patent leather pumps. "Did you know your shoes reflect up, Didi?"

"Help me, you simpering orangutan!"

She came upright easily enough when two more rescuers bore a hand, however. "Isn't it time you two started getting along?" Labib chastised. Jesus added, "This being a family crisis and all?" They got under Didi's arms on either side.

"Your father and I are *not* fighting," Didi objected. "Um, we're arranging a Marriage Encounter session with the bishop—"

She broke off and added her scream to the cacophony of yells, outcries, Troughite trills, and robotic distress tones as a string of explosions made *Crystal Harmonic* shudder from stem to stern.

* * *

Listening carefully to the explosions, Dante Bhang showed uncharacteristic ire. "*Di buttana*! Son of a bitches we wired to the Adit feeds were duds, I think, and the outer defensive systems as well." He peeked around a corner. "We aced internal security, on the other hand."

Feeling the ship roll glacially to port, Barnes swallowed spasmodically. "That sea hatch and the propulsion plant, too." He went back to picking the lock at a utility junction station. "Besides, the Adit's already offline, remember?"

"We need it to *stay* that way."

"Forget it for now!" Barnes got the door open and began looking over the lifeboat emergency launch systems. "One thing at a time. Jesus, I'm gettin' a friggin' migraine—oh, god!"

"Don't even think it," Dante dismissed. "The neurotoxin won't kick in for a good twelve hours yet, that can't be what's causing it—but work fast."

"It's hit and miss!" the Bygarian tech yelled. "The whole Trough's malfunctioning! Can't get a link to Adit Navel!" Lucky didn't need a specialist to explain, what with Adit equipment at the invasion command post blinking on and off unpredictably like lightning bugs. Something about the disappearance of the Outline balefire seemed to have kicked it off.

A nearby telecaster astrodynamics rig flashed holotext with an amazing originator code—the up-Trap SIs. BELIEVE ONGOING TROUGH MALFUNCTIONS CAUSED BY UP-TRAP PROBABILITY CONTAMINATION MODELED ON JUNKNOWITZ'S AND VECTORED THROUGH NANITE DAGGER. WILL ATTEMPT NEUTRALIZATION USING JUNKNOWITZ FADE.

Lucky looked at it askance. "What, are they gonna put me through an aura-wash?"

NO, USE YOU AS A LIGHTNING ROD TO VENT OUR OWN CONTAMINATION INTO THE TROUGH VIA ADIT TECHNOLOGY, MUCH THE SAME WAY YOUR CONTAMINATION HIT YOU IN THE FIRST PLACE—AFTER WHICH YOU SHOULD BE ABLE TO FADE TO EARTH. TROUGH WILL STABILIZE SOON AFTER. YOUR PROBABILITY CONTAMINATION WILL BE DISSIPATED AS WELL.

Wheeler glanced at the encroaching biomimetics and tactical holos that showed insurrectionist forces fleeing Light Trap as and when windows occurred. "You should give it a whirl, Howdy Doody; it's gonna get unhealthy for us around here soon." Sheena and Harley didn't contradict him.

With that the Adit fizzed to life and a new text flashed. EX-

PECT HIGH CONCENTRATIONS OF SYNCHRONISTIC ACTIVITY AT YOUR DESTINATION.

HANG TEN, EARTHMAN.

FIFTY-SEVEN

"WAIT, YOU FOOL!" Dante yelled, trying to slip past Randy Barnes as the police captain bulled his way back toward the galley stores locker. "The ship's dead in the water as planned and we can get the defensive weapons systems offline some other way! Damn you, more charges might send us to the bottom."

Even though they'd specified appropriate places, the Pesky Pizza taskmasters had stressed caution in planting any follow-up charges in an already weakened vessel.

Barnes was reaching for the mounds of explosive Pesky Pizza dough they hadn't used yet. "You want to sit there while your brain Swiss-cheeses? We can't get the antidote until the defenses are down, so they're goin' down if I haveta open this dinghy like a banana split!"

Needing Barnes's help, Dante tried one more appeal to sanity, trying to keep him from grabbing more detonators made from cannibalized action toys and the spare remote improvised from a fido cart's control unit. "Get a grip—"

Barnes, all inhibition lost in panic, skull-butted Dante, breaking his nose, and landed a flurry of punches that left him semiconscious on the deck. Gathering up all the rest of the explosive dough, Barnes charged off, sweating and wild-eyed, convinced he had only minutes to live and that the key to his survival was overkill.

Having gnawed the choicer cuts off Remora Barleycorn's skeleton, the creature that called itself Jason Duplex took another pull from a bottle of Cien Fuegos tequila and rose, weaving, to his feet. He was still hungry, being the periodic-gorge type. He left the linen closet in search of new prey, stepping on Remora's ripped bodice without noticing.

The string of explosions that thudded like body blows to the *Crystal Harmonic* was a mystery to almost everybody aboard, but its effects were more than obvious. Lights, power, ventilation, and other systems, including firefighting gear, were rendered inoperative in many places, fitful in others. Fortunately, the blazes in the Heave-Ho Room had been extinguished and the vessel was still seaworthy—not that that did much to palliate the shipwide panic of people and XTs searching for deliverance.

The majority of sophants on the Black Hole themer ship had been thrown into mental spin cycle, extra fluffy.

Most offworld gentry were even more stupefied and scared than the humans. Their wont in dealing with local unpleasantness was to fade elsewhere; the Trough was their guardian, their guarantor of superiority. They'd never seriously contemplated a situation in which it simply wasn't there.

But Yoo Sobek's use of the nanite dagger up-Trap had changed that. A common reaction was to seek lifeboat stations, but there were diverse others. A Vutrimir mall magnate abandoned his family and took to the air from the sports deck in his concealed and costly personal antigrav harness; some of the ship's systems were still functioning erratically, and he was targeted and blown to mist by a charged particle beam. A vacationing Maakik investment counselor dove confidently from the bow, having forgotten the difference in specific gravity between Earth's seawater and what the Maakik knew as an ocean; it sank like a bad penny stock.

A tacit truce sprang up among most Phoenixers and even between former victims, like the Sony-Neuhaus bunch and the XTs who'd been savoring their terror; all that was now secondary compared to survival. Many were terrified of what awaited them if the ship went under; its systems were no longer repelling sharks and other indig predators. Worse, the Ss-sarsassissians had all escaped and were presumably at large in their element, the gloomy reaches beneath and all around. And the sea dragons were known to hold revenge mandatory.

Tanabe was rolling with various punches. The explosions had been none of his doing or his people's and thus were worrisome. He had even more immediate priorities, however, since the ship seemed seaworthy for the time being. A team of Kamimura's *genin* had tried to commandeer the Kuril Islanders' submersible but it and the Kurils were gone; the gig that shuttled back and forth at anchorages had been taken by departing human crew members in one of the lesser-known traditions of the modern cruise industry, *caveat passenger*; even the Aquatics deck jetskis, sailboards, and such had been stowed, locked away somewhere. Like others, Tanabe and his people made for the promenade deck and the lifeboats; the Ss-sarsassissians were allies but there was no guaranteeing that the sea dragons would want or be able to tell friend from snack if the ship went down.

Asia and Brax got to the deck with Sinead, Lucky's parents, and Muldoon only to see the ugliest kind of bedlam. Human crew and staff were milling around empty lifeboat davits, and the boat cradles tilted over the side at the ends of their tracks, the falls dangling somewhere down in the nighted sea. "Somebody triggered the automatics!" a voice was yelling so shrilly that Asia couldn't tell whether it was a male or a female—or even whether it was human. "They're gone! All the boats were lowered away empty!"

"Where are the life jackets?" someone else demanded over and over, but no one had an answer. Brax had his doubts about that line of action anyway; even if those sea-snake aliens weren't in a vicious mood, sharks and hypothermia put a night swim over in the extreme options category. His first suspicion was that the lifeboat release had been a Black Hole tactic to confine unruly Phoenix factions and intruders, but that didn't hold water; the ship wasn't under *anybody's* control anymore. Witness the fact that Barb Steel could be seen scampering by the funnel with Llesh Llerrudz cradled in his arms, indecisive. What suspects did that leave?

There were already cries of "Where's the captain?" and "Let's get to the bridge!" but Brax didn't think the whiskery Kris Kringle skipper would have any answers and had no intention of getting himself, Asia, or the Junknowitzes caught up in the fleshgrinder again.

"Brax, you've been around the ship; what does that leave?" Asia coaxed him. "What's our best shot?"

But it was Muldoon who came up with an answer. "That Folatre fellow; if anyone has a fallback plan, it'll be him."

They started farther forward and belowdecks again; it was easier with most *Harmonicers* on deck and inclined to stay there. The most direct route to the bio-office lay through the off-limits area of the Adit, but with the ship in utter chaos and the Adit offline no security guards barred their way and hatches had been left open. Passing by, they heard a noise at the Pit Boss workstation and The Awesome Vogonskiy straightened from where he'd been jacking with it. Next to him was his malevolent little M'finti familiar, Tumi.

"Huh, *you* vermin, eh?" Either Vogonskiy wasn't one for crisis cease-fires or he thought the newcomers had come after him; he whipped his hands through hypertheatrical mystic passes, then splayed his fingers in a classic whammy. Combers of industrial-strength S/FX dazzled the humans and made them shrink back. Then Tumi went into a google-eyed windup of his own. Brax shrank from expected waves of malignant cell-dazzle, but although Vogonskiy's death-swipes were black demon clouds, the light in the background seemed to be getting *brighter*—a firmament of gemfires sparkled all across the Adit apparatus.

"Not this time, Monstro," a voice Brax recognized grated. There was bodily impact, and a pained grunt from Vogonskiy. Brax saw Sean Junknowitz recovering his balance after delivering what must have been an all-out dropkick and The Awesome Vogonskiy flying into a pile of check-through Trough luggage.

Rita and Alex called out their elder son's name with mixed joy and warning. Sean had to break off his follow-up attack on Vogonskiy as, alerted by his folks, he threw himself flat to avoid the Adit tool Tumi had plucked up and flung at him—some widget suggesting an antimatter lug wrench. At the same time, another figure emerged from the reactivated Adit. Sean was halfway back to his feet when Willy Ninja, fading in, tripped over him and they both went down again; in the meantime Tumi leapt from his perch, Vogonskiy bellied through the baggage, and the two made it through a side door. Eddie Ensign and Molly Riddle trod in a little more carefully and avoided the pileup, and just as they'd filed through, the Adit went dim once more.

Sean wanted to go inflict massive retribution on Vogonskiy and Tumi, but by then his mother was coming for him with open arms. "Mom, this is gonna have to wait—aw, *filho*!" He capitulated and embraced her back. "Hi, Mom; Dad. Um, sis." Gaunt and tattooed, he looked—as did Willy and Eddie—like a longtime POW out to settle a score. Alex and Rita wouldn't settle for anything less than a family hug that included a bemused Sinead and Lucky's three buddies, Brax included. A joyous music, heard mentally as much as aurally, emanated from Willy.

There was no solid explanation for the briefly successful

tunnel-vision connection that had let the End Zone group fade in after endless failure to get its Adit repaired. "There's a tidal wave of anomalous events building in the Trough." Molly shrugged. Nonetheless, the Adit was dark again; there'd be no fading off the *Crystal Harmonic*, even to End Zone, for the time being.

"Changes nothing," Sean pronounced. "I'm nailing that fatass walking carcinogen before he gets away again."

"You may have a hard time catching him," Asia warned, and gave them a rundown on prevailing circumstances.

Willy Ninja smiled oddly. "No sweat; I can find Vogonskiy no matter where he is." The mental-note music of Riiv's implant had a last-reel-showdown sound to it now.

Knowing there was no dissuading them, Molly held her slamtube at port arms. "Then, *my* priority's to find Charlie and the boys; Quick Fix solidarity, I suppose."

There'd been no further explosions, but the *Crystal Harmonic*, dead in the water, had taken on a decided list to port. A quick search failed to turn up Dr. Folatre. Sean told Brax, Asia, and his family to get abovedecks in case the *Harmonic* started to go down, which made Sinead bristle. "Still playing G.I. Joe? Makes you look like such a lout when you're wrong."

Sean's tattoos made his snarl more menacing. "Shouldn't you be in a mousehole somewhere?"

"Chil*dren*!" Rita Junknowitz's reprimand could still hit them where they lived. "Your father and I are going to be very disappointed in you if you don't stop this quarreling until we get Armageddon out of the way."

Phipps Hagadorn and what was left of his entourage had gone from nonfunctioning Adit to empty lifeboat davits and were now bound for the ship's planetary telecom center, hoping to summon indig rescue even though the signal techs hadn't been able to do so. His Watchmen had discarded the table they'd snatched up as cover in the Heave-Ho Room, but on the march they clustered tight around their patron, Secret-Service fashion; with the retinue shorthanded, even Keating Price was obliged to join the shield.

At the forward end of the Heave-Ho Room they had to skirt a throng of Tithists who were piling up a salvation mound. The true believers had put their faith in resurrection through good works and tithes and were, in their final moments, vying with one another to maximize their balance of payments. So they were heaping up purses, jewelry, bus tickets, shin plaster, and whatever else they could lay hands on. A few Tithists were wrestling strenuously with panicky fellow passengers, trying to escort old ladies out of the room, throw their coats across puddles, read to the unwell, or otherwise do a last good deed.

As Hagadorn and his party moved through the port-side-listing Jokers Wild Casino, the flat slap of a rifle shot changed Hagadorn's gameplan; one of the Watchmen, the side of his chest blown open, went stumbling over a roulette table. There was a brief clicking sound with which Phipps was familiar—Gilda recycling the Fortner bolt of a Daimler-Anschutz target weapon like the one she'd used to win Olympic gold. He heard her laugh in the emergency-light dimness, "Phipps? Let's talk settlement."

Hagadorn's Watchmen got him out of the Jokers Wild Casino with no further losses, but a harassing shot and echoing laughter let him know Gilda wasn't done with him yet.

"Now I know how Moby Dick felt!" he frothed to his entourage.

FIFTY-EIGHT

THE DISCOVERY OF brass speaking tubes connecting the Adit compartment to the bridge, just like old-time engine room tubes, decided them. Most of the group that now included Brax, Asia, the Junknowitzes, and the others could return to the relative safety of the deck or pursue their individual quests, able to check in by means of the tubes from bridge, engine room, or captain's cabin—but the catch was that at least one person was required to remain behind as coordinator and watch for reactivation of the Adit, lest they miss their best shot at escape.

Muldoon insisted on being the one to stand watch; he seemed to be enjoying his new role as hero. Brax didn't like leaving the little Man in Black behind, but at least Muldoon was armed, having accepted from Molly Riddle a diminutive gun that looked more like a plumbing fixture, a tech-*nouveau* faucet handle. Surprisingly, none of the other passengers, XTs *or* human, had come nosing around the Adit in search of a way out; perhaps it had something to do with loss of faith, or with fear of more explosions.

The subgroups split up and left; they were barely gone when Muldoon, poking aimlessly around the U of Pit Boss machinery, caught a flash of metal. Barb Steel was gliding into the compartment, with Llesh Llerrudz nowhere to be seen, glancing at all the metering to gauge the Adit's operational status.

Muldoon sprang at him, firing wildly. "Die, enemy of literature!" Unfortunately the energy derringer's pinbeam wasn't powerful enough to penetrate the metalflesh's faceplate, although it did pop one red lens eye like a bursting ember. Barb Steel returned fire with a dirklike finger, wounding Muldoon above the left hip, and took to his shiny heels. Ignoring all else—"Stand your ground and take what's coming to you, deconstructionist!"—Muldoon struggled after the metalflesh, taking no notice of the Adit equipment behind him coming alight.

"How can the Trough still be offline?" Llesh Llerrudz asked Barb Steel in dull befuddlement. "You must be wrong."

The gleamer sounded as prickly as his master usually did. "I make no mistakes; Adit operation is intermittent, irremediably so at present, as mad a situation as ours is on this ship."

"This ship!" That had brought a measure of heat back into the Nall. "I'll have my revenge on everyone aboard this detestable ship—everyone on this detestable planet! But first things first: since no conventional measures will suffice, I'll need other means to protect my person."

They were crouched behind the bar of the empty Davy Jones's Rocker disco, with sounds of conflict, major malfunction, and automatic alarms drifting through the various doorways. The entire crew and staff, including the captain, had reverted to an ethic of shameless self-interest; escape to some saner planet was impossible, and the systems that had made Llesh Llerrudz all but invulnerable aboard ship were inoperative in the wake of the inexplicable sabotage.

"Therefore," Llesh Llerrudz commanded, "reconfigure yourself for neurosquelch emission mode, yielding me direct fire control."

Barb Steel didn't move. "I deem that unwise. I would be less capable of quick or flexible response in that mode. In addition to the general run of rabble now abroad, a crazed MIB with delusions of wronged literary genius has targeted me."

"Be grateful I don't make you disengage your head for me to carry more conveniently! I'm weary of being borne under your arm; I'm giving you a direct order to reconfigure as I command."

Helpless to resist, Barb Steel shuddered and his body transformed like metalflesh origami. His back became concave and footrests came out of either calf; his arms locked back and his head shifted around, eyes sliding to either side as a single, multifacted cyclops lense emerged and handgrip controls sprouted where his ears should've been. His neck articulated, lengthened somewhat, and thinned out much.

As mechamorphosis went, it wasn't all that radical, but it so consumed the attention of both that they didn't notice a figure, watching from the portside entrance, sliding in to eavesdrop from behind a fallen Captain Hook statue. Llesh Llerrudz climbed up on the footrests and took the handgrips, Steel's locked-back arms enclosing him like a safety cage. Guiding his secretary's body around as if driving an exosuit, he test-fired a wan ray broad as a spotlight beam at the bulkhead. Barb Steel's oddly muffled voice said, "The first-intensity squelch will make of the target's brain a blank page. With it you can subdue whole groups in short order, though only at close range."

Llesh Llerrudz thumbed harder; the beam was harsher this time, narrower. "The second-intensity squelch slays, but uses up power reserves quickly and requires even closer range."

"No matter," Llesh Llerrudz said. "The first will do. Now, let us put these Phoenix—afff!"

Another interloper had arrived, this time through the starboard doorway and not taking trouble to conceal himself. Apterix Muldoon, outraged over Barb Steel's pureeing of his manuscript, charged in, waving the puny faucet-handle weapon Molly Riddle had given him. Llesh Llerrudz tried to slew the neurosquelch lens for a shot but wasn't as masterful an operator as he fancied himself to be. The little Man in Black dashed in close, firing, but the Nall was shielded by Barb Steel's body.

To save himself from being mind-expunged, Apterix Muldoon jammed the little gun up against the gleamer's skinnied-down neck and fired; there was an eruption that threw him back, made Llesh Llerrudz cry out, and blew Barb Steel's head off. But the gleamer's swaying body grabbed Muldoon with one hand, sliced and hacked and gutted him wide open with the other. It released him as it toppled over, bearing a trapped and squalling Llesh Llerrudz with it. The head rolled to a stop by the Captain Hook statue.

Gilda Hagadorn stood and, holding her rifle in one hand, picked up the decapitated cyclops head with the other. She'd been trying to outflank Phipps for a better line of fire when she happened on the scene in the disco.

Muldoon lay glassy-eyed in a spreading pool of his own blood and chopped viscera; the little handgun was a fused mass. Barb Steel was lifeless, too, and Llesh Llerrudz was struggling free of his secretary's derelict body. Gilda shouldered her rifle, held the heavy head in both hands, and, after a moment's fumbling, first-intensity-neurosquelched the Trough and Adits nabob. The Nall jerked a bit, then sat there almost as vacant-faced as Muldoon's corpse, staring at nothing and beginning to drool and make newborn-infant sounds.

Gilda held the late Barb Steel's cranium to her bosom. "What a head for business."

Fading aboard the *Crystal Harmonic*, Lucky was so surprised by the emergency lighting, the smell of smoke, the pronounced slope to the deck, and assorted distant sounds of strife that he caught only a glimpse of what he thought to be a figure in black slipping around the doorway. He was about to call to whoever it was when he was shoved to one side by Sheena Hec'k. "If you won't carry a weapon, at least stay out of the line of fire!"

"The first thing we need is some update, and dead men give no exposition," he chided her. The SIs had offered only fragmentary information on the shipboard summit. "Besides, with what's going on in Light Trap, I'm betting folks here'll be ready to talk sense—hello?"

With E. C. Wheeler and Harley Paradise safely faded in, the Adit had again shut down. Lucky spread his arms, beseeching the far-off Light Trap SIs. "Any time you're ready, we could use a little less happenstance." They had warned him it might take a while for the Trough to stabilize, and in the meantime there was a lot of probability distillate sloshing around out there.

"Planning to wait for an answer?" Wheeler taunted.

Lucky shook his head. "The Trough could be locked down for hours—days. We've got a lot of wheeling and dealing to do." With Black Hole in upheaval, their plan was to reshuffle the Phoenix deck with the promise that a new deal could be cut for Earth. SySobek's revelation of the galaxy's eight-ring secret, and the Silicon Intelligences' reformulated response to it, were going to reshape the sociopolitical landscape of the galaxy.

They sidled into the canted passageway. Harley, taking in the signs of mishap and damage, declared, "This is an improvement, after the stuff that was going on last time I was here."

Somewhere in the distance there was another explosion, and the vessel shifted somewhat more to port. From the direction of the bow came an interplanetary cross-section of shouts and caterwauls. "Wonder if it was such a bright idea, shooting your serendipity wad into the Trough," Wheeler frowned to Lucky. "We might need some. Which way, aft?"

Lucky fatalistically reached for and rolled the 8 Ball.

AS I
SEE IT
YES

"Let's do it."

They'd been gone only two minutes when the Adit gave another brief burp of space-time carbonation. Through it leapt a human body tattered and abused beyond any manufacturer's warranty. It capered like a marionette, swinging a scorched oblong from which shreds of leather wafted. "Junknowitz! We know you're here!"

"Prepare for Ultimate Audit!" added the briefcase.

Zastro Lint lurched into the passageway, following the targeting instinct that had led him back to Earth. His fade—accomplished largely through the briefcase's machinations—was the culmination of his harrowing escape from the indigs of Fair Game, whom Lint had inadvertantly caused to worship actuarial tables and dragoon him into the role of Oracle . . . but that's another story.

FIFTY-NINE

GILDA HAGADORN WAITED until Phipps's party was halfway across the Body Electric fitness room, among the workout machines—some of the Trough apparatus was as surreal as anything in the MoMA sculpture collection. The Watchmen were still clustered around their employer except for one who'd scouted ahead; Gilda, looking down from the observation deck, waited until that one was close enough, then irradiated her with a brief first-intensity neurosquelch beam from Barb Steel's decapitated head. The shot made the rest take cover among the interstellar exercise equipment, as Gilda had intended; the woman she'd lamped collapsed like an infant who hadn't learned to walk, gurgling and thrashing uncoordinatedly.

Gilda ducked down, and a hastily flung steak knife missed her. "Phipps, I really think we should talk reconciliation, don't you?" She was having such a good time that she didn't realize that an onlooker had appeared behind her at the observation deck doorway, weaving slightly.

Phipps recognized the gleamer's reconfigured cranium—having seen a demonstration once—and knew what it meant; Gilda's possession of a neurosquelch made Phipps's situation truly horrifying. It would be one thing for Gilda to try to claim his empire if she merely shot him and either deep-sixed the corpse or tried to shift the blame, but if she managed to get his mindwiped body home she stood a good chance of claiming power of attorney over her mentally incompetent spouse, overturning other legal arrangements by showing his mental incapacity. She could rule his domain while Phipps was relegated to a well-guarded, adult-size nursery.

Hagadorn moaned, then pulled his wits together; he made gestures to one of his Watchmen while talking. "Darling, you've made your point, but you've overlooked a few—"

The Watchman made a break for it, meaning to outflank her,

but one of those explosive .22s put him down for good. The rifle
had been smuggled aboard as assorted parts of Jiang Ding's entertainment troupe's maglev unicycles, but it shot true. Gilda
adroitly ducked a fusillade of tableware and dumbbell weights,
so flushed with triumph that she didn't sense movement behind
her. "You Watchmen! Bind my husband and back away, or
you'll all end up as babbling fetuses—*scheisse!*"

Hungry for more flesh, the abomination that was Jason Duplex lunged at Gilda from behind, throwing his tentacles around
her and fastening his feeding orifice to the side of her neck. The
tequila had thrown off his equilibrium, and he bore her over the
railing, plunging both of them to the fitness-room floor below.
Gilda wound up on the bottom; the sluglike Duplex's landing on
her finished the job of knocking her unconscious, and he began
devouring her. Barb Steel's head had bounced free; Phipps
pounced on it instantly and shouted in elation.

Gilda was as good as dead, half her throat and face gone; the
target rifle's light barrel lay bent under her, useless. Phipps considered squelching the obliviously feeding Duplex, but the creature might be extremely useful to his Earth takeover plan once
satiated.

"Close ranks! Stand ready!" he enjoined his Watchmen, hoist-
ing Barb Steel's head. "Tonight Earth is mine."

It didn't take the mirror-facebowled Peer Group trio long to
realize the incongruity of their fleeing the wrath of Mickey Formica and Nikkei. The TechSist leader dragged the other two to
a halt, the wrist pierced by Miss Sato's throwing cross still
bleeding freely. "Why should we fear a brace of naked indigs?
Lybaxx here is still strapped; let's char their primate butts!"

After a quick peppering of slagger shots, it was Nikkei and
Mickey racing before the hue and cry, high and low through the
ship. At length they swivel-hipped through the Stellar Winds Sa-
lon, hurdling a knot of all-purpose indig musicians working up
a psycho-grunge version of "Nearer My God to Thee."

Seconds later the Peers saw they had the two autochthons at
bay in an upholstered chamber off a main rec passageway.
Mickey and Nikkei were cowering behind a small rostrum that
offered scarcely any cover whatsoever. "Come out; we *need*
hostages like you," laughed the Peer Group leader as he and his
companions closed in.

The three were no sooner inside than they heard the hatch
close, and saw Mickey and Nikkei straightening as they worked

the rostrum's controls. The TechSists realized that they'd been lured into the High-Baller Room only when they were smashed upward by an antigrav system switched to full repulsor power—they were spreadeagled, and Lybaxx's slagger was pressed to the ceiling out of reach. Mickey and Nikkei remained in the charmed circle of the control rostrum, and Mickey was grinning. "Any last words?"

The Peer leader labored to speak. "Laugh now, you apes! Even if you kill us, Tanabe's handing you to Light Trap as hostages as soon as the Trough's back online, you and Sato! That was the deal all along, you dumbfuck indigs!"

A calculating note crept into his helmet-speaker voice. "So you'd better be nice to us; you're gonna need friends in Light Trap, monkey-boys."

"Same way you need friends in hell," Nikkei said, ramming the repulsors to the top. The Peer Group was flattened to pink giblets and red gravy on the ceiling and the slagger was pressed to junk; it all rained down when Mickey backed the controls off.

"Coulda used that gun, *homme*-icide," Mickey told his pard as they left the High-Baller.

"We don' need no steekeen' gones," Nikkei began with a headsman's grin. Mickey was fearing to hear what he had to say next—especially about Takuma and the hostage situation—when four Brazilian-trained Watchmen jumped them and Phipps Hagadorn sprang from hiding with Barb Steel's head in his hands.

NYPD captain Randy Barnes wasn't off-gassed; he knew he might not make it through, but he invoked mental survival techniques to focus on the job at hand—patting the last of the Pesky Pizza dough into a seam between the *Crystal Harmonic*'s aft collision bulkhead and a frame. A check of the improvised detonator told him the charge was primed to go.

He stood up, ignoring the cracking in his spine; now to suss out a safe way to play the angles, Phoenix against Black Hole against the pizzarino underground. There had to be some way for a savvy, ballsy guy like Randy Barnes to come out on top; the only reason he hadn't seen that sooner was because that Wog-Wop punk Bhang was such a pussy. While Barnes was re-assuring himself of this, he heard a voice cry out his name.

He threw himself into motion even as he realized it was Phipps Hagadorn, clutching a big metal lamp thing, his Brazilian goons backing and fronting him. A couple of them held

Tanabe's kid Nikkei and the other one, the gonzo AfricAm sidekick—Formica, that was his name—bound and gagged.

Too soon! The dough-charges were no kind of leverage if Barnes himself was sufficiently close to them to get blown to confetti; he took off running like a striped-assed ape.

"Get him!" Hagadorn thundered, taking up the chase himself. It was clear that Barnes—probably in cahoots with that mongrel Bhang—had caused the explosions and held the detonator controlling more. Here was another piece of the *Crystal Harmonic* convergence come to Hagadorn's hand; it confirmed the fact that he'd been chosen by Destiny to rule Earth and assume a central role in the drama of the Black Hole Travel Agency.

Which made it something of a shock to dash through a door into an engineering space and see an unconscious, possibly dying Randy Barnes at the feet of the legendary Kamimura, who held a length of ordinary marine chain *manriki-kusari* style.

Barnes's detonator was in the hand of Takuma Tanabe.

Something new had been added to the *Crystal Harmonic*'s passageway decor: an Yggdraasian guard in full vanity plate. The disarmed Ygg was fastened to the wall with great dollops of surgical epoxy, his helmet sealed shut and its transmitter ripped off. Further along, a downed surveillance remote was lying half-dissolved in a pool of pharmaceutical acid. A Skitterkin watchpet had been electrocuted with a portable charging unit and a Kammese staff supervisor was out cold with a broken graphite cricket bat nearby.

"What's all this about?" Harley wondered.

Lucky examined a small circular med-saw blade where it was embedded in a security lens it had split wide open, having apparently been flung like a *shuriken*. "I'd say Team Nihon's taken the field. We—"

The stream of incandescence that took Lucky, Sheena, Harley, and Wheeler from behind felt like a riot police water cannon firing liquid nitrogen; it downed them all and left them helpless before Zastro Lint and his cackling briefcase.

Lucky, out of tricks at last, gazed up in dull surrender. "Ya got me, Zas. Don't suppose it'd do any good to reiterate that I'm being framed?"

Lint, looking like a mixture of demon and concentration camp survivor, made a contemptuous sound; the briefcase extruded neural contacts, syringes, energy probes, and laser drills, gloating, "Step one: data confiscation. Say g'bye to all those fond memories, Opie!"

As the two were about to set to work on Lucky's noggin there came a stirring of the air and an invisible flurry. The briefcase was frisbeed at the bulkhead; Lint was spun like a gyroscope, to end up bound in an unbreakable tie-down strap. The briefcase landed in a Trough strongbox that somehow materialized nearby and the lid latched on it. "Cheaters!" Lint bellowed. "Damn all phasing!"

When the blur of activity slowed, Silvercup knelt to cradle Lucky's head. "Are you all right?"

"Comparatively. I thought you, I thought I was—"

She helped him up. "I encountered a fragmentary download of SELMI in Peterbuilt's body, who prompted me to reexamine how I felt about you."

"Yer ass is glassphalt, Tinsel Tits!" the smart-luggage screamed at Silvercup from its confinement.

"No," she corrected. "I think not." She assisted Sheena, Harley, and Wheeler to their feet. The two women looked the gleamer over; Harley turned a clinical gaze on Lucky, Sheena a puzzled one.

"Tell ya one thing, Zastro," Lucky said in order to avoid them. "Before anything else happens, you and I are gonna clear my name once and for all."

Having scouted the ship before, he knew what he needed was close by, so Lucky led the way to the unattended purser's office and a main data link. Silvercup effortlessly lugged Lint under one arm, the strongboxed briefcase under the other. "What *did* you and SELMI discuss?" Harley asked her in a neutral tone.

"A reappraisal of my desire to interact further with Lucky. I realized that in his absence I would be drawn to experiential rehashes, hypothetical conversations, extrapolations of our behaviors ... Fruitless speculations; only renewed contact will resolve my feelings, and Lucky's as well."

"And what *are* your feelings toward Lucky?" Sheena frankly wanted to know.

"Whoops! Here we are! Busy-busy!" Lucky singsonged idiotically to head off the reply.

Warning the ex-IRS man and his sulfurous briefcase, "Behave yourselves; what I did once I can do again," Silvercup dumped them by a multiplex interface terminal and flipped open the strongbox. It took a while to get them hooked up to the stricken ship's data systems.

"Power's down but that's no problem to you, huh, Zas?" Lucky observed. "Go on; phreak their files on you and me. Then we'll talk."

Lint's squandered life force had been drained to the lees, making the briefcase docile as well. "What choice have I? Very well." As the humans and the gleamer left, he and his symbiotic portmanteau began searching the data systems of Phoenix and Black Hole.

Tanabe's possession of the detonator was a shock but no real disheartenment to Hagadorn; more likely, he thought, it was one more test sent down by the Fates to certify his worthiness of power. "Ah-ah-ah, Takuma! That belongs to me," he said, at the same time indicating Nikkei, who had a Watchman's knifepoint at his throat. "*This* belongs to you; let's talk business."

He brought up Barb Steel's head, aiming the big lens of the neurosquelch projector at Tanabe's party. They'd both seen a demonstration of its power, and both knew Hagadorn could irradiate Tanabe's party before they could either withdraw or get inside attacking distance; Kamimura's possession of the *manriki-kusari* chain showed that Tanabe's bunch had no firearms. The redoubtable Miss Sato and some of the others had improvised *shuriken* and the like, but Hagadorn's wall of Watchmen and the fitful lighting made them of little use.

"Do stay, Taku! Just meet me halfway—we'll share the wealth! What profits we'll rake in from now on! Mr. Kamimura? Kindly don't buzz in your daimyo's ear; let him think."

But Kamimura had already passed on the crucial information: his trained sense of smell had picked up the faint aroma of Barnes's explosives, packed into the frame-bulkhead juncture in the middle of the engineering space. The detonator and the residue on Barnes's hands had made it pretty simple to sort out what the cop and Dante Bhang had been doing.

"Now," Hagadorn pressed, "I can either have that gadget from you in a gentlemanly way or take it once I've turned you into a neurosquelched imbecile. Which would you prefer?" He wasn't at all sure the ray's first-intensity range could reach across the compartment, but knew that if he could get Tanabe close he could kill the man with a close-up second-intensity charge and be rid of the troublesome swine for good.

"Tell you what: I'll meet you in the middle, send your son and his servant across, and accept the detonator. Then we can go our separate ways, fair? Or shall I have Nikkei carved up a bit while you consider?"

Tanabe held up the detonator. "By all means, Phipps, let's find common ground."

Both Miss Sato and Kamimura made moves to fetch the detonator, to shoulder the burden, but Hagadorn rejected that with an admonitory wave of the finger. "No, this is a top-echelon transaction." All casual ease, he stepped forth.

Hagadorn gestured, and Mickey and Nikkei were thrust stumbling at Tanabe's party, Miss Sato catching Nikkei. The two hadn't been of much importance to begin with, and in any case were within range of a first-intensity shot now along with the rest of Tanabe's party.

Tanabe himself met Hagadorn on the opposite side of Barb Steel's head, so close to the explosive charge that Tanabe marveled at the German's not smelling it. He knew Hagadorn intended to kill him and, at the very least, mindwipe the others in Tanabe's party. Absurd, how the Trough's going offline and the rest of it had ruined a perfectly executed plan and brought him to this moment—something to do with Lucky Junknowitz's probability contamination and the hyperdrama of synchronicity? In the end there was only one way to keep Earth out of the hands of Phipps Hagadorn and Black Hole.

"Don't look so glum, Taku," Hagadorn jollied him. "This is part of the natural order of things, after all—of competition and profit. *I* am become the invisible hand of the marketplace."

"Then maybe I am become the invisible hand of the hearth," Tanabe said mullingly, and triggered the detonator. At the same moment the explosion crushed him and Hagadorn against the opposite bulkhead, killing both instantly, the rest of Barnes's second, far greater string of explosion rocked the *Crystal Harmonic*, blew gaping holes in her bottom and sides, and started her settling into the ebon sea.

SIXTY

ALTHOUGH THE HELIPAD had tilted to port at a fifteen-degree list, a dazed assortment of passengers and crew members had straggled there in the vain hope of salvation from the sky.

The Awesome Vogonskiy hurdled one bunch, a circle of typically pessimistic Taavvt already twenty-six stanzas along in their highly formulaic death dirge, then dodged around a knot of Borzixx, litigious creatures who'd abandoned efforts to save themselves in order to prepare a legal brief they were going to stuff in a champagne bottle and toss overboard so that their heirs could sue Phoenix Enterprises.

The magician had shed his blaster-burnt and overloaded sorcerer's robes, bounding along now in close-fitting Chinese silks, each bound taking a harried *uhh!* out of him. He burst out onto the big, demarcated square of nonskid, sure in some corner of his ego that he would yet carry the day—unable to deal with the fact that superior predators were now on the boat. That he was less fleet, less empowered, less wolfish than they.

He was looking back over his shoulder as he leapt into the H-shaped landing guidemark; confirming that Vogonskiy's powers no longer held sway, Willy Ninja rose up out of the throng on one side and the man who considered himself most wronged of all, Sean Junknowitz, thrust apart the crowd on the other.

There were XTs present who'd parted seas and rearranged stellar systems, but all their power lay on the other side of a dead teleport system; they all drew back, even the sue-crazy Borzixx. If Vogonskiy expected any clemency from Willy Ninja, the look on Willy's face—as he recalled Riiv's death—disabused him of the idea.

Vogonskiy expanded himself like an intercontinental zeppelin and sprang through the stranded Troughers, nimble despite his size. Willy assumed a backup stance; Sean stepped to meet him. Vogonskiy laughed and death-swiped black killing clouds of ghost-energy at them.

Willy was lit with a corona of song that directed the attack away in windy vortices. Vogonskiy's best efforts couldn't get through the protections the two of them had acquired the hard way on End Zone; Sean went into a shuffling, finger-snapping shamanic dance and return-served at Vogonskiy the same moribund pall he'd thrown into so many victims. Vogonskiy groaned and fell to his knees, doubled over in agony as pitch-black smoke swirled into him and the last of his illusions fell away.

The End Zone escapees and everyone else there saw him as he truly was: a bloated apparition that resembled more strongly than anything else a walking tumor. He swelled, suppurated, went gangrenous and putrid; he burst in a dozen places to leak radiant ichors, Day-Glo discharges, pus like green lava. As they watched, he collapsed in on himself, shrinking. The Awesome Vogonskiy worked his last transformation, ending up as a puddle of necrotic alien tissues and bubbling rheum.

"Everybody must be on deck," Lucky told Sheena and Harley. "You go this way and Silv and me'll go that way. If you can't find anybody, for god's sake get to a lifeboat."

That suited Sheena, who was impatient to seek Sean. Harley had found she was all out of strong passions and so trailed after the redhead. But as she passed near the darkened Nostromo Tap Room, a voice said, "It's the Paradisical Harley!"

She turned to see Jason Duplex standing there—a markedly weird Jason Duplex, whose face looked bunched and askew somehow, and yet undeniably the ideal of billions. When he opened his mouth to speak to her, red drops found their way down from the corners. "Love what you've done with your hair! Harley, babe, I think I've found just the project for us to do together—with a starring role that will make you *somebody*!" Still ravenous, he sprang at her.

"I'm already somebody," Harley said, aiming the gaitmobe wearer's pistol and blazing away. It was a good thing the first two rounds hit his center of mass and killed him outright, because the third went wild as the *Crystal Harmonic* was jarred by Barnes's second round of explosives.

Bringing up the rear, a spectator as usual, Eddie Ensign thought, wriggling his way through the various species of helipad onlookers to rejoin Sean and Willy as they contemplated what was left of The Awful Vogonskiy. Eddie pondered the fact that he was nothing but excess baggage to neosuperheroes like

Sean and Willy—an unemployed star-stalker lacking all merit unless you counted a knack for spotting celebs trying to go incognito.

He shouldered past Shak Ilksingers, human cabin stewards, and one of the ship's supposed themers, E.T. the Extraterrestrial. At least Sean and Willy had reached a rapport. Eddie grinned and started to say, *Nobody important, guys; just me*—only to gape.

His star-stalker instincts—which caused him to scrutinize every viz he saw for hidden identities and camouflaged faces—had been running on autopilot, and had mug-shot him a face he had every reason to recall, especially there on the helipad where Vogonskiy had condemned Eddie, Willy, and Sean to End Zone. Eddie pirouetted, pointing at E.T. "It's Tumi!"

The M'finti had only halfway drawn a blaster when Sean, rolling his pelvis and shoulder-shaking, froze him with quick *ougan* voodoo passes. A blue Bunsen-burner flame rose up from Sean's right forefinger, and he flung it at Tumi as if flicking water from his fingertip; it engulfed Vogonskiy's familiar in fire. The crowd parted for him as he staggered to the rail and plunged over the side, a fireball meteor kicking its feet and screeching.

"I owe you a big one, Eduardo," Sean said.

"What were you about to say about nobody important?" Willy added.

"Forget it."

Sinead, Alex, and Rita finally caught up with them, with Brax and Asia trotting after, and at the same moment another, far stronger, series of explosions rocked the ship. Flotation bags that had been inflating from the hull pods were overwhelmed and the *Crystal Harmonic* began to go under. Life-forms of all kinds shrieked in dismay. But at least the ship was sinking slowly and into calm water; almost all aboard had had time to get topside, and now they were casting themselves to the waves.

Sean peered into the gloom. "There're small craft out there—somebody must've reached the lifeboats and brought 'em back. C'mon, we don't want to be sucked down when the ship goes under."

He went to scoop his mother up but she fended him off. "You know your father and I can take care of ourselves; it's Sinead who flunked junior drownproofing at summer camp."

Indisputably true and, with Alex and Rita calmly preparing to cope with survival afloat, Sean shrugged and swept his sister off her feet before she could get away, approaching the rail. "You may want to hold your nose here, sis."

"Sean, you macho fascist psychotic!"

"Hey, she's *our* meal ticket!" Labib yelled as he and his brother arrived, convoying Charlie and Didi; calmly leading the way was Sanpol Amsat, whose instincts of time and place were as finely attuned as ever. Molly Riddle appeared, too, discarding her heavy slamtube, and collected another kiss from Willy; Eddie Ensign was untying his jerkin.

Sinead had gotten control of the anger at Sean that she'd always found unmanageable before. "Want to know your flaw, brother dear? *You* think everything's a military problem. What you need to take on Black Hole from here on in's going to be a good, and I mean *top*, MBA."

Alex and Rita Junknowitz were looking on with as much wonder as they'd mustered for the aliens below.

"Well—with us as executive officers," Labib added, declaring his loyalty.

Jesus hastened to keep his hand in. "Yeah, I mean, we got in with Sinead on the ground floor, after all."

As Sean was wondering if he should dust off the brothers and considering the extremely troubling likelihood of what his sister was telling him, the cruise vessel listed more sharply than before and he and Sinead went over the rail.

He didn't have time to straighten them out before they hit the water and he felt something clip his head; the seawater all around him was a lot colder than he'd expected. He was weaker from his End Zone time than he'd realized, and couldn't make any headway against the dark water; he was about out of strength and hope when he felt himself yanked to the surface and revived a little to hear Sinead yell, "Somebody, help, please! He weighs a ton!"

The next thing he knew, he was belly down on an open boat deck, focusing on a face he knew.

"Lookin' green, gyrene." Skeeter chortled. Robyn, another of Sean's former Tiger Team mates, was bent down close, too; Sean had last seen them falling into the sea not far from the Micronesian island of Yap, back when Vogonskiy had captured himself, Eddie, and Willy. Sean upchucked brine, then asked hopefully, "V-Valhalla?"

Skeeter grinned rakishly. "Nope; Pesky Pizza Home Deliverance, our new employer."

* * *

Lucky and Silvercup were nearly floored by Barnes's second string of explosions. Lucky realized something and, appalled, turned to grab Silvercup by the shoulders. "This thing could go down! You—" He had no idea what her weight was, but knew she was denser than water. He was horrified at the idea of her plunging into the darkness with nothing to stop her until she sank into the floor of the Northwest Pacific Basin, or even the bottom of the Kuril Trench, more than five miles down. "Cripes, we gotta find a boat, make a raft—"

That was when a delayed charge somewhere close by nearly broke his eardrums with air pressure. Seawater seemed to surge at him from everywhere, not so much flooding in as simply rising, rising to every side, up to his chin before he knew it, more powerful than Silvercup. Swirling debris beat at and immobilized him as he tried to spot her; eerily, a number of sealed emergency lights were still functioning, throwing green radiance into the foaming confusion.

To his utter terror he saw that there was an entire section of hull gone—that he was looking down through the gaping side of the listing *Crystal Harmonic*, being plowed that way irresistibly by wreckage reluctantly answering the pull of gravity. There was no sign of Silvercup. He thought of what she must be feeling, thrashing like a metalflesh figurehead come to life as she plunged into one of the deepest places in all the oceans.

Then something had him around the chest, drawing him against the water's angry resistance to outrace the debris avalanche; he saw Silvercup's face strangely broadened, her eyes puffed almost shut but emitting faint beams that looked viridescent in that water. She towed him out and up toward the surface, her velocity and power telling him that she was kicking with at least partial phase speed.

Something long and sinewy slid by him in the opposite direction, and in a flash of hysteria he knew in his gut that it was a Ss-sarsassissian. But though the last ones he'd encountered underwater had conked and kidnapped him, this one wriggled by, disappearing toward the hole in the ship. Just as he was facing the fact that he couldn't hold his breath any longer, they broke the surface. Silvercup left the water like a sub-launched ballistic missile, bearing him up the lowered assault ramp of a U.S. Navy LCAC hovercraft of pre-Turn construction.

She held him upright and patted his back while he coughed out Pacific. Her naked form was slightly taller than usual and much more voluminous—but not bloated like a Thanksgiving parade balloon, exactly; she more suggested a socialist-heroic proletariat Earthmother statue, but of indubitable buoyancy. As he got his breath back, she reverted to what Lucky considered her true form.

They hadn't attracted all that much attention in the half-filled LCAC, where *Harmonic* crew members, other human rescuees, and varied XTs were being guarded by well-armed Earthers, including machinegunners atop the cabins. Not that all the firepower looked like it was going to be needed; the sea had taken the last intransigence out of the *Harmonic*ers. Lucky freely submitted to being patted down, so Silvercup did, too—to his vast relief and, though they didn't know it, the rescuers' great benefit.

The LCAC was brightly lit, as were the other craft in a mismatched flotilla ringing in the sinking cruise ship from all quarters. Teams on each rescue boat were busily camming the ship's demise and the survivors; Lucky concluded that somebody was planning on going worldwide with the story of the millennium. As he watched, Ss-sarsassissians nudged a group to an oceanographic vessel two hundred yards off—Asiatics, half of them naked. Silvercup, whose vision was far better than Lucky's, observed, "Those unclothed ones are terribly scarred, as if surgically mutilated and then healed. I wonder what it all means?"

"I guess we'll just have to wait and see." With the draining of his probability contamination, Lucky hoped he was drifting out of the spotlight in the drama of the Black Hole Travel Agency.

She took his hand; her touch was warm despite the survival swim. "What will you do now?"

Tough question, in one of his least favorite categories. As far as he knew, just about all the problems that had been facing him when he was kidnapped at PhenomiCon still existed. "Look for a new job, I guess—"

He was interrupted by another Ss-sarsassissian, who broke the surface to spit something onto the cargo deck. "This one said he wanted to talk to you, Lucky, so I followed your smell here."

"Oh. Thanks," Lucky said as the sea dragon dove back for more rescue work, realizing it must be one of the ones who'd grabbed him on way station Sierra, one of Plinisstro's wetwork specialists. What it had spit up on the deck was Zastro Lint's briefcase.

But when the case spoke, it was with Lint's voice. "Looks

like Lucky's a good name for you, Junknowitz; information we found in the data banks tentatively clears you of IRS violations."

Then the case's own rodent voice chimed in. "Yeah, can't win 'em all. On the positive side, however, we got leads for enough revenue-concealment cases to win the Field Agent of the Year award, no sweat."

"Lordy!" Lucky bent down for a closer look at the ripped, scorched, dinged-up case. "Your personalities have melded?"

"No, no, no, you blockhead!" Lint answered scornfully. "But with my body dying and the two of us interfaced through the ship's computer, this was the logical way to carry on with our assignment. Soon as we get back to D.C. we'll file preliminary forms to get you squared away. Shouldn't take more than a year or two, all told."

"The hell with him!" the briefcase protested in its own voice. "I bet he's still probability-toxined! Anyway, I say we buck for Agent Plenipotentiary status, take over the whole Phoenix–Black Hole prosecution!"

The briefcase fell into an acrimonious argument with itself. You gotta hand it to them, they never say die, Lucky thought, leading Silvercup aside.

"What were you about to tell me?" she reminded him. "About what you'll do next?"

Maybe things would work out after all. "Just take life one thing at a time, bioform style—very disorganized and paradigmatically human, and if that probability stuff's still giving me bad juju, so be it. Um, I don't suppose you'd care to try it for a while?"

"Yes, I would," she said, moving closer. "Even if it means living haplessly ever after."

EPILOGUE

THE EXTRANATIONAL PESKY Pizza flotilla that closed in around the *Crystal Harmonic* included seaplanes, a big-lifter aerostat, and a sub—but not the one belonging to the Kuril Islanders; they'd been suffered to escape. And so those of us who'd survived Crystal Night were saved.

Operation Home Deliverance had slam-dunked the biggest pie of all, and done what Sean Junknowitz's overly hasty attack had failed to do. But though the sinking of the ship had been a desperate pizzarino move prompted by Black Hole's accelerated campaign to openly subjugate and depopulate Earth, a clean win for the underground was prevented by the unforeseeable: the Trough's crash and the paralysis on Light Trap.

It's not my intention to make this a historical document; those were being spewed forth even before the attack on the cruise ship, and were soon being cranked out in unguessable volumes—albeit mostly for limited dissemination. Up and down the Trough, too, sentient species began trying to sort out what had happened.

This is simply a memoir fragment, if you will; a postcard from the initiating event of what is already being called the post-post-Turn, the Home Stretch, the New Vector.

As for Operation Home Deliverance, nothing the pizzarinos did before or after came close in magnitude, coordination of action, or scale of organization. Black Hole and Phoenix were reminded that, even on a befoolable tertiary world like ours, payback can be a bitch.

From Asia, Brax, the Junknowitzes, and the rest on the helipad to Nikkei Tanabe, straining to reach his dead father but pulled to safety by Mickey Formica, all of us who'd managed to live through the Cruise to Nowhere were hauled from the slowly rolling Pacific. Though neither had known that the other group was going to be active in rescue operations—the existence of

Takuma Tanabe's secret takeover op was something the underground hadn't even suspected—Pesky Pizza divers and Ss-sarsassissians cooperated in getting the survivors to safety. Otherwise it would've gone hard on the scuba teams, from what I saw.

The water foamed phosphorescent as the *Crystal Harmonic* slipped under the waves, taking with it Navel's Adit. Beings from distant star systems and the reigning powermongers of Earth were cowed before anonymous avengers—men, women, and children—as we survivors tallied losses.

Takuma Tanabe was dead and had taken Phipps Hagadorn along; they and Apterix Muldoon, who'd evinced in the end a reverence for the written word that humbled and instructed Braxmar Koddle, drifted down into the dark reaches not far from one another. Three ninjas—one a *kunoichi*, a female adept—had been among the Tanabe casualties. Barnes and other turncoats rode the long dark miles down and down, accompanied by what was left of Vogonskiy and Tumi, Gilda Hagadorn, Jason Duplex, and Barb Steel, as well as the neurosquelched and helpless Llesh Llerrudz and the Peer Group's remains.

The Pesky Pizzarinos were well prepared to prevent violence among the rescued factions, so that, for example, Didi Cola was restrained from garroting Papal Nuncio O'Dwyer with a lifeline when he suggested that she'd betrayed the Holy Father in Rome. The pizzarino craft began dispersing to preset and prepared destinations bearing Phoenix and Black Hole hostages.

The fate of Earth, the Trough, perhaps the universe pivoted on that one long day and night, and no one can yet say what those events will bring in the end. Of SySobek, Ka Shamok, and Miles Vanderloop, there's been no further word, and reports from Light Trap have it that the Outline hasn't been reignited. If Cosmosian government (do they *have* government?) grinds as slowly as its Earthly analogue, it may be millennia before those three even get a hearing. Or at any moment the sky could open up—but to initiate a more enlightened toxic-waste disposal policy, or to sterilize the dump site for good?

All we can do is wait, living our lives in the meantime as best we can. In that sense little has changed since humanity's earliest days; we always had a feeling about that, didn't we, in every time and clime—that the Last Days could come at any moment?

The raid on Light Trap was neither all success nor all failure; while many hostages were freed, the majority remain in the Sysops' keeping. A goodly number of Troughworld uprisings carried the day because the Agency lacked the means to rush in reinforcements. Although the Trough was functioning normally again—sort of—within days, freedom forces were by then entrenched on thousands of worlds, having overwhelmed occupying agencies and forces, recovered hostages from Light Trap, or both.

The fly in the ointment was that the vast majority of those planets found Aditless isolation far roughter than they'd anticipated—a damper on their economies and a psychological burden. FTL travel, with its obvious limitations and drawbacks, wouldn't serve, so most have resumed limited intercourse, at least, with the Trough; the crying need for technology, expertise, and other necessities to aid in rebuilding is motivation number one.

True to Lumber Jack's vision, the devastation wrought in those brief hours was unprecedented. Some of it will take years to set right, while other damage is irreparable. In scores of cases, fighting between rebels and local Black Hole puppet regimes escalated until doomsday weapons were used; many of those worlds are now worse off than Hazmat, at least a dozen being lifeless. For all of that, the galaxy was very fortunate that the Sysops' Red Giants were unusable.

As for Lumber, he's leading the long struggle to reestablish the immensely complex ecosystems of old-growth forest incinerated in the conflict on Wood Wind. By all accounts he's the right man for the job: his Head Start rebirth by the creosote bush, Earth's senior greenlife, gave him added status, but his decision not to assassinate Lucky gave him even more. The Light Trap raid would never have taken place without Lucky, and the appalling secret of the eight rings would still be hidden. Then there's the Wood Winder moral verdict that it would've been out-and-out wrong to kill an innocent man for self-preservation.

Back to the Trough. The unavoidable fact emerged that it can only be operated by the up-Trap SIs, and they in turn obey only Sysop users. The system is like an unphreakable toggle, ON/OFF, and the latter was quickly proclaimed by many to have even more drawbacks than the former. In short, the entities up-Trap still control the Trough, but they're best described as marching in place.

Fortunately, the effects of E. C. Wheeler's Limpidation pyramid scheme were counteracted by the devastating revelation of the eight rings' meaning. The trauma of the raid, the (attempted? partial?) discharge of Lucky's probability contamination, and, to a greater extent, the colloquy with SELMI also had their effects; thus, mercifully, the SIs won't be pushing the joys of Limpidation. Trough scuttlebutt has it that the SIs are oh-so-diplomatically dissuading, or perhaps I should say "deprogramming," the Fimblesector nanites from the scam.

Conditions down-Trap reflect those above. Management is beset by indecision and conflicting impulses, but the day-to-day business of the Trough goes on—in less malign fashion; the functionaries want to stay flexible, in case new standards of corporate ethics are instituted. In one sense, the galaxy's becoming a slightly less harrowing place thanks to sheer old-fashioned Cover Your Ass exec-think.

While the Sysops' countless subsidiaries and proxies are refraining from their usual subversion and machination, however, they continue to position themselves to Black Hole's advantage wherever possible. Still, Gipper's great tangerine isn't as omnipotent as it once was.

The revelation of the eight-ring secret hasn't exactly put sophant life on the side of the angels—did anybody think it would? It's all very well to tell factions in a generations-old species-purification war that the slaughter has been juiced at least in part by ineffable toxic karma from the great beyond, but that doesn't make peace automatic. The sad truth is, it's far easier for them to disbelieve, discount, or ignore you and go on warring. Much more pleasing to their id-side, too; it's what makes all us bioremediation microorganisms feel good.

Insurrection groups, independents like the Trauma Alliance and the pitifully few AzTekkers, nevertheless persist in trying to publicize the eight-rings secret and what it means. Some listen, like the Wood Winders. Other common responses are:

1. Absurd; get away from me, you religious nut.
2. Vengeance! Let's fry those Cosmosian bastards!
3. Hey, I've got my own problems.
4. Well, it may not be a perfect system, but at least it puts food on my table.
5. Blasphemer! Prepare to be cast into the converter!
6. Hmm . . . let's form a committee to look into this.

And so it goes. Will the Troughworlds tail eventually be able to wag the Light Trap dog? When, as most think will happen, the Sysops shake off their introspective paralysis, will it be to institute an enlightened new philosophy or to ring in an even more heavy-handed rule? Even Lucky's new 8 Ball gives conflicting answers. Personally, I think we're in for the status quo for a long time unless the Outline flares to life again and a Judgment is handed down—and I'm not so sure I'm eager for that.

While we wait, I'll give more personal updates—some two months after the Night to Remember.

Once again, matters on Earth are a kind of reflection of those in the Trough. Though it was thought that certain decisive actions and crucial events would bring resolution, they've instead rung in a new state of turmoil, antagonisms, and quandaries, and a new threat of catastrophe. It's been said that Pesky Pizza moved imprudently; surely Bhang and Barnes—particularly Barnes—weren't the optimal saboteurs. Who knows, perhaps it was more of Lucky Junknowitz's synchronicity at work, making Trough crash and *Harmonic* assault coincide.

In any case, other phases of the pizzarinos' enterprise didn't go as well as the *Crystal Harmonic* mission. Decapitating strikes at the rest of Phoenix failed and, corporate pragmatism being what it is, the top dogs were quickly replaced. The new ownership wasn't inclined to treat with the underground, and the Sysops were out of the picture because the Adit was gone. And the pizzarinos found themselves in indefinite possession of a bizarre medley of XTourists and superseded Terran kahunas.

Along with Agency personnel still at large, the Phoenix successors and a variety of coopted media and government powers fired up a massive disinformation campaign, a story of anarchists mounting an XT-invader hoax to capitalize on panic and upheaval. Alleged experts debunked the XT captives as animatronics, costumers, and gene-engineered fakes. The Vatican condemned the hoax and called for calm, as did the president of the United States, the king of England, and even—a first—the *Video Examiner*.

The underground made one attempt to show a press delegation a chained Ygg, at a gutted and quarantined RBMK nuclear power station in Lithuania. Just as the stunned newshounds were accepting the truth, a very dirty explosion blew the decaying thousand-ton core lid off like a flipped silver dollar, hurling flaming hunks of graphite hundreds of feet high along with a horrendous brew of cesium 137, iodine 131, and other fissionables.

It's impossible to say how Phoenix or some Agency network pulled it off—presuming it was their doing. Regardless, the underground was accused of producing nuclear-weapons-grade materials and didn't dare try anything of the sort again.

The Pizzarinos dispersed their hostages: a Nall indig-pacification expert was shackled at a Namibian Desert eco-research seitch on the Hoarusib River; a dominator triad of sue-happy Borzixx was penned up and howling legal threats to the Chang Tang sky at a Tibetan nomad camp; and a leading Kraam socialite couple was caged deep in a played-out South African diamond mine.

I should state here that Plinisstro and the Ss-sarsassissians were exempt from all this, as cobelligerents and valuable allies; moreover, they wouldn't have been too easy to corral. As it was, they took up temporary residence in a guarded stretch of ocean near the Tanegashima Space Center. Similarly, Molly Riddle, Charlie Cola, the Junknowitzes—all the rest of us who'd been fighting or victimized by Black Hole—were spared it.

Then began what the pizzarinos had planned as an all-out out-ing offensive, which became in effect an agitprop counterattack instead. Against Phoenix's control of most mass media, the pizzarinos marshaled their grassroots telecomm, their 'zine jun-gle drums, hacker neurosystem, counterculture caucuses, antiestablishment activists, and opposition intelligentsia.

Those with a stake in the status quo or terrified of change were almost impossible to sway. The lunatic fringe was quick to embrace the news about Black Hole, but that was more an em-barrassment than a victory. The uneven struggle for Earth's fate quickly boiled down to a contest to sway the huge middle group of independent thinkers. Public opinion shook out into broad camps that reflected Trough reaction to the eight-rings symbol.

Meanwhile, those of us who'd strayed all unknowingly into the whirlwind months before had gathered to lie doggo, compar-ing notes on what was and had been RGO. The loft posse, the Quick Fixers, the Junknowitzes, Silvercup, Sheena and E.C., Harley—we came together, matched stories, recuperated, gave what information we could to the pizzarinos' network, and sim-ply caught our breath. Meanwhile, the world moved closer to the ultimate breakdown.

The planetary row became moot, however, when the Trough reopened contact with Earth.

A month after the sinking, a new Adit was brought to Earth aboard a starship. Two factors had overcome the Sysops' aver-sion to reopening contact with unpredictable Adit Navel: their need to keep close surveillance on the place, and the demand of diverse Trough heavies that the stranded XTourists be succored.

Ss-sarsassiss had sent along an observer/assistance delegation to seek Plinisstro and his fellows. Other interested parties had demanded and been granted permission to embark similar deputations. The Sysops' ginger new attitude toward Earth was manifest in its assumption of a new public image and logo; hence, on a certain day in early October, a starship configured to look like a *Close Encounters* mother ship as built by Starfleet came down for a series of low, grand-progression passes over Earth, displaying a shifting all-languages holo: VENTURE CAPITAL INTERSTELLAR, INC.

Impervious to the all-out attacks launched by a number of different factions, it kissed the surface of the ocean just long enough to recover the Ss-sarsassissians; how it knew they were there is uncertain at this time.

The starship rumbled on grandly to hover over the island of Ra's al Ghar in the Arabian Sea, which was still radioactive from Gulf War II. The FTL foamed the place down with fast-evaporating stuff that cut the radiation low enough to meet EPA standards for a nursery basement. Then it dropped an autodeploy Adit installation—a cluster-module prefab that grew and shape-shifted into a Troughtech fortress-Parthenon. Impressive to the unanointed masses, food for thought for the bulk of the human race, but as workaday for the Trough and Adits division as reglassphalting a pothole.

Black Hole had been smart enough to know it would take extraordinary efforts to win even tentative acceptance from Earth. When the mighty portals of the Adit center swung silently aside and the telescopic cams focused in—no one wanting to get too close—the world saw a wide, gaudy gold ribbon stretched across the doorway. Into view stepped Harley Paradise, dressed like the Queen of the Oscars, carrying a large pair of scissors.

She gave a big spokesmodel smile, snipped the ribbon in half, tossed back those magnificent waves of auburn hair, and announced, "I hereby declare this doorway to the stars open for business!"

The real Harley, who was standing there watching the TV screen just like the rest of us, still shave-skulled and wearing her unigarb, fainted.

All was flux again and we homo sapiens were groping our way toward interim solutions. It was the kind of thing we're used to, the kind we've gone through after plagues, world wars, the fall of the USSR, the breakdowns of the Turn. We're a muddling-through kind of species, and we were back at our strong suit.

The most immediate benefit was that the underground had a venue for hostage repatriation. There've been endless difficulties and risks in holding and maintaining offworlders that, taken with the horrifying mini-Chernobyl in Ignalina, have convinced the pizzarinos that hostage-holding isn't their forte. Black Hole's inclined to deal and several releases have already occurred; the UN's doing a little of the brokering, but it's the major independent eco-groups the underground really trusts. Much of Black Hole's ransom payment is in Trough technology and assistance and there was also a major redevelopment package for Lithuania.

Granted, I can't answer any of the transcendent questions yet, but here, in no particular order, are the things I do know.

As I said, Earth wasn't reopened by any ordinary contact expedition. Because of the unique circumstances and the obvious need to engender trust in every way possible, the delegation had the strangest makeup of any in the annals of Trough and Adits. For one thing, all of Lucky's tourists—save Lumber Jack—had been bribed or convinced to sign on in one way or another.

They knew Earth somewhat but knew an Earth*man* quite well, and it was felt that their insights could prove invaluable. A prime inducement for them to accept employment was the fact that they'd found their former lives difficult to resume after misadventures with "Salty Waters." The Hono were regarded with suspicion as being less group-fixated than the rest of their race; the Rphians were spurned for claiming there were more things in life than the managerial fast track; and Dame Snarynxx couldn't bear to go back to her dowager putterings. Even phlegmatic Mr. Millmixx was there, insisting that efforts to mainstream him into Zillionite life were far too devitalizing. The Dimdwindles, who'd found existence on safe, secure planet FoolProof positively *bovine*, were a happy family again, except that GoBug was no longer a sickly larva but rather a miniature version of his parents with an even more voracious appetite for Pesky Pizza.

Those weren't the only familiar visages the Sysops had troubled themselves to recruit. Charlie Cola's old pal Mussh Kunwar, former Pit Boss on way station Sierra—"a good Joe, even if he is a Nall," as Charlie had said—had been reassigned to Earth with a healthy raise. Lucky's Occuumese acquaintance from way station Kloo, Puhn Jahnt, was coordinating manager, but the biggest shock lay in the identity of the Supervisory Liaison Administrator for Advisory Consultation.

"Thing," he said to Lucky darkly when they subsequently encountered one another on Ra's al Ghar, "I *knew* you would prove to be an unmitigated walking disaster."

"Thanks for your confidence in me, sir," Lucky told Mr. Undershort, the touchy little two-legged clam from Root Canal.

But while Undershort had played the good company man and accepted the job—and a promotion—to help lift Earth from tertiary status to secondary, he had his work cut out for him, as did the rest of the installation's complement. There were Upper Management types along to make sure, on the QT, that Earth didn't open too wide or progress too far; Black Hole wanted to appear benign and conciliatory without actually conceding any advantage.

Among humanity there was a rending row over whether to allow Black Hole on Earth, whether to allow Humans—and at that, *which* humans—to go offworld, whether to let UFOids walk among us openly—still anathema to many despite all the *Crystal Harmonic* themer jollity. On the other hand, Earth needed a lot of things the Trough could provide, and Black Hole wished to stay on Earth's good side and could also use a new tourist attraction—and we're at the height of our Theme Age.

The Agency had used the Harley Paradise simulacrum only because they couldn't get Harley herself; it had invested a lot of money and effort in image-identification, after all. The fact was bruited about by grapevinet that Harley could write her own ticket as *real* spokesmodel, but she sent back a demurral. Dedicating her life to that sort of thing didn't appeal to her anymore—besides which, we'd found out after she'd fainted, she was pregnant. At her request, the Agency stopped using her simulacrum.

Early word came from Wick Fourmoons, the ember-eyed, ebon-swathed, elongated drink of absinthe who'd met Lucky in a Confabulon restroom and saved his 'nads when Lint and Peterbuilt lugged him aboard the *Harmonic*. Owner-operator of Four Moons Connections, Inc., she's proved her business acumen by nailing down an exclusive contract for singles tours to male-rich Earth from female-abundant worlds in the Trough, and vice versa.

She's making a tidy little income just in nonrefundable

sign-up fees, and if the actual junkets ever get started she'll be wealthy. Here again, it's all too possible that Upper Management is just paying out slack in the hangman's rope, but she's bold enough to take the risk and dare the downside.

Australian authorities have been unsuccessful in locating the Intubis, and Ziggy Forelock has yet to reappear. Hearsay along the songlines has it that Gipper led them all on walkabout to inaccessible places. There's no talk of rebuilding DreamLand; leaks indicate that the commonwealth's moving quietly to revert control of Ayers Rock to Aborigine hands.

His father's self-sacrifice laid on Nikkei incalculable *on*, the Japanese "debt that cannot be repaid." This sufficiently denuded Nikkei of his indifference and alienation that he took up his burden as head of his small remaining family and assumed control over Takuma's global business interests. Of course, that didn't make him CEO of Nagoya or honcho of World Nihon, but he has enormous leverage, plus other lines of influence that accrue to him rather than to his father's corporate successors. Nagoya-Nihon are cautiously keeping him in the loop.

More importantly, he has Miss Tazuko Sato and Mickey Formica backing him, along with Kamimura's ninjas and other Tanabe retainers. Sato, I'm told, knew of the possibility that Takuma would offer Mickey and his own son as hostages to Light Trap—if that had been what it took to shore up Takuma's status as Phoenix overlord in the wake of his planned *Crystal Harmonic* coup. The real shock was that Sato herself was ready and willing to serve as hostage, too—and had been groomed for that purpose. It bears remembering that Takuma asked no greater sacrifices of others than he himself was prepared to make. I'm told the score from "West Side Story" has been heard in the executive section of the TAV *Beten-Sama Maru* when Nikkei and Sato are aboard.

One development hit us RGO fans like an Un-Gun. While a third of the human race was trying to conjure the means for a fade to the wonders and opportunities of the Trough—and the number of those who could actually do so without corporate or government sponsorship barely broke quadruple digits—every one of *us* was tendered that option by some circumstance or other. I suspect that, where other funding arrangements hadn't already serendipitously occurred, the Founders smurfed the traveling credit; we're their lab rats, or whatever metaphor you wish.

Lucky received an open ticket billed to the Fealty, and Silver already had one, of course. They emerged from hiding for a pilgrimage he'd been desperate to make. His brief sojourn on Wood Wind seems to have put Lucky's soul at ease in spite of the desolation there. The sight of new growth and the absolution of Lumber Jack's friendship healed something in him. I hope Lucky's come to grips with the fact that he did what he was fated to.

Molly Riddle was gifted a modest amount of travel debit by Jacob and Teleen, who'd come along on the Trough and Adits ship. Jacob has been put back on salary as consultant for the Earth mission, overjoyed to be working again. The Discipline Di incident, he and Upper Management dropped by tacit agreement.

Back to Molly. She didn't need her folks' largesse because the Teleportation Authority, citing some reg nobody'd ever heard of, presented the Quick Fixers with early-retirement compensatory packages. She's free to come and go and so accompanied Willy Ninja into the Trough.

Willy was sent an open round-trip ticket to Riiv's homeworld. Word of the fate of their premier life-singer had reached them, and, since a part of the Medusa-python still lived in Willy in the person of that incandescent filament implant, Riiv's people begged him to attend a memorial service. Molly rode shotgun, she insisted, because nobody with Willy's artistic temperament should wander the Trough unescorted. They joined in an elegy sung by an entire world and the hymns of beatification that followed; they've yet to return, but none of us fear for them or are surprised. Willy had told us he had a lot to learn.

Charlie Cola didn't need his retirement package either, since he was begged/pressured to accept the post of general indig ombudsman in the Navel Adit's top management. He divides his time between Ra's al Ghar and the East Hampton house, where Didi has also resumed residency. Word is, they spend a lot of time closeted together with SELMI; people have their fingers crossed.

Charlie's had one major disappointment. He asked the pizzarinos to try, for species treason, Dante Bhang—who'd been insisting suavely that there was nothing personal in his power play against Charlie, just business. The pizzarinos, who were supposedly ready to hand Bhang over, were for unclear reasons holding him off Corsica; what a surprise—he escaped. Charlie railed about it, but some say he was relieved at not having to preside over his old friend's funeral.

Bhang remains at large. As his phobias will preclude him from ever seeing the Trough, at least he has the consolation of being on a planet where there's going to be a lot of money to be made.

By regulation, Charlie's share of the buyout was divided among the others. Jesus and Labib are ecstatic, and plan to pool their resources to cover Sinead Junknowitz's traveling expenses to inveigle her into being their MBA muse. She doesn't appear to know quite what to think, but the notion of playing den mother to the likes of the boys is balanced by the opportunity to see a lot more of space than she'd ever dreamed of. They want her to help them take ecotourism to the stars; she says nothing doing, but spends a lot of time poring over Troughworld data.

Sanpol Amsat quietly stands by, and it's automatically assumed that he'll go, too. I don't claim to understand Amsat, this student of every Earthly belief system listed, from Animism to Zen, but it's clear that he's a spiritual seeker—which is what kept him working at Quick Fix—and will seek on.

As to Harley, she rejected any return to the Trough for the time being. Having conceived during her time with Packard, she must now have the privacy in which to mull over issues as difficult as any war. With the situation of the *Crystal Harmonic* survivors much freed up in the wake of the Adit Navel reopening, Asia convinced her to move in with Lynka and the other Femmes Fatales while she figures out her next move. Harley couldn't be in better company.

Other people had other priorities, but Eddie Ensign took it upon himself to visit End Zone and helped beat the bush to make sure the last of the victims there had been evacuated. Along the way, he was endowed with a one-baseline-year open ticket by something called the End Zone Resettlement Bureau. That confers upon him such breathtaking mobility in the Trough that his old employer Eye Spy is vying with just about every news service on Earth to hire him as the ultimate foreign correspondent, king of the lensmen, his byline writ so large it'll require two screens to read it.

A more dubious development came with the coded credit account set up for E. C. Wheeler and Sheena Hec'k by parties unknown. Both were perplexed. Then a bitty crystal thingamajig was delivered to E.C. at Meadow Suite; it reminded me of a glass onion when I saw it later.

When the crystal energized to E.C.'s touch, Bagbee appeared in a shielded one-time-only holo, saying that with Ka Shamok gone and its member forces dispersed and quiescent, the insurrection's core cadre could use help maintaining a functioning, viable secret command structure. As one who'd kicked up and down the galaxy and aided Ka Shamok in earlier days, Wheeler was solicited to lend whatever assistance he might see fit.

It was just after that that E.C. and Sheena faded to visit her mother on Foxal, taking Sean Junknowitz along. He and Sheena had started circling one another again in that primal way of theirs even before Pesky Pizza got them ashore; they had subsequently gotten down to mat work.

The three made the trip to Foxal, a joyous reunion was had—though Sheena's mother's new mate was relieved to see an end to it—and the trio departed for home. Way station Rass is where they managed to jump off the radar screen.

Sheena, at least, is too Troughwise to have been decoyed into a trap. If they really are with Bagbee and the rest, keeping an eye on events and preparing to act if the Founders' behavior takes a nasty swing, it seems to me that Sean's the most content of us all: an eternal rebel. However, I'd look for E.C. to get restless before very long and take to the Trough again, destination unknown, without saying good-bye.

Very roundabout reports from Hazmat say that the People and the Humanosaurs are trying their best to establish a permanent peace with one another and with the SIs reborn out of Warhead. Packard has managed to have himself appointed chancellor, but Commander DeSoto is now in total command of his praetorian guard. Check and balance.

Let's see, what else? Alex and Rita are back in Esmeralda, and the retired-hippy community gets a lot of cordiality from the *policía* these days. The aerospace truck disappeared in pieces from the Oaxaca impoundment yard; god alone knows what technology is about to emerge in that region.

At Sony-Neuhaus, Russell Print has deep-sixed all the Worlds Abound stuff and, what with his connections, has begun publishing a new line of nonfiction Trough and Black Hole related stuff—having first secured a promotion and a fat profit-sharing deal. Brax wished him well and returned to other endeavors.

In referring to Mickey Formica before, I forgot to mention what he said to Asia Boxdale on the deck of the NOAA vessel that had picked up her and Brax as well as the survivors of Takuma's party. "Happened to notice ol' Ding-Dong over there, convoying your little tush through the dustup." He had nodded to Brax, then he added, "When I saw the look on your face I knew it'd never happen between you and me. Just . . . when you dance your piece about *this* night, how'm I gonna look?"

She didn't take his hand, or give him any other false sign of intimacy, but said, "Human, Mickey. That's what I always shoot for. I think you'll like it."

"Thermal. Not as much as havin' you would be, but thermal anyway." He turned. "You take special care of her, ol' teabag Brax."

I said, "I will, Mickey. Always." And Asia gave me a smile I'll carry in my heart until my dying breath.

The place where our pizzarino escorts brought Asia and me, and where I write these words, was one I already knew. One of the first things I did was show Asia how, from my former room, you can see the sparkle of the swells off Philbin Beach. The rest of the posse and friends were billeted in or near Meadow Suite, too.

It was obvious, once I thought about it, that members of the Wampanoag tribe here in Gay Head would be in the pizzarino conspiracy. They know the virtues of patience and of action; now they've got their ancestral land back in physical fact and are insuring it stays that way in legal and legislative substance. With people like General Buckley Wakkendorf, Fatima Bebe, Keating Price, and other Hagadorn functionaries in hand, Pesky Pizza was well positioned to begin stripping Phoenix members of their plunder.

And secret lines of power now accrue to the pizzarino underground. Zastro Lint and his smart-briefcase are now at large in the datasphere, with SELMI acting as cyber-psychiatric counselor, and the Gay Head land grab by Phoenix is just the sort of thing the two of them love to leap on like rabid weasels. Major treaty violations, Bureau of Indian Affairs malfeasance, government collusion, and corporate misconduct have been thrust into the light.

There isn't a landholder or a lackey left up-island; the Wampanoags are regarded by the Phoenix successors as better left alone. From the Gay Head Cliffs to a boundary connecting the Menemsha Bight and Stonewall Pond, up-island is the tribe's.

From the time I arrived I've been working in a fever to put together as much of the story of Black Hole as I could; I'm going to call it *Gate Crashers*. With so many people telling me their parts of the story as they stay here or pass through—the loft posse, Silvercup, E.C. and Sheena, and many kinds of pizzarino—I feel at times like Bilbo at Elrond's house. Asia is working on her magnum opus, and I don't have to tell you what it's about; since she's been promised some rather extraordinary help, I can't wait to see what the special effects are going to be like.

Lucky and Silvercup have been staying up in the Gay Head lighthouse, which Buckley Wakkendorf had fitted out as a luxe hermitage. I go up there to talk to him when *Gate Crashers* feels like it's about to get the better of me.

Last night they, Asia, and I were sitting on the black iron walkway that encircles the lens housing itself, near the top of the red brick tower, watching the red and white beams sweep across the sea. Off to the left was the boarded-up White Visitation, and the parking area where the landholders had washed their cars; down below, I could see the spot near the Devil's Bridge where the helo almost riddled Gilda Hagadorn. Brightness gleamed off Silvercup's metalflesh.

I asked them something that had been bothering me. "D'you think there are others? Other dump sites the Cosmosians are using, other eight-ring galaxies? If we accept the model of landfills, doesn't it seem likely?"

It was Silvercup who answered. "We've talked about that, and believe you're right. But in order to contact them, it seems to me, we'll need Gipper Beidjie, or someone with the same powers on an even greater scale."

Asia was looking into the distance. "And how do we establish some connection?"

Silvercup gave that sterling smile of hers. "Let them see you dance, perhaps." Silver has lately become fascinated with Asia's art. "And give them a copy of *Gate Crashers*."

She touched Lucky's shoulder, a rare thing between them when there's anyone else around. "Shouldn't you tell Brax what you were saying?"

He mulled it over, then did. "Why should the order of things stop with those Cosmosians? They can't be *that* godlike, not with the polluter mind-set they've got. What if there's something beyond the cosmos?"

"As far above the Cosmosians as they are above us?" Asia asked. "Then what?"

"Then maybe all of existence is some kind of experiment, to see how we deal with this."

He pulled out his medallion, letting the light glimmer on the eight interlocking rings.

Also by
JACK McKINNEY